Date Due			

GREAT ILLUSTRATED CLASSICS

GREAT ILLUSTRATED CLASSICS

James Fenimore Cooper in his later years. Engraved for the *Democratic Review* by J. B. Forrest from a daguerreotype miniature.

AFLOAT AND ASHORE

BY JAMES FENIMORE COOPER

With biographical illustrations, pictures of con-
temporary scenes and drawings reproduced
from early editions together with an
introduction and captions by
Allen Klots, Jr.

NEW YORK · DODD, MEAD & COMPANY

AFLOAT AND ASHORE

PUBLISHED IN THE UNITED
STATES OF AMERICA, 1956
BY DODD, MEAD & COMPANY, INC.

PRINTED IN THE UNITED STATES OF AMERICA
BY THE CORNWALL PRESS, INC., CORNWALL, N. Y.

INTRODUCTION

Afloat and Ashore, published in 1844, seven years before James Fenimore Cooper's death, is based upon experiences of his youth and at the same time reflects the mature and dogmatic views of his fifty-five years.

Cooper knew the sea well as a result of his service in the merchant marine and the Navy. After he was expelled in his junior year from Yale, the college for which the hero of *Afloat and Ashore,* Miles Wallingford, was later to be intended, his father, Judge Cooper, sent him before the mast aboard a merchantman. He was destined for the Navy, but there being no naval academy, it was customary for potential midshipmen to serve an apprenticeship in the merchant marine. Judge Cooper was then a former member of Congress and a leader of the Federalist party, a position that stood to enhance the advancement of his son in a naval career.

But it was as an ordinary sailor that the young Cooper set out upon his first voyage on October 16, 1806, to England aboard the *Sterling,* carrying a freight of flour. The passage was stormy and long; forty days out of sight of land. Moreover, France and Britain were at each other's throats, and the Berlin Decree and Orders in Council respectively had established blockades to prevent neutrals from trading with either belligerent. As a consequence, American vessels found themselves preyed upon by both countries on the high seas. In addition, the British had taken to stopping American ships and impressing seamen on the charge that they were actually subjects of the crown posing as American citizens to escape military service. Indeed, so brazen had the English mariners become that in 1807 the British frigate *Leopard* intercepted the American frigate *Chesapeake* off the Norfolk Capes and removed four men to the fury of the populace whose home waters had been violated. It was onto such dangerous seas that Cooper ventured, and he knew at first hand the threat of impressment that haunted Miles Wallingford while in British territory.

Ashore, Cooper had time to wander around London with his shipmates as the young Miles does. In January 1807, he made voyages to the Mediterranean, returning to England from whence he had another rough trip to Philadelphia, lasting fifty-two days. In 1808, he was commissioned a midshipman and served for another three years mostly in inland waters, but the experience proved valuable for his later novels about the sea. It was his bride Susan Delancey, who persuaded him to foresake the Navy in 1811. She was later to challenge him to write his first novel *Precaution* on a dare that he could improve upon a mediocre English work he had been impatiently reading.

Some of the voyages of Miles Wallingford closely match the experiences of his creator and it is noticeable that Cooper dwells in greatest detail upon the ports that he had actually visited himself. As a storyteller, he is most at home in *Afloat and Ashore* when he writes of the sea. There is an aura of authenticity about and a genuine feeling for the life aboard ship that give to his descriptions of it a power before which his concern for the lives of his characters ashore pales.

The sense of competition seems to have been keen in Cooper. Even as he was provoked to write his first novel to prove that he could outdo one that he was reading, so he was induced to produce his first sea story to show that a writer with his experience as a sailor could create a more authentic story about the sea than a landlubber such as Walter Scott had done with *The Pirate*. As America's first great novelist to derive his sources from scenes at home, it was inevitable that Cooper should be compared with the leading English novelist of the time, and he was inordinately sensitive about being called the American Scott.

On setting out to surpass his English rival, he once more proved himself an innovator by instituting a new kind of fiction that showed adventures afloat could be put to use effectively as the basis of a novel. *The Pilot,* which was published as his fourth novel in January, 1824, became the precursor of a tradition of sea tales not only from Cooper's own pen but also followed by some of the titans of American literature. Cooper wrote more than a dozen sea stories including, in addition to *Afloat and Ashore, The Red Rover,* 1828; *The Water Witch,* 1830; *Homeward Bound,* 1838; *The Two Admirals,* 1842; *The Wing and Wing,* 1842; *Ned Myers,* 1843; *The Sea Lions,* 1849; as well as a history of the U. S. Navy which appeared in 1839. His maritime novels never became as well known as his famous stories of Indians and woodsmen that constitute the *Leatherstocking Tales,* but they are an important part of American literature and paved the way for such masterpieces in this genre as *Two Years Before the Mast, Moby Dick* and *The Sea Wolf.*

By the time Cooper came to write *Afloat and Ashore,* he had reversed the technique he had developed in the *Leatherstocking Tales* of involving his heroines directly in the skirmishes and adventures of his heroes. Lucy Hardinge and Grace Wallingford remain securely at home while Miles Wallingford ranges the deep and they do not intrude to temper the reality of a sailor's experiences in a man's world. Emily Merton becomes most closely involved as a participant in Miles' wanderings but even she manages to remain somewhat more aloof from them than the heroines in the earlier sea stories or the *Leatherstocking Tales* do from the affairs of their men.

Cooper, however, does involve himself in the course of his characters' lives. Miles Wallingford is an elderly man of sixty-five reviewing his past years, but the voice of the author, ten years his hero's junior, is at times thinly veiled behind the first person in which the narration is presented. Only eleven years before, Cooper had returned from seven years abroad to his home, Otsego Hall, in Cooperstown, New York. He found much wanting in his own land and was articulate in his criticism, launching forth upon a series of social and political tracts. He enraged his countrymen who answered his scathing attacks through the press, and Cooper retaliated with a battery of libel suits that absorbed much of his time and energy. Only a little more than two years before the appearance of *Afloat and Ashore,* he had further alienated his own neighbors by forbidding them their favorite picnic ground, Three Mile Point, which he owned.

By 1844, the tempest had somewhat subsided but occasional angry gusts remained reminiscent of it throughout the rest of his writing. His spokesman, Miles Wallingford, himself, shows a certain disagreeable arrogance about his own accomplishments, and Cooper cannot resist halting his narrative at times to trumpet his own prejudices. He is particularly unforgiving with contemporary journalists and never loses an opportunity to express his undying contempt for them, bewailing the passage of the day when "the citizen was supposed to have some rights, as put in opposition to the press." He rails against England ("She drove us into a war by the effects of her orders in council and paper blockades.") and satirizes New York society for its lingering respect for things English. Equally uncharitably he castigates his own land ("I will concede that money is the great end of American life—that there is little else to live for in the great model republic.") but widening the circumference of his scorn, he adds that "twenty Europeans can be bought with two ten-pound Bank of England notes much easier than two Americans." He decries an age "when the cant of a pretending irreligion is disposed to turn into ridicule the humbling of the person while asking for the blessing of the Almighty" and declares that on Sundays in the American towns "the old observances are giving way before the longings or weaknesses of human nature." In short, the writer of *Afloat and Ashore* reveals himself as an embittered man, wearied by his private battles. But when he reflects upon the adventures of his youth and recreates them in the voyages of Miles Wallingford at sea, the rancor falls away and the genius of the master narrator takes over to bring the story to life.

Afloat and Ashore is actually half a book, appearing originally as the first two of four volumes, with the life of Miles Wallingford developed to its logical conclusion in the later work that followed at the end of 1844, bearing his name. But the best of the narrative appears in *Afloat and Ashore* which, while important to an appreciation of *Miles Wallingford,* can stand alone as an absorbing tale of the sea.

ALLEN KLOTS, JR.

Principal Works of JAMES FENIMORE COOPER and Their Dates

Precaution—1820

The Spy—1821

The Pioneers—1823

The Pilot—1823

Lionel Lincoln—1825

The Last of the Mohicans—1826

The Prairie—1827

The Red Rover—1828

Notions of the Americans: Picked up by a Traveling Bachelor—1828

The Wept of Wishton-Wish—1829

The Water-Witch—1830

The Bravo—1831

A Letter to His Countrymen—1834

The Monikins—1835

Homeward Bound—1838

Home as Found—1838

The History of the Navy of the United States of America—1839

The Pathfinder—1840

The Deerslayer—1841

The Two Admirals—1842

The Wing-and-Wing—1842

Wyandotte—1843

Ned Myers—1843

Afloat and Ashore—1844

Satan's Toe—1845

The Chainbearer—1846

The Redskins—1846

The Crater—1847

The Ways of the Hour—1850

ILLUSTRATIONS

PREFACE

THE writer has published so much truth which the world has insisted was fiction, and so much fiction which has been received as truth, that, in the present instance, he has resolved to say nothing on the subject. Each of his readers is at liberty to believe just as much, or as little, of the matter here laid before him, or her, as may suit his or her notions, prejudices, knowledge of the world, or ignorance. If anybody is disposed to swear he knows precisely where Clawbonny is, that he was well acquainted with old Mr. Hardinge, nay, has often heard him preach—let him make his affidavit, in welcome. Should he get a little wide of the mark, it will not be the first document of that nature which has possessed the same weakness.

It is possible that certain captious persons may be disposed to inquire into the *cui bono* of such a book. The answer is this. Everything which can convey to the human mind distinct and accurate impressions of events, social facts, professional peculiarities, or past history, whether of the higher or more familiar character, is of use. All that is necessary is, that the pictures should be true to nature, if not absolutely drawn from living sitters. The knowledge we gain by our looser reading often becomes serviceable in modes and manners little anticipated in the moments when it is acquired.

Perhaps the greater portion of all our peculiar opinions have their foundation in prejudices. These prejudices are produced in consequence of its being out of the power of any one man to see, or know, everything. The most favored mortal must receive far more than half of all that he learns

on his faith in others ; and it may aid those who can never
be placed in positions to judge for themselves of certain
phases of men and things, to get pictures of the same, drawn
in a way to give them nearer views than they might otherwise obtain. This is the greatest benefit of all light literature in general, it being possible to render that which is
purely fictitious even more useful than that which is strictly
true, by avoiding extravagances, by portraying with fidelity, and, as our friend Marble might say, by "generalizing"
with discretion.

This country has undergone many important changes since
the commencement of the present century. Some of these
changes have been for the better ; others, we think out of all
question, for the worse. The last is a fact that can be known
to the generation which is coming into life by report only,
and these pages may possibly throw some little light on both
points, in representing things as they were. The population
of the republic is probably something more than eighteen
millions and a half to-day ; in the year of our Lord one thousand eight hundred, it was but a little more than five millions. In 1800, the population of New York was somewhat
less than six hundred thousand souls ; to-day it is probably a little less than two millions seven hundred thousand
souls. In 1800, the town of New York had sixty thousand
inhabitants ; whereas, including Brooklyn and Williams-
burg, which then virtually had no existence, it must have
at this moment quite four hundred thousand. These are
prodigious numerical changes, that have produced changes
of another sort. Although an increase of numbers does not
necessarily infer an increase of high civilization, it reasonably leads to the expectation of great melioration in the
commoner comforts. Such has been the result, and to those
familiar with facts as they now exist, the difference will
probably be apparent in these pages.

Although the moral changes in American society have not
kept pace with those that are purely physical, many that are
essential have nevertheless occurred. Of all the British possessions on this continent, New York, after its conquest from
the Dutch, received most of the social organization of the

mother country. Under the Dutch, even, it had some of these characteristic peculiarities in its patroons, the lords of the manor of the New Netherlands. Some of the southern colonies, it is true, had their caciques and other semi-feudal and semi-savage noblesse, but the system was of short continuance ; the peculiarities of that section of the country arising principally from the existence of domestic slavery on an extended scale. With New York it was different. A conquered colony, the mother country left the impression of its own institutions more deeply engraved than on any of the settlements that were commenced by grants to proprietors, or under charters from the crown. It was strictly a royal colony, and so continued to be, down to the hour of separation. The social consequences of this state of things were to be traced in her habits until the current of immigration became so strong as to bring with it those that were conflicting, if not absolutely antagonist. The influence of these two sources of thought is still obvious to the reflecting, giving rise to a double set of social opinions ; one of which bears all the characteristics of its New England and puritanical origin, while the other may be said to come of the usages and notions of the Middle States, proper.

This is said in anticipation of certain strictures that will be likely to follow some of the incidents of our story, it not being always deemed an essential in an American critic that he should understand his subject. Too many of them, indeed, justly the retort of the man who derided the claims to knowledge of life set up by a neighbor, that " had been to meetin' and had been to mill." We can all obtain some notions of the portion of a subject that is placed immediately before our eyes ; the difficulty is to understand that which we have no means of studying.

On the subject of the nautical incidents of this book, we have endeavored to be as exact as our authorities will allow. We are fully aware of the importance of writing what the world thinks, rather than what is true, and are not conscious of any very palpable errors of this nature.

It is no more than fair to appraise the reader that our tale is not completed in the first part, or the volumes that are now published. This the plan of the book would not permit; but we can promise those who may feel any interest in the subject, that the season shall not pass away, so far as it may depend on ourselves, without bringing the narrative to a close. Poor Captain Wallingford is now in his sixty-fifth year, and is naturally desirous of not being hung up long on the tenter-hooks of expectation so near the close of life. The old gentleman having seen much and suffered much, is entitled to end his days in peace. In this mutual frame of mind between the principal and his editors, the public shall have no cause to complain of unnecessary delay, whatever may be its rights of the same nature on other subjects.

The author—perhaps editor would be the better word—does not feel himself responsible for all the notions advanced by the hero of this tale, and it may be as well to say as much. That one born in the Revolution should think differently from the men of the present day, in a hundred things, is to be expected. It is in just this difference of opinion that the lessons of the book are to be found.

AFLOAT AND ASHORE

AFLOAT AND ASHORE.

CHAPTER I.

" And I—my joy of life is fled,
My spirit's power, my bosom's glow ;
The raven locks that graced my head,
Wave in a wreath of snow !
And where the star of youth arose
I deemed life's lingering ray should close ;
And those loved trees my tomb o'ershade,
Beneath whose arching bowers my childhood played."
MRS. HEMANS.

I WAS born in a valley not very remote from the sea. My father had been a sailor in youth, and some of my earliest recollections are connected with the history of his adventures and the recollections they excited. He had been a boy in the war of the Revolution, and had seen some service in the shipping of that period. Among other scenes he witnessed, he had been on board the Trumbull in her action with the Watt—the hardest-fought naval combat of that war—and he particularly delighted in relating its incidents. He had been wounded in the battle, and bore the marks of the injury in a scar that slightly disfigured a face that, without this blemish, would have been singularly handsome. My mother, after my poor father's death, always spoke of even this scar as a beauty-spot. Agreeably to my own recollections the mark scarcely deserved that commendation, as it gave one side of the face a grim and fierce appearance, particularly when its owner was displeased.

My father died on the farm on which he was born, and
which descended to him from his great-grandfather, an
English emigrant that had purchased it of the Dutch colo-
nist who had originally cleared it from the woods. The
place was called Clawbonny, which some said was good
Dutch, others bad Dutch ; and now and then a person ventured a conjecture that it might be Indian. Bonny it was,
in one sense at least, for a lovelier farm there is not on the
whole of the wide surface of the Empire State. What does
not always happen in this wicked world, it was as good as
it was handsome. It consisted of three hundred and
seventy-two acres of first-rate land, either arable or of rich
river bottom in meadows, and of more than a hundred of
rocky mountain side, that was very tolerably covered with
wood The first of our family who owned the place had
built a substantial one-story stone house, that bears the date
of 1707 on one of its gables ; and to which each of his suc-
cessors had added a little, until the whole structure got to
resemble a cluster of cottages thrown together without the
least attention to order or regularity. There were a porch,
a front door, and a lawn, however ; the latter containing
half a dozen acres of a soil as black as one's hat, and
nourishing eight or ten elms that were scattered about as
if their seeds had been sown broadcast. In addition to the
trees and a suitable garniture of shrubbery, this lawn was
coated with a sward that, in the proper seasons, rivalled all
I have read or imagined of the emerald and shorn slopes of
the Swiss valleys.

Clawbonny, while it had all the appearance of being the
residence of an affluent agriculturist, had none of the pretension of these later times. The house had an air of substantial comfort without, an appearance that its interior in
no manner contradicted. The ceilings were low, it is true,
nor were the rooms particularly large ; but the latter were
warm in winter, cool in summer, and tidy, neat, and respectable all the year round. Both the parlors had carpets,
as had the passages and all the better bedrooms ; and there
were an old-fashioned chintz settee, well stuffed and
cushioned, and curtains in the " big parlor," as we called

the best apartment—the pretending name of drawing-room
not having reached our valley as far back as the year 1796,
or that in which my recollections of the place, as it then
existed, are the most vivid and distinct.

We had orchards, meadows, and ploughed fields all
around us; while the barns, granaries, sties, and other
buildings of the farm, were of solid stone, like the dwelling,
and all in capital condition. In addition to the place, which
he inherited from my grandfather quite without any incum-
brance, well stocked and supplied with utensils of all sorts,
my father had managed to bring with him from sea some
fourteen or fifteen thousand dollars, which he carefully invested in mortgages in the county. He got twenty-seven
hundred pounds currency with my mother, similarly bestowed; and, two or three great landed proprietors and as
many retired merchants from York excepted, Captain Wallingford was generally supposed to be one of the stiffest
men in Ulster County. I do not know exactly how true
was this report; though I never saw anything but the
abundance of a better sort of American farm under the
paternal roof, and I know that the poor were never sent
away empty-handed. It is true that our wine was made of
currants; but it was delicious, and there was always a sufficient stock in the cellar to enable us to drink it three or
four years old. My father, however, had a small private
collection of his own, out of which he would occasionally
produce a bottle; and I remember to have heard Governor
George Clinton, afterward Vice President, who was an
Ulster County man, and who sometimes stopped at Clawbonny in passing, say that it was excellent East India
Madeira. As for clarets, burgundy, hock, and champagne,
they were wines then unknown in America, except on the
tables of some of the principal merchants, and here and
there on that of some travelled gentleman of an estate
larger than common. When I say that Governor George
Clinton used to stop occasionally and taste my father's
Madeira, I do not wish to boast of being classed with those
who then composed the gentry of the State. To this, in
that day, we could hardly aspire, though the substantial

hereditary property of my family gave us a local consideration that placed us a good deal above the station of ordinary
yeomen.   Had we lived in one of the large towns, our association would unquestionably have been with those who
are usually considered to be one or two degrees beneath the
highest class.   These distinctions were much more marked
immediately after the war of the Revolution than they are
to-day ; and they are more marked to-day, even, than all
but the most lucky or the most meritorious, whichever fortune dignifies, are willing to allow.

The courtship between my parents occurred while my
father was at home to be cured of the wounds he had received in the engagement between the Trumbull and the
Watt.   I have always supposed this was the moving cause
why my mother fancied that the grim-looking scar on the
left side of my father's face was so particularly becoming.
The battle was fought in June, 1780, and my parents were
married in the autumn of the same year.   My father did
not go to sea again until after my birth, which took place
the very day that Cornwallis capitulated at Yorktown.
These combined events set the young sailor in motion, for
he felt he had a family to provide for, and he wished to
make one more mark on the enemy in return for the
beauty-spot his wife so glorified in.   He accordingly got a
commission in a privateer, made two or three fortunate
cruises, and was able at the peace to purchase a prize-brig,
which he sailed as master and owner until the year 1790,
when he was recalled to the paternal roof by the death of
my grandfather.   Being an only son, the captain, as my
father was uniformly called, inherited the land, stock,
utensils, and crops, as already mentioned ; while the six
thousand pounds currency that were " at use," went to my
two aunts, who were thought to be well married to men in
their own class of life, in adjacent counties.

My father never went to sea after he inherited Clawbonny.
From that time down to the day of his death, he remained
on his farm, with the exception of a single winter passed in
Albany as one of the representatives of the county.   In his
day it was a credit to a man to represent a county, and to

hold office under the State ; though the abuse of the elective
principle, not to say of the appointing power, has since
brought about so great a change. Then a member of Congress was *somebody ;* now he is only—a member of Congress.

We were but two surviving children, three of the family
dying infants, leaving only my sister Grace and myself to
console our mother in her widowhood. The dire accident
which placed her in this, the saddest of all conditions for a
woman who had been a happy wife, occurred in the year
1794, when I was in my thirteenth year, and Grace was
turned of eleven. It may be well to relate the particulars.

There was a mill, just where the stream that runs through
our valley tumbles down to a level below that on which the
farm lies, and empties itself into a small tributary of the
Hudson. This mill was on our property, and was a source
of great convenience and of some profit to my father. There
he ground all the grain that was consumed for domestic
purposes for several miles around ; and the tolls enabled
him to fatten his porkers and beeves, in a way to give both
a sort of established character. In a word, the mill was the
concentrating point for all the products of the farm, there
being a little landing on the margin of the creek that put
up from the Hudson, whence a sloop sailed weekly for town.
My father passed half his time about the mill and landing,
superintending his workmen, and particularly giving directions about the fitting of the sloop, which was his property
also, and about the gear of the mill. He was clever, certainly, and had made several useful suggestions to the millwright who occasionally came to examine and repair the
works ; but he was by no means so accurate a mechanic as
he fancied himself to be. He had invented some new mode
of arresting the movement, and of setting the machinery
in motion when necessary ; what it was, I never knew, for
it was not named at Clawbonny after the fatal accident occurred. One day, however, in order to convince the millwright of the excellence of this improvement, my father
caused the machinery to be stopped, and then placed his
own weight upon the large wheel, in order to manifest the
sense he felt in the security of his invention. He was in

the very act of laughing exultingly at the manner in which the millwright shook his head at the risk he ran, when the arresting power lost its control of the machinery, the heavy head of water burst into the buckets, and the wheel whirled round, carrying my unfortunate father with it. I was an eye-witness of the whole, and saw the face of my parent, as the wheel turned it from me, still expanded in mirth. There was but one revolution made, when the wright succeeded in stopping the works. This brought the great wheel back nearly to its original position, and I fairly shouted with hysterical delight when I saw my father standing in his tracks, as it might be seemingly unhurt. Unhurt he would have been, though he must have passed a fearful keel-hauling, but for one circumstance. He had held on to the wheel with the tenacity of a seaman, since letting go his hold would have thrown him down a cliff of near a hundred feet in depth, and he actually passed between the wheel and the planking beneath it unharmed, although there was only an inch or two to spare ; but in rising from this fearful strait, his head had been driven between a projecting beam and one of the buckets, in a way to crush one temple in upon the brain. So swift and sudden had been the whole thing, that, on turning the wheel, his lifeless body was still inclining on its periphery, retained erect, I believe, in consequence of some part of his coat getting attached to the head of a nail. This was the first serious sorrow of my life. I had always regarded my father as one of the fixtures of the world ; as a part of the great system of the universe ; and had never contemplated his death as a possible thing. That another revolution might occur, and carry the country back under the dominion of the British crown, would have seemed to me far more possible than that my father could die. Bitter truth now convinced me of the fallacy of such notions.

It was months and months before I ceased to dream of this frightful scene. At my age, all the feelings were fresh and plastic, and grief took strong hold of my heart. Grace and I used to look at each other without speaking, long after the event, the tears starting to my eyes, and rolling down her cheeks, our emotions being the only communications between us, but communications that no uttered words could have made so plain. Even now, I allude to my mother's anguish with trembling. She was sent for to the house of the miller, where the body lay, and arrived unapprised of the extent of the evil. Never can I—never shall I forget the outbreakings of her sorrow, when she learned the whole of the dreadful truth. She was in fainting fits for hours, one succeeding another, and then her grief found tongue. There was no term of endearment that the heart of woman could dictate to her speech, that was not lavished on the lifeless clay. She called the dead "her Miles," "her beloved Miles," "her husband," "her own darling husband," and by such other endearing epithets. Once she seemed as if resolute to arouse the sleeper from his endless trance, and she said, solemnly, "Father—dear, dearest father!" appealing as it might be to the parent of her children, the tenderest and most comprehensive of all woman's terms of endearment—"Father, dear, dearest father! open your eyes and look upon your babes—your precious girl, and noble boy! Do not thus shut out their sight forever!"

But it was in vain. There lay the lifeless corpse, as insensible as if the spirit of God had never had a dwelling within it. The principal injury had been received on that much-prized scar; and again and again did my poor mother kiss both, as if her caresses might yet restore her husband to life. All would not do. The same evening, the body was carried to the dwelling, and three days later it was laid in the churchyard, by the side of three generations of forefathers, at a distance of only a mile from Clawbonny. That funeral service, too, made a deep impression on my memory. We had some Church of England people in the valley; and old Miles Wallingford, the first of the name, a substantial English franklin, had been influenced in his choice of a purchase by the fact that one of Queen Anne's churches stood so near the farm. To that little church, a tiny edifice of stone, with a high, pointed roof, without steeple, bell, or vestry-room, had three generations of us been taken to be christened, and three, including my father, had been taken to be buried. Excellent, kind-hearted, just-

minded Mr. Hardinge read the funeral service over the man
whom his own father had, in the same humble edifice,
christened. Our neighborhood has much altered of late
years ; but, then, few higher than mere laborers dwelt among
us, who had not some sort of hereditary claim to be beloved.
So it was with our clergyman, whose father had been his pre-
decessor, having actually married my grandparents. The
son had united my father and mother, and now he was
called on to officiate at the funeral obsequies of the first.
Grace and I sobbed as if our hearts would break, the whole
time we were in the church ; and my poor, sensitive, nervous little sister actually shrieked as she heard the sound of
the first clod that fell upon the coffin. Our mother was
spared that trying scene, finding it impossible to support it.
She remained at home, on her knees, most of the day on
which the funeral occurred.

Time soothed our sorrows, though my mother, a woman
of more than common sensibility, or, it were better to say,
of uncommon affections, never entirely recovered from the
effects of her irreparable loss. She had loved too well, too
devotedly, too engrossingly, ever to think of a second
marriage, and lived only to care for the interests of Miles
Wallingford's children. I firmly believe we were more
beloved because we stood in this relation to the deceased,
than because we were her own natural offspring. Her
health became gradually undermined, and, three years after
the accident of the mill, Mr. Hardinge laid her at my father's
side. I was now sixteen, and can better describe what
passed during the last days of her existence, than what
took place at the death of her husband. Grace and I
were apprised of what was so likely to occur, quite a month
before the fatal moment arrived ; and we were not so much
overwhelmed with sudden grief as we had been on the first
great occasion of family sorrow, though we both felt our loss
keenly, and my sister, I think I may almost say, inextin-
guishably. Mr. Hardinge had us both brought to the bedside, to listen to the parting advice of our dying parent, and to
be impressed with a scene that is always healthful, if rightly
improved. ''You baptized these two dear children, good

Mr. Hardinge," she said, in a voice that was already en-
feebled by physical decay, "and you signed them with the
sign of the cross, in token of Christ's death for them; and I
now ask of your friendship and pastoral care to see that they
are not neglected at the most critical period of their lives—
that when impressions are the deepest, and yet the most
easily made. God will reward all your kindness to the
orphan children of your friends." The excellent divine, a
man who lived more for others than for himself, made the
required promises, and the soul of my mother took its flight
in peace.

Neither my sister nor myself grieved as deeply for the loss
of this last of our parents, as we did for that of the first.
We had both seen so many instances of her devout goodness, had been witnesses of so great a triumph of her faith,
as to feel an intimate, though silent persuasion that her
death was merely a passage to a better state of existence
—that it seemed selfish to regret. Still, we wept and
mourned, even while, in one sense, I think we rejoiced. She
was relieved from much bodily suffering, and I remember, when I went to take a last look at her beloved face,
that I gazed on its calm serenity with a feeling akin to
exultation, as I recollected that pain could no longer exercise dominion over her frame, and that her spirit was then
dwelling in bliss. Bitter regrets came later, it is true, and
these were fully shared—nay, more than shared—by Grace.

After the death of my father, I had never bethought me
of the manner in which he had disposed of his property. I
heard something said of his will, and gleaned a little, acci-
dentally, of the forms that had been gone through in proving the instrument, and of obtaining its probate. Shortly
after my mother's death, however, Mr. Hardinge had a
free conversation with both me and Grace on the subject,
when we learned, for the first time, the disposition that had
been made. My father had bequeathed to me the farm,
mill, landing, sloop, stock, utensils, crops, etc., etc., in full
property; subject, however, to my mother's use of the
whole until I attained my majority; after which I was to
give her complete possession of a comfortable wing of the

house, which had every convenience for a small family within itself, certain privileges in the fields, dairy, sties, orchards, meadows, granaries, etc., and to pay her three hundred pounds currency, per annum, in money. Grace had four thousand pounds that were "at use," and I had all the remainder of the personal property, which yielded about five hundred dollars a year. As the farm, sloop, mill, landing, etc., produced a net annual income of rather more than a thousand dollars, besides all that was consumed in housekeeping, I was very well off, in the way of temporal things, for one who had been trained in habits as simple as those which reigned at Clawbonny.

My father had left Mr. Hardinge the executor, and my mother an executrix of his will, with survivorship. He had also made the same provision as respected the guardians. Thus Grace and I became the wards of the clergyman alone on the death of our last remaining parent. This was grateful to us both, for we both truly loved this good man, and, what was more, we loved his children. Of these there were two of ages corresponding very nearly with our own; Rupert Hardinge being not quite a year older than I was myself, and Lucy, his sister, about six months younger than Grace. We were all four strongly attached to each other, and had been so from infancy, Mr. Hardinge having had charge of my education as soon as I was taken from a woman's school.

I cannot say, however, that Rupert Hardinge was ever a boy to give his father the delight that a studious, well-conducted, considerate, and industrious child has it so much in his power to yield to his parent. Of the two, I was much the best scholar, and had been pronounced by Mr. Hardinge fit to enter college, a twelvemonth before my mother died; though she declined sending me to Yale, the institution selected by my father, until my school-fellow was similarly prepared, it having been her intention to give the clergyman's son a thorough education, in further-ance of his father's views of bringing him up to the church. This delay, so well and kindly meant, had the effect of changing the whole course of my subsequent life.

Cooper's manuscript of the first page of chapter xxix of *Afloat and Ashore*, showing the fine hand in which he wrote his novels. (*Courtesy of the Berg Collection, New York Public Library*)

My father, it seems, wished to make a lawyer of me, with the natural desire of seeing me advanced to some honorable position in the State. But I was adverse to anything like serious mental labor, and was greatly delighted when my mother determined to keep me out of college a twelvemonth, in order that my friend Rupert might be my classmate. It is true I learned quick, and was fond of reading; but the first I could not very well help, while the reading I liked was that which amused, rather than that which instructed me. As for Rupert, though not absolutely dull, but, on the other hand, absolutely clever in certain things, he disliked mental labor even more than myself, while he liked self-restraint of any sort far less. His father was sincerely pious, and regarded his sacred office with too much reverence to think of bringing up a " cosset-priest," though he prayed and hoped that his son's inclinations, under the guidance of Providence, would take that direction. He seldom spoke of the subject himself, but I ascertained his wishes through my confidential dialogues with his children. Lucy seemed delighted with the idea, looking forward to the time when her brother would officiate in the same desk where her father and grandfather had now conducted the worship of God for more than half a century; a period of time that to us young people seemed to lead us back to the dark ages of the country. And all this the dear girl wished for her brother, in connection with his spiritual rather than his temporal interests, inasmuch as the living was worth only a badly-paid salary of one hundred and fifty pounds currency per annum, together with a small but comfortable rectory, and a glebe of five-and-twenty acres of very tolerable land, which it was thought no sin, in that day, for the clergyman to work by means of two male slaves, whom, with as many females, he had inherited as part of the chattels of his mother.

I had a dozen slaves, also; negroes who, as a race, had been in the family almost as long as Clawbonny. About half of these blacks were singularly laborious and useful, namely, four males and three of the females; but several of the remainder were enjoying *otium*, and not altogethei without *dignitate*, as heir-looms to be fed, clothed, and lodged, for the good or evil they had done. There were some small-fry in our kitchens, too, that used to roll about on the grass, and munch fruit in the summer, *ad libitum;* and stand so close in the chimney-corners in cold weather, that I have often fancied they must have been, as a legal wit of New York once pronounced certain eastern coal mines to be, incombustible. These negroes all went by the patronymic of Clawbonny, there being among them Hector Clawbonny, Venus Clawbonny, Cæsar Clawbonny, Rose Clawbonny,—who was as black as a crow,—Romeo Clawbonny, and Julietta, commonly called Julee, Clawbonny; who were with Pharaoh, Potiphar, Samson, and Nebuchadnezzar, all Clawbonnys in the last resort. Neb, as the namesake of the herbivorous King of Babylon was called, was about my own age, and had been a sort of humble playfellow from infancy; and even now, when it was thought proper to set him about the more serious toil which was to mark his humble career, I often interfered to call him away to be my companion with the rod, the fowling-piece, or in the boat, of which we had one that frequently descended the creek and navigated the Hudson for miles at a time, under my command. The lad, by such means, and through an off-hand friendliness of manner that I rather think was characteristic of my habits at that day, got to love me as a brother or comrade. It is not easy to describe the affection of an attached slave, which has blended with it the pride of a partisan, the solicitude of a parent, and the blindness of a lover. I do think Neb had more gratification in believing himself particularly belonging to Master Miles, than I ever had in any quality or thing I could call my own. Neb, moreover, liked a vagrant life, and greatly encouraged Rupert and myself in idleness, and a desultory manner of misspending hours that could never be recalled. The first time I ever played truant was under the patronage of Neb, who decoyed me away from my books to go nutting on the mountain, stoutly maintaining that chestnuts were just as good as the spelling-book, or any primer that could be bought in York,

I have forgotten to mention that the death of my mother, which occurred in the autumn, brought about an immediate change in the condition of our domestic economy. Grace was too young, being only fourteen, to preside over such a household, and I could be of little use either in the way of directing or advising. Mr. Hardinge, who had received a letter to that effect from the dying saint, that was only put into his hand the day after the funeral, with a view to give her request the greater weight, rented the rectory, and came to Clawbonny to live, bringing with him both his children. My mother knew that his presence would be of the greatest service to the orphans she left behind her ; while the money saved from his own household expenses might enable this single-minded minister of the altar to lay by a hundred or two for Lucy, who, at his demise, might otherwise be left without a penny, as it was then said, cents not having yet come much into fashion.

This removal gave Grace and me much pleasure, for she was as fond of Lucy as I was of Rupert, and, to tell the truth, so was I, too. Four happier young people were not to be found in the State than we thus became, each and all of us finding in the arrangement exactly the association which was most agreeable to our feelings. Previously, we only saw each other every day ; now, we saw each other all day. At night we separated at an early hour, it is true, each having his or her room ; but it was to meet at a still earlier hour the next morning, and to resume our amusements in company. From study, all of us were relieved for a month or two, and we wandered through the fields, nutted, gathered fruit, or saw others gather it as well as the crops, taking as much exercise as possible in the open air, equally for the good of our bodies and the lightening of our spirits.

I do not think vanity, nor any feeling connected with self-love, misleads me, when I say it would have been difficult to find four young people more likely to attract the attention of a passer-by, than we four were, in the fall of 1797. As for Rupert Hardinge, he resembled his mother, and was singularly handsome in face, as well as graceful in movements. He had a native gentility of air, of which he knew how to make the most, and a readiness of tongue and a flow of spirits that rendered him an agreeable, if not a very instructive companion. I was not ill-looking myself, though far from possessing the striking countenance of my young associate. In manliness, strength, and activity, however, I had essentially the advantage over him, few youths of my age surpassing me in masculine qualities of this nature, after I had passed my twelfth year. My hair was a dark auburn, and it was the only thing about my face, perhaps, that would cause a stranger to notice it; but this hung about my temples and down my neck in rich ringlets, until frequent applications of the scissors brought it into something like subjection. It never lost its beauty entirely, and though now white as snow, it is still admired. But Grace was the one of the party whose personal appearance would be most likely to attract attention. Her face beamed with sensibility and feeling, being one of those countenances on which nature sometimes delights to impress the mingled radiance, sweetness, truth, and sentiment, that men ascribe to angels. Her hair was lighter than mine; her eyes of a heavenly blue, all softness and tenderness; her cheeks just of the tint of the palest of the colored roses; and her smile so full of gentleness and feeling, that, again and again, it has controlled my ruder and more violent emotions, when they were fast getting the mastery. In form, some persons might have thought Grace, in a slight degree, too fragile, though her limbs would have been delicate models for the study of a sculptor.

Lucy, too, had certainly great perfection, particularly in figure; though in the crowd of beauty that has been so profusely lavished on the youthful in this country, she would not have been at all remarked in a large assembly of young American girls. Her face was pleasing, nevertheless; and there was a piquant contrast between the raven blackness of her hair, the deep blue of her eyes, and the dazzling whiteness of her skin. Her color, too, was high, and changeful with her emotions. As for teeth, she had a set that one might have travelled weeks to meet with their equals; and, though she seemed totally unconscious of the advantage, she had a natural manner of showing them, that would have made a far less interesting face altogether agreeable. Her voice and laugh, too, when happy and free from care, were joyousness itself.

It would be saying too much, perhaps, to assert that any human being was ever totally indifferent to his or her personal appearance. Still, I do not think either of our party, Rupert alone excepted, ever thought on the subject, unless as it related to others, down to the period of which I am now writing. I knew, and saw, and felt that my sister was far more beautiful than any of the young girls of her age and condition that I had seen in her society; and I had pleasure and pride in the fact. I knew that I resembled her in some respects, but I was never coxcomb enough to imagine I had half her good looks, even allowing for difference of sex. My own conceit, so far as I then had any—plenty of it came, a year or two later—but my own conceit, in 1797, rather ran in the direction of my athletic properties—physical force, which was unusually great for sixteen—and stature. As for Rupert, I would not have exchanged these manly qualities for twenty times his good looks, and a thought of envy never crossed my mind on the subject. I fancied it might be well enough for a parson to be a little delicate, and a good deal handsome; for one who intended to knock about the world as I had it already in contemplation to do, strength, health, vigor, courage, and activity were much more to be desired than beauty.

Lucy I never thought of as handsome at all. I saw she was pleasing; fancied she was even more so to me than to any one else; and I never looked upon her sunny, cheerful, and yet perfectly feminine face, without a feeling of serenity and happiness. As for her honest eyes, they invariably met my own with an open frankness that said, as plainly as eyes could say anything, that there was nothing to be concealed.

CHAPTER II.

"Cease to persuade, my loving Proteus;
Home-keeping youth have ever homely wits;
I rather would entreat thy company
To see the wonders of the world abroad."
Two Gentlemen of—Clawbonny.

DURING the year that succeeded after I was prepared for Yale, Mr. Hardinge had pursued a very judicious course with my education. Instead of pushing me into books that were to be read in the regular course of that institution, with the idea of lightening my future labors, which would only have been providing excuses for future idleness, we went back to the elementary works, until even he was satisfied that nothing more remained to be done in that direction. I had my two grammars literally by heart, notes and all. Then we revised as thoroughly as possible, reading everything anew, and leaving no passage unexplained. I learned to scan, too, a fact that was sufficient to make a reputation for a scholar, in America, half a century since.[1] After this we turned our attention to mathematics, a science Mr. Hardinge rightly enough thought there was no danger of my acquiring too thoroughly. We mastered arithmetic, of which I had a good deal of previous knowl-

[1] The writer's master taught him to scan Virgil in 1801. This gentleman was a graduate of Oxford. In 1803, the class to which the writer then belonged in Yale was the first that ever attempted to scan in that institution. The quantities were in sad discredit in this country years after this, though Columbia and Harvard were a little in advance of Yale. All that was ever done in the last college, during the writer's time, was to scan the ordinary hexameter of Homer and Virgil.

edge, in a few weeks, and then I went through trigonometry, with some of the more useful problems in geometry. This was the point at which I had arrived when my mother's death occurred.

As for myself, I frankly admit a strong disinclination to be learned. The law I might be forced to study, but practising it was a thing my mind had long been made up never to do. There was a small vein of obstinacy in my disposition that would have been very likely to carry me through in such a determination, even had my mother lived, though deference to her wishes would certainly have carried me as far as the license. Even now she was no more, I was anxious to ascertain whether she had left any directions or requests on the subject, either of which would have been laws to me. I talked with Rupert on this matter, and was a little shocked with the levity with which he treated it. "What difference can it make to your parents, *now*," he said, with an emphasis that grated on my nerves, "whether you become a lawyer, or a merchant, or a doctor, or stay here on your farm, and be a farmer, like your father?"

"My father had been a sailor," I answered, quick as lightning.

"True; and a noble, manly, gentleman-like calling it is! I never see a sailor that I do not envy him his advantages. Why, Miles, neither of us has ever been in town even, while your mother's boatmen, or your own as they are now, go there regularly once a week. I would give the world to be a sailor."

"You, Rupert! Why, you know that your father intends, or rather wishes, that you should become a clergyman."

"A pretty appearance a young man of my figure would make in the pulpit, Miles, or wearing a surplice. No, no; there have been two Hardinges in the church in this century, and I have a fancy also to the sea. I suppose you know that my great-grandfather was a captain in the navy, and he brought his son up a parson; now turn about is fair play, and the parson ought to give a son back to a

2

man-of-war. I've been reading the lives of naval men, and it's surprising how many clergymen's sons, in England, go into the navy, and how many sailors' sons get to be priests.''

''But there is no navy in this country now—not even a single ship-of-war, I believe.''

'' That is the worst of it. Congress *did* pass a law two or three years since, to build some frigates, but they have never been launched. Now Washington has gone out of office I suppose we shall never have anything good in the country.''

I revered the name of Washington, in common with the whole country, but I did not see the *sequitur*. Rupert, however, cared little for logical inferences, usually asserting such things as he wished, and wishing such as he asserted. After a short pause, he continued the discourse.

''You are now substantially your own master,'' he said, ''and can do as you please. Should you go to sea and not like it, you have only to come back to this place, where you will be just as much the master as if you had remained here superintending cattle, cutting hay, and fattening pork, the whole time.''

''I am not my own master, Rupert, any more than you are, yourself. I am your father's ward, and must so remain for more than five years to come. I am just as much under his control as you, yourself.''

Rupert laughed at this, and tried to persuade me it would be a good thing to relieve his worthy father of all responsibility in the affair, if I had seriously determined never to go to Yale, or to be a lawyer, by going off to sea clandestinely, and returning when I was ready. If I ever was to make a sailor, no time was to be lost; for all with whom he had conversed assured him the period of life when such things were best learned, was between sixteen and twenty. This I thought probable enough, and I parted from my friend with a promise of conversing further with him on the subject at an early opportunity.

I am almost ashamed to confess that Rupert's artful sophism nearly blinded my eyes to the true distinction be-

tween right and wrong. If Mr. Hardinge really felt himself
bound by my father's wishes to educate me for the bar, and
my own repugnance to the profession was unconquerable,
why should I not relieve him from the responsibility at once
by assuming the right to judge for myself, and act accordingly? So far as Mr. Hardinge was concerned, I had little
difficulty in coming to a conclusion, though the profound
deference I still felt for my father's wishes, and more especially for those of my sainted mother, had a hold on my
heart, and an influence on my conduct, that was not so
easily disposed of. I determined to have a frank conversation with Mr. Hardinge, therefore, in order to ascertain how
far either of my parents had expressed anything that might
be considered obligatory on me. My plan went as far as to
reveal my own desire to be a sailor, and to see the world,
but not to let it be known that I might go off without his
knowledge, as this would not be so absolutely relieving the
excellent divine " from all responsibility in the premises,"
as was contemplated in the scheme of his own son.

An opportunity soon occurred, when I broached the subject by asking Mr. Hardinge whether my father, in his
will, had ordered that I should be sent to Yale, and there
be educated for the bar. He had done nothing of the sort.
Had he left any particular request, writing, or message on
the subject, at all? Not that Mr. Hardinge knew. It is
true, the last had heard his friend, once or twice, make some
general remark which would lead one to suppose that Captain Wallingford had some vague expectations I might go
to the bar, but nothing further. My mind felt vastly relieved
by these admissions, for I knew my mother's tenderness too
well to anticipate that she would dream of absolutely dictat-
ing in a matter that was so clearly connected with my own
happiness and tastes. When questioned on this last point,
Mr. Hardinge did not hesitate to say that my mother had
conversed with him several times concerning her views, as
related to my career in life. She wished me to go to Yale,
and then to read law, even though I did not practice. As
soon as this much was said, the conscientious servant of God
paused, to note the effect on me. Reading disappointment

in my countenance, I presume, he immediately added, "But your mother, Miles, laid no restraint on you, for she knew it was *you* who was to follow the career, and not herself. 'I should as soon think of commanding whom he was to marry, as to think of forcing a profession on him,' she added. ' He is the one who is to decide this, and he only. We may try to guide and influence him, but not go beyond this. I leave you, dear sir, to do all you think best in this matter, certain that your own wisdom will be aided by the providence of a kind Master.' "

I now plainly told Mr. Hardinge my desire to see the world, and to be a sailor. The divine was astounded at this declaration, and I saw that he was grieved. I believe some religious objections were connected with his reluctance to consent to my following the sea, as a calling. At any rate, it was easy to discover that these objections were lasting and profound. In that day few Americans travelled, by way of an accomplishment, at all ; and those few belonged to a class in society so much superior to mine, as to render it absurd to think of sending me abroad with similar views. Nor would my fortune justify such an expenditure. I was well enough off to be a comfortable and free housekeeper, and as independent as a king on my own farm ; living in abundance, nay, in superfluity, so far as all the ordinary wants were concerned ; but men hesitated a little about setting up for gentlemen at large, in the year 1797. The country was fast getting rich, it is true, under the advantage of its neutral position ; but it had not yet been long enough emancipated from its embarrassments to think of playing the nabob on eight hundred pounds currency a year. The interview terminated with a strong exhortation from my guardian not to think of abandoning my books for any project as visionary and useless as the hope of seeing the world in the character of a common sailor.

I related all this to Rupert, who, I now perceived for the first time, did not hesitate to laugh at some of his father's notions, as puritanical and exaggerated. He maintained that every one was the best judge of what he liked, and that the sea had produced quite as fair a proportion of saints as the land. He was not certain, considering the great difference there was in numbers, that more good men might not be traced in connection with the ocean, than in connection with any other pursuit.

"Take the lawyers, now, for instance, Miles," he said, "and what can you make out of them, in the way of religion, I should like to know? They hire their consciences out at so much *per diem*, and talk and reason just as zealously for the wrong as they do for the right."

"By George, that is true enough, Rupert. There is old David Dockett, I remember to have heard Mr. Hardinge say, always did double duty for his fee, usually acting as witness as well as advocate. They tell me he will talk by the hour of facts that he and his clients get up between them, and look the whole time as if he believed all he said to be true."

Rupert laughed at this sally, and pushed the advantage it gave him by giving several other examples to prove how much his father was mistaken by supposing that a man was to save his soul from perdition simply by getting admitted to the bar. After discussing the matter a little longer, to my astonishment, Rupert came out with a plain proposal that he and I should elope, go to New York, and ship as foremost-lads in some Indiaman, of which there were then many sailing, at the proper season, from that port. I did not dislike the idea, so far as I was myself concerned; but the thought of accompanying Rupert in such an adventure startled me. I knew I was sufficiently secure of the future to be able to risk a little at the present moment; but such was not the case with my friend. If I made a false step at so early an age, I had only to return to Clawbonny, where I was certain to find competence and a home; but, with Rupert, it was very different. Of the moral hazards I ran, I then knew nothing, and, of course, they gave me no concern. Like all inexperienced persons, I supposed myself too strong in virtue to be in any danger of contamination; and this portion of the adventure was regarded with the self-complacency with which the untried are apt to regard their own powers of endurance. I thought myself morally invulnerable.

But Rupert might find it difficult to retrace any serious error made at his time of life. This consideration would have put an end to the scheme, so far as my companion was concerned, had not the thought suggested itself that I should always have it in my own power to aid my friend. Letting something of this sort escape me, Rupert was not slow in enlarging on it, though this was done with great tact and discretion. He proved that, by the time we both came of age he would be qualified to command a ship, and that, doubtless, I would naturally desire to invest some of my spare cash in a vessel. The accumulations of my estate alone would do this much, within the next five years, and then a career of wealth and prosperity would lie open before us both.

"It is a good thing, Miles, no doubt," continued this tempting sophist, "to have money at use, and a large farm, and a mill, and such things; but many a ship nets more money in a single voyage than your whole estate would sell for. Those that begin with nothing, too, they tell me, are the most apt to succeed; and if we go off with our clothes only, we shall begin with nothing, too. Success may be said to be certain. I like the notion of beginning with nothing, it is so American!"

It is, in truth, rather a besetting weakness of America to suppose that men who have never had any means for qualifying themselves for particular pursuits, are the most likely to succeed in them; and especially to fancy that those who "begin poor" are in a much better way for acquiring wealth than they who commence with some means; and I was disposed to lean to this latter doctrine myself, though I confess I cannot recall an instance in which any person of my acquaintance has given away his capital, however large and embarrassing it may have been, in order to start fair with his poorer competitors. Nevertheless, there was something taking, to my imagination, in the notion of being the fabricator of my own fortune. In that day, it was easy to enumerate every dwelling on the banks of the Hudson that aspired to be called a seat, and I had often heard them named by those who were familiar with the river. I liked the thought of erecting a house on the Claw-bonny property that might aspire to equal claims, and to be the owner of a seat; though only after I had acquired the means myself, to carry out such a project. At present, I owned only a house; my ambition was to own a seat.

In a word, Rupert and I canvassed this matter in every possible way for a month, now leaning to one scheme, and now to another, until I determined to lay the whole affair before the two girls, under a solemn pledge of secrecy. As we passed hours in company daily, opportunities were not wanting to effect this purpose. I thought my friend was a little shy on this project; but I had so much affection for Grace, and so much confidence in Lucy's sound judgment, that I was not to be turned aside from the completion of my purpose. It is now more than forty years since the interview took place in which this confidence was bestowed; but every minute occurrence connected with it is as fresh in my mind as if the whole had taken place only yesterday.

We were all four of us seated on a rude bench that my mother had caused to be placed under the shade of an enormous oak that stood on the most picturesque spot, perhaps, on the whole farm, and which commanded a distant view of one of the loveliest reaches of the Hudson. Our side of the river, in general, does not possess as fine views as the eastern, for the reason that all our own broken, and in some instances magnificent background of mountains, fills up the landscape for our neighbors, while we are obliged to receive the picture as it is set in a humbler frame; but there are exquisite bits to be found on the western bank, and this was one of the very best of them. The water was as placid as molten silver, and the sails of every vessel in sight were hanging in listless idleness from their several spars, representing commerce asleep. Grace had a deep feeling for natural scenery, and she had a better mode of expressing her thoughts, on such occasions, than is usual with girls of fourteen. She first drew our attention to the view by one of her strong, eloquent bursts of eulogium; and Lucy met the remark with a truthful, simple answer that showed abundant sympathy with the sentiment, though

with less of exaggeration of manner and feeling, perhaps
I seized the moment as favorable for my purpose, and
spoke out.

"If you admire a vessel so much, Grace," I said, "you
will probably be glad to hear that I think of becoming a
sailor."

A silence of near two minutes succeeded, during which
time I affected to be gazing at the distant sloops, and then I
ventured to steal a glance at my companions. I found
Grace's mild eyes earnestly riveted on my face ; and, turning from their anxious expression with a little uneasiness, I
encountered those of Lucy looking at me as intently as if
she doubted whether her ears had not deceived her.

"A sailor, Miles !" my sister now slowly repeated ; "I
thought it settled you were to study law."

"As far from that as we are from England ; I 've fully
made up my mind to see the world if I can ; and Rupert,
here—"

"What of Rupert, here?" Grace asked, a sudden change
again coming over her sweet countenance, though I was
altogether too inexperienced to understand its meaning.
"He is certainly to be a clergyman—his dear father's
assistant, and, a long, long, very long time hence, his successor."

I could see that Rupert was whistling on a low key, and
affecting to look cool ; but my sister's solemn, earnest,
astonished manner had more effect on us both, I believe,
than either would have been willing to own.

"Come, girls," I said at length, putting the best face on
the matter, " there is no use in keeping secrets from you—
but remember that what I am about to tell you is a secret,
and on no account is to be betrayed."

"To no one but Mr. Hardinge," answered Grace. "If
you intend to be a sailor, he ought to know it."

"That comes of looking at our duties superficially,"—I
had caught this phrase from my friend,—"and not dis-
tinguishing properly between their shadows and their substance."

"Duties superficially ! I do not understand you, Miles.

Certainly Mr. Hardinge ought to be told what profession
you mean to follow. Remember, brother, he now fills the
place of a parent to you."

"He is not more my parent than Rupert's; I fancy you
will admit that much!"

"Rupert, again! What has Rupert to do with your
going to sea?"

"Promise me, then, to keep my secret, and you shall
know all; both you and Lucy must give me your words.
I know you will not break them, when once given."

"Promise him, Grace," said Lucy, in a low tone, and a
voice that, even at that age, I could perceive was tremulous.
"If we promise, we shall learn everything, and then may
have some effect on these headstrong boys by our advice."

"Boys! You cannot mean, Lucy, that Rupert is not to
be a clergyman—your father's assistant; that Rupert means
to be a sailor, too?"

"One never knows what boys will do. Let us promise
them, dear; then we can better judge."

"I do promise you, Miles," said my sister, in a voice so
solemn as almost to frighten me.

"And I, Miles," added Lucy; but it was so low, I had
to lean forward to catch the syllables.

"This is honest and right,"—it was honest, perhaps, but
very wrong,—"and it convinces me that you are both reasonable, and will be of use to us. Rupert and I have both
made up our minds, and intend to be sailors."

Exclamations followed from both girls, and another long
silence succeeded.

"As for the law, hang all law!" I continued, hemming,
and determined to speak like a man. "I never heard of a
Wallingford who was a lawyer."

"But you have both heard of Hardinges who were clergymen," said Grace, endeavoring to smile, though the expression of her countenance was so painful that even now
I dislike to recall it.

"And sailors, too," put in Rupert, a little more stoutly
than I thought possible. "My father's grandfather was an
officer in the navy."

"And my father was a sailor himself—in the navy, too."

"But there is no navy in this country now, Miles," returned Lucy, in an expostulating tone.

"What of that? There are plenty of ships. The ocean is just as big, and the world just as wide, as if we had a navy to cover the first. I see no great objection on that account—do you, Ru?"

"Certainly not. What we want is, to go to sea, and that can be done in an Indiaman, as well as in a man-of-war."

"Yes," said I, stretching myself with a little importance. "I fancy an Indiaman, a vessel that goes all the way to Calcutta, round the Cape of Good Hope, in the track of Vasquez de Gama, is n't exactly an Albany sloop."

"Who is Vasquez de Gama?" demanded Lucy, with so much quickness as to surprise me.

"Why, a noble Portuguese, who discovered the Cape of Good Hope, and first sailed round it, and then went to the Indies. You see, girls, even nobles are sailors, and why should not Rupert and I be sailors?"

"It is not that, Miles," my sister answered; "every honest calling is respectable. Have you and Rupert spoken to Mr. Hardinge on this subject?"

"Not exactly—not spoken—hinted only—that is, blindly —not so as to be understood, perhaps."

"He will never consent, boys!" and this was uttered with something very like an air of triumph.

"We have no intention of asking it of him, Grace. Rupert and I intend to be off next week, without saying a word to Mr. Hardinge on the subject."

Another long, eloquent silence succeeded, during which I saw Lucy bury her face in her apron, while the tears openly ran down my sister's cheek.

"You do not—cannot mean to do anything so cruel, Miles!" Grace at length said.

"It is exactly because it will not be cruel, that we intend to do it." Here I nudged Rupert with my elbow, as a hint that I wanted assistance; but he made no other reply than an answering nudge, which I interpreted into as much as if

he had said in terms, "You've got into the scrape in your own way, and you may get out of it in the same manner."
"Yes," I continued, finding succor hopeless, "yes, that's just it."

"What is just it, Miles? You speak in a way to show that you are not satisfied with yourself—neither you nor Rupert is satisfied with himself, if the truth were known."

"I not satisfied with myself! Rupert not satisfied with himself! You were never more mistaken in your life, Grace. If there ever were two boys in New York State that were well satisfied with themselves, they are just Rupert and I."

Here Lucy raised her face from her apron and burst into a laugh, the tears filling her eyes all the while.

"Believe them, dear Grace," she said. "They are precisely two self-satisfied, silly fellows, that have got some ridiculous notions in their heads, and then begin to talk about 'superficial views of duties,' and all such nonsense. My father will set it all right, and the boys will have had their talk."

"Not so fast, Miss Lucy, if you please. Your father will not know a syllable of the matter until you tell him all about it, after we are gone. We intend to 'relieve him from all responsibility in the premises.'"

This last sounded very profound, and a little magnificent, to my imagination; and I looked at the girls to note the effect. Grace was weeping, and weeping only; but Lucy looked saucy and mocking, even while the tears bedewed her smiling face, as rain sometimes falls while the sun is shining.

"Yes," I repeated, with emphasis, "'of all responsibility in the premises.' I hope that is plain English and good English, although I know that Mr. Hardinge has been trying to make you both so simple in your language, that you turn up your noses at a profound sentiment, whenever you hear one."

In 1797 the grandiose had by no means made the deep invasion into the every-day language of the country, that it has since done. Anything of the sublime, or of the recondite school was a good deal more apt to provoke a smile, than it is to-day—the improvement proceeding, as I have understood through better judges than myself, from the great melioration of mind and manners that is to be traced to the speeches in Congress, and to the profundities of the newspapers. Rupert, however, frequently ornamented his ideas, and, I may truly say, everything ambitious that adorned my discourse was derived from his example. I almost thought Lucy impertinent for presuming to laugh at sentiments which came from such a source, and, by way of settling my own correctness of thought and terms, I made no bones of falling back on my great authority, by fairly pointing him out.

" I thought so ! " exclaimed Lucy, now laughing with all her heart, though a little hysterically ; " I thought so, for this is just like Rupert, who is always talking to me about ' assuming the responsibility,' and ' conclusions in the premises,' and all such nonsense. Leave the boys to my father, Grace, and he will ' assume the responsibility ' of ' concluding the premises,' and the whole of the foolish scheme along with it ! "

This would have provoked me, had not Grace manifested so much sisterly interest in my welfare that I was soon persuaded to tell her—that minx Lucy overhearing every syllable, though I had half a mind to tell her to go away—all about our project.

" You see," I continued, " if Mr. Hardinge knows any thing about our plan, people will say he ought to have stopped us. ' He a clergyman, and not able to keep two lads of sixteen or seventeen from running away and going to sea ! ' they will say, as if it were so easy to prevent two spirited youths from seeing the world. Whereas, if he knew nothing about it, nobody can blame him. That is what I call ' relieving him from the responsibility.' Now, we intend to be off next week, or as soon as the jackets and trousers that are making for us, under the pretense of being boat dresses, are finished. We mean to go down the river in the sailboat, taking Neb with us to bring the boat back. Now you know the whole story, there will be no occasion to leave a letter for Mr. Hardinge ; for, three hours after we have sailed, you can tell him everything. We shall be gone a year ; at the end of that time you may look for us both ; and glad enough shall we all be to see each other. Rupert and I will be young men then, though you call us boys now.''

This last picture a good deal consoled the girls. Rupert, too, who had unaccountably kept back, throwing the laboring-oar altogether on me, came to the rescue, and, with his subtle manner and oily tongue, began to make the wrong appear the right. I do not think he blinded his own sister in the least, but I fear he had too much influence over mine. Lucy, though all heart, was as much matter-of-fact as her brother was a sophist. He was ingenious in glozing over truths ; she, nearly unerring in detecting them. I never knew a greater contrast between two human beings, than there was between these two children of the same parent, in this particular. I have heard that the son took after the mother, in this respect, and that the daughter took after the father ; though Mrs. Hardinge died too early to have had any moral influence on the character of her children.

We came again and again to the discussion of our subject during the next two or three days. The girls endeavored earnestly to persuade us to ask Mr. Hardinge's permission for the step we were about to undertake ; but all in vain. We lads were so thoroughly determined to '' relieve the divine from all the responsibility in the premises,'' that they might as well have talked to stones. We knew these just-minded, sincere, upright girls would not betray us, and continued obdurate to the last. As we expected, as soon as convinced their importunities were useless, they seriously set about doing all they could to render us comfortable. They made us duck bags to hold our clothes, two each, and mended our linen, stockings, etc., and even helped to procure us some clothes more suited to the contemplated expedition than most of those we already possessed. Our '' long togs,'' indeed, we determined to leave behind us, retaining just one suit each, and that of the plainest quality. In the course of a week everything was ready, our bags well lined, being concealed in the storehouse at the landing. Of this building I could at any moment procure the key, my authority as heir-apparent being very considerable, already, on the farm.

As for Neb, he was directed to have the boat all ready for the succeeding Tuesday evening, it being the plan to sail the day after the Wallingford of Clawbonny (this was the name of the sloop) had gone on one of her regular trips, in order to escape pursuit. I had made all the calculations about the tide, and knew that the Wallingford would go out about nine in the morning, leaving us to follow before midnight. It was necessary to depart at night and when the wharf was clear, in order to avoid observation.

Tuesday was an uneasy, nervous, and sad day for us all, Mr. Hardinge excepted. As the last had not the smallest distrust, he continued calm, quiet, and cheerful as was his wont. Rupert had a conscience-stricken and furtive air about him, while the eyes of the two dear girls were scarcely a moment without tears. Grace seemed now the most composed of the two, and I have since suspected that she had had a private conversation with my ingenious friend, whose convincing powers were of a very extraordinary quality, when he set about their use in downright earnest. As for Lucy, she seemed to me to have been weeping the entire day.

At nine o'clock it was customary for the whole family to separate, after prayers. Most of us went to bed at that early hour, though Mr. Hardinge himself seldom sought his pillow until midnight. This habit compelled us to use a good deal of caution in getting out of the house, in which Rupert and myself succeeded, however, without discovery, just as the clock struck eleven. We had taken leave of the girls in a hasty manner, in a passage, shaking hands, and each of us kissing his own sister, as he affected to retire for the night. To own the truth, we were much gratified to find how reasonably Grace and Lucy behaved on the occasion, and not a little surprised, for we had expected a scene, particularly with the former.

We walked away from the house with heavy hearts, few leaving the paternal roof for the first time, to enter upon the chances of the world, without a deep sense of the dependence in which they have hitherto lived. We walked fast and silently, and reached the wharf in less than half an hour, a distance of near two miles. I was just on the point of speaking to Neb, whose figure I could see in the boat, when I caught a glimpse of two female forms within six feet of me. There were Grace and Lucy, in tears, both waiting our arrival, with a view to see us depart ! I confess I was shocked and concerned at seeing these two delicate girls so far from their home, at such an hour ; and my first impulse was to see them both safely back before I would enter the boat ; but to this neither would consent. All my entreaties were thrown away, and I was obliged to submit.

I know not exactly how it happened, but of the fact I am certain ; odd as it may seem, at a moment like that, when about to separate, instead of each youth's getting his own sister aside to make his last speeches, and say his last say to, each of us got his friend's sister aside. I do not mean that we were making love, or anything of the sort ; we were a little too young, perhaps, for that ; but we obeyed an impulse which, as Rupert would have said, " produced that result."

What passed between Grace and her companion, I do not know. As for Lucy and myself, it was all plain sailing and fair dealing. The excellent creature forced on me six gold pieces, which I knew had come to her as an heirloom from her mother, and which I had often heard her declare she never meant to use, unless in the last extremity. She knew I had but five dollars on earth, and that Rupert had not one ; and she offered me this gold. I told her Rupert had better take it ; no, I had better take it. I should use it more prudently than Rupert, and would use it for the good of both. " Besides, you are rich," she said, smiling through her tears, " and can repay me—I lend them to you ; to Rupert I should have to give them." I could not refuse the generous girl, and took the money, all half-joes, with a determination to repay them with interest. Then I folded her to my heart, and kissed her six or eight times with fervor, the first time I had done such a thing in two years, and tore myself away. I do not think Rupert embraced Grace, but I confess I do not know, although we were standing within three or four yards of each other, the whole time.

"Write, Miles—write, Rupert," said the sobbing girls, leaning forward from the wharf, as we shoved off. It was not so dark but we could see their dear forms for several minutes, or until a bend in the creek put a dark mass of earth between us and them.

Such was the manner of my departure from Clawbonny, in the month of September, 1797. I wanted a few days of being seventeen ; Rupert was six months older, and Neb was his senior, again, by near a twelvemonth. Everything was in the boat but our hearts. Mine, I can truly say, remained with the two beloved creatures we left on the wharf ; while Rupert's was betwixt and between, I fancy— seldom absolutely deserting the dear tenement in which it was encased by nature.

CHAPTER III.

"There's a youth in this city, it were a great pity
That he from our lasses should wander awa';
For he's bonny and braw, weel-favored witha',
And his hair has a natural buckle and a',
His coat is the hue of his bonnet so blue;
His pocket is white as the new-driven snaw;
His hose they are blae, and his shoon like the slae,
And his clean siller buckles they dazzle us a'."

BURNS.

W E had selected our time well, as respects the hour of departure. It was young ebb, and the boat floated swiftly down the creek, though the high banks of the latter would have prevented our feeling any wind, even if there were a breeze on the river. Our boat was of some size, sloop-rigged and half-decked; but Neb's vigorous arms made her move through the water with some rapidity, and, to own the truth, the lad sprang to his work like a true runaway negro. I was a skilful oarsman myself, having received many lessons from my father in early boyhood, and being in almost daily practice for seven months in the year. The excitement of the adventure, its romance, or what for a short time seemed to me to be romance, and the secret apprehension of being detected, which I believe accompanies every clandestine undertaking, soon set me in motion also. I took one of the oars, and, in less than twenty minutes the Grace and Lucy, for so the boat was called, emerged from between two high, steep banks, and entered on the broader bosom of the Hudson.

Neb gave a half-suppressed, negro-like cry of exultation,

3

as we shot out from our cover, and ascertained that there was a pleasant and fair breeze blowing. In three minutes we had the jib and mainsail on the boat, the helm was up, the sheet was eased off, and we were gliding down-stream at the rate of something like five miles an hour. I took the helm, almost as a matter of course ; Rupert being much too indolent to do anything unnecessarily, while Neb was far too humble to aspire to such an office while Master Miles was there, willing and ready. In that day, indeed, it was so much a matter of course for the skipper of a Hudson River craft to steer, that most of the people who lived on the banks of the stream imagined that Sir John Jervis, Lord Anson, and the other great English admirals of whom they had read and heard, usually amused themselves with that employment out on the ocean. I remember the hearty laugh in which my unfortunate father indulged, when Mr. Hardinge once asked him how he could manage to get any sleep on account of this very duty. But we were very green, up at Clawbonny, in most things that related to the world.

The hour that succeeded was one of the most painful I ever passed in my life. I recalled my father, his manly frankness, his liberal bequests in my favor, and his precepts of respect and obedience ; all of which, it now seemed to me, I had openly dishonored. Then came the image of my mother, with her love and sufferings, her prayers, and her mild, but earnest exhortations to be good. I thought I could see both these parents regarding me with sorrowful, though not with reproachful countenances. They appeared to be soliciting my return with a species of silent, but not the less eloquent warnings of the consequences. Grace and Lucy, and their sobs, and admonitions, and entreaties to abandon my scheme, and to write, and not to remain away long, and all that tender interest had induced two warm-hearted girls to utter at our parting, came fresh and vividly to my mind. The recollection proved nearly too much for me. Nor did I forget Mr. Hardinge, and the distress he would certainly feel, when he discovered that he had not only lost his ward, but his only son. Then Clawbonny itself, the house, the orchards,

the meadows, the garden, the mill, and all that belonged to
the farm, began to have a double value in my eyes, and
to serve as so many cords attached to my heart-strings, and
to remind me that the rover

"Drags at each remove a lengthening chain."

I marvelled at Rupert's tranquillity. I did not then understand his character as thoroughly as I subsequently got to
know it. All that he most prized was with him in the
boat, in fact, and this lessened his grief at parting from
less beloved objects. Where Rupert was, there was his
paradise. As for Neb, I do believe his head was over his
shoulder, for he affected to sit with his face down-stream,
so long as the hills that lap in the rear of Clawbonny
could be at all distinguished. This must have proceeded
from tradition, or instinct, or some latent negro quality;
for I do not think the fellow fancied he was running away.
He knew that his two young masters were; but he was
fully aware he was my property, and, no doubt, thought,
as long as he stayed in my company, he was in the line of
his legitimate duty. Then it was my plan that he should
return with the boat, and, perhaps, these backward glances
were no more than the shadows of coming events, cast, in
his case, behind.

Rupert was indisposed to converse, for, to tell the truth,
he had eaten a hearty supper, and began to feel drowsy;
and I was too much wrapped up in my own busy thoughts
to solicit any communications. I found a sort of saddened
pleasure in setting a watch for the night, therefore, which
had an air of seaman-like duty about it, that in a slight
degree revived my old taste for the profession. It was
midnight, and I took the first watch myself, bidding my
two companions to crawl under the half-deck and go to
sleep. This they both did without any parley, Rupert
occupying an inner place, while Neb lay with his legs exposed to the night air.

The breeze freshened, and for some time I thought it
might be necessary to reef, though we were running dead
before the wind. I succeeded in holding on, however,

and I found the Grace and Lucy was doing wonders in my watch. When I gave Rupert his call at four o'clock, the boat was just approaching two frowning mountains, where the river was narrowed to a third or fourth of its former width ; and, by the appearance of the shores, and the dim glimpses I had caught of a village of no great size on the right bank, I knew we were in what is called Newburg Bay. This was the extent of our former journeyings south, all three of us having once before, and only once, been as low as Fishkill Landing, which lies opposite to the place that gives this part of the river its name.

Rupert now took the helm, and I went to sleep. The wind still continued fresh and fair, and I felt no uneasiness on account of the boat. It is true, there were two parts of the navigation before us of which I had thought a little seriously, but not sufficiently so to keep me awake. These were the Race, a passage in the Highlands, and Tappan Sea ; both points on the Hudson of which the navigators of that classical stream were fond of relating the marvels. The first I knew was formidable only later in the autumn, and, as for the last, I hoped to enjoy some of its wonders in the morning. In this very justifiable expectation, I fell asleep.

Neb did not call me until ten o'clock. I afterward discovered that Rupert kept the helm for only an hour, and then, calculating that from five until nine were four hours, he thought it a pity the negro should not have his share of the glory of that night. When I was awakened, it was merely to let me know that it was time to eat something,—Neb would have starved before he would precede his young master in that necessary occupation,—and I found Rupert in a deep and pleasant sleep at my side.

We were in the centre of Tappan, and the Highlands had been passed in safety. Neb expatiated a little on the difficulties of the navigation, the river having many windings, besides being bounded by high mountains ; but, after all, he admitted that there was water enough, and a road that was plain enough. From this moment, excitement kept us wide awake. Everything was new, and everything seemed delightful. The day was pleasant, the wind continued fair, and nothing occurred to mar our joy. I had a little map, one neither particularly accurate, nor very well engraved ; and I remember the importance with which, after having ascertained the fact myself, I pointed out to my two companions the rocky precipices on the western bank, as New Jersey ! Even Rupert was struck with this important circumstance. As for Neb, he was actually in ecstasies, rolling his large black eyes, and showing his white teeth, until he suddenly closed his truly coral and plump lips, to demand what New Jersey meant. Of course I gratified this laudable desire to obtain knowledge, and Neb seemed still more pleased than ever, now he had ascertained that New Jersey was a State. Travelling was not as much of an every-day occupation, at that time, as it is now ; and it was, in truth, something for three American lads, all under nineteen, to be able to say that they had seen a State, other than their own.

Notwithstanding the rapid progress we had made for the first few hours of our undertaking, the voyage was far from being ended. About noon the wind came out light from the southward, and, having a flood-tide, we were compelled to anchor. This made us all uneasy, for, while we were stationary, we did not seem to be running away. The ebb came again, at length, however, and then we made sail, and began to turn down with the tide. It was near sunset before we got a view of the two or three spires that then piloted strangers to the town. New York was not the "commercial emporium " in 1796 ; so high-sounding a title, indeed, scarce belonging to the simple English of the period, it requiring a very great collection of half-educated men to venture on so ambitious an appellation—the only emporium that existed in America, during the last century, being a slop-shop in Water Street, and on the island of Manhattan. Commercial emporium was a flight of fancy, indeed, that must have required a whole board of aldermen, and an extra supply of turtle, to sanction. What is meant by a literary emporium, I leave those editors who are "native and to the manor born," to explain.

We first saw the State prison, which was then new, and

a most imposing edifice, according to our notions, as we drew near the town. Like the gallows first seen by a traveller in entering a strange country, it was a pledge of civilization. Neb shook his head, as he gazed at it, with a moralizing air, and said it had "a wicked look." For myself, I own I did not regard it altogether without dread. On Rupert it made less impression than on any of the three. He was always somewhat obtuse on the subject of morals.[1]

New York, in that day, and on the Hudson side of the town, commenced a short distance above Duane Street. Between Greenwich, as the little hamlet around the State prison was called, and the town proper, was an interval of a mile and a half of open fields, dotted here and there with country-houses. Much of this space was in broken hills, and a few piles of lumber lay along the shores. St. John's Church had no existence, and most of the ground in its vicinity was in a low swamp. As we glided along the wharves, we caught sight of the first market I had ever seen—such proofs of an advanced civilization not having yet made their way into the villages of the interior. It was called "The Bear," from the circumstance that the first meat ever exposed for sale in it was of that animal ; but the appellation has disappeared before the intellectual refinement of these later times—the name of the soldier and statesman, Washington, having fairly supplanted that of the bear ! Whether this great moral improvement was brought about by the Philosophical Society, or the Historical Society, or "The Merchants," or the Aldermen of New York, I have never ascertained. If the latter, one cannot but admire their disinterested modesty in conferring this notable honor on the Father of his Country, inasmuch as all can see that there never has been a period when their own board has not possessed distinguished members, every way qualified to act as godfathers to the most illustrious markets of the republic. But Manhattan, in the way of taste, has

[1] It may be well to tell the European who shall happen to read this book, that in America a "state's prison" is not for prisoners of state, but for common rogues ; the term coming from the name borne by the local governments.

never had justice done it. So profound is its admiration for all the higher qualities, that Franklin and Fulton have each a market to himself, in addition to this bestowed on Washington. Doubtless there would have been Newton Market, and Socrates Market, and Solomon Market, but for the patriotism of the town, which has forbidden it from going out of the hemisphere in quest of names to illustrate. Bacon Market would doubtless have been too equivocal to be tolerated, under any circumstances. Then Bacon was a rogue, though a philosopher, and markets are always appropriated to honest people. At all events, I am rejoiced the reproach of having a market called "The Bear" has been taken away, as it was tacitly admitting our living near, if not absolutely in, the woods.

We passed the Albany basin, a large receptacle for North River craft, that is now in the bosom of the town and built on, and recognized in it the masthead of the Wallingford. Neb was shown the place, for he was to bring the boat round to it, and join the sloop, in readiness to return in her. We rounded the Battery, then a circular strip of grass, with an earthen and wooden breastwork running along the margin of the water, leaving a narrow promenade on the exterior. This brought us to Whitehall, since so celebrated for its oarsmen, where we put in for a haven. I had obtained the address of a better sort of sailor-tavern in that vicinity, and, securing the boat, we shouldered the bags, got a boy to guide us, and were soon housed. As it was near night, Rupert and I ordered supper, and Neb was directed to pull the boat round to the sloop, and to return to us in the morning ; taking care, however, not to let our lodgings be known.

The next day, I own I thought but little of the girls, Clawbonny, or Mr. Hardinge. Neb was at my bedside before I was up, and reported the Grace and Lucy safe alongside of the Wallingford, and expressed himself ready to wait on me in my progress in quest of a ship. As this was the moment of action, little was said, but we all breakfasted, and sallied forth, in good earnest, on the important business before us. Neb was permitted to follow, but at such a distance as to prevent his being suspected of belonging to our party—a gentleman with a serving-man at his heels, not being the candidate most likely to succeed in his application for a berth in the forecastle.

So eager was I to belong to some sea-going craft, that I would not stop even to look at the wonders of the town before we took the direction of the wharves. Rupert was for pursuing a different policy, having an inherent love of the genteeler gayeties of a town, but I turned a deaf ear to his hints, and this time I was master. He followed me with some reluctance, but follow he did, after some remonstrances that bordered on warmth. Any inexperienced eye that had seen us passing, would have mistaken us for two well-looking, smart young sailor-boys, who had just returned from a profitable voyage, and who, well-clad, tidy, and semi-genteel, were strolling along the wharves as *admirateurs*, not to say critics, of the craft. *Admirateurs* we were, certainly, or I was, at least; though knowledge was a point on which we were sadly deficient.

The trade of America was surprisingly active in 1797. It had been preyed upon by the two great belligerents of the period, England and France, it is true ; and certain proceedings of the latter nation were about to bring the relations of the two countries into a very embarrassed state ; but still the shipping interest was wonderfully active, and, as a whole, singularly successful. Almost every tide brought in or took out ships for foreign ports, and scarce a week passed that vessels did not arrive from, or sail for, all the different quarters of the world. An Indiaman, however, was our object ; the voyage being longer, the ships better, and the achievement greater, than merely to cross the Atlantic and return. We accordingly proceeded toward the Fly Market, in the vicinity of which, we had been given to understand, some three or four vessels of that description were fitting out. This market has since used its wings to disappear, altogether.

I kept my eyes on every ship we passed. Until the previous day, I had never seen a square-rigged vessel ; and no enthusiast in the arts ever gloated on a fine picture or statue with greater avidity than my soul drank in the

wonder and beauty of every ship I passed.   I had a large,
full-rigged model at Clawbonny ; and this I had studied
under my father so thoroughly, as to know the name of
every rope in it, and to have some pretty distinct notions
of their uses.   This early schooling was now of great use
to me, though I found it a little difficult, at first, to trace
my old acquaintances on the large scale in which they now
presented themselves, and amid the intricate mazes that were
drawn against the skies.   The braces, shrouds, stays, and
halyards, were all plain enough, and I could point to either,
at a moment's notice ; but when it came to the rest of the
running-rigging, I found it necessary to look a little, before
I could speak with certainty.

Eager as I was to ship, the indulgence of gazing at all I
saw was so attractive, that it was noon before we reached
an Indiaman.   This was a pretty little ship of about four
hundred tons, that was called the John.   Little, I say, for
such she would now be thought, though a vessel of her size
was then termed large.   The Manhattan, much the largest
ship out of the port, measured but about seven hundred
tons ; while few even of the Indiamen went much beyond
five hundred.   I can see the John at this moment, near
fifty years after I first laid eyes on her, as she then appeared.   She was not bright-sided, but had a narrow, cream-
colored streak, broken into ports.   She was a straight,
black-looking craft, with a handsome billet, low, thin bulwarks, and waistcloths secured to ridge-ropes.   Her larger
spars were painted the same color as her streak, and her
stern had a few ornaments of a similar tint.

We went on board the John, where we found the officers
just topping off with the riggers and stevedores, having
stowed all the provisions and water, and the mere trifle of
cargo she carried.   The mate, whose name was Marble, and
a well-veined bit of marble he was, his face resembling a
map that had more rivers drawn on it than the land could
feed, winked at the captain and nodded his head toward us
as soon as we met his eye.   The latter smiled, but did not
speak.

"Walk this way, gentlemen—walk this way, if you

please," said Mr. Marble, encouragingly, passing a ball of spun-yarn, all the while, to help a rigger serve a rope. " When did you leave the country ? "

This produced a general laugh, even the yellow rascal of a mulatto, who was passing into the cabin with some crockery, grinning in our faces at this salutation. I saw it was now or never, and determined not to be browbeaten, while I was too truthful to attempt to pass for that I was not.

" We left home last night, thinking to be in time to find berths in one of the Indiamen that is to sail this week."

" Not *this* week, my son—not till *next*," said Mr. Marble, jocularly. " Sunday is *the* day. We run from Sunday to Sunday—the better day, the better deed, you know. How do you leave father and mother ? "

" I have neither," I answered, almost choked. " My mother died a few months since, and my father, Captain Wallingford, has now been dead some years."

The master of the John was a man of about fifty, red-faced, hard-looking, pock-marked, square-rigged, and of an exterior that promised anything but sentiment. Feeling, however, he did manifest, the moment I mentioned my father's name. He ceased his employment, came close to me, gazed earnestly in my face, and even looked kind.

"Are you a son of Captain Miles Wallingford ? " he asked in a low voice, " of Miles Wallingford, from up the river ? "

" I am, sir ; his only son. He left but two of us, a son and a daughter ; and, though under no necessity to work at all, I wish to make this Miles Wallingford as good a seaman as the last, and, I hope, as honest a man."

This was said manfully, and with a spirit that must have pleased ; for I was shaken cordially by the hand, welcomed on board, invited into the cabin, and asked to take a seat at a table on which the dinner had just been placed. Rupert, of course, shared in all these favors. Then followed the explanations. Captain Robbins of the John, had first gone to sea with my father, for whom I believe he entertained a profound respect. He had even served with him once as

mate, and talked as if he felt that he had been under obligations to him. He did not question me very closely, seeming to think it natural enough that Miles Wallingford's only
son should wish to be a seaman.

As we sat at the table, even, it was agreed that Rupert
and I should join the ship, as green hands, the very next
morning, signing the articles as soon as we went on shore.
This was done accordingly, and I had the felicity of writing
Miles Wallingford to the *roll d'equipage*, to the tune of
eighteen dollars per month—seamen then actually receiving
thirty and thirty-five dollars per month—wages. Rupert
was taken also, though Captain Robbins cut him down
to thirteen dollars, saying, in a jesting way, that a parson's
son could hardly be worth as much as the son of one of the
best old shipmasters who ever sailed out of America. He
was a shrewd observer of men and things, this new friend
of mine, and I believe understood " by the cut of his jib,"
that Rupert was not likely to make a weather-earing man.
The money, however, was not of much account in our calculations; and lucky enough did I think myself in finding so
good a berth, almost as soon as looked for. We returned
to the tavern and stayed that night, taking a formal leave
of Neb, who was to carry the good news home, as soon as
the sloop should sail.

In the morning a cart was loaded with our effects, the bill
was discharged, and we left the tavern. I had the precaution not to go directly alongside the ship. On the contrary,
we proceeded to an opposite part of the town, placing the
bags on a wharf resorted to by craft from New Jersey, as if
we intended to go on board one of them. The cartman took
his quarter, and drove off, troubling himself very little about
the future movements of two young sailors. Waiting half
an hour, another cart was called, when we went to the John,
and were immediately installed in her forecastle. Captain
Robbins had provided us both with chests, paid for out of
the three months' advance, and in them we found the slops
necessary for so long a voyage. Rupert and I immediately
put on suits of these new clothes, with regular little round
tarpaulins, which so much altered us in appearance, even

from those produced by our Ulster County fittings, that we
scarce knew each other.

Rupert now went on deck to lounge and smoke a cigar,
while I went aloft, visiting every yard, and touching all three
of the trucks, before I returned from this, *my* exploring
expedition. The captain and mates and riggers smiled at
my movements, and I overheard the former telling his mate
that I was "old Miles over again." In a word all parties
seemed pleased with the arrangement that had been made.
I had told the officers aft of my knowledge of the names and
uses of most of the ropes ; and never did I feel so proud as
when Mr. Marble called out, in a loud tone,—

"D' ye hear there, Miles—away aloft and unreeve them
fore-topgallant halyards, and send an end down to haul up
this new rope, to reeve a fresh set."

Away I went, my head buzzing with the complicated
order, and yet I had a very tolerable notion of what was to
be done. The unreeving might have been achieved by any
one, and I got through that without difficulty ; and, the mate
himself helping me and directing me from the deck, the new
rope was rove with distinguished success. This was the
first duty I ever did in a ship, and I was prouder of it than
of any that was subsequently performed by the same individual. The whole time that I was thus occupied, Rupert
stood lounging against the foot of the main-stay, smoking
his cigar like a burgomaster. His turn came next, however,
the captain sending for him to the cabin, where he set him
to work to copy some papers. Rupert wrote a beautiful
hand, and he wrote rapidly. That evening I heard the
chief mate tell the dickey that the parson's son was likely
to turn out a regular "barber's clerk" to the captain.
"The old man," he added, "makes so many traverses himself on a bit of paper, that he hardly knows at which end to
begin to read it ; and I should n't wonder if he just stationed
this chap, with a quill behind his ear, for the v'y'ge."

For the next two or three days I was delightfully busy,
passing half the time aloft. All the sails were to be bent,
and I had my full share in the performance of this duty. I
actually furled the mizzen-royal with my own hands,—the

The river harbor off Canton, China, as it appeared to Wallingford

ship carrying standing royals,—and it was said to be very respectably done; a little rag-baggish in the bunt, perhaps, but secured in a way that took the next fellow who touched the gasket five minutes to cast the sail loose. Then it rained, and sails were to be loosened to dry. I let everything fall forward with my own hands, and, when we came to roll up the canvas again, I actually managed all three of the royals alone; one at a time, of course. My father had taught me to make a flat-knot, a bowline, a clove-hitch, two half-hitches, and such sort of things; and I got through with both a long and a short splice tolerably well. I found all this, and the knowledge I had gained from my model-ship at home, of great use to me; so much so, indeed, as to induce even that indurated bit of mortality, Marble, to say I "was the ripest piece of green stuff he had ever fallen in with."

All this time Rupert was kept at quill-driving. Once he got leave to quit the ship,—it was the day before we sailed, —and I observed he went ashore in his long togs, of which each of us had one suit. I stole away the same afternoon to find the post-office, and worked up-stream as far as Broadway, not knowing exactly which way to shape my course. In that day everybody who was anybody, and unmarried, promenaded the west side of this street, from the Battery to St. Paul's Church, between the hours of twelve and half past two, wind and weather permitting. There I saw Rupert in his country guise, nothing remarkable, of a certainty, strutting about with the best of them, and looking handsome in spite of his rusticity. It was getting late, and he left the street just as I saw him. I followed, waiting until we got to a private place before I would speak to him, however, as I knew he would be mortified to be taken for the friend of a Jack-tar in such a scene.

Rupert entered a door, and then reappeared with a letter in his hand. He, too, had gone to the post-office, and I no longer hesitated about joining him.

"Is it from Clawbonny?" I asked, eagerly. "If so, from Lucy, doubtless?"

"From Clawbonny—but from Grace," he answered, with

a slight change of color. " I desired the poor girl to let me know how things passed off after we left them : and, as for Lucy, her pot-hooks are so much out of the way, I never want to see them."

I felt hurt, offended, that my sister should write to any youngster but myself. It is true the letter was to a bosom friend,—a co-adventurer, one almost a child of the same family,—and I had come to the office expecting to get a letter from Rupert's sister, who had promised, while weeping on the wharf, to do exactly the same thing for me ; but there *is* a difference between one's sister writing to another young man, and another young man's sister writing to one's self. I cannot even now explain it ; but that there is a difference I am sure. Without asking to see a line that Grace had written, I went into the office, and returned in a minute or two, with an air of injured dignity, holding Lucy's epistle in my hand.

After all there was nothing in either letter to excite much sensibility. Each was written with the simplicity, truth, and feeling of a generous-minded, warm-hearted female friend, of an age not to distrust her own motives, to a lad who had no right to view the favor other than it was, as an evidence of early and intimate friendship. Both epistles are now before me, and I copy them as the shortest way of letting the reader know the effect our disappearance had produced at Clawbonny. That of Grace was couched in the following terms :—

DEAR RUPERT,—Clawbonny was in commotion at nine o'clock this morning, and well it might be ! When your father's anxiety got to be painful, I told him the whole, and gave him the letters. I am sorry to say he wept. I wish never to see such a sight again. The tears of two such silly girls as Lucy and I, are of little account—but, Rupert, to behold an aged man we love and respect like him, a minister of the gospel too, in tears ! It was a hard sight to bear. He did not reproach us for our silence, saying he did not see, after our promises, how we could well do otherwise. I gave your reasons about " responsibility in the premises " ; but I

don't think he understood them. Is it too late to return?
The boat that carried you down can bring you back ; and
oh ! how much rejoiced shall we all be to see you ! Wherever
you go and whatever you do, boys—for I write as much to one
as to the other, and only address to Rupert because he so earnestly desired it—but wherever you go, and whatever you do,
remember the instructions you have both received in youth,
and how much all of us are interested in your conduct and
happiness.

Affectionately yours,

GRACE WALLINGFORD.

To Mr. RUPERT HARDINGE.

Lucy had been less guarded, and possibly a little more
honest. She wrote as follows :—

DEAR MILES,—I believe I cried for one whole hour after
you and Rupert left us, and, now it is all over, I am vexed at
having cried so much about two such foolish fellows. Grace
has told you all about my dear, dear father, who cried too.
I declare, I don't know when I was so frightened ! I thought
it must bring you back, as soon as you hear of it. What
will be done I do not know ; but something, I am certain.
Whenever father is in earnest, he says but little. I know
he is in earnest now. I believe Grace and I do nothing but
think of you ; that is, she of you, and I of Rupert ; and a
little the other way, too—so now you have the whole truth.
Do not fail, on any account, to write before you go to sea,
if you do go to sea, as I hope and trust you will not.
Good-by.

LUCY HARDINGE.

To Mr. MILES WALLINGFORD.

P.S. Neb's mother protests, if the boy is not home by
Saturday night, she will go after him. No such disgrace as
a runaway ever befel her or hers, and she says she will not
submit to it. But I suppose we will see him soon, and with
him letters.

Now Neb had taken his leave, but no letter had been
trusted to his care. As often happens, I regretted the mis-

take when it was too late; and all that day I thought how
disappointed Lucy would be, when she came to see the negro
empty-handed.

Rupert and I parted in the street, as he did not wish to
walk with a sailor, while in his own long togs. He did not
say as much, but I knew him well enough to ascertain it
without his speaking. I was walking very fast in the direction of the ship, and had actually reached the wharves,
when, in turning a corner, I came plump upon Mr. Hardinge. My guardian was walking slowly, his face sorrowful
and dejected, and his eyes fastened on every ship he passed,
as if looking for his boys. He saw me, casting a vacant
glance over my person; but I was so much changed by dress,
and particularly by the little tarpaulin, that he did not know
me. Anxiety immediately drew his look toward the vessels,
and I passed him unobserved. Mr. Hardinge was walking
from, and I toward the John, and of course all my risk terminated as soon as out of sight.

That evening I had the happiness of being under way, in
a real full-rigged ship. It is true, it was under very short
canvas, and merely to go into the stream. Taking advantage of a favorable wind and tide, the John left the wharf
under her jib, main-topmast staysail, and spanker, and
dropped down as low as the Battery, when she sheered into
the other channel and anchored. Here I was, then, fairly
at anchor in the stream, half a mile from any land but the
bottom, and burning to see the ocean. That afternoon the
crew came on board, a motley collection of lately drunken
seamen, of whom about half were Americans, and the rest
natives of as many different countries as there were men.
Mr. Marble scanned them with a knowing look, and, to my
surprise, he told the captain there was good stuff among
them. It seems he was a better judge than I was myself,
for a more unpromising set of wretches, as to looks, I never
saw grouped together. A few, it is true, appeared well
enough; but most of them had the air of having been dragged
through—a place I will not name, though it is that which
sailors usually quote when describing themselves on such
occasions. But Jack, after he has been a week at sea, and

Jack coming on board to duty after a month of excesses on shore, are very different creatures, morally and physically.

I now began to regret that I had not seen a little of the town. In 1797, New York could not have had more than fifty thousand inhabitants, though it was just as much of a paragon then, in the eyes of all good Americans, as it is to-day. It is a sound patriotic rule to maintain that our best is always the best, for it never puts us in the wrong. I have seen enough of the world since to understand that we get a great many things wrong-end foremost in this country of ours ; undervaluing those advantages and excel- lences of which we have great reason to be proud, and boasting of others that, to say the least, are exceedingly equivocal. But it takes time to learn all this, and I have no intention of getting ahead of my story, or of my country ; the last being a most suicidal act.

We received the crew of a Saturday afternoon, and half of them turned in immediately. Rupert and I had a good berth, intending to turn in and out together, during the voyage ; and this made us rather indifferent to the move- ments of the rest of our extraordinary associates. The kid, at supper, annoyed us both a little ; the notion of seeing one's food in a round trough, to be tumbled over and cut from by all hands, being particularly disagreeable to those who have been accustomed to plates, knives and forks, and such other superfluities. I confess I thought of Grace's and Lucy's little white hands, and of silver sugar-tongs, and of clean plates and glasses, and table-cloths—napkins and sil- ver forks were then unknown in America, except on the very best tables, and not always on them, unless on high days and holidays—as we were going through the unsophis- ticated manipulations of this first supper. Forty-seven years have elapsed, and the whole scene is as vivid to my mind at this moment, as if it occurred last night. I wished my- self one of the long-snouted tribe, several times, in order to be in what is called " keeping."

I had the honor of keeping an anchor-watch in company with a grum old Swede, as we lay in the Hudson. The wind was light, and the ship had a good berth, so my asso-

4

ciate chose a soft plank, told me to give him a call should
anything happen, and lay down to sleep away his two hours
in comfort. Not so with me. I strutted the deck with as
much importance as if the weight of the state lay on my
shoulders—paid a visit every five minutes to the bows, to
see that the cables had not parted, and that the anchor did
not "come home,"—and then looked aloft, to ascertain
that everything was in its place. Those were a happy two
hours!

About ten next morning, being Sunday, and, as Mr.
Marble expressed it, "the better day, the better deed," the
pilot came off, and all hands were called to "up anchor."
The cook, cabin-boy, Rupert, and I were intrusted with the
duty of "fleeting jig" and breaking down the coils of the
cable, the handspikes requiring heavier hands than ours.
The anchor was got in without any difficulty, however,
when Rupert and I were sent aloft to loose the fore-topsail.
Rupert got into the top *via* the lubber's hole, I am sorry to
say, and the loosing of the sail on both yard-arms fell to my
duty. A hand was on the fore-yard, and I was next ordered up to loose the topgallant-sail. Canvas began to fall
and open all over the ship, the topsails were mastheaded,
and, as I looked down from the fore-topmast cross-trees,
where I remained to overhaul the clew-lines, I saw that the
ship was falling off, and that her sails were filling with a
stiff northwest breeze. Just as my whole being was en-
tranced with the rapture of being under way for Canton,
which was then called the Indies, Rupert called out to me
from the top. He was pointing at some object on the water,
and, turning, I saw a boat within a hundred feet of the
ship. In her was Mr. Hardinge, who at that moment
caught sight of us. But the ship's sails were now all full,
and no one on deck saw, or at least heeded, the boat. The
John glided past it, and, the last I saw of my venerated
guardian, he was standing erect, bareheaded, holding both
arms extended, as if entreating us not to desert him! Presently the ship fell off so much, that the after-sails hid him
from my view.

I descended into the top, where I found Rupert had

shrunk down out of sight, looking frightened and guilty. As for myself, I got behind the head of the mast, and fairly sobbed. This lasted a few minutes, when an order from the mate called us both below. When I reached the deck, the boat was already a long distance astern, and had evidently given up the idea of boarding us. I do not know whether I felt the most relieved or pained by the certainty of this fact.

CHAPTER IV.

"There is a tide in the affairs of men,
Which, taken at the flood, leads on to fortune.
Omitted, all the voyage of their life
Is bound in shallows and in miseries.
On such a full sea are we now afloat ;
And we must take the current when it serves,
Or lose our ventures."

Julius Cæsar.

IN four hours from the time when Rupert and I last saw Mr. Hardinge, the ship was at sea. She crossed the bar, and started on her long journey, with a fresh north-wester, and with everything packed on that she would bear. We took a diagonal course out of the bight formed by the coasts of Long Island and New Jersey, and sunk the land entirely by the middle of the afternoon. I watched the highlands of Navesink, as they vanished like watery clouds in the west, and then I felt I was at last fairly out of sight of land. But a foremast-hand has little opportunity for indulging in sentiment as he quits his native shore ; and few, I fancy, have the disposition. As regards the opportunity, anchors are to be got in off the bows, and stowed ; cables are to be unbent and coiled down ; studding-gear is to be hauled out and got ready ; frequently boom-irons are to be placed upon the yards, and the hundred preparations made, that render the work of a ship as ceaseless a round of activity as that of a house. This kept us all busy until night, when the watches were told off and set. I was in the larboard, or chief mate's watch, having actually been chosen by that hard-featured old seaman, the fourth man he named ; an honor for which I was indebted to the activity I had already manifested aloft. Rupert was less distinguished, being taken by the captain for the second mate's watch, the very last person chosen. That night Mr. Marble dropped a few hints on the subject, which let me into the secret of these two selections. "You and I will get along well together, I see that plainly, Miles," he said, "for there's quicksilver in your body. As for your friend in t' other watch, it's all as it should be; the captain has got one hand the most, and such as he is, he is welcome to him. He'll blacken more writing paper this v'y'ge, I reckon, than he'll tar down riggin'." I thought it odd, however, that Rupert, who had been so forward in all the preliminaries of our adventure, should fall so far astern in its first practical results.

It is not my intention to dwell on all the minute incidents of this, my first voyage to sea, else would it spin out the narrative unnecessarily, and render my task as fatiguing to the reader as it might prove to myself. One occurrence, however, which took place three days out, must be mentioned, as it will prove to be connected with important circumstances in the end. The ship was now in order, and was at least two hundred leagues from the land, having had a famous run off the coast, when the voice of the cook, who had gone below for water, was heard down among the casks, in such a clamor as none but a black can raise, with all his loquacity awakened.

"There's *two* niggers at that work!" exclaimed Mr. Marble, after listening an instant, glancing his eye round to make certain the mulatto steward was not in the discussion. "No *one* darkey ever could make all that outcry. Bear a hand below, Miles, and see if Africa has come aboard us in the night."

I was in the act of obeying, when Cato, the cook, was seen rising through the steerage-hatch, dragging after him the dark poll of another black, whom he had gripped by the wool. In an instant both were on deck, when, to my astonishment, I discovered the agitated countenance of Nebuchadnezzar Clawbonny. Of course the secret was out, the instant the lad's glistening features were recognized.

Neb, in a word, had managed to get on board the ship before she hauled out into the stream, and lay concealed among the water-casks, his pockets crammed with ginger-bread and apples, until discovered by the cook, in one of his journeys in quest of water. The food of the lad had been gone twenty-four hours, and it is not probable the fellow could have remained concealed much longer, had not this discovery taken place. The instant he was on deck, Neb looked eagerly around to ascertain how far the ship had got from the land, and, seeing nothing but water on every side of him, he fairly grinned with delight. This exasperated Mr. Marble, who thought it was adding insult to injury, and he gave the lad a cuff on the ear that would have set a white reeling. On Neb, however, this sharp blow produced no effect, falling as it did on the impregnable part of his system.

" Oh ! you 're a nigger, be you? " exclaimed the mate, waxing warmer and warmer, as he fancied himself baffled by the other's powers of endurance. " Take that, and let us see if you 're full-blooded ! "

A smart rap on the shin accompanying these words, Neb gave in on the instant. He begged for mercy, and professed a readiness to tell all, protesting he was not " a runaway nigger "—a term the mate used while applying the kicks.

I now interfered, by telling Mr. Marble, with all the respect due from a green hand to a chief mate, who Neb really was, and what I supposed to be his motives for following me to the ship. This revelation cost me a good deal in the end, the idea of Jack's having a " waiting-man " on board giving rise to a great many jokes at my expense during the rest of the voyage. Had I not been so active, and so willing, a great source of favor on board a ship, it is probable these jokes would have been much broader and more frequent. As it was, they annoyed me a good deal ; and it required a strong exercise of all the boyish regard I really entertained for Neb, to refrain from turning to and giving him a sound thrashing for his exploit, at the first good occasion. And yet, what was his delin-

quency compared to my own? He had followed his master
out of deep affection, blended somewhat, it is true, with a
love of adventure; while, in one sense, I had violated all
the ties of the heart, merely to indulge the latter passion.

The captain coming on deck, Neb's story was told, and,
finding that no wages would be asked in behalf of this
athletic, healthy young negro, he had no difficulty in receiving him into favor. To Neb's great delight, he was sent
forward to take his share on the yards and in the rigging,
there being no vacancy for him to fill about the caboose, or
in the cabin. In an hour the negro was fed, and he was
regularly placed in the starboard watch. I was rejoiced at
this last arrangement, as it put the fellow in a watch different from my own, and prevented his officious efforts to do my
work. Rupert, I discovered, however, profited often by his
zeal, employing the willing black on every possible occasion.
On questioning Neb, I ascertained that he had taken the boat
round to the Wallingford, and had made use of a dollar or
two, I had given him at parting, to board in a house suitable to his color, until the ship was ready for sea, when he
got on board, and stowed himself among the water-casks, as
mentioned.

Neb's apparition soon ceased to be a subject of discourse,
and his zeal quickly made him a general favorite. Hardy,
strong, resolute, and accustomed to labor, he was early of
great use in all the heavy drags; and aloft, even, though
less quick than a white would have been, he got to be serviceable and reasonably expert. My own progress— and I
say it without vanity, but simply because it was true—was
the subject of general remark. One week made me familiar
with the running-gear; and, by that time, I could tell a
rope by its size, the manner in which it led, and the place
where it was belayed, in the darkest night, as well as the
oldest seaman on board. It is true, my model-ship had
prepared the way for much of this expertness; but, free
from all sea-sickness, of which I never had a moment in
my life, I set about learning these things in good earnest,
and was fully rewarded for my pains. I passed the weather-
earing of the mizzen-topsail when we had been out a fort-

night, and went to those of the fore and main before we crossed the line. The mate put me forward on all occasions, giving me much instruction in private; and the captain neglected no opportunity of giving me useful hints, or practical ideas. I asked, and was allowed, to take my regular trick at the wheel before we got into the latitude of St. Helena; and from that time did my full share of seaman's duty on board, the nicer work of knotting, splicing, etc., excepted. These last required a little more time; but I am satisfied that, in all things but judgment, a clever lad, who has a taste for the business, can make himself a very useful and respectable mariner in six months of active service.

China voyages seldom produce much incident. If the moment of sailing has been judiciously timed, the ship has fair winds much of the way, and generally moderate weather. To be sure, there are points on the long road that usually give one a taste of what the seas sometimes are; but, on the whole, a Canton voyage, though a long one, cannot be called a rough one. As a matter of course, we had gales, and squalls, and the usual vicissitudes of the ocean, to contend with, though our voyage to Canton might have been called quiet, rather than the reverse. We were four months under our canvas, and, when we anchored in the river, the clewing up of our sails, and getting from beneath their shadows, resembled the rising of a curtain on some novel scenic representation. John Chinaman, however, has been so often described, particularly of late, that I shall not dwell on his peculiarities. Sailors, as a class, are very philosophical, so far as the peculiarities and habits of strangers are concerned, appearing to think it beneath the dignity of those who visit all lands, to betray wonder at the novelties of any. It so happened that no man on board the John, the officers, steward, and cook excepted, had ever doubled the Cape of Good Hope before this voyage; and yet our crew regarded the shorn polls, slanting eyes, long queues, clumsy dresses, high cheek-bones, and lumbering shoes of the people they now saw for the first time, with just as much indifference as they would have encountered a new fashion at home. Most of them, indeed, had seen, or fancied they had seen, much stranger sights, in the different countries they had visited; it being a standing rule with Jack to compress everything that is wonderful into the "last voyage"—that in which he is engaged for the present time being usually set down as commonplace, and unworthy of particular comment. On this principle, my Canton excursion ought to be full of marvels, as it was the progenitor of all that I subsequently saw and experienced as a sailor. Truth compels me to confess, notwithstanding, that it was one of the least wonderful of all the voyages I ever made, until near its close.

We lay some months in the river, getting cargo, receiving teas, nankins, silks, and other articles, as our supercargo could lay hands on them. In all this time, we saw just as much of the Chinese as it is usual for strangers to see, and not a jot more. I was much up at the factories with the captain, having charge of his boat; and, as for Rupert, he passed most of his working hours either busy with the supercargo ashore, or writing in the cabin. I got a good insight, however, into the uses of the serving-mallet, the fid, marlinspike, and winch, and did something with the needle and palm. Marble was very good to me, in spite of his nor'west face, and never let slip an occasion to give a useful hint. I believe my exertions on the outward-bound passage fully equalled expectations, and the officers had a species of pride in helping to make Captain Wallingford's son worthy of his honorable descent. I had taken occasion to let it be known that Rupert's great-grandfather had been a man-of-war captain; but the suggestion was met by a flat refusal to believe it from Mr. Kite, the second mate, though Mr. Marble remarked it might be so, as I admitted that both his father and grandfather had been, or were, in the church. My friend seemed fated to achieve nothing but the glory of a "barber's clerk."

Our hatches were got on and battened down, and we sailed for home early in the spring of 1798. The ship had a good run across the China Sea, and reached the Indies in rather a short passage. We had cleared all the islands, and were fairly in the Indian Ocean, when an adventure occurred, which was the first really worthy of being related that we met in the whole voyage. I shall give it, in as few words as possible.

We had cleared the Straits of Sunda early in the morning, and had made a pretty fair run in the course of the day, though most of the time in thick weather. Just as the sun set, however, the horizon became clear, and we got a sight of two small sail, seemingly heading in toward the coast of Sumatra, proas by their rig and dimensions. They were so distant, and were so evidently steering for the land, that no one gave them much thought, or bestowed on them any particular attention. Proas in that quarter were usually distrusted by ships, it is true; but the sea is full of them, and far more are innocent than are guilty of any acts of violence. Then it became dark soon after these craft were seen, and night shut them in. An hour after the sun had set, the wind fell to a light air, that just kept steerage-way on the ship. Fortunately, the John was not only fast, but she minded her helm, as a light-footed girl turns in a lively dance. I never was in a better-steering ship, most especially in moderate weather.

Mr. Marble had the middle watch that night, and, of course, I was on deck from midnight until four in the morning. It proved misty most of the watch, and for quite an hour we had a light drizzling rain. The ship the whole time was close-hauled, carrying royals. As everybody seemed to have made up his mind to a quiet night, one without any reefing or furling, most of the watch were sleeping about the decks, or wherever they could get good quarters, and be least in the way. I do not know what kept me awake, for lads of my age are apt to get all the sleep they can; but I believe I was thinking of Clawbonny, and Grace, and Lucy; for the latter, excellent girl as she was, often crossed my mind in those days of youth and comparative innocence. Awake I was, and walking in the weather-gangway, in a sailor's trot. Mr. Marble, he I do believe was fairly snoozing on the hen-coops, being, like the sails, as one might say, barely "asleep." At that moment I heard a noise, one familiar to seamen; that of an oar falling in a boat. So

completely was my mind bent on other and distant scenes,
that at first I felt no surprise, as if we were in a harbor
surrounded by craft of various sizes, coming and going at
all hours. But a second thought destroyed this illusion,
and I looked eagerly about me. Directly on our weather-
bow, distant, perhaps, a cable's length, I saw a small sail,
and I could distinguish it sufficiently well to perceive it was
a proa. I sang out "Sail ho! and close aboard!"

Mr. Marble was on his feet in an instant. He afterward
told me that when he opened his eyes, for he admitted this
much to me in confidence, they fell directly on the stranger.
He was too much of a seaman to require a second look in
order to ascertain what was to be done. "Keep the ship
away—keep her broad off!" he called out to the man at
the wheel. "Lay the yards square—call all hands, one of
you. Captain Robbins, Mr. Kite, bear a hand up; the
bloody proas are aboard us!" The last part of this call
was uttered in a loud voice, with the speaker's head down
the companion-way. It was heard plainly enough below,
but scarcely at all on deck.

In the meantime everybody was in motion. It is amazing
how soon sailors are wide awake when there is really anything to do! It appeared to me that all our people mustered
on deck in less than a minute, most of them with nothing
on but their shirts and trousers. The ship was nearly before
the wind by the time I heard the captain's voice; and then
Mr. Kite came bustling in among us forward, ordering
most of the men to lay aft to the braces, remaining himself
on the forecastle, and keeping me with him to let go the
sheets. On the forecastle, the strange sail was no longer
visible, being now abaft the beam; but I could hear Mr.
Marble swearing there were two of them, and that they
must be the very chaps we had seen to leeward, and standing in for the land at sunset. I also heard the captain
calling out to the steward to bring him a powder-horn. Immediately after, orders were given to let fly all our sheets
forward, and then I perceived that they were wearing ship.
Nothing saved us but the prompt order of Mr. Marble to
keep the ship away, by which means, instead of moving

toward the proas, we instantly began to move from them. Although they went three feet to our two, this gave us a moment of breathing time.

As our sheets were all flying forward, and remained so for a few minutes, it gave me leisure to look about. I soon saw both proas, and glad enough was I to perceive that they had not approached materially nearer. Mr. Kite observed this also, and remarked that our movements had been so prompt as to "take the rascals aback." He meant they did not exactly know what we were at, and had not kept away with us.

At this instant, the captain and five or six of the oldest seamen began to cast loose all our starboard, or weather guns, four in all, and sixes. We had loaded these guns in the Straits of Banca, with grape and canister, in readiness for just such pirates as were now coming down upon us; and nothing was wanting but the priming and a hot logger-head. It seems two of the last had been ordered in the fire, when we saw the proas at sunset; and they were now in excellent condition for service, live coals being kept around them all night by command. I saw a cluster of men busy with the second gun from forward, and could distinguish the captain pointing to it.

"There cannot well be any mistake, Mr. Marble?" the captain observed, hesitating whether to fire or not.

"Mistake, sir? Lord, Captain Robbins, you might cannonade any of the islands astern for a week, and never hurt an honest man. Let 'em have it, sir; I'll answer for it, you do good."

This settled the matter. The loggerhead was applied, and one of our sixes spoke out in a smart report. A breathless stillness succeeded. The proas did not alter their course, but neared us fast. The captain levelled his night-glass, and I heard him tell Kite, in a low voice, that they were full of men. The word was now passed to clear away all the guns, and to open the arm-chest, to come at the muskets and pistols. I heard the rattling of the boarding-pikes, too, as they were cut adrift from the spanker-boom, and fell upon the decks. All this sounded very ominous, and I began to think we should have a desperate engagement first, and then have all our throats cut afterward.

I expected now to hear the guns discharged in quick succession, but they were got ready only, not fired. Kite went aft, and returned with three or four muskets, and as many pikes. He gave the latter to those of the people who had nothing to do with the guns. By this time the ship was on a wind, steering a good full, while the two proas were just abeam, and closing fast. The stillness that reigned on both sides was like that of death. The proas, however, fell a little more astern ; the result of their own manœuvering, out of all doubt, as they moved through the water much faster than the ship, seeming desirous of dropping into our wake, with a design of closing under our stern, and avoiding our broadside. As this would never do, and the wind freshened so as to give us four or five knot way, a most fortunate circumstance for us, the captain determined to tack while he had room. The John behaved beautifully, and came round like a top. The proas saw there was no time to lose, and attempted to close before we could fill again ; and this they would have done with ninety-nine ships in a hundred. The captain knew his vessel, however, and did not let her lose her way, making everything draw again as it might be by instinct. The proas tacked, too, and, laying up much nearer to the wind than we did, appeared as if about to close on our lee-bow. The question was, now, whether we could pass them or not before they got near enough to grapple. If the pirates got on board us, we were hopelessly gone ; and everything depended on coolness and judgment. The captain behaved perfectly well in this critical instant, commanding a dead silence, and the closest attention to his orders.

I was too much interested at this moment to feel the concern that I might otherwise have experienced. On the forecastle, it appeared to us all that we should be boarded in a minute, for one of the proas was actually within a hundred feet, though losing her advantage a little by getting under the lee of our sails. Kite had ordered us to muster forward of the rigging, to meet the expected leap with a dis·

charge of muskets, and then to present our pikes, when I
felt an arm thrown around my body, and was turned in-
board, while another person assumed my place. This was
Neb, who had thus coolly thrust himself before me, in order
to meet the danger first. I felt vexed, even while touched with
the fellow's attachment and self-devotion, but had no time
to betray either feeling before the crews of the proas gave a
yell, and discharged some fifty or sixty matchlocks at us.
The air was full of bullets, but they all went over our heads.
Not a soul on board the John was hurt. On our side, we
gave the gentlemen the four sixes, two at the nearest and
two at the stern-most proa, which was still near a cable's
length distant. As often happens, the one seemingly farthest from danger, fared the worst. Our grape and canister
had room to scatter, and I can at this distant day still hear
the shrieks that arose from that craft! They were like the
yells of fiends in anguish. The effect on that proa was instantaneous ; instead of keeping on after her consort, she
wore short round on her heel, and stood away in our wake,
on the other tack, apparently to get out of the range of our
fire.

I doubt if we touched a man in the nearest proa. At
any rate, no noise proceeded from her, and she came up
under our bows fast. As every gun was discharged, and
there was not time to load them, all now depended on repel-
ling the boarders. Part of our people mustered in the waist,
where it was expected the proa would fall alongside, and
part on the forecastle. Just as this distribution was made,
the pirates cast their grapnel. It was admirably thrown,
but caught only by a ratlin. I saw this, and was about to
jump into the rigging to try what I could do to clear it,
when Neb again went ahead of me, and cut the ratlin with
his knife. This was just as the pirates had abandoned sails
and oars, and had risen to haul up alongside. So sudden
was the release, that twenty of them fell over by their own
efforts. In this state the ship passed ahead, all her canvas
being full, leaving the proa motionless in her wake. In
passing, however, the two vessels were so near, that those aft
in the John distinctly saw the swarthy faces of their enemies.

We were no sooner clear of the proas than the order was given, "Ready about!" The helm was put down, and the ship came into the wind in a minute. As we came square with the two proas, all our larboard guns were given to them, and this ended the affair. I think the nearest of the rascals got it this time, for away she went, after her consort, both running off toward the islands. We made a little show of chasing, but it was only a feint ; for we were too glad to get away from them, to be in earnest. In ten minutes after we tacked the last time, we ceased firing, having thrown some eight or ten round-shot after the proas, and were close-hauled again, heading to the southwest.

It is not to be supposed we went to sleep again immediately. Neb was the only man on board who did, but he never missed an occasion to eat or sleep. The captain praised us, and, as a matter of course in that day, he called all hands to "splice the main-brace." After this the watch was told to go below, as regularly as if nothing had happened. As for the captain himself, he and Mr. Marble and Mr. Kite went prying about the ship to ascertain if anything material had been cut by what the chief mate called "the bloody Indian matchlocks." A little running rigging had suffered, and we had to reeve a few new ropes in the morning ; but this terminated the affair.

I need hardly say, all hands of us were exceedingly proud of our exploit. Everybody was praised but Neb, who, being a " nigger," was in some way or other overlooked. I mentioned his courage and readiness to Mr. Marble, but I could excite in no one else the same respect for the poor fellow's conduct that I certainly felt myself. I have since lived long enough to know that as the gold of the rich attracts to itself the gold of the poor, so do the deeds of the unknown go to swell the fame of the known. This is as true of nations, and races, and families, as it is of individuals ; poor Neb belonging to a proscribed color, it was not in reason to suppose he could ever acquire exactly the same credit as a white man.

"Them darkeys do sometimes blunder on a lucky idee," answered Mr. Marble to one of my earnest representations,

" and I've known chaps among 'em that were almost as knowing as dullish whites; but everything out of the common way with 'em is pretty much chance. As for Neb, however, I will say this for him : that, for a nigger, he takes things quicker than any of his color I ever sailed with. Then he has no sa'ce, and that is a good deal with a black. White sa'ce is bad enough; but that of a nigger is unbearable."

Alas ! Neb. Born in slavery, accustomed to consider it arrogance to think of receiving even his food until the meanest white had satisfied his appetite, submissive, unrepining, laborious, and obedient—the highest eulogium that all these patient and unobtrusive qualities could obtain, was a reluctant acknowledgment that he had "no sa'ce." His quickness and courage saved the John, nevertheless; and I have always said it, and ever shall.

A day after the affair of the proas, all hands of us began to brag. Even the captain was a little seized with this mania ; and as for Marble, he was taken so badly, that had I not known he behaved well in the emergency, I certainly should have set him down as a Bobadil. Rupert manifested this feeling, too, though I heard he did his duty that night. The result of all the talk was to convert the affair into a very heroic exploit ; and it subsequently figured in the journals as one of the deeds that illustrate the American name.

From the time we were rid of the proas, the ship got along famously until we were as far west as about 52°, when the wind came light from the southward and westward, with thick weather. The captain had been two or three times caught in here, and he took it into his head that the currents would prove more favorable, could he stand in closer to the coast of Madagascar than common. Accordingly, we brought the ship on a bowline, and headed up well to the northward and westward. We were a week on this tack, making from fifty to a hundred miles a day, expecting hourly to see the land. At length we made it, enormously high mountains, apparently a long distance from us, though, as we afterward ascertained, a long dis-

tance inland ; and we continued to near it. The captain
had a theory of his own about the currents of this part of
the ocean, and, having set one of the peaks by compass, at
the time the land was seen, he soon convinced himself, and
everybody else whom he tried to persuade, Marble excepted,
that we were setting to windward with visible speed. Captain Robbins was a well-meaning, but somewhat dull man ;
and, when dull men become theorists, they usually make
sad work with the practice.

All that night we stood on to the northward and westward, though Mr. Marble had ventured a remonstrance
concerning a certain headland that was just visible, a little on
our weather-bow. The captain snapped his fingers at this,
however ; laying down a course of reasoning, which, if it
were worth anything, ought to have convinced the mate
that the weatherly set of the current would carry us ten
leagues to the southward and westward of that cape before
morning. On this assurance we prepared to pass a quiet
and comfortable night.

I had the morning watch, and when I came on deck, at
four, there was no change in the weather. Mr. Marble soon
appeared, and he walked into the waist, where I was leaning on the weather-rail, and fell into discourse. This he
often did, sometimes so far forgetting the difference in our
stations afloat—not ashore ; there I had considerably the advantage of him—as occasionally to call me "sir." I always
paid for this inadvertency, however, it usually putting a
stop to the communications for the time being. In one
instance he took such prompt revenge for this implied admission of equality, as literally to break off short in the discourse, and to order me, in his sharpest key, to go aloft and
send some studding-sails on deck, though they all had to be
sent aloft again and set, in the course of the same watch.
But offended dignity is seldom considerate, and not always
consistent.

"A quiet night, Master Miles "— this the mate could call
me, as it implied superiority on his part—" a quiet night,
Master Miles," commenced Mr. Marble, "and a strong
westerly current, accordin' to Captain Robbins. Well, to

my taste, gooseberries are better than currents, and I'd go about. That's my manner of generalizing."

"The captain, I suppose, sir, from that, is of a different opinion?"

"Why, yes, somewhatish—though I don't think he knows himself exactly what his own opinion is. This is the third v'y'ge I've sailed with the old gentleman, and he is half his time in a fog or a current. Now, it's his idee the ocean is full of Mississippi Rivers, and if one could only find the head of a stream, he might go round the world in it. More particularly does he hold that there is no fear of the land when in a current, as a stream never sets on shore. For my part, I never want any better hand-lead than my nose."

"Nose, Mr. Marble?"

"Yes, nose, Master Miles. Have n't you remarked how far we smelt the Injees, as we went through the islands?"

"It is true, sir, the Spice Islands, and all land, they say—"

"What the devil's that!" asked the mate, evidently startled at something he heard, though he appeared to smell nothing, unless, indeed, it might be a rat.

"It sounds like water washing on rocks, sir, as much as anything I ever heard in my life!"

"Ready about!" shouted the mate. "Run down and call the captain, Miles—hard a-lee—start everybody up, forward."

A scene of confusion followed, in the midst of which the captain, second mate, and the watch below, appeared on deck. Captain Robbins took command, of course, and was in time to haul the after-yards, the ship coming round slowly in so light a wind. Come round she did, however, and, when her head was fairly to the southward and east-ward, the captain demanded an explanation. Mr. Marble did not feel disposed to trust his nose any longer, but he invited the captain to use his ears. This all hands did, and, if sounds could be trusted, we had a pretty lot of breakers seemingly all around us.

"We surely can go out the way we came in, Mr. Marble?" said the captain, anxiously.

"Yes, sir, if there were no current; but one never knows where a bloody current will carry him in the dark."

"Stand by to let go the anchor!" cried the captain. "Let run and clew up, forward and aft. Let go as soon as you 'r ready, Mr. Kite."

Luckily, we had kept a cable bent as we came through the Straits, and, not knowing but we might touch at the Isle of France, it was still bent, with the anchor fished.

We had talked of stowing the latter in-board, but, having land in sight, it was not done. In two minutes it was a-cockbill, and, in two more, let go. None knew whether we should find a bottom; but Kite soon sang out to "snub," the anchor being down, with only six fathoms out. The lead corroborated this, and we had the comfortable assurance of being not only among breakers, but just near the coast. The holding-ground, however, was reported good, and we went to work and rolled up all our rags. In half an hour the ship was snug, riding by the stream, with a strong current, or tide, setting exactly northeast, or directly opposite to the captain's theory. As soon as Mr. Marble had ascertained this fact, I heard him grumbling about something, of which I could distinctly understand nothing but the words "bloody cape—bloody current."

CHAPTER V.

" They hurried us aboard a bark ;
    Bore us some leagues to sea ; where they prepared
    A rotten carcass of a boat, not rigged,
    Nor tackle, sail, nor mast : the very rats
    Instinctively have quit us."

Tempest.

THE hour that succeeded in the calm of expectation, was one of the most disquieting of my life. As soon as the ship was secured, and there no longer remained anything to do, the stillness of death reigned among us ; the faculties of every man and boy appearing to be absorbed in the single sense of hearing—the best, and indeed the only, means we then possessed of judging of our situation. It was now apparent that we were near some place or places where the surf was breaking on land ; and the hollow, not-to-be-mistaken bellowings of the element, too plainly indicated that cavities in rocks frequently received, and as often rejected, the washing waters. Nor did these portentous sounds come from one quarter only, but they seemed to surround us ; now reaching our ears from the known direction of the land, now from the south, the northeast, and, in fact, from every direction. There were instances when these moanings of the ocean sounded as if close under our stern, and then again they came from some point within a fearful proximity to the bows.

Happily the wind was light, and the ship rode with a moderate strain on the cable, so as to relieve us from the apprehension of immediate destruction. There was a long, heavy ground-swell rolling in from the southwest, but, the lead giving us eight fathoms, the sea did not break exactly

where we lay ; though the sullen washing that came to our
ears, from time to time, gave unerring notice that it was
doing so quite near us, independently of the places where it
broke upon rocks. At one time the captain's impatience
was so goading, that he had determined to pull round the
anchorage in a boat, in order to anticipate the approach of
light ; but a suggestion from Mr. Marble that he might unconsciously pull into a roller, and capsize, induced him to
wait for day.

The dawn appeared at last, after two or three of the longest hours I remember ever to have passed. Never shall I
forget the species of furious eagerness with which we gazed
about us. In the first place, we got an outline of the adjacent
land ; then, as light diffused itself more and more into the
atmosphere, we caught glimpses of its details. It was soon
certain we were within a cable's length of perpendicular cliffs
of several hundred feet in height, into whose caverns the sea
poured at times, producing those frightful, hollow moanings
that an experienced ear can never mistake. This cliff extended for leagues in both directions, rendering drowning
nearly inevitable to the shipwrecked mariner on that inhospitable coast. Ahead, astern, outside of us, and I might
almost say all around us, became visible, one after another,
detached ledges, breakers, and ripples ; so many proofs of
the manner in which Providence had guided us through the
hours of darkness.

By the time the sun appeared, for, happily, the day proved
bright and clear, we had obtained pretty tolerable notions of
the critical situation in which we were placed by means
of the captain's theory of currents. The very cape that we
were to drift past, lay some ten leagues nearly dead to windward, as the breeze then was ; while to leeward, far as the
eye could reach, stretched the same inhospitable barrier of
rock as that which lay on our starboard quarter and beam.
Such was my first introduction to the Island of Madagascar ;
a portion of the world, of which, considering its position,
magnitude, and productions, the mariners of Christendom
probably know less than of any other. At the time of which
I am writing, far less had been learned of this vast country

than is known to-day, though the knowledge of even our
own immediate contemporaries is of an exceedingly limited
character.

Now that the day had returned, the sun was shining on
us cheerfully, and the sea looked tranquil and assuring, the
captain became more pacified. He had discretion enough to
understand that time and examination were indispensable to
moving the ship with safety; and he took the wise course of
ordering the people to get their breakfasts, before he set us
at work. The hour that was thus employed forward, was
passed aft in examining the appearance of the water, and
the positions of the reefs around the ship. By the time we
were through, the captain had swallowed his cup of coffee
and eaten his biscuit; and, calling away four of the most
athletic oarsmen, he got into the jolly-boat, and set out on
the all-important duty of discovering a channel seaward.
The lead was kept moving, and I shall leave the party thus
employed for an hour or more, while we turn our attention
in-board.

Marble beckoned me aft, as soon as Captain Robbins was
in the boat, apparently with a desire to say something in
private. I understood the meaning of his eye, and followed
him down into the steerage, where all that was left of the
ship's water was now stowed, that on deck having been already used. The mate had a certain consciousness about
him that induced great caution, and he would not open his
lips until he had rummaged about below some time, affecting to look for a set of blocks that might be wanted for
some purpose or other, on deck. When this had lasted a
little time, he turned short round to me, and let out the secret
of the whole manœuvre.

"I'll tell you what, Master Miles," he said, making a
sign with a finger to be cautious, "I look upon this ship's
berth as worse than that of a city scavenger. We've plenty
of water all round us, and plenty of rocks, too. If we knew
the way back, there is no wind to carry us through it,
among these bloody currents, and there's no harm in getting
ready for the worst. So do you get Neb and the gentleman"
—Rupert was generally thus styled in the ship—"and clear

away the launch first. Get everything out of it that don't belong there; after which, do you put these breakers in, and wait for further orders. Make no fuss, putting all upon orders, and leave the rest to me."

I complied, of course, and in a few minutes the launch was clear. While busy, however, Mr. Kite came past, and desired to know "what are you at there?" I told him 't was Mr. Marble's orders, and the latter gave his own explanation of the matter.

"The launch may be wanted," he said, "for I 've no notion that jolly-boat will do to go out as far as we shall find it necessary to sound. So I am about to ballast the launch, and get her sails ready; there 's no use in mincing matters in such a berth as this."

Kite approved of the idea, and even went so far as to suggest that it might be well enough to get the launch into the water at once, by way of saving time. The proposition was too agreeable to be rejected, and, to own the truth, all hands went to work to get up the tackles with a will, as it is called. In half an hour the boat was floating alongside the ship. Some said she would certainly be wanted to carry out the stream-anchor, if for nothing else; others observed that half-a-dozen boats would not be enough to find all the channel we wanted; while Marble kept his eye, though always in an underhand way, on his main object. The breakers we got in, and stowed, filled with fresh water, by way of ballast. The masts were stepped, the oars were put on board, and a spare compass was passed down, lest the ship might be lost in the thick weather, of which there was so much, just in that quarter of the world. All this was said and done so quietly that nobody took the alarm; and when the mate called out, in a loud voice, "Miles, pass a bread-bag filled and some cold grub into that launch—the men may be hungry before they get back," no one seemed to think more was meant than was thus openly expressed. I had my private orders, however, and managed to get quite a hundred-weight of good cabin biscuit into the launch, while the cook was directed to fill his coppers with pork. I got some of the latter raw into the boat, too; raw pork being food that

sailors in no manner disdain. They say it eats like chestnuts.

In the meantime, the captain was busy in his exploring
expedition, on the return from which he appeared to think
he was better rewarded than has certainly fallen to the lot
of others employed on another expedition which bears the
same name. He was absent near two hours, and, when he
got back, it was to renew his theory of what Mr. Marble
called his "bloody currents."

"I 've got behind the curtain, Mr. Marble," commenced
Captain Robbins, before he was fairly alongside of the ship
again, whereupon Marble muttered, "Ay, ay, you 've got
behind the rocks, too!" "It 's all owing to an eddy that is
made in-shore by the main current, and we have stretched
a *leetle* too far in."

Even I thought to myself, what would have become of us
had we stretched a *leetle* farther in! The captain, however,
seemed satisfied that he could carry the ship out, and, as
this was all we wanted, no one was disposed to be very
critical. A word was said about the launch, which the mate
had ordered to be dropped astern, out of the way, and the
explanation seemed to mystify the captain. In the meanwhile, the pork was boiling furiously in the coppers.

All hands were now called to get the anchor up. Rupert
and I went aloft to loosen sails, and we stayed there until
the royals were mastheaded. In a very few minutes the
cable was up and down, and then came the critical part
of the whole affair. The wind was still very light, and it
was a question whether the ship could be carried past a
reef of rocks that now began to show itself above water, and
on which the long, heavy rollers, that came undulating from
the southwestern Atlantic, broke with a sullen violence that
betrayed how powerful was the ocean, even in its moments
of slumbering peacefulness. The rising and falling of its
surface was like that of some monster's chest, as he respired
heavily in sleep.

Even the captain hesitated about letting go his hold of the
bottom, with so strong a set of the water to leeward, and in
so light a breeze. There was a sort of bight on our starboard

bow, however, and Mr. Marble suggested it might be well
to sound in that direction, as the water appeared smooth
and deep. To him it looked as if there were really an eddy
in-shore, which might hawse the ship up to windward six or
eight times her length, and thus more than meet the loss that
must infallibly occur in first casting her head to seaward.
The captain admitted the justice of this suggestion, and I
was one of those who were told to go in the jolly-boat on this
occasion. We pulled in toward the cliffs, and had not gone
fifty yards before we struck an eddy, sure enough, which
was quite as strong as the current in which the ship lay.
This was a great advantage, and so much the more, because
the water was of sufficient depth, quite up to the edge of the
reef which formed the bight, and thus produced the change
in the direction of the set. There was plenty of room, too,
to handle the ship in, and, all things considered, the discovery was extremely fortunate. In the bottom of this
bight we should have gone ashore, the previous night, had
not our ears been so much better than our noses.

As soon as certain of the facts, the captain pulled back to
the ship, and gladdened the hearts of all on board with the
tidings. We now manned the handspikes cheerily, and began to heave. I shall never forget the impression made on
me by the rapid drift of the ship, as soon as the anchor was
off the bottom, and her bows were cast in-shore, in order to
fill the sails. The land was so near that I noted this drift by
the rocks, and my heart was fairly in my mouth for a few
seconds. But the John worked beautifully, and soon gathered way. Her bows did not strike the eddy, however, until
we got fearful evidence of the strength of the true current,
which had set us down nearly as low as the reef outside, to
windward of which it was indispensable for us to pass.
Marble saw all this, and he whispered me to tell the cook
to pass the pork into the launch at once—not to mind
whether it were particularly well done, or not. I obeyed,
and had to tend the fore-sheet myself, for my pains, when
the order was given to "ready about."

The eddy proved a true friend, but it did not carry us
up much higher than the place where we had anchored,

when it became necessary to tack. This was done in season, on account of our ignorance of all the soundings, and we had soon got the John's head off-shore again. Drawing a short distance ahead, the main-topsail was thrown aback, and the ship allowed to drift. In proper time, it was filled, and we got round once more, looking into the bight. The manœuvre was repeated, and this brought us up fairly under the lee of the reef, and just in the position we desired to be. It was a nervous instant, I make no doubt, when Captain Robbins determined to trust the ship in the true current, and run the gauntlet of the rocks. The passage across which we had to steer, before we could possibly weather the nearest reef, was about a cable's length in width, and the wind would barely let us lay high enough to take it at right angles. Then the air was so light, that I almost despaired of our doing anything.

Captain Robbins put the ship into the current with great judgment. She was kept a rap-full, until near the edge of the eddy, and then her helm was put nearly down, all at once. But for the current's acting, in one direction, on her starboard bow, and the eddy's pressing, in the other, on the larboard quarter, the vessel would have been taken aback ; but these counteracting forces brought her handsomely on her course again, and that in a way to prevent her falling an inch to leeward.

Now came the trial. The ship was kept a rap-full, and she went steadily across the passage, favored, perhaps, by a little more breeze than had blown most of the morning. Still, our leeward set was fearful, and, as we approached the reef, I gave all up. Marble screwed his lips together, and his eyes never turned from the weather-leeches of the sails. Everybody appeared to me to be holding his breath, as the ship rose on the long ground-swells, sending slowly ahead the whole time. We passed the nearest point of the rocks on one of the rounded risings of the water, just touching lightly as we glided by the visible danger. The blow was light, and gave little cause for alarm. Captain Robbins now caught Mr. Marble by the hand, and was in the very act of heartily shaking it, when the ship came down very much in the manner that a man unexpectedly lights on a stone, when he has no idea of having anything within two or three yards of his feet. The blow was tremendous, throwing half the crew down ; at the same instant, all three of the topmasts went to leeward.

One has some difficulty in giving a reader accurate notions of the confusion of so awful a scene. The motion of the vessel was arrested suddenly, as it might be by a wall, and the whole fabric seemed to be shaken to dissolution. The very next roller that came in, which would have undulated in toward the land but for us, meeting with so large a body in its way, piled up and broke upon our decks, covering everything with water. At the same time, the hull lifted, and, aided by wind, sea, and current, it set still farther on the reef, thumping in a way to break strong iron bolts, like so many sticks of sealing-wax, and cracking the solid live-oak of the floor-timbers as if they were made of willow. The captain stood aghast ! For one moment despair was painfully depicted in his countenance ; then he recovered his self-possession and seamanship. He gave the order to stand by to carry out to windward the stream-anchor in the launch, and to send a kedge to haul out by, in the jolly-boat. Marble answered with the usual " Ay, ay, sir ! " but before he sent us into the boats, he ventured to suggest that the ship had bilged already. He had heard timbers crack, about which he thought there could be no mistake. The pumps were sounded, and the ship had seven feet of water in her hold. This had made in about ten minutes. Still, the captain would not give up. He ordered us to commence throwing the teas overboard, in order to ascertain, if possible, the extent of the injury. A place was broken out in the wake of the main-hatch, and a passage was opened down into the lower hold, where we met the water. In the meantime, a South Sea man we had picked up at Canton, dove down under the lee of the bilge of the ship. He soon came back and reported that a piece of sharp rock had gone quite through the planks. Everything tending to corroborate this, the captain called a council of all hands on the quarter-deck, to consult as to further measures.

A merchantman has no claim on the services of her crew after she is hopelessly wrecked. The last have a lien in law on the ship and cargo for their wages; and it is justly determined that when this security fails, the claim for services ends. It followed, of course, that as soon as the John was given over, we were all our own masters; and hence the necessity for bringing even Neb into the consultation. With a vessel-of-war it would have been different. In such a case the United States pays for the service, ship or no ship, wreck or no wreck; and the seaman serves out his term of enlistment, be this longer or shorter. Military discipline continues under all circumstances.

Captain Robbins could hardly speak when we gathered round him on the forecastle, the seas breaking over the quarter-deck in a way to render that sanctuary a very uncomfortable berth. As soon as he could command himself, he told us that the ship was hopelessly lost. How it had happened, he could not very well explain himself, though he ascribed it to the fact that the currents did not run in the direction in which, according to all sound reasoning, they ought to run. This part of the speech was not perfectly lucid, though, as I understood our unfortunate captain, the laws of nature, owing to some inexplicable influence, had departed, in some way or other, from their ordinary workings expressly to wreck the John. If this were not the meaning of what he said, I did not understand this part of the address.

The captain was much more explicit after he got out of the current. He told us that the island of Bourbon was only about four hundred miles from where we then were, and he thought it possible to go that distance, find some small craft, and come back, and still save part of the cargo, the sails, anchors, etc., etc. We might make such a trip of it as would give us all a lift, in the way of salvage, that might prove some compensation for our other losses. This sounded well, and it had at least the effect to give us some present object for our exertions; it also made the danger we all ran of losing our lives less apparent. To land on the island of Madagascar in that day, was out of the ques-

"I shouted 'Land ho!'" Miles Wallingford sights the island of Bourbon from the jolly boat in company with Mr. Marble, Rupert, Neb and the cook, following the wreck of the *John* off the island of Madagascar. *Illustration by R. F. Zogbaum.*

(*p. 80*)

tion. The people were then believed to be far less civilized than in truth they were, and had a particularly bad character among mariners. Nothing remained, therefore, but to rig the boats, and make immediate dispositions for our departure.

Now it was that we found the advantage of the preparations already made. Little remained to be done, and that which was done was much better done than if we had waited until the wreck was half full of water, and the seas were combing in upon her. The captain took charge of the launch, putting Mr. Marble, Rupert, Neb, myself, and the cook into the jolly-boat, with orders to keep as close as possible to himself. Both boats had sails, and both were so arranged as to row in calms, or head winds. We took in rather more than our share of provisions and water, having two skilful caterers in the chief mate and cook; and, having obtained a compass, quadrant, and a chart for our portion of the indispensables, all hands were ready for a start in about two hours after the ship had struck.

It was just noon when we cast off from the wreck, and stood directly off the land. According to our calculations, the wind enabled us to run, with a clean full, on our true course. As the boats drew out into the ocean, we had abundant opportunities of discovering how many dangers we had escaped; and, for my own part, I felt deeply grateful, even then, as I was going out on the wide Atlantic in a mere shell of a boat, at the mercy we had experienced. No sooner were we fairly in deep water, than the captain and mate had a dialogue on the subject of the currents again. Notwithstanding all the difficulties his old theory had brought him into, the former remained of opinion that the true current set to windward, and that we should so find it as soon as we got a little into the offing; while the mate was frank enough to say he had been of opinion, all along, that it ran the other way. The latter added that Bourbon was rather a small spot to steer for, and it might be better to get into its longitude, and then find it by meridian observations, than to make any more speculations about matters of which we knew nothing.

The captain and Mr. Marble saw things differently, and we kept away accordingly, when we ought to have luffed all we could. Fortunately the weather continued moderate, or our little boat would have had a bad time of it. We out-sailed the launch with ease, and were forced to reef in order not to part company. When the sun set, we were more than twenty miles from the land, seeing no more of the coast, though the mountains inland were still looming up grandly in the distance. I confess, when night shut in upon us, and I found myself on the wide ocean, in a boat much smaller than that with which I used to navigate the Hudson, running every minute farther and farther into the watery waste, I began to think of Clawbonny, and its security, and quiet nights, and well-spread board, and comfortable beds, in a way I had never thought of either before. As for food, however, we were not stinted ; Mr. Marble setting us an example of using our teeth on the half-boiled pork, that did credit to his philosophy. To do this man justice, he seemed to think a run of four hundred miles in a jolly-boat no great matter, but took everything as regularly as if still on the deck of the John. Each of us got as good a nap as our cramped situations would allow.

The wind freshened in the morning, and the sea began to break. This made it necessary to keep still more away, to prevent filling at times, or to haul close up, which might have done equally well. But the captain preferred the latter course, on account of the current. We had ticklish work of it, in the jolly-boat, more than once that day, and were compelled to carry a whole sail in order to keep up with the launch, which beat us, now the wind had increased, Marble was a terrible fellow to carry on everything, ship or boat, and we kept our station admirably, the two boats never getting a cable's length asunder, and running most of the time within hail of each other. As night approached, however, a consultation was held on the subject of keeping in company. We had now been out thirty hours, and had made near a hundred and fifty miles, by our calculation. Luckily the wind had got to be nearly west, and we were running ahead famously, though it was as much as we could

do to keep the jolly-boat from filling. One hand was kept
bailing most of the time, and sometimes all four of us were
busy. These matters were talked over, and the captain
proposed abandoning the jolly-boat altogether, and to take
us into the launch, though there was not much vacant space
to receive us. But the mate resisted this, answering that
he thought he could take care of our boat a while longer,
at least. Accordingly, the old arrangement was maintained, the party endeavoring to keep as near together as
possible.

About midnight it began to blow in squalls, and two or
three times we found it necessary to take in our sails, out
oars, and pull the boat head to sea, in order to prevent her
swamping. The consequence was, that we lost sight of the
launch, and, though we always kept away to our course as
soon as the puffs would allow, when the sun rose we saw
nothing of our late companions. I have sometimes thought
Mr. Marble parted company on purpose, though he seemed
much concerned next morning when he had ascertained the
launch was nowhere to be seen. After looking about for
an hour, and the wind moderating, we made sail close on
the wind ; a direction that would soon have taken us away
from the launch, had the latter been close alongside when
we first took it. We made good progress all this day, and
at evening, having now been out fifty-four hours, we supposed ourselves to be rather more than half way on the
road to our haven. It fell calm in the night, and the next
morning we got the wind right aft. This gave us a
famous shove, for we sometimes made six and seven knots
in the hour. The fair wind lasted thirty hours, during
which time we must have made more than a hundred and
fifty miles, it falling nearly calm about an hour before
dawn, on the morning of the fourth day out. Everybody
was anxious to see the horizon that morning, and every eye
was turned to the east, with intense expectation, as the
sun rose. It was in vain ; there was not the least sign of
land visible. Marble looked sadly disappointed, but he endeavored to cheer us up with the hope of seeing the island
shortly. We were then heading due east, with a very ligh'

breeze from the northwest. I happened to stand up in the boat, on a thwart, and, turning my face to the southward, I caught a glimpse of something that seemed like a hummock of land in that quarter. I saw it but for an instant; but, whatever it was, I saw it plain enough. Mr. Marble now got on the thwart, and looked in vain to catch the same object. He said there was no land in that quarter—could be none—and resumed his seat to steer to the eastward, a little north. I could not be easy, however, but remained on the thwart until the boat lifted on a swell higher than common, and then I saw the brown, hazy-looking spot on the margin of the ocean again. My protestations now became so earnest, that Marble consented to stand for an hour in the direction I pointed out to him. "One hour, boy, I will grant you, to shut your mouth," the mate said, taking out his watch, "and that you need lay nothing to my door hereafter." To make the most of this hour, I got my companions at the oars, and we all pulled with hearty good-will. So much importance did I attach to every fathom of distance made, that we did not rise from our seats until the mate told us to stop rowing, for the hour was up. As for himself, he had not risen either, but kept looking behind him to the eastward, still hoping to see land somewhere in that quarter.

My heart beat violently as I got upon the thwart, but there lay my hazy object, now never dipping at all. I shouted "Land ho!" Marble jumped up on a thwart, too, and no longer disputed my word. It was land, he admitted, and it must be the island of Bourbon, which we had passed to the northward, and must soon have given a hopelessly wide berth. We went to the oars again with renewed life, and soon made the boat spin. All that day we kept rowing, till about five in the afternoon, when we found ourselves within a few leagues of the island of Bourbon, where we were met by a fresh breeze from the southward, and were compelled to make sail. The wind was dead on end, and we made stretches under the lee of the island, going about as we found the sea getting to be too heavy for us, as was invariably the case whenever we got too far east or west.

In a word a lee was fast becoming necessary. By ten, we were within a mile of the shore, but saw no place where we thought it safe to attempt a landing in the dark ; a long, heavy sea setting in round both sides of the island, though the water did not break much where we remained. At length the wind got to be so heavy, that we could not carry even our sail double-reefed, and we kept two oars pulling lightly in, relieving each other every hour. By daylight it blew tremendously, and glad enough were we to find a little cove where it was possible to get ashore. I had then never felt so grateful to Providence as I did when I got my feet on *terra firma*.

We remained on the island a week, hoping to see the launch and her crew ; but neither appeared. Then we got a passage to the Isle of France, on arriving at which place we found the late gale was considered to have been very serious. There was no American consul in the island, at that time ; and Mr. Marble, totally without credit or means, found it impossible to obtain a craft of any sort to go to the wreck in. We were without money, too, and, a home-ward-bound Calcutta vessel coming in, we joined her to work our passages home, Mr. Marble as dickey, and the rest of us in the forecastle. This vessel was called the Tigris, and belonged to Philadelphia. She was considered one of the best ships out of America, and her master had a high reputation for seamanship and activity. He was a little man of the name of Digges, and was under thirty at the time I first knew him. He took us on board purely out of a national feeling, for his ship was strong-handed with-out us, having thirty-two souls, all told, when he received us five. We afterwards learned that letters sent after the ship had induced Captain Digges to get five additional hands in Calcutta, in order to be able to meet the picaroons that were then beginning to plunder American vessels, even on their own coast, under the pretence of their having violated certain regulations made by the two great belliger-ents of the day, in Europe. This was just the commence-ment of the *quasi* war which broke out a few weeks later with France.

Of all these hostile symptoms, however, I then knew little and cared less. Even Mr. Marble had never heard of them, and we five joined the Tigris merely to get passages home, without entertaining second thoughts of running any risk, further than the ordinary dangers of the seas.

The Tigris sailed the day we joined her, which was the third after we reached Mauritius, and just fifteen days after we had left the wreck. We went to sea with the wind at the southward, and had a good run off the island, making more than a hundred miles that afternoon and in the course of the night. Next morning, early, I had the watch, and an order was given to set topgallant studding-sails. Rupert and I had got into the same watch on board this vessel, and we both went aloft to reeve the gear. I had taken up the end of the halyards, and had reeved them, and had overhauled the end down, when, in raising my head, I saw two small lug-sails on the ocean, broad on our weather-bow, which I recognized in an instant for those of the John's launch. I cannot express the feeling that came over me at that sight. I yelled, rather than shouted, "Sail ho !" and then, pushing in, I caught hold of a royal-backstay, and was on deck in an instant. I believe I made frantic gestures to windward, for Mr. Marble, who had the watch, had to shake me sharply before I could let the fact be known.

As soon as Marble comprehended me, and got the bearings of the boat, he hauled down all the studding-sails, braced sharp up on a wind, set the mainsail, and then sent down a report to Captain Digges for orders. Our new commander was a humane man, and having been told our whole story, he did not hesitate about confirming all that had been done. As the people in the launch had made out the ship some time before I saw the boat, the latter was running down upon us, and, in about an hour, the tiny sails were descried from the deck. In less than an hour after this, our main-yard swung round, throwing the topsail aback, and the well-known launch of the John rounded-to close under our lee ; a rope was thrown, and the boat was hauled alongside.

Everybody in the Tigris was shocked when we came to get a look at the condition of the strangers. One man, a powerful negro, lay dead in the bottom of the boat; the body having been kept for a dreadful alternative, in the event of his companions falling in with no other relief. Three more of the men were nearly gone, and had to be whipped on board as so many lifeless bales of goods. Captain Robbins and Kite, both athletic, active men, resembled spectres, their eyes standing out of their heads as if thrust from their sockets by some internal foe ; and when we spoke to them, they all seemed unable to answer. It was not fasting, or want of food, that had reduced them to this state, so much as want of water. It is true, they had no more bread left than would keep body and soul together for a few hours longer ; but of water they had tasted not a drop for seventy-odd hours ! It appeared that, during the gale, they had been compelled to empty the breakers to lighten the boat, reserving only one for their immediate wants. By some mistake, the one reserved was nearly half empty at the time ; and Captain Robbins believed himself then so near Bourbon, as not to go on an allowance until it was too late. In this condition had they been searching for the island quite ten days, passing it, but never hitting it. The winds had not favored them, and, the last few days, the weather had been such as to admit of no observation. Consequently, they had been as much out of their reckoning in their latitude as in their longitude.

A gleam of intelligence, and I thought of pleasure, shot athwart the countenance of Captain Robbins, as I helped him over the Tigris' side. He saw I was safe. He tottered as he walked, and leaned heavily on me for support. I was about to lead him aft, but his eye caught sight of a scuttle-butt, and the tin-pot on its head. Thither he went, and stretched out a trembling hand to the vessel. I gave him the pot as it was, with about a wine-glass of water in it. This he swallowed at a gulp, and then tottered forward for more. By this time Captain Digges joined us, and gave the proper directions how to proceed. All the sufferers had water in small quantities given them, and it is won-

derful with what expressions of delight they received the
grateful beverage. As soon as they understood the necessity of keeping it as long as possible in their mouths, and
on their tongues, before swallowing it, a little did them a
great deal of good. After this, we gave them some coffee,
the breakfast being ready, and then a little ship's biscuit
soaked in wine. By such means every man was saved,
though it was near a month before all were themselves again.
As for Captain Robbins and Kite, they were enabled to attend to duty by the end of a week, though nothing more
was exacted of them than they chose to perform.

CHAPTER VI.

*"The yesty waves
Confound and swallow navigation up."*

Macbeth.

POOR Captain Robbins! No sooner did he regain his bodily strength than he began to endure the pain of mind that was inseparable from the loss of his ship. Marble, who, now that he had fallen to the humbler condition of a second mate, was more than usually disposed to be communicative with me, gave me to understand that our old superior had at first sounded Captain Digges on the subject of proceeding to the wreck, in order to ascertain what could be saved; but the latter had soon convinced him that a first-rate Philadelphia Indiaman had something else to do besides turning wrecker. After a pretty broad hint to this effect, the John, and all that was in her, were abandoned to their fate. Marble, however, was of opinion that the gale in which the launch came so near being lost, must have broken the ship entirely to pieces, giving her fragments to the ocean. We never heard of her fate, or recovered a single article that belonged to her.

Many were the discussions between Captain Robbins and his two mates, touching the error in reckoning that had led them so far from their course. In that day, navigation was by no means as simple a thing as it has since become. It is true, lunars were usually attempted in India and China ships; but this was not an every-day affair, like the present morning and afternoon observations to obtain the time, and, by means of the chronometer, the longitude. Then we had so recently got clear of the islands, as to have no great need of any extraordinary head-work; and the "bloody currents" had acted their pleasure with us for eight or ten days before the loss of the ship. Marble was a very good navigator, one of the best I ever sailed with, in spite of the plainness of his exterior and his rough deportment; and, all things considered, he treated his old commander with great delicacy, promising to do all he could when he got home to clear the matter up. As for Kite, he knew but little, and had the discretion to say but little. This moderation rendered our passage all the more agreeable.

The Tigris was a very fast ship, besides being well found. She was a little larger than the John, and mounted twelve guns, nine-pounders. In consequence of the additions made to her crew, one way and another, she now mustered nearer fifty than forty souls on board. Captain Digges had certain martial tastes, and, long before we were up with the cape, he had us all quartered and exercised at the guns. He, too, had had an affair with some proas, and he loved to converse of the thrashing he had given the rascals. I thought he envied us our exploit, though this might have been mere imagination on my part, for he was liberal enough in his commendations. The private intelligence he had received of the relations between France and America quickened his natural impulses; and, by the time we reached St. Helena, the ship might have been said to be in good fighting order for a merchantman. We touched at this last-mentioned island for supplies, but obtained no news of any interest. Those who supplied the ship could tell us nothing but the names of the Indiamen who had gone out and home for the last twelvemonth, and the prices of fresh meat and vegetables. Napoleon civilized them seventeen years later.

We had a good run from St. Helena to the calm latitudes, but these last proved calmer than common. We worried through them after awhile, however, and then did very well until we got in the latitude of the Windward Islands. Marble one day remarked to me that Captain Digges was standing closer to the French island of Guadaloupe than was at all necessary or prudent, if he believed in his own

reports of the danger there existed to American commerce
in this quarter of the ocean.

I have lived long enough, and have seen too much of
men and things to fancy my country and countrymen right
in all their transactions, merely because newspapers, members of Congress, and Fourth of July orators are pleased
to affirm the doctrine. No one can go much to sea without reading with great distrust many of the accounts in the
journals of that day, of the grievous wrong done the commerce of America by the authorities of this or that port,
the seizure of such a ship, or the imprisonment of some
particular set of officers and men. As a rule, it is safer
to assume that the afflicted parties deserve all that has
happened to them, than to believe them immaculate ; and
quite likely much more, too. The habit of receiving such
appeals to their sympathies renders the good people of the
republic peculiarly liable to impositions of this nature ; and
the mother who encourages those of her children who fetch
and carry will be certain to have her ears filled with complaints and tattle. Nevertheless, it is a fact beyond all
dispute that the commerce of the country was terribly depre-
dated on by nearly all the European belligerents between
the commencement of the war of the French Revolution
and its close. So enormous were the robberies thus committed on the widely-extended trade of this nation, under
one pretence or another, as to give a coloring of retributive
justice, if not of moral right, to the recent failures of certain
States among us to pay their debts. Providence singularly
avenges all wrongs by its unerring course ; and I doubt
not, if the facts could be sifted to the bottom, it would be
found the devil was not permitted to do his work in either
case without using materials supplied by the sufferers in
some direct or indirect manner themselves. Of all the
depredations on American trade just mentioned, those of
the great sister republic, at the close of the last century,
were among the most grievous, and were of a character so
atrocious and bold, that I confess it militates somewhat
against my theory to admit that France owns very little
of the " suspended debt " · but I account for this last cir-

cumstance by the reparation she in part made by the treaty
of 1831. With England it is different. She drove us into
a war by the effects of her orders in council and paper
blockades, and compelled us to expend a hundred millions
to set matters right. I should like to see the books bal-
anced, not by the devil, who equally instigated the robberies
on the high seas, and the "suspension" or "repudiation"
of the State debts ; but by the great Accountant who keeps
a record of all our deeds of this nature, whether it be to
take money by means of cruising ships, or cruising scrip.
It is true these rovers encountered very different-looking
victims in the first place ; but it is a somewhat trite remark,
that the aggregate of human beings is pretty much the same
in all situations. There were widows and orphans as much
connected with the condemnation of prizes, as with the
prices of condemned stock ; and I do not see that fraud is
any worse when carried on by scriveners and clerks with
quills behind their ears than when carried on by gentlemen
wearing cocked hats and carrying swords by their sides.
On the whole, I am far from certain that the account-cur-
rent of honesty is not slightly—honesty very slightly
leavens either transaction—in favor of the non-paying
States, as men do sometimes borrow with good intentions,
and fail, from inability, to pay ; whereas, in the whole
course of my experience, I never knew a captor of a ship
who intended to give back any of the prize-money if he
could help it. But to return to my adventures.

We were exactly in the latitude of Guadaloupe, with the
usual breeze, when, at daylight, a rakish-looking brig was
seen in chase. Captain Digges took a long survey of the
stranger with his best glass—one that was never exhibited
but on state occasions—and then pronounced him to be a
French cruiser ; most probably a privateer. That he was
a Frenchman, Marble affirmed, was apparent by the height
of his topmasts and the shortness of his yards, the upper
spars, in particular, being mere apologies for yards. Everybody who had any right to an opinion, was satisfied the
brig was a French cruiser, either public or private.

The Tigris was a fast ship, and she was under topmast

and topgallant studding-sails at the time, going about seven
knots. The brig was on an easy bowline, evidently looking up for our wake, edging off gradually as we drew
ahead. She went about nine knots, and bade fair to close
with us by noon. There was a good deal of doubt, aft, as to
the course we ought to pursue. It was decided in the end,
however, to shorten sail and let the brig come up, as being
less subject to cavils, than to seem to avoid her. Captain
Digges got out his letters from home, and I saw him showing them to Captain Robbins, the two conning them over
with great earnestness. I was sent to do some duty near
the hen-coops, where they were sitting, and overheard a
part of their conversation. From the discourse, I gathered
that the proceedings of these picaroons were often equivocal,
and that Americans were generally left in doubt, until a
favorable moment occurred for the semi-pirates to effect their
purposes. The party assailed did not know when or how
to defend himself, until it was too late.

"These chaps come aboard you, sometimes, before you're
aware of what they are about," observed Captain Robbins.

"I'll not be taken by surprise in that fashion," returned
Digges, after a moment of reflection. "Here, you Miles,
go forward and tell the cook to fill his coppers with water,
and to set it boiling as fast as he can ; and tell Mr. Marble I
want him aft. Bear a hand, now, youngster, and give them
a lift yourself."

Of course I obeyed, wondering what the captain wanted
with so much hot water as to let the people eat their dinners off cold grub, rather than dispense with it ; for this
was a consequence of his decree. But we had not got the
coppers half filled, before I saw Mr. Marble and Neb lower-
ing a small ship's engine from the launch, and placing it
near the galley, in readiness to be filled. The mate told
Neb to screw on the pipe, and then half a dozen of the
men, as soon as we got through with the coppers, were told
to fill the engine with sea water. Captain Digges now came
forward to superintend the exercise, and Neb jumped on the
engine, flourishing the pipe about with the delight of a
"nigger." The captain was diverted with the black's

zeal, and he appointed him captain of the firemen on the spot.

"Now, let us see what you can do at that forward dead-eye, darkey," said Captain Digges, laughing. "Take it directly on the strap. Play away, boys, and let Neb try his hand."

It happened that Neb hit the dead-eye at the first jet, and he showed great readiness in turning the stream from point to point, as ordered. Neb's conduct on the night of the affair with the proas had been told to Captain Digges, who was so well pleased with the fellow's present dexterity, as to confirm him in office. He was told to stick by the engine at every hazard. Soon after, an order was given to clear for action. This had an ominous sound to my young ears, and, though I have no reason to suppose myself deficient in firmness, I confess I began to think again of Clawbonny, and Grace, and Lucy; ay, and even of the mill. This lasted but for a moment, however, and, as soon as I got at work, the feeling gave me no trouble. We were an hour getting the ship ready, and, by that time, the brig was within half a mile, luffing fairly up on our lee-quarter. As we shortened sail, the privateer manifested no intention of throwing a shot to make us heave-to. She seemed disposed to extend courtesy for courtesy.

The next order was for all hands to go to quarters. I was stationed in the main-top, and Rupert in the fore. Our duties were to do light work, in the way of repairing damages; and the captain, understanding that we were both accustomed to firearms, gave us a musket apiece, with orders to blaze away as soon as they began the work below. As we had both stood fire once, we thought ourselves veterans, and proceeded to our stations, smiling and nodding to each other as we went up the rigging. Of the two, my station was the best, since I could see the approach of the brig, the mizzen-topsail offering but little obstruction to vision after she got near; whereas the main-topsail was a perfect curtain, so far as poor Rupert was concerned. In the way of danger, there was not much difference as to any of the stations on board, the bulwarks of the ship being

little more than plank that would hardly stop a musket-
ball; and then the French had a reputation for firing into
the rigging.

As soon as all was ready, the captain sternly ordered silence. By this time the brig was near enough to hail. I could
see her decks quite plainly, and they were filled with men.
I counted her guns, too, and ascertained she had but ten,
all of which seemed to be lighter than our own. One circumstance that I observed, however, was suspicious. Her
forecastle was crowded with men, who appeared to be crouch-
ing behind the bulwarks, as if anxious to conceal their
presence from the eyes of those in the Tigris. I had a mind
to jump on a backstay and slip down on deck, to let this
threatening appearance be known ; but I had heard some sayings touching the imperative duty of remaining at quarters,
in face of the enemy, and I did not like to desert my station.
Tyros have always exaggerated notions both of their rights
and their duties, and I had not escaped the weakness. Still,
I think some credit is due for the alternative adopted. During the whole voyage, I had kept a reckoning, and paper
and pencil were always in my pocket, in readiness to catch a
moment to finish a day's work. I wrote as follows on a
piece of paper, therefore, as fast as possible, and dropped
the billet on the quarter-deck, by enclosing a copper in the
scrawl, cents then being in their infancy. I had merely
written, "The brig's forecastle is filled with armed men
hid behind the bulwarks!" Captain Digges heard the fall
of the copper, and looking up—nothing takes an officer's eye
aloft quicker than to find anything coming out of a top !—
he saw me pointing to the paper. I was rewarded for this
liberty by an approving nod. Captain Digges read what I
had written, and I soon observed Neb and the cook filling
the engine with boiling water. This job was no sooner
done than a good place was selected on the quarter-deck for
this singular implement of war, and then a hail came from
the brig.

"Vat zat sheep is?" demanded some one from the brig.

"The Tigris of Philadelphia, from Calcutta home. What
brig is that?"

"La Folie, corsaire Française. From vair you come?"

"From Calcutta. And where are you from?"

"Guadaloupe. Vair you go, eh?"

"Philadelphia. Do not luff so near me; some accident may happen."

"Vat you call 'accident'? Can nevair hear, eh? I will come tout près."

"Give us a wider berth, I tell you! Here is your jib-boom nearly foul of my mizzen-rigging."

"Vat mean zat, bert' vidair? eh! Allons, mes enfants, c'est le moment!"

"Luff a little, and keep his spar clear," cried our captain. "Squirt away, Neb, and let us see what you can do!"

The engine made a movement, just as the French began to run out on their bowsprit, and, by the time six or eight were on the heel of the jib-boom, they were met by the hissing hot stream, which took them *en echelon*, as it might be, fairly raking the whole line. The effect was instantaneous. Physical nature cannot stand excessive heat, unless particularly well supplied with skin; and the three leading Frenchmen, finding retreat impossible, dropped incontinently into the sea, preferring cold water to hot—the chances of drowning, to the certainty of being scalded. I believe all three were saved by their companions in-board, but I will not vouch for the fact. The remainder of the intended boarders, having the bowsprit before them, scrambled back upon the brig's forecastle as well as they could, betraying, by the random way in which their hands flew about, that they had a perfect consciousness how much they left their rear exposed on the retreat. A hearty laugh was heard in all parts of the Tigris, and the brig, putting her helm hard up, wore round like a top, as if she were scalded herself.[1]

We all expected a broadside now; but of that there was little apprehension, as it was pretty certain we carried the heaviest battery, and had men enough to work it. But the brig did not fire, I suppose, because we fell off a little ourselves, and she perceived it might prove a losing game. On

---

[1] This incident actually occurred in the war of 1798.

the contrary, she went quite round on her heel, hauling up
on the other tack far enough to bring the two vessels exactly
dos-à-dos. Captain Digges ordered two of the quarter-deck
nines to be run out of the stern-ports; and it was well he
did, for it was not in nature for men to be treated as our
friends in the brig had been served, without manifesting
certain signs of ill-humor. The vessels might have been
three cables' lengths asunder when we got a gun. The first
I knew of a shot was to hear it plunge through the mizzen-
topsail, then it came whistling through my top, between the
weather-rigging and the masthead, cutting a hole through
the main-topsail, and, proceeding onward, I heard it strike
something more solid than canvas. I thought of Rupert and
the fore-top in an instant, and looked anxiously down on
deck to ascertain if he were injured.

"Fore-top, there!" called out Captain Digges; "where
did that shot strike?"

"In the masthead," answered Rupert, in a clear, firm
voice. "It has done no damage, sir."

"Now's your time, Captain Robbins—give 'em a re-
minder."

Both our nines were fired, and a few seconds after, three
cheers arose from the decks of our ship. I could not see the
brig, now, for the mizzen-topsail; but I afterward learned
that we had shot away her gaff. This terminated the combat, in which the glory was acquired principally by Neb.
They told me, when I got down among the people again,
that the black's face had been dilated with delight the whole
time, though he stood fairly exposed to musketry, his mouth
grinning from ear to ear. Neb was justly elated with the
success that attended this exhibition of his skill, and described the retreat of our enemies with a humor and relish
that raised many a laugh at the discomfited privateersman.
It is certain that some of the fellows must have been nearly
parboiled.

I have always supposed this affair between La Folie and
the Tigris to have been the actual commencement of hostilities in the *quasi* war of 1798-99 and 1800. Other occurrences soon supplanted it in the public mind; but we of the

ship never ceased to regard the adventure as one of great national interest. It did prove to be a nine days' wonder in the newspapers.

From this time, nothing worthy of being noted occurred, until we reached the coast. We had got as high as the capes of Virginia, and were running in for the land, with a fair wind, when we made a ship in-shore of us. The stranger hauled up to speak us, as soon as we were seen. There was a good deal of discussion about this vessel, as she drew near, between Captain Digges and his chief mate. The latter said he knew the vessel, and that it was an Indiaman out of Philadelphia, called the Ganges, a sort of sister craft to our own ship ; while the former maintained, if it were the Ganges at all, she was so altered as scarcely to be recognized. As we got near, the stranger threw a shot under our fore-foot, and showed an American pennant and ensign. Getting a better look at her, we got so many signs of a vessel-of-war in our neighbor, as to think it wisest to heave-to, when the other vessel passed under our stern, tacked, and lay with her head-yards aback, a little on our weather-quarters. As she drew to windward, we saw her stern, which had certain national emblems, but no name on it. This settled the matter. She was a man-of-war, and she carried the American flag ! Such a thing did not exist a few months before, when we left home, and Captain Digges was burning with impatience to know more. He was soon gratified.

"Is not that the Tigris ? " demanded a voice, through a trumpet, from the stranger.

" Ay, ay ! What ship is that ? "

" The United States Ship Ganges, Captain Dale ; from the capes of the Delaware, bound on a cruise. You're welcome home, Captain Digges ; we may want some of your assistance under a cockade."

Digges gave a long whistle, and then the mystery was out. This proved to be the Ganges, as stated, an Indiaman bought into a new navy, and the first ship-of-war ever sent to sea under the government of the country, as it had existed since the adoption of the Constitution, nine years before. The privateers of France had driven the republic into an armament, and ships were fitting out in considerable numbers; some being purchased, like the Ganges, and others built expressly for the new marine. Captain Digges went on board the Ganges, and, pulling an oar in his boat, I had a chance of seeing that vessel also. Captain Dale, a compact, strongly-built, seaman-like looking man, in a blue and white uniform, received our skipper with a cordial shake of the hand, for they had once sailed together, and he laughed heartily when he heard the story of the boarding-party and the hot water. This respectable officer had no braggadocio about him, but he intimated that it would not be long, as he thought, before the rovers among the islands would have their hands full. Congress was in earnest, and the whole country was fairly aroused. Whenever that happens in America, it is usu- ally to take a new and better direction than to follow the ordinary blind impulses of popular feelings. In countries where the masses count for nothing, in the every-day working of their systems, excitement has a tendency to democracy; but, among ourselves, I think the effect of such a condition of things is to bring into action men and qualities that are commonly of little account, and to elevate, instead of depressing, public sentiment.

I was extremely pleased with the manly, benevolent countenance of Captain Dale, and had half a desire to ask leave to join his ship on the spot. If that impulse had been followed, it is probable my future life would have been very different from what it subsequently proved. I should have been rated a midshipman, of course; and, serving so early, with a good deal of experience already in ships, a year or two would have made me a lieutenant, and, could I have survived the pruning of 1801, I should now have been one of the oldest officers in the service. Providence directed otherwise; and how much was lost, or how much gained, by my continuance in the Tigris, the reader will learn as we proceed.

As soon as Captain Digges had taken a glass or two of wine with his old acquaintance, we returned to our own ship, and the two vessels made sail; the Ganges standing off to the northward and eastward, while we ran in for the capes of the Delaware. We got in under Cape May, or within five miles of it, the same evening, when it fell nearly calm. A pilot came off from the cape in a row-boat, and he reached us just at dark. Captain Robbins now became all impatience to land, as it was of importance to him to be the bearer of his own bad news. Accordingly, an arrangement having been made with the two men who belonged to the shore-boat, our old commander, Rupert and myself, prepared to leave the ship, late as it was. We two lads were taken for the purpose of manning two additional oars, but were to rejoin the ship in the bay, if possible; if not, up at town. One of the inducements of Captain Robbins to be off, was the signs of northerly weather. It had begun to blow a little in puffs from the northwest; and everybody knew, if it came on to blow seriously from that quarter, the ship might be a week in getting up the river, her news being certain to precede her. We hurried off accordingly, taking nothing with us but a change of linen, and a few necessary papers.

We got the first real blast from the northwest in less than five minutes after we had quitted the Tigris' side, and while the ship was still visible, or, rather, while we could yet see the lights in her cabin windows, as she fell off before the wind. Presently the lights disappeared, owing, no doubt, to the ship's luffing again. The symptoms now looked so threatening, that the pilot's men proposed making an effort, before it was too late, to find the ship; but this was far easier said than done. The vessel might be spinning away toward Cape Henlopen, at the rate of six or seven knots; and, without the means of making any signal in the dark, it was impossible to overtake her. I do believe that Captain Robbins would have acceded to the request of the men, had he seen any probability of succeeding; as it was, there remained no alternative but to pull in, and endeavor to reach the land. We had the light on the cape as our beacon, and the boat's head was kept directly for it, as the wisest course for us to pursue.

Changes of wind from southeast to northwest are very common on the American coast. They are almost always sudden; sometimes so much so, as to have taken ships aback; and the force of the breeze usually comes so early as to have produced the saying that a "nor'wester comes butt-end foremost." Such proved to be the fact in our case. In less than half an hour after it began to blow, the wind would have brought the most gallant ship that floated to double-reefed topsails, steering by, and to reasonably short canvas, running large. We may have pulled a mile in this half hour, though it was by means of a quick stroke and great labor. The Cape May men were vigorous and experienced, and they did wonders; nor were Rupert and I idle; but, as soon as the sea got up, it was as much as all four of us could do to keep steerage-way on the boat. There were ten minutes, during which I really think the boat was kept head to sea by means of the wash of the waves that drove past, as we barely held her stationary.

Of course it was out of the question to continue exertions that were as useless as they were exhausting. We tried the expedient, however, of edging to the northward, with the hope of getting more under the lee of the land, and, consequently, into smoother water, but it did no good. The nearest we ever got to the light must have considerably exceeded a league. At length Rupert, totally exhausted, dropped his oar, and fell panting on the thwart. He was directed to steer, Captain Robbins taking his place. I can only liken our situation at that fearful moment to the danger of a man who is clinging to a cliff, its summit and safety almost in reach of his hand, with the consciousness that his powers are fast failing him, and that he must shortly go down. It is true, death was not so certain by our abandoning the effort to reach the land, but the hope of being saved was faint indeed. Behind us lay the vast and angry Atlantic, without an inch of visible land between us and the Rock of Lisbon. We were totally without food of any sort, though, luckily, there was a small breaker of fresh water in the boat. The Cape May men had brought off their suppers with them, but they had made the meal;

whereas the rest of us had left the Tigris fasting, intend-ing to make comfortable suppers at the light.

At length Captain Robbins consulted the boatmen, and asked them what they thought of our situation. I sat be-tween these men, who had been remarkably silent the whole time, pulling like giants. Both were young, though, as I afterward learned, both were married ; each having a wife at that anxious moment waiting on the beach of the cape for the return of the boat. As Captain Robbins put the question, I turned my head, and saw that the man behind me, the oldest of the two, was in tears. I cannot describe the shock I experienced at this sight. Here was a man accustomed to hardships and dangers, who was making the stoutest and most manly efforts to save himself and all with him at the very moment, so strongly impressed with the danger of our situation, that his feelings broke forth in a way it is always startling to witness, when the grief of a man is thus exhibited in tears. The imagination of this husband was doubtless picturing to his mind the anguish of his wife at that moment, and, perhaps, the long days of sorrow that were to succeed. I have no idea he thought of himself, apart from his wife ; for a finer, more manly, resolute fellow never existed, as he subsequently proved to the fullest extent.

It seemed to me that the two Cape May men had a sort of desperate reluctance to give up the hope of reaching the land. We were a strong boat's crew, and we had a capital, though a light boat ; yet all would not do. About mid-night, after pulling desperately for three hours, my strength was quite gone, and I had to give up the oar. Captain Robbins confessed himself in a very little better state, and, it being impossible for the boatmen to do more than keep the boat stationary, and that only for a little time longer, there remained no expedient, but to keep off before the wind, in the hope of still falling in with the ship. We knew that the Tigris was on the starboard tack when we left her, and, as she would certainly endeavor to keep as close in with the land as possible, there was a remaining chance that she had wore ship to keep off Henlopen, and might be heading

up about north-northeast, and laying athwart the mouth of
the bay. This left us just a chance—a ray of hope; and it
had now become absolutely necessary to endeavor to profit
by it.

The two Cape May men pulled the boat round, and kept
her just ahead of the seas, so far as it was in their power;
very light touches of the oars sufficing for this where it could
be done at all. Occasionally, however, one of those chasing
waves would come after us at a racer's speed, invariably
breaking at such instants, and frequently half filling the
boat. This gave us new employment, Rupert and myself
being kept quite half the time bailing. No occupation,
notwithstanding the danger, could prevent me from looking
about the cauldron of angry waters, in quest of the ship.
Fifty times did I fancy I saw her, and as often did the delu-
sive idea end in disappointment. The waste of dark waters,
relieved by the gleaming of the combing seas, alone met the
senses. The wind blew directly down the estuary, and,
in crossing its mouth, we found too much swell to receive it
on our beam, and were soon compelled, most reluctantly
though it was, to keep dead away to prevent swamping.
This painful state of expectation may have lasted half an
hour, the boat sometimes seeming ready to fly out of the
water, as it drifted before the gale, when Rupert unexpectedly called out that he saw the ship.

There she was, sure enough, with her head to the northward and eastward, struggling along through the raging
waters, under her fore and main-topsails, close-reefed, and
reefed courses, evidently clinging to the land as close as she
could, both to hold her own and to make good weather. It
was barely light enough to ascertain these facts, though the
ship was not a cable's length from us when first discovered.
Unfortunately, she was dead to leeward of us, and was drawing ahead so fast as to leave the probability she would fore-
reach upon us, unless we took to all our oars. This was
done as soon as possible, and away we went, at a rapid rate,
aiming to shoot directly beneath the Tigris' lee-quarter, so
as to round-to under shelter of her hull, there to receive
a rope.

We pulled like giants. Three several times the water slapped into us, rendering the boat more and more heavy; but Captain Robbins told us to pull on, every moment being precious. As I did not look round,—could not well, indeed,—I saw no more of the ship until I got a sudden glimpse of her dark hull, within a hundred feet of us, surging ahead in the manner in which vessels at sea seem to take sudden starts that carry them forward at twice their former apparent speed. Captain Robbins had begun to hail, the instant he thought himself near enough, or at the distance of a hundred yards; but what was the human voice amid the music of the winds striking the various cords, and I may add chords, in the mazes of a square-rigged vessel's hamper, accompanied by the base of the roaring ocean! Heavens! what a feeling of despair was that, when the novel thought suggested itself almost simultaneously to our minds, that we should not make ourselves heard! I say simultaneously, for at the same instant the whole five of us set up a common, desperate shout to alarm those who were so near us, and who might easily save us from the most dreadful of all deaths—starvation at sea. I presume the fearful manner in which we struggled at the oars diminished the effect of our voices, while the effort to raise a noise lessened our power with the oars. We were already to leeward of the ship, though nearly in her wake, and our only chance now was to overtake her. The captain called out to us to pull for life or death, and pull we did. So frantic were our efforts, that I really think we should have succeeded, had not a sea come on board us, and filled us to the thwarts. There remained no alternative but to keep dead away, and to bail for our lives.

I confess I felt scalding tears gush down my cheeks, as I gazed at the dark mass of the ship just before it was swallowed up in the gloom. This soon occurred, and then, I make no doubt, every man in the boat considered himself as hopelessly lost. We continued to bail, notwithstanding; and, using hats, gourds, pots, and pans, soon cleared the boat, though it was done with no other seeming object than to avert immediate death. I heard one of the Cape May

men pray. The name of his wife mingled with his petitions
to God. As for poor Captain Robbins, who had so recently
been in another scene of equal danger in a boat, he remained
silent, seemingly submissive to the decrees of Providence.

In this state we must have drifted a league dead before
the wind, the Cape May men keeping their eyes on the
light, which was just sinking below the horizon, while the
rest of us were gazing seaward in ominous expectation of
what awaited us in that direction, when the hail of "Boat
ahoy!" sounded like the last trumpet in our ears. A
schooner was passing our track, keeping a little off, and
got so near as to allow us to be seen, though, owing to a
remark about the light which drew all eyes to windward,
not a soul of us saw her. It was too late to avert the
blow, for the hail had hardly reached us, when the
schooner's cut-water came down upon our little craft, and
buried it in the sea as if it had been lead. At such moments men do not think, but act. I caught at a bobstay,
and missed it. As I went down into the water, my hand
fell upon scme object to which I clung, and, the schooner
rising at the next instant, I was grasped by the hair by one
of the vessel's men. I had hold of one of the Cape May
men's legs. Released from my weight, this man was soon
in the vessel's head, and he helped to save me. When we
got in-board, and mustered our party, it was found that all
had been saved but Captain Robbins. The schooner wore
round, and actually passed over the wreck of the boat a
second time; but our old commander was never heard of
more!

CHAPTER VII.

"Oh! forget not the hour, when through forest and vale
We returned with our chief to his dear native halls!
Through the woody Sierra there sighed not a gale,
And the moonbeam was bright on his battlement walls;
And nature lay sleeping in calmness and light,
Round the house of the truants, that rose on our sight."

MRS. HEMANS.

WE had fallen on board an eastern coaster, called the Martha Wallis, bound from James River to Boston, intending to cross the shoals. Her watch had seen us, because the coasters generally keep better lookouts than Indiamen; the latter, accustomed to good offings, having a trick of letting their people go to sleep in the night-watches. I made a calculation of the turns on board the Tigris, and knew it was Mr. Marble's watch when we passed the ship; and I make no question he was, at that very moment, nodding on the hen-coops—a sort of trick he had. I cannot even now understand, however, why the man at the wheel did not hear the outcry we made. To me it appeared loud enough to reach the land.

Sailors ordinarily receive wrecked mariners kindly. Our treatment on board the Martha Wallis was all I could have desired, and the captain promised to put us on board the first coaster she should fall in with, bound to New York. He was as good as his word, though not until more than a week had elapsed. It fell calm as soon as the northwester blew its pipe out, and we did not get into the Vineyard Sound for nine days. Here we met a craft the skipper knew, and, being a regular Boston and New York coaster, we were put on board her, with a recommendation to good treatment. The people of the Lovely Lass received us just as we had been received on board the Martha Wallis ; all hands of us living aft, and eating codfish, good beef and pork, with duff (dough) and molasses, almost *ad libitum*. From this last vessel we learned all the latest news of the French war, and how things were going on in the country. The fourth day after we were put on board this craft, Rupert and I landed near Peck's Slip, New York, with nothing on earth in our possession, but just in what we stood. This, however, gave us but little concern—I had abundance at home, and Rupert was certain of being free from want, both through me and through his father.

I had never parted with the gold given me by Lucy, how-ever. When he got into the boat to land at the cape, I had put on the belt in which I kept this little treasure, and it was still round my body. I had kept it as a sort of memo-rial of the dear girl who had given it to me ; but I now saw the means of making it useful, without disposing of it alto-gether. I knew that the wisest course, in all difficulties, was to go at once to headquarters. I asked the address of the firm that owned, or rather had owned the John, and proceeded to the counting-house forthwith. I told my story, but found that Kite had been before me. It seems that the Tigris got a fair wind, three days after the blow, that carried her up to the very wharves of Philadelphia, when most of the John's people had come on to New York without delay. By communications with the shore at the cape, the pilot had learned that his boat had never returned, and our loss was supposed to have inevitably occurred. The accounts of all this were in the papers, and I began to fear that the distressing tidings might have reached Claw-bonny. Indeed, there were little obituary notices of Rupert and myself in the journals, inserted by some hand piously employed, I should think, by Mr. Kite. We were tenderly treated, considering our escapade ; and my fortune and pros-pects were dwelt on with some touches of eloquence that might have been spared.

In that day, however, a newspaper was a very different thing from what it has since become. Then, journals were created merely to meet the demand, and news was given as it actually occurred ; whereas, now, the competition has produced a change that any one can appreciate, when it is remembered to what a competition in news must infallibly lead. In that day, our own journals had not taken to imitating the worst features of the English newspapers—talents and education are not yet cheap enough in America to enable them to imitate the best—and the citizen was supposed to have some rights, as put in opposition to the press. The public sense of right had not become blunted by familiarity with abuses, and the miserable and craven apology was never heard for not enforcing the laws, that nobody cares for what the newspapers say. Owing to these causes, I escaped a thousand lies about myself, my history, my disposition, character, and acts. Still, I was in print ; and I confess it half frightened me to see my death announced in such obvious letters, although I had physical evidence of being alive and well.

The owners questioned me closely about the manner in which the John was lost, and expressed themselves satisfied with my answers. I then produced my half-joes, and asked to borrow something less than their amount on their security. To the latter part of the proposition, however, these gentlemen would not listen, forcing a check for a hundred dollars on me, desiring that the money might be paid at my own convenience. Knowing I had Clawbonny and a very comfortable income under my lee, I made no scruples about accepting the sum, and took my leave.

Rupert and I had now the means of equipping ourselves neatly, though always in sailor guise. After this was done we proceeded to the Albany basin, in order to ascertain whether the Wallingford were down or not. At the basin we learned that the sloop had gone out that very forenoon, having on board a black with his young master's effects ; a lad who was said to have been out to Canton with young Mr. Wallingford, and who was now on his way home to report all the sad occurences to the family in Ulster. This, then, was Neb, who had got thus far back in charge of our chests, and was about to return to slavery.

We had been in hopes that we might possibly reach Claw-bonny before the tidings of our loss. This intelligence was likely to defeat the expectation ; but, luckily, one of the fastest sloops on the river, a Hudson packet, was on the point of sailing, and, though the wind held well to the northward, her master thought he should be able to turn up with the tides as high as our creek, in the course of the next eight-and-forty hours. This was quite as much as the Wallingford could do I felt well persuaded ; and, making a bargain to be landed on the western shore, Rupert and I put our things on board this packet, and were under way in half an hour's time.

So strong was my own anxiety, I could not keep off the deck until we had anchored on account of the flood ; and much did I envy Rupert, who had coolly turned in as soon as it was dark, and went to sleep. When the anchor was down, I endeavored to imitate his example. On turning out next morning, I found the vessel in Newburg Bay, with a fair wind. About twelve o'clock I could see the mouth of the creek, and the Wallingford fairly entering it, her sails disappearing behind the trees just as I caught sight of them. As no other craft of her size ever went up to that landing, I could not be mistaken in the vessel.

By getting ashore half a mile above the creek, there was a farm-road that would lead to the house by a cut so short, as nearly to bring us there as soon as Neb could possibly arrive with his dire, but false intelligence. The place was pointed out to the captain, who had extracted our secret from us, and who, good-naturedly, consented to do all we asked of him. I do think he would have gone into the creek itself, had it been required. But we were landed with our bag of clothes—one answered very well for both—at the place I have mentioned, and, taking turn about to shoulder the wardrobe, away we went, as fast as legs could carry us. Even Rupert seemed to feel on this occasion, and I do think he had a good deal of contrition, as he must have recollected the pain he had occasioned his excellent father, and dear, good sister.

Clawbonny never looked more beautiful than when I first

cast eyes on it that afternoon. There lay the house in the secure retirement of its smiling vale, the orchards just beginning to lose their blossoms; the broad, rich meadows, with the grass waving in the south wind, resembling velvet; the fields of corn of all sorts; and the cattle, as they stood ruminating or enjoying their existence in motionless self-indulgence beneath the shade of trees, seemed to speak of abundance and considerate treatment. Everything denoted peace, plenty, and happiness. Yet this place, with all its blessings and security, had I wilfully deserted to encounter pirates in the Straits of Sunda, shipwreck on the shores of Madagascar, jeopardy in an open boat off the Isle of France, and a miraculous preservation from a horrible death on my own coast!

At no great distance from the house was a dense grove, in which Rupert and I had, with our own hands, constructed a rude summer-house, fit to be enjoyed on just such an afternoon as this on which we had returned. When distant from it only two hundred yards, we saw the girls enter the woods, evidently taking the direction of the seat. At the same moment I caught a glimpse of Neb moving up the road from the landing at a snail's pace, as if the poor fellow dreaded to encounter the task before him. After a moment's consultation, we determined to proceed at once to the grove, and thus anticipate the account of Neb, who must pass so near the summer-house as to be seen and recognized, We met with more obstacles than we had foreseen or remembered, and when we got to a thicket close in the rear of the bench, we found that the black was already in the presence of his two "young mistresses."

The appearance of the three, when I first caught a near view of them, was such as almost to terrify me. Even Neb, whose face was usually as shining as a black bottle, was almost of the color of ashes. The poor fellow could not speak, and, though Lucy was actually shaking him to extract an explanation, the only answer she could get was tears. These flowed from Neb's eyes in streams, and, at length, the fellow threw himself on the ground, and fairly began to groan.

"Can this be shame at having run away?" exclaimed Lucy, "or does it foretell evil to the boys?"

"He knows nothing of them, not having been with them --yet, I am terrified."

"Not on my account, dearest sister," I cried aloud ; "here are Rupert and I, God be praised, both in good health, and safe."

I took care to remain hid, as I uttered this, not to alarm more than one sense at a time ; but both the girls shrieked, and held out their arms. Rupert and I hesitated no longer, but sprang forward. I know not how it happened, though I found, on recovering my self-possession, that I was folding Lucy to my heart, while Rupert was doing the same to Grace. This little mistake, however, was soon rectified, each man embracing his own sister, as in duty bound, and as was most decorous. The girls shed torrents of tears, and assured us again and again, that this was the only really happy moment they had known since the parting on the wharf, nearly a twelvemonth before. Then followed looks at each other, exclamations of surprise and pleasure at the changes that had taken place in the appearance of all parties, and kisses and tears again in abundance.

As for Neb, the poor fellow was seen in the road, whither he had fled at the sound of my voice, looking at us like one in awe and doubt. Being satisfied in the end of our identity, as well as of our being in the flesh, the negro again threw himself on the ground, rolling over and over, and fairly yelling with delight. After going through this process of negro excitement, he leaped up on his feet, and started for the house, shouting at the top of his voice, as if certain the good intelligence he brought would secure his own pardon, —"Master Miles come home !—Master Miles come home !"

In a few minutes quiet was sufficiently restored among us four, who remained at the seat, to ask questions, and receive intelligible answers. Glad was I to ascertain that the girls had been spared the news of our loss. As for Mr. Hardinge, he was well, and busied, as usual, in discharging the duties of his holy office. He had told Grace and Lucy the name of the vessel in which we had shipped, but said nothing of the painful glimpse he had obtained of us, just as we lifted our anchor to quit the port. Grace, in a solemn manner, then demanded an outline of our adventures. As Rupert was the spokesman on this occasion, the question having been in a manner put to him as oldest, I had an opportunity of watching the sweet countenances of the two painfully interested listeners. Rupert affected modesty in his narration, if he did not feel it, though I remarked that he dwelt a little particularly on the shot which had lodged so near him, in the head of the Tigris' foremast. He spoke of the whistling it made as it approached, and the violence of the blow when it struck. He had the impudence, too, to speak of my good luck in being on the other side of the top, when the shot passed through my station; whereas I do believe that the shot passed nearer to me than it did to himself. It barely missed me, and by all I could learn, Rupert was leaning over by the topmast rigging when it lodged. The fellow told his story in his own way, however, and with so much unction that I observed it made Grace look pale. The effect on Lucy was different. This excellent creature perceived my uneasiness, I half suspected, for she laughed, and, interrupting her brother, told him, "There—that's enough about the cannon-ball; now let us hear of something else." Rupert colored, for he had frequently had such frank hints from his sister, in the course of his childhood; but he had too much address to betray the vexation I knew he felt.

To own the truth, my attachment for Rupert had materially lessened with the falling off of my respect. He had manifested so much selfishness during the voyage—had shirked so much duty, most of which had fallen on poor Neb—and had been so little of the man, in practice, whom he used so well to describe with his tongue—that I could no longer shut my eyes to some of his deficiencies of character. I still liked him, but it was from habit, and perhaps because he was my guardian's son, and Lucy's brother. Then I could not conceal from myself that Rupert was not, in a rigid sense, a lad of truth. He colored, exaggerated, glossed over, and embellished, if he did not absolutely

"The Grace and Lucy made one or two tolerably long cruises in the river." Miles and Rupert take their sisters for a trip on the Hudson River aboard the *Wallingford* following their return from their first sea voyage. *Drawing by J. Wheeler.*   (*p. 114*)

invent. I was not old enough then to understand that
most of the statements that float about the world are nothing but truths distorted, and that nothing is more rare than
unadulterated fact ; that truths and lies travel in company,
as described by Pope in his *Temple of Fame*, until

"This or that unmixed, no mortal e'er shall find."

In this very narration of our voyage, Rupert had left
false impressions on the minds of his listeners, in fifty
things. He had made far more of both our little skirmishes
than the truth would warrant, and he had neglected to
do justice to Neb in his account of each of the affairs.
Then he commended Captain Robbins' conduct in connection with the loss of the John, on points that could not be
sustained, and censured him for measures that deserved
praise. I knew Rupert was no seaman,—was pretty well
satisfied, by this time, he never would make one,—but I
could not explain all his obliquities by referring them to
ignorance. The manner, moreover, in which he represented himself as the principal actor, on all occasions, denoted so much address, that, while I felt the falsity of the
impressions he left, I did not exactly see the means necessary to counteract them. So ingenious, indeed, was his
manner of stringing facts and inferences together, or what
seemed to be facts and inferences, that I more than once
caught myself actually believing that which, in sober reality, I knew to be false. I was still too young, not quite
eighteen, to feel any apprehensions on the subject of Grace ;
and was too much accustomed to both Rupert and his sister
to regard either with any feelings very widely different from
those which I entertained for Grace herself.

As soon as the history of our adventures and exploits
was concluded, we all had leisure to observe and comment
on the alterations that time had made on our several persons. Rupert, being the oldest, was the least changed in
this particular. He had got his growth early, and was only
a little spread. He had cultivated a pair of whiskers at
sea, which rendered his face a little more manly,—an improvement, by the way,—but, the effects of exposure and

of the sun excepted, there was no very material change in
his exterior. Perhaps, on the whole, he was improved in
appearance. I think both the girl's fancied this, though
Grace did not say it, and Lucy only half admitted it, and
with many reservations. As for myself, I was also full-
grown, standing exactly six feet in my stockings, which was
pretty well for eighteen. But I had also spread; a fact
that is not common for lads at that age. Grace said I had
lost all delicacy of appearance; and as for Lucy, though
she laughed and blushed, she protested I began to look like
a great bear. To confess the truth, I was well satisfied
with my own appearance, did not envy Rupert a jot, and
knew I could toss him over my shoulder whenever I chose.
I stood the strictures on my appearance, therefore, very
well; and, though no one was so much derided and laughed
at as myself, in that critical discussion, no one cared less
for it. Just as I was permitted to escape, Lucy said, in an
undertone,—

"You should have stayed at home, Miles, and then the
changes would have come so gradually, no one would have
noticed them, and you would have escaped being told how
much you are altered, and that you are a bear."

I looked eagerly round at the speaker, and eyed her intently. A look of regret passed over the dear creature's
face, her eyes looked as penitent as they did soft, and
the flush that suffused her countenance rendered this last
expression almost bewitching. At the same instant she
whispered, "I did not really mean that."

But it was Grace's turn, and my attention was drawn to
my sister. A year had made great improvements in Grace.
Young as she was, she had lost much of the girlish air in
the sedateness and propriety of the young woman. Grace
had always something more of these last than is common;
but they had now completely removed every appearance of
childish, I might almost say of girlish frivolity. In person
her improvement was great; though an air of exceeding
delicacy rather left an impression that such a being was
more intended for another world than this. There was
even an air of fragility and of pure intellectuality about

my poor sister, that half disposed one to fancy that she would one day be translated to a better sphere in the body precisely as she stood before human eyes. Lucy bore the examination well. She was all woman, there being nothing about her to create any miraculous expectations or fanciful pictures ; but she was evidently fast getting to be a very lovely woman. Honest, sincere, full of heart, overflowing with the feelings of her sex, gentle, yet spirited, buoyant, though melting with the charities ; her changeful, but natural, and yet constant feelings in her, kept me incessantly in pursuit of her playful mind and varying humors. Still, a more high-principled being, a firmer or more consistent friend, or a more accurate thinker on all subjects that suited her years and became her situation than Lucy Hardinge, never existed. Even Grace was influenced by her judgment, though I did not then know how much my sister's mind was guided by her simple and less pretending friend's capacity to foresee things, and to reason on their consequences.

We were more than an hour uninterruptedly together before we thought of repairing to the house. Lucy then reminded Rupert that he had not yet seen his father, whom she had just before observed alighting from his horse at the door of his own study. That he had been apprised of the return of the runaways, if not prodigals, was evident, she thought, by his manner ; and it was disrespectful to delay seeking his forgiveness and blessing. Mr. Hardinge received us both without surprise, and totally without any show of resentment. It was about the time he expected our return, and no surprise was felt at finding this expectation realized, as a matter of course, while resentment was almost a stranger to his nature. We all shed tears, the girls sobbing aloud ; and we were both solemnly blessed. Nor am I ashamed to say I knelt to receive that blessing, in an age when the cant of a pretending irreligion—there is as much cant in self-sufficiency as in hypocrisy, and they very often go together—is disposed to turn into ridicule the humbling of the person while asking for the blessing of the Almighty through the ministers of his altars ; for kneel I did, and weep I did, and, I trust, the one in humility and the other in contrition.

When we had all become a little calm, and a substantial meal was placed before us adventurers, Mr. Hardinge demanded an account of all that had passed. He applied to me to give it, and I was compelled to discharge the office of an historian, somewhat against my inclination. There was no remedy, however, and I told the story in my own simple manner, and certainly in a way to leave very different impressions from many of those made by the narrative of Rupert. I thought once or twice, as I proceeded, Lucy looked sorrowful, and Grace looked surprised. I do not think I colored in the least as regarded myself, and I know I did Neb no more than justice. My tale was soon told, for I felt the whole time as if I were contradicting Rupert, who, by the way, appeared perfectly unconcerned—perfectly unconscious, indeed—on the subject of the discrepancies in the two accounts. I have since met with men who did not know the truth when it was even placed very fairly before their eyes.

Mr. Hardinge expressed his heartfelt happiness at having us back again, and soon after he ventured to ask if we were satisfied with what we had seen of the world. This was a home question, but I thought it best to meet it manfully. So far from being satisfied, I told him it was my ardent desire to get on board one of the letters-of-marque, of which so many were then fitting out in the country, and to make a voyage to Europe. Rupert, however, confessed he had mistaken his vocation, and that he thought he could do no better than to enter a lawyer's office. I was thunderstruck at this quiet admission of my friend of his incapacity to make a sailor, for it was the first intimation I heard of his intention. I had remarked a certain want of energy in various situations that required action in Rupert, but no want of courage ; and I had ascribed some portion of his lassitude to the change of condition, and, possibly, of food ; for, after all, that godlike creature, man, is nothing but an animal, and is just as much influenced by his stomach and digestion as a sheep or a horse.

Mr. Hardinge received his son's intimation of a prefer-
ance of intellectual labors to a more physical state of existence, with a gratification my own wishes did not afford
him.   Still, he made no particular remark to either at the
time, permitting us both to enjoy our return to Clawbonny,
without any of the drawbacks of advice or lectures.   The
evening passed delightfully, the girls beginning to laugh
heartily at our own ludicrous accounts of the mode of living
on board ship, and of our various scenes in China, the Isle
of Bourbon, and elsewhere.   Rupert had a great deal of
humor, and a very dry way of exhibiting it ; in short, he
was almost a genius in the mere superficialities of life ; and
even Grace rewarded his efforts to entertain us, with laughter to tears.   Neb was introduced after supper, and the
fellow was both censured and commended ; censured for
having abandoned the household gods, and commended for
not having deserted their master.   His droll descriptions of
the Chinese, their dress, pigtails, shoes, and broken English,
diverted even Mr. Hardinge, who, I believe, felt as much
like a boy on this occasion, as any of the party.   A happier
evening than that which followed in the little tea-parlor, as
my dear mother used to call it, was never passed in the century that the roof had covered the old walls of Clawbonny.

Next day I had a private conversation with my guardian,
who commenced the discourse by rendering a sort of account
of the proceeds of my property during the past year.   I
listened respectfully, and with some interest ; for I saw the
first gave Mr. Hardinge great satisfaction, and I confess the
last afforded some little pleasure to myself.   I found that
things had gone on very prosperously.   Ready money was
accumulating, and I saw that, by the time I came of age,
sufficient cash would be on hand to give me a ship of my
own, should I choose to purchase one.   From that moment
I was secretly determined to qualify myself to command her
in the intervening time.   Little was said of the future, beyond an expression of the hope, by my guardian, that I
would take time to reflect before I came to a final decision
on the subject of my profession.   To this I said nothing
beyond making a respectful inclination of the head.

For the next month, Clawbonny was a scene of uninter-
rupted merriment and delight. We had few families to
visit in our immediate neighborhood, it is true; and Mr.
Hardinge proposed an excursion to the Springs,—the country was then too new, and the roads too bad, to think of
Niagara—but to this I would not listen. I cared not for the
Springs,—knew of, and cared less for fashion,—and loved
Clawbonny to its stocks and stones. We remained at home,
then, living principally for each other. Rupert read a good
deal to the girls, under the direction of his father; while I
passed no small portion of my time in athletic exercises.
The Grace and Lucy made one or two tolerably long cruises
in the river, and at length I conceived the idea of taking
the party down to town in the Wallingford. Neither of the
girls had ever seen New York, or much of the Hudson; nor
had either ever seen a ship. The sloops that passed up and
down the Hudson, with an occasional schooner, were the
extent of their acquaintance with vessels; and I began to
feel it to be matter of reproach that those in whom I took so
deep an interest, should be so ignorant. As for the girls
themselves, they both admitted, now I was a sailor, that
their desire to see a regular, three-masted, full-rigged ship,
was increased seven-fold.

Mr. Hardinge heard my proposition, at first, as a piece of
pleasantry; but Grace expressing a strong desire to see a
large town, or what was thought a large town in this
country, in 1799, and Lucy looking wistful, though she remained silent under an apprehension her father could not
afford the expense of such a journey, which her imagination
rendered a great deal more formidable than it actually
proved to be, the excellent divine finally acquiesced. The
expense was disposed of in a very simple manner. The
journey, both ways, would be made in the Wallingford;
and Mr. Hardinge was not so unnecessarily scrupulous as to
refuse passages for himself and children in the sloop, which
never exacted passage-money from any who went to or
from the farm. Food was so cheap, too, as to be a matter
of no consideration; and, being entitled legally to receive
that at Clawbonny, it made no great difference whether it

were taken on board the vessel, or in the house. Then
there was a Mrs. Bradfort in New York, a widow lady of
easy fortune, who was a cousin-german of Mr. Hardinge's,
—his father's sister's daughter,—and with her he always
stayed in his own annual visits to attend the convention of
the Church,—I beg pardon, of the Protestant Episcopal
Church, as it is now *de rigueur* to say ; I wonder some ultra
does not introduce the manifest improvement into the
Apostles' Creed of saying, " I believe in the Holy Protestant
Episcopal Catholic Church," etc.,—but, the excellent divine,
in his annual attendance on the conventions, was accustomed
to stay with his kinswoman, who often pressed him to bring
both Lucy and Grace to see her ; her house in Wall Street
being abundantly large enough to accommodate a much more
numerous party. " Yes," said Mr. Hardinge, " that shall
be the arrangement. The girls and I will stay with Mrs.
Bradfort, and the young men can live at a tavern. I dare
say this new City Hotel, which seems to be large enough to
contain a regiment, will hold even them. I will write this
very evening to my cousin, so as not to take her by surprise."

In less than a week after this determination, an answer
was received from Mrs. Bradfort ; and, the very next day,
the whole party, Neb included, embarked in the Wallingford. Very different was this passage down the Hudson
from that which had preceded it. Then I had the sense
of error about me, while my heart yearned toward the two
dear girls we had left on the wharf ; but now everything
was above-board, sincere, and by permission. It is scarcely
necessary to say that Grace and Lucy were enchanted with
everything they saw. The Highlands, in particular, threw
them both into ecstasies, though I have since seen so much
of the world as to understand, with nearly all experienced
tourists, that this is relatively the worst part of the scenery
of this beautiful river. When I say relatively, I mean as
comparing the bolder parts of our stream with those of
others,—speaking of them as high lands,—many other portions of this good globe having a much superior grandeur,
while very few have so much lovely river scenery compressed

into so small a space as is to be found in the other parts of the Hudson.

In due time we arrived in New York, and I had the supreme happiness of pointing out to the girls the State's prison, the Bear Market, and the steeples of St. Paul's and Trinity—old Trinity, as it was so lately the fashion to style a church that was built only a few years before, and which, in my youth, was considered as magnificent as it was venerable. That building has already disappeared; and another edifice, which is now termed splendid, *vast*, and I know not what, has been reared in its place. By the time this is gone, and one or two generations of buildings have succeeded, each approaching nearer to the high standard of church architecture in the old world, the Manhattanese will get to understand something of the use of the degrees of comparison on such subjects. When that day shall arrive, they will cease to be provincial, and—not till then.

What a different thing was Wall Street, in 1799, from what it is to-day! Then, where so many Grecian temples are now reared to Plutus, were rows of modest provincial dwellings; not a tittle more provincial, however, than the thousand meretricious houses of bricks and marble that have since started up in their neighborhood, but far less pretending, and in so much the more creditable. Mrs. Bradfort lived in one of these respectable abodes, and thither Mr. Hardinge led the way, with just as much confidence as one would now walk into Bleecker Street, or the Fifth Avenue. Money-changers were then unknown, or, if known, were of so little account that they had not sufficient force to form a colony and a league by themselves. Even the banks did not deem it necessary to be within a stone's throw of each other,—I believe there were but two,—as it might be in self-defence. We have seen all sorts of expedients adopted, in this sainted street, to protect the money-bags, from the little temple that was intended to be so small as only to admit the dollars and those who were to take care of them, up to the edifice that might contain so many rogues, as to render things safe on the familiar principle of setting a thief to catch a thief. All would not do. The difficulty has been found to be unconquerable, except in those cases in which the homely and almost worn-out expedient of employing honest men has been resorted to. But, to return from the gossipings of old age to an agreeable widow, who was still under forty.

Mrs. Bradfort received Mr. Hardinge in a way to satisfy us all that she was delighted to see him. She had prepared a room for Rupert and myself, and no apologies or excuses would be received. We had to consent to accept of her hospitalities. In an hour's time all were established, and I believe all were at home.

I shall not dwell on the happiness that succeeded. We were all too young to go to parties, and, I might almost add, New York itself was too young to have any ; but in the last I should have been mistaken, though there were not as many children's balls in 1799, perhaps, after allow-ing for the difference in population, as there are to-day. If too young to be company, we were not too young to see sights. I sometimes laugh as I remember what these were at that time. There was such a museum as would now be thought lightly of in a Western city of fifteen or twenty years' growth—a circus kept by a man of the name of Richetts—the theatre in John Street, a very modest Thespian edifice—and a lion, I mean literally the beast, that was kept in a cage quite out of town, that his roaring might not disturb people, somewhere near the spot where the triangle that is called Franklin Square now is. All these we saw, even to the theatre ; good, indulgent Mr. Hardinge seeing no harm in letting us go thither under the charge of Mrs. Bradfort. I shall never forget the ecstasy of that night ! The novelty was quite as great to Rupert and myself as it was to the girls ; for though we had been to China, we had never been to the play.

Well was it said, " Vanity, vanity—all is vanity ! " He that lives as long as I have lived, will have seen most of his opinions, and I think I may add, all his tastes, change. Nothing short of revelation has a stronger tendency to con-vince us of the temporary character of our probationary state in this world, than to note for how short a period,

and for what imperfect ends, all our hopes and success in
life have been buoying us up, and occupying our minds.
After fifty, the delusion begins to give way ; and, though
we may continue to live, and even to be happy, blind indeed must be he who does not see the end of his road, and
foresee some of the great results to which it is to lead.   But
of all this, our quartette thought little in the year 1799.

CHAPTER VIII.

"Thou art the same eternal sea!
The earth hath many shapes and forms
Of hill and valley, flower and tree;
Fields that the fervid noontide warms,
Or Winter's rugged grasp deforms,
Or bright with Autumn's golden store;
Thou coverest up thy face with storms,
)r smilest serene—but still thy roar
And dashing foam go up to vex the sea-beat shore.
                                                    LUNT.

I HAD a free conversation with my guardian, shortly
after we reached town, on the subject of my going
to sea again. The whole country was alive with the
armament of the new marine; and cocked hats, blue
coats and white lappels, began to appear in the streets, with
a parade that always marks the new officer and the new
service. Now, one meets distinguished naval men at every
turn, and sees nothing about their persons to denote the
profession, unless in actual employment afloat, even the
cockade being laid aside; whereas in 1799 the harness was
put on as soon as the parchment was received, and only laid
aside to turn in. Ships were building or equipping in all
parts of the country; and it is matter of surprise to me that
I escaped the fever, and did not apply to be made a midshipman. Had I seen another captain who interested me as
much as Captain Dale, I make no doubt my career would
have been quite different; but, as things were, I had im-
bibed the prejudice that Southey, in his very interesting, but,
in a professional sense, very worthless, *Life of Nelson*,
has attributed to that hero: "Aft, the more honor; forward,

the better man.'' Thus far, I had not got into the cabin windows, and, like all youngsters who fairly begin on the forecastle, felt proud of my own manhood and disdain of hazards
and toil. I determined, therefore, to pursue the course I
had originally pointed out to myself, and follow in the footsteps of my father.

Privateers were out of the question in a war with a country that had no commerce. Nor do I think I would have
gone in a privateer under any circumstances. The business
of carrying on a warfare merely for gain, has ever struck me
as discreditable ; though it must be admitted the American
system of private-armed cruisers has always been more
respectable and better conducted than that of most other
nations. This has been owing to the circumstance that men
of a higher class than is usual in Europe, have embarked in
the enterprises. To a letter-of-marque, however, there could
be no objection ; her regular business is commerce ; she
arms only in self-defence, or, if she capture anything, it is
merely such enemies as cross her path, and who would
capture her if they could. I announced to Mr. Hardinge,
therefore, my determination not to return to Clawbonny, but
to look for a berth in some letter-of-marque, while then in
town.

Neb had received private instructions, and my sea dunnage, as well as his own, was on board the Wallingford,—
low enough the wreck had reduced both to be,—and
money obtained from Mr. Hardinge was used to purchase
more. I now began to look about me for a ship, determined to please my eye as to the vessel, and my judgment
as to the voyage. Neb had orders to follow the wharves
on the same errand. I would sooner trust Neb than Rupert
on such a duty. The latter had no taste for ships ; felt no
interest in them ; and I have often wondered why he took a
fancy to go to sea at all. With Neb it was very different.
He was already an expert seaman ; could hand, reef, and
steer, knot and splice, and was as useful as nine men in ten
on board a vessel. It is true, he did not know when it
became necessary to take in the last reef—had no notion of
stowing a cargo so as to favor the vessel, or help her sailing ;

but he would break out a cask sooner than most men I ever met with. There was too much "nigger" in him for head-work of that sort, though he was ingenious and ready enough in his way. A sterling fellow was Neb, and I got in time to love him very much as I can conceive one would love a brother.

One day, after I had seen all the sights, and had begun to think seriously of finding a ship, I was strolling along the wharves on the latter errand, when I heard a voice I knew cry out, "There, Captain Williams, there's just your chap; he'll make as good a third mate as can be found in all America." I had a sort of presentiment this applied to me, though I could not, on the instant, recall the speaker's name. Turning to look in the direction of the sounds, I saw the hard countenance of Marble, alongside the weather-beaten face of a middle-aged shipmaster, both of whom were examining me over the nettings of a very promising-looking armed merchantman. I bowed to Mr. Marble, who beckoned me to come on board, where I was regularly introduced to the master.

This vessel was called the Crisis, a very capital name for a craft in a country where crisises of one sort or another occur regularly as often as once in six months. She was a tight little ship of about four hundred tons, had hoop-pole bulwarks, as I afterward learned, with nettings for ham-mocks and old junk, principally the latter; and showed ten nine-pounders, carriage-guns, in her batteries. I saw she was loaded, and was given to understand that her shipping-articles were then open, and the serious question was of procuring a third mate. Officers were scarce, so many young men were pressing into the navy; and Mr. Marble ventured to recommend me, from near a twelvemonth's knowledge of my character. I had not anticipated a berth aft quite so soon, and yet I had an humble confi-dence in my own ability to discharge the duty. Captain Williams questioned me for fifteen or twenty minutes, had a short conversation with Mr. Marble alone, and then frankly offered me the berth. The voyage was to be round the world, and it took my fancy at the very sound. The

ship was to take a cargo of flour to England ; there, she was
to receive a small assorted cargo for the northwest coast, and
some of the sandal-wood islands ; after disposing of her toys
and manufactures in barter, she was to sail for Canton,
exchange her furs, wood, and other articles for teas, etc.,
and return home. To engage in this voyage, I was offered
the berth I have mentioned, and thirty dollars a month.
The wages were of little moment to me, but the promotion
and the voyage were of great account. The ship, too, carried
out letters of marque and reprisal with her, and there were
the chances of meeting some Frenchman in the European
waters, at least.

I examined the vessel, the berth I was to occupy, made
a great many shy glances at the captain, to ascertain his
character by that profound expedient, analyzing his looks,
and finally determined to ship, on condition Neb should be
taken as an ordinary seaman. As soon as Marble heard
this last proposal, he explained the relation in which the
black stood to me, and earnestly advised his being received
as a seaman. The arrangement was made accordingly,
and I went at once to the notary and signed the articles.
Neb was also found, and he was shipped too ; this time
regularly, Mr. Hardinge attending and giving his sanction
to what was done. The worthy divine was in excellent
spirits, for that very day he had made an arrangement
with a friend at the bar to place Rupert in his office, Mrs.
Bradfort insisting on keeping her young kinsman in her
house, as a regular inmate. This left on the father no
more charge than to furnish Rupert with clothes, and a
few dollars of pocket money. But I knew Rupert too
well to suppose he would, or could, be content with the
little he might expect from the savings of Mr. Hardinge.
I was not in want of money. My guardian had supplied
me so amply, that not only had I paid my debt to the
owners of the John, and fully equipped myself for the
voyage, but I actually possessed dollars enough to supply
all my probable wants during the expected absence.
Many of the officers and men of the Crisis left behind
them orders with their wives and families to receive their

wages, in part, during their absence, as letters from time to time apprised the owners that these people were on board, and in discharge of their several duties. I determined on giving Rupert the benefit of such an arrangement. First presenting him with twenty dollars from my own little store, I took him with me to the counting-house, and succeeded, though not without some difficulty, in obtaining for my friend a credit of twenty dollars a month, promising faithfully to repay any balance that might arise against me in consequence of the loss of the ship, or of any accident to myself. This I was enabled to do on the strength of my credit as the owner of Clawbonny ; for, as is usual in these cases, I passed for being much richer than I really was, though far from being poor.

I will acknowledge that, while I felt no reluctance at making this arrangement in favor of Rupert, I felt mortified he should accept it. There are certain acts we may all wish to perform, and yet which bring regrets when successfully performed. I was sorry that my friend, Lucy's brother, Grace's admirer,—for I was quick enough in perceiving that Rupert began to entertain fancies of that sort,—had not pride enough to cause him to decline receiving money which must be earned by the sweat of my brow, and this, moreover, in a mode of life he had not himself sufficient resolution to encounter a second time. But he accepted the offer, and there was an end of it.

As everything was alive in 1798, the Crisis was ready to sail in three days after I joined her. We hauled into the North River, as became the dignity of our voyage, and got our crew on board. On the whole, we mustered a pretty good body of men, ten of them being green ; fellows who had never seen the ocean, but who were young, healthy, and athletic, and who promised to be useful before a great while. Including those aft, we counted thirty-eight souls on board. The ship was got ready in hopes of being able to sail of a Thursday, for Captain Williams was a thoughtful man, and was anxious to get the ship fairly at sea, with the first work done, previously to the next Sabbath. Some small matters, however, could

not be got through with in time ; and as for sailing of a
Friday, that was out of the question. No one did that,
in 1798, who could help it. This gave us a holiday, and I
got leave to pass the afternoon and evening ashore.

Rupert, Grace, Lucy, and I took a long walk into the
country that evening ; that is, we went into the fields, and
along the lanes, for some distance above the present site
of Canal Street. Lucy and I walked together most of the
time, and we both felt sad at the idea of so long a separation as was now before us. The voyage might last three
years ; and I should be legally a man, my own master, and
Lucy a young woman of near nineteen, by that time.
Terrible ages in perspective were these, and which seemed
to us pregnant with as many changes as the life of a man.

" Rupert will be admitted to the bar when I get back,"
I casually remarked, as we talked the matter over.

" He will, indeed," the dear girl answered. " Now
you are to go, Miles, I almost regret my brother is not to
be in the ship ; you have known each other so long, love
each other so much, and have already gone through such
frightful trials in company."

" Oh ! I shall do well enough—there 'll be Neb ; and
as for Rupert, I think he will be better satisfied ashore
than at sea. Rupert is a sort of natural lawyer."

By this I merely meant he was good at a subterfuge,
and could tell his own story.

" Yes, but Neb is not Rupert, Miles," Lucy answered,
quick as thought, and I fancied a little reproachfully.

" Very true—no doubt I shall miss your brother, and
that, too, very much, at times ; but all I meant in speaking of Neb was, as you know, that he and I like each
other, too, and have been through just the same trials together, you understand, and have known each other as
long as I can remember."

Lucy was silent, and I felt embarrassed and a little at a
loss what to say next. But a girl approaching sixteen,
and who is with a youth who possesses her entire confidence, is not apt to be long silent. Something she will
say ; and how often is that something warm with natural

feeling, instinct with truth, and touching from its confiding simplicity !

"You will sometimes think of us, Miles?" was Lucy's next remark, and it was said in a tone that induced me to look her full in the face, when I discovered that her eyes were suffused with tears.

"Of that you may be very certain, and I hope to be rewarded in kind. But now I think of it, Lucy, I have a debt to pay you, and, at the same time, a little interest. Here are the half-joes you forced me to take last year, when we parted at Clawbonny. See, they are exactly the same pieces ; for I would as soon have parted with a finger as with one of them."

"I had hoped they might have been of use to you, and had quite forgotten them. You have destroyed an agreeable illusion."

"Is it not quite as agreeable to know we had no occasion for them ? No, here they are ; and, now I go with Mr. Hardinge's full approbation, you very well know I can be in no want of money. So, there is your gold ; and here, Lucy, is some interest for the use of it."

I made an effort to put something into the dear girl's hand as I spoke, but all the strength I could properly apply was not equal to the purpose. So tightly did she keep her little fingers compressed, that I could not succeed without a downright effort at force.

"No, no, Miles," she said, hurriedly, almost huskily ; "that will never do ! I am not Rupert ; you may prevail with him—never with me !"

"Rupert ! What can Rupert have to do with such a thing as this locket ? Youngsters don't wear lockets."

Lucy's fingers separated as easily as an infant's, and I put my little offering into her hand without any more resistance. I was sorry, however, to discover that, by some means unknown to me, she had become acquainted with the arrangement I had made as respected the twenty dollars a month. I afterwards ascertained that this secret had leaked out through Neb, who had it from one of the clerks of the counting-house who had visited the ship, and

repeated it to Mrs. Bradfort's black maid in one of his
frequent visits to the house. This is a common channel
of information, though it seldom proves as true as it did in
this instance.

I could see that Lucy was delighted with her locket.
It was a very pretty ornament, in the first place, and it
had her own hair, that of Grace, Rupert, and my own,
very prettily braided together, so as to form a wreath,
made like a rope, or a grummet, encircling a combination
of letters that included all our initials. In this there was
nothing that was particular, while there was much that was
affectionate. Had I not consulted Grace on the subject,
it is possible I should have been less cautious, though I
declare I had no thought of making love. All this time
I fancied I felt for, and trusted Lucy as another sister. I
was shrewd enough to detect Rupert's manner and feeling
toward my own sister, and I felt afraid it was, or soon would
be fully reciprocated; but as to imagining myself in love
with Lucy Hardinge, or any one else, the thought never
crossed my mind, though the dear girl herself so often did!

I saw Lucy's smile, and I could not avoid noticing the
manner in which, once or twice, unconsciously to herself,
I do believe, this simple-minded, sincere creature, pressed
the hand which retained the locket to her heart; and yet
it made no very lively impression on my imagination at
the time. The conversation soon changed, and we began
to converse of other things. I have since fancied that
Grace had left us alone in order that I might return the
half-joes to Lucy, and offer the locket; for, looking round
and seeing the latter in its new owner's hand, while Lucy
was bestowing on it one of the hundred glances of grateful pleasure it received that afternoon, she waited until we
came up, when she took my arm, remarking, as this was
to be our last evening together, she must come in for her
share of the conversation. Now, I solemnly affirm that
this was the nearest approach to anything like a love-scene
that had ever passed between Lucy Hardinge and myself.

I would gladly pass over the leave-taking, and shall say
but little about it. Mr. Hardinge called me into his room,

when we got back to the house.   He spoke earnestly and
solemnly to me, recalling to my mind many of his early
and more useful precepts.   He then kissed me, gave me
his blessing, and promised to remember me in his prayers.
As I left him—and I believe he went on his knees as
soon as my back was turned—Lucy was waiting for me
in the passage.   She was in tears, and paler than common,
but her mind seemed made up to sustain a great sacrifice
like a woman.   She put a small, but exceedingly neat copy
of the Bible into my hand, and uttered, as well as emotion
would permit, " There, Miles ; that is my keepsake.   I do
not ask you to think of me when you read ; but think of
God."   She then snatched a kiss, and flew into her room
and locked the door.   Grace was below, and she wept on
my neck like a child, kissing me again and again, and calling me " her brother—her dear, her only brother."   I
was obliged actually to tear myself away from Grace.
Rupert went with me to the ship, and passed an hour or
two on board.   As we crossed the threshold, I heard a
window open above my head, and, looking up, I saw Lucy,
with streaming eyes, leaning forward to say, " Write, Miles
—write as often as you possibly can."

Man must be a stern being by nature, to be able to tear
himself from such friends, in order to encounter enemies,
hardships, dangers and toil, and all without any visible
motive.   Such was my case, however, for I wanted not
for a competency, or for most of those advantages which
might tempt one to abandon the voyage.   Of such a
measure, the possibility never crossed my mind.   I believed that it was just as necessary for me to remain third
mate of the Crisis, and to stick by the ship while she would
float, as Mr. Adams thinks it necessary for him to present
abolition petitions to a Congress which will not receive them.
We both of us, doubtless, believed ourselves the victims of
fate.

We sailed at sunrise, wind and tide favoring.   We had
anchored off Courtlandt Street, and as the ship swept past
the Battery I saw Rupert, who had only gone ashore in
the pilot's boat at daylight, with two females, watching

our movements. The girls did not dare to wave their handkerchiefs; but what cared I for that? I knew that their good wishes, kind wishes, tender wishes, went with me; and this little touch of affection, which woman knows so well how to manifest, made me both happy and sad for the remainder of the day.

The Crisis was an unusually fast ship, faster even than the Tigris; coppered to the bends, copper-fastened, and with a live-oak frame. No better craft sailed out of the republic. Uncle Sam had tried to purchase her for one of his new navy; but the owners, having this voyage in view, refused his tempting offers. She was no sooner under her canvas, than all hands of us perceived we were in a traveller; and glad enough were we to be certain of the fact, for we had a long road before us. This, too, was with the wind free, and in smooth water; whereas those who knew the vessel asserted her *forte* was on a bowline and in a sea—that is to say, she would sail relatively faster than most other craft, under the latter circumstances.

There was a strange pleasure to me, notwithstanding all I had suffered previously, all the risks I had run, and all I had left behind me, in finding myself once more on the broad ocean. As for Neb, the fellow was fairly enraptured. So quickly and intelligently did he obey orders, that he won a reputation before we crossed the bar. The smell of the ocean seemed to imbue him with a species of nautical inspiration, and even I was astonished with his readiness and activity. As for myself, I was in every way at home. Very different was this exit from the port from that of the previous year. Then everything was novel, and not a little disgusting. Now I had little, almost nothing, to learn—literally nothing, I might have said, were it not that every shipmaster has certain ways of his own, that it behooves all his subordinates to learn as quickly as possible. Then I lived aft, where we not only had plates, and table-cloths, and tumblers, and knives and forks, but comparatively clean articles of the sort. I say comparatively, the two other degrees being usually wanting in northwest traders.

The Crisis went to sea with a lively breeze at south-west, the wind shifting after she had got into the lower bay. There were a dozen sail of us altogether, and in our little fleet were two of Uncle Sam's men, who felt disposed to try their hands with us. We crossed the bar, all three of us, within a cable's length of each other, and made sail in company, with the wind a trifle abaft the beam. Just as Navesink disappeared, our two men-of-war merchantmen altered, hauled up on bowlines, and jogged off toward the West Indies, being at the time about a league astern of us. This success put us all in high good-humor, and had such an effect on Marble in particular, that he began to give it as his opinion that our only superiority over them would not be found confined to sailing on an experiment. It is very convenient to think favorably of one's self, and it is certainly comfortable to entertain the same notion as respects one's ship.

I confess to a little awkwardness at first, in acting as an officer. I was young, and commanded men old enough to be my father—regular sea-dogs, who were as critical in all that related to the niceties of the calling, as the journalist who is unable to appreciate the higher qualities of a book is hypercritical on its minor faults. But a few days gave me confidence, and I soon found I was obeyed as readily as the first mate. A squall struck the ship in my watch about a fortnight out, and I succeeded in getting in sail and saving everything, canvas and spars, in a way that did me infinite service aft. Captain Williams spoke to me on the subject, commending the orders I had given, and the coolness with which they had been issued; for, as I afterward understood, he remained some time in the companion-way, keeping the other two mates back, though all hands had been called, in order to see how I could get along by myself in such a strait. On this occasion, I never saw a human being exert himself like Neb. He felt that my honor was concerned. I do really think the fellow did two men's duty the whole time the squall lasted. Until this little incident occurred, Captain Williams was in the habit of coming on deck to examine the heavens, and see how things were getting on in **my** night-watches ; but after this, he paid no more visits of this sort to me than he paid to Mr. Marble. I had been gratified by his praises ; but this quiet mode of showing confidence gave me more happiness than I can express.

We had a long passage out, the wind hanging to the eastward near three weeks. At length we got moderate southerly breezes, and began to travel on our course. Twenty-four hours after we had got the fair wind, I had the morning watch, and made, as the day dawned, a sail directly abeam of us, to windward, about three leagues distant, or just hull down. I went into the main-top, and examined her with a glass. She was a ship seemingly of about our own size. and carrying everything that would draw. I did not send word below until it was broad daylight, or for near half an hour ; and in all that time her bearings did not vary any perceptible distance.

Just as the sun rose, the captain and chief mate made their appearance on deck. At first they agreed in supposing the stranger a stray English West Indiaman, bound home ; for at that time few merchant vessels were met at sea that were not English or American. The former usually sailed in convoys, however, and the captain accounted for the circumstance that this was not thus protected, by the fact of her sailing so fast. She might be a letter-of-marque, like ourselves, and vessels of that character did not take convoy. As the two vessels lay exactly abeam of each other, with square yards, it was not easy to judge of the sparring of the stranger, except by means of his masts. Marble, judging by the appearance of his topsails, began to think our neighbor might be a Frenchman, he had so much hoist to the sails. After some conversation on the subject, the captain ordered me to brace forward the yards, as far as our studding-sails would allow, and to luff nearer to the stranger. While the ship was thus changing her course, the day advanced, and our crew got their breakfast.

As a matter of course, the strange ship, which kept on the same line of sailing as before, drew ahead of us a

little, while we neared her sensibly. In the course of
three hours we were within a league of her, but well on
her lee-quarter. Marble now unhesitatingly pronounced
her to be a Frenchman, there being no such thing as mistaking the sails. To suppose an Englishman would go to
sea with such triangles of royals, he held to be entirely
out of the question; and then he referred to me to know
if I did not remember the brig "we had licked in the
West Indies, last v'y'ge, which had just such r'yals as
the chap up there to windward?" I could see the resemblance, certainly, and had remarked the same peculiarity
in the few French vessels I had seen.

Under all the circumstances, Captain Williams determined
to get on the weather-quarter of our neighbor, and take a
still nearer look at him. That he was armed, we could
see already; and, as near as we could make out, he carried
twelve guns, or just two more than we did ourselves. All
this was encouraging; sufficiently so, at least, to induce us
to make a much closer examination than we had yet done.

It took two more hours to bring the Crisis, fast as she
sailed, on the weather-quarter of her neighbor, distant about
a mile. Here our observations were much more to the purpose, and even Captain Williams pronounced the stranger
to be a Frenchman, "and, no doubt, a letter-of-marque, like
ourselves." He had just uttered these words, when we saw
the other vessel's studding-sails coming down, her royals
and topgallant-sails clewing up, and all the usual signs of
her stripping for a fight. We had set our ensign early in
the day, but, as yet, had got no answering symbol of na-
tionality from the chase. As soon as she had taken in all
her light canvas, however, she clewed up her courses, fired a
gun to windward, and hoisted the French tricolor, the most
graceful flag among the emblems of Christendom, but one
that has been as remarkably unsuccessful in the deeds it has
witnessed on the high seas, as it has been remarkable for the
reverse on land. The French have not been wanting in
excellent sailors,—gallant seamen, too; but the results of
their exploits afloat have ever borne a singular disproportion to the means employed,—a few occasional exceptions

just going to prove that the causes have been of a character as peculiar, as these results have, in nearly all ages, been
uniform. I have heard the want of success in maritime exploits, among the French, attributed to a want of sympathy,
in the nation, with maritime things. Others, again, have
supposed that the narrow system of preferring birth to
merit, which pervaded the whole economy of the French
marine, as well as of its army, previously to the Revolution,
could not fail to destroy the former, inasmuch as a man of
family would not consent to undergo the toil and hardships
that are unavoidable to the training of the true seaman.
The last reason, however, can scarcely be the true one, as
the young English noble has often made the most successful naval officer; and the marine of France, in 1798, had
surely every opportunity of perfecting itself, by downright
practice, uninjured by favoritism, as that of America. For
myself, though I have now reflected on the subject for years,
I can come to no other conclusion than that national character has some very important agency,—or, perhaps, it might
be safer to say, has had some very important agency,—
through some cause or other, in disqualifying France from
becoming a great naval power, in the sense of skill; in that
of mere force, so great a nation must always be formidable.
Now she sends her princes to sea, however, we may look for
different results.

Notwithstanding the fact that an Englishman, or an
American, rarely went alongside of a Frenchman, in 1798,
without a strong moral assurance of victory, he was sometimes disappointed. There was no lack of courage in their
enemies, and it occasionally happened that there was no
lack of skill. Every manifestation that the experience of
our captain could detect, went to show that we had fallen in
with one of these exceptions. As we drew nearer to our
enemy, we perceived that he was acting like a seaman. His
sails had been furled without haste or confusion; an infalli-
ble evidence of coolness and discipline when done on the eve
of battle, and signs that the watchful seaman, on such occasions, usually notes as unerring indications of the sort of
struggle that awaits him. It was consequently understood,

among us on the quarter-deck, that we were likely to have
a warm day's work of it.   Nevertheless, we had gone too
far to retreat without an effort, and we began, in our turn,
to shorten sail, in readiness for the combat.   Marble was a
prince of a fellow, when it came to anything serious.   I
never saw him shorten sail so coolly and readily as he did
that very day.   We had everything ready in ten minutes
after we began.

It was rare, indeed, to see two letters-of-marque set to as
coolly and as scientifically as were the facts with the Crisis
and La Dame de Nantes ; for so, as we afterwards ascertained, was our antagonist called.   Neither party aimed at
any great advantage by manœuvring ; but we came up
alongside of "The Lady," as our men subsequently nicknamed the Frenchman, the two vessels delivering their
broadsides nearly at the same instant.   I was stationed on
the forecastle, in charge of the head-sheets, with orders to
attend generally to the braces and the rigging, using a musket in moments that were not otherwise employed.   Away
went both my jib-sheet blocks at the beginning, giving me
a very pretty job from the outset.   This was but the commencement of trouble ; for, during the two hours and a
half that we lay battering La Dame de Nantes, and she lay
battering us, I had really so much to attend to in the way
of reeving, knotting, splicing, and turning in afresh, that I
had scarcely a minute to look about me in order to ascertain how the day was going.   I fired my musket but twice.
The glimpses I did manage to take were far from satisfactory, however ; several of our people being killed or
wounded, one gun fairly crippled by a shot, and our rigging
in a sad plight.   The only thing encouraging was Neb's
shout, the fellow making it a point to roar almost as loud
as his gun, at each discharge.

It was evident from the first that the Frenchman had
nearly twice as many men as we carried.   This rendered
any attempt at boarding imprudent, and, in the way of
pounding, our prospects were by no means flattering.   At
length I heard a rushing sound over my head, and, looking
up, I saw that the main-topmast, with the yards and sails,

had come down on the fore-braces, and might shortly be expected on deck. At this point, Captain Williams ordered all hands from the guns to clear the wreck. At the same instant, our antagonist, with a degree of complaisance that I could have hugged him for, ceased firing also. Both sides seemed to think it was very foolish for two merchantmen to lie within a cable's length of each other, trying which could do the other the most harm; and both sides set about the by this time very necessary duty of repairing damages. While this was going on, the men at the wheel, by a species of instinctive caution, did their whole duty. The Crisis luffed all she was able, while La Dame de Nantes edged away all she very conveniently could, placing more than a mile of blue water between the two vessels, before we, who were at work aloft, were aware they were so decidedly running on diverging lines.

It was night before we got our wreck clear; and then we had to look about us, to get out spare spars, fit them, rig them, point them, and sway them aloft. The last operation, however, was deferred until morning. As it was, the day's work had been hard, and the people really wanted rest. Rest was granted them at eight o'clock; at which hour our late antagonist was visible about a league distant, the darkness beginning to envelop her. In the morning the horizon was clear, owing to the repulsion which existed in so much force between the two vessels. It was not our business to trouble ourselves about the fate of our adversary, but to take heed of our own. That morning we got our spars, crossed the yards, and made sail again. We had several days' work in repairing all our damages; but, happening to be found for a long voyage, and well found, too, by the end of a week the Crisis was in as good order as if we had not fought a battle. As for the combat, it was one of those in which either side might claim the victory, or not, as it suited tastes. We had very ingenious excuses for our failure, however; and I make no doubt the French were just as ready, in this way, as we were ourselves.

Our loss in this engagement amounted to two men killed outright, and to seven wounded, two of whom died within a

few days. The remaining wounded all recovered, though
the second mate, who was one of them, I believe never got
to be again the man he had been. A canister-shot lodged
near his hip, and the creature we had on board as a surgeon
was not the hero to extract it. In that day, the country
was not so very well provided with medical men on the
land, as to spare many good ones to the sea. In the new
navy, it was much the fashion to say, "If you want a leg
amputated, send for the carpenter; he does know how to
use a saw, while it is questionable whether the doctor knows
how to use anything." Times, however, are greatly altered
in this respect; the gentlemen who now compose this
branch of the service being not only worthy of commendation for their skill and services, but worthy of the graduated
rank which I see they are just now asking of the justice
of their country, and which, as that country ordinarily
administers justice, I am much afraid they will ask in vain.

CHAPTER IX.

"If we
Cannot defend our own door from the dog,
Let us be worried ; and our nation lose
The name of hardiness, and policy."

Henry V.

THE combat between the Crisis and La Dame de Nantes took place in 42° 37′ 12″ north latitude, and 34° 16′ 43″ west longitude, from Greenwich. This was very near the centre of the northern Atlantic, and gave us ample time to get our ship in good condition before we drew in with the land. Shortly after the affair, the wind came out light at northeast, forcing us down nearer to the Bay of Biscay than was at all convenient, when bound to London. The weather grew foggy, too, which is not usual on the coast of Europe, with the wind at east, and the nights dark. Just a fortnight after the action, I was awakened early one morning by a rough shake of the shoulder from Marble, who had the watch, but who was calling me at least an hour before the time. "Bear a hand and turn out," he said ; "I want you on deck, Mr. Wallingford." I obeyed, of course, and soon stood in the presence of the chief mate, rubbing my eyes diligently, as if they had to be opened by friction.

It was just six bells, or seven o'clock, and one of the watch was on the point of making the bell proclaim as much, when Mr. Marble ordered him not to strike the hour. The weather was thick, or rather foggy, and the wind light, with very little sea going. All this I had time to notice, to listen to the unusual order about the bell, and to gape twice, before the mate turned to me. He seized my arm, carried

me on the lee side of the quarter-deck, shook his finger at a
vacant spot in the fog, and said,—

"Miles, my boy, down yonder, within half a mile of this
very spot, is our friend the Frenchman!"

"How is it possible you can know that, Mr. Marble?"
I demanded in surprise.

"Because I have seen him, with these two good-looking
eyes of mine. This fog opens and shuts like a playhouse-
curtain, and I got a peep at the chap, about ten minutes
since. It was a short look, but it was a sure one; I would
swear to the fellow in any admiralty court in Christendom."

"And what do you intend to do, Mr. Marble? We found
him a hard subject in clear weather; what can we do with
him in thick?"

"That depends on the old man; his very natur' is over-
laid by what has happened already, and I rather think he
will be for a fresh skrimmage;" Marble was an uneducated
Kennebunk man, and by no means particular about his
English. "There'll be good picking in that French gentleman, Master Miles, for those who come in at the beginning
of the plunder!"

The chief mate then told me to go below and turn up all
hands, making as little rumpus about it as possible. This I
did; and when I returned to the deck, I found the fingers
of Marble going again, with Captain Williams for his audi-
tor, just as they had gone to me, a few minutes earlier.
Being an officer, I made no scruples about joining the party.
Marble was giving his account of the manner in which he
had momentarily seen the enemy, the canvas he was under,
the course he was steering, and the air of security that
prevailed about him. So much, he insisted he had noted,
though he saw the ship for about twenty seconds only. All
this, however, might be true, for a seaman's eye is quick,
and he has modes of his own for seeing a great deal in a
brief space of time. Marble now proposed that we should
go to quarters, run alongside of the Frenchman, pour in a
broadside, and board him in the smoke. Our success would
be certain, could we close with him without being seen;
and it would be almost as certain, could we engage him with

ours guns by surprise. The chief mate was of opinion we had dosed him in the other affair, in a way to sicken him; this time we should bring him to with a round turn!

The "old man" was pleased with the notion, I saw at a glance; and I confess it took my fancy also. We all felt very sore at the result of the other attempt, and here it seemed as if fortune gave us a good occasion for repairing the evil.

"There can be no harm in getting ready, Mr. Marble," the captain observed; "and when we are ready ourselves, we shall know better what to think of the matter."

This was no sooner said, than away we went to clear ship. Our task was soon done; the tompions were got out, the guns cast loose, ammunition was brought up, and a stand of grape was put in over the shot in every piece in both batteries. As the men were told the motive, they worked like dray-horses; and I do not think we were ten minutes before the ship was ready to go into action at a moment's notice.

All this time Captain Williams refused to keep the ship away. I believe he wanted to get a look at our neighbor himself, for he could not but foresee what might be the consequences, should he run down in the fog, and engage a heavier vessel than his own, without the ceremony of a hail. The sea was covered with Englishmen, and one of their cruisers might not very easily pardon such a mistake, however honestly made. But preparation seems to infer a necessity for performance. When everything was ready, all eyes were turned aft in a way that human nature could hardly endure, and the captain was obliged to yield. As Marble, of all on board, had alone seen the other vessel, he was directed to conn the Crisis in the delicate operation she was about to undertake.

As before, my station was on the forecastle. I had been directed to keep a bright lookout, as the enemy would doubtless be first seen from forward. The order was unnecessary, however, for never did human beings gaze into a fog more anxiously than did all on board our ship on this occasion. Calculating by the distance, and the courses

steered, we supposed ten or fifteen minutes would bring us
square alongside of Mr. Marble's ship; though some among
us doubted his having seen any vessel at all. There was
about a five-knot breeze, and we had all our square-sails set,
knowing it was necessary to go a little faster than our
adversary to catch up with him. The intense expectation,
not to say anxiety, of such a scene, is not easily described.
The surrounding fog, at times, seemed filled with ships ; but
all vanished into *thick* air, one after another, leaving nothing
but vapor. Severe orders had been given for no one to call
out, but, the minute the ship was seen, for the discoverer to
go aft and report. At least a dozen men left their quarters
on this errand, all returning in the next instant, satisfied
they had been deceived. Each moment, too, increased the
expectation ; for each moment must we be getting nearer
and nearer to her, if any vessel were really there. Quite
twenty minutes, however, passed in this manner, and no
ship was seen. Marble continued cool and confident, but the
captain and second mate smiled, while the people began to
shake their heads, and roll the tobacco into their cheeks.
As we advanced, our own ship luffed by degrees, until we
had got fairly on our old course again, or were sailing close
upon the wind. This change was made easily, the braces
not having been touched ; a precaution that was taken
expressly to give us this advantage. When we found ourselves once more close upon the wind, we gave the matter
up forward, supposing the mate had been deceived. I saw
by the expression of the captain's face that he was about to
give the order to secure the guns, when, casting my eyes
forward, there was a ship sure enough, within a hundred
yards of us ! I held up both arms, as I looked aft, and
luckily caught the captain's eye. In an instant, he was on
the forecastle.

It was easy enough to see the stranger now. There he
was in the fog, looking mystical and hazy ; but there he
was, under his main-topgallant-sail, close-hauled, and moving ahead in all the confidence of the solitude of the ocean.
We could not see his hull, or so faintly as only to distinguish
its mass : but, from his tops up, there was no mistaking the

objects. We had shot away the Frenchman's mizzen-royal-mast. It was a pole, and there the stump stood, just as it was when we had last seen him on the evening of the day of the combat. This left no doubt of the character of our neighbor, and it at once determined our course. As it was, we were greatly outsailing him, but an order was immediately given to set the light staysails. As Captain Williams passed aft, he gave his orders to the men in the batteries. In the meantime the second mate, who spoke very good New York French, came upon the forecastle in readiness to answer the expected hail. As the Crisis was kept a little free in order to close, and as she sailed so fast, it was apparent we were coming up with the chase, hand over hand.

The two ships were not more than a hundred feet asunder when the Frenchman first saw us. This blindness was owing to several circumstances. In the first place, ten men look forward in a ship where one looks aft. Those who looked aloft, too, were generally on the quarter-deck, and this prevented them from looking astern. Then the Frenchman's crew had just gone to their breakfasts, most of them eating below. She was so strong-handed, moreover, as to give a forenoon's watch below, and this still left many of the sluggards in their hammocks. In that day, even a French ship-of-the-line was no model of discipline or order, and a letter-of-marque was consequently worse. As it afterwards appeared, we were first seen by the mate of the watch, who ran to the taffrail, and, instead of giving an order to call all hands, he hailed us. Mr. Forbank, our second mate, answered; mumbling his words so that, if they were bad French, they did not sound like good English. He got out the name "Le Hasard, de Bordeaux," pretty plainly, however; and this served to mystify the mate for a few seconds. By the end of that time our bows were doubling on the Frenchman's quarter, and we were sheering into him so fast as quite to distract the Nantes man. The hail had been heard below, however, and the Frenchmen came tumbling up by the dozen, forward and aft.

Captain Williams was a prime seaman, and one of the coolest men that ever lived. Everything that day was done

A contemporary drawing of the London waterfront as it appeared to Wallingford when he delivered there his first command, the brig *Amanda*, following her rescue from French captors. *Drawing by T. Malton. (Courtesy of The Old Print Shop)*

at precisely the proper moment. The Frenchman attempted to keep off, but our wheel was so touched as to keep us lapping in nearly a parallel line with them the whole time; and our forward sails soon becalmed even their mainsail. Of course, we went two feet to their one. Marble came on the forecastle just as our cathead was abreast of "The Lady's" forward rigging. Less than a minute was required to take us so far forward, and that minute was one of great confusion among the French. As soon as Marble got on the forecastle, he made a signal, the ensign was run up, and the order was given to fire. We let fly all five of our nine-pounders, loaded with two round and a stand of grape, at the same moment. At the next instant the crash of the ships coming foul of each other was heard. Marble shouted "Come on, boys!" and away he, and I, and Neb, and all hands of us went on board of the Frenchman like a hurricane. I anticipated a furious hand-to-hand conflict; but we found the deck deserted, and had no difficulty whatever in getting possession. The surprise, the rush, and the effect of the broadside gave us an easy victory. The French captain had been nearly cut in two by a nine-pound shot, moreover, and both of the mates were severely wounded. These accidents contributed largely to our success, causing the enemy to abandon the defence as hopeless. We had not a soul hurt.

The prize proved to be the ship I have mentioned, a letter-of-marque from Guadaloupe, bound to Nantes. She was a trifle larger than the Crisis, mounted twelve French nines, and had eighty-three souls on board when she sailed. Of these, however, no less than twenty-three had been killed and wounded in our previous affair with her, and several were absent in a prize. Of the wounded, nearly all were still in their hammocks. Among the remainder, some sixteen or eighteen suffered by our close and destructive broadside on the present occasion, reducing the efficient part of her crew to about our own numbers. The vessel was new and valuable, and her cargo was invoiced at something like sixty thousand dollars, having some cochineal among it.

As soon as assured of our victory, the Crisis' main-topsail was braced aback, as well as it could be, and her helm put down. At the same time, the Dame was kept away, and the two ships went clear of each other. Little injury had been done by the collision, or the grinding : and, in consequence of our guns having been so much shotted, no damage whatever was done the lower masts of the prize. The shot had just force enough to pass through the bulwarks, make splinters, and to lodge. This left both vessels in good condition for going into port.

At first it was determined to leave me in La Dame de Nantes, as prize-master, with directions to follow the Crisis into Falmouth, whither she was bound for orders. But, on further examination, it was discovered that the crew of an American brig was on board the prize as prisoners ; La Dame de Nantes having captured the vessel only two days before we met the former the first time, taken out her people, manned her, and ordered her for Nantes. These Americans, including the master and two mates, amounted to thirteen souls in all, and they enabled us to make a different disposition of the prize. The result of an hour or two's deliberation was as follows :—

Our old second mate, whose hurt was likely to require better care than could be had on the northwest coast, was put on board the French ship as prize-master, with orders to make the best of his way to New York. The master and chief mate of the American brig agreed to act under him, and to assist in carrying La Dame across the ocean. Three or four of our invalids were sent home also, and the liberated Americans took service for the passage. All the French wounded were left in the ship, under the charge of their own surgeon, who was a man of some little merit, though a good deal of a butcher, as was too much the fashion of that day.

It was dark before all the arrangements were made, when La Dame de Nantes turned short round on her heel, and made sail for America. Of course our captain sent in his official report by her, and I seized a moment to write a short letter to Grace, which was so worded as to be addressed to the whole family. I knew how much happiness a line from me would bestow, and I had the pleasure to inform them,

also, that I was promoted to be second mate—the second
mate of the American brig having shipped as my successor
in the rank of third officer.

The parting on the wide ocean, that night, was solemn,
and, in some respects, sad. We knew that several who
were in La Dame de Nantes would probably be left behind,
as she travelled her long, solitary path, in the depths of the
ocean ; and there were the chances that she, herself, might
never arrive. As respects the last, however, the odds were
in her favor, the American coast being effectually cleared
of French privateers by that time ; and I subsequently
received eleven hundred and seventy-three dollars for my
share in that exploit. How I was affected by the circumstance, and what I did with the money, will appear in the
sequel.

The Crisis made a sail on a bowline, at the same moment
her prize filled away for America ; Miles Wallingford a
much more important personage than he had been a few
hours before. We put the prisoners below, keeping a good
watch over them, and hauled off to the northward and westward, in order to avoid any French cruisers that might be
hovering on their own coast. Captain Williams seemed
satisfied with the share of glory he had obtained, and
manifested no further disposition to seek renown in arms.
As for Marble, I never knew a man more exalted in his own
esteem, than he was by the results of that day's work. It
certainly did him great credit ; but, from that hour, woe to
the man who pretended to dispute with him concerning
the character of any sail that happened to cross our path.

The day after we parted company with our prize, we
made a sail to the westward, and hauled up to take a look
at her, the wind having shifted. She was soon pronounced
to be an American ; but, though we showed our colors, the
stranger, a brig, manifested no disposition to speak us.
This induced Captain Williams to make sail in chase, more
especially as the brig endeavored to elude us by passing
ahead, and the run was pretty nearly on our course. At
four P.M., we got near enough to throw a nine-pound shot
between the fellow's masts, when the chase hove-to, and

permitted us to come up. The brig proved to be the prize of La Dame de Nantes, and we took possession of her forthwith. As this vessel was loaded with flour, pot and pearl ashes, etc., and was bound to London, I was put in charge of her with a young man of my own age, of the name of Roger Talcott, for my assistant, having six men for my crew. Of course the Frenchmen, all but one who acted as cook and steward excepted, were received on board the Crisis. Neb went with me, through his own and my earnest entreaties, though spared by Marble with great reluctance.

This was my first command; and proud enough did I feel on the occasion, though almost dying with the apprehension of doing something wrong. My orders were, to make the Lizard light, and to crawl along up channel, keeping close in with the English coast; Captain Williams anticipating instructions to go to the same port to which the Amanda (the brig) was bound, and expecting to overtake us, after he had called at Falmouth for his orders. As the Crisis could go four feet to the Amanda's three, before sunset our old ship was hull down ahead of us.

When I took charge of the deck the next morning, I found myself on the wide ocean, with nothing in sight, at the age of eighteen, and in the enemy's seas, with a valuable vessel to care for, my way to find into narrow waters that I had never entered, and a crew on board, of whom just one half were now on their first voyage. Our green hands had manifested the aptitude of Americans, and had done wonders in the way of improvement; but a great deal still remained to be learned. The Crisis' complement had been too large to employ everybody at all sorts of work, as is usually done in a merchant-vessel with her ordinary number of hands, and the landsmen had to take their chances for instruction. Notwithstanding, the men I got were stout, healthy, willing and able to pull and haul with the oldest salts.

By the arrangement that had been made, I was now thrown upon my own resources. Seamanship, navigation, address, prudence, all depended on me. I confess I was, at first, nearly as much depressed by the novelty and responsi-

bility of my command, as Neb was delighted. But it is surprising how soon we get accustomed to changes of this sort.
The first five or six hours set me quite at my ease, though
it is true nothing occurred in the least out of the usual way ;
and, by the time the sun set, I should have been happy
could I have got over the uneasiness produced by the darkness. The wind had got round to southwest, and blew fresh.
I set a lower and a topmast studding-sail, and by the time
the light had entirely vanished, the brig began to drag after
her canvas in a way to keep me wide awake. I was at a
loss whether to shorten sail or not. On the one hand, there
was the apprehension of carrying away something ; and, on
the other, the fear of seeming timid in the eyes of the two of
three seamen I had with me. I watched the countenances
of these men, in order to glean their private sentiments,
but, usually, Jack relies so much on his officers, that he
seldom anticipates evils. As for Neb, the harder it blew, the
greater was his rapture. He appeared to think the wind
was Master Miles', as well as the ocean, the brig, and himself. The more there was of each, the richer I became. As
for Talcott, he was scarcely as good a seaman as myself,
though he was well educated, had good manners, was well
connected, and had been my original competitor for the
office of third mate. I had been preferred only through the
earnest recommendations of Marble. Talcott, however, was
as expert a navigator as we had in the ship, and had been
placed with me on that account ; Captain Williams fancying
two heads might prove better than one. I took this young
man into the cabin with me, not only as a companion, but to
give him consideration with the people forward. On shore,
though less fortunate in the way of estate, he would have
been considered as fully my equal in position.

Talcott and myself remained on deck together nearly the
whole of the first night, and the little sleep I did get was
caught in a topmast studding-sail that lay on the quarter-
deck, and which I had determined not to set, after rowsing
it up for that purpose. When daylight returned, however,
with a clear horizon, no increase of wind, and nothing in
sight, I was so much relieved as to take a good nap until

10

eight. All that day we started neither tack nor sheet, nor touched a brace. Toward evening I went aloft myself to look for land, but without success, though I knew, from our observation at noon, it could not be far off. Fifty years ago the longitude was the great difficulty with navigators. Both Talcott and myself did very well with the lunars, it is true; but there was no chance to observe, and even lunars soon get out of their reckoning among currents and tides. Glad enough, then, was I to hear Neb sing out "Light ahead!" from the fore-topsail-yard. This was about ten o'clock. I knew this light must be the Lizard, as we were too far to the eastward for Scilly. The course was changed so as to bring the light a little on the weather-bow; and I watched for its appearance to us on deck with an anxiety I have experienced since, only in the most trying circumstances. Half an hour sufficed for this, and then I felt comparatively happy. A new beginner even is not badly off with the wind fresh at southwest, and the Lizard light in plain view on his weather-bow, if he happen to be bound up channel. That night, consequently, proved to be more comfortable than the previous.

Next morning there was no change, except in the brig's position. We were well in the channel, had the land as close aboard as was prudent, and could plainly see, by objects ashore, that we were travelling ahead at a famous rate. We went within a mile of the Eddystone, so determined was I to keep as far as possible from the French privateers. Next morning we were up abreast of the Isle of Wight; but the wind had got round to the southward and eastward, becoming much lighter, and so scant as to bring us on a taut bowline. This made England a lee-shore, and I began to be as glad to get off it, as I had lately been to hug it.

All this time, it will easily be understood, that we kept a sharp lookout, on board the brig, for enemies. We saw a great many sail, particularly as we approached the Straits of Dover, and kept as much aloof from all as circumstances would allow. Several were evidently English vessels-of-war, and I felt no small concern on the subject of having

some of my men impressed; for at that period, and for
many years afterward, ships of all nations that traded with
the English lost many of their people by this practice, and
the American craft more than any other. I ascribed to
our sticking so close to the coast, which we did as long as
it was at all safe, the manner in which we were permitted
to pass unnoticed, or, at least, undetained. But as we
drew nearer to the narrow waters, I had little hope of
escaping without being boarded. In the meanwhile, we
made short stretches off the land, and back again, all one
day and night, working slowly to the eastward. We still
met with no interruption. I was fast getting confidence in
myself; handling the Amanda, in my own judgment, quite
as well as Marble could have done it, and getting my green
hands into so much method and practice, that I should not
have hesitated about turning round and shaping our course
for New York, so far as the mere business of navigating the
vessel was concerned.

The lights on the English coast were safe guides for
our movements, and they let me understand how much we
made or lost on a tack. Dungeness was drawing nearer
slowly, to appearances, and I was beginning to look out
for a pilot, when Talcott, who had the watch, about three
in the morning, came with breathless haste into the cabin,
to tell me there was a sail closing with us fast, and, so far
as he could make her out in the darkness, she was lugger-
rigged. This was startling news indeed, for it was almost
tantamount to saying the stranger was a Frenchman. I
did not undress at all, and was on deck in a moment.
The vessel in chase was about half a mile distant on our
lee-quarter, but could be plainly enough distinguished, and
I saw at a glance she was a lugger. There were certainly
English luggers; but all the traditions of the profession
had taught me to regard a vessel of that particular rig as
a Frenchman. I had heard of privateers from Dunkirk,
Boulogne, and various other ports in France, running over
to the English coast in the night, and making prizes, just
as this fellow seemed disposed to serve us. Luckily, our
head was toward the land, and we were looking about a

point and a half to windward of the light on Dungeness, being also favored with a flood tide, so far as we could judge by the rapid drift of the vessel to windward.

My decision was made in a minute. I knew nothing of batteries, or where to seek protection; but there was the land, and I determined to make for it as fast as I could. By keeping the brig a good full, and making all the sail she could carry, I thought we might run ashore before the lugger could get alongside us. As for her firing, I did not believe she would dare to attempt that, as it might bring some English cruiser on her heels, and France was some hours' sail distant. The fore and mizzen topgallant-sails were set as fast as possible, the weather-braces pulled upon a little, the bowlines eased, and the brig kept a rap-full. The Amanda was no flyer, certainly; but she seemed frightened as much as we were ourselves, that night. I never knew her to get along so fast, considering the wind; and really there was a short time when I began to think she held her own, the lugger being jammed up as close as she could be. But this was all delusion, that craft coming after us more like a sea-serpent than a machine carried ahead by canvas. I was soon certain that escape from such a racer by sailing, was altogether out of the question.

The land and light were now close aboard us, and I expected every moment to hear the brig's keel grinding on the bottom. At this instant I caught a faint glimpse of a vessel at anchor to the eastward of the point, and apparently distant about a quarter of a mile. The thought struck me that she might be an English cruiser, for they frequently anchored in such places; and I called out, as it might be instinctively, "Luff!" Neb was at the helm, and I knew by his cheerful answer that the fellow was delighted. It was lucky we luffed as we did, for, in coming to the wind, the vessel gave a scrape that was a fearful admonisher of what would have happened in another minute. The Amanda minded her helm beautifully, however, and we went past the nearest land without any further hints, heading up just high enough to fetch a little to windward of the vessel at anchor. At the next moment, the lugger,

then about a cable's length from us, was shut in by the
land. I was now in great hopes the Frenchman would be
obliged to tack; but he had measured his distance well,
and felt certain, it would seem, that he could lay past.
He reasoned, probably, as Nelson is said to have reasoned
at the Nile, and as some of his captains unquestionably did
reason; that is, if there was water enough for us, there
was water enough for him. In another minute I saw him
jammed nearly into the wind's eye, luffing past the point,
and falling as easily into our wake as if drawn by attraction.

All this time, the night was unbroken by any sound. Not
a hail, nor a call, our own orders excepted, and they had
been given in low tones, had been audible on board the
Amanda. As regards the vessel at anchor, she appeared to
give herself no concern. There she lay, a fine ship, and, as I
thought, a vessel-of-war, like a marine bird asleep on its
proper element. We were directly between her and the
lugger, and it is possible her anchor-watch did not see the
latter. The three vessels were not more than half a cable's
length asunder; that is, we were about that distance from
the ship, and the lugger was a very little farther from us.
Five minutes must determine the matter. I was on the brig's
forecastle, anxiously examining all I could make out on
board the ship, as her size, and shape, and rig became slowly
more and more distinct; and I hailed:

"Ship ahoy!"

"Hilloa! What brig's that?"

"An American, with a French privateer-lugger close on
board me, directly in my wake. You had better be stirring!"

I heard the quick exclamation of "The devil there is!"
"Bloody Yankees!" came next. Then followed the call of
"All hands." It was plain enough my notice had set everything in motion in that quarter. Talcott now came running
forward to say he thought, from some movements on board
the lugger, that her people were now first apprised of the
vicinity of the ship. I had been sadly disappointed at the
call for all hands on board the ship, for it was in the manner of a merchantman, instead of that of a vessel-of-war

But we were getting too near to remain much longer in doubt. The Amanda was already sweeping up on the Englishman's bows, not more than forty yards distant.

"She is an English West Indiaman, Mr. Wallingford," said one of my oldest seamen, "and a running ship; some vessel that has deserted or lost her convoy."

"Do you know anything of the lugger?" demanded an officer from on board the ship, in a voice that was not very amicable.

"No more than you see; she has chased me, close aboard, for the last twenty minutes."

There was no reply to this for a moment, and then I was asked, "to tack, and give us a little chance, by drawing him away for a few minutes. We are armed, and will come out to your assistance."

Had I been ten years older, experience in the faith of men, and especially of men engaged in the pursuit of gain, would have prevented me from complying with this request; but, at eighteen, one views these things differently. It did appear to me ungenerous to lead an enemy in upon a man in his sleep, and not endeavor to do something to aid the surprised party; I answered "Ay, ay!" therefore, and tacked directly alongside of the ship. But the manœuvre was too late, the lugger coming in between the ship and the brig, just as we began to draw ahead again, leaving him room, and getting a good look at us both. The Englishman appeared the most inviting, I suppose, for she up helm and went on board of him on his quarter. Neither party used their guns. We were so near, however, as plainly to understand the whole, to distinguish the orders, and even to hear the blows that were struck by hand. It was an awful minute to us in the brig. The cries of the hurt reached us in the stillness of that gloomy morning, and oaths mingled with the clamor. Though taken by surprise, John Bull fought well; though we could perceive that he was overpowered, however, just as the distance, and the haze that was beginning to gather thick around the land, shut in the two vessels from our view.

The disappearance of the two combatants furnished me

with a hint how to proceed. I stood out three or four minutes longer, or a sufficient distance to make certain we
should not be seen, and tacked again. In order to draw as
fast as possible out of the line of sight, we kept the brig off
a little, and then ran in toward the English coast, which was
sufficiently distant to enable us to stand on in that direction
some little time longer. This expedient succeeded perfectly ;
for, when we found it necessary to tack again, day began to
dawn. Shortly after, we could just discern the West Indiaman and the lugger standing off the land, making the best
of their way toward the French coast. In 1799, it is possible
that this bold Frenchman got his prize into some of his own
ports, though three or four years later it would have been a
nearly hopeless experiment. As for the Amanda, she was
safe ; and Nelson did not feel happier, after his great ac-
chievement at the Nile, than I felt at the success of my own
expedient. Talcott congratulated me and applauded me ;
and I believe all of us were a little too much disposed to ascribe to our own steadiness and address, much that ought
fairly to have been imputed to chance.

Off Dover we got a pilot, and learned that the ship captured was the Dorothea, a valuable West Indiaman that had
stolen away from her convoy, and come in alone, the previous evening. She anchored under Dungeness at the first
of the ebb, and. it seems, had preferred taking a good night's
rest to venturing out in the dark, when the flood made.
Her berth was a perfectly snug one, and the lugger would
probably never have found her, had we not led her directly
in upon her prey.

I was now relieved from all charge of the brig ; and a relief I found it, between shoals, enemies, and the tides, of
which I knew nothing. That day we got into the Downs,
and came-to. Here I saw a fleet at anchor ; and a pretty
stir it made among the men-of-wars'-men, when our story
was repeated among them. I do think twenty of their
boats were alongside of us, to get the facts from the original
source. Among others who thus appeared, to question me,
was one old gentleman, whom I suspected of being an admiral. He was in shore-dress, and came in a plain way ;

the men in his boat declining to answer any questions ; but they paid him unusual respect. This gentleman asked me a great many particulars, and I told him the whole story frankly, concealing or coloring nothing. He was evidently much interested. When he went away, he shook me cordially by the hand, and said : "Young gentleman, you have acted prudently and well. Never mind the grumbling of some of our lads; they think only of themselves. It was your right and your duty to save your own vessel, if you could, without doing anything dishonorable ; and I see nothing wrong in your conduct. But it's a sad disgrace to us to let these French rascals be picking up their crumbs in this fashion, right under our hawse-holes."

CHAPTER X.

"How pleasant and how sad the turning tide
    Of human life, when side by side
    The child and youth begin to glide
        Along the vale of years ;
    The pure twin-being for a little space,
    With lightsome heart, and yet a graver face,
        Too young for woe, though not for tears."

ALLSTON.

W ITH what interest and deference most Americans of any education regarded England, her history, laws, and institutions, in 1799 ! There were a few exceptions,—warm political partisans, and here and there an individual whose feelings had become embittered by some particular incident of the Revolution,—but surprisingly few, when it is recollected that the country was only fifteen years from the peace. I question if there ever existed another instance of as strong provincial admiration for the capital, as independent America manifested for the mother country, in spite of a thousand just grievances, down to the period of the war of 1812. I was no exception to the rule, nor was Talcott. Neither of us had ever seen England before we made the Lizard on this voyage, except through our mind's eyes ; and these had presented quantities of beauties and excellences that certainly vanished on a nearer approach. By this I merely mean that we had painted in too high colors, as is apt to be the case when the imagination holds the pencil ; not that there was any unusual absence of things worthy to be commended. On the contrary, even at this late hour, I consider England as a model for a thousand advantages, even to our own inappreciable selves. Nevertheless, much delusion was blended with our admiration.

English history was virtually American history; and everything on the land, as we made our way toward town, which the pilot could point out, was a source of amusement and delight. We had to tide it up to London, and had plenty of leisure to see all there was to be seen. The Thames is neither a handsome nor a very magnificent river; but it was amazing to witness the number of vessels that then ascended or descended it. There was scarce a sort of craft known to Christendom, a few of the Mediterranean excepted, that was not to be seen there; and as for the colliers, we drifted through a forest of them that seemed large enough to keep the town a twelvemonth in firewood, by simply burning their spars. The manner in which the pilot handled our brig, too, among the thousand ships that lay in tiers on each side of the narrow passage we had to thread, was perfectly surprising to me; resembling the management of a coachman in a crowded thoroughfare, more than the ordinary working of a ship. I can safely say I learned more in the Thames, in the way of keeping a vessel in command, and in doing what I pleased with her, than in the whole of my voyage to Canton and back again. As for Neb, he rolled his dark eyes about in wonder, and took an occasion to say to me, "He 'll make her talk, Masser Miles, afore he have done." I make no doubt the navigation from the Forelands to the bridges, as it was conducted thirty years since, had a great influence on the seamanship of the English. Steamers are doing away with much of this practice, though the colliers still have to rely on themselves. Coals will scarcely pay for tugging.

I had been directed by Captain Williams to deliver the brig to her original consignee, an American merchant established in the modern Babylon, reserving the usual claim for salvage. This I did, and that gentleman sent hands on board to take charge of the vessel, relieving me entirely from all further responsibility. As the captain in his letter had, inadvertently I trust, mentioned that he had put " Mr, Wallingford, his third mate," in charge, I got no invitation

to dinner from the consignee; though the affair of the cap-
ture under Dungeness found its way into the papers, *via*
Deal, I have always thought, with the usual caption of
"Yankee Trick."

Yankee trick! This phrase, so often carelessly used, has
probably done a great deal of harm in this country. The
young and ambitious—there are all sorts of ambition, and,
among others, that of being a rogue; as a proof of which,
one daily hears people call envy, jealousy, covetousness,
avarice, and half of the meaner vices, ambition—the young
and ambitious, then, of this country too often think to do a
good thing that shall have some of the peculiar merit of a
certain other good thing that they have heard laughed at
and applauded under this designation. I can account in no
other manner for the great and increasing number of "Yankee tricks" that are of daily occurrence among us. Among
other improvements in taste, not to say in morals, that
might be introduced into the American press, would be the
omission of the histories of these rare inventions. As two
thirds of the editors of the whole country, however, are Yankees, I suppose they must be permitted to go on exulting
in the cleverness of their race. We are indebted to the
Puritan stock for most of our instructors,—editors and
schoolmasters,—and when one coolly regards the prodigious progress of the people in morals, public and private
virtue, honesty, and other estimable qualities, he must, indeed, rejoice in the fact that our masters so early discovered
"a church without a bishop."

I had an opportunity while in London, however, of ascertaining that the land of our fathers, which, by the way,
has archbishops, contains something besides an unalloyed virtue in its bosom. At Gravesend we took on board two custom-house officers (they always set a rogue to watch a rogue
in the English revenue system), and they remained in the
brig until she was discharged. One of these men had been
a gentleman's servant, and he owed his place to his former
master's interest. He was a miracle of custom-house integ-
rity and disinterestedness, as I discovered in the first hour
of our intercourse. Perceiving a lad of eighteen in charge

of the prize, and ignorant that this lad had read a good deal of Latin and Greek under excellent Mr. Hardinge, besides being the heir of Clawbonny, I suppose he fancied he would have an easy time with him.   The man's name was Sweeney. Perceiving in me an eager desire to see everything, the brig was no sooner at her moorings than he proposed a cruise ashore.   It was Sweeney who showed me the way to the consignee's, and, that business accomplished, he proposed that we should proceed on and take a look at St. Paul's, the Monument, and, as he gradually found my tastes more intel-lectual than he at first supposed, the wonders of the West End.   I was nearly a week under the pilotage of the "Ad-mirable Sweeney."   After showing me the exteriors of all the things of mark about the town, and the interiors of a few that I was disposed to pay for, he descended in his tastes, and carried me through Wapping, its purlieus and its scenes of atrocities.   I have always thought Sweeney was sounding me, and hoping to ascertain my true character by the course he took ; and that he betrayed his motives in a proposition which he finally made, and which brought our intimacy to a sudden close.   The result, however, was to let me into secrets I should probably have never learned in any other manner.   Still, I had read and heard too much to be easily duped ; and I kept myself not only out of the power of my tempter, but out of the power of all that could injure me, remaining simply a curious observer of what was placed before my eyes.   Good Mr. Hardinge's lessons were not wholly forgotten ; I could run away from him much easier than from his precepts.

I shall never forget a visit I made to a house called the Black Horse, in St. Catherine's Lane.   This last was a nar-row street that ran across the site of the docks that now bear the same name ; and it was the resort of all the local infamy of Wapping.   I say local infamy ; for there were portions of the West End that were even worse than any-thing which a mere port could produce.   Commerce, that parent of so much that is useful to man, has its dark side, as everything else of earth ; and, among its other evils, it drags after it a long train of low vice ; but this train is neither so long nor so broad as that which is chained to the chariot-wheels of the great. Appearances excepted, and they are far less than might be expected, I think the West End could beat Wapping out and out in every essential vice; and, if St. Giles be taken into the account, I know of no salvo in favor of the land over the sea.

Our visit to the Black Horse was paid of a Sunday, that being the leisure moment of all classes of laborers, and the day when, being attired in their best, they fancied themselves best prepared to appear in the world. I will here remark, that I have never been in any portion of Christendom that keeps the Sabbath precisely as it is kept in America. In all other countries, even the most rigorously severe in their practices, it is kept as a day of recreation and rest, as well as of public devotion. Even in American towns, the old observances are giving away before the longings or weaknesses of human nature ; and Sunday is no longer what it was. I have witnessed scenes of brawling, blasphemy, and rude tumult in the suburbs of New York, on Sundays, within the last few years, that I have never seen in any other part of the world on similar occasions ; and serious doubts of the expediency of the high-pressure principle have beset me, whatever may be the just constructions of doctrine. With the last I pretend not to meddle ; but, in a worldly point of view, it would seem wise, if you cannot make men all that they ought to be, to aim at such social regulations as shall make them as little vile as possible. But, to return to the Black Horse in St. Catherine's Lane— a place whose very name was associated with vileness.

It is unnecessary to speak of the characters of its female visitors. Most of them were young, many of them were still blooming and handsome, but all of them were abandoned. "I need tell you nothing of these girls," said Sweeney, who was a bit of a philosopher in his way, ordering a pot of beer, and motioning me to take a seat at a vacant table ; "but, as for the men you see here, half are house-breakers and pickpockets, come to pass the day genteelly among you gentlemen-sailors. There are two or three faces here that I have seen at the Old Bailey, myself ; and how they have remained in the country, is more than I can tell you. You perceive these fellows are just as much at their ease, and the landlord who receives and entertains them is just as much at his ease, as if the whole party were merely honest men.''

"How happens it," I asked, "that such known rogues are allowed to go at large, or that this innkeeper dares receive them?''

"Oh! you're a child yet, or you would not ask such a question! You must know, Master Wallingford, that the law protects rogues as well as honest men. To convict a pickpocket, you must have witnesses, and jurors to agree, and prosecutors, and a sight of things that are not as plenty as pocket-handkerchiefs, or even wallets and Bank of England notes. Besides, these fellows can prove an *alibi* any day in the week. An *alibi*, you must know—''

"I know very well what an *alibi* means, Mr. Sweeney.''

"The deuce you do!" exclaimed the protector of the king's revenue, eying me a little distrustfully. "And pray, how should one as young as you, and coming from a new country like America, know that?''

"Oh!" said I, laughing, "America is just the country for *alibis*—everybody is everywhere, and nobody anywhere. The whole nation is in motion, and there is every imaginable opportunity for *alibis*.''

I believed I owed the development of Sweeney's "ulterior views" to this careless speech. He had no other idea of the word than its legal signification; and it must have struck him as a little suspicious that one of my apparent condition in life, and especially of my years, should be thus early instructed in the meaning of this very useful professional term. It was a minute before he spoke again, having been all that time studying my countenance.

"And pray, Master Wallingford," he then inquired, "do you happen to know what *nolle prosequi* means, too?''

"Certainly; it means to give up the chase. The French lugger under Dungeness entered a *nolle prosequi* as respects my brig, when she found her hands full of the West India-man.''

"So, so; I find I have been keeping company all this

time with a knowing one, and I such a simpleton as to fancy
him green ! Well, that I should live to be done by a raw
Jonathan !''

" Poh, poh, Mr. Sweeney, I can tell you a story of two
of our naval officers, that took place just before we sailed ·
and then you will learn that all hands of us, on the other
side of the Big Pond, understood Latin. One of these
officers had been engaged in a duel, and he found it necessary to lie hid. A friend and shipmate, who was in his
secret, came one day in a great hurry to tell him that the
authorities of the State in which the parties fought had
'entered a *nolle prosequi*' against the offenders. He had
a newspaper with the whole thing in it, in print. ' What 's
a *nolle prosequi*, Jack?' asked Tom. 'Why, it 's Latin, to
be sure, and it means some infernal thing or other. We
must contrive to find out, for it 's half the battle to know
who and what you 've got to face.' 'Well, you know lots
of lawyers, and dare show your face ; so, just step out and
ask one.' ' I 'll trust no lawyer ; I might put the question
to some chap who had been fee'd. But we both studied a
little Latin when boys, and between us we 'll undermine
the meaning.' Tom assented, and to work they went.
Jack had the most Latin ; but, do all he could, he was not
able to find a ' *nolle* ' in any dictionary. After a great deal
of conjecture, the friends agreed it must be the root of
' knowledge,' and that point was settled. As for ' *prosequi*,'
it was not so difficult, as ' *sequor* ' was a familiar word ;
and, after some cogitation, Jack announced his discoveries.
' If this thing were in English, now,' he said, ' a fellow
might understand it. In that case, I should say that the
sheriff's men were in " pursuit of knowledge " ; that is,
hunting after *you;* but Latin, you remember, was always
an inverted sort of stuff, and that " *pro* " alters the whole
signification. The paper says they 've " entered a *nolle
prosequi* " ; and the " entered " explains the whole. " Entered a *nolle* " means, have entered on the knowledge, got
a scent ; you see it is law English ; " *pro* " means " how,"
and " *sequi*," " to give chase." The amount of it all is,
Tom, that they are on your heels, and I must go to work

and send you off, at once, two or three hundred miles into the interior, where you may laugh at them and their " *nolle prosequis* " together.' " [1]

Sweeney laughed heartily at this story, though he clearly did not take the joke, which I presume he fancied lay concealed under an American flash tongue ; and he proposed, by way of finishing the day, to carry me to an entertainment where, he gave me to understand, American officers were fond of sometimes passing a few minutes. I was led to a Wapping assembly-room, on entering which I found myself in a party composed of some forty or fifty cooks and stewards of American vessels, all as black as their own pots, with partners of the usual color and bloom of English girls. I have as few prejudices of color as any American well can have ; but I will confess this scene struck me as being painfully out of keeping. In England, however, nothing seemed to be thought of it ; and I afterwards found that marriages between English women, and men of all colors of the rainbow, were very common occurrences.

When he had given me this ball as the climax of his compliments, Sweeney betrayed the real motive of all his attentions. After drinking a pot of beer, extra well laced with gin, he offered his services in smuggling anything ashore that the Amanda might happen to contain, and which I, as the prize-master, might feel a desire to appropriate to my own particular purposes. I met the proposal with a little warmth, letting my tempter understand that I considered his offer so near an insult, that it must terminate our acquaintance. The man seemed astounded. In the first place, he evidently thought all goods and chattels were made to be plundered, and then he was of opinion that plundering was a very common "Yankee trick." Had I been an Englishman, he might possibly have understood my conduct ; but, with him, it was so much a habit to fancy an American a rogue, that, as I afterward discovered, he was trying to persuade the leader of a press-gang that I was the half-educated and illegitimate son of some English merchant, who wished to pass himself off for an American. I pretend

[1] There is said to be foundation for this story.

not to account for the contradiction, though I have often met with the same moral phenomena among his country-men ; but here was as regular a rogue as ever cheated, who pretended to think roguery indigenous to certain nations, among whom his own was not included.

At length I was cheered with the sight of the Crisis, as she came drifting through the tiers, turning and twisting, and glancing along, just as the Amanda had done before her. The pilot carried her to moorings quite near us ; and Talcott, Neb and I were on board her before she was fairly secured. My reception was very favorable, Captain Wil-liams having seen the account of the " Yankee trick " in the papers ; and, understanding the thing just as it had hap-pened, he placed the most advantageous construction on all I had done. For myself, I confess I never had any misgiv-ings on the subject.

All hands of us were glad to be back in the Crisis again. Captain Williams had remained at Falmouth longer than he expected, to make some repairs that could not be thoroughly completed at sea, which alone prevented him from getting into the river as soon as I did myself. Now the ship was in, we no longer felt any apprehension of being impressed, Sweeney's malignancy having set several of the gang upon the scent after us. Whether the fellow actually thought I was an English subject or not, is more than I ever knew ; but I felt no disposition myself to let the point be called in question before my Lord Chief Justice of a Rendezvous. The King's Bench was more governed by safe principles, in its decisions, than the gentlemen who presided in these marine courts of the British navy.

As I was the only officer in the ship who had ever seen anything of London, my fortnight's experience made me a notable man in the cabin. It was actually greater prefer-ment for me than when I was raised from third to be second mate. Marble was all curiosity to see the English capital, and he made me promise to be his pilot, as soon as duty would allow time for a stroll, and to show him everything I had seen myself. We soon got out the cargo, and then took in ballast for our northwest voyage ; the articles we

11

intended to traffic with on the coast, being too few and too light to fill the ship. This kept us busy for a fortnight, after which we had to look about us to obtain men to supply the places of those who had been killed, or sent away in La Dame de Nantes. Of course we preferred Americans ; and this so much the more, as Englishmen were liable to be pressed at any moment. Fortunately, a party of men that had been taken out of an American ship, a twelvemonth before, by an English cruiser, had obtained their discharges ; and they all came to London, for the double purpose of getting some prize money, and of obtaining passages home. These lads were pleased with the Crisis and the voyage, and, instead of returning to their own country, sailor-like, they took service to go nearly round the world. These were first-rate men,—Delaware River seamen,—and proved a great accession to our force. We owed the windfall to the reputation the ship had obtained by her affairs with the letter-of-marque ; an account of which, copied from the log-book, and a little embellished by some one on shore, the consignee had taken care should appear in the journals. The history of the surprise, in particular, read very well ; and the English were in a remarkably good humor, at that time, to receive an account of any discomfiture of a Frenchman. At no period since the year 1775, had the American character stood so high in England as it did just then ; the two nations, for a novelty, fighting on the same side. Not long after we left London, the underwriters at Lloyd's actually voted a handsome compliment to an American commander for capturing a French frigate. Stranger things have happened than to have the day arrive when English and American fleets may be acting in concert. No one can tell what is in the womb of time ; and I have lived long enough to know that no man can foresee who will continue to be his friends, or a nation what people may become its enemies.

The Crisis at length began to take in her baîes and boxes for the northwest coast, and, as the articles were received slowly, or a few packages at a time, it gave us leisure for play. Our captain was in such good-humor with us, on account of the success of the outward-bound passage, that

he proved very indulgent. This disposition was probably
increased by the circumstance that a ship arrived in a very
short passage from New York, which spoke our prize ; all
well, with a smacking southerly breeze, a clear coast, and a
run of only a few hundred miles to make. This left the
almost moral certainty that La Dame de Nantes had arrived safe, no Frenchman being likely to trust herself on
that distant coast, which was now alive with our own
cruisers, going to or returning from the West Indies.

I had a laughable time in showing Marble the sights of
London. We began with the wild beasts in the Tower, as
in duty bound ; but of these our mate spoke very dis-
paragingly. He had been too often in the East "to be
taken in by such animals"; and, to own the truth, the
cockneys were easily satisfied on the score of their *ména-
gerie*. We next went to the Monument ; but this did not
please him. He had seen a shot-tower in America—there
was but one in that day—that beat it out and out as to height,
and he thought in beauty, too. There was no reasoning
against this. St. Paul's rather confounded him. He frankly
admitted there was no such church at Kennebunk ; though
he did not know but Trinity, New York, "might stand up
alongside of it." "Stand up alongside of it !" I repeated
laughing. "Why, Mr. Marble, Trinity, steeple and all,
could stand up in it—under that dome—and then leave
more room in this building than all the other churches in
New York contain, put altogether."

It was a long time before Marble forgave this speech.
He said it was "unpatriotic"; a word which was less used
in 1799 than it is used to-day, certainly, but which, nevertheless, was used. It often meant then, as now, a thick and
thin pertinacity in believing in provincial marvels ; and, in
this, Marble was one of the most patriotic men with whom
I ever met. I got him out of the church, and along Fleet
Street, through Temple Bar, and into the Strand, however,
in peace ; and then we emerged into the arena of fashion,
aristocracy, and the court. After a time we worked our
way into Hyde Park, where we brought up, to make our
observations.

Marble was deeply averse to acknowledging all the admiration he really felt at the turnouts of London, as they were exhibited in the Park, of a fine day, in their season. It is probable the world elsewhere never saw anything approaching the beauty and magnificence that is here daily seen, at certain times, so far as beauty and magnificence are connected with equipages, including carriages, horses, and servants. Unable to find fault with the *tout ensemble*, our mate made a violent attack on the liveries. He protested it was indecent to put a "hired man"—the word *help* never being applied to the male sex, I believe, by the most fastidious New England purist—in a cocked-hat; a decoration that ought to be exclusively devoted to the uses of ministers of the gospel, governors of States, and militia officers. I had some notions of the habits of the great world, through books, and some little learned by observation and listening; but Marble scouted at most of my explanations. He put his own construction on everything he saw; and I have often thought, since, could the publishers of travels have had the benefit of his blunders, how many would have profited by them. Gentlemen were just then beginning to drive their own coaches; and I remember in a particular instance, an ultra in the new mode had actually put his coachman in the inside, while he occupied the dickey in person. Such a gross violation of the proprieties was unusual, even in London; but there sat Jehu, in all the dignity of cotton-lace, plush, and a cocked-hat. Marble took it into his head that this man was the king, and no reasoning of mine could persuade him to the contrary. In vain I pointed out to him a hundred similar dignitaries, in the proper exercise of their vocation, on the hammer-cloths; he cared not a straw—this was not showing him one inside; and a gentleman inside of a carriage, who wore so fine a coat, and a cocked-hat in the bargain, could be nothing less than some dignitary of the empire; and why not the king! Absurd as all this will seem, I have known mistakes, connected with the workings of our own institutions, almost as great, made by theorists from Europe.

While Marble and I were wrangling on this very point,

a little incident occurred, which led to important consequences in the end. Hackney-coaches, or any other public conveyance, short of post-chaises and post-horses, are
not admitted into the English parks. But glass-coaches
are ; meaning by this term, which is never used in America,
hired carriages that do not go on the stands. We encountered one of these glass-coaches in a very serious
difficulty. The horses had got frightened by means of a
wheelbarrow, aided, probably, by some bad management of
the driver, and had actually backed the hind wheels of the
vehicle into the water of the canal. They would have soon
had the whole carriage submerged, and have followed it
themselves, had it not been for the chief mate and myself.
I thrust the wheelbarrow under one of the forward wheels,
just in time to prevent the final catastrophe ; while Marble
grasped the spoke with his iron gripe, and, together, he and
the wheelbarrow made a resistance that counterbalanced
the backward tendency of the team. There was no foot-
man ; and, springing to the door, I aided a sickly-looking,
elderly man, a female, who might very well have been his
wife, and another that I took for his daughter, to escape.
By my agency all three were put on the dry land, without
even wetting their feet, though I fared worse myself. No
sooner were they safe, than Marble, who was up to his
shoulders in the water, and who had made prodigious efforts
to maintain the balance of power, released his hold, the
wheelbarrow gave way at the same moment, and the whole
affair, coach and horses, had their will, and went, stern foremost, overboard. One of the horses was saved, I believe,
and the other drowned ; but, a crowd soon collecting, I paid
little attention to what was going on in the carriage, as soon
as its cargo was discharged.

The gentleman we had saved pressed my hand with
fervor, and Marble's, too ; saying that we must not quit
him—that we must go home with him. To this we consented readily enough, thinking we might still be of use.
As we all walked toward one of the more private entrances
of the Park, I had an opportunity of observing the people
we had served. They were very respectable in appearance ;

but I knew enough of the world to see that they belonged to what is called the middle class in England. I thought the man might be a soldier; while the two females had an air of great respectability, though not in the least of fashion. The girl appeared to be nearly as old as myself, and was decidedly pretty. Here, then, was an adventure! I had saved the life of a damsel of seventeen, and had only to fall in love to become the hero of a romance.

At the gate, the gentleman stopped a hackney-coach, put the females in, and desired us to follow. But to this we would not consent, both being wet, and Marble particularly so. After a short parley, he gave us an address in Norfolk Street, Strand; and we promised to stop there on our way back to the ship. Instead of following the carriage, however, we made our way on foot into the Strand, where we found an eating-house, turned in and eat a hearty dinner each, the chief mate resorting to some brandy in order to prevent his taking cold. On what principle this is done, I cannot explain, though I know it is often practised, and in all quarters of the world.

As soon as we had dined and dried ourselves, we went into Norfolk Street. We had been told to ask for Major Merton, and this we did. The house was one of those plain lodging-houses, of which most of that part of the town is composed; and we found the major and his family in the occupation of the first floor, a mark of gentility on which some stress is laid in England. It was plain enough, however, to see that these people were not rolling in that splendor of which we had just seen so much in the Park.

"I can trace the readiness and gallantry of the English tar in your conduct," observed the major, after he had given us both quite as warm a reception as circumstances required, at the same time taking out his pocket-book, and turning over some bank notes. "I wish, for your sakes, I was better able than I am to reward you for what you have done; but twenty pounds is all I can now offer. At some other time circumstances may place it in my power to give further and better proofs of my gratitude."

As this was said, the major held two ten-pound notes

toward Marble, doubtless intending that I should receive one of them as a fair division of the spoils. Now, according to all theory, and the established opinion of the Christian world, America is *the* avaricious country; the land, of all others, in which men are the most greedy of gain; in which human beings respect gold more, and themselves less, than in any other portion of this globe. I never dispute anything that is settted by the common consent of my fellow-creatures, for the simple reason that I know the decision must be against me; so I will concede that money is the great end of American life—that there is little else to live for in the great model republic. Politics have fallen into such hands, that office will not even give social station; the people are omnipotent, it is true; but, though they can make a governor, they cannot make gentlemen and ladies; even kings are sometimes puzzled to do that; literature, arms, arts, and fame of all sorts are unattainable in their rewards among us, as in other nations, leaving the puissant dollar in its undisturbed ascendency; still, as a rule, twenty Europeans can be bought with two ten-pound Bank of England notes much easier than two Americans. I leave others to explain the phenomenon; I only speak of the fact.

Marble listened to the major's speech with great attention and respect, fumbling in his pocket for his tobacco-box the whole time. The box was opened just as the major ended, and even I began to be afraid that the well-known cupidity of Kennebunk was about to give way before the temptation, and the notes were to be stowed alongside of the tobacco; but I was mistaken. Deliberately helping himself to a quid, the chief mate shut the box again, and then he made his reply.

"Quite ginerous in you, major," he said, "and all shipshape and right. I like to see things done just in that way. Put up the money; we thank you as much as if we could take it, and that squares all accounts. I would just mention, however, to prevent mistakes, as the other idee might get us impressed, that this young man and I are both born Americans—he from up the Hudson somewhere, and I from York city, itself, though edicated Down East."

" Americans ! " resumed the major, drawing himself up a
little stiffly ; " then you, young man," turning to me, and
holding out the notes, of which he now seemed as anxious to
be rid, as I had previously fancied he was sorry to see go,
" you will do me the favor to accept this small token of my
gratitude."

"It is quite impossible, sir," I answered respectfully.
" We are not exactly what we seem, and you are probably
deceived by our roundabouts ; but we are the first and second officers of a letter-of-marque."

At the word "officers," the major drew back his hand,
and hastily apologized. He did not understand us even
then, I could plainly see ; but he had sufficient sagacity to
understand that his money would not be accepted. We
were invited to sit down, and the conversation continued.

" Master Miles, there," resumed Marble," has an estate,
a place called Clawbonny, somewhere up the Hudson ; and he
has no business to be sailing about the world in jacket and
trousers, when he ought to be studying law, or trying his
hand at college. But as the old cock crows, the young 'un
l'arns ; his father was a sailor before him, and I suppose
that 's the reason on 't."

This announcement of my position ashore did me no
harm, and I could see a change in the deportment of the
whole family—not that it had ever treated me haughtily,
or even coldly ; but it now regarded me as more on a level
with itself. We remained an hour with the Mertons, and I
promised to repeat the call before we sailed. This I did a
dozen times, at least ; and the major, finding, I suppose,
that he had a tolerably well-educated youth to deal with,
was of great service in putting me in a better way of seeing
London. I went to both theatres with the family, taking
care to appear in a well-made suit of London clothes, in
which I made quite as respectable a figure as most of the
young men I saw in the streets. Even Emily smiled when
she first saw me in my long togs, and I thought she blushed.
She was a pretty creature ; gentle and mild in her ordinary
deportment, but full of fire and spirit at the bottom, as I
could see by her light blue, English eye. Then she had

been well educated ; and in my young ignorance of life, I fancied she knew more than any girl of seventeen I had ever met with. Grace and Lucy were both clever, and had been carefully taught by Mr. Hardinge ; but the good divine could not give two girls, in the provincial retirement of America, the cultivation and accomplishments that were within the reach of even moderate means in England. To me, Emily Merton seemed a marvel in the way of attainments ; and I often felt ashamed of myself, as I sat at her side, listening to the natural and easy manner in which she alluded to things, of which I then heard for the first time.

CHAPTER XI.

" ' Boatswain !
  ' Here, master : what cheer ? '
  ' Good : speak to the mariners ; fall to 't
Yarely, or we run ourselves aground : bestir, bestir.' "

Tempest.

AS Captain Williams wished to show me some favor for the manner in which I had taken care of the brig, he allowed me as much time ashore as I asked for. I might never see London again ; and, understanding I had fallen into good company, he threw no obstacle in the way of my profiting by it. So careful was he, indeed, as to get one of the consul's clerks to ascertain who the Mertons were, lest I should become the dupe of the thousands of specious rogues with which London abounds. The report was favorable, giving us to understand that the major had been much employed in the West Indies, where he still held a moderately lucrative, semi-military appointment, being then in England to settle certain long and vexatious accounts, as well as to take Emily, his only child, from school. He was expected to return to the old, or some other post, in the course of a few months. A portion of this I gleaned from Emily herself, and it was all very fairly corroborated by the account of the consul's clerk. There was no doubt that the Mertons were persons of respectable position ; without having any claims, however, to be placed very high. From the major, moreover, I learned he had some American connections, his father having married in Boston.

For my part, I had quite as much reason to rejoice at the chance which threw me in the way of the Mertons, as they had. If I was instrumental in saving their lives, as was undeniably the case, they taught me more of the world, in the ordinary social sense of the phrase, than I had learned in all my previous life. I make no pretensions to having seen London society ; that lay far beyond the reach of Major Merton himself, who was born the son of a merchant, when merchants occupied a much lower position in the English social scale than they do to-day, and had to look to a patron for most of his own advancement. But he was a gentleman ; maintained the notions, sentiments, and habits of the caste ; and was properly conscious of my having saved his life when it was in great jeopardy. As for Emily Merton, she got to converse with me with the freedom of a friend ; and very pleasant it was to hear pretty thoughts expressed in pretty language, and from pretty lips. I could perceive that she thought me a little rustic and provincial ; but I had not been all the way to Canton to be browbeaten by a cockney girl, however clever and handsome. On the whole—and I say it without vanity, at this late day—I think the impression left behind me, among these good people, was favorable. Perhaps Clawbonny was not without its influence ; but, when I paid my last visit, even Emily looked sorrowful, and her mother was pleased to say they should all miss me much. The major made me promise to hunt him up, should I ever be in Jamaica, or Bombay ; for one of which places he expected to sail himself, with his wife and daughter, in the course of a few months. I knew he had had one appointment, thought he might receive another, and hoped everything would turn out for the best.

The Crisis sailed on her day ; and she went to sea from the Downs, a week later, with a smacking southerly wind. Our Philadelphians turned out a noble set of fellows ; and we had the happiness of beating an English sloop-of-war, just as we got clear of the channel, in a fair trial of speed. To lessen our pride a little, a two-decker that was going to the Mediterranean, treated us exactly in the same manner, only three days later. What made this last affair more mortifying, was the fact that Marble had just satisfied himself, and all hands, that, a sloop-of-war being the fastest description of vessel, and we having got the better of one of them, it might be fairly inferred we could outsail the whole British navy.   I endeavored to console him, by reminding him that "the race was not always to the swift." He growled out some sort of an answer, denouncing all sayings, and desiring to know out of what book I had picked up that nonsense.

I have no intention of dwelling on every little incident that occurred on the long road we were now travelling. We touched at Madeira, and landed an English family that went there for the benefit of an invalid; got some fruit, fresh meat, and vegetables, and sailed again.   Our next stopping place was Rio, whither we went for letters from home, the captain being taught to expect them. The ship's letters were received, and they were filled with eulogiums on our good conduct, having been written after the arrival of La Dame de Nantes ; but great was my disappointment on finding there was not even a scrawl for myself.

Our stay at Rio was short, and we left port with a favorable slant of wind, running as far south as 50° in a very short time.   As we drew near to the southern extremity of the American continent, however, we met with heavy weather and foul winds.   We were now in the month that corresponds to November in the northern hemisphere, and had to double the Horn at that unpropitious season of the year, going westward.   There is no part of the world of which navigators have given accounts so conflicting, as of this celebrated passage.   Each man appears to have described it as he found it, himself, while no two seem to have found it exactly alike.   I do not remember to have ever heard of calms off Cape Horn ; but light winds are by no means uncommon, though tempests are undoubtedly the predominant characteristic.   Our captain had already been round four times, and he held the opinion that the season made no difference, and that it was better to keep near the land.   We shaped our course accordingly for Staten Land, intending to pass through the Straits of Le

A map of South America, drawn about the time that Miles Wallingford sailed around Cape Horn. *(Courtesy of The Old Print Shop)*

Maire, and hug the Horn as close as possible in doubling it.   We made the Falkland Islands, or West Falkland rather, just as the sun rose, one morning, bearing a little on our weather-quarter, with the wind blowing heavily at the eastward.   The weather was thick, and, what was still worse, there was so little day, and no moon, that it was getting to be ticklish work to be standing for a passage as narrow as that we aimed at.   Marble and I talked the matter over, between ourselves, and wished the captain could be persuaded to haul up and try to go to the eastward of the island, as was still possible, with the wind where it was.   Still, neither of us dared propose it; I, on account of my youth, and the chief mate, as he said, on account of "the old fellow's obstinacy."   "He likes to be poking about in such places," Marble added, "and is never so happy as when he is running round the ocean in places where it is full of unknown islands, looking for sandal-wood and *bêche-la-mer!*   I 'll warrant you, he 'll give us a famous time of it, if he ever gets us up on the northwest coast."   Here the consultation terminated, we mates believing it wiser to let things take their course.

I confess to having seen the mountains on our weather-quarter disappear, with melancholy forebodings.   There was little hope of getting any observation that day; and to render matters worse, about noon the wind began to haul more to the southward.   As it hauled, it increased in violence, until, at midnight, it blew a gale; the commencement of such a tempest as I had never witnessed in any of my previous passages at sea.   As a matter of course, sail was reduced as fast as it became necessary, until we had brought the ship down to a close-reefed main-topsail, the fore-topmast staysail, the fore-course, and the mizzen staysail. This was old-fashioned canvas; the more recent spencer being then unknown.

Our situation was now far from pleasant. The tides and currents, in that high latitude, run with great velocity; and then, at a moment when it was of the greatest importance to know precisely where the ship was, we were left in the painful uncertainty of conjecture, and

theories that might be very wide of the truth. The captain had nerve enough, notwithstanding, to keep on the
larboard tack until daylight, in the hope of getting in
sight of the mountains of Terra del Fuego. No one now
expected we should be able to fetch through the straits
but it would be a great relief to obtain a sight of the land
as it would enable us to get some tolerably accurate notions of our position. Daylight came at length, but it
brought no certainty. The weather was so thick, between
a drizzling rain, sea-mist, and the spray, that it was seldom we could see a league around us, and frequently, not
half a mile. Fortunately, the general direction of the
eastern coast of Terra del Fuego is from northwest to
southeast, always giving us room to wear off shore, provided we did not unexpectedly get embarrassed in some
one of the many deep indentations of that wild and inhospitable shore.

Captain Williams showed great steadiness in the trying
circumstances in which we were placed. The ship was
just far enough south to render it probable she could
weather Falkland Islands on the other tack, could we rely
upon the currents; but it would be ticklish work to undertake such a thing in the long, intensely dark nights we
had, and thus run the risk of finding ourselves on a lee-
shore. He determined, therefore, to hold on as long as
possible, on the tack we were on, expecting to get through
another night without coming upon the land, every hour
now giving us the hope that we were drawing near to the
termination of the gale. I presume he felt more emboldened to pursue this course, by the circumstance that the
wind evidently inclined to haul, little by little, more to the
southward, which was not only increasing our chances of
laying past the islands, but lessened the danger from Terra
del Fuego.

Marble was exceedingly uneasy during that second
night. He remained on deck with me the whole of the
morning watch; not that he distrusted my discretion in the
least, but because he distrusted the wind and the land. I
never saw him in so much concern before, for it was his

habit to consider himself a timber of the ship, that was to sink or swim with the craft.

"Miles," said he, "you and I know something of these 'bloody currents,' and we know they take a ship one way, while she looks as fiercely the other as a pig that is dragged aft by the tail. If we had run down the 50th degree of longitude, now, we might have had plenty of sea-room, and been laying past the cape with this very wind; but no, the old fellow would have had no islands in that case, and he never could be happy without half a dozen islands to bother him."

"Had we run down the 50th degree of longitude," I answered, "we should have had twenty degrees to make to get round the Horn; whereas, could we only lay through the Straits of Le Maire, six or eight of those very same degrees would carry us clear of everything."

"Only lay through the Straits of Le Maire, on the 10th November, or, what is the same thing in this quarter of the world, of May, and with less than nine hours of daylight! And such daylight too! Why, our Newfoundland fogs, such stuff as I used to eat when a youngster and a fisher-man, are high noon to it! Soundings are out of the question hereabouts; and before one has hauled in the deep-sea, with all its line out, his cut-water may be on a rock. This ship is so weatherly and drags ahead so fast, that we shall see *terra firma* before any one has a notion of it. The old man fancies, because the coast of Fuego trends to the northwest, that the land will fall away from us as fast as we draw toward it. I hope he may live long enough to persuade all hands that he is right!"

Marble and I were conversing on the forecastle at the time, our eyes turned to the westward, for it was scarcely possible for him to look in any other direction, when he interrupted himself by shouting out, "Hard up with the helm—spring to the after-braces, my lads—man mizzen-staysail downhaul!" This set everybody in motion, and the captain and third mate were on deck in a minute. The ship fell off, as soon as we got the mizzen staysail in, and the main-topsail touching. Gathering way fast, as she got the wind more aft, her helm threw her stern up, and away she went like a top. The fore-topmast staysail-sheet was tended with care, and yet the cloth emitted a sound like the report of a swivel, when the sail first filled on the other tack. We got the starboard fore-tack forward, and the larboard sheet aft, by two tremendously severe drags, the blocks and bolts seeming fairly to quiver as they felt the strains. Everything succeeded, however, and the Crisis began to drag off from the coast of Terra del Fuego, of a certainty ; but to go whither, no one could precisely tell. She headed up nearly east, the wind playing about between south-and-by-east, and south-east-and-by-south. On that course, I own I had now great doubt whether she could lay past the Falkland Islands, though I felt per- suaded we must be a long distance from them. There was plenty of time before us to take the chances of a change.

As soon as the ship was round, and trimmed by the wind on the other tack, Captain Williams had a grave con- versation with the chief mate, on the subject of his reason for what he had done. Marble maintained that he had caught a glimpse of the land ahead—"just as you know I did of La Dame de Nantes, Captain Williams," he con- tinued ; "and seeing there was no time to be lost, I or- dered the helm hard up, to wear off shore." I distrusted this account, even while it was in the very process of com- ing out of the chief mate's mouth, and, Marble afterward admitted to me, quite justly ; but the captain either was satisfied, or thought it prudent to seem so. By the best calculations I afterwards made, I suppose we must have been from fifteen to twenty leagues from the land when we wore ship ; but, as Marble said, when he made his private confessions, "Madagascar was quite enough for me, Miles, without breaking our nose on this sea-gull coast ; and there may be 'bloody currents' on this side of the Cape of Good Hope, as well as on the other. We've got just so much of a gale and a foul wind to weather, and the ship will do both quite as well with her head to the eastward, as with her head to the westward."

All that day the Crisis stood on the starboard tack, dragging through the raging waters as it might be by violence; and just as night shut in again, she wore round, once more, with her head to the westward. So far from abating, the wind increased, and toward evening we found it necessary to furl our topsail and fore-course. Mere rag of a sail as the former had been reduced to, with its four reefs in, it was a delicate job to roll it up. Neb and I stood together on the bunt, and never did I exert myself more than on that occasion. The foresail, too, was a serious matter, but we got both in without losing either. Just as the sun set, or as night came to increase the darkness of that gloomy day, the fore-topmast staysail went out of the bolt-rope, with a report that was heard all over the ship, disappearing in the mist like a cloud driving in the heavens. A few minutes later, the mizzen staysail was hauled down in order to prevent it from travelling the same road. The jerks even this low canvas occasionally gave the ship, made her tremble from her keel to her trucks.

For the first time I now witnessed a tempest at sea. Gales, and pretty hard ones, I had often seen; but the force of the wind on this occasion as much exceeded that in ordinary gales of wind, as the force of these had exceeded that of a whole-sail breeze. The seas seemed crushed, the pressure of the swooping atmosphere, as the currents of the air went howling over the surface of the ocean, fairly preventing them from rising; or, where a mound of water did appear, it was scooped up and borne off in spray, as the axe dubs inequalities from the log. In less than an hour after it began to blow the hardest there was no very apparent swell—the deep breathing of the ocean is never entirely stilled—and the ship was as steady as if hove half out, her lower yard-arms nearly touching the water, an inclination at which they remained as steadily as if kept there by purchases. A few of us were compelled to go as high as the futtock-shrouds to secure the sails, but higher it was impossible to get. I observed that when I thrust out a hand to clutch anything, it was necessary to make the movement in such a direction as to allow for lee-way, precisely as a boat quarters the stream in crossing against a current. In

12

ascending it was difficult to keep the feet on the ratlins, and in descending it required a strong effort to force the body down toward the centre of gravity. I make no doubt, had I groped my way up to the cross-trees, and leaped overboard, my body would have struck the water thirty or forty yards from the ship. A marlinspike falling from either top would have endangered no one on deck.

When the day returned, a species of lurid, sombre light was diffused over the watery waste, though nothing was visible but the ocean and the ship. Even the sea-birds seemed to have taken refuge in the caverns of the adjacent coast, none reappearing with the dawn. The air was full of spray, and it was with difficulty that the eye could penetrate as far into the humid atmosphere as half a mile. All hands mustered on deck as a matter of course, no one wishing to sleep at a time like that. As for us officers, we collected on the forecastle, the spot where danger would first make itself apparent, did it come from the side of the land.

It is not easy to make a landsman understand the embarrassments of our situation. We had had no observations for several days, and had been moving about by dead reckoning, in a part of the ocean where the tides run like a mill-tail, with the wind blowing a little hurricane. Even now, when her bows were half submerged, and without a stitch of her canvas exposed, the Crisis drove ahead at the rate of three or four knots, luffing as close to the wind as if she carried after-sail. It was Marble's opinion that, in such smooth water, do all we could, the vessel would drive toward the much-dreaded land again, between sun and sun of that short day, a distance of from thirty to forty miles. "Nor is this all, Miles," he added to me, in an aside; "I no more like this 'bloody current,' than that we had over on the other side of the pond, when we broke our back on the rocks of Madagascar. You never see as smooth water as this, unless when the wind and current are travelling in the same direction." I made no reply, but there all four of us, the captain and his three mates, stood looking anxiously into the vacant mist on our lee-bow, as if we expected every moment to behold our homes. A silence of ten minutes succeeded, and I was still gazing in the same direction, when by a sort of mystic rising of the curtain, I fancied I saw a beach of long extent, with a dark-looking waste of low bottom extending inland, for a considerable distance. The beach did not appear to be distant half a knot, while the ship seemed to glide along it, as compared with visible objects on shore, at a rate of six or eight miles the hour. It extended almost in a parallel line with our course, too, as far as could be seen, both astern and ahead.

"What a strange delusion is this !" I thought to myself, and turned to look at my companions, when I found all looking one at the other, as if to ask a common explanation.

"There is no mistake here," said Captain Williams, quietly. "That is land, gentlemen."

"As true as gospel," answered Marble, with the sort of steadiness despair sometimes gives. "What is to be done, sir ?"

"What can be done, Mr. Marble ? We have not room to wear, and, of the two, there seems, so far as I can judge, more sea-room ahead than astern."

This was so apparent, there was no disputing it. We could see the land, looking low, chill, and of the hue of November ; and we could also perceive that ahead, if anything, it fell off a little toward the northward, while astern it seemingly stretched in a due line with our course. That we passed it with great velocity, too, was a circumstance that our eyes showed us too plainly to admit of any mistake. As the ship was still without a rag of sail, borne down by the wind as she had been for hours, and burying to her hawse-holes forward, it was only to a racing tide, or current of some sort, that we could be indebted for our speed. We tried the lead, and got bottom in six fathoms !

The captain and Marble now held a serious consultation. That the ship was entering some sort of an estuary was certain, but of what depth, how far favored by a holding-ground, or how far without any anchorage at all, were facts that defied our inquiries. We knew that the land called Terra del Fuego was, in truth, a cluster of islands, intersected by various channels and passages, into which ships had occasionally ventured, though their navigation had never led to any other results than some immaterial discoveries in geography. That we were entering one of these passages, and under favorable circumstances, though so purely accidental, was the common belief; and it only remained to look out for the best anchorage, while we had daylight. Fortunately, as we drove into the bay, or passage, or whatever it was, the tempest lifted less spray from the water, and, owing to this and other causes, the atmosphere gradually grew clearer. By ten o'clock, we could see fully a league, though I can hardly say that the wind blew less fiercely than before. As for the sea, there was none, or next to none; the water being as smooth as in a river.

The day drew on, and we began to feel increased uneasiness at the novelty of our situation. Our hope and expectation were to find some anchorage; but to obtain this it was indispensable also to find a lee. As the ship moved forward, we still kept the land in view, on our starboard hand, but that was a lee, instead of a weather-shore; the last alone could give our ground-tackle any chance whatever in such a tempest. We were drawing gradually away from this shore, too, which trended more northerly, giving us additional sea-room. The fact that we were in a powerful tide's way, puzzled us the most. There was but one mode of accounting for the circumstance. Had we entered a bay, the current must have been less, and it seemed necessary there should be some outlet to such a swift accumulation of water. It was not the mere rising of the water, swelling in an estuary, but an arrow-like glancing of the element as it shot through a pass. We had a proof of this last fact about eleven o'clock, that admitted of no dispute. Land was seen directly ahead, at that hour, and great was the panic it created. A second look, however, reassured us, the land proving to be merely a rocky islet of some six or eight acres in extent. We gave it a berth, of course, though we examined closely for an anchorage near it, as we approached. This islet was too low and too small to make any lee, nor did we like the looks of the holding-ground.

The notion of anchoring there was subsequently abandoned; but we had now some means of noting our progress. The ship was kept a little away, in order to give this island a berth, and the gale drove her through the water at the rate of seven or eight knots. This, however, was far from being our whole speed, the tide sweeping us onward at a furious rate, in addition. Even Captain Williams thought we must be passing that rock at the rate of fifteen knots!

It was noon, and there was no abatement in the tempest, no change in the current, no means of returning, no chance of stopping; away, we were driven, like events ruled by fate. The only change was the gradual clearing up of the atmosphere, as we receded from the ocean, and got farther removed from its mists and spray. Perhaps the power of the gale had, in a small degree, abated, by two o'clock, and it would have been possible to carry some short sail; but, there being no sea to injure us, it was unnecessary, and the ship continued to drive ahead, under bare poles. Night was the time to dread.

There was now but one opinion among us, and that was this: we thought the ship had entered one of the passages that intersect Terra del Fuego, and that there was the chance of soon finding a lee, as these channels were known to be very irregular and winding. To run in the night seemed impossible; nor was it desirable, as it was almost certain we should be compelled to return by the way we had entered, to extricate ourselves from the dangers of so intricate a navigation. Islands began to appear, moreover, and we had indications that the main passage itself was beginning to diminish in width. Under the circumstances, therefore, it was resolved to get everything ready, and to let go two anchors as soon as we could find a suitable spot. Between the hours of two and four, the ship passed seventeen islets, some of them quite near; but they afforded no shelter. At last, and it was time, the sun beginning to fall very low, as we could see by the waning light, we saw an island of some height and size ahead, and we hoped it might afford us a lee. The tide had changed too, and that was in our favor. Turning to windward, however, was out of the question, since we could carry no sail, and the night was near. Anchor, then, we must, or continue to drive onward in the darkness, sheered about in all directions by a powerful adverse current. It is true, this current would have been a means of safety, by enabling us to haul up from rocks and dangers ahead, could we carry any canvas ; but it still blew too violently for the last. To anchor, then, it was determined.

I had never seen so much anxiety in Captain Williams' countenance, as when he was approaching the island mentioned. There was still light enough to observe its outlines and shores, the last appearing bold and promising. As the island itself may have been a mile in circuit, it made tolerable lee, when close to it. This was then our object, and the helm was put to starboard as we went slowly past, the tide checking our speed. The ship sheered into a sort of roadstead—a very wild one it was—as soon as she had room. It was ticklish work, for no one could tell how soon we might hit a rock ; but we went clear, luffing quite near to the land, where we let go both bowers at the same instant. The ship's way had been sufficiently deadened, by throwing her up as near the wind as she could be got, and there was no difficulty in snubbing her. The lead gave us seven fathoms, and this within pistol-shot of the shore. We knew we were temporarily safe. The great point was to ascertain how the vessel would tend, and with how much strain upon her cables. To everybody's delight, it was found we were in a moderate eddy, that drew the ship's stern from the island, and allowed her to tend to the wind, which still had a fair range from her topsail-yards to the trucks. Lower down, the tempest scuffled about, howling and eddying, and whirling first to one side and then to the other, in a way to prove how much its headlong impetuosity was broken and checked by the land. It is not easy to describe the relief we felt at these happy chances. It was like giving foothold to some wretch who thought a descent of the precipice was inevitable.

The ship was found to ride easily by one cable, and the hands were sent to the windlass to heave up the other anchor, as our lead told us we had rocks beneath us, and the captain was afraid of the chafing. The larboard bower anchor was catted immediately, and there it was left suspended, with a range of cable overhauled, in readiness to let go at a moment's notice. After this the people were told to get their suppers. As for us officers, we had other things to think of. The Crisis carried a small quarter-boat, and this was lowered into the water; the third mate and myself manned its oars, and away we went to carry the captain round the ship, in order that he might ascertain the soundings, should it be necessary to get under way in the night. The examination was satisfactory on all points but one, that of the holding-ground; and we returned to the. vessel, having taken good care to trust ourselves in neither the wind nor the current. An anchor-watch was set, with a mate on deck, four hours and four hours, and all hands turned in.

I had the morning watch. What occurred from seven o'clock (the captain keeping the dog-watches himself) until a few minutes before four, I cannot tell in detail, though I understood generally, that the wind continued to blow in the same quarter, though it gradually diminished in violence, getting down to something like a mere gale, by midnight. The ship rode more easily; but when the flood came in, there was no longer an eddy, the current sucking round each side of the island in a very unusual manner. About ten minutes before the hour when it was my regular watch on deck, all hands were called; I ran on deck, and found the ship had struck adrift, the cable having parted. Marble had got the vessel's head up to the wind, under bare poles as before, and we soon began to heave in the cable. It was found that the mischief had been done by the rocks, the strands being chafed two thirds through. As soon as the current took the vessel's hull with force, the cable parted. We lost our anchor, of course, for there was no possible way of getting back to the island at present, or until the ebb again made.

It wanted several hours of day, and the captain called a council. He told us, he made no doubt that the ship had got into one of the Terra del Fuego passages, guided by Providence ; and as he supposed we must be almost as far south of Staten Land, he was of opinion we had made an important discovery ! Get back we could not, so long as the wind held where it was, and he was disposed to make sail, and push the examination of the channel, as far as circumstances would allow. Captain Williams had a weakness on this point, that was amiable and respectable perhaps, but which hardly comported with the objects and prudence of a trading shipmaster. We were not surprised, therefore, at hearing his suggestion ; and, in spite of the danger, curiosity added its impulses to our other motives of acquiescing. We could not get back as the wind then was, and we were disposed to move forward. As for the dangers of the navigation, they seemed to be lessening as we advanced, fewer islands appearing ahead, and the passage itself grew wider. Our course, however, was more to the southward, bringing the ship close up by the wind once more.

The morning promised to be lighter than we had found the weather for several days, and we even experienced some benefit from the moon. The wind, too, began to back round to the eastward again, as we approached the dawn ; and we got the three topsails, close-reefed, the fore-course, and a new fore-topmast staysail, on the ship. At length day appeared, and the sun was actually seen struggling among dark masses of wild-looking, driving clouds. For the first time since we entered those narrow waters, we now got a good look around us. The land could be seen in all directions.

The passage in which we found the Crisis, at sunrise on the morning of the second of these adventurous days, was of several leagues in width ; and bounded, especially on the north, by high, precipitous mountains, many of which were covered with snow.

The channel was unobstructed ; and not an island, islet, or rock was visible. No impediment to our proceeding offered, and we were still more encouraged to push on. The course we were steering was about south-southwest, and the captain predicted we should come out into the ocean to the westward of the Straits of Le Maire, and somewhere near the cape itself. We should unquestionably make a great discovery! The wind continued to back round, and soon got to be abaft the beam. We now shook our reefs out, one after another, and we had whole topsails on the vessel by nine o'clock. This was carrying hard, it must be owned; but the skipper was determined to make hay while the sun shone. There were a few hours, when I think the ship went fifteen knots by the land, being so much favored by the current. Little did we know the difficulties toward which we were rushing!

Quite early in the day, land appeared ahead, and Marble began to predict that our rope was nearly run out. We were coming to the bottom of a deep bay. Captain Williams thought differently; and when he discovered a narrow passage between two promontories, he triumphantly predicted our near approach to the cape. He had seen some such shape to the mountains inland, in doubling the Horn, and the hill-tops looked like old acquaintances. Unfortunately, we could not see the sun at meridian, and got no observation. For several hours we ran southwesterly, in a passage of no great width, when we came to a sudden bend in our course, which led us away to the northwest. Here we still had the tide with us, and we then all felt certain that we had reached a point where the ebb must flow in a direction contrary to that in which we had found it in the other parts of the passage. It followed, that we were now half way through to the ocean, though the course we were steering predicted a sinuous channel. We were certainly not going now toward Cape Horn.

Notwithstanding the difficulties and doubts which beset us, Captain Williams packed on the ship, determined to get ahead as fast as he could, while there was light. It no longer blew a gale, and the wind was hauling more to the southward again. It soon got to be right aft, and before sunset it had a little westing in it. Fortunately, it moderated, and we set our mainsail and topgallant-sails. We had carried a lower and topmast studding-sails nearly all day.

The worst feature in our situation, now, was the vast number of islands, or islets, we met. The shore on each side was mountainous and rude, and deep indentations were constantly tempting us to turn aside. But, rightly judging that the set of the tide was a fair index to the true course, the captain stood on.

The night that followed was one of the most anxious I ever passed. We were tempted to anchor a dozen times, in some of the different bays, of which we passed twenty ; but could not make up our minds to risk another cable. We met the flood a little after sunset, and got rid of it before morning. But the wind kept hauling, and at last it brought us fairly on a taut bowline ; under topgallant-sails, however. We had come too far to recede, or now would have been the time to turn round, and retrace our steps. But we hoped every moment to reach some inclination south, again, that would carry us into the open sea. We ran a vast many chances of shipwreck, passing frightfully near several reefs ; but the same good Providence which had so far protected us, carried us clear. Never was I so rejoiced as when I saw day returning.

We had the young ebb, and a scant wind, when the sun rose next day. It was a brilliant morning, however, and everybody predicted an observation at noon. The channel was full of islands, still, and other dangers were not wanting ; but, as we could see our way, we got through them all safely. At length our course became embarrassed, so many large islands, with passages between them, offering on different sides.   One headland, however, lay before us ; and, the ship promising to weather it, we held on our way. It was just ten o'clock as we approached this cape, and we found a passage westward that actually led into the ocean ! All hands gave three cheers as we became certain of this fact, the ship tacking as soon as far enough ahead, and setting seaward famously with the tide.

Captain Williams now told us to get our quadrants, for the heavens were cloudless, and we should have a horizon in time for the sun. He was anxious to get the latitude of our discovery. Sure enough, it so fell out, and we prepared to

observe ; some predicting one parallel, some another.   As
for the skipper himself, he said he thought we were still to
the eastward of the cape ; but he felt confident that we had
come out to the westward of Le Maire.   Marble was silent ;
but he had observed, and made his calculations, before either
of the others had commenced the last.   I saw him scratch
his head, and go to the chart which lay on the companion-
way.   Then I heard him shout,—

" In the Pacific, by St. Kennebunk ! "—he always swore
by this pious individual when excited.   " We have come
through the Straits of Magellan without knowing it ! "

CHAPTER XII.

"Sound trumpets, ho!—weigh anchor—loosen sail!
The seaward-flying banners chide delay;
As if 't were heaven that breathes this kindly gale,
Our life-like bark beneath it speeds away."

PINKNEY.

THE stout ship Crisis had, like certain persons, done a good thing purely by chance. Had her exploit happened in the year 1519, instead of that of 1800, the renowned passage we had just escaped from would have been called the Crisis Straits, a better name than the mongrel appellation it now bears; which is neither English nor Portuguese. The ship had been lost, like a man in the woods, and came nearer home than those in her could have at all expected. The "bloody currents" had been at the bottom of the mistake, though this time they did good, instead of harm. Any one who has been thoroughly lost on a heath, or in a forest, or even in a town, can comprehend how the head gets turned on such occasions, and will understand the manner in which we had mystified ourselves.

I shall remember the feelings of delight with which I looked around me, as the ship passed out into the open ocean, to my dying day. There lay the vast Pacific, its long, regular waves rolling in toward the coast, in mountain-like ridges, it is true, but under a radiant sun, and in a bright atmosphere. Everybody was cheered by the view, and never did order sound more pleasant in my ears, than when the captain called out in a cheerful voice, "to man the weather-braces." This command was given the

instant it was prudent; and the ship went foaming past
the last cape, with the speed of a courser. Studding-sails
were then set, and, when the sun was dipping, we had a
good offing, were driving to the northward under everything we could carry, and had a fair prospect of an excellent run from the neighborhood of Terra del Fuego, and
its stormy seas.

It is not my intention to dwell on our passage along
the western coast of South America. A voyage to the
Pacific was a very different thing in the year 1800, however, from what it is to-day. The power of Spain was
then completely in the ascendant, intercourse with any
nation but the mother country being strictly prohibited.
It is true, a species of commerce, that was called the
"forced trade on the Spanish Main," existed under that
code of elastic morals which adapts the maxim of "your
purse or your life" to modern diplomacy as well as to the
habits of the highwayman. According to divers masters
in the art of ethics now flourishing among ourselves, more
especially in the atmosphere of the journals of the commercial communities, the people that "can trade and won't
trade must be made to trade." At the commencement of
the century, your mercantile moralists were far less manly
in the avowal of their sentiments, though their practices
were in no degree wanting in the spirit of our more modern
theories. Ships were fitted out, armed, and navigated, on
this just principle, quite as confidently and successfully as
if the tongue had declared all that the head had conceived.

Guarda-costas were the arguments used, on the other
side of this knotty question, by the authorities of Spain;
and a very insufficient argument, on the whole, did they
prove to be. It is an old saying that vice is twice as active
as virtue; the last sleeping, while the former is hard at
work. If this be true of things in general, it is thrice true
as regards smugglers and custom-house officers. Owing to
this circumstance, and sundry other causes, it is certain that
English and American vessels found the means of plundering the inhabitants of South America, at the period of which
I am writing, without having recourse to the no longer

reputable violence of Dampier, Wood, Rogers, or Drake. As I feel bound to deal honestly with the reader, whatever I may have done by the Spanish laws, I shall own that we made one or two calls as we proceeded north, shoving ashore certain articles purchased in London, and taking on board dollars in return for our civility. I do not know whether I am bound, or not, to apologize for my own agency in these irregular transactions,—regular would be quite as apposite a word,—for, had I been disposed to murmur, it would have done my morals no good, nor the smuggling any harm. Captain Williams was a silent man, and it was not easy to ascertain precisely what he thought on the subject of smuggling; but in the way of practice, I never saw any reason to doubt that he was a firm believer in the doctrine of Free Trade. As for Marble, he put me in mind of a certain renowned editor of a well-known New York journal, who evidently thinks that all things in heaven and earth, sun, moon, and stars, the void above, and the caverns beneath us, the universe, in short, was created to furnish materials for newspaper paragraphs; the worthy mate just as confidently believing that coasts, bays, inlets, roadsteads, and havens were all intended by nature as means to run goods ashore wherever the duties or prohibitions render it inconvenient to land them in the more legal mode. Smuggling, in his view of the matter, was rather more creditable than the regular commerce, since it required greater cleverness.

I shall not dwell on the movements of the Crisis for the five months that succeeded her escape from the Straits of Magellan. Suffice it to say, that she anchored at as many different points on the coast; that all which came up the main-hatch, went ashore; and all that came over the bulwarks, was passed down into the run. We were chased by guarda-costas seven times, escaping from them on each occasion, with ease; though we had three little running fights. I observed that Captain Williams was desirous of engaging these emissaries of the law as easily as possible, ordering us to fire altogether at their spars. I have since thought that this moderation proceeded from a species of principle that is common enough—a certain half-way code of right and wrong—which encouraged him to smuggle, but which caused him to shrink from taking human life. Your half-way rogues are the bane of honesty.

After quitting the Spanish coast, altogether, we proceeded north, with the laudable intention of converting certain quantities of glass beads, inferior jack-knives, frying-pans, and other homely articles of the same nature, into valuable furs. In a word, we shaped our course for that district which bids fair to set the mother and daughter by the ears, one of these days, unless it shall happen to be disposed of à la Texas, or what is almost as bad, à la Maine, ere long. At that time the whole northwest coast was unoccupied by white men, and I felt no scruples about trading with the natives who presented themselves with their skins as soon as we had anchored, believing that they had the best right to the country and its products. We passed months in this traffic, getting, at every point where we stopped, something to pay us for our trouble.

We went as far north as 53°, and that is pretty much all I ever knew of our last position. At the time, I thought we had anchored in a bay on the mainland, but I have since been inclined to think it was in one of the many islands that line that broken coast. We got a very secure berth, having been led to it by a native pilot who boarded us several leagues at sea, and who knew enough English to persuade our captain that he could take us to a point where sea-otter skins might be had for the asking. Nor did the man deceive us, though a more unpromising-looking guide never had charge of smuggling Christians. He carried us into a very small bay, where we found plenty of water, capital holding-ground, and a basin as smooth as a dock. But one wind—that which blew from the northwest—could make any impression on it, and the effects of even that were much broken by a small island that lay abreast of the entrance; leaving good passages, on each side of it, out to sea. The basin itself was rather small, it is true, but it did well enough for a single ship. Its diameter may have been three hundred yards, and I never saw a sheet of natural water that was so near a circle. Into a place like this, the reader will imagine, we did not venture without taking the proper precautions. Marble was sent in first, to reconnoitre and sound, and it was on his report that Captain Williams ventured to take the ship in.

At that time, ships on the northwest coast had to use the greatest precautions against the treachery and violence of the natives. This rendered the size of our haven the subject of distrust ; for, lying in the middle of it, where we moored, we were barely an arrow's flight from the shore, in every direction but that which led to the narrow entrance. It was a most secure anchorage, as against the dangers of the sea, but a most insecure one as against the dangers of the savages. This we all felt, as soon as our anchors were down ; but, intending to remain only while we bartered for the skins which we had been told were ready for the first ship that should offer, we trusted to vigilance as our safeguard in the interval.

I never could master the uncouth sounds of the still more uncouth savages of that distant region. The fellow who carried us in had a name of his own, doubtless, but it was not to be pronounced by a Christian tongue, and he got the *sobriquet* of the Dipper from us, owing to the manner in which he ducked at the report of our muskets, which had been discharged by Marble merely with the intention to renew the cartridges. We had hardly got into the little basin, before the Dipper left us, returning in an hour, however, with a canoe loaded to the water's edge with beautiful skins, and accompanied by three savages as wild-looking, seemingly as fierce, and certainly as avaricious as he was himself. These auxiliaries, through various little circumstances, were known among us that same afternoon, by the several appellations of Smudge, Tin-pot, and Slit-nose. These were not heroic names, of a certainty, but their owners had as little of the heroic in their appearance as usually falls to the lot of a man in the savage state. I cannot tell the designation of the tribes to which these four worthies belonged, nor do I know any more of their history and pursuits than the few facts which came under my own immediate observation. I did ask some questions of the captain, with a view to obtain a few ideas on this subject, but all he knew was, that these people put a high value on blankets, beads, gunpowder, frying-pans, and old hoops, and that they set a remarkably low price on sea-otter skins, as well as on the external coverings of sundry other animals. An application to Mr. Marble was still less successful, being met by the pithy answer that he was "no naturalist, and knew nothing about these critturs, or any wild beasts, in general." Degraded as the men certainly were, however, we thought them quite good enough to be anxious to trade with them. Commerce, like misery, sometimes makes a man acquainted with strange bed-fellows.

I had often seen our own Indians after they had become degraded by their intercourse with the whites and the use of rum, but never had I beheld any beings so low in the scale of the human race, as the northwestern savages appeared to be. They seemed to be the Hottentots of our own continent. Still, they were not altogether without the means of commanding our respect. As physical men they were both active and strong, and there were gleams of ferocity about them, that all their avarice and art could not conceal. I could not discover in their usages, dress, or deportment, a single trace of that chivalrous honor which forms so great a relief to the well-established cruelty of the warriors of our own part of the continent. Then, these sea-otter dealers had some knowledge of the use of fire-arms, and were too well acquainted with the ships of us civilized men to have any superstitious dread of our power.

The Dipper, and his companions, sold us one hundred and thirty-three sea-otter skins the very afternoon we anchored. This, of itself, was thought to be a sufficient reward for the trouble and risk of coming into this unknown basin. Both parties seemed pleased with the results of the trading, and we were given to understand that, by remaining at anchor, we might hope for six or eight times our present number of skins. Captain Williams was greatly gratified with the success with which he had already met, and having found that all the Dipper had promised came true, he determined to remain a day or two, in his present berth, in order to wait for more bargains. This resolution was no sooner communicated to the savages than they expressed their delight, sending off Tin-pot and Slit-nose with the intelligence, while the Dipper and Smudge remained in the ship, apparently on terms of perfect good-fellowship with everybody on board. The gentry of the northwest coast being flagrant thieves, however, all hands had orders to keep a good lookout on our two guests, Captain Williams expressing his intention to flog them soundly, should they be detected in any of their usual light-fingered dexterity.

Marble and myself observed that the canoe, in which the messengers left us, did not pull out to sea, but that it entered a small stream, or creek, that communicated with the head of the bay. As there was no duty on board, we asked the captain's permission to explore this spot; and, at the same time, to make a more thorough examination of our haven, generally. The request being granted, we got into the yawl, with four men, all of us armed, and set out on our little expedition. Smudge, a withered, gray-headed old Indian, with muscles, however, that resembled whip-cord, was alone on deck, when this movement took place. He watched our proceedings narrowly, and, when he saw us descend into the boat, he very coolly slipped down the ship's side, and took his place in the stern-sheets, with as much quiet dignity as if he had been captain. Marble was a good deal of a ship's martinet in such matters, and he did not more than half like the familiarity and impudence of the procedure.

"What say you, Miles," he asked, a little sharply, "shall we take this dried ourang-outang ashore with us, or shall we try to moisten him a little, by throwing him overboard?"

"Let him go, by all means, Mr. Marble. I dare say the man wishes to be of use, and he has only a bad manner of showing it."

"Of use! He is worth no more than the carcass of a whale that has been stripped of its blubber. I say, Miles, there would be no need of the windlass to heave the blanket off of this fish ! ''

This professional witticism put Marble in good-humor with himself, and he permitted the fellow to remain. I remember the thoughts that passed through my mind, as the yawl pulled toward the creek, on that occasion, as well as if it had all occurred yesterday. I sat looking at the semi-human being who was seated opposite, wondering at the dispensation of divine Providence which could leave one endowed with a portion of the ineffable nature of the Deity, in a situation so degraded. I had seen beasts in cages that appeared to me to be quite as intelligent, and members of the diversified family of human caricatures, or of the baboons and monkeys, that I thought were quite as agreeable objects to the eye. Smudge seemed to be almost without ideas. In his bargains, he had trusted entirely to the vigilance of the Dipper, whom we supposed to be some sort of a relation ; and the articles he received in exchange for his skins failed to arouse in his grim, vacant countenance, the smallest signs of pleasure. Emotion and he, if they had been acquainted, now appeared to be utter strangers to each other ; nor was this apathy in the least like the well-known stoicism of the American Indian, but had the air of downright insensibility. Yet this man assuredly had a soul, a spark of the never-dying flame that separates man from all the other beings of earth !

The basin in which the Crisis lay was entirely fringed with forest. The trees in most places even overhung the water, forming an impenetrable screen to everything inland, at the season when they were in leaf. Not a sign of a habitation of any sort was visible ; and, as we approached the shore, Marble remarked that the savages could only resort to the place at the moments when they had induced a ship to enter, in order to trade with them.

'' No, no,'' added the mate, turning his head in all directions, in order to take a complete survey of the bay ; '' there are no wigwams or papooses hereabouts. This is only a trading-post ; and luckily for us, it is altogether without custom-house officers.''

"Not without smugglers, I fancy, Mr. Marble, if contriving to get other people's property without their knowledge, can make a smuggler. I never say a more thorough-looking thief than the chap we have nicknamed the Dipper. I believe he would swallow one of our iron spoons, rather than not get it!"

"Ay, there's no mistake about him, 'Master Mile,' as Neb calls you. But this fellow here has n't brains enough to tell his own property from that of another man. I would let him into our bread-lockers, without any dread of his knowing enough to eat. I never saw such a vacancy in a human form; a Down East idiot would wind him up in a trade as handily as a pedler sets his wooden clocks in motion."

Such was Marble's opinion of the sagacity of Mr. Smudge, and, to own the truth, such, in a great measure, was my own. The men laughed at the remarks,—seamen are a little apt to laugh at chief mates' wit,—and their looks showed how thoroughly they coincided with us in opinion. All this time the boat had been pushing ahead, and it soon reached the mouth of the little creek.

We found the inlet deep, but narrow and winding. Like the bay itself, it was fringed with trees and bushes, and this in a way to render it difficult to get a view of anything on the land, more especially as the banks were ten or fifteen feet in height. Under the circumstances, Marble proposed that we should land on both sides of the creek, and follow its windings on foot, for a short distance, in order to get a better opportunity to reconnoitre. Our dispositions were soon made. Marble and one of the boat's crew, each armed, landed on one side of the inlet, while Neb and myself, similarly provided, went ashore on the other. The two remaining men were ordered to keep abreast of us in the boat, in readiness to take us on board again, as soon as required.

"Leave that Mr. Smudge in the boat, Miles," Marble called out across the creek, as I was about to put foot on the ground. I made a sign to that effect to the savage, but when I reached the level ground on the top of the bank, I perceived the fellow was at my elbow. It was so difficult to make such a creature understand one's wishes without the aid of speech, that, after a fruitless effort or two to send him back by means of signs, I abandoned the attempt, and moved forward so as to keep the whole party in the desired line. Neb offered to catch the old fellow in his arms and to carry him down to the yawl; but I thought it more prudent to avoid anything like violence. We proceeded, therefore, accompanied by this escort.

There was nothing, however, to excite alarm or awaken distrust. We found ourselves in a virgin forest, with all its wildness, dampness, gloomy shadows, dead and fallen trees, and unequal surface. On my side the creek there was not the smallest sign of a footpath, and Marble soon called out to say he was equally without any evidences of the steps of man. I should think we proceeded quite a mile in this manner, certain that the inlet would be a true guide on our return. At length a call from the boat let us know there was no longer water enough to float it, and that it could proceed no farther. Marble and myself descended the banks at the same moment, and were taken in, intending to return in the yawl. Smudge glided back to his old place with his former silence.

"I told you to leave the ourang-outang behind," Marble carelessly observed, as he took his own seat, after assisting in getting the boat round with its head toward the bay. "I would rather have a rattlesnake for a pet, than such a cub."

"It is easier said than done, sir. Master Smudge stuck to me as close as a leech."

"The fellow seems all the better for his walk—I never saw him look half as amiable as he does at this moment."

Of course this raised a laugh, and it induced me to look round. For the first time I could detect something like a human expression in the countenance of Smudge, who seemed to experience some sensation a little akin to satisfaction.

"I rather think he had taken it into his head we were about to desert the coppers," I remarked, "and fancied he might lose his supper. Now he must see we are going back, he probably fancies he will go to bed on a full stomach.''

Marble assented to the probability of this conjecture, and the conversation changed. It was matter of surprise to us that we had met no traces of anything like a residence near the creek, not the smallest sign of man having been discovered by either. It was reasonable to expect that some traces of an encampment at least, would have been found. Everybody kept a vigilant lookout at the shore as we descended the creek ; but, as on the ascent, not even a footprint was detected.

On reaching the bay, there being still several hours of daylight, we made its entire circuit, finding nowhere any proof of the former presence of man. At length Marble proposed pulling to the small wooded island, that lay a little without the entrance of the haven, suggesting that it was possible the savages might have something like an encampment there, the place being more convenient as a lookout into the offing than any point within the bay itself. In order to do this it was necessary to pass the ship, and we were hailed by the captain, who wished to know the result of our examinations. As soon as he learned our present object, he told us to come alongside, intending to accompany us to the island in person. On getting into the boat, which was small and a little crowded by the presence of Smudge, Captain Williams made a sign for that personage to quit the yawl. He might as well have intimated as much to one of the thwarts ! Laughing at the savage's stupidity, or obstinacy, we scarce knew which to term it, the boat was shoved off, and we pulled through the entrance, two hundred yards outside perhaps, until our keel grated against the low rocks of this islet.

There was no difficulty in landing ; and Neb, who preceded the party, soon gave a shout, the proof that he had made some discovery. Every man among us now looked to his arms, expecting to meet an encampment of savages; but we were disappointed. All that the negro had discovered were the unequivocal traces of a former bivouac ; and,

judging from a few of the signs, that of no very recent occupation. The traces were extensive, covering quite half
of the interior of the island ; leaving an extensive curtain
of trees and bushes, however, so as completely to conceal
the spot from any eyes without. Most of the trees had been
burnt down, as we at first thought, in order to obtain fuel ;
but further examination satisfied us that it had been done as
much by accident as by design.

At first nothing was discovered in this encampment,
which had every appearance of not having been extensively
used for years, though the traces of numerous fires, and the
signs of footsteps, and a spring in the centre, indicated the
recent occupation, of which I have just spoken. A little
further scrutiny, however, brought to light certain objects
that we did not note without much wonder and concern.
Marble made the first discovery. It was impossible for seamen to mistake the object, which was the head of a rudder,
containing the tiller-hole, and which might have belonged
to a vessel of some two hundred and fifty or three hundred
tons. This set all hands of us at work, and in a few minutes we found, scattered about, fragments of plank, top-
timbers, floor-timbers, and other portions of a ship, all more
or less burnt, and stripped of every particle of metal. Even
the nails had been drawn by means of perseverance and
labor. Nothing was left but the wood, which proved to be
live-oak, cedar, and locust, the proofs that the unfortunate
craft had been a vessel of some value. We wanted no assurance of this, however, as none but a northwest trader could
well have got as high up the coast, and all vessels of that
class were of the best description. Then the locust, a wood
unknown to the shipbuilders of Europe, gave us nearly
certain assurance that the doomed craft had been a countryman.

At first, we were all too much occupied with our interesting discovery to bethink us of Smudge. At length, I
turned to observe its effect on the savage. He evidently
noted our proceedings ; but his feelings, if the creature had
any, were so deeply buried beneath the mask of dulness,
as completely to foil my penetration. He saw us take up

fragment after fragment, examine them, heard us converse over them, though in a language he could not understand, and saw us throw them away, one after another, with seemingly equal indifference. At length he brought a half burned billet to the captain, and held it before his eyes, as if he began to feel some interest in our proceedings. It proved to be merely a bit of ordinary wood, a fragment of one of the beeches of the forest that lay near an extinguished pile; and the act satisfied us all, the fellow did not comprehend the reason of the interest we betrayed. He clearly knew nothing of the strange vessel.

In walking around this deserted encampment, the traces of a pathway to the shore were found. They were too obvious to be mistaken, and led us to the water in the passage opposite to that by which the Crisis had been carried in by the Dipper, and at a point that was not in view from her present anchorage. Here we found a sort of landing, and many of the heavier pieces of the wreck; such as it had not been thought necessary to haul up to the fires, having no metal about them. Among other things of this sort, was a portion of the keel quite thirty feet long, the keelson bolts, keelson, and floor-timbers all attached. This was the only instance in which we discovered any metal; and this we found, only because the fragment was too strong and heavy to be manageable. We looked carefully, in all directions, in the hope of discovering something that might give us an insight into the nature of the disaster that had evidently occurred, but, for some time, without success. At length I strolled to a little distance from the landing, and took a seat on a flat stone, which had been placed on the living rock that faced most of the island, evidently to form a resting-place. My seat proved unsteady, and in endeavoring to adjust it more to my mind, I removed the stone, and discovered that it rested on a common log-slate. This slate was still covered with legible writing, and I soon had the whole party around me, eager to learn the contents. The melancholy record was in these precise words, namely :—

"The American brig Sea Otter, John Squires, master, coaxed into this bay, June 9th, 1797, and seized by savages on the morning of the 11th. Master, second mate, and seven of the people killed on the spot. Brig gutted first, then hauled up here, and burnt to the water's edge for the iron. David King, first mate, and six others, namely, George Lunt, Henry Webster, Stephen Stimpson, and John Harris, seamen, Bill Flint, cook, and Peter Doolittle, boy, still living, but God only knows what is to be our fate. I shall put this slate beneath the stone I now sit on, in the hope it may one day let our friends learn what has happened.''

We looked at each other, astounded. Both the captain and Marble remembered to have heard that a brig in this trade, called the Sea Otter, was missing ; and here, by a communication that was little short of miraculous, we were let into the secret of her disappearance.

"Coaxed in," repeated the captain, running his eye over the writing, which had been thus singularly preserved, and that, in a situation where one would think it might have been discovered a thousand times. "Yes, yes—I now begin to understand the whole matter. If there were any wind, gentlemen, I would go to sea this very night."

"That would be hardly worth our while, Captain Williams," the chief mate answered, "since we are now on our guard, and I feel pretty certain that there are no savages in our neighborhood. So far, the Dipper and his friends have traded with us fairly enough, and it is likely they have more skins to dispose of. This chap, whom the people have christened Smudge, takes matters so coolly, that I hardly think he knows anything about the Sea Otter, which may have been cut off by another gang, altogether."

There was good reason in these remarks, and they had their effect on the captain. The latter, however, determined to put Smudge to the proof, by showing him the slate, and otherwise bringing him under such cross-examination as signs alone could effect. I dare say, an indifferent spectator would have laughed at witnessing our efforts to confound the Indian. We made grimaces, pointed, exclaimed, hallooed, swore, and gesticulated in vain. Smudge was as unmoved at it all, as the fragment of keel to which he was

confronted. The fellow either did not, or would not understand us. His stupidity defied our tests ; and Marble gave
the matter up in despair, declaring that "the beast knows
nothing of anything, much less of the Sea Otter." As for
the slate, he did not seem to have the smallest notion what
such a thing meant.

We returned to the ship, carrying with us the slate, and
the report of our discoveries. All hands were called, and
the captain made us a speech. It was sufficiently to the
point, though it was not in the least of the "godlike"
character. We were told how ships were lost by the carelessness of their crews ; reminded we were on the northwest
coast, where a vessel with a few boxes of beads and bales of
blankets, to say nothing of her gunpowder, firearms, and
metals, was as valuable, as a vessel laden with gold dust
would be in one of our ports. Vigilance, while on watch,
and obedience to the orders of the vessel, in the event of an
alarm, were the principal things dwelt on. By observing
these two great requisites, we should all be safe enough ;
whereas, by disregarding them, we should probably share
the fate of the people of the brig, of which we had just discovered some of the remains.

I will confess, I passed an uncomfortable night. An unknown enemy is always a formidable enemy ; and I would
rather have fought three guarda-costas at once, than lie
where we did, in a bay as smooth as a looking-glass, surrounded by forests as silent as a desert, and in a well-armed
ship, that was prepared at all points to meet her foes, even
to her boarding-nettings.

Nothing came of it all. The Dipper and Smudge eat
their supper with the appetites of injured innocence, and
slept like tops. If guilty, we all agreed that they must be
utterly destitute of consciences. As for ourselves, we were
on the alert until near morning, the very moment when the
danger would probably be the greatest, provided there were
any at all ; and then weariness overcame all who were not
on the lookout, and some who were. Still, nothing happened. The sun returned to us in due season, gilding the
tree-tops with its beams ; our little bay began to bask in its

glory, and with the cheerfulness that usually accompanies such a scene, vanished most of our apprehensions for the moment. A night of reflection had quieted our fears, and we all woke up next morning, as indifferent to the fate of the Sea Otter as was at all decent.

CHAPTER XIII.

"The monarch wind—the mystery of commanding,
The godlike power—the art Napoleon,
Of winning, fettering, moulding, wielding, banding
The hearts of millions, till they move as one :
Thou hast it."

HALLECK.

SMUDGE and the Dipper behaved admirably all next
day. Beef, pork, and bread—those great *desiderata*
of life, which the European is apt to say form the
primun mobile of American existence—seemed to
engross their thought ; and when they were not eating, they
were busy with sleep. At length we grew ashamed of
watching such mere animals, and turned our thoughts to other
subjects. We had understood from the Dipper that eight-
and-forty hours must elapse before we might expect to see
any more skins ; and Captain Williams passing from alarm
to extreme security, determined to profit by a lovely day, and
send down, or rather strip, all three of the topmasts, and
pay some necessary attention to their rigging. At nine
o'clock, accordingly, the hands were turned-to, and before
noon the ship was pretty thoroughly *en deshabille*. We sent
as little down as possible, keeping even the topsail-yards
aloft, though without their lifts or braces, steadying them
by guys ; but the topmasts were lowered as far as was found
possible, without absolutely placing the lower yards on the
hammock-cloths. In a word, we put the ship in the most un-
manageable position, without absolutely littering our decks.
The security of the haven, and the extreme beauty of the
weather, emboldened the captain to do this ; apprehension
of every sort appearing to have quite taken leave of him.

"The whole had been done so suddenly, and yet with so much skill that I was a helpless prisoner as it might be in a single instant!" The savages Smudge and Dipper seize Wallingford aboard the *Crisis* off the northwest coast of North America. *Drawing by F. O. C. Darley.*
(*p. 207*)

The work proceeded merrily. We had not only a strong crew, but we had a good crew; and our Philadelphians were in their element the moment there was a question of the rigging. By sunset, the chafes were examined, and parcelled, and served anew; and the topmast rigging was all got up and put over the mastheads again, and every-thing was ready to sway upon in the morning. But an uncommonly active day required a good night's rest; and the people were all ordered to turn in, as soon as they had supped. The ship was to be left to the vigilance of the captain and the three mates during the night.

The anchor-watch was set at eight, and ran from two hours to two hours. My turn commenced at midnight, and was to last until two; Marble succeeding me from two until four, when all hands were to be called to get our sticks aloft. When I turned out at twelve, I found the third mate conversing, as well as he could, with the Dipper; who, with Smudge, having slept so much of the day, appeared dis-posed to pass the night in smoking.

"How long have these fellows been on deck?" I asked of the third mate, as he was about to go below.

"All my watch; I found them with the captain, who passed them over to me for company. If that chap, the Dipper, only knew anything of a human language, he would be something of society; but I'm as tired of making signs to him, as I ever was with a hard day's work."

I was armed, and felt ashamed of manifesting fear of an unarmed man. Then the two savages gave no additional cause of distrust; the Dipper having taken a seat on the windlass, where he was smoking his pipe with an appear-ance of philosophy that would have done credit to the gravest-looking baboon. As for Smudge, he did not appear to be sufficiently intellectual to smoke—an occupation that has at least the merit of affecting the air of wisdom and reflection. I never could discover whether your great smokers were actually wiser than the rest of the race, or not; but, it will be admitted, they occasionally seem to be so. It was a pity Smudge did not have recourse to the practice, as it might have given the fellow an appearance of sometimes cogitating. As it was, while his companion was enjoying his pipe at the windlass, he kept strolling about the deck, much as a pig would have wandered in the same place, and seemingly with the same object.

I took charge of the decks with a very lively sense of the peculiarity of our situation. The security that prevailed on board struck me as unnatural; and yet I could detect no particular reason for immediate alarm. I might be thrown overboard or murdered by the two savages on deck, it was very true; but of what use would it be to destroy me, since they could not hope to destroy all the rest on board without being discovered? The night was star-lit, and there was little chance of a canoe's approaching the ship without my seeing it; a circumstance that, of itself, in a great measure, removed the danger. I passed the first quarter of an hour in reflecting on these things; and then, as use accustomed me to my situation, I began to think less of them and to revert to other subjects.

Clawbonny, Grace, Lucy, and Mr. Hardinge, often rose before my mind's eye, in those distant seas. It was seldom I passed a tranquil watch at night without revisiting the scenes of my boyhood, and wandering through my own fields, accompanied by my beloved sister and her quite as well beloved friend. How many hours of happiness had I thus passed on the trackless wastes of the Pacific and the Atlantic, and with how much fidelity did memory recall the peculiar graces, whether of body or mind, of each of the dear girls in particular. Since my recent experience in London, Emily Merton would occasionally adorn the picture, with her more cultivated discourse and more finished manner; and yet I do not remember to have ever given her more than a third place on the scale of my admiration.

On the present occasion I was soon lost in ruminations on the past, and in imagining events for the future. I was not particularly expert at building castles in the air; but what youth of twenty, or maiden of sixteen, never reared some sort of a fabric of this nature? These fanciful structures are the results of inexperience building with the materials of hope. In my most imaginative moments, I could

even fancy Rupert an industrious, staid lawyer, adorning his
profession, and rendering both Lucy and Grace happy.
Beyond this it was not easy for the human faculties to conceive.

Lucy sang sweetly.   At times her songs fairly haunted
me, and for hours I could think of nothing but their tender
sentiment and their touching melody.   I was no nightingale
myself, though I sometimes endeavored to hum some one of
the airs that floated in my recollection, like beautiful visions
of the past.   This night, in particular, my thoughts recurred
to one of these songs that told of affection and home ; and
I stood for several minutes, leaning over the railing forward,
humming the tune to myself, while I endeavored to recall
not only the words but the sweet voice that was wont to
give them so much thrilling pathos.   I did this sometimes
at Clawbonny ; and time and again had Lucy placed her
soft little hand on my mouth, as she would laughingly say,
"Miles, Miles, do not spoil so pretty a song ! You will
never succeed with music, so work the harder with your
Latin."   Sometimes she would steal behind me—I fancied
I could hear her breathing at my shoulder, even as I leaned
over the rail—and would apply her hand slyly to my lips,
in her many attempts of this nature.   So vivid did one of
these scenes become, that I thought I really felt the soft,
smooth hand on my mouth, and I was actually about to kiss
it, when something that was smooth enough, certainly, but
which was very far from being soft, passed between my
teeth, and I felt it drawn so tight as completely to prevent
my calling out.   At the same moment my arms were seized
from behind, and held as if grasped by a vice.   Turning, as
well as I was able, I found that rascal Smudge had been
breathing within an inch of my ear, while he passed the
gag ; and the Dipper was busy in lashing my arms together
behind my back.   The whole had been done so suddenly,
and yet with so much skill, that I was a helpless prisoner
as it might be, in a single instant !

Resistance being as much out of my power as it was to
give any alarm, I was soon secured, hands and feet, and
placed carefully in the waist, a little out of the way ; for I

probably owed my life solely to the wish of Smudge to keep me as his slave. From that instant every appearance of stupidity vanished from this fellow's countenance and manner, and he became the moving spirit, and I might say the soul, of all the proceedings of his companions. As for myself, there I sat lashed to a spar, utterly unable to help myself, an unwilling witness of all that followed. I felt the imminent danger of our situation, but I think I felt the disgrace of having such a surprise occur in my watch, more even than the personal risks I ran !

In the first place, I was disarmed. Then the Dipper took a lantern which stood on the binnacle, lighted it, and showed it, for half a minute, above the taffrail. His signal must have been instantly answered, for he soon extinguished the light, and moved about the deck, in attentive watchfulness to seize any straggler, who might happen to come on deck. Little fear of that, however, weariness chaining the men to their berths as closely as if they had been bolted down with iron. I now expected to see the fellows fill the yawl with effects, and run away with them, for, as yet, I could not believe that two men would have the hardihood to attack such a ship's company as ours.

I reckoned without my host. It might have been ten minutes after I was seized, that dark-looking figures began to climb the ship's sides, until more than thirty of them were on her decks. This was done so noiselessly, too, that the most vigilant attention on my part gave no notice of their approach, until they stood among us. All these men were armed ; a few with muskets, others with clubs, and some with bows and arrows. So far as I could discover, each had some sort of a knife, and a few had hatchets, or tomahawks. To my great regret, I saw that three or four were immediately stationed at the companion-way, aft, and as many more at the booby-hatch, forward. This was effectually commanding the only two passages by which the officers and men would be likely to ascend, in the event of their attempting to come on deck. It is true, the mainhatch, as well as that of the steerage, was used by day, but both had been covered over night, and no one would think of using either unless aware of the danger that existed on deck.

I suffered a good deal both from the gag and the ropes that bound my limbs, and yet I hardly thought of the pain, so intense was my curiosity as to what was to follow. After the savages were all on board, the first quarter of an hour passed in making their dispositions. Smudge—the stupid, inanimate, senseless Smudge—acting as leader, and manifesting not only authority, but readiness and sagacity. He placed all his people in ambush, so that one appearing from below, would not at once he apprised of the charge that had taken place on deck, and thus give the savages time to act. After this, another quarter of an hour passed, during which the fall of a pin might almost have been heard, so profound was the silence. I shut my eyes in this terrific interval, and endeavored to pray.

"On deck, here—forward, there!" said a voice, suddenly, that, at once, I knew to be the captain's. I would have given the world to be able to answer, in order to warn him of the danger, but this was impossible. I did groan, and I believe the captain heard me; for he moved away from the cabin door, and called out, "Mr. Wallingford—where have you got to, Mr. Wallingford?" He was without his hat, having come on deck half clad, simply to ascertain how went the night, and it makes me shudder, even now, to write about the blow that fell on his unprotected skull. It would have felled an ox, and it crushed him on the spot. The caution of his murderers prevented his falling, however, for they did not wish to alarm the sleepers below; though the plash on the water that followed could not fail to reach ears which took in every sound with the avidity of mine. Thus perished Captain Williams, a mild, well-meaning man, an excellent seaman, and one whose principal fault was want of caution. I do not think the water was necessary to complete his fate, as nothing human could have survived such a blow.

Smudge had been the principal actor in this frightful scene; and as soon as it was over, he caused his men to return to their ambushes. I now thought the officers and men were to be murdered in this manner, as one by one they appeared on deck. It would soon be time for Marble to turn out, though there was the hope he might not unless called, and I could not do this office, situated as I was. But I was mistaken. Instead of enticing any men on deck, the savages pursued a different course. Having destroyed the captain, they closed the doors of the companion-way, drew over the booby-hatch, and adopted the safe expedient of making all below prisoners. This was not done altogether without noise, and the alarm was evidently given by the means taken to secure the fastenings. I heard a rush at the cabin doors, which was soon followed by one at the booby-hatch; but Smudge's ingenuity had been sufficient to prevent either from being successful.

As soon as certain that their prisoners were safe, the savages came and loosened the ropes of my arms sufficiently to put me more at my ease. They removed those which bound my feet entirely, and, at the same instant, the gag was taken from my mouth. I was then led to the companion-way, and, by a sign, given to understand I might communicate with my friends below. In the management of all this, I found that Smudge, the semi-human, dull, animal-seeming Smudge, was at the head. I also came to the conclusion my life was to be spared, for a time at least, and for some purpose that, as yet, baffled my conjectures. I did not call out immediately, but waited until I heard a movement on the ladder, when I complied with the orders of my captors and masters.

"Mr. Marble," I cried, loud enough to be heard below, "is that you?"

"Ay, ay; and is that you, Master Miles?"

"This is I. Be cautious how you act, Mr. Marble. The savages are in possession of the upper deck, and I am their prisoner. The people are all below, with a strong watch at the fore-scuttle."

I heard a long, low whistle within the companion-way doors, which it was easy enough to interpret into an expression of the chief mate's concern and wonder. For myself, I saw no use in attempting concealment, but was resolved to speak out fully, even though it might be at the risk of betraying some of my feelings to my captors, among whom I thought it probable there might be more than one who understood something of English.

"We miss Captain Williams below, here," Marble resumed, after a short delay. "Do you know anything of his movements?"

"Alas! Mr. Marble—poor Captain Williams can be of no service to any of us, now."

"What of him?" was demanded in a clear, full voice, and as quick as lightning. "Let me know at once."

"He has been killed by a blow from a club, and is thrown overboard."

A dead silence followed, and it lasted near a minute.

"Then it has fallen to my duty to decide what is to be done!" Marble at length exclaimed. "Miles, are you at liberty? Dare you say what you think?"

"I am held here by two of the savages, whose prisoner I certainly am. Still, Mr. Marble, they encourage me to speak; but I fear some among them understand what we say."

There was another pause, during which the mate was doubtless reflecting on the best course to pursue.

"Harkee, Miles," Marble continued; "we know each other, and can tell what is meant without blabbing. How old are you, out there, on deck?"

"Quite thirty years, Mr. Marble—and good stout years they are, too!"

"Well provided for, with sulphur and the pills, or only with Indian tools, such as our boys sometimes play with?"

"A little of the first—half a dozen, perhaps; with some of the last, and a plenty of carvers."

An impatient push from the Dipper warned me to speak plainer, and satisfied me that the fellow could comprehend what passed, so long as we confined ourselves to a straight-forward discourse. This discovery had the effect to put me still more on my guard.

"I understand you, Miles," Marble answered, in a thoughtful manner; "we must be on our guard. Do you think they mean to come below?"

"I see no signs at present; but *understanding*,"—em-

phasizing the word—"is more general than you imagine,
and no secrets must be told.   My advice is, ' Millions for
defence, and not a cent for tribute."

As this last expression was common in the mouths of
the Americans of the day, having been used on the occasion of the existing war with France, I felt confident it
would be understood.   Marble made no answer, and I was
permitted to move from the companion-way, and to take a
seat on the hen-coops.   My situation was sufficiently remarkable.   It was still dark ; but enough light fell from
the stars to permit me to see all the swarthy and savage
forms that were gliding about the decks, and even to observe
something of the expression of the countenances of those
who, from time to time, came near to stare me in the face.
The last seemed ferociously disposed ; but it was evident
that a master-spirit held all these wild beings in strict subjection ; quelling the turbulence of their humors, restraining
their fierce disposition to violence, and giving concert and
design to all their proceedings.   This master-spirit was
Smudge !   Of the fact, I could not doubt ; his gestures, his
voice, his commands, giving movement and method to everything that was done.   I observed that he spoke with authority
and confidence, though he spoke calmly.   He was obeyed
without any particular marks of deference, but he was
obeyed implicitly.   I could also see that the savages considered themselves as conquerors ; caring very little for the men
under hatches.

Nothing   material   occurred   until   the   day   dawned.
Smudge—for so I must continue to call this revolting-look-
ing chief, for want of his true name—would permit nothing
to be attempted until the light became sufficiently strong to
enable him to note the proceedings of his followers.   I subsequently ascertained, too, that he waited for reinforcements,
a yell being raised in the ship, just as the sun appeared,
which was answered from the forest.   The last seemed fairly
alive with savages ; nor was it long before canoes issued
from the creek, and I counted one hundred and seven of
these wretches on board the ship.   This was their whole
force, however, no more ever appearing.

All this time, or for three hours, I had no more communication with our own people. I was certain, however, that they were all together, a junction being easy enough, by means of the middle deck, which had no other cargo than the light articles intended for the northwest trade, and by knocking down the forecastle bulkhead. There was a sliding board in the last, indeed, that would admit of one man's passing at a time, without having recourse to this last expedient. I entertained no doubt Marble had collected all hands below; and, being in possession of plenty of arms, the men having carried their muskets and pistols below with them, with all the ammunition, he was extremely formidable. What course he would pursue, I was obliged to conjecture. A sortie would have been very hazardous, if practicable at all; and it was scarcely practicable, after the means taken by Smudge and the Dipper to secure the passages. Everything, so far as I was concerned, was left to conjecture.

The manner in which my captors treated me, excited my surprise. As soon as it was light, my limbs were released, and I was permitted to walk up and down the quarter-deck to restore the circulation of the blood. A clot of blood, with some fragments of hair, marked the spot where poor Captain Williams had fallen; and I was allowed to dash a bucket of water over the place, in order to wash away the revolting signs of the murder. For myself, a strange recklessness had taken the place of concern, and I became momentarily indifferent to my fate. I expected to die, and I am now ashamed to confess that my feelings took a direction toward revenge, rather than toward penitence for my past sins. At times, I even envied Marble, and those below, who might destroy their enemies at a swoop, by throwing a match into the magazine. I felt persuaded, indeed, it would come to that before the mate and men would submit to be the captives of such wretches as were then in possession of the deck. Smudge and his associates, however, appeared to be perfectly indifferent to this danger, of the character of which they were probably ignorant. Their scheme had been very cunningly laid; and, thus far, it was perfectly successful.

The sun was fairly up, and the savages began to think seriously of securing their prize, when the two leaders, Smudge and the Dipper, approached me in a manner to show they were on the point of commencing operations. The last of these men I now discovered had a trifling knowledge of English, which he had obtained from different ships. Still, he was a savage, to all intents and purposes, the little information thus gleaned, serving to render his worse propensities more dangerous, rather than, in any manner, tempering them. He now took the lead, parading all his men in two lines on the deck, making a significant gesture toward his fingers, and uttering, with emphasis, the word "count." I did count the wretches, making, this time, one hundred and six, exclusively of the two leaders.

"Tell him, down there," growled the Dipper, pointing below.

I called for Mr. Marble, and when he had reached the companion-way, the following conversation took place between us :—

"What is it now, Miles, my hearty?" demanded the chief mate.

"I am ordered to tell you, sir, that the Indians number one hundred and eight, having just counted them for this purpose."

"I wish there were a thousand, as we are about to lift the deck from the ship, and send them all into the air. Do you think they can understand what I say, Miles?"

"The Dipper does, sir, when you speak slow and plain. He has only half a notion of what you now mean, as I can see by his countenance."

"Does the rascal hear me now—is he anywhere near the companion-way?"

"He does, and is; he is standing at this moment on the larboard side of the companion-way, kneeling one knee on the forward end of the hen-coop."

"Miles," said Marble, in a doubting sort of a voice.

"Mr. Marble—I hear what you say."

"Suppose—eh—lead through the companion-way—eh— what would happen to you?"

" I should care little for that, sir, as I 've made up my mind to be murdered. But it would do no good just now, and might do harm. I will tell them, however, of your intention to blow them up, if you please ; perhaps that may make them a little shy.''

Marble assented, and I set about the office as well as I could. Most of my communications had to be made by means of signs ; but, in the end, I succeeded in making the Dipper understand my meaning. By this man the purport was told to Smudge, in terms. The old man listened with grave attention, but the idea of being blown up produced no more effect on him than would have been produced by a message from home to tell him that his chimney was on fire, supposing him to have possessed such a civilized instrument of comfort.

That he fully comprehended his friend, I could see by the expression of his ourang-outang-looking countenance. But fear was a passion that troubled him very little ; and, sooth to say, a man whose time was passed in a condition as miserable as that in which he habitually dwelt, had no great reason to set a very high value on his life. Yet these miserable wretches never commit suicide ! That is a relief reserved rather for those who have become satiated with human enjoyments, nine pampered sensualists dying in this mode for one poor wretch whose miseries have driven him to despair.

I was astonished at seeing the intelligence that gleamed in the baboon-like face of Smudge, as he listened to his friend's words. Incredulity was the intellectual meaning in his eye, while indifference seemed seated in his whole visage.

It was evident the threat had made no impression, and I managed to let Marble understand as much, and that in terms which the Dipper could not very well comprehend. I got no answer, a death-like stillness reigning below decks, in lieu of the bustle that had so lately been heard there. Smudge seemed struck with the change, and I observed he was giving orders to two or three of the elder savages, apparently to direct a greater degree of watchfulness. I confess to some uneasiness myself, for expectation is an unpleasant guest in a scene like that, and more especially when accompanied by uncertainty.

Smudge now seemed to think it time to commence his operations in earnest. Under the direction of the Dipper a quantity of line was thrown into the yawl, studding-halyards, and such other rope of convenient size as could be found in the launch, and the boat was towed by two or three canoes to the island. Here the fellows made what seamen call a "guess-warp" of their rope, fastening one end to a tree, and paying out line as the yawl was towed back again to the ship. The Dipper's calculation proved to be sufficiently accurate, the rope reaching from the vessel to the tree.

As soon as this feat was accomplished, and it was done with sufficient readiness, though somewhat lubberly, twenty or thirty of the savages clapped on the warp until they had tautened it to as great a strain as it would bear. After this they ceased pulling, and I observed a search around the galley in quest of the cook's axe, evidently with a design to cut the cables. I thought this a fact worth communicating to Marble, and I resolved to do so at any risk of my life.

"The Indians have run a line to the island, and are about to cut the cables, no doubt intending to warp the ship ashore, and that, too, at the very spot where they once had the Sea Otter."

"Ay, ay,—let them go on; we'll be ready for them in time," was the only answer I received.

I never knew whether to ascribe the apathy the savages manifested to this communication, to a wish that the fact might be known to the people below, or to indifference. They certainly proceeded in their movements with just as much coolness as if they had the ship all to themselves. They had six or eight canoes, and parties of them began to move round the vessel with precisely the same confidence as men would do it in a friendly port. What most surprised me were the quiet and submission to orders they observed. At length the axe was found secreted in the bows of the launch, and Marble was apprised of the use to which it was immediately applied by the heavy blows that fell upon the cables.

"Miles," said the chief mate, "these blows go to my heart! Are the blackguards really in earnest?"

"The larboard bower is gone, sir, and the blows you now hear are on the starboard, which is already half in two—that finishes it ; the ship now hangs only by the warp."

"Is there any wind, boy ?"

"Not a breath of it in the bay, though I can see a little ripple on the water outside."

"Is it rising or falling water, Miles ?"

"The ebb is nearly done—they 'll never be able to get the ship up on the shelving rock where they had the Sea Otter, until the water rises ten or twelve feet."

"Thank God for that ! I was afraid they might get her on that accursed bed, and break her back at once."

"Is it of any importance to us, Mr. Marble? What hope can we have of doing anything against such odds, and in our circumstances ?"

"The odds I care nothing for, boy. My lads are screwed up so tight, they 'd lick the whole northwest coast, if they could only get on deck without having their fashion-pieces stove in. The circumstances, I allow, must count for a great deal."

"The ship is moving fast towards the island—I see no hope for us, Mr. Marble."

"I say, Miles, it is worth some risk to try and save the craft—were it not for fear of you, I would have played the rascals a trick half an hour since."

"Never mind me, sir—it was my fault it has happened, and I ought to suffer for it ; do what duty and discretion tell you is best."

I waited a minute after this in intense expectation, not knowing what was to follow, when a report made me fancy for an instant some attempt was making to blow up the deck. The wails and cries that succeeded, however, soon let me into the real state of the case. A volley of muskets had been fired from the cabin windows, and every individual in two canoes that were passing at the time, to the number of eleven, were shot down like bullocks. Three were killed dead, and the remainder received wounds that promised to be mortal. My life would have been the instant sacrifice of this act. had it not been for the stern

authority of Smudge, who ordered my assailants off, with
a manner and tone that produced immediate compliance.
It was clear I was reserved for some peculiar fate.

Every man who could, rushed into the remaining canoes
and the ship's yawl, in order to pick up the killed and
wounded, as soon as the nature of the calamity was known.
I watched them from the taffrail, and soon ascertained that
Marble was doing the same from the windows below me.
But the savages did not dare venture in a line with a fire
that had proved so fatal, and were compelled to wait until
the ship had moved sufficiently ahead to enable them to
succor their friends without exposing their own lives. As
this required some distance as well as time, the ship was
not only left without a canoe or boat of any sort, in the
water, but with only half her assailants on board of her.
Those who did remain, for want of means to attack any
other enemy, vented their spite on the ship, expending all
their strength in frantic efforts on the warp. The result
was, that while they gave great way to the vessel, they
finally broke the line.

I was leaning on the wheel with Smudge near me, when
this accident occurred. The tide was still running ebb and
with some strength, and the ship was just entering the narrow passage between the island and the point that formed
one termination of the bay, heading, of course, toward the
tree to which the warp had been secured. It was an im-
pulsive feeling, rather than any reason, that made me give
the vessel a sheer with the helm, so as to send her directly
through the passage, instead of letting her strike the rocks.
I had no eventual hope in so doing, nor any other motive
than the strong reluctance I felt to have the good craft hit
the bottom. Luckily, the Dipper was in the canoes, and
it was not an easy matter to follow the ship, under the fire
from her cabin windows, had he understood the case and
been disposed to do so. But like all the rest in the canoes, he
was busy with his wounded friends, who were all carried off
toward the creek. This left me master of the ship's movements
for five minutes, and by that time she had drawn through the
passage, and was actually shooting out into the open ocean.

This was a novel, and in some respects an embarrassing situation. It left a gleam of hope, but it was a hope without a direction and almost without an object. I could perceive that none of the savages on board had any knowledge of the cause of our movement, unless they might understand the action of the tide. They had expected the ship to be run ashore at the tree ; and here she was gliding into the ocean, and was already clear of the passage. The effect was to produce a panic, and fully one half of those who had remained in the ship, jumped overboard and began to swim for the island. I was momentarily in hope all would take this course ; but quite five-and-twenty remained, more from necessity than choice, as I afterwards discovered, for they did not know how to swim. Of this number was Smudge, who probably still remained to secure his conquest.

It struck me the moment was favorable, and I went to the companion-way and was about to remove its fastenings, thinking the ship might be recovered during the prevalence of the panic. But a severe blow, and a knife gleaming in the hands of Smudge, admonished me of the necessity of greater caution. The affair was not yet ended, nor was my captor a man as easily disconcerted as I had incautiously supposed. Unpromising as he seemed, this fellow had a spirit that fitted him for great achievements, and which, under other circumstances, might have made him a hero. He taught me the useful lesson of not judging of men merely by their exteriors.

CHAPTER XIV.

"*Court.* Brother John Bates, is not that the morning which breaks
yonder?
Bates. I think it be; but we have no great cause to desire the
approach of day.
Will. We see yonder the beginning of the day; but I think we
shall never see the end of it."

Henry V.

THE ship did not lose her steerage way. As soon
as past the point of the island a gentle southerly
breeze was felt, and acting on the spars and hull
it enabled me, by putting the helm a little up, to
keep her head off shore, and thus increase her distance from
the bay. The set of the tide did more for her than the wind,
it is true, but the two acting in unison, carried her away
from the coast at a rate that nearly equalled two knots in
the hour. This was slow moving, certainly, for a vessel in
such a strait; but it would require fifteen or twenty minutes
for the canoes to return from the creek, and make the circuit
of the island by the other channel. By that time we should
be near half a mile at sea.

Smudge, beyond a question, understood that he was in a
dilemma, though totally ignorant of some of the leading
difficulties of his case. It was plain to me he could not
comprehend why the ship took the direction of the offing,
for he had no conception of the power of the rudder. Our
tiller worked below, and it is possible this circumstance
mystified him; more small vessels in that day managing
their helms without the aid of the wheel, than with it. At
length the movement of the vessel became too palpable to
admit of further delay; and this savage approached me
with a drawn knife, and a manner that proved natural affec-

tion had not been the motive of his previous moderation. After flourishing his weapon fiercely before my eyes, and pressing it most significantly, once or twice, against my breast, he made signs for me to cause the ship to turn round and re-enter the port. I thought my last moment had come, but naturally enough pointed to the spars, giving my master to understand that the vessel was not in her usual trim. I believe I was understood as to this part of my excuses, it being too apparent that our masts and yards were not in their usual places, for the fact to be overlooked even by a savage. Smudge, however, saw that several of the sails were bent, and he pointed to those, growling out his threats should I refuse to set them. The spanker, in particular, being near him, he took hold of it, shook it, and ordered me to loosen it forthwith.

It is scarcely necessary to say, I obeyed this order with secret joy. Casting loose the brails, I put the out-hauler in the hands of a dozen of the savages, and set the example of pulling. In a minute we had this sail spread, with the sheet a little eased off. I then led a party forward, and got the fore and main staysails on the ship. To these were added the mizzen staysail, the only other piece of canvas we could show, until the topmasts were fidded. The effect of these four sails, however, was to add at least another knot to the way of the ship, and to carry her out sooner to a point where she felt the full force of the light breeze that was blowing from the southeast. By the time the four sails were set, we were fully a quarter of a mile from the island, every instant getting more fairly into the true currents of the air.

Smudge watched me with the eyes of a hawk. As I had obeyed his own orders in making sail, he could not complain of that; but the result evidently disappointed him. He saw we were still moving in the wrong direction, and as yet, not a canoe was visible. As for these last, now the vessel had way on her, I was not without hopes of being able to keep them exposed to the fire from the cabin windows, and, finally, of getting rid of them by drawing off the land to a distance they would not be likely to follow.

The Dipper, however, I was aware, was a bold fellow,— knew something of vessels,—and I was determined to give a hint to Marble to pick him off, should he come within range of his muskets.

In the meantime the alarm and impatience of Smudge and his companions very sensibly increased. Five minutes were an age, in the circumstances in which they were placed, and I saw that it would soon be necessary to adopt some new expedient, or I might expect to be sacrificed to the resentment of these savages. Necessity sharpens the wits, and I hit upon a scheme which was not entirely without the merit of ingenuity. As it was, I suppose I owed my life to the consciousness of the savages that they could do nothing without me.

Smudge, with three or four of the fiercest of his companions, had begun again to menace me with the knife, making signs, at the same time, for me to turn the ship's head toward the land. I asked for a little room and then, described a long circle on the deck, pointing to the four sails we had set, and this in a way to tell them that under the canvas we carried, it would be necessary to go a great distance in order to turn round. When I had succeeded in communicating this idea, I forthwith set about giving them to understand that by getting up the topmasts, and making more sail, we might return immediately. The savages understood me, and the explanation appearing reasonable to them, they went aside and consulted together. As time pressed, it was not long before Smudge came to me with signs to show him and his party how to get the remainder of the sails set. Of course, I was not backward in giving the desired information.

In a few minutes, I had a string of savages hold of the mast-rope, forward, a luff-tackle being applied. As everything was ready aloft, all we had to do was to pull, until, judging by the eye, I thought the spar was high enough, when I ran up the rigging and clapped in the fid. Having the topmast out of the way, without touching any of its rigging, I went down on the fore-yard, and loosened the sail. This appeared so much like business, that the savages

gave sundry exclamations of delight; and by the time I
got on deck, they were all ready to applaud me as a good
fellow. Even Smudge was completely mystified; and
when I set the others at work at the jeer-fall to sway up
the fore-yard, he was as active as any of them. We soon
had the yard in its place, and I went aloft to secure it,
touching the braces first so as to fill the sail.

The reader may rest assured I did not hurry myself, now
I had things in so fair a way. I could perceive that my
power and importance increased with every foot we went
from the land; and the ship steering herself under such
canvas, the wheel being a trifle up, there was no occasion
for extraordinary exertion on my part. I determined now
to stay aloft as long as possible. The yard was soon secured and then I went up into the top, where I began to set
up the weather-rigging. Of course, nothing was very thoroughly done, though sufficiently so for the weather we had.

From the top I had a good view of the offing, and of
the coast for leagues. We were now quite a mile at sea,
and, though the tide was no longer of any use to us, we
were drawing through the water quite at the rate of two
knots. I thought that the flood had made, and that it took
us a little on our lee-bow, hawsing us up to windward.
Just as I had got the last lanyard fastened, the canoes
began to appear, coming round the island by the farther
passage, and promising to overtake us in the course of the
next twenty minutes. The crisis demanded decision, and I
determined to get the jib on the ship. Accordingly, I was
soon on deck.

Having so much the confidence of the savages, who now
fancied their return depended on me, I soon had them at
work, and we had the stay set up in two or three minutes.
I then ran out and cast off the gaskets, when my boys began to hoist at a signal from me. I have seldom been so
happy as when I saw that large sheet of canvas open to
the air. The sheet was hauled in and belayed as fast as
possible, and then it struck me I should not have time to
do any more before the canoes would overtake us. It was
my wish to communicate with Marble. While passing aft,

to effect this object, I paused a moment to examine the movement of the canoes; old Smudge, the whole time, expressing his impatience that the ship did not turn round. I make no doubt I should have been murdered a dozen times, had I lives enough, were it not that the savages felt how dependent they were on me for the government of the vessel. I began to see my importance, and grew bold in proportion.

As for the canoes, I took a look at them through a glass. They were about half a mile distant, had ceased paddling, and were lying close together, seemingly in consultation. I fancied the appearance of the ship, under canvas, had alarmed them, and that they began to think we had regained the vessel, and were getting her in sailing condition again, and that it might not be prudent to come too near. Could I confirm this impression, a great point would be gained. Under the pretence of making more sail, in order to get the ship's head round, a difficulty I had to explain to Smudge by means of signs some six or eight times, I placed the savages at the main-topmast mast-rope, and told them to drag. This was a task likely to keep them occupied, and what was more, it kept them all looking forward, leaving me affecting to be busied aft. I had given Smudge a cigar too, to put him in good-humor, and I had also taken the liberty to light one for myself.

Our guns had all been primed, levelled, and had their tompions taken out the night before, in readiness to repel any assault that might be made. I had only to remove the apron from the after-gun, and it was ready to be discharged. Going to the wheel, I put the helm hard up, until our broadside bore on the canoes. Then glancing along my gun, until I saw it had a tolerable range, I clapped the cigar to the priming, springing back to the wheel, and putting the helm down. The explosion produced a general yell among the savages, several of whom actually leaped into the chains ready to go overboard, while Smudge rushed toward me, fiercely brandishing his knife. I thought my time had come! but, perceiving that the ship was luffing fast, I motioned eagerly forward, to draw the attention of my assailant in that quarter. The vessel was coming-to,

and Smudge was easily induced to believe it was the com‧
mencement of turning round. The breathing time allowed
me to mystify him with a few more signs; after which,
he rejoined his people, showed them exultingly the ship
still luffing, and I make no doubt, he thought himself, and
induced the rest to think, that the gun had a material agency
in producing all these apparent changes. As for the canoes,
the grape had whistled so near them, that they began to paddle
back, doubtless under the impression that we were again masters of the ship, and had sent them this hint to keep aloof.

Thus far I had succeeded beyond my most sanguine expectations; and I began to entertain lively hopes of not
only saving my life, but of recovering the command of the
vessel. Could I manage to get her out of sight of land,
my services would be so indispensable, as almost to insure
success. The coast was very low, and a run of six or eight
hours would do this, provided the vessel's head could be
kept in the right direction. The wind, moreover, was
freshening, and I judged that the Crisis had already four
knots' way on her. Less than twenty miles would put all
the visible coast under water. But it was time to say something to Marble. With a view to lull distrust, I called
Smudge to the companion-way, in order that he might hear
what passed, though I felt satisfied, now that the Dipper
was out of the ship, not a soul remained among the savages
who could understand a syllable of English, or knew anything of vessels. The first call brought the mate to the
door. "Well, Miles; what is it?" he asked; "what
meant the gun, and who fired it?"

"All right, Mr. Marble. I fired the gun to keep off the
canoes, and it has had the effect I wished."

"Yes; my head was out of the cabin window at the time,
for I believed the ship was wearing, and thought you had
given up, and were going back into port. I saw the round-
shot strike within twenty fathoms of the canoes, and as for
the grape, some of it flew beyond them. Why, we are more
than half a league from the land, boy! Will Smudge stand
that much longer?"

I then told Marble precisely how we were situated on

deck, the sail we were under, the number of savages we had on board, and the notion the savages entertained on the subject of turning the ship round. It is not easy to say which listened with the most attention, Marble or Smudge. The latter made frequent gestures for me to turn the ship toward the coast, for by this time she had the wind abeam again, and was once more running in a straight line. It was nec· essary, on more accounts than one, to adopt some immediate remedy for the danger that began to press on me anew. Not only must Smudge and his associates be pacified, but, as the ship got into the offing, she began to feel the ground-swell, and her spars aloft were anything but secure. The main-topmast was about half up, and it was beginning to surge and move in the cap in a way I did not like. It is true, there was not much danger yet ; but the wind was rising, and what was to be done ought to be done at once. I was not sorry, however, to perceive that five or six of the savages, Smudge among the number, began to betray signs of sea-sickness. I would have given Clawbonny at the moment to have had all the rascals in rough water !

I now endeavored to make Smudge understand the necessity of my having assistance from below, both to assist in turning the vessel, and in getting the yards and masts into their places. The old fellow shook his head and looked grave at this. I saw he was not sick enough yet to be indifferent about his life. After a time, however, he pronounced the names of Neb and Yo, the blacks having attracted the attention of the savages, the last being the cook. I under· stood him he would suffer these two to come to my assist· ance, provided it could be done without endangering his own ascendency. Three unarmed men could hardly be danger· ous to twenty-five who were armed ; and then I suspected that he fancied the negroes would prove allies to himself, in the event of a struggle, rather than foes. As for Neb, he made a fatal mistake ; nor was he much nearer the truth in reward to Joe,—or Yo, as he called him,—the cook feeling quite as much for the honor of the American flag, as the fairest-skinned seaman in the country. It is generally found that the loyalty of the negroes is of proof.

I found means to make Smudge understand the manner in which these two blacks could be got on deck without letting up the rest. As soon as he fairly comprehended the means to be used, he cheerfully acquiesced, and I made the necessary communication to Marble. A rope was sent down over the stern-boat to the cabin windows, and Neb took a turn round his body ; when he was hauled up to the gunwale of the boat, into which he was dragged by the assistance of the savages. The same process was used with Joe. Before the negroes were permitted to go aloft, however, Smudge made them a brief oration, in which oracular sentences were blended with significant gestures, and indications of what they were to expect in the event of bad behavior. After this, I sent the blacks into the main-top, and glad enough I thought they were both to get there.

Thus reinforced, we had the main-topmast fidded in a very few minutes. Neb was then directed to set up the rigging, and to clear away the yard, so it might be got into its place. In a word, an hour passed in active exertions, at the end of which we had everything rove, bent, and in its place, on the mainmast, from the topmast-head to the deck. The topgallant-mast was lying fore and aft in the waist, and could not then be touched ; nor was it necessary. I ordered the men to loosen both sails, and to overhaul down their rigging. In the eyes of Smudge, this looked highly promising ; and the savages gave a yell of delight when they saw the topsail fairly filled and drawing. I added the mainsail to the pressure, and then the ship began to walk off the coast, at a rate that promised all I hoped for. It was now necessary for me to stick by the wheel, of the uses of which Smudge began to obtain some notions. At this time, the vessel was more than two leagues from the island, and objects began to look dim along the coast. As for the canoes, they could no longer be seen, and chasing us any farther was quite out of the question. I felt that the crisis was approaching.

Smudge and his companions now became more and more earnest on the subject of turning the ship round. The indistinctness of the land began seriously to alarm them, and

seasickness had actually placed four of their number flat on
the deck. I could see that the old fellow himself was a good
deal affected, though his spirit, and the risks he ran, kept
him in motion, and vigilantly on the watch. It was necessary to seem to do something; and I sent the negroes up
into the fore-top, to get the topsail-yard in its place, and
the sail set. This occupied another hour, before we were
entirely through, when the land was getting nearly awash.
As soon as the mizzen-topsail was set, I braced sharp up,
and brought the ship close upon the wind. This caused the
Indians to wilt down like flowers under a burning sun, just
as I expected; there being, by this time, a seven-knot breeze,
and a smart head-sea on. Old Smudge felt that his forces
were fast deserting him, and he now came to me, in a manner that would not be denied, and I felt the necessity of doing something to appease him. I got the savages stationed
as well as I could, hauled up the mainsail, and put the ship
in stays. We tacked better than I could have believed possible, and when my wild captors saw that we were actually
moving in the direction of the land again, their delight was
infinite. Their leader was ready to hug me; but I avoided
this pleasure in the best manner I could. As for the consequences, I had no apprehensions, knowing we were too
far off to have any reason to dread the canoes, and being
certain it was easy enough to avoid them in such a breeze.

Smudge and his companions were less on the alert, as soon
as they perceived the ship was going in the proper direction.
They probably believed the danger in a measure over, and
they began to yield a little to their physical sufferings. I
called Neb to the wheel, and leaning over the taffrail, I
succeeded in getting Marble to a cabin window, without
alarming Smudge. I then told the mate to get all his forces
in the forecastle, having observed that the Indians avoided
that part of the vessel, on account of the heavy plunges
she occasionally made, and possibly because they fancied
our people were all aft. As soon as the plan was understood, I strolled forward, looking up at the sails, and touching a rope, here and there, like one bent on his ordinary
duty. The savage stationed at the fore-scuttle was as sick

as a dog, and with streaming eyes, he was paying the landsmen's tribute to the sea. The hatch was very strong, and
it was secured simply by its hasp and a bit of iron thrust
through it. I had only to slip my hand down, remove the
iron, throw open the hatch, when the ship's company
streamed up on deck, Marble leading.

It was not a moment for explanations. I saw at a glance,
that the mate and his followers regarded the situation of the
ship very differently from what I did myself. I had now
been hours with the savages, had attained a little of their
confidence, and knew how dependent they were on myself
for their final safety ; all of which, in a small degree, disposed me to treat them with some of the lenity I fancied I
had received from them, in my own person. But Marble
and the crew had been chafing below, like caged lions, the
whole time, and, as I afterwards learned, had actually taken
an unanimous vote to blow themselves up, before they would
permit the Indians to retain the control of the vessel. Then
poor Captain Williams was much beloved forward, and his
death remained to be avenged. I would have said a word
in favor of my captors, but the first glance I got at the
flushed face of the mate, told me it would be useless. I
turned, therefore, to the sick savage who had been left
as a sentinel over the fore-scuttle, to prevent his interference. This man was armed with the pistols that had
been taken from me, and he showed a disposition to use
them. I was too quick in my motions, however, falling
upon him so soon as to prevent one who was not expert
with the weapons from using them. We clenched, and fell
on the deck together, the Indian letting the pistols fall to
meet my grasp.

As this occurred, I heard the cheers of the seamen ; and
Marble, shouting out to "revenge Captain Williams," gave
the order to charge. I soon had my own fellow perfectly at
my mercy, and got him so near the end of the jib downhaul, as to secure him with a turn or two of that rope. The
man made little resistance, after the first onset ; and, catching up the pistols, I left him, to join in what was doing aft.
As I lay on the deck, I heard several plunges into the

water, and then half a dozen of most cruelly crushing blows succeeded. Not a shot was fired by either party, though some of our people, who had carried all their arms below the night the ship was seized, used their pikes with savage freedom. By the time I got as far aft as the mainmast, the vessel was our own. Nearly half the Indians had thrown themselves into the sea; the remaining dozen had either been knocked in the head like beeves, or were stuck, like so many porkers. The dead bodies followed the living into the sea. Old Smudge alone remained, at the moment of which I have spoken.

The leader of the savages was examining the movements of Neb, at the moment the shout was raised; and the black, abandoning the wheel, threw his arms around those of the old man, holding him like a vice. In this situation he was found by Marble and myself, who approached at the same instant, one on each side of the quarter-deck.

"Overboard with the blackguard!" called out the excited mate; "overboard with him, Neb, like a trooper's horse!"

"Hold!" I interrupted; "spare the old wretch, Mr. Marble; he spared me."

A request from me would, at any moment outweigh an order from the captain, himself, so far as the black was concerned, else Smudge would certainly have gone into the ocean, like a bundle of straw. Marble had in him a good deal of the indifference to bodily suffering that is generated by habit, and, aroused, he was a dangerous, and sometimes a hard man; but in the main, he was not cruel; and then he was always manly. In the short struggle which had passed, he had actually dropped his pike, to knock an Indian down with his fist; bundling the fellow through a port without ceremony, ere he had time to help himself. But he disdained striking Smudge, with such odds against him; and he went to the helm, himself, bidding Neb secure the prisoner. Glad of this little relief to a scene so horrible, I ran forward, intending to bring my own prisoner aft, and to have the two confined together, below. But I was too late. One of the Philadelphians had just got the poor wretch's head and shoulders through the bow-port, and I was barely in time to see his feet disappear.

Not a cheer was given for our success. When all was over, the men stood gazing at each other, stern, frowning, and yet with the aspects of those who felt they had been, in a manner, disgraced by the circumstances which led them to the necessity of thus regaining the command of their own vessel. As for myself, I ran and sprang upon the taffrail to look into the ship's wake. A painful sight met me, there! During the minute or two passed in the brief struggle, the Crisis had gone steadily ahead, like the earth moving in its orbit, indifferent to the struggles of the nations that are contending on its bosom. I could see heads and arms tossing in our track for a hundred fathoms, those who could not swim struggling to the last to preserve their existence. Marble, Smudge, and Neb were all looking in the same direction, at that instant. Under an impulse I could not control, I ventured to suggest that we might yet tack and save several of the wretches.

"Let them drown, and be d——d!" was the chief mate's sententious answer.

"No, no, Masser Mile," Neb ventured to add, with a remonstrating shake of the head, "dat will nebber do—no good ebber come of Injin. If you don't drown him, he sartain drown you."

I saw it was idle to remonstrate, and by this time one dark spot after another began to disappear, as the victims sank in the ocean. As for Smudge, his eye was riveted on the struggling forms of his followers, in a manner to show that traces of human feelings are to be found, in some aspect or other, in every condition of life. I thought I could detect workings of the countenance of this being, indurated as his heart had become by a long life of savage ferocity, which denoted how keenly he felt the sudden destruction that had alighted on his tribe. He might have had sons and grandsons among those struggling wretches, on whom he was now gazing for the last time. If so, his self-command was almost miraculous; for while I could see that he felt, and felt intensely, not a sign of weakness escaped him. As the last head sunk from view I could see him shudder, a suppressed groan escaped him, then he turned his face toward the bulwarks, and stood immovable as one of the pines of his own forests, for a long time. I asked Marble's permission to release the old man's arms, and the mate granted it, though not without growling a few curses on him, and on all who had been concerned in the late occurrences on board the ship.

There was too much duty to be done, to render all secure, to suffer us to waste much time in mere sympathy. All the topmast rigging, backstays, etc., had to be set up afresh, and gangs were sent about this duty, forward and aft. The blood was washed from the decks, and a portion of the crew got along the topgallant-masts, and pointed them. The topsails were all close reefed, the courses hauled up, the spanker and jib taken in, and the ship hove-to. It wanted but two hours of sunset when Mr. Marble had got things to his mind. We had crossed royal-yards, and had everything set that would draw, from the trucks down. The launch was in the water towing astern; the ship was then about a mile from the southern passage into the bay, toward which she was steering, with the wind very much as it had been since an hour after sunrise, though slightly falling. Our guns were loose, and the crew was at quarters. Even I did not know what the new captain intended to do, for he had given his orders in the manner of one whose mind was too immovably made up to admit of consultation. The larboard battery was manned, and orders had been given to see the guns on that side levelled and ready for firing. As the ship brushed past the island, in entering the bay, the whole of this broad-side was delivered in among its bushes and trees. We heard a few yells in reply, that satisfied us that the grape had told, and that Marble had not miscalculated the position of some of his enemies, at least.

When the ship entered the little bay, it was with a moderate and steady movement, the breeze being greatly broken by the forests. The main-yard was thrown aback, and I was ordered into the launch, with its crew armed. A swivel was in the bows of the boat, and I pulled into the creek in order to ascertain if there were any signs of the savages.

In entering the creek the swivel was discharged, according to orders, and we soon detected proofs that we disturbed a bivouac. I now kept loading and firing this little piece into the bushes, supporting it with occasional volleys of musketry, until pretty well satisfied that we had swept the shore effectually. At the bivouac I found the canoes and our own yawl, and what was some little revenge for what had happened, I also found a pile of no less than six hundred skins, which had doubtless been brought to trade with us, if necessary, in order to blind our eyes until the favorable moment for the execution of the conspiracy should offer. I made no scruple about confiscating these skins, which were taken on board the ship.

I next went to the island, on which I found one man dying with a grape-shot wound, and evidence that a considerable party had left it, as soon as they felt our fire. This party had probably gone outside the island, but it was getting too late to follow. On my return I met the ship coming out, Captain Marble being determined not to trust her inside another night. The wind was getting light, and the tides running fiercely in that high latitude, we were glad to make an offing again while there was still day. The success with the skins greatly mollified the new captain, who declared to me that after he had hanged Smudge in sight of his own shores, he should "feel something like himself again."

We passed the night under our topsails, standing off and on, with the wind steady, but light at the southward. Next morning, the duty of the ship went on as usual, until the men had breakfasted, when we stood again into the bay. This time, we hove-to so as to get one of the buoys, when we dropped the stream, leaving the topsails set. We then hove up the anchor, securing the range of cable that was bent to it. Both of the anchors, and their ranges of cable, were thus recovered ; the ends of the last being entered at the hawse-holes, and the pieces spliced. This work may have occupied us four hours ; after which, the stream anchor was hove up, catted, and fished. Marble then ordered a whip rove at the fore-yard-arm.

I was on the quarter-deck when this command was suddenly given. I wished to remonstrate, for I had some tolerably accurate notions of legality, and the rights of persons. Still, I did not like to say anything ; for Captain Marble's eye and manner were not the least in the trifling mood, at that instant. The whip was soon rove, and the men stood looking aft, in silent expectation.

"Take that murdering blackguard forward, fasten his arms behind his back, place him on the third gun, and wait for orders," added our new captain, sternly.

No one dared hesitate about obeying these orders, though I could see that one or two of the lads disliked the business.

"Surely," I ventured to say, in a low voice, " you are not in earnest, Mr. Marble ! "

"Captain Marble, if you please, Mr. Wallingford. I am now master of this vessel, and you are her chief mate. I intend to hang your friend, Smudge, as an example to the rest of the coast. These woods are full of eyes at this moment ; and the sight they 'll presently see, will do more good than forty missionaries, and threescore and ten years of preaching. Set the fellow up on the gun, men, as I ordered. This is the way to generalize with an Indian."

In a moment, there stood the hapless wretch, looking about him with an expression that denoted the consciousness of danger, though it was not possible he could comprehend the precise mode of his execution. I went to him, and pressed his hand, pointing upward, as much as to say his whole trust was now in the Great Spirit. The Indian understood me, for from that instant he assumed an air of dignified composure, like one every way prepared to meet his fate. It is not probable, with his habits, that he saw any peculiar hardship in his own case ; for he had, doubt-less, sacrificed many a prisoner under circumstances of less exasperation than that which his own conduct had provoked.

"Let two of the ' niggers' take a turn with the end of the whip round the chap's neck," said Marble, too dignified to turn Jack Ketch in person, and unwilling to set any of the white seamen at so ungracious an office. The cook, Joe, and another black soon performed this revolting duty, from the odium of which a sailor seldom altogether escapes.

I now perceived Smudge looking upward, seeming to comprehend the nature of the fate that awaited him. The deeply-seated principle within him caused a dark shadow to pass over a countenance already so gloomy and wrinkled by suffering and exposure ; and he turned his look wistfully toward Marble, at whose command each order in succession had been obeyed. Our new captain caught that gaze, and I was, for a single moment, in hope he would relent, and let the wretch go. But Marble had persuaded himself he was performing a great act of nautical justice ; nor was he aware, himself, how much he was influenced by a feeling allied to vengeance.

" Sway away ! " he called out ; and Smudge was dangling at the yard-arm in a few seconds.

A block of wood could not have been more motionless than the body of this savage, after one quivering shudder of suffering had escaped it. There it hung, like a jewel-block, and every sign of life was soon taken away. In a quarter of an hour, a man was sent up, and, cutting the rope, the body fell, with a sharp plunge, into the water, and disappeared.

At a later day, the account of this affair found its way into the newspapers at home. A few moralists endeavored to throw some doubts over the legality and necessity of the proceedings, pretending that more evil than good was done to the cause of sacred justice by such disregard of law and principles ; but the feeling of trade, and the security of ships when far from home, were motives too powerful to be put down by the still, quiet remonstrances of reason and light. The abuses to which such practices would be likely to lead, in cases in which one of the parties constituted himself the law, the judge, and the executioner, were urged in vain against the active and ever-stimulating incentive of a love of gold. Still, I knew that Marble wished the thing undone when it was too late, it being idle to think of quieting the suggestions of that monitor God has implanted within us, by the meretricious and selfish approbation of those who judge of right and wrong by their own narrow standard of interest.

CHAPTER XV.

THE Crisis was tacked as soon as the body of Smudge was cut down, and she moved slowly, her crew maintaining a melancholy silence, out of the little haven. I never witnessed stronger evidence of sadness in the evolutions of a vessel ; the slow and stately departure resembling that of mourners leaving the grave on which they had just heard the fall of the clod. Marble told me afterwards he had been disposed to anchor, and remain until the body of poor Captain Williams should rise, as it probably would within the next forty-eight hours ; but the dread of a necessity of sacrificing more of the natives induced him to quit the fatal spot, without paying the last duties to our worthy old commander. I always regretted we did not remain, for I think no Indian would have come near us, had we continued in the harbor a month.

It was high noon when the ship once more issued into the broad bosom of the Pacific. The wind was at southeast, and as we drew off from the land, it came fresh and steady. About two, having an offing of ten or twelve miles, orders were issued to set all the larboard studding-sails, and we stood to the southward and westward under a press of canvas. Every one saw in this change a determination to quit the coast ; nor did we regret the measure, for our

The author of *Afloat and Ashore*. Engraved by Thomson from an original drawing and published in the *New Monthly Magazine*, London, April 1, 1831.

trade had been quite successful, down to the moment of the seizure, but could hardly be prosperous after what had passed. I had not been consulted in the affair at all, but the second mate having the watch, I was now summoned to the cabin, and let into the secret of our future movements. I found Marble seated at the cabin table, with Captain Williams' writing-desk open before him, and sundry papers under examination.

"Take a seat, Mr. Wallingford," said the new master, with a dignity and manner suited to the occasion. "I have just been overhauling the old man's instructions from the owners, and find I have done right in leaving these hang-gallows rascals to themselves, and shaping our course to the next point of destination. As it is, the ship has done surprisingly well. There are $67,370 good Spaniards down in the run, and that for goods which I see are invoiced at just $26,240; and when you consider that no duties, port-charges, or commissions are to be deducted, but that the dollars under our feet are all our own, without any drawbacks, I call the operation a good one. Then that blundering through the straits, though it must never be talked of in any other light than a bold push for a quick passage, did us a wonderful deal of good, shoving us ahead near a month in time. It has put us so much ahead of our calculations, indeed, that I would cruise for Frenchmen for five or six weeks, were there the least probability that one of the chaps was to the westward of the Horn. Such not being the fact, however, and there still being a very long road before us, I have thought it beat to push for the next point of destination. Read that page of the owners' idees, Mr. Wallingford, and you will get their advice for just such a situation as that in which we find ourselves."

The passage pointed out by Captain Marble was somewhat parenthetical, and was simply intended to aid Captain Williams, in the event of his not being able to accomplish the other objects of his voyage. It had a place in the instructions, indeed, solely on account of a suggestion of Marble's himself, the project being one of those favorite schemes of the mate, that men sometimes maintain through thick and thin, until they get to be ruling thoughts. On Captain Williams it had not weighed a feather ; his intention having been to proceed to the Sandwich Islands for sandal-wood, which was the course then usually pursued by north-west traders, after quitting the coast. The parenthetical project, however, was to touch at the last island, procure a few divers, and proceed in quest of certain islands where it was supposed the pearl fishery would succeed. Our ship was altogether too large, and every way too expensive, to be risked in such an adventure, and so I told the ex-mate without any scruple. But this fishery was a "fixed idea," a quick road to wealth, in the new captain's mind, and find-ing it in the instructions, though simply as a contingent course, he was inclined to regard it as the great object of the voyage. Such it was in his eyes, and such it ought to be, as he imagined, in those of the owners.

Marble had excellent qualities in his way, but he was not fit to command a ship. No man could stow her better, fit her better, sail her better, take better care of her in heavy weather, or navigate her better ; and yet he wanted the judgment necessary to manage the property that must be committed to his care, and he had no more ideas of com-mercial thrift than if he had never been employed in any of the concerns of commerce. This was, in truth, the reason he had never risen any higher in his profession, the mercan-tile instinct—one of the liveliest and most acute to be found in natural history—forewarning his different owners that he was already in the berth nature and art had best quali-fied him to fill. It is wonderful how acute even dull men get to be, on the subject of money !

I own my judgment, such as it was at nineteen, was opposed to the opinion of the captain. I could see that the contingency contemplated by the instructions had not arisen, and that we should be acting more in conformity with the wishes of the owners, by proceeding to the Sandwich Islands in quest of sandal-wood, and thence to China, after a cargo of teas. Marble was not to be convinced, however, though I think my arguments shook him a little. What might have been the result, it is difficult to say, had not

chance befriended the views of each of us, respectively. It
is proper to add, that Marble availed himself of this opportunity to promote Talcott, who was brought into the cabin
as third mate. I rejoiced greatly in this addition to our
little circle on the quarter-deck, Talcott being a man of education, much nearer my own age than the two others, and
united to me by unusual ties since our common adventure
in the prize. I was not only rejoiced to be able to associate
with him, but to hear him called *Mr.* Talcott.

We had a long, but mild passage to the Sandwich Islands.
This group occupied a very different place, in the opinions
of the world, in the year 1800, from that it fills to-day.
Still it had made some small advances in civilization since
the time of Cook. I am told there are churches, taverns,
billiard tables, and stone dwellings in these islands now,
which are fast turning to the Christian religion, and obtaining the medley of convenience, security, vice, roguery, law,
and comfort, that is known as civilization. It was far different then, our reception being by men who were but a small
degree removed from savages. Among those who first came
on board us, however, was the master of an American brig,
belonging to Boston, whose vessel had got on a reef, and
bilged. He intended to remain by the wreck, but wished
to dispose of a considerable amount of sandal-wood that was
still in his vessel, and for the safety of which he was under
great concern, as the first gale of wind might scatter it to
the winds of the ocean. If he could obtain a fresh stock of
goods to trade on, he proposed remaining on the islands until another vessel belonging to the same owners, which was
expected in a few months, should arrive, on board which
vessel he intended to embark with everything he could save
from the wreck, and such wood as he could purchase in the
interim. Captain Marble rubbed his hands with delight,
when he returned from a visit to the wreck, his arrangements all completed.

"Luck is with us, Master Miles," he said, "and we'll be
off for them pearl fisheries next week. I have bought all
the sandal-wood in the wreck, paying in trumpery, and at
prices only about double Indian trade, and we will heave up,

and carry the ship round to the wreck, and begin to take in this afternoon. There is capital holding-ground inside the reef, and the ship can be safely carried within a hundred fathoms of her cargo !''

All turned out as Marble had hoped and predicted, and the Crisis was back at her anchorage in front of the village, which is now the city of Honolulu, within the week named. We got our supply of hogs, and having procured four of the best divers going, we sailed in quest of Captain Marble's Eldorado of Pearls. I was less opposed to the scheme than I had been, for we were now so much in advance of our time, that we could afford to pass a few weeks among the islands, previously to sailing for China. Our course was to the southwest, crossing the line in about 170° west longitude. There was a clear sea for more than a fortnight while we were nearing the equator, the ship making but little progress. Glad enough was I to hear the order given to turn more to the northward again, for the heat was oppressive, and this was inclining toward our route to China. We had been out from Owyhee, as it was then usual to call the island where Cook was killed—Hawaii, as it is called to-day—we had been out from the island about a month, when Marble came up to me one fine moonlight evening, in my watch, rubbing his hands, as was his custom when in good-humor, and broke out as follows :—

"I 'll tell you what, Miles," he said, "you and I have been salted down by Providence for something more than common ! Just look back at all our adventures in the last three years, and see what they come to. Firstly, there was shipwreck over here on the coast of Madagascar," jerking his thumb over a shoulder in a manner that was intended to indicate about two hundred degrees of longitude, that being somewhat near our present distance from the place he mentioned, in an air-line; "then followed the boat business under the Isle of Bourbon, and the affair with the privateer off Guadaloupe. Well, as if that were n't enough, we ship together again in this vessel, and a time we had of it with the French letter-of-marque. After that, a devil of a passage we made through the Straits of Magellan. Then came the

melancholy loss of Captain Williams, and all that business ;
after which we got the sandal-wood out of the wreck, which
I consider the luckiest transaction of all.''

" I hope you don't set down the loss of Captain Williams
among our luck, sir ! ''

" Not I, but the stuff is all logged together, you know ;
and in overhauling for one idee, in such a mess, a fellow is
apt to get hold of another.   As I was saying, we have been
amazingly lucky, and I expect nothing else but we shall discover an island yet !''

" Can that be of any great service to us?   There are so
many owners ready to start up and claim such discoveries,
that I question if it would do us any great benefit.''

" Let them start up—who cares for them?   We 'll have
the christening and that 's half the battle.   Marble Land,
Wallingford Bay, Talcott Hills, and Cape Crisis, would look
well on a chart—ha ! Miles ?''

" I have no objection to see it, sir.''

" Land ho !'' cried the lookout on the forecastle.

" There it is now, by George !'' cried Marble, springing
forward.   " I overhauled the chart half an hour since, and
there ought to be nothing within six hundred miles of us.''

There it was, sure enough, and much nearer to us than
was at all desirable.   So near, indeed, that the wash of the
breakers on the reef that so generally lies off from the low
coral islands of the Pacific, was distinctly audible from the
ship.   The moon gave a strong light, it is true, and the
night was soft and balmy, but the air, which was very light,
blew directly toward this reef, and then there were always
currents to apprehend.   We sounded, but got no bottom.

" Ay, this is one of your coral reefs, where a man goes on
the rocks from off soundings, at a single jump,'' muttered
Marble, ordering the ship brought by the wind on the best
tack to haul off-shore.   " No notice, and a wreck.   As for
anchoring in such a place, a fellow might as well run a line
out to Japan ; and could an anchor find the bottom, the
cable would have some such berth as a man who slept in a
hammock filled with open razors.''

All this was true enough ; and we watched the effect of
16

our change of course with the greatest anxiety. All hands were called, and the men were stationed in readiness to work the ship. But a few minutes satisfied us the hope of clawing off in so light an air was to the last degree vain. The vessel set in fast toward the reef, the breakers on which now became apparent, even by the light of the moon, the certain sign they were fearfully near.

This was one of those moments in which Marble could show himself to be a true man. He was perfectly calm and self-possessed ; and stood on the taffrail, giving his orders, with a distinctness and precision I had never seen surpassed. I was kept in the chains, myself, to watch the casts of the lead. " No bottom," however, was the never-failing report ; nor was any bottom expected ; it being known that these reefs were quite perpendicular on their seaward side. The captain called out to me, from time to time, to be active and vigilant, as our set in-shore was uncontrollable, and the boats, if in the water, as the launch could not be for twenty minutes, would be altogether useless. I proposed to lower the yawl, and to pull to leeward, to try the surroundings, in order to ascertain if it were not possible to find bottom at some point short of the reef, on which we should hopelessly be set, unless checked by some such means, in the course of the next fifteen or twenty minutes.

" Do it at once, sir," cried Marble. " The thought is a good one, and does you credit, Mr. Wallingford."

I left the ship in less than five minutes, and pulled off, under the ship's lee-bow, knowing that tacking or wearing would be out of the question under the circumstances. I stood up in the stern-sheets, and made constant casts with the hand-lead, with a short line, however, as the boat went foaming through the water. The reef was now plainly in sight, and I could see, as well as hear, the long, formidable ground-swells of the Pacific, while, fetching up against these solid barriers, they rolled over, broke, and went beyond the rocks in angry froth. At this perilous instant, when I would not have given the poorest acre of Clawbonny to have been the owner of the Crisis, I saw a spot to leeward that was comparatively still, or in which the water did not break. It was not fifty fathoms from me when first discovered, and toward it I steered, animating the men to redoubled exertions. We were in this narrow belt of smooth water, as it might be, in an instant, and the current sucked the boat through it so fast as to allow time to make but a single cast of the lead. I got bottom ; but it was in six fathoms !

The boat was turned, and headed out again, as if life and death depended on the result. The ship was fortunately within sound of the voice, steering still by the wind, though setting three feet toward the reef, for one made in the desired direction ; and I hailed.

" What now, Mr. Wallingford ? " demanded Marble, as calmly as if anchored near a wharf at home.

" Do you see the boat, sir ? "

" Quite plainly ; God knows you are near enough to be seen."

" Has the ship steerage-way on her, Captain Marble ? "

" Just that, and nothing more to boast of."

" Then ask no questions ; but try to follow the boat. It is the only hope ; and it may succeed."

I got no answer ; but I heard the deep, authoritative voice of Marble, ordering the " helm up," and the men " to man the weather-braces." I could scarcely breathe, while I stood looking at the ship's bows, as they fell off, and noted her slow progress ahead. Her speed increased sensibly, however, and I kept the boat far enough to windward to give the vessel room fairly to enter the pass. At the proper moment, we moved toward the inlet, the Crisis keeping more and more away, in order to follow. I was soon in the pass itself, the water breaking within ten fathoms on each side of me, sending portions of its foam to the very blades of our oars ; but the lead still gave me six fathoms. At the next cast, I got ten ; and then the ship was at the point where I had just before found six. The breakers were roaring behind me, and I pulled round, and waited for the ship, steering to the southward, sounding as I went. I could see that the ship hauled up, and that I was already behind the reef. Straining my voice, I now called out,—

" Anchor, sir—bear a hand and anchor, as soon as possible."

Not a word came back ; but up went the courses, followed by the topgallant-sails, after which down went the jib. I heard the fore and main-topsail halyards overhauling themselves, spite of the roar of the breakers, and then the ship luffed into the wind. Glad enough was I to hear the heavy plunge of one of the bowers, as it fell from the cat-head into the water. Even then I remained stationary, to note the result. The ship took her scope of cable freely, after which I observed that she was brought up. The next moment I was on board her.

"A close shave, Mr. Wallingford," said Marble, giving me a squeeze of the hand, that said more for his feelings than any words such a being could utter ; "and many thanks for your piloting. Is not that land I see, away here to leeward—more to the westward, boy?"

"It is, sir, beyond a doubt. It must be one of the coral islands ; and this is the reef that usually lies to seaward from them. There is the appearance of trees ashore !"

"It's a discovery, youngster, and will make us all great names! Remember, this passage I call ' Miles' Inlet ' ; and to the reef, I give the name of ' Yawl Reef.' "

I could not smile at this touch of Marble's vanity, for concern left me no thoughts but for the ship. The weather was now mild and the bay smooth ; the night was fine, and it might be of the last importance to us to know something more of our situation. The cable might chafe off, probably would, so near a coral reef ; and I offered to pull in toward the land, sounding as I went, and otherwise gaining the knowledge that might be necessary to our security. After a little reflection, the captain consented, ordering me to take provisions and water in the boat, as the duty might detain me until morning.

I found the bay between the reef and the island about a league in breadth, and across its entire width the soundings did not vary much from ten fathoms. The outer barrier of rock, on which the sea broke, appeared to be an advanced wall, that the indefatigable little insects had erected, as it might be, in defence of their island, which had probably been raised from the depths of the ocean, a century or two ago,

by some of their own ancestors. The gigantic works completed by these little aquatic animals, are well known to
navigators, and give us some tolerably accurate notions of
the manner in which the face of the globe has been made to
undergo some of its alterations. I found the land easy of
access, low, wooded, and without any sign of habitation.

The night was so fine that I ventured inland, and after
walking more than a mile, most of the distance in a grove
of cocoa and bananas, I came to the basin of water that is
usually found in the islands of this particular formation.
The inlet from the sea was at no great distance, and I sent
one of the men back to the yawl, with orders for the boat
to proceed thither. I next sounded the inlet and the bay,
and found everywhere a sandy bottom, and about ten
fathoms of water. As I expected, the shoalest spot was the
inlet, but in this, which I sounded thoroughly, there was
nowhere less than five. It was now midnight; and I should
have remained on the island until morning, to make further
surveys by daylight, had we not seen the ship under her
canvas, and so much nearer to us than we had supposed possible, as to satisfy me she was drifting in fast toward the
land. Of course I did not hesitate, but pulled on board.

It was as I suspected. The rocks so near the reef had
chafed off the cable; the ship struck adrift, and Marble was
under his canvas waiting my return, in order to ascertain
where he might anchor anew. I told him of the lagoon in
the centre of the island, and gave him every assurance of
there being water enough to carry in any craft that floats.
My reputation was up, in consequence of the manner the
ship had been taken through the first inlet, and I was
ordered to conn her into this new haven.

The task was not difficult. The lightness of the wind
and uncertainty about the currents proving the only source
of embarrassment, I succeeded in finding the passage, after
a short trial; and sending the boat ahead, under Talcott, as
an additional precaution, soon had the Crisis floating in the
very centre of this natural dock. Sail was shortened as we
came in, and the ship made a flying moor; after which we
lay as securely, as if actually in some basin wrought by art

It is my opinion, the vessel would have ridden out the hardest gale, or anything short of a hurricane, at single anchor, in that place. The sense of security was now so strong upon us, that we rolled up our canvas, set an anchor-watch of only one man, and turned in.

I never laid my head down, on board ship, with greater satisfaction than I did that night. Let the truth be frankly stated. I was perfectly satisfied with myself. It was owing to my decision and vigilance that the ship was saved, when outside the reef, out of all question; and I think she would have been lost after she had struck adrift, had I not discovered her present berth. There she was, however, with land virtually all round her, a good bottom, plenty of water, and well moored. As I have said already, she could not be better secured in an artificial dock. In the midst of the Pacific, away from all custom-house officers, in a recently discovered and uninhabited island, there was nothing to fear. Men sleep soundly in such circumstances, and I should have been in a deep slumber in a minute after I was in my berth, had not Marble's conversation kept me awake, quite unwillingly, on my part, for five minutes. His state-room door was open, and through it, the following discourse was held.

" I think, on the whole," commenced the captain, " it will be better to generalize a little more; " this was a favorite expression of the ex-mate's, and one he often used without exactly knowing its application himself. " Yes, to generalize a little more; it shall be Marble Land, Wallingford Bay, Yawl Reef, Talcott Inlet, Miles' Anchorage— and a d——d bad anchorage it was, Miles; but never mind, we must take the good with the bad in this wicked world."

" Very true, sir; but, as for taking that anchorage, you must excuse me, as I shall never take it again."

" Perhaps not. Well, this is what I call comfort—ha ! Talcott? Is Talcott asleep, Miles? "

" He and the second mate are hard at it, sir—full and by, and going ten knots," I muttered, wishing my tormentor in Japan, at the moment.

" Ay ; they are rackers at a sleep ! I say, Miles, such a

discovery as this will make a man's fortune! The world generalizes in discoveries, altogether, making no great matter of distinction between your Columbuses, Cooks, or Marbles. An island is an island, and he who first discovers it, has the credit. Poor Captain Williams! he would have sailed this ship for a whole generation, and never found anything in the way of novelty."

"Except the straits," I muttered, very indistinctly, breathing deep and hard.

"Ay, that was an affair! Had n't you and I been aboard, the ship never would have done that. We are the very offspring of luck! There was the affair of the wreck off Madagascar—there are bloody currents in the Pacific, too, I find, Miles."

"Yes, sir—hard-a-weather—"

"The fellow's dreaming. One word, boy, before you cut loose from all reason and reflection. Don't you think it would be a capital idea to poke in a little patriotism among the names! patriotism goes so far in our part of the world. Congress Rocks would be a good title for the highest part of the reef, and Washington Sands would do for the landing you told me of. Washington should have a finger in the pie."

"Crust is n't down, sir."

"The fellow's off, and I may as well follow, though it is not easy to sleep on the honor of a discovery like this. Good night, Miles!"

"Ay, ay, sir!"

Such was the account Marble afterward gave me of the termination of the dialogue. Sleep, sleep, sleep! Never did men enjoy their rest more than we did for the next five hours, the ship being as silent as a church on a week day during the whole time. For myself, I can safely say I heard nothing, or knew nothing, until I was awakened by a violent shake of the shoulder. Supposing myself to have been aroused for an ordinary watch at sea, I was erect in an instant, and found the sun's rays streaming into my face through the cabin windows. This prevented me for a moment from seeing that I had been disturbed by Captain

Marble himself. The latter waited until he perceived I could understand him, and then he said in a grave, meaning manner,—

"Miles, there is a mutiny in the ship! Do you understand me, Mr. Wallingford?—a bloody mutiny!"

"A mutiny, Captain Marble! You confound me, sir—I had thought our people perfectly satisfied."

"Umph! one never knows whether the copper will come up head or tail. I thought when I turned in last night, it was to take the surest nap I ever tasted afloat; and here I awake, and find a mutiny!"

I was on my feet and dressing in an instant, as a matter of course, having first gone to the berths of the two other mates, and given each a call.

"But how do you know this, Captain Marble?" I resumed, as soon as there was a chance. "I hear no disturbance, and the ship is just where we left her," glancing through the cabin windows; "I think you must be mistaken, sir."

"Not I. I turned out ten minutes since, and was about to go on deck to get a look at your basin, and breathe the fresh air, when I found the companion-door fastened, precisely Smudge-fashion. I suppose you will allow that no regular ship's company would dare to fasten the officers below, unless they intended to seize the craft."

"This is very extraordinary! Perhaps some accident has befallen the doors. Did you call out, sir?"

"I thumped like an admiral, but got no answer. When on the point of trying the virtue of a few kicks, I overheard a low laugh on deck, and that let me into the secret of the state of the nation at once. I suppose you will all admit, gentlemen, when sailors laugh at their officers, as well as batten them down, that they must be somewhat near a state of mutiny."

"It does look so, indeed, sir. We had better arm the moment we are dressed, Captain Marble."

"I have done that already, and you will each find loaded pistols in my state-room."

In two minutes from that moment, all four of us were in

a state for action, each man armed with a brace of ship's pistols, well loaded and freshly primed. Marble was for making a rush at the cabin doors at once, but I suggested the improbability of the steward or Neb's being engaged in any plot against the officers, and thought it might be well to ascertain what had become of the two blacks before we commenced operations. Talcott proceeded instantly to the steerage where the steward slept, and returned in a moment to report that he had found him sound asleep in his berth.

Reinforced by this man, Captain Marble determined to make his first demonstration by way of the forecastle, where, by acting with caution, a surprise on the mutineers might be effected. It will be remembered that a door communicated with the forecastle, the fastenings of which were on the side of "'twixt decks." Most of the cargo being in the lower hold there was no difficulty in making our way to this door, where we stopped and listened, in order to learn the state of things on the other side of the bulkhead. Marble had whispered to me, as we groped our way along in the sort of twilight which pervaded the place, the hatches being on and secured, that "them bloody Philadelphians" must be at the bottom of the mischief, as our old crew were a set of as "peaceable, well-disposed chaps as ever eat duff (dough) out of a kid."

The result of the listening was to produce a general surprise. Out of all question, snoring, and that on no small scale of the gamut of Morpheus, was unequivocally heard. Marble instantly opened the door, and we entered the forecastle, pistols in hand. Every berth had its tenant and all hands were asleep! Fatigue, and the habit of waiting for calls, had evidently kept each of his seamen in his berth, until that instant. Contrary to usage, in so warm a climate, the scuttle was on, and a trial soon told us it was fast.

"To generalize on this idee, Miles," exclaimed the captain, "I should say we are again battened down by savages!"

"It does indeed look so, sir; and yet I saw no sign of the island's being inhabited. It may be well, Captain Marble, to muster the crew, that we may learn who 's who."

"Quite right—do you turn 'em up, and send 'em all aft into the cabin, where we have more daylight."

I set about awakening the people, which was not difficult, and in a few minutes everybody was sent aft. Following the crew, it was soon found that only one man was missing, and he was the very individual whom we had left on deck, when we had all gone below on securing the ship. Every soul belonging to the vessel was present in the cabin or steerage, but this solitary man—Philadelphians and all !

"It can never be that Harris has dared to trifle with us," said Talcott; "and yet it does look surprisingly like it."

"Quite sure, Miles, that Marble Land is an uninhabited island?" said the captain, interrogatively.

"I can only say, sir, that it is as much like all the other uninhabited coral islands we have passed, as one pea is like another ; and that there were no signs of a living being visible last night. It is true we saw but little of the island, though to all appearances there was not much to see."

"Unluckily all the men's arms are on deck, in the arm-chest, or strapped to the boom or masts. There is no use, however, in dillydallying against one man ; so I will make a rumpus that will soon bring the chap to his bearings."

Hereupon Marble made what he called a rumpus in good earnest. I thought, for a minute, he would kick the cabin doors down.

"'Andzomelee—'andzomelee," said some one on deck. "Vat for you make so much kick?"

"Who the devil are you?" demanded Marble, kicking harder than ever. "Open the cabin doors, or I'll kick them down, and yourself overboard."

"Monsieur—sair," rejoined another voice, "tenez—you air prisonnier. Comprenez-vous—prisonair, eh?"

"These are Frenchmen, Captain Marble," I exclaimed, "and we are in the hands of the enemy."

This was astounding intelligence, so much so, that all had difficulty in believing it. A further parley, however, destroyed our hopes, little by little, until we entered into an arrangement with those on deck, to the following effect ; I was to be permitted to go out, in order to ascertain the

real facts of our situation ; while Marble and the remainder
of the crew were to remain below, passive, until the result
should be reported.   Under this arrangement, one of the
cabin doors was opened, and I sallied forth.

Astonishment almost deprived me of the power of vision,
when I looked around me.   Quite fifty armed white men,
sailors and natives of France, by their air and language,
crowded round me, as curious to see me, as I could possibly
be to see them.   In their midst was Harris, who approached
me with an embarrassed and sorrowful air.

"I know I deserve death, Mr. Wallingford," this man
commenced ; "but I fell asleep after so much work, and
everything looking so safe and out-of-harm's-way like ;
and when I woke up, I found these people on board, and
in possession of the ship."

"In the name of wonder, whence come they, Harris?
Is there a French ship at the island?"

"By all I can learn and see, sir, they are a crew of a
wrecked letter-of-marque—an Indiaman of some sort or
other ; and finding a good occasion to get off the island,
and make a rich prize, they have helped themselves to the
poor Crisis—God bless her ! say I, though she is now under
the French flag, I suppose."

I looked up at the gaff, and sure enough, there was flying
the tricolor.

CHAPTER XVI.

"The morning air blows fresh on him:
The waves dance gladly in his sight;
The sea-birds call, and wheel, and skim—
Oh, blessed morning light!
He doth not hear their joyous call; he sees
No beauty in the wave, nor feels the breeze."

DANA.

TRUTH is, truly, often stranger than fiction. The history of the circumstances that brought us into the hands of our enemies will fully show this. La Pauline was a ship of six hundred tons, that carried letters-of-marque from the French government. She sailed from France a few weeks after we had left London, bound on a voyage somewhat similar to our own, though neither sea-otter skins, sandal-wood, nor pearls, formed any part of her contemplated bargains. Her first destination was the French islands off Madagascar, where she left part of her cargo, and took in a few valuables in return. Thence she proceeded to the Philippine Islands, passing in the track of English and American traders, capturing two of the former, aud sinking them after taking out such portions of cargo as suited her own views. From Manilla, La Pauline shaped her course for the coast of South America, intending to leave certain articles brought from France, others purchased at Bourbon, the Isle of France, and the Philippines, and divers bales and boxes found in the holds of her prizes, in that quarter of the world, in exchange for the precious metals. In effecting all this, Monsieur Le Compte, her commander, relied, firstly, on the uncommon sailing of his ship; secondly, on his own uncommon

boldness and dexterity, and, thirdly, on the well-known
disposition of the South Americans to smuggle. Doub-
loons and dollars taking up but little room, he reserved
most of the interior of his vessel, after his traffic on the
"Main," for such property as might be found in the six or
eight prizes he calculated, with certainty, on making, after
getting to the eastward of the Horn. All these well-
grounded anticipations had been signally realized down
to a period of just three months to a day, prior to our own
arrival at this unhappy island.

On the night of the day just mentioned, La Pauline,
without the smallest notice of the vicinity of the danger,
running in an easy bow-line, and without much sea, had
brought up on another part of the very reef from which
we had made so narrow an escape. The rocks being
coral, there was little hope for her ; and, in fact, they appeared through her bottom within two hours after she
struck. The sugars taken in at the Isle of France as a
ground tier of ballast, were soon rendered of doubtful
value, as a matter of course, but the weather remaining
pleasant, Captain Le Compte succeeded, by means of his
boats in getting everything else of value on the island,
and forthwith set about breaking up the wreck, in order
to construct a craft that might carry himself and his people to some civilized land. Having plenty of tools, and
something like sixty men, great progress had been made
in the work, a schooner of about ninety tons being then
so far completed, as to be nearly ready to be put in the
water. Such was the state of things, when, one fine night,
we arrived in the manner already related. The French
kept constant lookouts, and it seems we were seen, a distant speck on the ocean, just as the sun set, while the low
trees of the island eluded our vigilance. By the aid of a
good night-glass, our movements were watched, and a boat
was about to be sent out to warn us of our danger, when
we passed within the reef. Captain Le Compte knew
the chances were twenty to one that we were an enemy,
and he chose to lie concealed to watch the result. As
soon as we had anchored within the basin, and silence

prevailed in the ship, he manned his own gig, and pulled with muffled oars up under our bows, to reconnoitre. Finding everything quiet, he ventured into the fore-chains, and thence on deck, accompanied by three of his men. He found Harris snoring, with his back supported against a gun carriage, and immediately secured him. Then it only remained to close the fore-scuttle and the cabin doors, and to fasten them, to have us all prisoners below. The boat was sent for more men, and hours before any of us in the berths were awake, the ship had effectually changed masters. Harris told our story, and the captors knew our whole history, from the day of sailing down to the present time.

Much of this I learned in subsequent conversations with the French, but enough of it was related to me then to let me understand the outlines of the truth. My eyes also let me into many secrets. I found the island, by daylight, substantially as I had supposed it to be. It was not so large, however, as it had seemed to me by the aid of the moon, though its general character was the same. The basin in which the ship lay might have covered a hundred and fifty acres in extent, the belt of land which encircled it, varying in breadth from a quarter of a mile to three miles. Most of the island was an open grove, lying at an elevation of from ten to thirty feet above the ocean ; and we ascertained there were several springs of the sweetest water on it. Nature, by one of its secret processes, had covered the earth with a beautiful short grass; and the French, with their usual attention to the table, and their commendable activity, had already several materials for salads, etc., in full growth. String-beans might be had for asking, and *petits pois* were literally a drug. I saw the tents of the French extending in a line beneath the shades of the trees ; and there was La Petite Pauline (the schooner) on her ways, actually undergoing the process of receiving her first coat of paint. As for La Pauline herself, I could just discover her lower mastheads, inclining at an angle of forty-five degrees from the perpendicular through a vista in the trees.

There was a good-humored common-sense in all the proceedings of Monsieur Le Compte, that showed he was a philosopher in the best sense of the word. He took things without repining himself, and wished to make others as happy as circumstances would allow. At his suggestion I invited Marble on deck ; and after making my own commander acquainted with the state of the facts, we both listened to the propositions of our captor. Monsieur Le Compte, all his officers, and not a few of his men, had been prisoners, some time or other, in England, and there was no difficulty in carrying on the negotiations in our mother tongue.

"Votre bâtiment—your sheep, shall become French— bien entendu," commenced our captor; "vid her cargaison —rig, and tout cela. Bien ; c'est convenu. I shall not exact rigueur in mes conditions. If you shall have possible to take your sheep from nous autres Français—d'accord. Every man for himself et sa nation. Zere is the pavillon Français—and zere it shall fly, so long as we shall not help —mais—parole d'honneur, ze prize come cheep, and shall be sell very dear—entendez-vous? Bien. Now, sair, I shall put you and all your peepl' on ze island, vere you shall take our place, while we take your place. Ze arm shall be in our hand while ze sheep stay, but we leave you fusils, poudre, et tout cela, behind."

This was, nearly verbatim, the programme of capitulation as laid down by Captain Le Compte. As for Marble, it was not in his nature to acquiesce in such an arrangement without much cavilling and contention. But *cui bono ?* We were in Monsieur Le Compte's hands ; and, though disposed to deal very handsomely by us, it was easy enough to see he was determined to make his own conditions. I succeeded, at last, in making Marble understand that resistance was useless ; and he submitted, though with some such grace as a man who has not been mesmerized, submits to an amputation—those who have, are said rather to delight in the amusement.

The terms of the capitulation—and they differed but little from surrendering at discretion—were no sooner agreed to, than our people were ordered into the fore-castle, whence they were transferred to the boats, in readiness to be sent ashore. All the chests and private effects were moved out, in the most honorable manner, and sent into La Pauline's boats, which lay prepared to receive them. As for us officers, we were put in the gig, Neb and the cabin steward being charged with the duty of looking after our private property. When everybody, the blacks excepted, was in a boat, we shoved off and proceeded toward the landing, as chopfallen and melancholy a party as ever took possession of a newly-discovered country. Marble affected to whistle, for he was secretly furious at the nonchalance manifested by Captain Le Compte; but I detected him in getting parts of Monny Musk and the Irish Washerwoman, into the same strain. To own the truth, the ex-mate was morally much disturbed. As for myself, I considered the affair as an incident of war, and cared much less.

"Voilà, Messieurs," exclaimed Monsieur Le Compte, flourishing his arms, with an air of unsurpassed generosity; "you shall be master here, so soon after we shall go away, and take our leetl' property wid us!"

"He's d——d generous, Miles," growled Marble, in my ear. "He'll leave us the island, and the reef, and the cocoa-nuts, when he has gone off with our ship, and her cargo. I'll bet all I'm worth, he tows off his bloody schooner, in the bargain."

"There is no use in complaining, sir; and by keeping on good terms with the French, we may fare the better."

The truth of this was soon apparent. Captain Le Compte invited us to share his breakfast, and we repaired to the tent of the French officers, with that purpose. In the meantime, the French sailors were transferring the few articles they intended to carry away, to the ship, with the generous object of leaving their own tents to the immediate occupation of us prisoners. As Monsieur Le Compte's plan was to proceed to the Spanish Main, in order to complete his contemplated traffic in that quarter, no sooner were the tents prepared, than the French began also to ship such articles

of their own, as it had originally been proposed to exchange
for Spanish dollars. In the meantime, we sat down to
breakfast.

"C'est la fortune de guerre!—vat you call fortune of
war, Messieurs," observed Captain Le Compte, whirling
the stick in a vessel of chocolate, in a very artistical manner, all the while. "Bon—c'est excellent. Antoïn."

Antoin appeared in the shape of a well-smoked, copper-
colored cabin-boy. He was told to take a small pitcher
of the chocolate, with Captain Le Compte's compliments,
to Mademoiselle, and to tell her there was now every prospect of their quitting the island in a very few days, and of
seeing la belle France in the course of the next four or
five months. This was said in French, and rapidly, with
the vehemence of one who felt all he uttered, and more
too, but I knew enough of the language to understand its
drift.

"I suppose the fellow is generalizing on our misfortunes,
in his d——d lingo," growled Marble; "but let him look
out—he's not home yet, by many a thousand miles!"

I endeavored to explain it all to Marble; but it was
useless; he insisted the Frenchman was sending chocolate
from his own table, to his crew, in order to play the mag-
nifico, on the score of his own good luck. There was no
use in "kicking against the pricks," and I let Marble enjoy
the pleasure of believing the worst of his captor; a sort of
Anglo-Saxon propensity, that has garnished many a page
in English and American history—to say nothing of the
propensities and histories of others, among the great family
of nations.

When breakfast was over, Monsieur Le Compte led me
aside, in a walk under the trees, to explain his views and
intentions. He gave me to understand I had been selected
for this communication, on account of his observing the
state of mind of my captain. I also comprehended a little
French, which was quite convenient in a conversation with
one who interlarded his English so much with phrases
taken from his mother tongue. I was given to understand that the French would put the schooner into the

water that very evening, and that we should find her masts, rigging, and sails all fitted for her. With activity, she could be ready to quit the island in a fortnight, at the farthest. A portion of our own provisions would be landed, as better suited to our habits than those which had been taken from La Pauline ; while a portion of the last would be transferred to the Crisis, for the same reason, as applied to the French. As for water-casks, etc., they were all arranged ; everything of the sort having been taken from the wreck, with little or no difficulty, immediately after the loss of the ship. In a word, we should have little more to do, than to step the masts, rig our craft, stow her hold, and proceed at once to the nearest friendly port.

"I zink you shall go to Canton," added Monsieur Le Compte. "Ze distance shall not be much more than to Sout' America ; and zere you shall find plenty of your compatriotes. Of course, you can sleep and go chez vous —vat you call 'home,' with toute la facilité. Oui—cet arrangement est admirable."

So the arrangement might appear to him, though I confesss to a decided preference to remaining in the "blind Crisis," as our men had got to call her, after her blundering through the Straits of Magellan.

"Allons !" exclaimed the French captain, suddenly. "We are near ze tent of Mademoiselle—we shall go and demand how she carry herself ce beau matin !"

On looking up, I saw two small tents within fifty yards of us. They were beautifully placed, in the midst of a thicker portion of the grove than usual, and near a spring of the most exquisitely limpid water I ever beheld. These tents were made of new canvas, and had been fashioned with care and skill. I could see that the one we first approached was carpeted over, and that it had many of the appliances of a comfortable abode. Monsieur Le Compte, who was really a good-looking fellow under forty, put on his most amiable appearance as he got near the canvas door ; and he hemmed once or twice, as respectfully as he could, by way of letting his presence be known. In an instant, a maid-servant came out to receive him. The moment I laid eyes on this woman, it struck me her face was familiar, though I could not recall the place, or time, where, or when, we had before met. The occurrence was so singular, that I was still ruminating on it, when I unexpectedly found myself standing in the tent, face to face with Emily Merton and her father !

We recognized each other at a glance, and, to Monsieur Le Compte's amazement, hearty greetings passed between us, as old acquaintances. Old acquaintances, however, we could scarce be called ; but, on an uninhabited island in the South Seas, one is glad to meet any face that he has ever met before. Emily looked less blooming than when we had parted, near a twelvemonth before, in London ; but she was still pretty and pleasing. Both she and her father were in mourning, and, the mother not appearing, I at once guessed the truth. Mrs. Merton was an invalid when I knew her, though I had not anticipated for her so speedy a death.

I thought Captain Le Compte appeared vexed at my reception. Still, he did not forget his good manners ; and he rose, saying he would leave me with my friends to make mutual explanations, while he proceeded to overlook the duty of the day. On taking his leave, I was not pleased to see him approach and kiss Emily's hand. The act was done respectfully, and not entirely without grace ; but there were a feeling and manner in it that could not well be mistaken. Emily blushed, as she wished him good-morning, and turning to look at me, in spite of a kind of dog-in-the-manger sensation, I could not forbear smiling.

"Never, Mr. Wallingford, never !" Emily said, with emphasis, the instant her admirer was out of hearing. "We are at his mercy, and must keep terms with him ; but I can never marry a foreigner."

"That is poor encouragement for Wallingford, my dear," said her father, laughing, "should he happen to take a fancy to you himself."

Emily looked confused, but what, for the circumstances, was better still, she looked concerned.

"I am sure, dear sir," she answered, with a quickness I

thought charming, "I am sure Mr. Wallingford will not suppose I meant anything so rude. Then, he is no importunate suitor of mine, like this disagreeable Frenchman, who always seems to me more like a Turkish master, than like one who really respects a woman. Besides—"

"Besides what, Miss Merton?" I ventured to ask, perceiving that she hesitated.

"Besides, Americans are hardly foreigners to us," added Emily, smiling; "for we have even American relatives, you know, father."

"Quite true, my dear, and came near being Americans ourselves. Had my father established himself where he married, as had been his first intention, such would have been our national character. But Monsieur Le Compte has given us a moment to tell our stories to each other, and I think it will not be a very long moment. Let one of us commence, if we wish the offices done without unpleasant listeners."

Emily urged me to begin, and I did not hesitate. My story was soon told. Major Merton and his daughter understood all about the capture of the ship in the basin, though they were ignorant of the vessel's name. I had only to relate our voyage on the main, and the death of Captain Williams, therefore, to have my whole story told. I made it all the shorter, from an impatience to hear the circumstances which had thrown my friends into their present extraordinary position.

"It seems extraordinary enough, beyond doubt," Major Merton began, the moment I left him an opening by my closing remark, "but it is all very simple when you commence at the right end of the sad story, and follow events in the order in which they occurred. When you left us in London, Wallingford, I supposed we were on the point of sailing for the West Indies, but a better appointment soon after offering in the East, my destination was changed to Bombay. It was important that I should reach my port at as early a day as possible, and no regular Indiaman being ready, I took passage in a licensed running vessel, a ship of no size or force. Nothing occurred until we had got within three or four days' sail of our port, when we fell in with La Pauline, and were captured. At first, I think Captain Le Compte would have been willing to let me go on parole, but no opportunity offered, and we went with the ship to Manilla. While there the melancholy loss happened, which, no doubt, you have comprehended from our mourning; and I was strongly in hopes of making some arrangements that would still enable me to save my situation. But by this time Monsieur Le Compte had become an open admirer of Emily, and I suppose it is hopeless to expect any liberation, so long as he can invent excuses to frustate it."

"I trust he does not abuse his power in any way, and annoy Miss Merton with importunities that are unpleasant to her."

Emily rewarded me for the warmth with which I spoke, with a sweet smile, and a slight blush.

"Of that I cannot accuse him, in one sense at least," resumed Major Merton. "Monsieur Le Compte does all for us that his sense of delicacy can suggest; and it was not possible for passengers to be more comfortable or retired on board ship, than we were in the Pauline. That vessel had a poop, and its cabin was given up entirely to our use. At Manilla I was permitted to go at large on a mere verbal assurance of returning, and on all other particulars we have been treated as well as circumstances would very well allow. Nevertheless, Emily is too young to admire a suitor of forty, too English to admire a foreigner, and too well-born to accept one who is merely a merchant sailor—I mean one who is nothing, and has nothing, but what his ship makes him or can give him."

I understood Major Merton's distinction; he saw a difference between the heir of Clawbonny, pursuing his adventures for the love of the sea, and a man who pursued the sea as an adventurer. It was not very delicately made, but it was pretty well, as coming from an European to an American—the latter being assumed, *ex gratiâ*, to be a being of an inferior order, morally, politically, physically, socially, and in every other sense but the pecuniary. Thank

Heaven! the American dollar is admitted, pennyweight for pennyweight, to a precedency immediately next to that of the metal dollar of Europe. It even goes before the paper thaler of Prussia.

"I can readily imagine Miss Merton would look higher than Captain Le Compte, for various reasons," I answered making a sort of acknowledgment for the distinction in my favor by bowing involuntarily, "and I should hope the gentleman would cease to be importunate as soon as convinced he cannot succeed."

"You do not know a Frenchman, Mr. Wallingford," rejoined Emily. "He is the hardest creature on earth to persuade into the notion that he is not adorable."

"I can hardly believe that this weakness extends as far as the sailors," said I, laughing. "At all events, you will be released the instant you reach France."

"Sooner too, I trust, Wallingford," resumed the father. "These Frenchmen can have their own way out here in the solitude of the Pacific, but once in the Atlantic I shall expect some British cruiser to pick us up, long ere we can reach France."

This was a reasonable expectation, and we conversed about it for some time. I shall not repeat all that passed, but the reader can have no difficulty in understanding that Major Merton and myself communicated to each other every fact that was likely to be of interest to men in our situation. When I thought it prudent to take my leave he walked some distance with me, holding his way to a point on the outer side of the island, where I could get a view of the wreck. Here he left me for the moment, while I proceeded along the beach, ruminating on all that had passed.

The process by which nature uses her materials to found islands in the midst of oceans like the Pacific, is a curious study. The insect that forms the coral rock must be an industrious little creature, as there is reason to think that some of the reefs that have become known to navigators within the last sixty or seventy years, have since been converted into islands bearing trees, by their labors. Should the work go on, a part of this vast sea will yet be converted

into a continent; and who knows but a railroad may yet
run across that portion of our globe, connecting America
with the Old World? I see that Captain Beechy, in his
voyage, speaks of a wreck that occurred in 1792, on a reef,
where in 1826 he found an island near three leagues long,
bearing tall trees. It would be a curious calculation to
ascertain, if one family of insects can make an island three
leagues long, in thirty-four years, how many families it
would take to make the grading of the railroad I have mentioned. Ten years since, I would not have ventured a hint
of this nature, for it might have set speculation in motion,
and been the instrument of robbing more widows and
orphans of their straitened means; but, Heaven be praised!
we have at length reached a period in the history of the country, when a man may venture on a speculation in the theory
of geography without incurring the risk of giving birth to
some wild—if not unprincipled—speculation in dollars and
cents.

As I drew near the outer shore of the island, opposite to
the wreck, I came unexpectedly on Marble. The poor fellow was seated on a raised projection of coral rock, with his
arms folded, and was in so thorough a brown study, that he
did not even hear my footsteps in approaching, though I
purposely trod heavily, in order to catch his ear. Unwilling
to disturb him, I stood gazing at the wreck myself, for some
little time, the place affording a much better view of it than
any other point from which it had met my eye. The French
had made far greater inroads upon their vessel, than the elements. She had struck to leeward of the island, and lay in
a spot where, indeed, it might take years to break her entirely up, in that placid sea. Most of her upper works, however, were gone; and I subsequently discovered that her
own carpenters had managed to get out even a portion of
her floor-timbers, leaving the fabric bound together by those
they left. Her lower masts were standing, but even her
lower yards had been worked up, in order to make something useful for the schooner. The beach, at no great distance, was still strewed with objects brought from the reef,
and which it had not yet been found necessary to use.

At length a movement of mine attracted Marble's attention, and he turned his head toward me. He seemed glad I had joined him, and expressed himself happy, also that he saw me alone.

"I have been generalizing a little on our condition, Miles," he said, "and look at it which end forward I may, I find it bad enough; almost enough to overcome me. I loved that ship, Mr. Wallingford, as much as some folks love their parents—of wife or children, I never had any—and the thought that she has fallen into the hands of a Frenchman, is too much for my natur'. Had it been Smudge, I could have borne up against it; but to haul down one's colors to a wrack, and a bloody French wrack, too, it is superhuman!"

"You must remember all the circumstances, Captain Marble, and you will find consolation. The ship was surprised, as we surprised the Lady of Nantes."

"That's just it—put that on a general principle, now, and where are you? Surprisers must n't be surprised. Had we set a quarter-watch, sir, it never could have happened; and nothing less than a quarter-watch should have been set in a strange haven. What mattered it, that it was an uninhabited island, and that the ship was land-locked and well moored, and the holding-ground was capital? It is all of no account when you come to look at the affair in the way of duty. Why, old Robbins, with his rivers in the ocean, would never have been caught in this miserable manner."

Then Marble fairly gave in, placed his two hard hands on his face, and I could see tears trickling from beneath them, as if water were squeezed from a stone.

"The chances of the sea, Captain Marble," I said, greatly shocked at such an exhibition, coming from such a quarter— "the chances of the sea are sometimes too much for the best sailors. We should look at this loss, as we look at the losses occasioned by a gale; then there is some hope left, after all."

"I should like to know what—to me there is no land ahead."

"Surprisers may not only be surprised, but they may

carry on their old trade again, and surprise once more, in their turn."

"What do you mean by that, Miles?" said Marble, looking up eagerly, and speaking as quick as lightning; "are you generalizing, or have you any particular project in view?"

"Both, sir. Generalizing, so far as taking the chances of war are concerned, and particularizing, as to a certain notion that has come into my head."

"Out with the last, Miles—out with it, boy; the Lord made you for something uncommon."

"First, let me know, Captain Marble, whether you have had any further conversation with Monsieur Le Compte? whether he has said any more on the subject of our future proceedings?"

"I just left the grinning rascal—those amiable smiles of his, Miles, are only so many grins thrown into our faces to let us feel his good luck; but, d——n him, if I ever get home, I'll fit out a privateer and be after him, if there's a fast-going schooner to be had in all America for love or money. I think I'd turn pirate to catch the villain!"

Alas! poor Marble. Little would he, who never got higher than a mate, unless by accident, be likely to persuade your cautious ship-owners to intrust him with a vessel of any sort, to go tilting against windmills afloat in that fashion.

"But why go to America for a schooner, Captain Marble, when the French are polite enough to give us one here, exactly where we are?"

"I begin to understand you, my boy. There is a little consolation in the idee, but this Frenchman has already got my commission, and without the document we should be no better than so many pirates."

"I doubt that, sir, even were a ship to act generally, provided she actually sailed with a commission, and lost it by accident. Commissions are all registered, and proof of our character could be found at home."

"Ay, for the Crisis, but not for this 'Pretty Polly';" for so Marble translated Petite Pauline. "The commission is only good for the vessel that is named in it."

"I don't know that, Captain Marble. Suppose our ship had been sunk in an action in which we took our enemy, could we not continue our voyage in the prize, and fight anything that came in our way afterward?"

"By George, that does look reasonable. Here was I just threatening to go out as a pirate, yet hesitating about taking my own."

"Do not the crews of captured vessels often rise upon their captors, and recapture their own vessels? and were any of them ever called pirates? Besides, nations at war authorize almost every sort of hostile act against their enemies."

"Miles, I have been mistaken—you are a good seaman, but natur' meant you for a lawyer! Give me your hand, boy; I see a gleam of hope ahead, and a man can live on less hope than food."

Marble then told me the substance of the conversation he had held with Captain Le Compte. The latter had expressed a sudden and violent impatience to be off. I understood the cause in a moment; he wished to separate Emily from her old acquaintance, as soon as possible, intending to put the schooner into the water for us that very afternoon, and to sail himself in the morning. This was a sudden resolution, and the French were moving heaven and earth to carry it into effect. I confess to some little regret at hearing it, for it was pleasant to meet the Mertons in that unexpected manner, and the influence of woman in such a solitude is unusually great. I now told Marble of my discovery, and, when he had got through with his expressions of wonder, I carried him to the tents, and led him into the presence of his old acquaintances. In consequence of this visit, I enjoyed another half hour's *tête-à-tête* with Emily, Marble soon taking the major to walk with him beneath the trees.

We were both recalled to a sense of our real situation by the reappearance of Monsieur Le Compte. I cannot say that our conqueror behaved in the least unhandsomely toward us, notwithstanding his evident jealousy. He had the tact to conceal most of his feelings, and owing either to liberality or to art, he assumed an air of generous confidence, that would be much more likely to touch the feelings of the maid he sought than any acts of severity. First asking permission of Miss Merton, he even invited us and himself to dine with the major, and on the whole we had an agreeable entertainment. We had turtle and champagne, and both of a quality that was then out of the reach of all the aldermen of London or New York ; begging pardon of the Sir Peters and Sir Johns of Guildhall, for putting them, in any sense, on a level with the "gentleman from the Fourth Ward" or the "gentleman from the Eleventh Ward" ; though, if the truth must be told, the last very often eat the best dinners, and drink, out of all comparison, the best wines. Who pays, is a fact buried in the arcana of aldermanic legerdemain. It was late before we left the table, though Monsieur Le Compte quitted us early.

At five o'clock precisely we were summoned to witness the launch. Champagne and claret had brought Marble into good-humor, nor was I at all out of spirits, myself. Emily put on her hat, and took her parasol, just as she would have done at home, and accepting my arm, she walked to the ship-yard, like all the rest of us. Getting her a good place for the sight, I accompanied Marble to take a look at the "Pretty Poll," which had not as yet attracted as much of our attention as she ought. I had suggested to him the probability of an occasion offering to rise upon the Frenchmen, while their attention was taken up by the schooner ; but Monsieur Le Compte warily kept quite half his men in the ship, and this put the attempt out of the question, since the guns of the Crisis would have swept any part of the island.

The French mechanics deserved great credit for the skill they had manifested in the construction of La Petite Pauline. She was not only a safe and commodious craft for her size, but, what was of great importance to us, her lines promised that she would turn out to be a fast sailer. I afterwards ascertained that Captain Le Compte had been her draftsman, possessing not only much taste for, but a good deal of practice in, the art. The ship in which the Mertons had taken passage to Bombay, had the copper for a teak-built frigate and sloop-of-war in her, and this had been transferred, among other articles, to La Pauline, before the prize was burned. Availing himself of this circumstance, Monsieur Le Compte had actually coppered his schooner, and otherwise he had made her as neat and commodious as possible. I make no doubt he intended to surprise his friends at Marseilles, by showing what clever mariners, wrecked on an island of the Pacific, could do on an emergency. Then, doubtless, he found it pleasant to linger on this island, eating fresh cocoa-nuts, with delicious turtle, and making love to Emily Merton. Some of the charms of " Pretty Poll " were fairly to be attributed to the charms of the young lady.

The men began to wedge up the moment we were all present, and this portion of the labor was soon completed. Monsieur Le Compte then took his station in the head of the schooner. Making a profound bow to Emily, as if to ask her permission, the signal was given ; the spur-shores were knocked away, and the little craft slid off into the water so easily, making so little ripple as she shot a hundred fathoms into the bay, as to give the assurance she would prove a fast vessel. Just as she was water-borne, Le Compte dashed a bottle against the tiller, and shouted at the top of his voice, " Succès à La Belle Emilie."

I turned to Emily, and saw by the blush that she understood French, while the manner in which she pouted her pretty plump lip betrayed the humor in which the compliment had been received.

In a few minutes Captain Le Compte landed, and, in a set speech, he gave up the schooner to our possession. We were told not to consider ourselves as prisoners, our captor handsomely admitting that he had gained no laurels by his victory.

" We shall go away good friend," he concluded, " mais, suppose we shall meet, and nos deux républiques shall not be at peace, then each must fight for son pavillon ! "

This was a good concluding sentiment for such a scene.

"Then Marble fairly gave in, placed his two hard hands on his face, and I could see tears trickling from beneath them as if water were squeezed from a stone." Captain Marble succumbs to despair at having been surprised aboard the *Crisis* by the French off a lonely South Pacific island. *Drawing by F. O. C. Darley.*   (*p. 264*)

Immediately after, the Mertons and their domestics, of whom there were a man and a woman, embarked. I took leave of them on the beach, and either my observation or my vanity induced me to think Emily got into the boat with reluctance. Many good wishes were exchanged, and the major called out to us, " We shall meet again, gentlemen— there has been a Providence in our previous intercourse. Adieu, until then."

The French were now in a great bustle. Most of the articles they intended to carry away were already on board the ship, and by the time it was dusk they had closed their communication with the land. When Captain Le Compte took his leave of us, I could not but thank him for his many civilities. He had certainly dealt generously by us, though I still think his sudden departure, which made us fall heirs to many things we otherwise might not have so done, was owing to his wish to remove Emily Merton, as quickly as possible, from my sight.

At daylight next morning, Neb came to the officers' tents to say the ship was getting her anchors. I was up and dressed in a moment. The distance to the inlet was about a mile, and I reached it just as the Crisis was cast. In a few minutes she came sweeping into the narrow pass, under her topsails, and I saw Emily and her father leaning over the hammock-cloths of the quarter-deck. The beautiful girl was so near that I could read the expression of her soft eyes, and I fancied they were filled with gentle concern. The major called out, " God bless you, dear Wallingford ! " then the ship swept past, and was soon in the outer bay. Half an hour later, or before I left the spot, she was at sea, under everything that would draw from her trucks down.

CHAPTER XVII.

"I better brook the loss of brittle life,
Than those proud titles thou hast won of me;
They wound my thoughts, worse than thy sword my flesh."
SHAKESPEARE.

HALF-WAY between this inlet and the ship-yard I found Marble, standing with his arms folded, gazing after the receding ship. His countenance was no longer saddened; but it was fierce. He shook his hand menacingly at the French ensign, which was flying at our old gaff, and said,—"Ay, d——n you, flutter away; you quiver and shake now like one of your coxcombs pigeon-winging; but where will you be this day two months? Miles, no man but a bloody Frenchman would cast away a ship there, where this Mister Count has left the bones of his vessel; though here, where we came so nigh going, it's a miracle any man could escape. Had n't we brought the Crisis through that opening first, he never would have dared to go out by it."

I confess I saw little about Monsieur Le Compte's management but skill and good seamanship; but nothing is more painful to most men than to admit the merit of those who have obtained an advantage over them. Marble could not forget his own defeat, and the recollection jaundiced his eyes and biased his judgment.

"I see our people are busy already, sir," I remarked, by way of drawing the captain's attention to some other subject. "They have hauled the schooner up to the yard, and seem to be getting along spars for shores."

"Ay, ay; Talcott has his orders, and I expect you will

bestir yourself. I shall step the masts myself, and you will get all the rigging ready to be put into its place, the moment it is possible. That Frenchman calculated, he told me to my face, that we might get to sea in a fortnight; I will let him see that a set of Yankees can rig and stow his bloody schooner in three days, and then leave themselves time to play."

Marble was not a man of idle vaunts. He soon had everybody at work, with a system, order, silence, and activity, that proved he was master of his profession. Nor was the language which might sound so boastful to foreign ears, altogether without its justification. Forty Americans were a formidable force; and, well directed, I make no doubt they would accomplish far more than the ordinary run of French seamen, as they were governed and managed in the year 1800, and counting them man for man, would have accomplished in double the time. Our crew had now long acted together, and frequently under the most trying circumstances; and they showed their training, if men ever did, on the present occasion. Everybody was busy; and we had the shears up, and both masts stepped, in the course of a few hours. By the time the mainmast was in, I had the foremast rigged, the jib-boom in its place, the spritsail yard crossed—everything carried a spar under its bowsprit then— and the lower yard up. It is true, the French had got every- thing ready for us; and when we turned the hands to, after dinner, we actually began to strike in cargo, water, pro- visions, and such other things as it was intended to carry away. At dusk, when we knocked off work, the Emily looked like a sea-going craft, and there was every prospect of our having her ready for sea by the following evening. But the duty had been carried on in silence. Napoleon said there had been more noise made in the little schooner which carried him from L'Orient to Basque Roads, than was made on board the line-of-battle ship that conveyed him to St. Helena, during the whole passage. Since that memorable day, the French have learned to be silent on board ship, and the fruits remain to be seen.

That night, Marble and myself consulted together on the

aspect of things—or, as he expressed it, "we generalized over our prospects." Monsieur Le Compte had done one thing which duty required of him. He did not leave us a kernel of the gunpowder belonging to either ship; nor could we find a boarding-pike, cutlass, or weapon of any sort, except the officers' pistols. We had a canister of powder, and a sufficiency of bullets for the last, which had been left us, out of an *esprit de corps*, or the feelings of an officer which told him he might possibly need these means to keep our own crew in order. Such was not the fact, however, with the particular people we happened to have; a more orderly and reasonable set of men never sailing together. But Monsieur Le Compte knew it was his duty to put it out of their power to trouble us, so far as it lay in his; but, at the same time, while he left us the means of safety, he provided against our doing any further injury to his own countrymen. In this he had pretty effectually succeeded, so far as armament was concerned.

The next morning I was up with the appearance of the dawn, and, having suffered much from the heat the preceding day, I walked to a suitable spot, threw off my clothes, and plunged into the basin. The water was transparent almost as air; and I happened to select a place where the coral grew within a few yards of the surface. As I dove, my eye fell on a considerable cluster of large oysters that were collected on the rock, and, reaching them, I succeeded in bringing up half a dozen that clung to each other. These dives I repeated, during the next quarter of an hour, until I had all the oysters, sixty or eighty in number, safe on the shore. That they were the pearl oysters, I knew immediately; and beckoning to Neb, the fellow soon had them snug in a basket, and put away in a place of security. The circumstance was mentioned to Marble, who, finding no more heavy drags to be made, ordered the Sandwich Islanders to take a boat and pass a few hours in their regular occupation, on account of the owners—if, indeed, the last had any further claim on our services. These men met with tolerable success, though, relatively, nothing equal to mine. What, just then, was of far more importance, they made a discovery of an arm-chest lying on the bottom of the basin, at the anchorage of the Crisis, and which had doubtless been sunk there by the French. We had all La Pauline's boats but the captain's gig. I went in one of them with a gang of hands, and, the divers securing a rope to the handles of the chest, we soon got it in. It turned out to be one of the arm-chests of the Crisis, which the French had found in their way and thrown overboard, evidently preferring to use weapons to which they were accustomed. They had done better by carrying the chest out to sea, and disposing of it in fifty or a hundred fathoms of water.

The prize was turned over to the gunner, who reported that it was the chest in which we kept our cutlasses and pistols, of both of which there was a sufficient supply to give every man one of each. There were also several horns of powder, and a bag of bullets; but the first was ruined by the water. As for the arms, they were rubbed dry, oiled, and put away again in the chest, after the last had stood a whole day in the hct sun open. Thus, through the agency of men brought for a very different purpose, we were put in possession of the means of achieving the exploit, which might now be said to form the great object of our lives.

That day we got everything on board the schooner that it was thought desirable to take with us. We left much behind that was valuable, it is true, especially the copper; but Marble wisely determined that it was inexpedient to put the vessel deeper than good ballast-trim, lest it should hurt her sailing. We had got her fairly to her bearings, and this was believed to be as low as was expedient. It is true, a great deal remained to be stowed; the deck being littered, and the hold, the ground tier excepted, in great confusion. But our bread, water, beef, pork, and other eatables, were all there, and in abundance; and, though not to be had for the asking, they were still to be had. The sails were bent, and the only anchor, La Pauline's stream, with her two largest kedges, was on our bows. While in this condition, Marble gave the unexpected order for all

18

hands to come on board, and for the shore-fasts to be cast off.

Of course, there was no dissenting to so positive a command. We had signed new shipping-articles for the schooner, extending the engagements made when we entered on board the Crisis, to this new vessel, or any other she might capture. The wind was a steady trade, and when we showed our mainsail and jib to it, the little craft glided athwart the basin like a duck. Shooting through the pass, Marble tacked her twice, as soon as he had an offing ; and everybody was delighted with the quickness with which she was worked. There was barely light enough to enable us to find our way through the opening in the reef ; and just thirty-eight hours after the Crisis sailed, we were on her track. We had only conjecture to guide us as to the ship's course, with the exception of the main fact of her having sailed for the west coast of South America ; but we had not failed to notice that she disappeared in the northeast trades, on a bowline. We put the schooner as near as possible on the same course, making a proper allowance for the difference in the rig of the two vessels.

The distance run that night satisfied us all that Monsieur Le Compte was a good draftsman. The schooner ran 106 miles in twelve hours, against a very respectable sea, which was at least ten or fifteen more than the Crisis could have done under the same circumstances. It is true, that what was close-hauled for her, was not close-hauled for us ; and, in this respect, we had the advantage of her. Marble was so well pleased with our night's work, that when he came on deck next morning, the first thing he did was to order a bottle of rum to be brought him, and then all hands to be called. As soon as the people were up, he went forward, got into the head, and commanded everybody to muster on the forecastle. Marble now made a speech.

" We have some good, and some bad luck this v'y'ge, men," he said ; " and when we generalize on the subject, it will be found that good luck has usually followed the

bad luck. Now, the savages, with that blackguard
Smudge, knocked poor Captain Williams in the head, and
threw him overboard, and got the ship from us; then
came the good luck of getting her back again. After this,
the French did us that unhandsome thing; now, here
comes the good luck of their leaving us a craft that will
overhaul the ship, when I need n't tell you what will come
of it." Here all hands, as in duty bound, gave three
cheers. "Now, I neither sail nor fight in a craft that
carries a French name. Captain Count christened the
schooner the—Mr. Wallingford, will you tell her exact
name?"

"La Belle Emilie," said I, "or the Beautiful Emily."

"None of your belles for me, nor your Beautiful Emilys
either," cried Marble, smashing the bottle over the schooner's
nose; "so here goes three cheers again, for the 'Pretty
Poll,' which was the name the craft was born to, and the
name she shall bear, as long as Moses Marble sails her."

From that moment, the schooner was known by the name
of the "Pretty Poll." I met with portions of our crew
years afterward, and they always spoke of her by this appellation; sometimes familiarly terming her the "Poll," or the
"Polly."

All the first day out, we were busy in making ourselves
comfortable, and in getting the Polly's trim. We succeeded
so well in this last, that, according to our calculations, we
made a knot an hour more than the Crisis could have done
under the same circumstances, fast as the ship was known
to be. As the Crisis had about thirty-eight hours the start
of us, and ran, on an average, about seven knots the hour
for all that time, it would require about ten days to overtake
her. Of course this could only happen, according to our own
calculations, when we were from eighteen hundred to two
thousand miles from the island. For my own part, I sincerely hoped it would not occur at all, at sea; feeling satisfied our only chances of success depended on surprise. By
following the vessel into some port, it might be possible to
succeed; but for an unarmed schooner to attack a ship like
the Crisis, with even a large crew on board, it seemed rash-

ness to think of it. Marble, however, would not listen to my remonstrances. He insisted we had more than powder enough to load all our pistols half a dozen times each, and, laying the ship plump aboard, the pistols would do the rest. I was silenced, quite as a matter of course, if not convinced.

The fifth day out, Neb came to me, saying, "Master Miles, somet'ing must be done wid 'em 'ere 'ysters! Dey smell onaccountable; and de people swear they will t'row 'em overboard, if I don't eat 'em. I not hungry enough for dat, sir."

These were the pearl oysters, already mentioned, which had been hastening to dissolution and decomposition, by the heat of the hold. As the captain was as much concerned in this portion of the cargo, as I was myself, I communicated the state of things to him, and he ordered the bags and barrels on deck, forthwith. It was well something was done, or I doubt not a disease would have been the consequence. As decomposition was the usual process by which to come at the treasures of these animals, however, everything was exactly in the state we wished.

An uninterested observer would have laughed at seeing the employment on the quarter-deck for the next four hours. Marble, and two mates, attacked a barrel belonging to the captain, while Neb and I had my own share to ourselves. It was a trying occupation, the odor far exceeding in strength that of the Spice Islands. We stood it, however— for what will not man endure for the sake of riches? Marble foresaw the difficulties, and had once announced to the mates that they then would "open on shares." This had a solacing influence, and amid much mirth and sundry grimaces, the work went on with tolerable rapidity. I observed, however, that Talcott threw one or two subjects, that doubtless were tougher than common, overboard, after very superficial examinations.

The first seven oysters I examined contained nothing but seed pearl, and not many of these. Neb opened, and I examined; and the latter occupation was so little to my taste, that I was just on the point of ordering the whole lot thrown overboard, when Neb handed me another. This oyster contained nine beautiful pearls, of very uniform dimensions, and each about as large as a good-sized pea. I dropped them into a bowl of fresh water, whence they came out sweet, pearly, and lustrous. They were of the sort known as the "white water," which is the kind most prized among Christian nations, doubtless on account of their harmonizing so well with the skins of their women. No sooner was my luck known, than it brought all the other "pearl fishermen" around me; Marble, with his nostrils plugged with oakum, and a quid of tobacco in his mouth, that was as large as a small potato.

"By George, Miles, that looks like business," the captain exclaimed, going back to his work, with renovated zeal, "though it is a calling fit only for hogs and scavengers! Did I embark in it largely, I would keep as many clerks as a bank. What do you suppose, now, these nine chaps may be worth?"

"Some fifty dollars, or thereabouts; you see, sir, they are quite large—much larger than it is usual to see our women wear."

The ninth of my oysters produced eleven pearls, and all about the size and quality of the first. In a few minutes I had seventy-three just such pearls, besides a quantity of seed pearl. Then followed a succession of barren shells; a dozen not giving a pearl. The three that succeeded them gave thirty-one more; and another yielded four pearls, each of which was as large as a small cherry. After that, I got one that was almost as large as a common hickory-nut, and six more of the size of the cherry-sized pearls. In addition to these, I got in all, one hundred and eighty-seven of the size of peas, besides a large handful of the seed pearl. I afterward ascertained that the pearls I had thus obtained were worth in the market about eighteen hundred dollars; as they were far more remarkable for their beauty than for their size.

Notwithstanding the oakum plugs, and the tobacco, and the great number of shells his divers had found, for they had brought up something like two hundred and fifty oysters in the course of a day, the party of the captain found, in all, but thirty-six pearls, the seed excepted, though they obtained some beautiful specimens among the shells. From that moment Marble discontinued the trade, and I never heard him say anything more on the subject of pursuing it. My own beauties were put carefully away, in reserve for the time when I might delight the eyes of certain of my female friends with them. I never intended to sell one, but they were very precious to me on other accounts. As for the crew, glad enough were they to be rid of such uncomfortable shipmates. As I gazed on the spotless and lustrous pearls, and compared them with the revolting tenements from which they had just been redeemed, I likened them to the souls of the just escaping from their tenements of clay, to enjoy hereafter an endless existence of purity.

In the meantime, the Pretty Poll continued to find her way along miles and miles of the deserted track across the Pacific. Marble had once belonged to a Baltimore clipper, and he sailed our craft probably much better than she would have been sailed by Monsieur Le Compte, though that officer, as I afterwards learned, had distinguished himself in command of a lugger-privateer, in the British Channel. Our progress was generally from a hundred and fifty to two hundred and twenty miles in twenty-four hours; and so it continued to be for the first ten days, or the period, when, according to our own calculations, we ought to be near the Crisis had that vessel steered a course resembling our own. For my own part, I neither wished nor expected to see the ship, until we reached the coast of South America, when we might ascertain her position by communicating with the shore. As for the guarda-costas, I knew we could easily elude them, and there might be a small chance of regaining the vessel, something like the way in which we had lost her. But Marble's impatience, and the keenness with which he felt our disgrace, would not make terms even with the elements; and I do believe he would have run alongside of the Crisis in a gale of wind, could he have come up with her. The chance of our having sailed so far, however, on a line so nearly resembling that of the chase as to bring us together, was so very small, that few of us thought it worth our consideration.

On the morning of the eleventh day, the lookout we had kept on the fore-topsail-yard, sang out " Sail ho ! " Marble and myself were soon on the yard, there being nothing visible from the deck. The upper sails, topgallant-sails and royals, of the ship were visible on our weather quarter, distant from fifteen to twenty miles. As we were now in the track of whalers, of which there were a good many in that part of the Pacific, I thought it was probable this was one ; but Marble laughed at the notion, asking if I had ever heard of a whaler's carrying royals on her cruising ground. He affirmed it was the Crisis, heading the same way we were ourselves, and which had only got to windward of us, by keeping a better luff. We had calculated too much on the schooner's weatherly qualities, and had allowed her to fall off more than was necessary, in the night-watches.

The Pretty Poll was now jammed up on a wind, in the hope of closing with the chase in the course of the night. But the wind had been growing lighter and lighter for some hours, and by noon, though we had neared the chase so much as to be able to see her from deck, there was every prospect of its falling calm ; after which, in the trades, it would be surprising if we did not get a blow. To make the most of our time, Marble determined to tack, when we had just got the chase a point off our weather bow. An hour after tacking, an object was seen adrift on the ocean, and keeping away a little to close with it, it was ascertained to be a whale-boat adrift. The boat was American-built, had a breaker of water, the oars, and all the usual fittings in it ; and the painter being loose, it had probably been lost, when towing in the night, in consequence of having been fastened by three half-hitches.

The moment Marble ascertained the condition of this boat, he conceived his plan of operations. The four Sandwich Islanders had been in whalers, and he ordered them into the boat, put in some rum and some food, gave me his orders, got in himself, and pulled ahead, going off at five knots the hour, leaving the schooner to follow at the rate of two. This was about an hour before sunset, and by the time it was dark, the boat had become a mere speck on the water, nearly half-way between us and the ship, which was now some fifteen miles distant, heading always in the same direction.

My orders had been very simple. They were, to stand on the same course until I saw a light from the boat, and then tack so as to run on a parallel line with the ship. The signal was made by Marble about nine o'clock. It was immediately answered from the schooner. The light in the boat was concealed from the ship, and our own was shown only for a few seconds, the disappearance of Mr. Marble's telling us in that brief space that our answer was noted. I tacked immediately, and taking in the foresail stood on the directed course. We had all foreseen a change in the weather, and probably a thunder-squall. So far from its giving Marble any uneasiness, he anticipated the blow with pleasure, as he intended to lay the Crisis aboard in its height. He fancied that success would then be the most certain. His whole concern was at not being able to find the ship in the darkness, and it was to obviate this difficulty that he undertook to pilot us up to her in the manner I have just mentioned.

After getting round, a sharp lookout was kept for the light. We caught another view of it directly on our weather-beam. From this we inferred that the ship had more wind than we felt, inasmuch as she had materially altered her position, while we had not moved a mile since we tacked. This was on the supposition that Marble would endeavor to follow the movements of the ship. At ten the tempest broke upon us with tropical violence, and with a suddenness that took everybody by surprise. A squall had been expected, but no one anticipated its approach for several hours, and we had all looked for the return of the whale-boat ere that moment should come. But come it did when least expected, the first puff throwing our little schooner down in a way to convince us the elements were in earnest. In fifteen minutes after the first blast was felt I had the schooner under a reefed foresail, and with that short canvas

there were instants, as she struggled up to the summit of
the waves, that it seemed as if she were about to fly out of
the water. My great concern, however, was for the boat,
of which nothing could now be seen. The orders left by
Marble anticipated no such occurrence as this tempest, and
the concert between us was interrupted. It was naturally
inferred among us, in the schooner, that the boat would
endeavor to close as soon as the danger was foreseen;
and as this would probably be done by running on a con-
verging line, all our efforts were directed to keeping the
schooner astern of the other party, in order that they might
first reach the point of junction. In this manner there was
a chance of Marble's finding the schooner, while there was
little of our finding the boat. It is true we carried several
lights, but as soon as it began to rain even a bonfire would
not have been seen at a hundred yards. The water poured
down upon us, as if it fell from spouts, occasionally ceasing
and then returning in streams.

I had then never passed so miserable a night; even that
in which Smudge and his fellows murdered Captain Williams and seized the ship, being happiness in comparison.
I loved Marble. Hardy, loose in some respects, and unnur-
tured as he was in others, the man had been steadily my
friend. He was a capital seaman, a sort of an instinctive
navigator, true as the needle to the flag, and as brave as a
lion. Then I knew he was in his present strait on account
of mortified feeling, and the rigid notions he entertained of
his duty to his owners. I think I do myself no more than
justice, when I say that I would gladly have exchanged
places with him any time that night.

We held a consultation on the quarter-deck, and it was
determined that our only chance of picking up the boat was
by remaining as nearly as possible at the place where her
crew must have last seen the schooner. Marble had a
right to expect this, and we did all that lay in our power to
effect the object, wearing often, and gaining on our tacks
what we lost in coming round. In this manner we passed
a painful and most uncomfortable night; the winds howling
about us a sort of requiem for the dead, while we hardly

knew when we were wallowing in the seas or not, there being so much water that came down from the clouds, as nearly to drown us on deck.

At last the light returned, and soon after the tempest broke, appearing to have expended its fury. An hour after the sun had risen, we got the trade-wind again, the sea became regular once more, and the schooner was under all her canvas. Of course, every one of us officers was aloft, some forward, some aft, to look out for the boat; but we did not see her again. What was still more extraordinary, nothing could be seen of the ship! We kept all that day cruising around the place, expecting to find at least the boat; but without success.

My situation was now altogether novel to me. I had left home rather more than a twelvemonth before, the third officer of the Crisis. From this station, I had risen regularly to be her first officer; and now, by a dire catastrophe, I found myself in the Pacific, solely charged with the fortunes of my owners, and those of some forty human beings. And this, too, before I was quite twenty years old.

Marble's scheme of attacking the ship had always seemed to me to be wild and impracticable. This was while it was his project, not my own. I still entertained the same opinion, as regards the assault at sea; but I had, from the first, regarded an attempt on the coast as a thing much more likely to succeed. Then Emily, and her father, and the honor of the flag, and the credit I might personally gain, had their influence; and, at sunset, all hope of finding the boat being gone, I ordered sail made on our course.

The loss of the whale-boat occurred when we were about two thousand miles from the western coast of South America. We had a long road before us, consequently; and, as I had doubted whether the ship we had seen was the Crisis, it was necessary to be in motion, if anything was to be effected with our old enemies. The reader may feel some desire to know in what manner my succession to the command was received by the people. No man could have been more implicitly obeyed. I was now six feet and an inch in height, of a powerful and active frame, a good sea-

man, and had the habit of command, through a twelvemonth's experience. The crew knew me, having seen me
tried, from the weather-earings down; and it is very likely
I possessed more of their confidence than I deserved. At
all events, I was as implicitly obeyed as if I had sailed from
New York at their head. Everybody regretted Marble;
more, I think, than we regretted poor Captain Williams,
though it must have been on account of the manner we saw
him disappear, as it might be, from before our eyes; since,
of the two, I think the last was the most estimable man.
Nevertheless, Marble had his strong points, and they were
points likely to take with seamen; and they had particularly
taken with us. As for the four Sandwich Islanders, I do
not know that they occupied any of our minds at all. We
had been accustomed to regard them as strange beings, who
came from that ocean to which they had thus suddenly
returned.

Fifteen days after the loss of the whale-boat, we made the
peaks of the Andes, a very few degrees to the southward
of the equator. From some casual remarks made by the
French, and which I had overheard, I had been led to believe they intended to run for Guayaquil, or its vicinity; and
I aimed at reaching the coast near the same point. We
had been in, ourselves, at several bays and roadsteads, moreover, on this part of the shore, on our way north; and I
felt at home among them. We had acquaintances, too, who
could not fail to be of use to us; and everything conspired
to render this an advantageous landfall.

On the evening of the twenty-ninth day after quitting
the island, we took the schooner into an open roadstead,
where we had carried on some extensive traffic in the ship,
about eight months before, and where I fancied we should
still be recognized. As was expected, we had scarcely
anchored, before a Don Pedro Something, a fellow with a
surprising string of names, came off to us in a boat, in order
to ascertain who we were, and what we wanted. Perhaps
it would be better to say, what we had that he wanted. I
knew the man at a glance, having delivered to him, myself,
three boat-loads of goods, and received a small bag of doub-

loons in exchange. A very few words, half English, half Spanish, served to renew our acquaintance; and I gave our old friend to understand that I was in search of the ship, from which I had been separated on some extra duty. After beating around the bush to discover all he could, the Don Pedro gave me to understand that a ship had gone in behind an island that was only ten miles to the southward of us, that very afternoon; that he had seen her himself, and had supposed she might be his old friend the Crisis, until he saw the French ensign at her gaff. This was sufficient, and I made inquiries for a pilot. A man qualified to carry us to the place was found in one of the boatmen. As I feared the news of the arrival of a schooner might be carried to the ship, much as we had got our intelligence, no time was lost, but we were under way by ten o'clock. At midnight we entered the pass between the main and the island; there I got into a boat, and pulled ahead, in order to reconnoitre. I found the ship lying close under a high bluff, which made a capital lee, and with every sign about her of tranquillity. Still, I knew a vessel that was always in danger from the guarda-costas, and which relied on the celerity of its movements for its safety, would have a vigilant lookout. Accordingly, I took a cool and careful examination of the ship's position, landing and ascending the bluff, in order to do this at my ease. About two o'clock in the morning, I returned to the schooner.

When I put my foot on the Polly's deck again, she was quite near the point, or bluff, having set down toward it during my absence. All hands were on deck, armed, and in readiness. Expectation had got to be so keen, that we had a little difficulty in keeping the men from cheering; but silence was preserved, and I communicated the result of my observations in as few words as possible. The orders were then given, and the schooner was brought under short sail, for the attack. We were so near our side of the bluff, while the ship lay so near the other, that my principal apprehension was of falling to leeward, which might give the French time to muster, and recollect themselves. The canvas, accordingly, was reduced to the foresail, though the jib, mainsail, and topsail, were all loose, in readiness to be set, if wanted. The plan was to run the ship aboard, on her starboard bow, or off-side, as respected the island; and to do this with as little of a shock as possible.

When everything was ready, I went aft, stood by the man at the helm, and ordered him to bear up. Neb placed himself just behind me. I knew it was useless to interfere, and let the fellow do as he pleased. The pilot had told me the water was deep, up to the rocks of the bluff; and we hugged the land as close as possible, in rounding the point. At the next moment the ship was in sight, distant less than a hundred fathoms. I saw we had good way, and, three minutes later, I ordered the foresail brailed. At the same instant I walked forward. So near were we, that the flapping of the canvas was heard in the ship, and we got a hail.

A mystified answer followed, and then crash came our bows along those of the Crisis. "Hurrah! for the old craft!" shouted our men, and aboard we tumbled in a body. Our charge was like the plunge of a pack of hounds as they leap through a hedge.

The scene that followed was one of wild tumult. Some twenty pistols were fired, and a good many hard blows were struck; but the surprise secured us the victory. In less than three minutes, Talcott came to report to me that our lads had complete possession of the deck, and that the French asked for quarter. At first, the enemy supposed they had been seized by a guarda-costa, for the impression had been general among them that we intended to quit the island for Canton. Great was the astonishment among them when the truth came to be known. I heard a great many "*sacr-r-r-es!*" and certain other maledictions in low French, that it is scarcely worth while to repeat.

Harris, one of the Philadelphians, and the man who had got us into the difficulty by falling asleep on his watch, was killed; and no less than nine of our men, myself among the number, were hurt in this brisk business. All the wounds, however, were slight; only three of the injuries taking the parties off duty. As for the poor fellow who fell, he owed his death to risking too much, in order to recover the ground he had lost.

The French fared much worse than ourselves. Of those killed outright, and those who died before morning, there were no less than sixteen; our fellows having fired a volley into a group that was rushing on deck, besides using their cutlasses with great severity for the first minute or two. This was on the principle that the first blow was half the battle. There were few wounded; most of those who fell being cut or thrust at by several at the same time—a species of attack that left little chance for escape. Poor Monsieur Le Compte was found stone-dead at the cabin doors, having been shot in the forehead, just as he put his foot on the deck. I heard his voice once in the fray, and feared it boded no good; but the silence which succeeded was probably caused by his just then receiving the fatal bullet. He was in his shirt.

CHAPTER XVIII.

" *1st. Witch.* Hail !
2d. Witch. Hail !
3d. Witch. Hail !
1st. Witch. Lesser than Macbeth, and greater.
2d. Witch. Not so happy, yet much happier."

Macbeth.

I HOPE I shall be believed in saying, if Marble had been with us when we retook the ship, I should have been perfectly happy. He was not, however, and regret was left to mingle in our triumph. I had a hasty interview with Major Merton that night, and communicated all that was necessary to quiet the apprehensions of his daughter. Emily was in her state-room, and had been alarmed, as a matter of course ; but when she learned that all was over, and had terminated successfully, her fears yielded to reason. Of course, both she and her father felt it to be a great relief that they were no longer prisoners.

We were no sooner fairly in command of our old ship again, than I had all hands called to get the anchor. We hove up, and passed out to sea without delay, it being necessary to cover our movements with as much mystery as possible, in order to prevent certain awkward demands from the Spanish government, on the subject of the violation of neutral territory. A hint from Major Merton put me on my guard as respected this point, and I determined to disappear as suddenly as we had arrived, in order to throw obstacles in the way of being traced. By daylight, therefore, both the ship and schooner were four leagues from the land, and on the " great highway of nations"; a road, it may be said in passing, that was then greatly infested by foot-pads and other robbers.

Just as the sun rose, we buried the dead. This was done decently, and with the usual ceremony, the triumph of victory giving place to the sad reflections that are so apt to succeed to the excited feelings of most of our struggles. I saw poor Le Compte disappear from sight with regret, and remembered his recent hopes, his generous treatment, his admiration of Emily, and all that he had so lately thought and felt, as a warning of the fragile nature of life, and that which life can bestow. Thus terminated an acquaintance of a month ; but a month that had been pregnant with incidents of great importance to myself.

It now became necessary to decide on our future course. I had the ship, just as the French got her from us, with the addition of those portions of their own cargo with which they had intended to trade on the coast of South America. These consisted of silks and various fancy articles, with a little wine, and would be nearly as valuable at home as they were in Spanish America. I was strongly averse to smuggling, and the ship having already followed out her original instructions on this point, I saw no necessity for pursuing the ungrateful trade any further. Could I return to the island, and get the articles of value left on it by the French, such as the copper they had not used, and divers bales received from the Bombay ship, which had been abandoned by us all under a tent, more profit would accrue to my owners than by any illicit commerce we could now possibly carry into effect on the coast.

While Talcott, and the new chief mate, and myself were discussing these points, the cry of "Sail ho!" was heard. A large ship had suddenly hove up out of the morning's mist, within a mile of us, and I thought at first we had got under the guns of a Spanish man-of-war. A second look at her, however, satisfied us all that, though heavy and armed, she was merely one of those clumsy traders that sailed periodically from the colonies to Spain. We went to quarters, and cleared ship, but made no effort to avoid the stranger. The Spaniards, of the two, were the most uneasy,

I believe, their country being then at war with England;
but we spoke each other without coming to blows. As
soon as the strangers saw the American ensign, they expressed a wish to communicate with us ; and, unwilling to
let them come on board us, I volunteered a visit to the
Spanish captain. He received me with formal politeness,
and, after some preliminary discourse, he put into my hands
some American newspapers, which contained a copy of the
treaty of peace between the United States and France. On
looking over the articles of this new compact, I found that
had our recapture of the Crisis been delayed to that very
day, at noon, it would have been illegal. The two nations,
in fact, were at peace when the French seized the ship, but
the customary provisions as to captures in distant seas, just
brought us within the saving clauses. Such is war, and its
concomitants !

In the course of half an hour's conversation, I discovered
that the Spaniard intended to touch at Valparaiso, and
called, in order to get men, his own having suffered, up the
coast, with the small-pox. His ship was large, carried a
considerable armament, and he should not deem her safe
from the smaller English cruisers, unless he doubled the
Cape much stronger handed than he then was. I caught at
the idea, and inquired what he thought of Frenchmen ?
They would answer his purpose, for France and Spain had
a common enemy, and nothing would be easier than to send
the French from Cadiz to Marseilles. A bargain was consequently struck on the spot.

When I got back on board the Crisis, I had all the
prisoners mustered on deck. They were made acquainted
with the offers of the Spanish captain, with the fact that
peace now existed between our respective countries, and
with the chance that presented itself, so opportunely, for
them to return home. The proposition was cheerfully accepted, anything being better than captivity. Before parting, I endeavored to impress on the French the necessity
of prudence on the subject of our recapturing the Crisis in
Spanish waters, inasmuch as the circumstance might induce
an inquiry as to what took the ship there ; it being well

19

understood that the mines were the punishment of those who were taken in the contraband trade in that quarter of the world. The French promised fairly. Whether they kept their words I never knew, but, if they did not, no consequences ever followed from their revelations. In such a case, indeed, the Spanish government would be very apt to consider the question one that touched the interests of smugglers alike, and to feel great indifference between the parties. At all events, no complaints were ever made to the American government; or, if made, they never reached my ears, or those of my owners. It is most probable nothing was ever said on the subject.

About noon we had got rid of our prisoners. They were allowed to take away with them all their own effects, and, as usually happens in such cases, I make little doubt some that belonged to other persons. The ships then made sail, each on her own course; the Spaniard running down the coast, while we spread our studding-sails for the island. As soon as this was done, I felt relieved from a great burden, and had leisure to think of other matters. I ought to mention, however, that I put the second mate, or him who had become chief mate by my own advancement, in command of the "Pretty Poll," giving him two experienced seamen as his own mates, and six men, to sail her. This made Talcott the Crisis' first officer, and glad was I to see him in a station a little suited to his attainments.

That evening, just as the sun was setting, I saw Emily again, for the first time since she had stood leaning over the rail as the Crisis shot through the inlet of the lagoon. The poor girl was pale, and it was evident, while she could not but rejoice at her liberation, and her release from the solicitations of the unfortunate Le Compte, that his death had cast a shade of sadness over her pretty features. It could not well be otherwise, the female breast ever entertaining its sympathies for those who submit to the influence of its owner's charms. Then, poor Le Compte had some excellent qualities, and he treated Emily, as she admitted to me herself, with the profoundest respect and delicacy. His admiration could scarce be an offence in her eyes, however disagreeable it proved, in certain points of view.

Our meeting partook of the character of our situation, being a mixture of melancholy and happiness. I rejoiced in our success, while I regretted Marble, and even our late enemies, while the major and his daughter could not but remember all the gloomy particulars of their late, and, indeed, of their present position.

"We seem to be kept like Mahomet's coffin, sir," Emily observed, as she looked affectionately at her father, "suspended between heaven and earth—the Indies and America —not knowing on which we are to alight. The Pacific is our air, and we are likely to breathe it, to our heart's content."

"True, love; your comparison is not an unhappy one. But, Wallingford, what has become of Captain Marble in these stirring times? You have not left him, Sancho Panza like, to govern Barataria, while you have come to recover his ship?"

I told my passengers of the manner in which our old friend had disappeared, and inquired if anything had been seen of the whale-boat, or the schooner, on the night of the tropical tempest.

"Nothing," answered the major. "So far from expecting to lay eyes on the 'Beautiful Emily,' again, we supposed you would be off for Canton by the end of the fortnight that succeeded our own departure. At least, that was poor Le Compte's version of the matter. I am certain, however, that no sail was seen from this ship, during the whole passage; nor had we any storm like that you have described. More beautiful weather, I never met at sea."

Upon this, I sent for the log-book, and ascertained, by day and date, that the Crisis was not within fifty leagues of the spot where we encountered the thunder-squall. Of course the ship we saw was a stranger; most probably a whaler. This destroyed any little hope that was left concerning Marble's fate.

But it is time that I should mention a *galanterie* of poor Le Compte's. He was well provided with shipwrights—

better, indeed, than with seamen—as was apparent by the readiness with which he had constructed the schooner. During the passage from Marble Land, he had set these workmen about building a poop on the Crisis' quarter-deck, and I found the work completed. There was a very pretty, airy cabin, with two state-rooms communicating with light quarter-galleries, and everything that is customary with such accommodations. Furniture had been made, with French dexterity and taste, and the paint was just dry to receive it. Emily and her father were to take possession of these new accommodations the very day succeeding that in which the ship fell again into our hands. This alteration was not such as I would have made, as a seaman ; and I wonder Monsieur Le Compte, who had the gauntlet to run through the most formidable navy in the world, should have ventured on it, since it sensibly affected the ship's sailing on a wind. But, now it was peace, I cared little about it, and determined to let it remain, so long, at least, as Miss Merton continued on board.

That very night, therefore, the major occupied one of the state-rooms, and his daughter the other. Imitating poor Le Compte's gallantry, I gave them a separate table, though I took quite half my meals with them, by invitation. Emily did not absolutely dress my wound, a flesh injury in the shoulder, that office falling to her father's share, who had seen a good deal of service, and was familiar with the general treatment of hurts of this nature ; but she could, and did, show many of those gentle and seductive attentions, that the tenderness of her sex can alone bestow, with full effect, on man. In a fortnight my hurt was cured, though Emily had specifics to recommend, and advice to bestow, until we were both ashamed to allude to the subject any longer.

As for the passage, it was just such a one as might be expected to occur, in the trades of the Pacific. The ship was under studding-sails nearly the whole time, making, day in and day out, from a hundred and twenty to two hundred miles in the twenty-four hours. The mates kept the watches, and I had little to do, but to sit and chat with the major and his daughter, in the cool, airy cabin that Le Compte had provided for us ; listen to Emily's piano, which had been transferred from the prize, and subsequently saved from the wreck, or read aloud out of some of the two or three hundred beautifully-bound and sweetly-scented volumes that composed her library. In that day, people read Pope, and Young, and Milton, and Shakespeare, and that sort of writers ; a little relieved by Mrs. Radcliffe, and Miss Burney, and Monk Lewis, perhaps. As for Fielding and Smollet, they were well enough in their place, which was not a young lady's library, however. There were still more useful books, and I believe I read everything in the ship, before the voyage ended. The leisure of a sea life, in a tranquil, well-ordered vessel, admits of much study ; and books ought to be a leading object in the fitting out that portion of a vessel's equipment which relate chiefly to the welfare of her officers and crew.

Time passed pleasantly enough with a young fellow who had certainly some reason to be satisfied with his own success thus far in life, and who could relieve the tedium of ship's duty in such society. I cannot say I was in love, though I often thought of Emily when she was not before my eyes, and actually dreamt of her three times in the first fortnight after the recapture of the ship. What was a little remarkable, as I conceive, I often found myself drawing comparisons between her and Lucy, though I hardly knew why, myself. The result was very much after this sort— Emily had vastly the advantage in all that related to art, instruction, training—I am wrong, Mr. Hardinge had given his daughter a store of precise, useful knowledge, that Emily did not possess ; and then I could not but see that Lucy's tact in moral feeling was much of the highest order of the two. But in purely conventional attainments, in most that relates to the world, its usages, its *finesse* of feeling and manner, I could see that Emily was the superior. Had I known more myself, I could have seen that both were provincial—for England, in 1801, was but a province as to mere manners, though on a larger scale than America is even now—and that either would have been remarked for peculiarities in the more sophisticated circles of the continent of Europe. I dare say half my own countrymen would have preferred Lucy's nature to the more artificial manner of Emily; but it will not do to say that even female deportment, however delicate and feminine nature may have made it, cannot be improved by certain general rules for the government of that which is even purely conventional. On the whole, I wished that Lucy had a little of Emily's art, and Emily a good deal more of Lucy's nature. I suppose the perfection in this sort of thing is to possess an art so admirable that it shall appear to be nature in all things immaterial, while it leaves the latter strictly in the ascendant in all that is material.

In person, I sometimes fancied Emily was the superior, and sometimes, when memory called me back to certain scenes that had occurred during my last visit to Clawbonny, that it was Lucy. In complexion, and perhaps in eyes, the English girl beat her rival; possibly, also, in the teeth—though Lucy's were even and white; but in the smile, in the outline of the face, most especially in the mouth, and in the hands, feet, and person generally, I think nine judges in ten would have preferred the American. One peculiar charm was common to both; and it is a charm, though the strongest instance I ever saw of it in my life was in Italy, that may be said to belong, almost exclusively, to the Anglo-Saxon race; I mean that expression of the countenance which so eminently betokens feminine purity and feminine tenderness united; the look which artists love to impart to the faces of angels. Each of the girls had much of this, and I suppose it was principally owing to their heavenly blue eyes. I doubt if any woman with black or hazel eyes, notwithstanding all the brilliancy of their beauty, ever possessed this charm in the highest degree. It belonged to Grace even more than to Lucy or Emily; though of the last two I think the English girl possessed it in a slight degree the most, so far as it was connected with mere shading and color, while the American exhibited the most of it in moments of feeling and emotion. Perhaps this last advantage was owing to Lucy's submitting most to nature and to her impulses. It must be remembered, however, that I had not seen Lucy now for near two years, and two of the most important years of a young female's life, as respected her personal appearance.

As relates to character, I will not now speak as plainly as I shall be called on to do hereafter. A youth of twenty is not the best judge of such things, and I shall leave events to tell their own story in this particular.

We had been at sea a fortnight, when happening to allude to the pearl fishery, I bethought me of my own prizes. A ship that carries a numerous crew is a sort of *omnium gatherum* of human enjoyments. For ordinarily manned craft, seamen are necessary ; but ships-of-war, privateers, and letters-of-marque can afford, as poor Marble would express it, to generalize. We had several tradesmen in the Crisis—mechanics, who found the restraints of a ship necessary for their own good—and, among others, we happened to have a goldsmith. This man had offered to perforate my pearls, and to string them ; an operation to which I consented. The fellow had performed his task as well as could be desired, and supplying from his own stores a pair of suitable clasps, had formed the whole into a simple, but as beautiful a necklace, as I ever laid eyes on. He had put the largest pearl of all directly in the centre, and then arranged the remainder, by placing several of the smaller together separated by one of the second size, until the whole formed a row that would much more than encircle my own neck, and which, of course, would drop gracefully round that of a female.

When I produced this beautiful ornament, one that a woman of rank might have coveted, Emily did not endeavor to conceal her admiration. Unaccustomed, herself, to the highest associations of her own country, she had never seen a necklace of the same value, and she even fancied it fit for a queen. Doubtless, queens usually possess much more precious pearls than those of mine, and yet it was to be supposed they would not disdain to wear even such as they. Major Merton examined the necklace carefully, and I could see by his countenance, he was surprised and pleased.

On the whole, I think it may be questioned, if any other man enjoys as many physical advantages with the same means, as the American. I speak more of his habits, than of his opportunities; but I am of opinion, after seeing a good deal of various parts of the world, that the American of moderate fortune has more physical indulgences than any other man. While this is true, however, as a whole, there are certain points on which he signally fails. He fails often, when it comes to the mere outward exhibition; and it is probable there is not a single well-ordered household —meaning for the purposes of comfort and representation united—in the whole country. The particular deficiency, if deficiency it be, applies in an almost exclusive degree to the use of precious stones, jewelry, and those of the more valuable metals in general. The ignorance of the value of precious stones is so great, that half the men, meaning those who possess more or less of fortune, do not even know the names of those of the commoner sorts. I doubt if one educated American in twenty could, even at this moment, tell a sapphire from an amethyst, or a turquoise from a garnet; though the women are rather more expert as lapidaries. Now, I was a true American in this respect, and, while I knew I possessed a very beautiful ornament, I had not the smallest idea of its value as an article of commerce. With the major it was different. He had studied such things, and he had a taste for them. The reader will judge of my surprise, therefore, when I heard him say,—

"That necklace, in the hands of Rundle and Bridges, would bring a thousand pounds, in London!"

"Father!" exclaimed Emily.

"I do think it. It is not so much the size of the pearls, though these largest are not common even in that particular, but it is their extreme beauty; their color and transparency—their water, as it is called."

"I thought that a term applied only to diamonds," observed Emily, with an interest I wished she had not manifested.

"It is also applied to pearls—there are pearls of what is called the 'white water,' and they are of the sort most

prized in Europe. The 'yellow water,' are more esteemed
among nations of darker skins; I suppose that is the secret.
Yes, I think if you send this necklace to London, Wallingford, you will get six or eight hundred pounds for it."

"I shall never sell it, sir—at least, not as long as I can
avoid it." I saw that Emily looked at me, with an earnestness for which I could not account.

"Not sell it!" repeated her father. "Why, what in the
name of Neptune can you do with such an ornament?"

"Keep it. It is strictly my own. I brought it up from
the bottom of the sea with my own hands; removed the
pearls from what the editors would call their 'native
homes' myself, and I feel an interest in them, that I never
could feel in any ornament that was purchased."

"Still, this will prove rather an expensive taste. Pray,
what interest do you obtain for money, in your part of the
world, Wallingford?"

"Six per cent, in New York, sir, perhaps, on the better
sort of permanent securities."

"And how much is sixty pounds sterling, when turned
into dollars?"

"We usually say five for one, though it is not quite that;
from two hundred and eighty to two hundred and ninety,
all things considered—though two hundred and sixty-six,
nominally, or thereabouts."

"Well, even two hundred and sixty-six dollars a year is a
good deal for a young man like you to pay for the pleasure
of saying he owns a pearl necklace that he cannot use."

"But it cost me nothing, sir, and of course I can lose
nothing by it."

"I rather think you will lose what I tell you, if the
ornament can be sold for that sum. When a man has
property from which he might derive an income, and does
not, he is, in one sense, and that the most important, a
loser."

"I have a sister, Major Merton; I may possibly give it
to her—or, should I marry, I would certainly give it to
my wife."

I could see a smile struggling about the mouth of the

major, which I was then too young, and I may add, too American, to understand. The incongruity of the wife of a man of two thousand, or five-and-twenty hundred dollars a year wearing two years' income round her neck, or of being magnificent in only one item of her dress, household, or manner of living, never occurred to my mind. We can all laugh when we read of Indian chiefs wearing uniform coats, and cocked-hats, without any other articles of attire ; but we cannot imagine inconsistencies in our own cases, that are almost as absurd in the eyes of highly sophisticated and conventional usages. To me, at that age, there was noth- ing in the least out of the way, in Mrs. Miles Wallingford's wearing the necklace, her husband being unequivocally its owner. As for Emily, she did not smile, but continued to hold the necklace in her own very white, plump hand, the pearls making the hand look all the prettier, while the hand assisted to increase the lustre of the pearls. I ventured to ask her to put the necklace on her neck. She blushed slightly, but she complied.

"Upon my word, Emily," exclaimed the gratified father, "you become each other so well, that I am losing a preju- dice, and begin to believe even a poor man's daughter may be justified in using such an ornament."

The sight was certainly sufficient to justify anything of the sort. The dazzling whiteness of Miss Merton's skin, the admirable outlines of her throat and bust, and the flush which pleasure gave her cheeks, contributed largely to the beauty of the picture. It would have been difficult to say whether the charms of the woman ornamented the pearls, or those of the pearls ornamented the woman ! I remember I thought, at the time, my eyes had never dwelt on any object more pleasing than was Miss Merton during the novelty of that spectacle. Nor did the pleasure cease on the instant ; for I begged her to continue to wear the neck- lace during the remainder of the day—a request with which she had the good-nature to comply. Which was most gratified by this exhibition, the young lady or myself, it might be difficult to say ; for there is a mutual satisfaction in admiring, and in being admired.

When I went into the cabin to say good night, I found
Emily Merton, with the necklace in her hand, gazing at it,
by the light of a powerful lamp, with eyes as liquid and
soft as the pearls themselves. I stood still to admire her,
for never before had I seen her so bewitchingly beautiful.
Her countenance was usually a little wanting in intellectual
expression, though it possessed so much of that which I
have described as angelic; but on this occasion it seemed
to me to be full of ideas. Can it be possible, whispered
conceit—and what very young man is entirely free from
it?—can it be possible she is now thinking how happy a
woman Mrs. Miles Wallingford will one day be? Am I in
any manner connected with that meditating brow, that
reflecting air, that fixed look, that pleased, and yet doubting
expression?

"I was about to send for you, Captain Wallingford," said
Emily, the instant she saw me, and confirming my conceited
conjectures, by blushing deeper than I had seen her before,
in the whole of that blushing, sensitive, and enjoyable day;
"about to send for you, to take charge of your treasure."

"And could you not assume that much responsibility, for
a single night?"

"'T would be too great—it is an honor reserved for Mrs.
Wallingford, you know."

This was smilingly said, I fancied sweetly and kindly,
and yet it was said not altogether without something that
approached to an equivoque; a sort of manner that the
deep, natural feeling of Grace, and needle-like truth of
Lucy, had rendered unpleasant to me. I took the necklace,
shook the young lady's hand for good-night,—we always
did that, on meeting and parting for the day,—paid my
compliments to the father, and withdrew.

I was dressing next morning, when Neb came bolting
into my state-room, with his Clawbonny freedom of manner,
his eyes looking lobsters, and his necklace of pearls, glit-
tering between a pair of lips that might have furnished a
cannibal two famous steaks. As soon as fairly established
in command, I had brought the fellow aft, berthing him in
the steerage, in order to have the benefit of more of his

personal service than I could obtain while he was exclusively
a foremast Jack. Still, he kept his watch; for it would
have been cruel to deprive him of that pleasure.

"Oh! Masser Mile!" exclaimed the black, as soon as he
could speak; "'e boat—'e boat!"

"What of the boat? Is any one overboard?"

"'E whale-boat, sir!—poor Captain Marble—'e whale-
boat, sir!"

"I understand you, Neb; go on deck, and desire the
officer of the watch to heave-to the ship, as soon as it is
proper; I will come up, the instant I can."

Here, then, I thought, Providence has brought us on the
track of the unfortunate whale-boat; and we shall doubtless
see the mutilated remains of some of our old companions—
poor Marble, doubtless, from what Neb said—well, the will
of God be done. I was soon dressed; and, as I went up the
cabin ladder, the movement on deck denoted the nature of
the excitement that now prevailed generally, in the ship.
Just as I reached the quarter-deck, the mainyard swung
round, and the sails were brought aback. The whole crew
was in commotion, and it was some little time before I could
learn the cause.

The morning was misty, and the view round the ship,
until within a few minutes, had been confined to a circle of
less than a mile in diameter. As the sun rose, however,
the mist broke away gradually, and then the watch caught
a view of the whale-boat mentioned by Neb. Instead of
being floating about on the ocean, with the remains of its
unfortunate crew lying in its bottom, as I had expected to
see it, when I caught the first glimpse of the unlooked-for
object, it was not a mile distant, pulling briskly for us, and
containing not only a full, but a strong and animated crew.

Just at that instant, some one cried out "Sail ho!" and
sure enough, a ship was seen some four or five miles to leeward, a whaler evidently, turning to windward, under easy
canvas, in order to rejoin her boat, from which she had
lately been separated by the night and the fog. This, then,
was no more than a whaler and her boat; and, on sweeping
the horizon with a glass, Talcott soon discovered, a mile

to windward of the boat, a dead whale, with another boat lying by it, in waiting for the approach of the ship, which promised to fetch as far to windward, on its next tack.

"They desire to speak us, I suppose, Mr. Talcott," I remarked. "The ship is probably an American ; it is likely the captain is in the boat, and he wishes to send letters or messages home."

A shout came from Talcott, at the next instant—then he cried out,—

"Three cheers, my lads ; I see Captain Marble in that boat, as plainly as I see the boat itself ! "

The cheers that followed were a spontaneous burst of joy. They reached the approaching boat, and gave its inmate an earnest of his reception. In three more minutes, Marble was on the deck of his old ship. For myself, I was unable to speak ; nor was poor Marble much better off, though more prepared for the interview.

"I knew you, Miles ; I knew you, and the bloody ' Pretty Poll,' " he at last got out, the tears running down his cheeks like water, "the moment the fog lifted, and gave me a fair glimpse. They 've got her—yes, d——n her—God bless her, I mean—they 've got her, and the bloody Frenchmen will not go home with *that* feather in their caps. Well, it could n't have happened to a cleverer fellow ; and I 'm just as happy as if I had done it myself ! "

There he stood, sound, safe, and sturdy as ever; and the four Sandwich Islanders were all in the boat, just as well as if they never quitted the ship. Every man of the crew had to shake hands with Marble, congratulations were to be exchanged, and a turbulent quarter of an hour passed before it was possible to get a coherent account from the man of what had befallen him. As soon as practicable, however, he motioned for silence, and told his own story aloud for the benefit of all hands.

"You know how I left you, men," Marble commenced, swabbing his eyes and cheeks, and struggling to speak with something like an appearance of composure, "and the errand on which I went. The last I saw of you was about half an hour before the gust broke. At that time I was so near the ship as to make out she was a whaler; and, nothing doubting of being in sight of you in the morning, I thought it safer to pull alongside of her, than to try to hunt for the schooner in the dark. I found an old shipmate in the whaler's captain, who was looking for a boat that had struck adrift the night before; and both parties were pleased. There was not much time for compliments, however, as you all know. The ship bore up to speak you, and then she bore up, again and again, on account of the squalls. While Mr. Wallingford was probably hugging the wind in order to find me, we were running off to save our spars; and next morning we could see nothing of you. How else we missed each other is more than I can say; for I 've no idee you went off and left me out here, in the middle of the ocean—''

'' We cruised for you, within five miles of the spot, for a whole day!'' I exclaimed eagerly.

'' No, no, Captain Marble,'' the men put in, in a body, '' we did all that men could do, to find you.''

'' I know it! I could swear to it, without a word from one of you. Well, that 's the whole story. We could not find you, and I stuck by the ship as a matter of course, as there was no choice between that and jumping overboard; and here has the Lord brought us together again, though we are every inch of five hundred miles from the place where we parted.''

I then took Marble below, and related to him all that had occurred since the separation. He listened with the deepest interest, manifesting the strongest sympathy in our success. Nothing but expressions of gratification escaped him, until I remarked, as I concluded my account,—

'' And here is the old ship for you, sir, just as we lost her; and glad am I to see her once more in so good hands.''

'' Who put that bloody poop on her, you or the Frenchman, Miles?''

'' The Frenchman. Now it is peace, however, it is no great matter; and the cabin is very convenient for the major and his daughter.''

"It's just like 'em! Spoiling the neatest quarter-deck on the ocean with a bloody supernumerary cabin!"

"Well, sir, as you are master now, you can have it all cut away again, if you think proper."

"I! I cut away anything! I take the command of this ship from the man who has so fairly won it! If I do, may I be d——d!"

"Captain Marble! You astonish me by this language, sir; but it is nothing more than a momentary feeling, of which your own good sense—nay, even your duty to the owners—will cause you to get rid."

"You never were more mistaken in your life, Master Miles Wallingford," answered Marble, solemnly. "I thought of all this the moment I recognized the ship, and that was as soon as I saw her, and my mind was made up from that instant. I cannot be so mean as to come in at the seventh hour, and profit by your courage and skill. Besides, I have no legal right to command here. The ship was more than twenty-four hours in the enemy's hands, and she comes under the usual laws of recapture and salvage."

"But the owners, Captain Marble—remember there is a cargo to be taken in at Canton, and there are heavy interests at stake."

"By George, that would make me so much the more firm. From the first I have thought matters would be better in your hands than mine; you have an edication, and that's a wonderful thing, Miles. As to sailing a ship, or stowing her, or taking care of her in heavy weather, or finding my way across an ocean, I'll turn my back on no man; but it's a different thing when it comes to figures and calculations."

"You disappoint me greatly in all this, sir; we have gone through so much together—"

"We did not go through the recapture of this vessel together, boy."

"But it was your thought, and but for an accident, would have been your deed."

"I don't know that; I have reflected coolly in the matter, after I got over my mortification; and I think we should have been flogged, had we attacked the French at sea. Your own plan was better, and capitally carried out. Harkee, Miles, this much will I do, and not a jot more. You are bound to the island, I take it for granted, to pick up odds and ends ; and then you sail for Canton ? ''

'' Precisely—I am glad you approve of it, as you must by seeing into it so readily.''

'' Well, at the island, fill up the schooner with such arti- cles as will be of no use at Canton. Let her take in the copper, the English goods, and the like of that, and I will carry her home ; while you can pursue the v'y'ge in the ship, as you alone have a right to do.''

No argument of mine could turn Marble from his resolu- tion. I fought him all day on the subject, and at night he was put in command of the '' Pretty Poll,'' with our old second mate for his first officer.

CHAPTER XIX.

"Thou shalt seek the beach of sand,
  Where the water bounds the elfin land ;
  Thou shalt watch the oozy brine,
  Till the sturgeon leaps in the light moonshine."

DRAKE.

THERE is but a word to say of the whaler. We spoke her, of course, and parted, leaving her her boat. She passed half an hour close to us, and then went after her whale. When we lost sight of her, she was cutting in the fish, as coolly as if nothing had happened. As for ourselves, we made the best of our way for the island.

Nothing worth relating occurred during the remainder of the passage. We reached our place of destination ten days after we found Marble, and carried both the ship and schooner into the lagoon, without any hesitation or difficulty. Everything was found precisely as we had left it ; two months having passed as quietly as an hour. The tents were standing, the different objects lay where they had been hastily dropped at our hurried departure, and everything denoted the unchangeable character of an unbroken solitude. Time and the seasons could alone have produced any sensible alteration. Even the wreck had neither shifted her bed, nor suffered injury. There she lay, seemingly an immovable fixture on the rocks, and as likely to last as any other of the durable things around her.

It is always a relief to escape from the confinement of a ship, even if it be only to stroll along the vacant sands of some naked beach. As soon as the vessels were secured we poured ashore in a body, and the people were given a holiday. There was no longer an enemy to apprehend, and we all enjoyed the liberty of movement and the freedom from care that accompanied our peculiar situation. Some prepared lines and commenced fishing ; others hauled the seine ; while the less industriously disposed lounged about, selected the fruit of the cocoa-nut tree, or hunted for shells—of which there were many, and those extremely beautiful, scattered along the inner and outer beaches, or lying visible just within the wash of the water. I ordered two or three of the hands to make a collection for Clawbonny ; paying them, as a matter of course, for their extra services. Their success was great, and I still possess the fruits of their search, as memorials of my youthful adventures.

Emily and her maid took possession of their old tents, neither of which had been disturbed ; and I directed that the necessary articles of furniture should be landed for their use. As we intended to remain eight or ten days at Marble Land, there was a general disposition to make ourselves comfortable ; and the crew were permitted to bring such things ashore as they desired, care being had for the necessary duties of the ships. Since quitting London, we had been prisoners, with the short interval of our former visit to this place, and it was now deemed wisest to give the people a little relaxation. To all this I was advised by Marble ; who, though a severe, and so often seemingly an obdurate man, was in the main disposed to grant as much indulgence, at suitable moments, as any officer I ever sailed with. There was an ironical severity, at times, about the man, which misled superficial observers. I have heard of a waggish boatswain in the navy, who, when disposed to menace the crew with some of his official visitations, used to cry out, "Fellow-citizens, I'm coming among you" ; and the anecdote never recurs to my mind, without bringing Marble back to my recollections. When in spirits, he had much of this bitter irony in his manner ; and his own early experience had rendered him somewhat insensible to professional suffering ; but, on the whole, I always thought him a humane man.

We went into the lagoon before the sun had risen ; and,

before the breakfast hour of those who lived aft, we had everything landed that was necessary, and were in possession of our tents. I had ordered Neb to attend particularly to the wants of the Mertons, and precisely as the bell of the ship struck eight, which, at that time of day, meant eight o'clock, the black came with the major's compliments, inviting " Captain " Wallingford and " Captain " Marble to breakfast.

" So it goes, Miles," added my companion, after promising to join the party in a few moments. " This arrangement about the schooner leaves us both captains, and prevents anything like your downhill work, which is always unpleasant business. Captain Marble and Captain Wallingford sound well ; and I hope they may long sail in company. But natur' or art never meant me for a captain."

" Well, admitting this, where there are *two* captains, one must outrank the other, and the senior commands. You should be called Commodore Marble."

" None of your pleasantry, Miles," returned Marble, with a severe look and shake of the head ; "it is by your favor, and I hope by your good opinion, that I am master of even that little, half-blooded, part French, part Yankee, schooner. It is my second, and I think it will be my last command. I have generalized over my life, upon a large scale, within the last ten days, and have come to the conclusion that the Lord created me to be your mate, and not you to be mine. When natur' means a man for anything partic'lar, she does n't set him adrift among human beings, as I was set adrift."

" I do not understand you, sir—perhaps you will give me an outline of your history ; and then all will be plain."

" Miles, oblige me in one particular—it will cost you no great struggle, and will considerably relieve my mind."

" You have only to name it, sir, to be certain it will be done."

" Drop that bloody *sir*, then ; it 's unbecoming now, as between you and me. Call me Marble, or Moses ; as I call you Miles."

" Well, be it so. Now for this history of yours, which

you have promised to give me, by the way, any time these two years."

"It can be told in a few words; and I hope it may be of service. A human life, properly generalized on, is at any time as good as most sermons. It is full of what I call the morality of idees. I suppose you know to what I owe my names?"

"Not I—to your sponsors in baptism, like all the rest of us, I suppose."

"You're nearer the truth than you may imagine, this time, boy. I was found, a child of a week old, they tell me, lying in a basket, one pleasant morning, in a stone-cutter's yard, on the North River side of the town, placed upon a bit of stone that was hewing out for the head of a grave, in order, as I suppose, that the workmen would be sure to find me, when they mustered at their work. Although I have passed for a Down-Easter, having sailed in their craft in the early part of my life, I'm in truth York born."

"And is this all you know of your origin, my dear Marble?"

"All I want to know, after such a hint. A man is never anxious to make the acquaintance of parents who are afraid to own him. I dare say, now, Miles, that you knew, and loved, and respected your mother?"

"Love, and respect her! I worshipped her, Marble; and she deserved it all, if ever human being did!"

"Yes, yes; I can understand that," returned Marble, making a hole in the sand with his heel, and looking both thoughtful and melancholy. "It must be a great comfort to love and respect a mother! I've seen them, particularly young women, that I thought set quite as much store by their mothers, as they did by themselves. Well, no matter; I got into one of poor Captain Robbins' bloody currents at the first start, and have been drifting about ever since, just like the whale-boat with which we fell in, pretty much as the wind blew. They had n't the decency to pin even a name—they might have got one out of a novel or a story-book, you know, to start a poor fellow in life with—to my shirt; no—they just set me afloat on that bit of tombstone,

and cast off the standing part of what fastened me to anything human. There they left me, to generalize on the
'arth and its ways, to my heart's content."

"And you were found next morning, by the stone-cutter,
when he came, again, to use his chisel."

"Prophecy could n't have better foretold what happened.
There I was found, sure enough; and there I made my first
escape from destruction. Seeing the basket, which it seems
was one in which he had brought his own dinner, the day
before, and forgotten to carry away with him, he gave it a
jerk to cast away the leavings, before he handed it to the
child who had come to take it home, in order that it might
be filled again, when out I rolled on the cold stone. There
I lay, as near the grave as a tombstone, when I was just a
week old."

"Poor fellow—you could only know this by report, however. And what was done with you?"

"I suppose, if the truth were known, my father was
somewhere about that yard; and little do I envy the old
gentleman his feelings, if he reflected much over matters
and things. I was sent to the almshouse, however; stone-
cutters being nat'rally hard-hearted, I suppose. The fact
that I was left among such people, makes me think so much
the more that my own father must have been one of them,
or it never could have happened. At all events, I was soon
rated on the almshouse books; and the first thing they did
was to give me some name. I was No. 19, for about a week;
at the age of fourteen days I became Moses Marble."

"It was an odd selection that your 'sponsors in baptism'
made!"

"Somewhat—Moses came from the Scriptur's, they tell
me; there being a person of that name, as I understand, who
was turned adrift pretty much as I was myself."

"Why, yes—so far as the basket and the abandonment
were concerned; but he was put afloat fairly, and not clapped
on a tombstone, as if to threaten him with the grave at the
very outset."

"Well, Tombstone came very near being my name. At
first they thought of giving me the name of the man for

whom the stone was intended ; but, that being Zollickoffer, they though I never should be able to spell it. Then came Tombstone, which they thought melancholy, and so they called me Marble ; consaiting, I suppose, it would make me tough.''

"How long did you remain in the almhouse, and at what age did you first go to sea ?''

"I stayed among them the public feeds, until I was eight years old, and then I took a hazy day to cut adrift from charity. At that time, Miles, our country belonged to the British—or they treated it as if they did, though I 've heard wiser men than myself say, it was always our own, the King of England only happening to be our king—but I was born a British subject, and being now just forty, you can understand I went to sea several years before the Revolution.''

"True—you must have seen service in that war ; on one side or the other?''

"If you say both sides, you 'll not be out of the way. In 1775, I was a foretop-man in the Romney 50, where I remained until I was transferred to the Connecticut 74—''

"The what ?'' said I, in surprise. "Had the English a line-of-battle ship called the Connecticut?''

"As near as I could make it out; I always thought it a big compliment for John Bull to pay the Yankees.''

"Perhaps the name of your ship was the Carnatic? The sounds are not unlike.''

"Blast me, if I don't thing you 've hit it, Miles. Well I 'm glad of it, for I run from the ship, and I should n't half like the thought of serving a countryman such a trick. Yes, I then got on board of one of our sloops, and tried my hand at settling the account with my old masters. I was taken prisoner for my pains, but worried through the war without getting my neck stretched. They wanted to make it out on board the old Jarsey, that I was an Englishman, but I told 'em just to prove it. Let 'em only prove where I was born, I said, and I would give it up. I was ready to be hanged if they could only prove where I was born. D——e, but I sometimes thought I never was born at all ''

"You are surely an American, Marble? A Manhattan-ese, born and educated?"

"Why, as it is not likely any person would import a child a week old, to plant it on a tombstone, I conclude I am. Yes, I must be that; and I have sometimes thought of laying claim to the property of Trinity Church, on the strength of my birthright. Well, as soon as the war was over, and I got out of prison, and that was shortly after you were born, Captain Wallingford, I went to work regularly, and have been ever since sarving as dickey, or chief mate, on board some craft or other. If I had no family bosom to go into as a resting-place I had my bosom to fill with solid beef and pork, and that is not to be done by idleness.

" And all this time, my good friend, you have been living, as it might be, alone in the world, without a relative of any sort?"

"As sure as you are there. Often and often have I walked through the streets of New York, and said to my-self, Among all these people, there is not one that I can call a relation. My blood is in no man's veins but my own."

This was said with a bitter sadness that surprised me. Obdurate, and insensible to suffering as Marble had ever appeared to me, I was not prepared to find him giving such evidence of feeling. I was then young, but now I am old, and one of the lessons learned in the years that have inter-vened, is not to judge of men by appearances. So much sensibility is hidden beneath assumed indifference, so much suffering really exists behind smiling countenances, and so little does the exterior tell the true story of all that is to be found within, that I am now slow to yield credence to the lying surfaces of things. Most of all have I learned to condemn that heartless injustice of the world, that renders it so prompt to decide, on rumor and conjectures, constitut-ing itself a judge from which there shall be no appeal, in cases which it has not taken the trouble to examine, and in which it has not even the power to examine evidence.

" We are all of the same family, my friend," I answered, with a good design, at least, "though a little separated by time and accidents."

"Family! Yes, I belong to my own family. I'm a more important man in my family, than Bonaparte is in his, for I am all in all—ancestors, present time, and posterity!"

"It is at least your own fault you are the last; why not marry and have children?"

"Because my parents did not set me the example," answered Marble, almost fiercely. Then clapping his hand on my shoulder in a friendly way, as if to soothe me after so sharp a rejoinder, he added in a gentler tone, "Come, Miles, the major and his daughter will want their breakfasts, and we had better join them. Talking of matrimony, there's the girl for you, my boy, thrown into your arms almost nat'rally, as one might say."

"I am far from being so sure of that, Marble," I answered, as both began to walk slowly toward the tent. "Major Merton might not think it an honor, in the first place, to let his daughter marry a Yankee sailor."

"Not such a one as myself, perhaps; but why not one like you? How many generations have there been of you now at the place you call Clawbonny?"

"Four, from father to son, and all of us Miles Wallingfords."

"Well, the old Spanish proverb says 'it takes three generations to make a gentleman'; and here you have four to start upon. In my family, all the generations have been on the same level, and I count myself old in my sphere."

"It is odd that a man like you should know anything of old Spanish proverbs!"

"What? Of such a proverb, think you, Miles? A man without even a father or mother—who never had either, as one may say—and he not remember such a proverb! Boy, boy, I never forget anything that so plainly recalls the tombstone, and the basket, and the almshouse, and Moses, and the names!"

"But Miss Merton might object to the present generation," I resumed, willing to draw my companion from his bitter thoughts, "however favorably disposed her father might prove to the last."

"That will be your own fault, then. Here you have

her, out on the Pacific Ocean, all to yourself; and if you
cannot tell your own story, and that in a way to make her
believe it, you are not the lad I take you for."

I made an evasive and laughing answer; but, being quite
near the tent by this time, it was necessary to change the
discourse. The reader may think it odd, but that was the
very first time the possibility of my marrying Emily Merton ever crossed my mind. In London, I had regarded
her as an agreeable acquaintance, with just as much of the
coloring of romance and of the sentimental about our intercourse, as is common with youths of nineteen and girls a little younger; but as nothing more. When we met on the
island, Emily appeared to me like a friend—a female friend
—and, of course, one to be viewed with peculiarly softened
feelings; still, as only a friend. During the month we had
just passed in the same ship, this tie had gradually strength-
ened; and I confess to a perfect consciousness of there being
on board a pretty girl in her nineteenth year, of agreeable
manners, delicate sentiments, and one whose presence gave
the Crisis a charm she certainly never enjoyed during poor
Captain Williams' time. Notwithstanding all this, there
was something—though what that something was, I did
not then know myself—which prevented me from absolutely falling in love with my fair guest. Nevertheless,
Marble's suggestion was not unpleasant to me; but, on the
other hand, it rather conduced to the satisfaction of my
present visit.

We were kindly received by our hosts, who always
seemed to remember the commencement of our acquaintance, when Marble and myself visited them together. The
breakfast had a little of the land about it; for Monsieur Le
Compte's garden still produced a few vegetables, such as
lettuce, pepper-grass, radishes, etc.; most of which, however,
had sown themselves. Three or four fowls, too, that he
had left on the island in the hurry of his departure, had
begun to lay; and Neb having found a nest, we had the
very unusual treat of fresh eggs. I presume no one will
deny that they were sufficiently "country laid."

"Emily and myself consider ourselves as old residents

here," the major observed, as he gazed around him, the table being set in the open air, under some trees; "and I could almost find it in my heart to remain on this beautiful island for the remainder of my days—quite, I think, were it not for my poor girl, who might find the society of her old father rather dull work, at her time of life."

"Well, major," said Marble, "you have only to let your taste be known, to have the ch'ice among all our youngsters to be her companion. There is Mr. Talcott, a well-edicated and mannerly lad enough, and of good connections, they tell me; and as for Captain Wallingford here, I will answer for him. My life on it, he would give up Clawbonny, and property on which he is the fourth of his name, to be king, or Prince of Wales of this island, with such company!"

Now it was Marble, and not I, who made this speech; and yet I heartily wished it unsaid. It made me feel foolish, and I dare say it made me look foolish; and I know it caused Emily to blush. Poor girl! she, who blushed so easily, and was so sensitive, and so delicately situated—she was entitled to have more respect paid to her feelings. The major and Marble, however, took it all very coolly, continuing the discourse as if nothing out of the way had been said.

"No doubt—no doubt," answered the first; "romance always finds votaries among young people, and this place may well excite romantic feelings in those who are older than these young men. Do you know, gentlemen, that ever since I have known this island, I have had a strong desire to pass the remainder of my days on it? The idea I have just mentioned to you, therefore, is by no means one of a moment's existence."

"I am glad, at least, dear sir," observed Emily, laughing, "that the desire has not been so strong as to induce you to make formal proposals on the subject."

"You, indeed, are the great obstacle; for what could I do with a discontented girl, whose mind would be running on balls, theatres, and other amusements? We should not have even a church."

"And, Major Merton," I put in, "what could you, or

any other man, do with himself, in a place like this, without companions, books, or occupation?"

"If a conscientious man, Miles, he might think over the past ; if a wise one, he would certainly reflect on the future. I should have books, since Emily and I could muster several hundred volumes between us ; and with books, I should have companions. What could I do? I should have everything to create, as it might be, and the pleasure of seeing everything rising up under my own hand. There would be a house to construct—the materials of that wreck to collect—ropes, canvas, timber, tar, sugar, and divers other valuables that are still out on the reef, or which lie scattered about on the beach, to gather together, and save against a rainy day. Then I would have a thought for my poultry ; and possibly you might be persuaded to leave me one or two of these pigs, of which I see the French forgot half a dozen, in their haste to cheat the Spaniards. Oh ! I should live like a prince, and be a prince *regnant* in the bargain."

"Yes, sir, you would be captain and all hands, if that would be any gratification ; but I think you would soon weary of your government, and be ready to abdicate."

"Perhaps so, Miles ; yet the thought is pleasant to me ; but for this dear girl, it would be particularly so. I have very few relatives ; the nearest I have being, oddly enough, your own country-people, gentlemen. My mother was a native of Boston, where my father, a merchant, married her ; and I came very near being a Yankee myself, having been born but a week after my parents landed in England. On my father's side, I have not five recognized relatives, and they are rather distant ; while those on my mother's are virtually all strangers. Then I never owned a foot of this earth on which we live, in my life—"

" Nor I," interrupted Marble, with emphasis.

" My father was a younger son ; and younger sons in England are generally lack-lands. My life has been such, and, I may add, my means such, that I have never been in the way of purchasing even enough earth to bury me in ; and here, you see, is an estate that can be had for asking. How much land do you fancy there is in this island, gentlemen? I mean, apart from the beach, the sands and rocks; but such as has grass, and bears trees —ground that might be tilled, and rendered productive, without much labor?"

"A hundred thousand acres," exclaimed Marble, whose calculation was received with a general laugh.

"It seems rather larger to me, sir," I answered, "than the farm at Clawbonny. Perhaps there may be six or eight hundred acres of the sort of land you mention; though the whole island must contain several thousands—possible four or five."

"Well, four or five thousand acres of land make a good estate—but, as I see Emily is getting frightened, and is nervous under the apprehension of falling heir to such extensive possessions, I will say no more about them."

No more was said, and we finished our breakfasts, conversing of the past, rather than of the future. The major and Marble went to stroll along the groves, in the direction of the wreck; while I persuaded Emily to put on her hat and stroll—the other way.

"This is a singular notion of my father's," my fair companion remarked, after a moment of musing; "nor is it the first time, I do assure you, on which he has mentioned it. While we were here before, he spoke of it daily."

"The scheme might do well enough for two ardent lovers," said I, laughing; "but would scarcely be wise for an elderly gentleman and his daughter. I can imagine that two young people, warmly attached to each other, might get along in such a place for a year or two, without hanging themselves; but I fancy even love would tire out, after a while, and they would set about building a boat, in which to be off."

"You are not very romantic, I perceive, Mr. Wallingford," Emily answered, and I thought a little reproachfully. "Now, I own that to my taste, I could be happy anywhere —here, as well as in London, surrounded by my nearest and dearest friends."

"Surrounded! Ay, that would be a very different matter. Let me have your father, yourself, honest Marble, good Mr. Hardinge, Rupert, dear, dear Grace and Lucy, with Neb, and some others of my own blacks, and I should ask no better home. The island is only in twenty, has plenty of shade, some delicious fruits, and would be easily tilled—one might do here, I acknowledge, and it would be pleasant to found a colony."

"And who are all these people you love so well, Mr. Wallingford, that their presence would make a desert island pleasant?"

"In the first place, Major Merton is a half-pay officer in the British service, who has been appointed to some civil station in India," I answered gallantly. "He is a respectable, agreeable, well-informed gentleman, a little turned of fifty, who might act as judge and chancellor. Then he has a daughter—"

"I know more of her and her bad qualities than you do yourself, sire; but who are Rupert, and Grace, and Lucy—dear, dear Grace, especially?"

"Dear, dearest Grace, madam, is my sister—my only sister—all the sister I ever can have, either by marriage, or any other means, and sisters are usually dear to young men, I believe."

"Well—I knew you had a sister, and a dear sister, but I also knew you had but one. Now as to Rupert—"

"He is not another sister, you may be well assured. I have mentioned to you a friend from childhood, who went to sea with me, at first, but, disliking the business, has since commenced the study of the law."

"That, then, is Rupert. I remember some such touches of his character, but did not know the name. Now, proceed on to the next—"

"What, Neb! You know him almost as well as I do myself. He is yonder feeding the chickens, and will save his passage money."

"But you spoke of another—that is—was there not a Mr.—Hardinge was the name, I think?"

"Oh! true—I forgot Mr. Hardinge and Lucy, though they would be two of the most important of the colonists.

Mr. Hardinge is my guardian, and will continue to be so a few months longer, and Lucy is his daughter—Rupert's sister. The old gentleman is a clergyman, and would help us to keep Sundays as one should, and might perform the marriage ceremony, should it ever be required."

"Not much danger of that, I fancy, on your desert island—your Barataria," observed Miss Merton, quickly.

I cannot explain the sensitiveness of certain young ladies on such points, unless it be through their consciousness. Now, had I been holding this idle talk with Lucy, the dear, honest creature would have laughed, blushed ever so little, possibly, and nodded her head in frank assent; or, perhaps, she would have said "Oh! certainly," in a way to show that she had no desire to affect so silly a thing as to wish one to suppose she thought young people would not get married at Marble Land, as well as Clawbonny, or New York. Miss Merton, however, saw fit to change the discourse, which soon turned on her father's health. On this subject she was natural and full of strong affection. She was anxious to get the major out of the warm latitudes. His liver had been touched in the West Indies, but he had hoped that he was cured, or he never would have accepted the Bombay appointment. Experience, however, was giving reason to suspect the contrary, and Emily wished him in a cold climate as soon as possible, and that with an earnestness that showed she regarded all that had been said about the island as sheer pleasantry. We continued the conversation for an hour, when, returning to the tent, I left my fair companion with a promise to be as active as possible, in order to carry the ship into a higher latitude. Still I did not deem the island a particularly dangerous place, notwithstanding its position; the trades and sea breezes, with its ample shades, rendering the spot one of the most delightful tropical abodes I had ever been in.

After quitting Emily, I went to join Marble, who was alone, pacing a spot beneath the trees, that poor Le Compte had worn into a path, and which he had himself called his "quarter-deck."

"This Major Merton is a sensible man, Miles," the ex-

mate began, as soon as I dropped in alongside of him, and
joined in his semi-trot; "a downright, sensible sort of a
philosopher-like man, accordin' to my notion."

"What has he been telling you, now, that has seized
your fancy so much stronger than common?"

"Why, I was thinking of this idee of his, to remain on
the island, and pass the remainder of the v'y'ge here, without slaving day and night to get up two or three rounds
of the ladder of promotion, only to fall down again."

"And did the major speak of such things? I know of
no disappointments of his, to sour him with the world."

"I was not speaking for Major Merton, but for myself,
Miles. To tell you the truth, boy, this idee seems just
suited to me, and I have almost made up my mind to remain
behind here, when you sail."

I looked at Marble with astonishment; the subject on
which the major had spoken in pleasantry, rather than
with any real design of carrying his project into execution,
was one that my old messmate regarded seriously! I had
noted the attention with which he listened to our discourse,
during breakfast, and the strong feeling with which he
spoke at the time, but had no notion of the cause of either.
I knew the man too well, not to understand at once that
he was in sober earnest, and had too much experience of
his nature, not to foresee the greatest difficulty in turning
him from his purpose. I understood the true motive to
be professional mortification at all that had occurred since
he succeeded Captain Williams in command; for Marble
was much too honest and too manly, to think for a moment
of concealing his own misfortunes behind the mantle offered
by my success.

"You have not thought of this matter sufficiently, my
friend," I answered evasively, knowing the folly of
attempting to laugh this matter off; "when you have
slept on it a night, you will see things differently."

"I fancy not, Miles. Here is all I want, and just what
I want. After you have taken away everything that can
be required for the vessels, or desirable to the owners, there
will be enough left to keep me a dozen lives."

"It is not on account of food that I speak—the island alone, in its fruits, fish, and birds, to say nothing as to the seeds, and fowls, and pigs we could leave you, would be sufficient to keep fifty men ; but think of the solitude, the living without object, the chances of sickness, the horrible death that would follow to one unable to rise and assist himself, and all the other miseries of being alone. Depend on it, man was not created to live alone. Society is indispensable to him, and—"

"I have thought of it all, and find it entirely to my taste. I tell you, Miles, I should be exactly in my sphere in this island, and that as a hermit. I do not say I should not like some company, if it could be yourself, or Talcott, or the major, or even Neb ; but no company is better than bad ; and as for asking, or allowing any one to stay with me, it is out of the question. I did, at first, think of keeping the Sandwich Islanders ; but it would be bad faith, and they would not be likely to remain quiet after the ship had sailed. No, I will remain alone. You will probably report the island when you get home, and that will induce some vessel, which may be passing near, to look for me, so I shall hear of you all, every four or five years."

"Gracious Heaven ! Marble, you cannot be serious in so mad a design ?"

"Just look at my situation, Miles, and decide for yourself. I am without a friend on earth—I mean nat'ral friend—I know what sort of friend you are, and parting with you will be the toughest of all—but I have not a relation on the wide earth—no property, no home, no one to wish to see me return, not even a cellar to lay my head in. To me all places are alike, with the exception of this, which, having discovered, I look upon as my own."

"You have a country, Marble, and that is the next thing to family and home—overshadows all."

"Ay, and I'll have a country here. This will be America, having been discovered by Americans, and in their possession. You will leave me the buntin', and I'll show the stars and stripes of a Fourth of July, just as you

will show 'em in some other part of the world. I was
born Yankee, at least, and I'll die Yankee. I've sailed
under that flag, boy, ever since the year '77, and will not
sail under another, you may depend on it."

"I never could justify myself to the laws for leaving a
man behind me in such a place."

"Then I'll run, and that will make all right. But you
know well enough, boy, that leaving a captain is one thing,
and leaving a man another."

"And what shall I tell all your acquaintances, those who
have sailed with you so often and so long, has become of
their old shipmate?"

"Tell 'em that the man who was once found is now
lost," answered Marble, bitterly. "But I'm not such a
fool as to think myself of so much importance as you seem
to imagine. The only persons who will consider the transaction of any interest will be the newspaper gentry, and
they will receive it only as news, and thank you about
half as much as they would for a murder or a robbery, or
the poisoning of a mother and six little children."

"I think, after all, you would scarcely find the means
of supporting yourself," I added, looking round in affected
doubt; for I felt at each instant how likely my companion
was to adhere to his notion, and this from knowing him
so well. "I doubt if the cocoa is healthy all the year
round, and there must be seasons when the trees do not
bear."

"Have no fear of that sort. I have my own fowling-
piece, and you will leave me a musket or two, with some
ammunition. Transient vessels, now the island is known,
will keep up the supply. There are two hens setting at
this moment, and a third has actually hatched. Then one
of the men tells me there is a litter of pigs near the
mouth of the bay. As for the hogs and the poultry, the
shell-fish and berries will keep them; but there are fifteen
hogsheads of sugar on the beach, besides thirty or forty
more in the wreck, and all above water. There are casks
of beans and peas, the sea-stores of the French, besides
lots of other things. I can plant, and fish, and shoot, and

21

make a fence from the ropes of the wreck, and have a large garden, and all that a man can want. Our own poultry, you know, has long been out, but there is still a bushel of Indian corn left that was intended for their feed. One quart of that will make me a rich man in such a climate as this, and with soil like that on the flat between the two groves. I own a chest of tools, and am, ship-fashion, both a tolerable carpenter and blacksmith; and I do not see that I shall want for anything. You must leave half the things that are scattered about, and so far from being a man to be pitied I shall be a man to be envied. Thousands of wretches in the greatest thoroughfares of London would gladly exchange their crowded streets and poverty for my solitude and abundance.''

I began to think Marble was not in a state of mind to reason with, and changed the subject. The day passed in recreation as had been intended, and next morning we set about filling up the schooner. We struck in all the copper, all the English goods, and such portions of the Frenchman's cargo as would be most valuable in America. Marble, however, had announced to others his determination to remain behind, to abandon the seas, and to turn hermit. As his first step, he gave up the command of the Pretty Poll, and I was obliged to restore her, again, to our old third mate, who was every way competent to take care of her. At the end of the week the schooner was ready, and despairing of getting Marble off in her, I ordered her to sail for home, *via* Cape Horn, giving especial instructions not to attempt Magellan. I wrote to the owners, furnishing an outline of all that had occurred, and of my future plans, simply remarking that Mr. Marble had declined acting, out of motives of delicacy, since the recapture of the ship, and that in future their interests must remain in my care. With these despatches the schooner sailed. Marble and I watched her until her sails became a white speck on the ocean, after which she suddenly disappeared.

As for the ship, she was all ready; and my only concern now was in relation to Marble. I tried the influence of Major Merton; but, unfortunately, that gentleman had

already said too much in favor of our friend's scheme, in
ignorance of its effect, to gain much credit when he turned
round, and espoused the other side. The arguments of
Emily failed, also. In fact, it was not reason, but feeling
that governed Marble; and, in a bitter hour, he had determined to pass the remainder of his days where he was.
Finding all persuasion useless, and the season approaching
when the winds rendered it necessary to sail, I was compelled
to yield, or resort to force. The last I was reluctant to think
of, nor was I certain the men would have obeyed me had I
ordered them to use it. Marble had been their commander
so long, that he might, at any moment, have reassumed the
charge of the ship; and it was not probable his orders would
have been braved under any circumstances that did not involve illegality or guilt. After a consultation with the
major, I found it necessary to yield to this whim, though I
did so with greater reluctance than I ever experienced on
any other occasion.

CHAPTER XX.

" Pass on, relentless world! I grieve
No more for all that thou has riven!
Pass on, in God's name—only leave
The things thou never yet hast given."

LUNT.

AFTER every means had been uselessly exhausted to persuade Marble from his design, it only remained to do all we could to make him comfortable and secure. Of enemies, there was no danger, and care was not necessary for defence. We got together, however, some of the timber, planks, and other materials that were remaining at the ship-yard, and built him a cabin, that offered much better shelter against the tropical storms that sometimes prevailed, than any tent could yield. We made this cabin as wide as a plank is long, or twelve feet, and some five or six feet longer. It was well sided and tightly roofed, having three windows and a door. The lights of the wreck supplied the first, and her cabin door the last. We had hinges, and everything that was necessary to keep things in their place. There was no chimney required, fire being unnecessary for warmth in that climate; but the French had brought their caboose from the wreck, and this we placed under a proper covering at a short distance from the hut, the strength of one man being insufficient to move it. We also enclosed, by means of ropes, and posts made of ribs of the wreck, a plot of ground of two acres in extent, where the land was the richest and unshaded, so as to prevent the pigs from injuring the vegetables; and, poor Marble knowing little of gardening, I had a melancholy pleasure in seeing the whole piece dug, or

324

rather hoed up, and sown and planted myself, before we
sailed. We put in corn, potatoes, peas, beans, lettuce,
radishes, and several other things, of which we found the
seeds in the French garden. We took pains, moreover, to
transport from the wreck, many articles that it was thought
might prove of use, though they were too heavy for Marble
to handle. As there were near forty of us, all busy in this
way for three or four days, we effected a great deal, and may
be said to have got the island in order. I felt the same
interest in the duty, that I should in bestowing a child
for life.

Marble, himself, was not much among us all this time.
He rather complained that I should leave him nothing to
do, though I could see he was touched by the interest we
manifested in his welfare. The French launch had been
used as the means of conveyance between the wreck and the
beach, and we found it where it had been left by its original
owners, anchored to leeward of the island, and abreast of
the ship. It was the last thing I meddled with, and it was
my care to put it in such a state that, at need, it might be
navigated across that tranquil sea, to some other island,
should Marble feel a desire to abandon his solitude. The
disposition I made of the boat was as follows :—

The launch was large and coppered, and it carried two
lug-sails. I had both masts stepped, with the yards, sails,
sheets, etc., prepared, and put in their places ; a stout rope
was next carried round the entire boat, outside, and a few
inches below the gunwale, where it was securely nailed.
From this rope, led a number of lanyards, with eyes turned
into their ends. Through these eyes I rove a sort of ridge-
rope, leading it also through the eyes of several stancheons
that were firmly stepped on the thwarts. The effect, when
the ridge-rope was set up, was to give the boat the protection
of this waist-cloth, which inclined inboard, however, sufficiently to leave an open passage between the two sides, of
only about half the beam of the boat. To the ridge-rope
and lanyards, I had tarpaulins firmly attached, tacking their
lower edges strongly to the outer sides of the boat. By this
arrangement, when all was in its place, and properly secured,

a sea might break, or a wave slap against the boat, without her taking in much water. It doubled her security in this particular, more than answering the purposes of a half-deck and washboard. It is true, a very heavy wave might carry all away; but very heavy waves would probably fill the boat, under any circumstances. Such a craft could only find safety in her buoyancy; and we made her as safe as an undecked vessel very well could be.

Marble watched me while I was superintending these changes in the boat, with a good deal of interest; and one evening—I had announced an intention to sail next morning, the major and Emily having actually gone on board— that evening, he got my arm, and led me away from the spot, like a man who has urgent business. I could see that he was much affected, and had strong hopes he intended to announce a change of purpose. His hand actually trembled, the whole time he grasped my arm.

"God bless you, Miles! God bless you, dear boy!" he said, speaking with difficulty, as soon as we were out of ear-shot from the others. "If any being could make me pine for the world, it would be such a friend as you. I could live on without father or mother, brother or sister, ship or confidence of my owners, good name even, were I sure of meeting such a lad as yourself in only every thousandth man I fell in with. But, young as you are, you know how it is with mankind; and no more need be said about it. All I ask now is, that you will knock off with this 'making him comfortable,' as you call it, or you'll leave me nothing to do for myself. I can fit out that boat as well as e'er a man in the Crisis, I'd have you to know."

"I am well aware of that, my friend; but I am not so certain that you would. In that boat, I am in hopes you will follow us out to sea, and come on board again, and take your old place as master."

Marble shook his head, and I believe he saw by my manner that I had no serious expectations of the sort I named. We walked some distance farther, in silence, before he again spoke. Then he said suddenly, and in a way to show how much his mind was troubled,—

" Miles, my dear boy, you must let me hear from you ! "

" Hear from me ! By what means, pray ? You cannot expect the Postmaster-General will make a mail route be-tween New York and this island ? "

" Poh ! I 'm getting old, and losing my memory. I was generalizing on friendship, and the like of that, and the idee ran away with me. I know, of course, when you are out of sight, that I shall be cut off from the rest of the world—probably shall never see a human face again. But what of that ? My time cannot be long now, and I shall have the fish, fowls, and pigs to talk to. To tell you the truth, Miles, Miss Merton gave me her own Bible yesterday, and, at my request, she pointed out that part which gives the account about Moses in the bulrushes, and I 've just been looking it over ; it is easy enough, now, to understand why I was called Moses."

" But Moses did not think it necessary to go and live in a desert, or on an uninhabited island, merely because he was found in those bulrushes."

" That Moses had no occasion to be ashamed of his parents. It was fear, not shame, that sent him adrift. Nor did Moses ever let a set of lubberly Frenchmen seize a fine, stout ship, like the Crisis, with a good, able-bodied crew of forty men on board her."

" Come, Marble, you have too much sense to talk in this manner. It is, fortunately, not too late to change your mind ; and I will let it be understood that you did so at my persuasion."

This was the commencement of a final effort on my part to induce my friend to abandon his mad project. We conversed quite an hour, until I had exhausted my breath, as well as my arguments, indeed ; and all without the least success. I pointed out to him the miserable plight he must be in, in the event of illness ; but it was an argument that had no effect on a man who had never had even a headache in his life. As for society, he cared not a straw for it when ashore, he often boasted ; and he could not yet appreciate the effects of total solitude. Once or twice, remarks escaped him as if he thought it possible I might one day return ;

but they were ventured in pleasantry, rather than with any appearance of seriousness. I could see that the self-devoted hermit had his misgivings, but I could obtain no verbal concession from him to that effect. He was reminded that the ship must positively sail next day, since it would not do to trifle with the interests of the owners any longer.

"I know it, Miles," Marble answered, "and no more need be said on the subject. Your people are through with their work, and here comes Neb to report the boat ready to go off. I shall try my hand ashore to-night, alone; in the morning, I suppose you would like to take an old ship-mate by the hand for the last time, and you will nat'rally look for me at the water-side. Good night! Before we part, however, I may as well thank you for the supply of clothes I see you have put in my hut. It was scarcely wanted, as I have enough needles and thread to supply a slop-shop; and the old duck left by the French will keep me in jackets and trousers for the remainder of my days. Good night, my dear boy! God bless you—God bless you!"

It was nearly dark, but I could see that Marble's eyes looked moist, and feel that his hand again trembled. I left him, not without the hope that the solitude of this night, the first in which he had been left by himself, would have the effect to lessen his desire to be a hermit. When I turned in, it was understood that all hands were to be called at day-light, and the ship unmoored.

Talcott came to call me, at the indicated moment. I had made him chief mate, and taken one of the Philadelphians for second officer; a young man who had every requisite for the station, and one more than was necessary, or a love of liquor. But drunkards do tolerably well on board a ship in which reasonable discipline is maintained. For that matter, Neptune ought to be a profound moralist, as youths are very generally sent to sea to cure most of the ethical ailings. Talcott was directed to unmoor, and heave short. As for myself, I got into a boat and pulled ashore, with an intention of making a last and strong appeal to Marble.

No one was visible on the island when we reached it. The pigs and fowls were already in motion, however, and were gathering near the door of the hut, where Marble was accustomed to feed them about that hour ; the fowls on sugar, principally. I proceeded to the door, opened it, entered the place, and found it empty ! Its late inmate was then up, and abroad. He had probably passed a sleepless night, and sought relief in the fresh air of the morning. I looked for him in the adjacent grove, on the outer beach, and in most of his usual haunts. He was nowhere visible. A little vexed at having so long a walk before me, at a moment when we were so much pressed for time, I was about to follow the grove to a distant part of the island, to a spot I knew Marble frequented a good deal, when moody ; but my steps were arrested by an accidental glance at the lagoon. I missed the Frenchman's launch, or the boat I had myself caused to be rigged with so much care, the previous day, for the intended hermit's especial advantage. This was a large boat ; one that had been constructed to weigh a heavy anchor, and I had left her moored between a grapnel and the shore, so securely, as to forbid the idea she could have been moved, in so quiet a time, without the aid of hands. Rushing to the water, I got into my own boat, and pulled directly on board.

On reaching the ship, a muster of all hands was ordered. The result proved that everybody was present, and at duty. It followed that Marble, alone, had carried the boat out of the lagoon. The men who had had the anchor-watches during the past night, were questioned on the subject ; but no one had seen or heard anything of a movement in the launch. Mr. Talcott was told to continue his duty, while I went aloft myself, to look at the offing. I was soon in the main-topmast cross-trees, where a view was commanded of the whole island, a few covers excepted, of all the water within the reef, and of a wide range without. Nowhere was the boat or Marble to be seen. It was barely possible that he had concealed himself behind the wreck, though I did not see how even this could be done, unless he had taken the precaution to strike the launch's masts.

By this time, our last anchor was aweigh, and the ship was clear of the bottom. The topsails had been hoisted before I went aloft, and everything was now ready for filling away. Too anxious to go on deck, under such circumstances, and a lofty position being the best for ascertaining the presence of rocks, I determined to remain where I was, and conn the ship through the passes, in my own person. An order was accordingly given to set the jib, and to swing the head-yards, and get the spanker on the ship. In a minute, the Crisis was again in motion, moving steadily toward the inlet. As the lagoon was not entirely free from danger, coral rocks rising in places, quite near the surface of the water, I was obliged to be attentive to the pilot's duty until we got into the outer bay, when this particular danger in a great measure disappeared. I could then look about me with more freedom. Though we so far changed our position, as respected the wreck, as to open new views of it, no launch was to be seen behind it. By the time the ship reached the passage through the reef, I had little hope of finding it there.

We had got to be too familiar with the channels to have any difficulty in taking the ship through them ; and we were soon fairly to windward of the reef. Our course, however, lay to leeward ; and we passed round the southern side of the rocks, under the same easy canvas, until we got abreast, and within half a cable's length of the wreck. To aid my own eyes, I had called up Talcott and Neb ; but neither of us could obtain the least glimpse of the launch. Nothing was to be seen about the wreck ; though I took the precaution to send a boat to it. All was useless. Marble had gone out to sea, quite alone, in the Frenchman's launch ; and, though twenty pairs of eyes were now aloft, no one could even fancy that he saw anything in the offing that resembled a boat.

Talcott and myself had a private interview on the subject of Marble's probable course. My mate was of opinion that our friend had made the best of his way for some of the inhabited islands, unwilling to remain here when it came to the pinch, and yet ashamed to rejoin us. I could hardly believe this ; in such a case, I thought he would have waited until we had sailed ; when he might have left the island also, and nobody been the wiser. To this Talcott answered that Marble probably feared our importunities ; possibly, compulsion. It seemed singular to me, that a man who regretted his hasty decision, should adopt such a course ; and yet I was at a loss to explain the matter much more to my own satisfaction. Nevertheless, there was no remedy. We were as much in the dark as it was possible to be with a knowledge of the circumstance that the bird had flown.

We hovered around the reef for several hours, most of which time I passed in the cross-trees, and some of it on the royal-yard. Once, I thought I saw a small speck on the ocean, dead to windward, that resembled a boat's sail ; but there were so many birds flying about, and glancing beneath the sun's rays, that I was reluctantly compelled to admit it was probably one of them. At meridian, therefore, I gave the order to square away, and to make sail on our course. This was done with the greatest reluctance, how-ever, and not without a good deal of vacillation of purpose. The ship moved away from the land rapidly, and by two o'clock, the line of cocoa-nut trees that fringed the horizon astern, sunk entirely beneath the rolling margin of our view. From that moment, I abandoned the expectation of ever seeing Moses Marble again, though the occurrence left all of us sad for several days.

Major Merton and his daughter were on the poop nearly the whole of this morning. Neither interfered in the least ; for the old soldier was too familiar with discipline to venture an opinion concerning the management of the ship. When we met at dinner, however, the conversation naturally turned on the disappearance of our old friend.

" It is a thousand pities that pride should have prevented Marble from acknowledging his mistake," observed the major, " and thus kept him from getting a safe passage to Canton, where he might have left you, and joined another ship, had he thought it necessary."

" Where we shall do the same thing, I suppose, dear sir,"

added Emily, with a manner that I thought marked, "and thus relieve Captain Wallingford from the encumbrance of our presence."

"Me! call your delightful society anything but an encumbrance, I beg of you, Miss Merton," I rejoined in haste. "Now that Mr. Le Compte has furnished this comfortable cabin, and you are no longer at any inconvenience to yourselves, I would not be deprived of the advantage and pleasure of this association for more than I dare mention."

Emily looked gratified; while her father appeared to me to be thoughtful. After a brief pause, however, the major resumed the discourse.

"I should certainly feel myself bound to make many apologies for the trouble we are giving," he said, "especially, since I understand from Wallingford, he will not accept, either for himself or his owners, anything like compensation even for the food we consume, were it not that we are here by constraint, and not by any agency of our own. As soon as we reach Canton, however, I shall feel it a duty to get on board the first English ship that will receive us."

I stole a glance at Emily, but could not understand the expression of her countenance, as she heard this announcement. Of course, I made an earnest protest against the major's doing anything of the sort; and yet I could not well find any sufficient reason for urging him to remain where he was, beyond my own gratification. I could not go to either England or Bombay; and I took it for granted Major Merton wished to proceed at once, to one, if not to both of these places. We conversed, a little generally perhaps, on the subject for some time longer; and when I left the cabin, it struck me Emily's melancholy had in no degree lessened.

It is a long road to traverse over half of the Pacific. Weeks and weeks were thus occupied; Talcott and myself profiting by every suitable occasion, to enjoy the advantages of the association chance had thus thrown in our way. I make no doubt I was greatly benefited by my constant communications with the Mertons; the major being a cultivated, though not a particularly brilliant man; while I conceive it to be utterly impossible for two young men, of our time of

A contemporary plan of New York City in the days when Miles Wallingford visited it between his ocean voyages.

life and profession, to be daily, almost hourly, in the company of a young woman like Emily Merton, without losing some of the peculiar roughness of the sea, and getting, in its place, some small portion of the gentler qualities of the saloon. I date a certain *aplomb*, an absence of shyness in the company of females, from this habitual intercourse with one of the sex who had, herself, been carefully educated in the conventionalities of respectable, if not of very elegant or sophisticated society.

At length we reached the China seas, and falling in to windward, we made a quick run to Canton. It now became necessary for me to attend to the ship and the interests of my owners ; suffering my passengers to land at Whampoa, with the understanding we were to meet before either party sailed. I soon disposed of the sandal-wood and skins, and found no difficulty in procuring teas, nankins, china-ware, and the other articles pointed out in the instructions to poor Captain Williams. I profited by the occasion, also, to make certain purchases on my own account, that I had a presentiment would be particularly agreeable to the future mistress of Clawbonny, let that lady turn out to be whomsoever she might. The dollars obtained on the west coast of South America enabled me to do this ; my instructions giving the necessary authority to use a few of them on private account. My privilege as master rendered all proper.

In a word, the residence of six or eight weeks at Canton proved a very advantageous affair for those whose money was embarked in the Crisis. Sandal-wood and sea-otter skins brought particularly high prices ; while teas, and the manufactures of the country, happened to be low. I had no merit in this—not a particle ; and yet I reaped the advantage, so far as advantage was connected with the mere reputation of the voyage—success being of nearly as great account in commerce as in war. It is true, I worked like a dog ; for I worked under an entirely novel sense of responsibility, and with a feeling, I am certain, that could never have oppressed me in the care of my own property, and I deserved some portion of the credit subsequently obtained.

At all events I was heartily rejoiced when the hatches were on, and the ship was once more ready for sea.

It now became a duty, as well as a pleasure, to seek Major Merton, whom I had seen but once or twice during the last two months. He had passed that time at Whampoa, while I had been either at the factories or on board. The major was occupied when I called, and Emily received me alone. When she learned that I was ready to sail for home, and had come to take my leave, it was easy to see that she was uneasy if not distressed. I felt unhappy at parting, too, and perhaps I had less scruple about saying as much.

" God only knows, Miss Merton, whether we are ever to be permitted to see each other again," I remarked, after the preliminary explanations had been made.

The reader will remember that I am now an old man, and that vanity no longer has any of that influence over me which it might be supposed to possess over one of more juvenile hopes and feelings ; that I relate facts, without reference to their effect on myself, beyond the general salvo of some lingering weaknesses of humanity. I trust, therefore, I shall be understood in all my necessary allusions to the estimation in which I was apparently held by others. Emily fairly started when I made this remark concerning the probable duration of the approaching separation, and the color left her cheek. Her pretty white hand shook, so that she had difficulty in using her needle ; and there was an appearance of agitation and distress about the charming girl, that I had never before witnessed in one whose manner was usually so self-possessed and calm. I now know the reason why I did not throw myself on my knees, and beg the charming girl to accompany me to America, though I wondered at myself afterward, when I came to reflect coolly on all that had passed, for my stoicism. I will not affirm that I fancied Emily's agitation to be altogether owing to myself, but I confess to an inability to account for it in any other manner as agreeable to myself. The appearance of Major Merton at that instant, however, prevented everything like a scene, and probably restored us both to a consciousness of the necessity of seeming calm. As for the

major himself, he was evidently far from being unconcerned, something having occurred to disturb him.   So very
apparent was this, that I commenced the discourse by asking
if he were unwell.

"Always that, I fear, Miles," he answered; "my physician has just told me frankly, unless I get into a cold climate as soon as possible, my life will not be worth six
months' purchase."

"Then sail with me, sir," I cried, with an eagerness and
heartiness that must have proved my sincerity.   "Happily,
I am not too late to make the offer; and, as for getting
away, I am ready to sail to-morrow!"

"I am forbidden to go near Bombay," continued the
major, looking anxiously at his daughter; "and that appointment must be abandoned.   If I could continue to
hold it, there is no probability of a chance to reach my
station this half year."

"So much the better for me, sir.   In four or five months
from this moment, I will land you in New York, where you
will find the climate cold enough for any disease.   I ask
you as friends, as guests, not as passengers; and to prove
it, the table of the upper cabin, in future, shall be mine.   I
have barely left room in the lower cabin to sleep or dress in,
having filled it with my own private venture, as is my right."

"You are as generous as kind, Miles; but what will
your owners think of such an arrangement?"

"They have no right to complain.   The cabin and passengers, should any of the last offer, after deducting a very
small allowance for the ship's portion of the food and water,
are mine by agreement.   All the better food I find at my
own charge; and should you insist on remunerating the
owners for the coarser, or such as they find, you can do so
—it will be less than a hundred dollars at the most."

"On these conditions, then, I shall thankfully profit by
your offer, attaching, however, one more that I trust you
may be permitted to fulfil.   It is important to me that I
reach England—can you touch at St. Helena?"

"Willingly, if it be your wish.   The health of the crew,
moreover, may render it desirable."

"There, then, I will quit you, if an opportunity offer to proceed to England. Our bargain is made, dear Miles; and to-morrow I shall be ready to embark."

I think Emily never looked more beautiful than she did while listening to this arrangement. It doubtless relieved her mind on the painful subject of her father's health, and I fancied it relieved it also on the subject of our own immediate separation. Months must elapse before we could reach St. Helena ; and who could foresee what those months might bring forth? As I had a good deal to do at such a moment, I took my leave with my feelings lightened, as it might be, of a burden. The reader will at once infer I was in love. But he will be mistaken. I was not in love, though my imagination, to use a cant phrase of some of the sects, was greatly exercised. Lucy, even then, had a hold of my heart in a way of which I was ignorant myself; but it was not in nature for a youth, just approaching his majority, to pass months and months, almost alone, in the society of a lovely girl who was a year or two his junior, and not admit some degree of tenderness toward her in his feelings. The circumstances were sufficient to try the constancy of the most faithful swain that ever lived. Then it must be remembered that I had never professed to love Lucy—was not at all aware that she entertained any other sentiment toward me than that she entertained toward Rupert; whereas Emily—but I will not prove myself a coxcomb on paper, whatever I might have been, at the moment, in my own imagination.

Next day, at the appointed hour, I had the happiness to receive my old passengers. It struck me that Talcott was as much gratified as I was myself, for he, too, had both pleasure and improvement in Emily Merton's society. It has often been said that the English East-India ships are noted for quarrelling and making love. The quarrels may be accounted for on the same principle as the love-making, namely, propinquity ; the same proximity producing hostility in those sterner natures, that, in others of a gentler cast, produces its opposite feeling.

We sailed, and it is scarcely necessary to tell the reader

how much the tedium of so long a voyage, and the monot-
ony of a sea-voyage, was relieved by the graces and gentle
intercourse of our upper cabin. The other apartment being
so crowded and hot, I passed most of my time in the poop,
which was both light and airy. Here I generally found the
father and daughter, though often the latter alone. I played
reasonably well on the flute and violin, and had learned to
accompany Emily on her piano, which, it will be remembered, Monsieur Le Compte had caused to be transferred
from the Bombay ship to his own vessel, and which had
subsequently been saved from the wreck.

Talcott played also on the flute, far better than I did
myself, and we frequently made a trio, producing very
respectable sea-music—better, indeed, than Neptune often
got for his smiles. In this manner, then, we travelled our
long road, sometimes contending with head-winds and cross-
seas, sometimes becalmed, and sometimes slipping along at
a rate that rendered everybody contented and happy.

In passing the Straits of Sunda, I related to Major Merton
and Emily the incidents of the John's affair with the proas,
and her subsequent loss on the island of Madagascar ; and
was rewarded by the interest they took in the tale. We all
spoke of Marble, as indeed we often did, and expressed
our regrets at his absence. The fate of my old shipmate
was frequently discussed among us, there being a great
diversity of opinion on the subject. As for the major, he
thought poor Marble must be lost at sea, for he did not
perceive how any one man could manage a boat all alone
by himself. Talcott, who had juster notions of what a seaman could do, was of opinion that our late commander had
run to leeward, in the hope of finding some inhabited island,
preferring the association of even cannibals, when it came
to the trying moment, to total solitude. I thought he had
gone to windward, the boat being so well equipped for that
service, and that Marble was in the expectation of falling
in with some of the whalers, who were known to be cruising in certain latitudes. I was greatly struck, however, by
a remark made by Emily, on the evening of the very day
when we passed the Straits of Sunda.

22

"Should the truth be ever known, gentlemen," she said, "I am of opinion it will be found that poor Mr. Marble only left the island to escape from your importunities, and returned to it after the ship disappeared; and that he is there at this moment, enjoying all the happiness of a hermit."

This might be true, and from that hour the thought would occasionally recur to my mind. As I looked forward to passing at least several more years at sea, I secretly determined to ascertain the fact for myself, should occasion ever offer. In the meantime, the Crisis had reached a part of the ocean where, in those days, it was incumbent on those who had the charge of a ship to keep a vigilant lookout for enemies. It seems we were not fated to run the gauntlet of these pirates entirely unharmed.

Early on the following morning, I was awoke by Talcott's giving me a hearty shake of the shoulder.

"Turn out at once, Captain Wallingford!" cried my mate; "the rascals are closing around us like crows about a carcass. As bad luck will have it, we have neither room nor breeze to spare. Everything looks like a busy morning for us, sir."

In just three minutes from that moment, I was on deck, where all hands were soon collected, the men tumbling up, with their jackets in their hands. Major Merton was already on the poop, surveying the scene with a glass of his own; while the two mates were clearing away the guns, and getting the ship in a state to make a suitable defence. To me, the situation was altogether novel. I had been six times in the presence of enemies before, and twice as commander; but never under circumstances that called so imperiously for seamanship and good conduct. The ocean seemed covered with enemies, Major Merton declaring that he could count no less than twenty-eight proas, all full of men, and some of them armed with artillery. These chaps were ahead, astern, to windward, and to leeward; and what was worse, they had just wind enough to suit their purposes, there being about a five-knot breeze. It was evident that the craft acted in concert, and that they were desperately

bent on our capture, having closed around us in this manner
in the night. Nevertheless, we were a warm ship for a merchantman; and not a man in the Crisis betrayed any feeling
that indicated any other desire than a wish to resist to the
last. As for Neb, the fellow was in a broad grin, the whole
time; he considered the affair as a bit of fun. Yet this
negro was afraid to visit certain places about the farm in
the dark, and could not have been induced to cross a
churchyard alone, under a bright sun, I feel well persuaded.
He was the oddest mixture of superstitious dread and lion-
hearted courage I ever met with in my life.

It was still early, when the proas were near enough to
commence serious operations. This they did, by a nearly
simultaneous discharge of about a dozen guns, principally
sixes, that they carried mounted in their bows. The shot
came whistling in among our spars and rigging, literally
from every direction, and three struck, though they were
not of a size to do any serious injury. Our people were
at quarters, having managed to man both batteries, though
it left scarcely any one to look after the braces and rigging,
and none but the officers with small-arms.

Mr. Merton must have felt that his and his daughter's
liberty, if not their lives, were in the keeping of a very
youthful commander; still, his military habits of subordina-
tion were so strong, he did not venture even a suggestion.
I had my own plan, and was just of an age to think it de-
rogatory to my rank to ask advice of any one. The proas
were strongest ahead and on both bows, where they were
collecting to the number of near twenty, evidently with the
intention of boarding, should an opportunity offer; while,
astern, and on our quarter, they were much fewer, and far
more scattered. The reason of all this was apparent by
our course, the pirates naturally supposing we should continue to stand on.

Orders were given to haul up the mainsail and to man
the spanker-brails. The men were taken from the starboard battery, exclusively, to perform this work. When
all was ready, the helm was put up, and the ship was
brought as short round on her heel as possible, hauling up,

on an easy bowline, on the other tack. In coming round, we delivered all our larboard guns among the crowd of enemies, well crammed with grape; the distance being just right for scattering, this broadside was not without effect. As soon as braced up, on the other tack, we opened, starboard and larboard, on such of the chaps as came within range; clearing our way as we went. The headmost proas all came round in chase; but being from half a mile to a mile astern, we had time to open a way out of the circle, and to drive all the proas who were now ahead of us, to take refuge among the crowd of their fellows. The manœuvre was handsomely executed; and in twenty minutes we ceased firing, having all our enemies to the westward of us, and in one group; this was an immense advantage, as it enabled us to fight with a single broadside, prevented our being raked, and rendered our own fire more destructive, by exposing to it a more concentrated, and, at the same time, a larger object. I ought to have said before, that the wind was at the southward.

The Crisis now tacked, setting the courses and royals. The ship lay up well, and the proas having collected round their admiral, there was a prospect of her passing to windward of everything. Six of the fellows, however, seemed determined to prevent this, by hauling close on a wind, and attempting to cross our bows, firing as they did so. The ship stood on, apparently as if to intercept them; when, finding ourselves near enough, we kept away about three points; and swept directly down in the very centre of the main body of the proas. As this was done, the enemy, taken by surprise, cleared a way for us, and we passed the whole of them, delivering grape and canister, as fast as we could deal it out. In the height of the affair, and the thickest of the smoke, three or four of the proas were seen quite near us, attempting to close; but I did not think it necessary to call the people from the guns, which were worked with great quickness, and did heavy execution. I fancy the pirates found it hotter than they liked, for they did not keep on with us; though our lofty sails gave us an advantage, and would have enabled us to leave them, had

they pursued a different course. As it was, we were clear
of them, in about five minutes; and the smoke beginning
to rise, we soon got a view of what had been done in that
brief space. In order to increase our distance, however,
we kept still away, running pretty fast through the water.

By the confusion which prevailed among the pirates, the
rascals had been well peppered. One had actually sunk,
and five or six were round the spot, endeavoring to pick up
the crew. Three more had suffered in their spars, and the
movements indicated that all had enough. As soon as satisfied of this, I hauled the ship up to her course, and we
continued to leave the cluster of boats, which remained
around the spot where their consort had gone down. Those
of the fellows to windward, however, did not seem disposed
to give it up, but followed us for two hours, by which time
the rest of their flotilla were hull down. Believing there
was now plenty of room, I tacked toward these persevering
gentry, when they went about like tops, and hauled off
sharp on a wind. We tacked once more to our course,
and were followed no farther.

The captain of a pepper ship afterwards told me that our
assailants lost forty-seven men, mostly killed, or died of
their hurts, and that he had understood that the same officer
commanded the Crisis that had commanded the John, in
her affair, near the same spot. We had some rigging cut,
a few of our spars slightly injured, and two men hurt, one
of whom happened to be Neb. The man most hurt died
before we reached the Cape, but more from the want of
surgical assistance than from the original character of his
wound. As for Neb, he went to duty before we reached
St. Helena. For my part, I was surprised one of the proas
did not get down his throat, his grin being wide enough,
during the whole affair, to admit of the passage of a two-
decker.

We went into the island, as had been agreed, but no ship
offering and none being expected soon, it became necessary
for my passengers to continue on with us to New York.
Emily had behaved uncommonly well in the brush with
the pirates, and everybody was glad to keep her in the

ship. The men swore she brought good luck, forgetting that the poor girl must have met with much ill luck, in order to be in the situation in which she was actually placed.

Nothing occurred on the passage from St. Helena to New York, worthy of being specially recorded. It was rather long, but I cannot say it was unpleasant. At length our reckoning told us to look out for land. The major and Emily were on deck, all expectation, and ere long we heard the welcome cry. A hazy cloud was just visible on our lee-bow. It grew more and more dense and distinct, until it showed the hues and furrows of a mountain-side. The low point of the Hook, and the higher land beyond, then came in view. We glided past the light, doubled the Spit, and got into the upper bay, just an hour before the sun of a beautiful day in June was setting. This was in the year of our Lord 1802.

CHAPTER XXI.

" Drink ! drink ! to whom shall we drink?
　To a friend or a mistress?—Come, let me think !
　To those who are absent, or those who are here?
　To the dead that we loved, or the living still dear?
　Alas ! when I look I find none of the last !
　The present is barren—let 's drink to the past."

PAULDING.

THOUGH strictly a Manhattanese as a sailor, I shall not run into rhapsody on the subject of the beauties of the inner or outer bay of this prosperous place. No man but one besotted with provincial conceit could ever think of comparing the harbor of New York with the Bay of Naples ; nor do I know two places, that have the same great elements of land and water, that are less alike. The harbor of New York is barely pretty—not a particle more, if quite as much ; while the Bay of Naples is almost what its owners so fondly term it, "a little bit of heaven, fallen upon earth." On the other hand, however, Naples, as a haven, is not to be mentioned in the same breath with the great American mart, which, as a port, has no competitor within the circle of my knowledge, Constantinople alone excepted. I wish my semi-townsmen, the Manhattanese, could be persuaded of these facts, as when they do brag, as the wisest of mortals sometimes will, they might brag of their strong, and not of their weak points, as is now too often the case.

The major, Emily, and myself stood on the poop, regarding the scene, as the ship glided onward, before a good southeast breeze. I watched the countenances of my companions with interest, for I had the nervousness of a tyro

and a provincial on the subject of the opinions of the people
of other lands concerning everything that affected my own.
I could see that the major was not particularly struck ; and
I was disappointed, then, whatever may be my opinion now.
Emily better answered my hopes. Whether the charming
girl really felt the vast contrast between a view of the unbroken expanse of the ocean, and the scene before her, or
was disposed to please her host, she did not hesitate to express delight. I let her understand how much I was gratified ; and thus our long, long voyage, and that, so far as
degrees of longitude were concerned, nearly embraced the
circuit of the earth, may be said to have terminated with
the kindest feeling.

The ship was off Bedloe's, and the pilot had begun to
shorten sail, when a schooner crossed our fore-foot, beating
down. I had been too much occupied with the general
movement of the bay, to notice one small craft ; but, this
vessel happening to tack quite near us, I could not but turn
my eyes in her direction. At that instant I heard a shout
from Neb, who was furling one of the royals. It was one
of those irrepressible "nigger gollies" that often escaped
from the fellow involuntarily.

"What do you mean by that uproar, on the mizzen-royal-
yard," I called out angrily ; for the style of my ship had
now become an object of concern with me. "Keep silence,
sir, or I'll find a way to instruct you in the art."

"Lord ! Masser Mile," cried the negro, pointing eagerly
toward the schooner, "there go Pretty Poll."

It was our old craft, sure enough, and I hailed her, incontinently.

"Pretty Polly, ahoy !"

"Halloo !"

"Where are you bound, sir ; and when did that schooner
get in from the Pacific?"

"We are bound to Martinique—the Poll got home from
the South Seas about six months since. This is her third
voyage to the West Indies, since."

Here then was the certainty that the cargo sent home,
and the letter with it, were all safe. I must be expected,

and the owners would soon hear of my arrival. We were not kept long in doubt ; for, as the ship entered the Hudson, a boat approached, and in her were two of the principal members of our firm. I had seen them, and that is all ; but my own letters, and the report of the officer who brought home the schooner, had told them all about me. Could Nelson, after his victory of the Nile, have walked into the King of England's private cabinet with the news of his own success, his reception would not have been more flattering than that I now received. I was "Captain Wallingforded" at every sentence ; and commendations were so intermixed with inquiries about the value of the cargo, that I did not know which to answer first. I was invited to dine the very next day by both the gentlemen in the same breath ; and when I raised some objections connected with the duty of the ship, the invitations were extended from day to day for a week. So very welcome is he who brings us gold !

We went alongside of a North River wharf, and had everything secure, just as the sun was setting. The people were then allowed to go ashore for the night. Not a soul of them asked for a dollar, but the men walked up the wharf attended by a circle of admiring landlords, that put them all above want. The sailor who has three years' pay under his lee, is a sort of Rothschild on Jack's Exchange. All the harpies about our lads knew that the Crisis and her teas, etc., were hypothecated to meet their own ten and twenty dollar advances.

I dressed myself hurriedly, and ordered Neb to imitate my example. One of the owners had kindly volunteered to see Major Merton and Emily to a suitable residence, with an alacrity that surprised me. But the influence of England and Englishmen, in all America, was exceedingly great forty years since. This was still more true in New York than in the country generally, and a half-pay English major was a species of nobleman among the better sort of Manhattanese of that day. How many of these *quasi* lords have I seen, whose patents of nobility were merely the commissions or captains and lieutenants, signed by the Majesty of England !

In that day—it is nonsense to deny it—the man who had served against the country, provided he was a "British officer," was a better man than he who had served in our own ranks. This was true, however, only as regarded society; the ballot-boxes and the people giving very different indications of their sentiments on such subjects. Nor is this result, so far as New York was concerned, as surprising as at first sight it may possibly appear. Viewed as a class, the gentry of New York took sides with the crown. It is true, that the portion of this gentry which might almost be called *baronial*—it was strictly manorial—was pretty equally divided, carrying with them their collaterals; but the larger portion of this entire class of the *élite* of society took sides with the crown, and the peace of '83 found no small part of them in possession of their old social stations, the confiscations affecting few beyond the most important and the richest of the delinquents. I can give an instance within my own immediate knowledge of the sort of justice of these confiscations.

The head of one of the most important of all the colonial families was a man of indolent habits, and was much indisposed to any active pursuits. This gentleman was enormously rich, and his estates were confiscated and sold. Now this attainted traitor had a younger brother who was actually serving in the British army in America, his regiment sharing in the battles of Bunker Hill, Brandywine, Monmouth, etc. But the major was a younger son, and in virtue of that republican merit, he escaped the consequences of his adhesion to the service of the crown, and after the Revolution the cadet returned to his native country, and took quiet possession of a property of no inconsiderable amount; while his senior passed his days in exile, paying the bitter penalty of being rich in a revolution. It was a consequence of the peculiarities first mentioned, that the Manhattanese society set so high a value on English connection. They still admired, as the provincial only can admire, and they worshipped, as the provincial worships; or, at a safe distance. The strange medley of truth, cant, selfishness, sophistry, and good faith, that founded the political hostility to the move-

ments of the French Revolution, had as ardent believers in
this country as it had in England itself; and this contributed
to sustain the sort of feeling I have described. Of the fact
there can be no doubt, as any one will testify who knew
New York society forty years ago.

No wonder, then, that Major Merton and Emily fared
well on their sudden arrival in the country. Some romance,
moreover, was attached to their adventures; and I had no
great reason to give myself any anxiety on their account.
There was little doubt of their soon being much more at
home than I could hope to be, though in my native land.

Neb soon reported himself ready for shore-duty, and I
ordered him to follow me. It was my intention to proceed
to the counting-house of the owners, to receive some letters
that awaited me, and after writing short answers, to despatch
the black at once to Clawbonny with the intelligence of my
return. In 1802, the Battery was the court-end of the town,
and it was a good deal frequented by the better classes, particularly at the hour at which I was now about to cross it.
I have never returned from a voyage, especially to Europe,
without being particularly struck with two things in the
great Western Emporium—since the common councils and
the editors insist on the word—namely, the provincial appearance of everything that meets the eye, and the beauty
of the younger females; meaning, however, by the last, the
true, native portion of the population, and not the throng
from Ireland and Germany, who now crowd the streets, and
who certainly, as a body, are not in the least remarkable for
personal charms. But an American can tell an American
man or woman as soon as he lays eyes on either; and there
were few besides native girls on the Battery at the time of
which I am writing. As there were many children taking
their evening walk, and black servants were far more common than now, Neb had his share of delights, too, and I
heard him exclaim " Golly ! " twice, before we reached the
centre of the Battery. This exclamation escaped him on
passing as many sable Venuses, each of whom bridled up at
the fellow's admiration, and doubtless was as much offended
as the sex is apt to be on such occasions.

I must have passed twenty young women that evening,
either of whom would induce a youth to turn round to look
again; and, for a moment, I forgot my errand. Neither
Neb nor I was in a hurry. We were strolling along, in this
manner, gazing right and left, when a party approached,
under the trees, that drew all my attention to itself. In front
walked a young man and young woman, who were dressed
simply, but with a taste that denoted persons of the better
class. The former was remarkable for nothing, unless it
might be a rattling vivacity, of which large doses were ad-
ministered to his fair companion, who, seemingly, swallowed
it less reluctantly than doses of another sort are so often
received. At least, I thought so while the two were at a
distance, by the beautiful glistening teeth that were shining
like my own spotless pearls, between lips of coral. The air,
beauty, figure, and, indeed, all connected with this singularly
lovely young creature, struck my imagination at once. It
was not so much her beauty, though that was decided and
attractive, as the admixture of feminine delicacy with blooming health; the walk, so natural, and yet so full of lightness and grace; the laugh, so joyous, and still so quiet and
suited to her sex; and the entire air and manner, which
denoted equally buoyant health and happiness, the graceful-
ness of one who thought not of herself, and the refinement
which is quite as much the gift of native sentiment as the
fruit of art and association. I could not tell what her companion was saying; but as they approached, I fancied them
acknowledged lovers, on whom fortune, friends, and circumstances smiled alike. A glance aside told me that even Neb
was struck by the being before him, and that he had ceased
looking at the sable Venuses, to gaze at this.

I could not keep my gaze off the face of this lovely creature, who did not let me get a good look of her dark-blue
eyes, however, until I was quite near, when they were
naturally turned toward the form that approached. For a
few seconds, while in the very act of passing, we looked intently at each other, and the charm said to be possessed by
certain animals, was not more powerful than was our mutual
gaze. In this manner we had actually passed each other,

and I was still in a sort of mystified trance, when I heard suddenly, in a voice and tone that caused every nerve to thrill within me, the single word—

" Miles ! "

Turning, and taking another look, it was impossible any longer to mistake. Lucy Hardinge stood before me, trembling, uncertain, her face now pale as death, now flushed to scarlet, her hands clasped, her look doubting, eager, shrinking, equally denoting hope and fear, and all so blended, as to render her the most perfect picture of female truth, feeling, diffidence, and natural modesty I had ever beheld.

"Lucy—is it—can it be possible? It is, then, you, I thought so gloriously beautiful, and that without knowing you, too."

I take it for granted, had I studied a week, I should not have composed a more graceful salutation than this, which burst forth in a way that set all the usual restraints of manners at defiance. Of course, I felt bound to go through with the matter as prosperously as I had commenced, and in spite of the publicity of the place, in spite of half a dozen persons, who heard what passed, and had turned, smiling, to see what would come next, in spite of the grave-looking gentleman who had so lately been all vivacity and gayety, I advanced, folded the dear girl to my heart, and gave her such a kiss, as I 'll take upon myself to say, she had never before received. Sailors usually do not perform such things by halves, and I never was more in earnest in my life. Such a salutation, from a young fellow who stood rather more than six feet in his stockings, had a pair of whiskers that had come all the way from the Pacific with very little trimming, and who possessed a manliness about him of which mere walking up and down Broadway would have robbed a young Hercules, had the effect to cover poor Lucy with blushes and confusion.

"There—that will do, Miles," she said, struggling to get free ; " a truce, I pray you. See, yonder are Grace and my father, and Rupert."

There they all were, sure enough, the whole family having come out, to take an evening walk, in company with a certain Mr. Andrew Drewett, a young gentleman who was a fellow-student of Rupert's, and who, as I afterward ascertained, was a pretty open admirer of Rupert's sister. There was a marked difference in the manner in which I was received by Grace and Lucy. The first exclaimed " Miles ! " precisely as the last had exclaimed ; her color heightened, and tears forced themselves into her eyes, but she could not be said to blush. Instead of first manifesting an eagerness to meet my salute, and then shrinking sensitively from it, she flung her delicate arms round my neck, without the slightest reserve, both arms too, kissed me six or eight times without stopping, and then began to sob, as if her heart would break. The spectators, who saw in all this the plain, honest, natural, undisguised affection of a sister, had the good taste to walk on, though I could see that their countenances sympathized with so happy a family meeting. I had but a moment to press Grace to my heart, before Mr. Hardinge's voice drew my attention to him. The good old man forgot that I was two inches taller than he was himself; that I could, with ease, have lifted him from the earth, and carried him in my arms, as if he were an infant ; that I was bronzed by a long voyage, and had Pacific Ocean whiskers ; for he caressed me as if I had been a child, kissed me quite as often as Grace had done, blessed me aloud, and then gave way to his tears, as freely as both the girls. But for this burst of feeling on the part of a grayheaded old clergyman, I am afraid our scene would not altogether have escaped ridicule. As it was, however, this saved us. Clergymen were far more respected in America, forty years ago, than they are to-day, though I think they have still as much consideration here as in most other countries ; and the general respect felt for the class would have insured us from any manifestations of the sort, without the nature and emotion which came in its aid. As for myself, I was glad to take refuge in Rupert's hearty but less sentimental shake of the hand. After this, we all sought a seat, in a less public spot, and were soon sufficiently composed to converse. As for the gentleman named Drewett, he waited long enough to inquire of Lucy who I was, and then he had suffi-

cient tact to wish us all good evening. I overheard the little dialogue which produced this explanation.

"A close friend, if not a near relation, Miss Hardinge?"
he observed, inquiringly.

"Oh, yes," answered the smiling, weeping girl, with the
undisguised truth of her honest nature, "both friend and
relative."

"May I presume to ask the name?"

"The name, Mr. Drewett! Why it is Miles—dear Miles
—you surely have heard us speak of Miles—but I forget;
you never were at Clawbonny. Is it not a most joyful
surprise, dearest, dearest Grace?"

Mr. Andrew Drewett waited, I thought, with most commendable patience, for Grace to squeeze Lucy's hand, and to
murmur her own felicitations, when he ventured to add,—

"You were about to say something, Miss Hardinge?"

"Was I—I declare I have forgotten what it was. Such
a surprise—such a joyful, blessed surprise—I beg pardon,
Mr. Drewett—ah! I remember now; I was about to say that
this is Mr. Miles Wallingford, of Clawbonny, the gentleman
who is my father's ward—Grace's brother, you know."

"And how related to yourself, Miss Hardinge?" the
gentleman continued, a little perseveringly.

"To me! Oh! very, very near—that is—I forget so much
this evening—why, not at all."

It was at this moment Mr. Drewett saw fit to make his
parting salutations with studied decorum, and to take his
leave in a manner so polite, that, though tempted, I could
not, just at the moment, stop the current of my feelings, to
admire. No one seemed to miss him, however, and we five,
who remained, were soon seated in the spot I have mentioned, and as much abstracted from the scene around us,
as if we had been on the rustic bench, under the old elm,
on the lawn—if I dare use so fine a word, for so unpretend-
ing a place—at Clawbonny. I had my station between Mr.
Hardinge and Grace, while Lucy sat next her father, and
Rupert next to my sister. My friend could see me without
difficulty, owing to his stature, while I saw the glistening
eyes of Lucy, riveted on my face, as, leaning on her father's

knee, she bent her graceful form forward, in absorbed attention.

"We expected you; we have not been taken altogether by
surprise!" exclaimed good Mr. Hardinge, clapping his hand
on my shoulder, as if to say he could now begin to treat
me like a man. "I consented to come down, just at this
moment, because the last Canton ship that arrived brought
the intelligence that the Crisis was to sail in ten days."

"And you may judge of our surprise," said Rupert,
"when we read the report in the papers, 'The Crisis, Captain Wallingford.'"

"I supposed my letters from the island had prepared you
for this," I observed.

"In them, you spoke of Mr. Marble, and I naturally
concluded, when it came to the pinch, the man would resume the command, and bring the ship home. Duty to the
owners would be apt to induce him."

"He did not," I answered, a little proudly perhaps, forgetting poor Marble's probable situation, for an instant, in
my own vanity. "Mr. Marble understood well, that if I
knew nothing else, I knew how to take care of a ship."

"So it seems, my dear boy, indeed, so it doth seem!"
said Mr. Hardinge, kindly. "I hear from all quarters,
your conduct commended; and the recovery of the vessel
from the French, was really worthy of Truxtun himself."

At that day, Truxtun was the great gun of American
naval idolatry, and had as much local reputation, as Nelson
himself enjoyed in England. The allusion was a sore assault on my modesty; but I got along with it, as well as I
could.

"I endeavored to do my duty, sir," I answered, trying
not to look at Lucy, and seem meek; "and it would have
been a terrible disgrace to have come home, and been obliged
to say the French got the ship from us when we were all
asleep."

"But you took a ship from the French, in that manner,
and kept her too!" said a soft voice, every intonation of
which was music to me.

I looked round and saw the speaking eyes of Lucy, just

clear of the gray coat of her father, behind which she instinctively shrank, the instant she caught my glance.

"Yes," I answered, "we did something of that sort, and were a little more fortunate than our enemies. But, you will recollect, we were much favored by the complaisance of poor Monsieur Le Compte, in leaving us a schooner to work our mischief in."

"I have always thought that part of your story, Miles, a little extraordinary," observed Mr. Hardinge; "though I suppose this Frenchman's liberality was, in some measure, a matter of necessity, out there, in the middle of the Pacific."

"I hardly think you do Captain Le Compte justice, sir. He was a chivalrous fellow, and every way a gallant seaman. It is possible, he was rather more in a hurry than he might have been, but for his passengers—that is all—at least, I have always suspected that the wish to have Miss Merton all to himself, induced him to get rid of us as soon as possible. He evidently admired her, and could have been jealous of a dead-eye."

"Miss Merton!" exclaimed Grace. "Jealous!"

"Miss Merton!" put in Rupert, leaning forward curiously.

"Miss Merton! And jealous of dead-eyes, and wishing to get rid of us!" said Mr. Hardinge, smiling. "Pray who is Miss Merton? and who are the us? and what are the dead-eyes?"

Lucy was silent.

"Why, sir, I thought I wrote you all about the Mertons. How we met them in London, and then found them prisoners to Monsieur Le Compte, and that I intended to carry them to Canton in the Crisis?"

"You told us some of this, certainly; but though you may have written 'all about' a Major Merton, you forgot to tell us 'about all' the Mertons. This is the first syllable I have ever had about a Miss Merton. How is it, girls—did Miles ever speak of any one but the major in his letters?"

"Not a syllable to me, sir, of any young lady, I can

23

assure you," replied Grace, laughing. "How was it to you, Lucy?"

"Of course he would not tell me that which he thought fit to conceal from his own sister," said Lucy, in a low voice.

"It is odd I should have forgotten to mention her," I cried, endeavoring to laugh it off. "Young men do not often forget to write about young ladies."

"This Miss Merton is young, then, brother?"

"About your own age, Grace."

"And handsome, and agreeable, and accomplished?"

"Something like yourself, my dear."

"But handsome, I take it for granted, Miles," observed Mr. Hardinge, "by the manner in which you have omitted to speak of her charms, in your letters!"

"Why, sir, I think most persons, that is, the world in general, I mean such as are not over-fastidious, would consider Miss Merton particularly handsome; agreeable in person and features, I would be understood to say."

"Oh! you are sufficiently explicit; everybody can understand you," added my laughing guardian, who had no more thought of getting me married to his own daughter than to a German princess of a hundred and forty-five quarterings, if there are any such things; "some other time we will have the particulars of her eyes, hair, teeth, etc., etc."

"Oh! sir, you may save me the trouble by looking at her yourself, to-morrow, since she and her father are both here."

"Here!" exclaimed all four in a breath; Lucy's extreme surprise extorting the monosyllable from her reserve even a little louder than from the rest.

"Certainly, here; father, daughter, and servants. I dare say I omitted to speak of the servants in my letters, too, but a poor fellow who has a great deal to do cannot think of everything in a minute. Major Merton has a touch of the liver-complaint, and it would not do to leave him in a warm climate. So, no other chance offering, he is proceeding to England, by the way of America."

"And how long had you these people on board your ship, Miles?" Grace asked, a little gravely.

"Actually on board with myself, about nine months, I

should think ; but including the time in London, at Canton, and on the island, I should call our aquaintance one of rather more than a year's standing.''

'' Long enough, certainly, to make a young lady sufficiently obvious to a young gentleman's memory, not to be forgotten in his letters.''

After this pointed speech there was a silence, which Mr. Hardinge broke by some questions about the passage home from Canton. As it was getting cool on the Battery, however, we all moved away, proceeding to Mrs. Bradfort's. This lady, as I afterward discovered, was much attached to Lucy, and had insisted on giving her these opportunities of seeing the world. She was quite at her ease in her circumstances, and belonged to a circle a good deal superior to that into which Grace and myself could have claimed admission in right of our own social position. Lucy had been well received as her relative, and as a clergyman's daughter, and Grace on her own account, as I afterward learned. It would be attaching too much credit to Clawbonny to say that either of the girls had not improved by this association, though it was scarcely possible to make Grace more feminine and lady-like than she had been made by nature. The effect on Lucy was simply to put a little reserve on her native frankness and sturdy honesty ; though candor compels me to say, that mingling with the world, and especially the world to which they had been introduced by Mrs. Bradfort, had certainly increased the native charm of manner that each possessed. I began to think Emily Merton, so far from possessing any advantage over the two girls, might now improve a little herself by associating with them.

At the house, I had to tell my whole story, and to answer a multitude of questions. Not a syllable more was said about Miss Merton ; and even Lucy had smiles to bestow and remarks to make, as before. When we got to the lights where the girls could remove their shawls and hats, I made each of them stand before me, in order to ascertain how much time had altered them. Grace was now nineteen ; and Lucy was only six months her junior. The greatest change was in the latter. Her form had ripened into something as near as possible to girlish perfection. In this respect she had the advantage of Grace, who was a little too slight and delicate; whereas Lucy, without any of the heaviness that so often accompanies a truly rounded person, and which was perhaps a slight defect in Emily Merton's figure, was without an angle of any sort in her entire outline. Grace, always so handsome, and so intellectual in the expression of her countenance, had improved less in this respect, than Lucy, whose eyes had obtained a tenderness and feeling that rendered them, to me, even more attractive than those of my own dear sister. In a word, any man might have been proud, at finding two such admirable creatures interested in him, as interested, every look, smile, syllable, and gesture of these girls, denoted they were in me.

All this time, Neb had been overlooked. He had followed us to the house, however, and was already engaged in a dark-colored flirtation with a certain Miss Chloe Clawbonny, his own second-cousin, in the kitchen; a lady who had attracted a portion of his admiration, before we sailed, and who had accompanied her young mistress to town. As soon as it was ascertained the fellow was below, Lucy, who was quite at home in her kinswoman's house, insisted on his being introduced. I saw by the indulgent smile of Mrs. Bradfort, that Lucy was not exceeding her conceded privileges, and Neb was ordered up forthwith. Never was there a happier fellow than this "nigger" appeared to be on that occasion. He kept rolling his tarpaulin between his fingers, shifting his weight from leg to leg, and otherwise betraying the confusion of one questioned by his betters; for in that day, a negro was ready enough to allow he had his betters, and did not feel he was injured in so doing. At the present time, I am well aware that the word is proscribed even in the State's prisons; everybody being just as good as everybody else; though some have the misfortune to be sentenced to hard labor, while others are permitted to go at large. As a matter of course, the selections made through the ballot-boxes, only go to prove that "one man is as good as another."

Our party did not separate until quite late. Suppers

were eaten in 1802 ; and I was invited to sit down with the rest of the family, and a gay set we were. It was then the fashion to drink toasts ; gentlemen giving ladies, and ladies gentlemen. The usage was singular, but very general ; more especially in the better sort of houses. We men drank our wine, as a matter of course ; while the ladies sipped theirs, in that pretty manner in which females moisten their lips on such occasions. After a time, Mrs. Bradfort, who was very particular in the observance of forms, gayly called on Mr. Hardinge for his toast.

"My dear Mrs. Bradfort," said the divine, good-humoredly, "if it were not in your own house, and contrary to all rule to give a person who is present, I certainly should drink to yourself. Bless me, bless me, whom shall I give? I suppose I shall not be permitted to give our new bishop, Doctor Moore?"

The cry of " No bishop! " was even more unanimous than it is at this moment, among those who, having all their lives dissented from episcopal authority, fancy it an evidence of an increasing influence to join in a clamor made by their own voices ; and this, moreover, on a subject that not one in a hundred among them has given himself the trouble even to skim. Our opposition— in which Mrs. Bradfort joined, by the way—was of a very different nature, however ; proceeding from a desire to learn what lady Mr. Hardinge could possibly select, at such a moment. I never saw the old gentleman so confused before. He laughed, tried to dodge the appeal, fidgeted, and at last fairly blushed. All this proceeded, not from any preference for any particular individual of the sex, but from natural diffidence, the perfect simplicity and nature of his character, which caused him to be abashed at even appearing to select a female for a toast. It was a beautiful picture of masculine truth and purity ! Still, we would not be put off ; and the old gentleman, composing his countenance five or six times in vain efforts to reflect, then looking as grave as if about to proceed to prayer, raised his glass, and said,—

" Peggy Perott ! "

A general laugh succeeded this announcement, Peggy Perott being an old maid who went about tending the sick for hire, in the vicinity of Clawbonny, and known to us all as the ugliest woman in the country.

"Why do you first insist on my giving a toast, and then laugh at it when given?" cried Mr. Hardinge, half amused, half serious in his expostulations. "Peggy is an excellent woman, and one of the most useful I know."

"I wonder, my dear sir, you did not think of adding a sentiment!" cried I, a little pertly.

"And if I had, it would have been such a one as no woman need be ashamed to hear attached to her name. But enough of this; I have given Peggy Perott, and you are bound to drink her;" that we had done already; "and now, cousin, as I have passed through the fiery furnace—"

"Unscathed?" demanded Lucy, laughing ready to kill herself.

"Yes, unscathed, Miss; and now, cousin, I ask of you to honor us with a toast."

Mrs. Bradfort had been a widow many years, and was fortified with the panoply of her state. Accustomed to such appeals, which, when she was young and handsome, had been of much more frequent occurrence than of late, she held her glass for the wine with perfect self-possession, and gave her toast with the conscious dignity of one who had often been solicited in vain "to change her condition."

"I will give you," she said, raising her person and her voice, as if to invite scrutiny, "my dear old friend, good Dr. Wilson."

It was incumbent on a single person to give another who was also single; and the widow had been true to the usage; but "good Dr. Wilson" was a half superannuated clergyman, whom no one could suspect of inspiring anything beyond friendship.

"Dear me—dear me!" cried Mr. Hardinge, earnestly, "how much more thoughtful, Mrs. Bradfort, you are than myself! Had I thought a moment, I might have given the doctor; for I studied with him, and honor him vastly."

This touch of simplicity produced another laugh—how easily we all laughed that night!—and it caused a little more confusion in the excellent divine. Mrs. Bradfort then called on me, as was her right; but I begged that Rupert might precede me, he knowing more persons, and being now a sort of man of the world.

"I will give the charming Miss Winthrop," said Rupert, without a moment's hesitation, tossing off his glass with an air that said, "How do you like that?"

As Winthrop was a highly respectable name, it denoted the set in which Rupert moved; and as for the young lady, I dare say she merited his eulogium, though I never happened to see her. It was something, however, in 1802, for a youngster to dare to toast a Winthrop, or a Morris, or a Livingston, or a De Lancey, or a Stuyvesant, or a Beekman, or a Van Rensselaer, or a Schuyler, or a Rutherford, or a Bayard, or a Watts, or a Van Cortlandt, or a Verplanck, or a Jones, or a Walton, or any of that set. They, and twenty similar families, composed the remnant of the colonial aristocracy, and still made head, within the limits of Manhattan, against the inroads of the Van—something elses. Alas! alas! how changed is all this, though I am obliged to believe it is all for the best.

"Do you know Miss Winthrop?" I asked of Grace, in a whisper.

"Not at all; I am not much in that set," she answered quietly. "Rupert and Lucy have been noticed by many persons whom I do not know."

This was the first intimation I got, that my sister did not possess all the advantages in society that were enjoyed by her friend. As is always the case where it is believed to be our loss, I felt indignant at first; had it been the reverse, I dare say I should have fancied it all very right. Consequences grew out of these distinctions which I could not then foresee, but which will be related in their place. Rupert now called on Grace for her toast, a lady commonly succeeding a gentleman. My sister did not seem in the least disconcerted; but after a moment's hesitation, she said,—

"Mr. Edward Marston."

This was a strange name to me, but I afterwards ascertained it belonged to a respectable young man who visited Mrs. Bradfort's, and who stood very well with all his acquaintances. I looked at Rupert, to note the effect; but Rupert was as calm as Grace herself had been when he gave Miss Winthrop.

"I believe I have no one to call upon but you, Miles," said Grace, smiling.

"Me! Why, you all know I am not acquainted with a soul. Our Ulster County girls have almost all gone out of my recollection; besides, no one would know them here, should I mention twenty."

"You strangely forget, brother, that most of us are Ulster County folk. Try if you can recall no young lady—"

"Oh! easily enough, for that matter; a young fellow can hardly have lived nine months in the same cabin with Emily, and not think of her when hard pushed; I will give you Miss Emily Merton."

The toast was drunk, and I thought Mr. Hardinge looked thoughtful, like one who had a guardian's cares, and that Grace was even grave. I did not dare look at Lucy, though I could have toasted her all night, had it been in rule to drink a person who was present. We began to chat again, and I had answered some eight or ten questions, when Mrs. Bradfort, much too precise to make any omissions, reminded us that we had not yet been honored with Miss Lucy Hardinge's toast. Lucy had enjoyed plenty of time to reflect; and she bowed, paused a moment as if to summon resolution, and then mentioned—

"Mr. Andrew Drewett."

So, then, Lucy Hardinge toasted this Mr. Drewett—the very youth with whom she had been in such animated discourse when I first met the party! Had I been more familiar with the world, I should have thought nothing of a thing that was so common; or, did I understand human nature better, I might have known that no sensitive and delicate woman would betray a secret that was dear to her, under so idle a form. But I was young, and ready myself to toast the girl I preferred before the universe; and I could not make suitable allowances for difference of sex and temperament. Lucy's toast made me very uncomfortable for the rest of the evening; and I was not sorry when Rupert reminded me that it was eleven, and that he would go with me to a tavern, in order to look for a room.

The next morning was passed in transacting the business of the ship. I found myself much noticed among the merchants and shipmasters; and one of my owners took me on 'Change, that I might see and be seen. As the papers had spoken of the recapture of the Crisis, on the arrival of the Pretty Poll, and had now each an article on the arrival of the ship, I had every reason to be satisfied with my reception. There are men so strong in principle, as well as intellect, I do suppose, that they can be content with the approbation of their own consciences, and who can smile at the praises or censure of the world alike; but I confess to a strong sympathy with the commendation of my fellow-creatures, and as strong a distaste for their disapprobation. I know this is not the way to make a very great man; for he who cannot judge, feel, and act for himself, will always be in danger of making undue sacrifices to the wishes of others; but you can have no more of a cat than the skin; and I was sufficiently proud at finding myself a miniature hero, about the lower end of Wall Street, and in the columns of the newspapers. As for these last, no one can complain of their zeal in extolling everything national. To believe them, the country never was wrong, or defeated, or in a condition to be defeated, except when a political opponent could be made to suffer by an opposite theory; and then nothing was ever right. As to fame, I have since discovered they consider that of each individual to be public property, in which each American has a part and parcel, the editors, themselves, more than the man who has thrown the article into the common lot. But I was young in 1802, and even a paragraph in my praise in a newspaper had a certain charm for me, that I will not deny. Then I had done well, as even my enemies, if I had any, must have admitted.

CHAPTER XXII.

"Ships are but boards, sailors but men; there be land-rats and water-rats, water-thieves and land-thieves—I mean pirates; and then there is the peril of waters, winds, and rocks; the man is, notwithstanding, sufficient;—three thousand ducats;—I think I may take his bond."—*Merchant of Venice.*

I SAW Grace, and Lucy, and Rupert, and good Mr. Hardinge, every day, but I could not find time to call on the Mertons until near the close of a week. I then paid them a visit, and found them glad to see me, but not at all in want of my attentions to make them comfortable. The major had exhibited his claims to the British consul, who happened to be a native Manhattanese, and was well connected, a circumstance that then gave him an influence in society that his commission alone would not have conferred. Colonel Barclay, for so was this gentleman called, had taken the Mertons by the hand as a matter of course, and his example being followed by others, I found that they were already in the best circle of the place. Emily mentioned to me the names of several of those with whom she had exchanged visits, and I knew at once, through Lucy's and Grace's conversation, and from my own general knowledge of the traditions of the colony and State, that they were among the leading people of the land, socially if not politically; a class altogether above any with whom I had myself ever associated. Now I knew that the master of a merchantman, whatever might be his standing with his owner or consignee, or the credit he had gained among his fellows, was not likely to get admission into this set; and there was the comfortable prospect before me, of having my own sister and the two other girls I admired most and loved best in the world—next to Grace, of course—visiting round in houses, of which the doors were shut against myself. This is always unpleasant, but in my case it turned out to be more.

When I told Emily that Grace and Lucy were in town, and intended coming to see her that very morning, I thought she manifested less curiosity than would have been the case a month before.

"Is Miss Hardinge a relative of Mr. Rupert Hardinge, the gentleman to whom I was introduced at dinner, yesterday?" she demanded, after expressing the pleasure it would give her to see the ladies.

I knew that Rupert had dined out the day before, and there being no one else of the same name, I answered in the affirmative.

"He is the son of a respectable clergyman, and of very good connections, I hear."

"The Hardinges are so considered among us; both Rupert's father and grandfather were clergymen, and his great-grandfather was a seaman—I trust you will think none the worse of him for that."

"A sailor! I had supposed, from what some of those present said—that is, I did not know it."

"Perhaps they told you that his great-grandfather was a British officer?"

Emily colored, and then she laughed faintly, admitting, however, that I had guessed right.

"Well, all this was true," I added, "though he was a sailor. Old Captain Hardinge—or Commodore Hardinge, as he used to be called, for he once commanded a squadron —was in the English navy."

"Oh! that sort of a sailor!" cried Emily, quickly. "I did not know that it was usual to call gentlemen in the navy, seamen."

"They would make a poor figure if they were not, Miss Merton; you might as well say that a judge is no lawyer."

This was enough, however, to satisfy me that Miss Merton no longer considered the master of the Crisis the first man in the world.

A ring announced the arrival of the two girls. They were shown up, and I soon had the satisfaction of seeing these three charming young women together. Emily received her two guests very courteously, and was frank, nay warm, in the expression of her gratitude for all that I had done for herself and her father. She even went back so far as to speak of the occurrence in the Park, at London, and was gracious enough to declare that she and her parents owed their lives to my interference. All this gave her listeners great pleasure, for I believe neither ever tired of hearing my praises. After this opening, the conversation turned on New York, its gayeties, and the different persons known to them mutually. I saw that the two girls were struck with the set Miss Merton was in, which was a shade superior even to that of Mrs. Bradfort's, though the fusion which usually accompanies that sort of thing brought portions of each circle within the knowledge of the other. As the persons named were utter strangers to me, I had nothing to say, and sat listening in silence. The opportunity was improved by comparing the girls with each other.

In delicacy of appearance, Grace and Lucy each had the advantage of the English beauty. Their hands and feet were smaller, their waists finer, and their *tournures*, generally, I thought the most pleasing. Emily had the advantage in complexion, though her color had less fineness and delicacy. Perhaps her teeth were the most brilliant; though Grace and Lucy, particularly the latter, had very fine teeth. The English girl's shoulders and bust, generally, would have been more admired than those of most American—particularly than most New York—girls; but it was not possible to surpass those of Lucy. As a whole, Emily's countenance had the most spirit. Lucy's the most finesse and feeling. I make no comparison with the expression of Grace's countenance, which was altogether too remarkable for its intellectual character, to be included in anything like a national classification. I remember I thought, as they sat there in a row conversing frankly and cheerfully together, Lucy the handsomest, in

"One had actually sunk, and five or six were round the spot endeavoring to pick up the crew." The *Crisis* emerges victorious from a battle with twenty-eight proas. *Drawing by R. W. Van Boskerck.* (p. 341)

her pretty neat morning dress; while I had my doubts whether Emily would not have extorted the most applause in a ball-room. This distinction is mentioned, because I believe it national.

The visit lasted an hour; for I had expressed a wish to all parties that they would become acquainted, and the girls seemed mutually pleased. As they chatted, I listened to the tones of their voices, and fancied, on the whole, that Emily had slightly the advantage in intonation and accent; though it was scarcely perceptible, and it was an advantage that was attended by a slight sacrifice of the charm of natural utterance. She was a little more artificial in this respect than her companions, and in so much less pleasing; though, had the comparison been made with the Manhattan style of the present day, the odds would have been immensely in her favor. In 1802, however, some attention was still paid to the utterance, tones of voice, and manner of speaking of young ladies. The want of it all, just now, is the besetting vice of the whole of our later instruction of the sex; it being almost as rare a thing, nowadays, to find a young American girl who speaks her own language gracefully, as it is to find one who is not of pleasing person.

When the young ladies parted, it was with an understanding that they were soon to meet again. I shook hands with Emily, English fashion, and took my leave at the same time.

"Well, Miles," said Grace, as soon as we were in the street, "you have certainly been of service to a very charming young woman—I like her, excessively."

"And you, Lucy—I hope you agree with Grace, in thinking my friend, Emily Merton, a charming young woman?"

Lucy did not speak as frankly, or as decidedly as Grace, so far as manner was concerned; though she coincided in words.

"I am of the same opinion," she said, in a tone that was far less cheerful than her usually very cheerful manner. "She is one of the loveliest creatures I ever saw; and it is no wonder—"

"What is no wonder, dear?" asked Grace, observing that her friend hesitated to proceed.

"Oh ! I was about to say something silly, and had better not finish the speech. But what a finished manner Miss Merton possesses ; do you not think so, Grace?"

"I wish she had a little less of it, dear ; that is precisely what I should find fault with in her deportment. It is manner ; and, though we all must have some, it strikes me it ought not to be seen. I think all the Europeans we saw in town, last winter, Lucy, had more or less of this manner."

"I dare say it would seem so to us ; notwithstanding, it may be very agreeable to those who are used to it—a thing to miss when one gets much accustomed to it."

As Lucy made this remark I detected a furtive and timid glance at myself. I was mystified at the time, and was actually so silly as to think the dear girl was talking at me, and to feel a little resentment. I fancied she wished to say, "There, Master Miles, you have been in London, and on a desert island in the South Seas—the very extremes of human habits—and have got to be so sophisticated, so very un-Clawbonnyish, as to feel the necessity of a manner, in the young ladies with whom you associate." The notion nettled me to a degree that induced me to pretend duty, and to hurry down to the ship. Whom should I meet, in Rector Street, but Mr. Hardinge, who had been across to the Hudson in search of me.

"Come hither, Miles," said the excellent old man, "I wish to converse with you seriously."

As Lucy was uppermost in my thoughts at the moment, I said to myself, "What can the dear old gentleman have to say, now?"

"I hear from all quarters the best accounts of you, my dear boy," Mr. Hardinge continued, "and I am told you make a very superior seaman. It is a feather in your cap, indeed, to have commanded an Indiaman a twelvemonth before you are of age. I have been conversing with my old friend John Murray, of the house of John Murray & Sons, one of the very best merchants in America, and he says. 'Push the boy ahead, when you find the right stuff in him.

Get him a ship of his own, and that will put him on the true
track.   Teach him early to have an eye to his own interests,
and it will make a man of him, at once.'   I have thought
the matter over, have had a vessel in my eye, for the last
month, and will purchase her at once, if you like the
plan."

"But have I money enough for such a thing, my dear sir
—after having sailed in the John, and the Tigris, and the
Crisis, I should not like to take up with any of your B's,
No. 2."

"You have forgotten to mention the ' Pretty Poll,' Miles,"
said the divine, smiling.   "Be under no fear, however, for
your dignity ; the vessel I have in treaty is all you could
wish, they tell me, having made but one voyage, and is sold
on account of the death of her owner.   As for money, you
will remember I have thirteen thousand dollars of your
income invested in stocks, and stocks that cost but ten.   The
peace has brought everything up, and you are making money,
right and left.   How have your own pay and private venture turned out ?"

"Perfectly well, sir.   I am near three thousand dollars
in pocket, and shall have no need to call on you for my
personal wants.   Then I have my prize money to touch.
Even Neb, wages and prize money, brings me nine hundred
dollars.   With your permission, sir, I should like to give the
fellow his freedom."

"Wait till you are of age, Miles, and then you can do as
you please.   I hold four thousand dollars of your invested
money, which has been paid in, and I have placed it in
stocks.   Altogether, I find we can muster in solid cash,
more than twenty thousand dollars, while the price of the
ship, as she stands, almost ready for sea, is only fifteen.
Now, go and look at the vessel ; if you like her, I will close
the bargain at once."

"But, my dear Mr. Hardinge, do you think yourself
exactly qualified to judge of the value of a ship?"

"Poh ! poh ! don't imagine I am so conceited as to purchase on my own knowledge.   I have taken some of the
very best advice of the city.   There is John Murray, to

begin with—a great ship-holder, himself, and Archibald
Gracie, and William Bayard—all capital judges, have
taken an interest in the affair. Three others of my friends
have walked round to look at the vessel, and all approve—
not a dissenting voice."

"May I ask, sir, who have seen her, besides the gentlemen you have named? They, I admit, are, indeed, good
judges."

"Why—why—yes—do you happen to know anything of
Doctor Benjamin Moore, now, Miles?"

"Never heard of him, sir, in my life; but a physician
can be no great judge of a ship."

"No more of a physician than yourself, boy—Doctor
Benjamin Moore, the gentleman we elected bishop, while
you were absent—"

"Oh! he you wished to toast, instead of Miss Peggy
Perott," cried I, smiling. "Well, what does the bishop
think of her—if he approve, she must be orthodox."

"He says she is the handsomest vessel he ever laid eyes
on, Miles; and let me tell you, the favorable opinion of so
good a man as Doctor Moore, is of value, even though it be
about a ship."

I could not avoid laughing, and I dare say most of the
readers will also, at this touch of simplicity; and yet, why
should not a bishop know as much of ships as a set of
ignoramuses who never read a theological book in their
lives, some of them not even the Bible, should know about
bishops? The circumstance was not a tittle more absurd
than many that are occurring daily before our eyes, and to
which, purely from habit, we submit, very much as a matter of course.

"Well, sir," I replied, as soon as I could, "I will look
at the ship, get her character, and give you an answer at
once. I like the idea, for it is pleasant to be one's own
master."

In that day, $15,000 would buy a very excellent ship, as
ships went. The vessel I was taken to see was coppered
and copper-fastened, butt-bolted, and she measured just five
hundred tons. She had a great reputation as a sailer, and,

what was thought a good deal of in 1802, was Philadelphia
built. She had been one voyage to China, and was little
more than a year old, or the best possible age for a vessel.
Her name was the "Dawn," and she carried an "Aurora"
for her figure-head. Whether she were, or were not inclined to Puseyism, I never could ascertain, although I can
affirm she had the services of the Protestant Episcopal
Catholic Church read on board her afterward, on more
than one occasion.

The result of my examination and inquiries was favorable,
and, by the end of the week, the Dawn was purchased.
The owners of the Crisis were pleased to express their
regrets, for they had intended that I should continue in the
command of their vessel, but no one could object to a man's
wishing to sail in his own employment. I made this important acquisition at what was probably the most auspicious
moment of American navigation. It is a proof of this that,
the very day I was put in possession of the ship, good
freights were offered to no less than four different parts of
the world. I had my choice between Holland, France,
England, and China. After consulting with my guardian, I
accepted that to France, which not only paid the best, but
I was desirous of seeing more of the world than had yet
fallen to my share. I could make a voyage to Bordeaux
and back in five months, and by the end of that time I
should be of age, and, consequently, my own master. As I
intended to have great doings at Clawbonny on that occasion,
I thought it might be well not to go too far from home.
Accordingly, after shipping Talcott and the Philadelphian,
whose name was Walton, for my mates, we began to take in
cargo as soon as possible.

In the meantime I bethought me of a visit to the paternal
home. It was a season of the year when most people, who
were anybodies, left town, and the villas along the shores
of the Hudson had long been occupied. Mr. Hardinge, too,
pined for the country and his flock. The girls had had
enough of town, which was getting to be very dull, and
everybody, Rupert excepted, seemed anxious to go up the
river. I had invited the Mertons to pass part of the sum-

24

mer at the farm, moreover, and it was time the invitation should be renewed, for the major's physicians had advised him to choose some cooler residence than the streets of a hot, close town could furnish during the summer months. Emily had been so much engrossed with the set into which she had fallen since her landing, and which it was easy for me to see was altogether superior to that in which she had lived at home, that I was surprised at the readiness with which she urged her father to redeem his promise.

"Mr. Hardinge tells me, sir, that Clawbonny is really a pretty spot," she said, "and the country around it is thought to be very healthy. You cannot get answers from home [she meant England] for several months, and I know Captain Wallingford will be happy to receive us. Besides, we are pledged to accept this additional favor from him."

I thought Major Merton felt some of my own surprise at Emily's earnestness and manner, but his resistance was very feeble. The old gentleman's health, indeed, was pretty thoroughly undermined, and I began to have serious doubts of his living even to return to Europe. He had some relatives in Boston, and had opened a correspondence with them, and I had thought, more than once, of the expediency of apprising them of his situation. At present, however, nothing better could be done than to get him into the country.

Having made all the arrangements with the others, I went to persuade Rupert to be of the party, for I thought it would make both Grace and Lucy so much the happier.

"Miles, my dear fellow," said the young student, gaping, "Clawbonny is certainly a capitalish place, but you will admit it is somewhat stupid after New York. My good kinswoman, Mrs. Bradfort, has taken such a fancy to us all, and has made me so comfortable—would you believe it, boy, she has actually given me six hundred a year, for the last two years, besides making Lucy presents fit for a queen. A sterling woman is she, this cousin Margaret of ours!"

I heard this, truly, not without surprise; for, in settling with my owners, I found Rupert had drawn every cent to which he was entitled, under the orders I had left when I last went to sea.

As Mrs. Bradfort was more than at her ease, however, had no nearer relative than Mr. Hardinge, and was much attached to the family, I had no difficulty in believing it true, so far as the lady's liberality was concerned. I heartily wished Rupert had possessed more self-respect; but he was, as he was!

"I am sorry you cannot go with us," I answered, "for I counted on you to help amuse the Mertons—"

"The Mertons! Why, surely, they are not going to pass the summer at Clawbonny?"

"They quit town with us, to-morrow. Why should not the Mertons pass the summer at Clawbonny?"

"Why, Miles, my dear boy, you know how it is with the world—how it is with these English, in particular. They think everything of rank, you know, and are devotees of style and appearance, and all that sort of thing, you know, as no one understands better than myself; for I pass most of my time in the English set, you know."

I did not then understand what had come over Rupert, though it is all plain enough to me now. He had, truly enough, got into what was then called the English set. Now, there is no question, that, so far as the natives themselves were concerned, this was as good a set as ever existed in this country; and it is also beyond all cavil, that many respectable English persons, of both sexes, were occasionally found in it; but it had this great defect: every Englishman who wore a good coat, and had any of the slang of society, made his way into the outskirts, at least, of this set; and Rupert, whose own position was not yet thoroughly confirmed, had fallen a great deal into the association of these accidental comers and goers. They talked large, drank deep, and had a lofty disdain for everything in the country, though it was very certain they were just then in much better company where they were, than they had ever been at home. Like most tyros, Rupert fancied these blustering gentry persons to imitate; and, as they seldom conversed ten minutes without having something to say of my Lord A—— or Sir John B——, persons they had read of, or seen in the streets, he was weak enough to imagine they knew all about the dignitaries of the British empire. As Rupert was really a gentleman, and had good manners naturally, it was a grievous thing to see him fashioning himself anew, as it might be, on such very questionable models.

"Clawbonny is not a stylish place, I am ready to allow," I answered, after a moment of hesitation; "still, it is respectable. There is a good farm, a valuable mill, and a good, old, comfortable, straggling, stone house."

"Very true, Miles, my dear fellow, and all as dear to me, you know, as the apple of my eye—but farmish; young ladies like the good things that come from farms, but do not admire the homeliness of the residence. I speak of young English ladies, in particular. Now, you see, Major Merton is a field-officer, and that is having good rank in a respectable profession, you know—I suppose you understand, Miles, that the king puts most of his sons into the army, or navy—all this makes a difference, you understand?"

"I understand nothing about it; what is it to me where the King of England puts his sons?"

"I wish, my dear Miles, if the truth must be said, that you and I had been a little less boyish, when we were boys, than happened to be the case. It would have been all the better for us both."

"Well, I wish no such thing. A boy should be a boy, and a man a man. I am content to have been a boy, while I was a boy. It is a fault in this country, that boys fancy themselves men too soon."

"Ah! my dear fellow, you will not, or do not understand me. What I mean is, that we were both precipitate in the choice of a profession—I retired in time, but you persevere; that is all."

"You did retire in season, my lad, if truth is what you are after; for had you stayed a hundred years on board ship, you never would have made a sailor."

When I said this I fancied I had uttered a pretty severe thing. Rupert took it so coolly, however, as to satisfy me at once that he thought differently on the subject.

"Clearly, it is not my vocation. Nature intended me for something better, I trust, and I mistook a boyish inclination for a taste. A little experience taught me better, and I am now where I feel I ought to be. I wish, Miles, you had come to the study of the law, at the time you went to sea. You would have been, by this time, at the bar, and would have had a definite position in society."

"I am very glad I did not. What the deuce should I have done as a lawyer; or what advantage would it have been to me to be admitted to the bar?"

"Advantage! Why, my dear fellow, every advantage in the world. You know how it is in this country, I suppose, in the way of society, my dear Miles?"

"Not I; and, by the little I glean from the manner you sheer about in your discourse, I wish to know nothing. Do young men study law merely to be genteel?"

"Do not despise knowledge, my boy; it is of use, even in trifles. Now in this country, you know, we have very few men of mere leisure—heirs of estates to live on their incomes, as is done in Europe; but nine tenths of us must follow professions, of which there are only half a dozen suitable for a gentleman. The army and navy are nothing, you know; two or three regiments scattered about in the woods, and half a dozen vessels. After these there remain the three learned professions, divinity, law, and physic. In our family divinity has run out, I fear. As for physic, 'Throw physic to the dogs,' as Miss Merton says—"

"Who?" I exclaimed, in surprise. "'Throw physic to the dogs'—why that is Shakespeare, man!"

"I know it, and it is Miss Emily Merton's, too. You have made us acquainted with a charming creature, at least, Miles, by this going to sea. Her notions on such subjects are as accurate as a sun-dial."

"And has Miss Emily Merton ever conversed with you on the subject of my profession, Rupert?"

"Indeed she has, and regretted it, again and again. You know as well as I do, Miles, to be a sailor, other than in a navy, is not a genteel profession!"

I broke out into a fit of laughter at this remark. It struck me as infinitely droll, and as somewhat silly. I knew my precise position in society, perfectly; had none of the silly swaggering about personal merit, and of "one man's being as good as another," that has since got into such general use among us ; and understood perfectly the useful and unavoidable classifications that take place in all civilized communities, and which, while they are attended by certain disadvantages as exceptions, produce great bene- fits as a whole, and was not disposed at all to exaggerate my claims or to deny my deficiencies. But the idea of attaching any considerations of gentility to my noble, manly, daring profession, sounded so absurd I could not avoid laughing. In a few moments, however, I became grave.

"Harkee, Rupert," said I; "I trust Miss Merton does not think I endeavored to mislead her as to my true posi- tion, or to make her think I was a greater personage than I truly am?"

"I'll not answer for that. When we were first ac- quainted, I found she had certain notions about Clawbonny, and your estate, and all that, which were rather English, you know. Now in England, an estate gives a man a cer- tain consideration, whereas land is so plenty with us, that we think nothing of the man who happens to own a little of it. Stock, in America, as it is so much nearer ready money, is a better thing than land, you know."

How true was this, even ten years since ; how false is it to-day! The proprietor of tens of thousands of acres was, indeed, under the paper-money *régime*, a less important man than the owner of a handful of scrip, which has had all its value squeezed out of it, little by little. That was truly the age when the representative of property was of far more importance than the property itself ; and all be- cause the country existed in a fever that set everything in motion. We shall see just such times again, I fear.

"But what had Emily Merton to do with all this?"

"Miss Merton? Oh! she is English, you know, and felt as English persons always do, at the sound of acres. I set it all right, however, and you need be under no concern."

"The devil you did! And, pray, in what manner was this done? How was the matter set right?"

Rupert took the cigar from his mouth, suffered the smoke to issue, by a small, deliberate jet, cocking his nose up at the same time as if observing the stars, and then deigned to give me an answer. Your smokers have such a disdainful, ultra-philosophical manner, sometimes!

"Why, just in this way, my fine fellow. I told her Clawbonny was a farm, and not an estate, you know; that did a good deal, of itself. Then, I entered into an explanation of the consideration of farmers in this country, you know, and made it all as plain as A B C. She is a quick girl, is Emily, and takes a thing remarkably soon."

"Did Miss Merton say anything to induce you to suppose she thought the less of me, for these explanations."

"Of course not—she values you, amazingly—quite worships you, as a sailor—thinks you a sort of merchant-captain Nelson, or Blake, or Truxtun, and all that sort of thing. All young ladies, however, are exceedingly particular about professions, I suppose you know, Miles, as well as I do myself."

"What, Lucy, Rupert? Do you imagine Lucy cares a straw about my not being a lawyer, for instance?"

"Do I? Out of all question. Don't you remember how the girls wept—Grace as well as Lucy—when we went to sea, boy? It was all on account of the ungentility of the profession, if a fellow can use such a word."

I did not believe this, for I knew Grace better, to say the least; and thought I understood Lucy sufficiently, at that time, to know she wept because she was sorry to see me go away. Still, Lucy had grown from a very young girl, since I sailed in the Crisis, into a young woman, and might view things differently, now, from what she had done three years before. I had not time, however, for further discussion at that moment, and I cut the matter short.

"Well, Rupert, what am I to expect?" I asked; "Clawbonny, or no Clawbonny?"

"Why, now you say the Mertons are to be of the party, I suppose I shall have to go; it would be inhospitable else. I do wish, Miles, you would manage to establish visiting relations with some of the families on the other side of the river. There are plenty of respectable people within a few hours' sail of Clawbonny.''

'' My father, and my grandfather, and my great-grandfather managed, as you call it, to get along, for the last hundred years, well enough on the west side ; and, although we are not quite as genteel as the east, we will do well enough. The Wallingford sails early in the morning, to save the tide ; and I hope your lordship will turn out in season, and not keep us waiting. If you do, I shall be ungenteel enough to leave you behind.''

I left Rupert with a feeling in which disgust and anger were blended. I wish to be understood, more particularly as I know I am writing for a stiff-necked generation. I never was guilty of the weakness of decrying a thing because I did not happen to possess it myself. I knew my own place in the social scale perfectly ; nor was I, as I have just said, in the least inclined to fancy that one man was as good as another. I knew very well that this was not true, either in nature or in the social relations ; in political axioms, any more than in political truths. At the same time, I did not believe nature had created men unequal, in the order of primogeniture from male to male. Keeping in view all the facts, I was perfectly disposed to admit that habits, education, association, and sometimes chance and caprice, drew distinctions that produced great benefits, as a whole ; in some small degree qualified, perhaps, by cases of individual injustice. This last exception, however, being applicable to all things human, it had no influence on my opinions, which were sound and healthful on all these points ; practical, common-sense like, and in conformity with the decisions of the world from the time of Moses, down to our own, or, I dare say, of Adam himself, if the truth could be known ; and, as I have said more than once in these rambling memoirs, I was not disposed to take a false view of my own social position. I belonged, at most, to the class of small proprietors, as they existed in the last century, and filled a very useful and respectable niche between the yeoman and gentleman, considering the last strictly in reference to the upper class of that day. Now,

it struck me that Emily Merton, with her English notions,
might very well draw the distinctions Rupert had mentioned ; nor am I conscious of having cared much about it,
though she did. If I were a less important person on *terra
firma*, with all the usages and notions of ordinary society
producing their influence, than I had been when in command of the Crisis, in the centre of the Pacific, so was Miss
Merton a less important young lady, in the midst of the
beauty of New York, than she had been in the isolation of
Marble Land. This I could feel very distinctly. But
Lucy's supposed defection did more than annoy me. I felt
humbled, mortified, grieved. I had always known that
Lucy was better connected than I was myself, and I had
ever given Rupert and her the benefit of this advantage, as
some offset to my own and Grace's larger means ; but it had
never struck me that either the brother or sister would be
disposed to look down upon us in consequence. The world
is everywhere—and America, on account of its social vicissitudes, more than most other countries—constantly exhibiting
pictures of the struggles between fallen consequence and
rising wealth. The last may, and does have the best of it,
in the mere physical part of the strife ; but in the more
moral, if such a word can be used, the quiet ascendency of
better manners and ancient recollections is very apt to over-
shadow the fussy pretensions of the vulgar aspirant, who
places his claims altogether on the almighty dollar. It is
vain to deny it ; men ever have done it, and probably ever
will defer to the past, in matters of this sort—it being much
with us, in this particular, as it is with our own lives, which
have had all their greatest enjoyments in bygone days. I
knew all this—felt all this—and was greatly afraid that
Lucy, through Mrs. Bradfort's influence, and her town associations, might have learned to regard me as Captain Wallingford of the merchant-service, and the son of another
Captain Wallingford of the same line in life. I determined,
therefore, to watch her with jealous attention, during the
few days I was to remain at Clawbonny. With such generous intentions, the reader is not to be surprised if I found
some of that for which I so earnestly sought—people being

very apt to find precisely the thing for which they look,
when it is not lost money.

The next morning we were all punctual, and sailed at the
proper hour. The Mertons seemed pleased with the river,
and, having a fresh southerly wind in our favor, with a
strong flood-tide, we actually landed at the mill the same
afternoon. Everything is apt to be agreeable when the
traveller gets on famously ; and I thought I never saw
Emily in better spirits than she was when we first reached
the top of the ascent that lies above the landing. I had
given her my arm, as due to hospitality, while the others
got up as they could ; for I observed that Rupert assisted
no one. As for Lucy, I was still too much vexed with her,
and had been so all day, to be as civil as I ought. We
were soon at a point that commanded a view of the house,
meadows, orchards, and fields.

"This, then, is Clawbonny!" exclaimed Emily, as soon
as I pointed out the place to her. "Upon my word, a very
pretty farm, Captain Wallingford. Even prettier than you
represented it to be, Mr. Rupert Hardinge."

"Oh ! I always do justice to everything of Wallingford's,
you know. We were children together, and became so
much attached in early life, that it's no wonder we remain so
in these our later days."

Rupert was probably nearer the truth than he imagined,
when he made this speech ; my regard for him, by this time,
being pretty much reduced to habit ; and certainly it had no
increase from any fresh supplies of respect. I began to hope
he might not marry Grace, though I had formerly looked
forward to the connection as a settled thing. "Let him get
Miss Merton, if he can," I said to myself; "it will be no
great acquisition, I fancy, to either side."

How different was it with his father, and, I may add, with
Lucy ! The old gentleman turned to me, with tears in his
eyes ; pointed to the dear old house, with a look of delight ;
and then took my arm, without reference to the wants of
Miss Merton, and led me on, conversing earnestly of my
affairs, and of his own stewardship. Lucy had her father's
arm, on the other side ; and the good divine was too much

accustomed to her, to mind the presence of his daughter. Away we three went, therefore, leading the way, while Rupert took charge of Emily and Grace. Major Merton followed, leaning on his own man.

"It is a lovely—it is a lovely spot, Miles," said Mr. Hardinge; "and I do most sincerely hope you will never think of tearing down that respectable-looking, comfortable, substantial, good old-fashioned house, to build a new one."

"Why should I, dear sir? The house, with an occasional addition, all built in the same style, has served us a century, and may very well serve another. Why should I wish for more, or a better house?"

"Why, sure enough? But now you are a sort of a merchant, you may grow rich, and wish to be the proprietor of a seat."

The time had been, when such thoughts often crossed my mind; but I cared less for them, then. To own a seat, was the great object of my ambition in boyhood; but the thought had weakened by time and reflection.

"What does Lucy think of the matter? Do I want, or indeed deserve, a better house?"

"I shall not answer either question," replied the dear girl, a little saucily, I thought. "I do not understand your wants, and do not choose to speak of your deservings. But I fancy the question will be settled by a certain Mrs. Wallingford, one of these days. Clever women generally determine these things for their husbands."

I endeavored to catch Lucy's eye, when this was said, by leaning a little forward myself; but the girl turned her head in such a manner as prevented my seeing her face. The remark was not lost on Mr. Hardinge, however, who took it up with warmth, and all the interest of a most pure and disinterested affection.

"I suppose you will think of marrying, one of these days, Miles," he said; "but, on no account, marry a woman who will desert Clawbonny, or who would wish materially to alter it. No good-hearted woman, indeed— no true-hearted woman—would ever dream of either. Dear me! dear me! the happy days and the sorrowful days—

the gracious mercies of Providence, and the chastening afflictions—that I myself have seen, and felt, and witnessed, under these same roofs!"

This was followed by a sort of enumeration of the events of the last forty years, including passages in the lives of all who had dwelt at the farm; the whole concluding with the divine's solemnly repeating, "No, no, Miles! do not think, even, of marrying a woman who would wish you to desert, or materially alter, Clawbonny."

CHAPTER XXIII.

" **If thou be'st rated by thy estimation,**
Thou dost deserve enough ; and yet enough
May not extend so far as to the lady.''
Merchant of Venice.

NEXT morning, I was early afoot, and I found Grace as much alive to the charms of home, as I was myself. She put on a gypsy, and accompanied me into the garden, where, to my surprise, I found Lucy. It looked like old times to be in that spot, again, with those two dear girls. Rupert alone was wanting to complete the picture ; but I had an intimate conviction that Rupert, as he had been at least, could never come within the setting of the family group again. I was rejoiced, however, to see Lucy, and more so, just where I found her, and I believe told her as much with my eyes. The charming girl looked happier than she had appeared the day before, or for many previous days indeed, and I felt less apprehension than of late, concerning her having met with any agreeable youth of a more genteel profession than that of a merchant-captain.

"I did not expect to find you here, Miss Lucy,'' cried Grace, "eating half-ripe currants, too, or my eyes deceive me, at this early hour in the morning. It is not twenty minutes since you were in your own room, quite unadorned.''

"The green fruit of dear Clawbonny is better than the ripe fruit of those vile New York markets !'' exclaimed Lucy, with a fervor so natural as to forbid any suspicion of acting. "I should prefer a Clawbonny potato to a New York peach !''

Grace smiled, and as soon as Lucy's animation had a little subsided, she blushed.

"How much better would it be, Miles," my sister resumed, "could you be induced to think and feel with us, and quit the seas, to come and live for the rest of your days on the spot where your fathers have so long lived before you. Would it not, Lucy?"

"Miles will never do that," Lucy answered, with emphasis. "Men are not like us females, who love everything we love at all with our whole hearts. Men prefer wandering about, and being shipwrecked, and left on desert islands, to remaining quietly at home on their own farms. No, no, you 'll never persuade Miles to do that."

"I am not astonished my brother thinks desert islands such pleasant abodes, when he can find companions like Miss Merton on them."

"You will remember, sister of mine, in the first place, that Marble Land is very far from being a desert island at all; and in the next, I found Miss Merton in Hyde Park, London, almost in the canal, for that matter."

"I think it a little odd that Miles never told us all about this in his letters at the time, Lucy. When young gentlemen drag young ladies out of canals, their friends at home have a right to know something of the matter."

How much unnecessary misery is inflicted by unmeaning expressions like this. Grace spoke lightly, and probably without a second thought about the matter; but the little she said not only made me thoughtful and uneasy, but it drove everything like a smile from the usually radiant countenance of her friend. The conversation dragged, and soon after we returned together to the house.

I was much occupied that morning in riding about the place with Mr. Hardinge, and listening to his account of his stewardship. With the main results I was already acquainted, nay, possessed them in the Dawn, but the details had all to be gone over with the most minute accuracy. A more simple-minded being there was not on the earth than Mr. Hardinge; and that my affairs turned out so well was the result of the prosperous condition of the country at that day, the system my father had adopted in his lifetime, and the good qualities of the different agents he had chosen—every one of whom remained in the situation in which he was at the sad moment of the fatal accident at the mill. Had matters really depended on the knowledge and management of the most excellent divine, they would soon have been at sixes and sevens.

"I am no believer in miracles, my dear Miles," observed my guardian, with amusing self-complacency; "but I do think a change has been wrought in me, to meet the emergencies of a situation in which the interests of two orphans have been so suddenly intrusted to my guidance and care. God be thanked! everything prospers; your affairs, as well as those of my dear Grace. It is wonderful, boy, how a a man of my habits has been directed in his purchases of wheat, for instance; I, who never bought a bushel until the whole responsibility of your mills fell upon my shoulders. I take no credit to myself for it—no credit to myself."

"I hope the miller has not been backward, my dear sir, in giving you all the assistance in his power."

"Morgan? yes, he is always ready; and you know I never forget to send him into the market to both buy and sell. Really his advice has been so excellent, that to me it has the appearance of being almost miraculous—prophetic, I should say, were it not improper. We should avoid all exaggeration in our gratitude, boy."

"Very truly, sir. And in what manner have you managed to get along so well with the crops on the place itself?"

"Favored by the same great adviser, Miles. It is really wonderful, the crops we have had, and the judgment that has been so providentially shown in the management of the fields as well as of the mills!"

"Of course, sir, old Hiram [Neb's uncle] has always been ready to give you his aid? Hiram has a great deal of judgment in his way."

"No doubt, no doubt. Hiram and I have done it all, led by a providential counsel. Well, my boy, you ought to be satisfied with your earthly lot, for everything seems to prosper that belongs to you. Of course you will marry, one of these days, and transmit this place to your son, as it has been received from your fathers ? "

" I keep that hope in perspective, sir ; or as we sailors say for a sheet-anchor."

" Your hope of salvation, boy, is your sheet-anchor, I trust. Nevertheless, we are not to be too hard on young men, and must let them have a little romance in their compositions. Yes, yes ; I trust you will not become so much wedded to your ship, as not to think of taking a wife one of these days. It will be a happy hour to me when I can see another Mrs. Miles Wallingford at Clawbonny. She will be the third ; for I can remember your grandmother."

" Can you recommend to me a proper person to fill that honorable station, sir ? " said I, smiling to myself, and exceedingly curious to hear the answer.

" What do you think of this Miss Merton, boy ? She is handsome, and that pleases young men ; clever, and that pleases old ones ; well educated, and that will last when the beauty is gone ; and, so far as I can judge, amiable ; and that is as necessary to a wife as fidelity. Marry no woman, Miles, that is not amiable ! "

" May I ask what you call amiable, sir ? and, when that question is answered, I may venture to go so far as to inquire whom you call amiable ? "

" Very sensible distinctions, and such as are entitled to fair answers ; at least the first. I do not call levity, amiability ; nor mere constitutional gayety. Some of the seemingly most light-hearted women I have ever known, have been anything but amiable. There must be an unusual absence of selfishness—a person must live less for herself, than others —or rather, must find her own happiness in the happiness of those she loves, to make a truly amiable woman. Heart and principle are at the bottom of what is truly amiable ; though temperament and disposition undoubtedly contribute. As for the whom, your own sister Grace is a truly amiable young woman. I never knew her do anything to hurt another's feelings in my life."

" I suppose you will admit, sir, I cannot very well marry Grace ? "

" I wish you could, with all my heart—yes, with all my heart ! Were not you and Grace brother and sister, I should consider myself well quit of the responsibility of my guardianship, in seeing you man and wife."

" As that is out of the question, I am not without hopes you can mention another who will do just as well so far as I am concerned."

" Well, there is Miss Merton—though I do not know her well enough to venture absolutely on a recommendation. Now, I told Lucy, no later than yesterday, while we were on the river, and as you were pointing out to Miss Merton the forts in the Highlands, that I thought you would make one of the handsomest couples in the State ; and moreover, I told her—bless me, how this corn grows ! The plants will be in tassel in a few days, and the crops must turn out most beneficent—truly, truly there is a Providence in all things ; for, at first, I was for putting the corn on yonder hill-side, and the potatoes here ; but old Hiram was led by some invisible agency to insist on this field for the corn, and the hill-side for the potatoes ; and, now, look and see what crops are in promise ! Think of a nigger's blundering on such a thing ! "

In 1802, even well-educated and well-intentioned clergy-men had no scruples in saying " nigger."

" But, sir, you have quite forgotten to add what else you told Lucy."

" True, true—it is very natural that you should prefer hearing me talk about Miss Merton, to hearing me talk about potatoes. I 'll tell that to Lucy, too, you may depend on it."

" I sincerely hope you will do no such thing, my dear sir," I cried, in no little alarm.

" Ah ! that betrays guilt—consciousness, I should say : for what guilt can there be in a virtuous love ? and rely on it, both the girls shall know all about it. Lucy and I often talk over your matters, Miles ; for she loves you as well as your own sister. Ah ! my fine fellow, you blush at it, like a girl of sixteen ! But there is nothing to be ashamed of, and there is no occasion for blushes."

"Well, sir, letting my blushes—the blushes of a ship-master !—but setting aside my blushes, for mercy's sake what more did you tell Lucy ? "

"What more ? Why I told her how you had been on a desert island, quite alone, as one might say, with Miss Merton, and how you had been at sea, living in the same cabin, as it were, for nine months ; and it would be wonderful, wonderful indeed, if two so handsome young persons should not feel an attachment for each other. Country might make some difference, to be sure—"

"And station, sir ? What do you think would be the influence of the difference of station, also ? "

"Station ! Bless me, Miles ; what difference in station is there between you and Miss Merton, that it should cause any obstacle to your union ? "

"You know what it is, sir, as well as I do myself. She is the daughter of an officer in the British army, and I am the master of a ship. You will admit, I presume, Mr. Hardinge, that there is such a thing as a difference in station ? "

"Beyond all question. It is exceedingly useful to remember it ; and I greatly fear the loose appointments of magistrates and other functionaries, that are making round the country, will bring all our notions on such subjects into great confusion. I can understand that one man is as good as another in rights, Miles ; but I cannot understand he is any better, because he happens to be uneducated, ignorant, or a blackguard."

Mr. Hardinge was a sensible man in all such distinctions, though so simple in connection with other matters.

"You can have no difficulty, however, in understanding that in New York, for instance, I should not be considered the equal of Major Merton—I mean socially altogether, and not in personal merit or the claims which years give —and, of course, not the equal of his daughter ? "

"Why—yes—I know what you mean, now. There may be some little inequality in that sense, perhaps ; but Clawbonny, and the ship, and the money at use, would be very apt to strike a balance."

"I am afraid not, sir. I should have studied law, sir, had I wished to make myself a gentleman."

"There are lots of vulgar fellows getting into the law, Miles; men who have not half your claims to be considered gentlemen. I hope you do not think I wished you and Rupert to study law in order to make gentlemen of you?"

"No, sir; it was unnecessary to take that step as regards Rupert, who was fully born in the station. Clergymen have a decided position all over the world, I believe; and then you are extremely well-connected otherwise, Mr. Hardinge. Rupert has no occasion for such an assistance; with me it was a little different."

"Miles, Miles, this is a strange fancy to come over a young man in your situation—and who, I am afraid, has been the subject of envy, only too often, to Rupert."

"If the truth were known, Mr. Hardinge, I dare say both Rupert and Lucy, in their secret hearts, think they possess advantages in the way of social station that do not belong to Grace and myself."

Mr. Hardinge looked hurt, and I was soon sorry that I had made this speech. Nor would I have the reader imagine that what I had said proceeded in the least from that narrow, selfish feeling which, under the blustering pretension of equality, presumes to deny the existence of a very potent social fact; but simply from the sensitiveness of feelings which on this subject were somewhat in danger of becoming morbid, through the agency of the most powerful passion of the human heart, or that which has well been called the master-passion. Nevertheless, Mr. Hardinge was much too honest a man to deny a truth, and much too sincere to wish even to prevaricate about it, however unpleasant it might be to acknowledge it in all its unpleasant bearings.

"I now understand you, Miles; and it would be idle to pretend that there is not some justice in what you say, though I attach very little importance to it, myself. Rupert is not exactly what I could wish him to be in all things, and possibly he may be coxcomb enough, at times, to fancy he has this slight advantage over you; but as for Lucy, I'll engage she never thinks of you but as a second brother, and that she loves you exactly as she loves Rupert.''

Mr. Hardinge's simplicity was of proof, and it was idle to think of making any impression on it. I changed the subject, therefore, and this was easy enough done by beginning again to talk about the potatoes. I was far from being easy, nevertheless; for I could not avoid seeing that the good divine's restlessness might readily widen the little breach which had opened between his daughter and myself.

That day, at dinner, I discovered that Grace's winter in town had led to a sensible melioration of the domestic economy; most especially as related to the table. My father and mother had introduced some changes, which rendered the Clawbonny household affairs a little different from those of most other of the Ulster County families near our own class; but their innovations, or improvements, or whatever they might be called, were far from being as decided as those introduced by their daughter. Nothing, perhaps, sooner denotes the condition of people, than the habits connected with the table. If eating and drinking be not done in a certain way, and a way founded in reason, too, as indeed are nearly all the customs of polished life, whatever may be the cant of the ultras of reason —but, if eating and drinking be not done in a certain way, your people of the world perceive it sooner than almost anything else. There is, also, more of common-sense and innate fitness, in the usages of the table, so long as they are not dependent on mere caprice, than in almost any other part of our deportment; for everybody must eat, and most persons choose to eat decently. I had been a little nervous on the subject of the Mertons, in connection with the Clawbonny table, I will confess; and great was my delight when I found the breakfast going off so well. As for the major, himself by no means familiar with the higher classes of his own country, he had that great stamp of a gentleman, simplicity; and he was altogether above the cockney distinctions of eating and drinking; those about cheese and malt liquors, and such vulgar niceties;

nor was he a man to care about the silver-forkisms; but
he understood that portion of the finesse of the table
which depended on reason and taste, and was accustomed
to observe it. This I knew from near a twelvemonth's
intercourse, and I had feared we might turn out to be a
little too rustic.

Grace had made provisions against all this, with a tact
and judgment for which I could have worshipped her. I
knew the viands, the vegetables, and the wines would all
be good of their kind, for in these we seldom failed; nor
did I distrust the cookery, the English-descended families
of the Middle States, of my class, understanding that to
perfection; but I feared we should fail in those little
incidents of style and arrangement, and in the order of the
service, that denote a well-regulated table. This is just
what Grace had seen to; and I found that a great revolution had been quietly effected in this branch of our domestic economy during my absence; thanks to Grace's
observations while at Mrs. Bradfort's.

Emily seemed pleased at dinner, and Lucy could again
laugh and smile. After the cloth was removed, the major
and Mr. Hardinge discussed a bottle of Madeira, and that
too of a quality of which I had no reason to be ashamed;
while we young people withdrew together to a little
piazza, that was in the shade at that hour, and took seats,
for a chat. Rupert was permitted to smoke, on condition
that he would not approach within fifteen feet of the party.
No sooner was this little group thus arranged, the three
girls in a crescent, than I disappeared.

"Grace, I have not yet spoken to you of a necklace of
pearls possessed by your humble servant," I cried, as my
foot again touched the piazza. "I would not say a word
about it—"

"Yet Lucy and I heard all about it," answered Grace,
with provoking calmness, "but would not ask to see it,
lest you should accuse us of girlish curiosity. We waited
your high pleasure in the matter."

"You and Lucy heard I had such a necklace!"

"Most unquestionably: I. Grace Wallingford, and she,

Lucy Hardinge. I hope it is no infringement on the rights of Mr. Miles Clawbonny ''—so the girls often called me, when they affected to think I was on my high ropes— '' I hope it is no infringement on the rights of Mr. Miles Clawbonny to say as much ? ''

'' And pray how could you and Lucy know anything about it ? ''

'' That is altogether another question ; perhaps we may accord an answer, after we have seen the necklace.''

'' Miss Merton told us, Miles,'' said Lucy, looking at me with gentleness, for she saw I really wished an answer ; and what could Lucy Hardinge ever refuse me, that was right in itself, when she saw my feelings were really interested ?

'' Miss Merton? Then I have been betrayed, and the surprise I anticipated is lost.''

I was vexed, and my manner must have shown it in a slight degree. Emily colored, bit her lip, and said nothing ; but Grace made her excuses with more spirit than it was usual for her to show.

'' You are rightly punished, Master Miles,'' she cried ; '' for you had no business to anticipate surprises. They are vulgar things at best, and they are worse than that when they come from a distance of fifteen thousand miles—from a brother to a sister. Besides, you have surprised us sufficiently once, already, in connection with Miss Merton.''

'' I ! '' I exclaimed.

'' Me ! '' added Emily.

'' Yes, I and me ; did you tell us one word about her, in your letters ? and have you not now both surprised and delighted us, by making us acquainted with so charming a person? I can pardon such a surprise, on account of its consequences ; but nothing so vulgar as a surprise about pearls.''

Emily blushed now ; and in her it was possible to tell the difference between a blush and the suffusion that arose from a different feeling ; but she looked immensely superior to anything like explanations.

'' Captain Wallingford ''—how I disliked that Captain —'' Captain Wallingford can have but little knowledge

of young ladies," she said coldly, "if he supposes such
pearls as he possesses would not form the subject of their
conversation."

I was coxcomb enough to fancy Emily was vexed that
I had neglected to be more particular about her being on
the island, and her connection with the ship. This might
have been a mistake, however.

"Let us see the pearls, Miles; and that will plead your
apology," said Lucy.

"There, then—your charming eyes, young ladies, never
looked on pearls like those, before."

Female nature could not suppress the exclamations of
delight that succeeded. Even Rupert, who had a besetting weakness on the subject of all personal ornaments,
laid aside his cigar, and came within the prescribed distance, the better to admire. It was admitted all round,
New York had nothing to compare with them. I then
mentioned that they had been fished up by myself from
the depths of the sea.

"How much that adds to their value!" said Lucy, in a
low voice, but in her warm, sincere manner.

"That was getting them cheap, was it not, Miss Wallingford?" inquired Emily, with an emphasis I disliked.

"Very; though I agree with Lucy, it makes them so
much the more valuable."

"If Miss Merton will forget my charge of treason, and
condescend to put on the necklace, you will all see it to
much greater advantage than at present. If a fine necklace embellishes a fine woman, the advantage is quite
reciprocal. I have seen my pearls once already on her
neck, and know the effect."

A wish of Grace's aided my application, and Emily
placed the ornaments around her throat. The dazzling
whiteness of her skin gave a lustre to the pearls that they
certainly did not previously possess. One scarcely knew
which to admire the most—the ornaments, or their setting.

"How very, very beautiful they are now!" cried Lucy,
in generous admiration. "Oh! Miss Merton, pearls should
ever be your ornaments."

"Those pearls, you mean, Lucy," put in Rupert, who was always extremely liberal with other people's means; "the necklace ought never to be removed."

"Miss Merton knows their destination," I said gallantly, "and the terms of ownership."

Emily slowly undid the clasp, placed the string before her eyes, and looked at it long and silently.

"And what is this destination, Miles? What these terms of ownership?" my sister asked.

"Of course he means them for you, dear," Lucy remarked in haste. "For whom else can he intend such an ornament?"

"You are mistaken, Miss Hardinge. Grace must excuse me for being a little selfish this time, at least. I do not intend those pearls for Miss Wallingford, but for Mrs. Wallingford, should there ever be such a person."

"Upon my word, such a double temptation, my boy, I wonder Miss Merton ever had the fortitude to remove them from the enviable position they so lately occupied," cried Rupert, glancing meaningly toward Emily, who returned the look with a slight smile.

"Of course, Miss Merton understood that my remark was ventured in pleasantry," I said stiffly, "and not in presumption. It was decided, however, when in the Pacific, that these pearls ought to have that destination. It is true, Clawbonny is not the Pacific, and one may be pardoned for seeing things a little differently here, from what they appeared there. I have a few more pearls, however, very inferior in quality, I confess, to those of the necklace; but, such as they are, I should esteem it a favor, ladies, if you would consent to divide them equally among you. They would make three very pretty rings, and as many breastpins."

I put into Grace's hands a little box containing all the pearls that had not been placed on the string. There were many fine ones among them, and some of very respectable size, though most were of the sort called seed. In the whole, there were several hundreds.

"We will not balk his generosity," said Grace, smiling;

"so, Miss Merton, we will separate the pearls into three parcels, and draw lots for them. Here are handsome ornaments among them!"

"They will have one value with you, at least, Grace, and quite likely with Lucy, while they might possibly possess another with Miss Merton. I fished up every one of those pearls with my own hands."

"Certainly, that will give them value with both Lucy and me, dearest Miles, as would the simple fact that they are your gift; but what is to give them their especial value with Miss Merton?"

"They may serve to remind Miss Merton of some of her hairbreadth escapes, of the weeks passed on the island, and of scenes that, a few years hence, will probably possess the colors of a dream, in her recollection."

"One pearl I will take, with this particular object," said Emily, with more feeling than I had seen her manifest since she had got back into the world, "if Miss Wallingford will do me the favor to select it."

"Let it be enough for a ring, at least," Grace returned, in her own sweetest manner. "Half a dozen of the finest of these pearls, of which one shall be on Miles' account, and five on mine."

"On those conditions, let it, then, be six. I have no occasion for pearls to remind me how much my father and myself owe to Captain Wallingford."

"Come, Rupert," added Grace, "you have a taste in these things, let us have your aid in the selection."

Rupert was by no means backward in complying, for he loved to be meddling in such matters.

"In the first place," he said, "I shall at once direct that the number be increased to seven; this fine one in the centre, and three on each side, gradually diminishing in size. We must look to quality, and not to weight, for the six puisné judges, as we should call them in the courts. The chief justice will be a noble-looking fellow, and the associates ought to be of good quality to keep his honor's company."

"Why do you not call your judges, 'my lord,' as we do

in England, Mr. Hardinge?" inquired Emily, in her prettiest manner.

"Why, sure enough! I wish with all my heart we did, and then a man would have something worth living for."

"Rupert!" exclaimed Lucy, coloring, "you know it is because our government is republican, and that we have no nobles among us. Nor do you say exactly what you think; you would not be ' my lord,' if you could."

"As I never shall be a ' my lord,' and I am afraid never a ' your honor.' There, Miss Merton—there are numbers two and three—observe how beautifully they are graduated as to size."

"Well, ' your honor,' " added Grace, who began to be a little uneasy at the manner Rupert and Emily exhibited toward each other—"well, ' your honor,' what is to come next?"

"Numbers four and five, of course; and here they are, Miss Merton, as accurately diminished as if done by hand. A beautiful ring it will make. I envy those who will be recalled to mind by so charming an object."

"You will now be one of those yourself, Mr. Hardinge," observed Emily, with great tact; " for you are fully entitled to it by the trouble you are giving yourself, and the taste and judgment you possess."

Lucy looked petrified. She had so long accustomed herself to think of Grace as her future sister, that the open admiration expressed in Rupert's countenance, which was too manifest to escape any of us, first threw a glimmering of light on suspicions of the most painful nature. I had long seen that Lucy understood her brother's character better than any of us—much better, indeed, than his simple-minded father; and as for myself, I was prepared to expect anything but consistency and principle in his conduct. Dearly as I prized Lucy, and by this time the slight competition that Emily Merton had presented to my fancy, had entirely given way to the dear creature's heart and nature—but, dearly as I prized Lucy, I would greatly have preferred that my sister should not marry her brother; and, so far from feeling resentment on account of his want of fidelity, I was rather disposed to rejoice at it. I could appreciate his want of merit, and his unfitness to be the husband of such a woman as Grace, even at my early age; but, alas! I could not appreciate the effects of his inconstancy on a heart like that of my sister. Could I have felt as easy on the subject of Mr. Andrew Drewett, and of my own precise position in society, I should have cared very little, just then, about Rupert and his caprices.

The pearls for the ring were soon selected by Rupert, and approved of by Grace, after which I assumed the office of dividing the remainder myself. I drew a chair, took the box from Rupert, and set about the task.

"I shall make a faithful umpire, girls," I observed, as pearl after pearl was laid, first on one spot, then on another, "for I feel no preference between you—Grace is as Lucy, Lucy is as Grace, with me."

"That may be fortunate, Miss Hardinge, since it indicates no preference of a particular sort, that might require repressing," said Emily, smiling significantly at Lucy. "When gentlemen treat young ladies as sisters, it is a subject of rejoicing. These sailors need severe lessons, to keep them within the rules of the land."

Why this was said, I did not understand; but Rupert laughed at it, as if it were a capital thing. To mend the matter, he added, a little boisterously for him,—

"You see, Miles, you had better have taken to the law—the ladies cannot appreciate the merits of you tars."

"So it would seem," I returned, a little dryly, "after all Miss Merton has experienced and seen of the trade."

Emily made no reply, but she regarded her pearls with a steadiness that showed she was thinking more of their effect than that of either her own speech or mine. I continued to divide the pearls, and soon had the work complete.

"What am I to do, now?" I asked. "Will you draw lots, girls, or will you trust to my impartiality?"

"We will certainly confide in the last," answered Grace. "The division is so very equitable that I do not well see how you can defraud either."

"That being the case, this parcel is for you, Lucy; and, Grace, that is yours."

Grace rose, put her arms affectionately around my neck, and gave me one of the hundred kisses that I had received, first and last, for presents of one sort and another. The deep attachment that beamed in her saint-like eyes, would of itself have repaid me for fifty such gifts. At the moment, I was almost on the point of throwing her the necklace in the bargain; but some faint fancies about Mrs. Miles Wallingford prevented me from so doing. As for Lucy, not a little to my surprise, she received the pearls, muttered a few unintelligible words, but did not even rise from her chair. Emily seemed to tire of this, so she caught up her gypsy, said the evening was getting to be delightful, and proposed a walk. Rupert and Grace cheerfully acquiesced, and the three soon left the place, Lucy preparing to follow, as soon as a maid could bring her hat, and I excusing myself on the score of business in my own room.

"Miles," said Lucy, as I was about to enter the house, she herself standing on the edge of the piazza, on the point of following the party, but holding toward me the little paper box in which I had placed her portion of the pearls.

"Do you wish me to put them away for you, Lucy?"

"No, Miles—not for me, but for yourself—for Grace—for Mrs. Miles Wallingford, if you prefer that."

This was said without the slightest appearance of any other feeling than a gentle request. I was surprised, and scarce knew what to make of it; at first, I refused to take the box.

"I hope I have done nothing to merit this, Lucy?" I said, half affronted, half grieved.

"Remember, Miles," the dear girl answered, "we are no longer children, but have reached an age when it is incumbent on us to respect appearances a little. These pearls must be worth a great deal of money, and I feel certain my father, when he came to think of it, would scarce approve of my receiving them."

"And this from you, dear Lucy!"

"This from me, dear Miles," returned the precious girl,

tears glistening in her eyes, though she endeavored to smile. "Now take the box, and we will be just as good friends as ever."

"Will you answer me one question as frankly and as honestly as you used to answer all my questions?"

Lucy turned pale, and she stood reflecting an instant before she spoke.

"I can answer no question before it is asked," was at length her answer.

"Have you thought so little of my presents as to have thrown away the locket I gave you, before I sailed for the northwest coast?"

"No, Miles; I have kept the locket, and shall keep it as long as I live. It was a memorial of our childish regard for each other, and in that sense is very dear to me. You will let me keep the locket, I am sure!"

"If it were not you, Lucy Hardinge, whom I know to be truth itself, I might be disposed to doubt you; so many strange things exist, and so much caprice, especially in attachments, is manifested here, ashore!"

"You need doubt nothing I tell you, Miles; on no account would I deceive you."

"That I believe—nay, I see it is your present object to undeceive me. I do not doubt anything you tell me, Lucy. I wish I could see that locket, however; show it to me, if you have it on your person."

Lucy made an eager movement, as if about to produce the locket; then she arrested the impetuous indication, while her cheeks fairly burned with the blushes that suffused them.

"I see how it is, Lucy; the thing is not to be found. It is mislaid, the Lord knows where, and you do not like to avow it."

The locket at that moment lay as near the blessed creature's heart as it could be placed, and her confusion proceeded from the shame of letting that fact be known. This I could not see, and consequently did not know. A very small and further indication of feeling on my part might have betrayed the circumstance, but pride prevented it, and I took the still extended box, I dare say in a somewhat dramatic manner. Lucy looked at me earnestly; I saw it was with difficulty that she kept from bursting into tears.

"You are not hurt, Miles?" she said.

"I should not be frank if I denied it. Even Emily Merton, you saw, consented to accept enough pearls for a ring."

"I did perceive it; and yet you remember she felt the impropriety of receiving such large gifts from gentlemen. Miss Merton has gone through so much, so much in your company, Miles, that no wonder she is willing to retain some little memorial of it all, until—"

She hesitated, but Lucy chose not to finish the sentence. She had been pale, but her cheeks were now like the rose again.

"When Rupert and I first went to sea, Lucy, you gave me your little treasure in gold; every farthing you had on earth, I fancy."

"I am glad I did, Miles; for we were very young then, and you had been so kind to me, I rejoice I had a little gratitude. But we are now in situations," she added, smiling so sweetly as to render it difficult for me to refrain from catching her in my arms and folding her to my heart, "that place both of us above the necessity of receiving aid of this sort."

"I am glad to hear this, though I shall never part with the dear recollection of the half-joes."

"Or I with that of the locket. We will retain these, then, as keepsakes. My dear Mrs. Bradfort, too, is very particular about Rupert or myself receiving favors of this sort from any but herself. She has adopted us in a manner, and I owe to her liberality the means of making the figure I do. Apart from that, Miles, we are all as poor as we have ever been."

I wished Rupert had half his sister's self-respect and pride of character. But he had not; for in spite of his kinswoman's prohibitions, he had not scrupled to spend nearly three years of the wages that accrued to me as third mate of the Crisis. For the money I cared not a stiver; it was a very different thing as to the feeling.

As for Lucy, she hastened away, as soon as she had induced me to accept the box ; and I had no choice but to
place all the pearls together, and put them in Grace's
room, as my sister desired me to do with her own property
before proceeding on her walk.

I determined I would converse confidentially with Grace,
that very evening, about the state of affairs in general,
and, if possible, learn the worst concerning Mr. Andrew
Drewett's pretensions.   Shall I frankly own the truth ?   I
was sorry that Mrs. Bradfort had made Lucy so independent ;
as it seemed to increase the chasm that I fancied was opening
between us.

CHAPTER XXIV.

"Your name abruptly mentioned, casual words
Of comment on your deeds, praise from your uncle,
News from the armies, talk of your return,
A word let fall touching your youthful passion,
Suffused her cheek, called to her drooping eye
A momentary lustre."

HILLHOUSE.

I HAD no difficulty in putting my project of a private interview with Grace in execution, in my own house. There was one room at Clawbonny, that, from time immemorial, had been appropriated exclusively to the use of the heads of the establishment. It was called the "family room," as one would say "family pictures" or "family plate." In my father's time, I could recollect that I never dreamed of entering it, unless asked or ordered; and even then, I always did so with some such feelings as I entered a church. What gave it a particular and additional sanctity in our eyes, also, was the fact that the Wallingford dead were always placed in their coffins, in this room, and thence they were borne to their graves. It was a very small triangular room, with the fireplace in one corner, and possessing but a single window, that opened on a thicket of rose-bushes, syringas, and lilacs. There was also a light external fence around this shrubbery, as if purposely to keep listeners at a distance. The apartment had been furnished when the house was built, being in the oldest part of the structures, and still retained its ancient inmates. The chairs, tables, and most of the other articles had actually been brought from England, by Miles the First, as we used to call the emigrant; though he was thus only in reference to the Clawbonny dynasty, having been something

like Miles the Twentieth, in the old country. My mother
had introduced a small settee, or some such seat as the
French would call a *causeuse;* a most appropriate article,
in such a place.

In preparation for the interview I had slipped into Grace's
hand a piece of paper, on which was written, "Meet me in
the family room, precisely at six!" This was sufficient;
at the hour named, I proceeded to the room, myself. The
house of Clawbonny, in one sense, was large for an American residence; that is to say, it covered a great deal of
ground, every one of the three owners who preceded me,
having built; the last two leaving entire the labors of the
first. My turn had not yet come, of course; but the reader
knows already that I, most irreverently, had once contemplated abandoning the place, for a "seat" nearer the
Hudson. In such a *suite* of constructions, sundry passages
became necessary, and we had several more than was usual
at Clawbonny, besides having as many pairs of stairs. In
consequence of this ample provision of stairs, the chambers
of the family were totally separated from those of all the
rest of the house.

I began to reflect seriously on what I had to say, and how
it was to be said, as I walked through the long passage
which led to the "family room," or the "triangle," as my
own father had nicknamed the spot. Grace and I had
never yet held what might be termed a family consultation;
I was too young to think of such a thing, when last at
home, and no former occasion had offered since my return.
I was still quite young, and had more diffidence than might
have been expected in a sailor. To me, it was far more
embarrassing to open verbal communications of a delicate
nature, than it would have been to work a ship in action.
But for this *mauvaise honte*, I do think I should have been
explicit with Lucy, and not have parted from her on the
piazza, as I did, leaving everything in just as much doubt
as it had been before a word passed between us. Then I
entertained a profound respect for Grace; something more
than the tenderness of a brother for a sister; for, mingled
with my strong affection for her, was a deference, a species

26

of awe of her angel-like character and purity, that made me far more disposed to receive advice from her, than to bestow it. In the frame of mind which was natural to all these blended feelings, I laid my hand on the old-fashioned brass latch, by which the door of the "triangle" was closed. On entering the room, I found my sister seated on the *causeuse*, the window open to admit air, and the room looking snug but cheerful, and its occupant's sweet countenance expressive of care, not altogether free from curiosity. The last time I had been in that room, it was to look on the pallid features of my mother's corpse, previously to closing the coffin. All the recollections of that scene rushed upon our minds at the same instant; and taking a place by the side of Grace, I put an arm around her waist, drew her to me, and receiving her head on my bosom, she wept like a child. My tears could not be altogether restrained, and several minutes passed in profound silence. No explanations were needed; I knew what my sister thought and felt, and she was equally at home as respects my sensations. At length we regained our self-command, and Grace lifted her head.

"You have not been in this room since, brother?" she observed, half inquiringly.

"I have not, sister. It is now many years—many for those who are as young as ourselves."

"Miles, you will think better about that 'seat,' and never abandon Clawbonny—never destroy this blessed room!"

"I begin to think and feel differently on the subject, from what I once did. If this house were good enough for our forefathers, why is it not good enough for me? It is respectable and comfortable, and what more do I want?"

"And so warm in winter, and so cool in summer; with good thick stone walls; while everything they build now is a shingle palace! Besides, you can add your portion, and each addition has already been a good deal modernized. It is so pleasant to have a house that partakes of the usages of different periods!"

"I hardly think I shall ever abandon Clawbonny, my dear; for I find it growing more and more precious as other ties and expectations fail me."

Grace drew herself entirely from my arms, and looked intently, and, as I fancied, anxiously at me, from the other corner of the settee. Then she affectionately took one of my hands in both her own, and pressed it gently.

"You are young to speak of such things, my dear brother," she said, with a tone and air of sadness I had never yet remarked in her voice and manner; "much too young for a man; though I fear we women are born to know sorrow!"

I could not speak if I would, for I fancied Grace was about to make some communications concerning Rupert. Notwithstanding the strong affection that existed between my sister and myself, not a syllable had ever been uttered by either, that bore directly on our respective relations with Rupert and Lucy Hardinge. I had long been certain that Rupert, who was never backward in professions, had years before spoken explicitly to Grace, and I made no doubt they were engaged, though probably subject to some such conditions as the approval of his father and myself; approvals that neither had any reason for supposing would be withheld. Still, Grace had never intimated anything of the sort, and my conclusions were drawn from conjectures founded as I imagined on sufficient observation. On the other hand, I had never spoken to Grace of my love for Lucy. Until within the last month, indeed, when jealousy and distrust came to quicken the sentiment, I was unconscious myself, with how much passion I did actually love the dear girl; for, previously to that, my affection had seemed so much a matter of course, was united with so much that was fraternal, in appearance at least, that I had never been induced to enter into an inquiry as to the nature of this regard. We were both, therefore, touching on hallowed spots in our hearts, and each felt averse to laying bare the weakness.

"Oh! you know how it is with life, Grace," I answered, with affected carelessness, after a moment's silence; "now all sunshine, and now all clouds—I shall probably never marry, my dear sister, and you, or your children, will inherit Clawbonny; then you can do as you please with the house. As a memorial of myself, however, I will leave orders for stone to be got out this fall, and, next year, I will put up the south wing, of which we have so much talked, and add three or four rooms in which one will not be ashamed to see his friends.''

"I hope you are ashamed of nothing that is at Claw-bonny, now, Miles—as for your marrying, my dear brother, that remains to be seen; young men do not often know their own minds on such a subject, at your age.''

This was said not altogether without pleasantry, though there was a shade of sadness in the countenance of the beloved speaker, that from the bottom of my heart I wished were not there. I believe Grace understood my concern, and that she shrunk with virgin sensitiveness from touching further on the subject, for she soon added,—

"Enough of this desponding talk. Why have you particularly desired to see me, here, Miles?''

"Why? Oh! you know I am to sail next week, and we have never been here; and, now we are both of an age to communicate our thoughts to each other, I supposed—that is—there must be a beginning of all things, and it is as well to commence now as any other time. You do not seem more than half a sister, in the company of strangers like the Mertons, and Hardinges!''

"Strangers, Miles! How long have you regarded the last as strangers?''

"Certainly not strangers in the way of acquaintance, but strangers to our blood. There is not the least connection between us and them.''

"No, but much love; and love that has lasted from childhood. I cannot remember the time when I have not loved Lucy Hardinge.''

"Quite true—nor I. Lucy is an excellent girl, and one is almost certain of always retaining a strong regard for her. How singularly the prospects of the Hardinges are changed by this sudden liking of Mrs. Bradfort!''

"It is not sudden, Miles. You have been absent years, and forget how much time there has been to become intimate and attached. Mr. Hardinge and Mrs. Bradfort are sisters' children; and the fortune of the last, which, I am told, exceeds six thousand a year, in improving real estate in town, besides the excellent and valuable house in which she lives, came from their common grandfather, who cut off Mrs. Hardinge with a small legacy, because she married a clergyman. Mr. Hardinge is Mrs. Bradfort's heir-at-law, and it is by no means unnatural that she should think of leaving the property to those who, in one sense, have as good a right to it as she has herself."

"And is it supposed she will leave Rupert her heir?"

"I believe it is—at least—I think—I am afraid—Rupert himself imagines it; though doubtless Lucy will come in for a fair share. The affection of Mrs. Bradfort for Lucy is very strong—so strong, indeed, that she offered, last winter, openly to adopt her, and to keep her with her constantly. You know how true and warm-hearted a girl Lucy is, and how easy it is to love her."

"This is all new to me—why was not the offer accepted?"

"Neither Mr. Hardinge nor Lucy would listen to it. I was present at the interview in which it was discussed, and our excellent guardian thanked his cousin for her kind intentions; but, in his simple way, he declared, as long as life was spared him, he felt it a duty to keep his girl; or, at least, until he committed her to the custody of a husband, or death should part them."

"And Lucy?"

"She is much attached to Mrs. Bradfort, who is a good woman in the main, though she has her weaknesses about the world, and society, and such things. Lucy wept in her cousin's arms, but declared she never could leave her father. I suppose you do not expect," added Grace, smiling, "that she had anything to say about a husband."

"And how did Mrs. Bradfort receive this joint declaration of resistance to her pleasure, backed, as the last was, by dollars?"

"Perfectly well. The affair terminated by Mr. Hardinge's consenting to Lucy's passing each winter in town, until she marry. Rupert, you know, lives there as a stu-

dent at law, at present, and will become established there.
when admitted to the bar.''

"And I suppose the knowledge that Lucy is likely to
inherit some of the old Bleecker estate, has not in the least
diminished her chance of finding a husband to remove her
from the paternal custody of her father?''

"No husband could ever make Lucy anything but Mr.
Hardinge's daughter; but you are right, Miles, in suppos,
ing that she has been sought. I am not in her secrets, foi
Lucy is a girl of too much principle to make a parade of hei
conquests, even under the pretence of communicating them
to her dearest friend—and in that light, beyond all question,
does she regard me; but I feel as morally certain as one can
be, without actually knowing the facts, that Lucy refused
one gentleman, winter before last, and three last winter.''

"Was Mr. Andrew Drewett of the number?" I asked,
with a precipitation of which I was immediately ashamed.

Grace started a little at the vivacity of my manner, and
then she smiled, though I still thought sadly.

"Of course not," she answered, after a moment's thought,
"or he would not still be in attendance. Lucy is too frank
to leave an admirer in doubt an instant after his declaration
is made, and her own mind made up; and not one of all
those who, I am persuaded, have offered, has ever ventured
to continue more than a distant acquaintance. As Mr.
Drewett never has been more assiduous than down to the
last moment of our remaining in town, it is impossible he
should have been rejected. I suppose you know Mr. Hardinge has invited him here?''

"Here? Andrew Drewett? And why is he coming
here?''

"I heard him ask Mr. Hardinge's permission to visit us
here; and you know how it is with our dear, good guardian
—the milk of human kindness himself, and so perfectly
guileless that he never sees more than is said in such matters, it was impossible he could refuse. Besides, he likes
Drewett, who, apart from some fashionable follies, is both
clever and respectable. Mr. Drewett has a sister married
into one of the best families on the other side of the river,

and is in the habit of coming into the neighborhood every
summer ; doubtless he will cross from his sister's house to
Clawbonny.''

I felt indignant for just one minute, and then reason
resumed its sway. Mr. Hardinge, in the first place, had
the written authority, or request, of my mother that he
would invite whom he pleased, during my minority, to the
house ; and, on that score, I felt no disapprobation. But
it seemed so much like braving my own passion, to ask an
open admirer of Lucy's to my own house, that I was very
near saying something silly. Luckily I did not, and Grace
never knew what I suffered at this discovery. Lucy had
refused several offers—that was something ; and I was
dying to know what sort of offers they were. I thought I
might at least venture to ask that question.

"Did you know the four gentleman that you suppose
Lucy to have refused?" said I, with as indifferent an air as
I could assume, affecting to destroy a cobweb with my
rattan, and even carrying my acting so far as to make an
attempt at a low whistle.

"Certainly ; how else should I know anything about it?
Lucy has never said a word to me on the subject ; and,
though Mrs. Bradfort and I have had our pleasantries on
the subject, neither of us is in Lucy's secrets.''

"Ay, your pleasantries on the subject ! That I dare say.
There is no better fun to a woman than to see a man make
a fool of himself in this way ; little does she care how much
a poor fellow suffers ! ''

Grace turned pale, and I could see that her sweet countenance became thoughtful and repentant.

"Perhaps there is truth in your remark, and justice in
your reproach, Miles. None of us treat this subject with
as much seriousness as it deserves, though I cannot suppose any woman can reject a man whom she believes to
be seriously attached to her, without feeling for him. Still,
attachments of this nature affect your sex less than ours,
and I believe few men die of love. Lucy, moreover, never
has, and I believe never would encourage any man whom
she did not like ; this principle must have prevented any

of that intimate connection, without which the heart never can get much interested. The passion that is produced without any exchange of sentiment or feeling, Miles, cannot be much more than imagination or caprice."

"I suppose those four chaps are all famously cured by this time, then?" said I, pretending again to whistle.

"I cannot answer for that; it is so easy to love Lucy, and to love her warmly. I only know they visit her no longer, and when they meet her in society behave just as I think a rejected admirer would behave when he has not lost his respect for his late flame. Mrs. Bradfort's fortune and position may have had their influence on two, but the others, I think, were quite sincere."

"Mrs. Bradfort is quite in a high set, Grace, altogether above what we have been accustomed to."

My sister colored a little, and I could see she was not at her ease. Still, Grace had too much self-respect, and too much character, ever to feel an oppressive inferiority where it did not exist in essentials; and she had never been made to suffer, as the more frivolous and vain often suffer, by communications with a class superior to their own—especially when that class, as always happens, contains those who, having nothing else to be proud of, take care to make others feel their inferiority.

"This is true, Miles," she answered; "or I might better say both are true. Certainly I never have seen as many well-bred persons as I meet in her circle; indeed, we have little around us at Clawbonny to teach us any distinctions in such tastes. Mr. Hardinge, simple as he is, is so truly a gentleman, that he has not left us altogether in the dark as to what was expected of us; and I fancy the higher people truly are in the world, the less they lay stress on anything but what is substantial in these matters."

"And Lucy's admirers—and Lucy herself—"

"How, Lucy herself?"

"Was she well received—courted—admired? Met as an equal, and treated as an equal? And you, too?"

"Had you lived more in the world, Miles, you would not have asked the question. But Lucy has been always re

ceived as Mrs. Bradfort's daughter would have been received; and as for myself, I have never supposed it was not
known exactly who I am."

"*Captain* Miles Wallingford's daughter, and *Captain*
Miles Wallingford's sister," said I, with a little bitterness on
each emphasis.

"Precisely; and a girl proud of her connections with
both," rejoined Grace, with strong affection.

"I wish I knew one thing, Grace; and I think I ought to
know it, too."

"If you can make the last appear, Miles, you may rest
assured you shall know it, if it depend on me."

"Did any of these gentry—these soft-handed fellows—
ever think of offering to you?"

Grace laughed, and she colored so deeply—oh! how
heavenly was her beauty, with that roseate tint on her
cheek!—but she colored so deeply that I felt satisfied that
she, too, had refused her suitors. The thought appeased
some of my bitter feelings, and I had a sort of semi-savage
pleasure in believing that a daughter of Clawbonny was not
to be had for the asking, by one of that set. The only
answers I got were these disclosures by blushes.

"What are the fortune and position of this Mr. Drewett,
since you are resolved to tell me nothing of your own
affairs?"

"Both are good, and such as no young lady can object
to; he is even said to be rich."

"Thank God! He then is not seeking Lucy in the hope
of getting some of Mrs. Bradfort's money?"

"Not in the least. It is so easy to love Lucy for Lucy's
sake, that even a fortune-hunter would be in danger of being caught in his own trap. But Mr. Drewett is above the
necessity of practising so vile a scheme for making money."

Here, that the present generation may not be misled, and
imagine fortune-hunting has come in altogether within the
last twenty years, I will add that it was not exactly a trade
in this country—a regular occupation—in 1802, as it has become in 1844. There were such things then, certainly, as
men or women who were ready to marry anybody who

would make them rich, but I do not think theirs was a calling to which either sex served regular apprenticeship, as is
practised to-day. Still, the business was carried on, to speak
in the vernacular, and sometimes with marked success.

"You have not told me, Grace," I resumed, "whether
you think Lucy is pleased or not with the attentions of this
gentleman."

My sister looked at me intently, for a moment, as if to
ascertain how far I could, or could not, ask such a question
with indifference. It will be remembered that no verbal
explanations had ever taken place between us on the subject
of our feelings toward the companions of our childhood, and
that all that was known to either was obtained purely by
inference. Between myself and Lucy nothing had ever
passed, indeed, which might not have been honestly referred
to our long and early association, so far as the rules of intercourse were concerned, though I sometimes fancied I
could recall a hundred occasions, on which Lucy had formerly manifested deep attachment for myself; nor did I
doubt her being able to show similar proofs by reversing the
picture. This, however, was, or I had thought it to be,
merely the language of the heart; the tongue having never
spoken. Of course, Grace had nothing but conjecture on
this subject, and, alas! she had begun to see how possible
it was for those who lived near each other to change their
views on such subjects; no wonder, then, if she fancied it
still easier for those who had been separated for years.

"I have not told you, Miles," Grace answered, after a
brief delay, "because it would not be proper to communicate the secrets of my friend to a young man, even to you,
were it in my power, as it is not, since Lucy never has
made to me the slightest confidential communications of any
sort or nature, touching love."

"Never!" I exclaimed—reading my fancied doom in the
startling fact; for I conceived it impossible, had she ever
really loved me, that the matter should not have come up
in conversation between two so closely united. "Never!
What, no girlish—no childish preference—have you never
had any mutual preferences to reveal?"

"Never," answered Grace, firmly, though her very temples seemed illuminated. "Never. We have been satisfied with each other's affection, and have had no occasion to enter into any unfeminine and improper secrets, if any such existed."

A long, and I doubt not a mutually painful pause succeeded.

"Grace," said I at length, "I am not envious of this probable accession of fortune to the Hardinges, but I think we should all have been much more united—much happier —without it."

My sister's color left her face, she trembled all over, and she became as pale as death.

"You may be right in some respects, Miles," she answered, after a time. "And yet it is hardly generous to think so. Why should we wish to see our oldest friends— those who are so very dear to us, our excellent guardian's children, less well off than we are ourselves? No doubt, no doubt, it may seem better to *us* that Clawbonny should be the castle and we its possessors; but others have their rights and interests as well as ourselves. Give the Hardinges money, and they will enjoy every advantage known in this country—more than money can possibly give us— why, then, ought we to be so selfish as to wish them deprived of this advantage? Place Lucy where you will, she will alway be Lucy ; and as for Rupert, so brilliant a young man needs only an opportunity to rise to anything the country possesses ! "

Grace was so earnest, spoke with so much feeling, appeared so disinterested, so holy I had almost said, that I could not find in my heart the courage to try her any further. That she began to distrust Rupert, I plainly saw, though it was merely with the glimmerings of doubt. A nature as pure as hers, and a heart so true, admitted with great reluctance the proofs of the unworthiness of one so long loved. It was evident, moreover, that she shrunk from revealing her own great secret, while she had only conjectures to offer in regard to Lucy ; and even these she withheld, as due to her sex, and the obligations of friend-

ship. I forgot that I had not been ingenuous myself, and
that I made no communication to justify any confidence on
the part of my sister. That which would have been treachery in her to say, under this state of the case, might have
been uttered with greater frankness on my own part. After
a pause, to allow my sister to recover from her agitation, I
turned the discourse to our own more immediate family
interests, and soon got off the painful subject altogether.

"I shall be of age, Grace," I said, in the course of my
explanations, "before you see me again. We sailors are
always exposed to more chances and hazards than people
ashore ; and I now tell you, should anything happen to me,
my will may be found in my secretary ; signed and sealed,
the day I attain my majority. I have given orders to have
it drawn up by a lawyer of eminence, and shall take it to
sea with me, for that very purpose."

"From which I am to infer that I must not covet Clawbonny," answered Grace, with a smile that denoted how little she cared for the fact. "You give it to our cousin, Jack
Wallingford, as a male heir, worthy of enjoying the honor."

"No, dearest, I give it to you. It is true, the law would
do this for me ; but I choose to let it be known that I wish
it to be so. I am aware my father made that disposition of
the place, should I die childless before I became of age ;
but, once of age, the place is all mine ; and that which is
all mine, shall be all thine, after I am no more."

"This is melancholy conversation, and, I trust, useless.
Under the circumstances you mention, Miles, I never should
have expected Clawbonny, nor do I know I ought to possess
it. It comes as much from Jack Wallingford's ancestors, as
from our own ; and it is better it should remain with the
name. I will not promise you, therefore, I will not give it
to him, the instant I can."

This Jack Wallingford, of whom I have not yet spoken,
was a man of five-and-forty, and a bachelor. He was a
cousin-german of my father's, being the son of a younger
brother of my grandfather's, and somewhat of a favorite.
He had gone into what was called the new countries, in that
day, or a few miles west of Cayuga Bridge, which put him

into Western New York. I had never seen him but once, and that was on a visit he paid us on his return from selling quantities of pot and pearl ashes in town; articles made on his new lands. He was said to be a prosperous man, and to stand little in need of the old paternal property.

After a little more conversation on the subject of my will, Grace and I separated, each more closely bound to the other, I firmly believed, for this dialogue in the "family room." Never had my sister seemed more worthy of all my love; and, certain I am, never did she possess more of it. Of Clawbonny she was as sure as my power over it could make her.

The remainder of the week passed as weeks are apt to pass in the country, and in summer. Feeling myself so often uncomfortable in the society of the girls, I was much in the fields; always possessing the good excuse of beginning to look after my own affairs. Mr. Hardinge took charge of the major, an intimacy beginning to spring up between these two respectable old men. There were, indeed, so many points of common feeling, that such a result was not at all surprising. They both loved the Church—I beg pardon, the Holy Catholic Protestant Episcopal Church. They both disliked Bonaparte—the major hated him, but my guardian hated nobody—both venerated Billy Pitt, and both fancied the French Revolution was merely the fulfilment of prophecy, through the agency of the devils. As we are now touching upon times likely to produce important results, let me not be misunderstood. As an old man, aiming, in a new sphere, to keep enlightened the generation that is coming into active life, it may be necessary to explain. An attempt has been made to induce the country to think that Episcopalian and tory were something like synonymous terms, in the "times that tried men's souls." This is sufficiently impudent *per se*, in a country that possessed Washington, Jay, Hamilton, the Lees, the Morrises, the late Bishop White, and so many other distinguished patriots of the Southern and Middle States; but men are not particularly scrupulous when there is an object to be obtained, even though it be pretended that heaven is an incident of that object. I shall, therefore, confine my explanations to what I have said about Billy Pitt and the French.

The youth of this day may deem it suspicious that an Episcopal divine—Protestant Episcopal, I mean; but it is so hard to get the use of new terms as applied to old thoughts, in the decline of life!—may deem it suspicious that a Protestant Episcopal divine should care anything about Billy Pitt, or execrate infidel France; I will, therefore, just intimate that, in 1802, no portion of the country dipped more deeply into similar sentiments than the descendants of those who first put foot on the rock of Plymouth, and whose progenitors had just before paid a visit to Geneva, where, it is "said or sung," they had found a "church without a bishop, and a state without a king." In a word, admiration of Mr. Pitt, and execration of Bonaparte, were by no means such novelties in America, in that day, as to excite wonder. For myself, however, I can truly say, that, like most Americans who went abroad in those stirring times, I was ready to say with Mercutio, "A plague on both your houses"; for neither was even moderately honest, nor even decently respectful to ourselves. Party feeling, however, the most inexorable, and the most unprincipled, of all tyrants, and the bane of American liberty, notwithstanding all our boasting, decreed otherwise; and, while one half the American republic was shouting hosannas to the Great Corsican, the other half was ready to hail Pitt as the "Heaven-born Minister." The remainder of the nation felt and acted as Americans should. It was my own private opinion, that France and England would have been far better off, had neither of these worthies ever had a being.

Nevertheless, the union of opinion between the divine and the major was a great bond of union in friendship. I saw they were getting on well together, and let things take their course. As for Emily, I cared very little about her, except as she might prove to be connected with Rupert, and through Rupert with the happiness of my sister. As for Rupert, himself, I could not get entirely weaned from one whom I had so much loved in boyhood, and who, moreover, possessed the rare advantage of being Lucy's brother and Mr. Hardinge's son. "Sidney's sister, Pembroke's mother," gave him a value in my eyes that he had long ceased to possess on his own account.

" You see, Neb," I said, toward the end of the week, as the black and I were walking up from the mill in company, " Mr. Rupert has altogether forgotten that he ever knew the name of a rope in a ship. His hands are as white as a young lady's!"

"Nebber mind dat, Masser Mile. Masser Rupert nebber feel a saterfaction to be wracked away, or to be prisoner to Injin! Golly! No gentleum to be envy, sir, 'em does n't enjoy dat!"

" You have a queer taste, Neb, from all which I conclude you expect to return to town with me in the Wallingford, this evening, and to go out in the Dawn?"

"Sartain, Masser Mile. How you t'ink of goin' to sea, and leave nigger at home?"

Here Neb raised such a laugh that he might have been heard a hundred rods, seeming to fancy the idea he had suggested was so preposterous as to merit nothing but ridicule.

" Well, Neb, I consent to your wishes; but this will be the last voyage in which you will have to consult me on the subject, as I shall make out your freedom papers the moment I am of age."

"What dem?" demanded the black, quick as lightning.

"Why, papers to make you your own master—a free man; you surely know what that means. Did you never hear of free niggers?"

"Sartain—awful poor debble dey be, too. You catch Neb, one day, at being a free nigger, gib you leave to tell him of it, Masser Mile!"

Here was another burst of laughter that sounded like a chorus in merriment.

"This is a little extraordinary, Neb! I thought, boy, all slaves pined for freedom?"

"P'rhaps so; p'rhaps not. What good he do, Masser

Mile, when heart and body well satisfy as it is? Now, how long a Wallingford family lib, here, in dis berry spot?" Neb always talked more like a "nigger," when within hearing of the household gods, than he did at sea.

"How long? About a hundred years, Neb—just one hundred and seven, I believe, to be accurate."

"And how long a Clawbonny family, at 'e same time, Masser Mile?"

"Upon my word, Neb, your pedigree is a little confused, and I cannot answer quite as certainly. Eighty or ninety, though, I should think, at least; and, possibly, a hundred, too. Let me see—you called old Pompey your grandfather; did you not, Neb?"

"Sartain; berry good grandfader, too, Masser Mile. Ole Pomp a won'erful black!"

"Oh! I say nothing touching the quality; I dare say he was as good as another. Well, I think that I have heard old Pompey's grandfather was an imported Guinea, and that he was purchased by my great-grandfather, about the year 1700."

"Dat just as good as gospel! Who want to make up lie about poor debble of nigger? Well, den, Masser Mile, in all dem 1700 year, did he ebber hear of a Clawbonny that want to be a free nigger? Tell me dat, once, an' I hab an answer."

"You have asked me more than I can answer, boy; for I am not in the secret of your own wishes, much less in those of all your ancestors."

Neb pulled off his tarpaulin, scratched his wool, rolled his black eyes at me, as if he enjoyed the manner in which he had puzzled me; after which he set off on a tumbling excursion, in the road, going like a wheel on his hands and feet, showing his teeth like rows of pearls, and concluding the whole with roar the third, that sounded as if the hills and valleys were laughing, in the very fatness of their fertility. The physical *tour de force* was one of those feats of agility in which Neb had been my instructor, ten years before.

"S'pose I free, who do sich matter for you, Masser Mile?" cried Neb, like one laying down an unanswerable proposition. "No, no, sir—I belong to you, you belong to me, and we belong to one anodder."

This settled the matter for the present, and I said no more. Neb was ordered to be in readiness for the next day; and at the appointed hour, I met the assembled party to take my leave, on this, my third departure from the roof of my fathers. It had been settled the major and Emily were to remain at the farm until July, when they were to proceed to the Springs, for the benefit of the water, after living so long in a hot climate. I had passed an hour with my guardian alone, and he had no more to say, than to wish me well, and to bestow his blessing. I did not venture an offer to embrace Lucy. It was the first time we had parted without this token of affection; but I was shy, and I fancied she was cold. She offered me her hand, as frankly as ever, however, and I pressed it fervently, as I wished her adieu. As for Grace, she wept in my arms, just as she had always done; and the major and Emily shook hands cordially with me, it being understood I should find them in New York, at my return. Rupert accompanied me down to the sloop.

"If you should find an occasion, Miles, let us hear from you," said my old friend. "I have a lively curiosity to learn something of the Frenchmen; nor am I entirely without the hope of soon gratifying the desire, in person."

"You! If you have any intention to visit France, what better opportunity, than to go in my cabin? Is it business, that will take you there?"

"Not at all; pure pleasure. Our excellent cousin thinks a gentleman of a certain class ought to travel; and I believe she has an idea of getting me attached to the legation, in some form or other."

This sounded so odd to me! Rupert Hardinge, who had not one penny to rub against another, so lately, was now talking of his European tour, and of legations! I ought to have been glad of his good fortune, and I fancied I was. I said nothing, this time, concerning his taking up any portion of my earnings, having the sufficient excuse of not being on pay myself. Rupert did not stay long in the sloop, and we were soon under way. I looked eagerly along the high banks of the creek, fringed as it was with bushes, in hopes of seeing Grace, at least; nor was I disappointed. She and Lucy had taken a direct path to the point where the two waters united, and were standing there, as the sloop dropped past. They both waved their handkerchiefs, in a way to show the interest they felt in me; and I returned the parting salutations by kissing my hand again and again. At this instant, a sail-boat passed our bows, and I saw a gentleman standing up in it, waving his handkerchief, quite as industriously as I was kissing my hand. A look told me it was Andrew Drewett, who directed his boat to the point, and was soon making his bows to the girls in person. His boat ascended the creek, no doubt with his luggage; while the last I saw of the party it was walking off in company, taking the direction of the house.

CHAPTER XXV.

" Or feeling, as the storm increases,
  The love of terror nerve thy breast,
  Didst venture to the coast ;
To see the mighty war-ship leap
From wave to wave upon the deep,
Like chamois goat from steep to steep,
  Till low in valley lost."

ALLSTON.

ROGER TALCOTT had not been idle during my absence. Clawbonny was so dear to me, that I had stayed longer than was proposed in the original plan ; and I now found the hatches on the Dawn, a crew shipped, and nothing remaining but to clear out. I mean the literal thing, and not the slang phrase, one of those of which so many have crept into the American language, through the shop, and which even find their way into print ; such as " charter coaches," " on a boat," " on board a stage," and other similar elegancies. " *On* a boat " always makes me ——, even at my present time of life. The Dawn was cleared the day I reached town.

Several of the crew of the Crisis had shipped with us anew, the poor fellows having already made away with all their wages and prize money, in the short space of a month ! This denoted the usual improvidence of sailors, and was thought nothing out of the common way. The country being at peace, a difficulty with Tripoli excepted, it was no longer necessary for ships to go armed. The sudden excitement produced by the brush with the French had already subsided, and the navy was reduced to a few vessels that had been regularly built for the service ; while the lists of

419

officers had been curtailed of two thirds of their names. We were no longer a warlike, but were fast getting to be a strictly commercial, body of seamen. I had a single six-pounder, and half a dozen muskets, in the Dawn, besides a pair or two of pistols, with just ammunition enough to quell a mutiny, fire a few signal-guns, or to kill a few ducks.

We sailed on the 3d of July. I have elsewhere intimated that the Manhattanese hold exaggerated notions of the comparative beauty of the scenery of their port, sometimes presuming to compare it even with Naples; to the bay of which it bears some such resemblance as a Dutch canal bears to a river flowing through rich meadows, in the freedom and grace of nature. Nevertheless, there are times and seasons when the bay of New York offers a landscape worthy of any pencil. It was at one of these felicitous moments that the Dawn cast off from the wharf, and commenced her voyage to Bordeaux. There was barely air enough from the southward to enable us to handle the ship, and we profited by a morning ebb to drop down to the Narrows, in the midst of a fleet of some forty sail; most of the latter, however, being coasters. Still we were a dozen ships and brigs, bound to almost as many different countries. The little air there was, seemed scarcely to touch the surface of the water; and the broad expanse of bay was as placid as an inland lake, of a summer's morning. Yes, yes—there are moments when the haven of New York does present pictures on which the artist would seize with avidity; but the instant nature attempts any of her grander models, on this, a spot that seems never to rise much above the level of commercial excellences, it is found that the accessories are deficient in sublimity, or even beauty.

I have never seen our home waters so lovely as on this morning. The movements of the vessels gave just enough of life and variety to the scene to destroy the appearance of sameness; while the craft were too far from the land to prevent one of the most unpleasant effects of the ordinary landscape scenery of the place—that produced by the disproportion between the tallness of their spars, and the low character of the adjacent shores. As we drew near the

Narrows, the wind increased ; and forty sail, working through the pass in close conjunction, terminated the piece with something like the effect produced by a *finale* in an overture. The brightness of the morning, the placid charms of the scenery, and the propitious circumstances under which I commenced the voyage, in a commercial point of view, had all contributed to make me momentarily forget my private griefs, and to enter cheerfully into the enjoyment of the hour.

I greatly disliked passengers. They appeared to me to lessen the dignity of my position, and to reduce me to the level of an innkeeper, or one who received boarders. I wished to command a ship, not to take in lodgers ; persons whom you are bound to treat with a certain degree of consideration, and in one sense, as your superiors. Still, it had too much of an appearance of surliness, and a want of hospitality, to refuse a respectable man a passage across the ocean, when he might not get another chance in a month, and that, too, when it was important to himself to proceed immediately. In this particular instance, I became the dupe of a mistaken kindness on the part of my former owners. These gentlemen brought to me a Mr. Brigham—Wallace Mortimer Brigham was his whole name, to be particular—as a person who was desirous of getting to France with his wife and his wife's sister, in order to proceed to Italy for the health of the married lady, who was believed to be verging on a decline. These people were from the eastward, and had fallen into the old error of Americans, that the south of France and Italy had residences far more favorable for such a disease, than our own country. This was one of the provincial notions of the day, that were entailed on us by means of colonial dependency. I suppose the colonial existence is as necessary to a people, as childhood and adolescence are to the man ; but as my Lady Mary Wortley Montagu told her friend, Lady Rich—" Nay ; but look you, my dear madam, I grant it a very fine thing to continue always fifteen ; that, everybody must approve of—it is quite fair ; but, indeed, one need not be five years old.''

I was prevailed on to take these passengers, and I got a

specimen of their characters even as we dropped down the bay, in the midst of the agreeable scene to which I have just alluded. They were *gossips;* and that, too, of the lowest, or personal cast. Nothing made them so happy as to be talking of the private concerns of their fellow-creatures; and, as ever must happen where this propensity exists, nine tenths of what they said rested on no better foundation than surmises, inferences drawn from premises of questionable accuracy, and judgments that were entered up, without the authority, or even the inclination, to examine witnesses. They had also a peculiarity that I have often remarked in persons of the same propensity; most of their gossiping arose from a desire to make apparent their own intimacy with the private affairs of people of mark—overlooking the circumstance that, in thus making the concerns of others the subjects of their own comments, they were impliedly admitting a consciousness of their own inferiority; men seldom condescending thus to busy themselves with the affairs of any but those of whom they feel it to be a sort of distinction to converse. I am much afraid good-breeding has more to do with the suppression of this vice, than good principles, as the world goes. I have remarked that persons of a high degree of self-respect, and a good tone of manners, are quite free from this defect of character; while I regret to be compelled to say that I have been acquainted with divers very saintly professors, including one or two parsons, who have represented the very *beau idéal* of scandal.

My passengers gave me a taste of their quality, as I have said, before we had got a mile below Governor's Island. The ladies were named Sarah and Jane; and between them and Wallace Mortimer, what an insight did I obtain into the private affairs of sundry personages of Salem, in Massachusetts, together with certain glimpses in at Boston folk; all, however, referring to qualities and facts that might be classed among the real or supposed. I can, at this distant day, recall Scene 1st, Act 1st, of the drama that continued while we were crossing the ocean, with the slight interruption of a few days, produced by sea-sickness.

"Wallace," said Sarah, "did you say yesterday, that John Viner had refused to lend his daughter's husband twenty thousand dollars, to get him out of his difficulties, and that he failed in consequence?"

"To be sure. It was the common talk through Wall Street yesterday, and everybody believes it"—there was no more truth in the story, than in one of the forty reports that have killed General Jackson so often, in the last twenty years. "Yes, no one doubts it—but all the Viners are just so! All of us, in our part of the world, know what to think of the Viners."

"Yes, I suppose so," drawled Jane. "I've heard it said this John Viner's father ran all the way from the Commons in Boston, to the foot of State Street, to get rid of a dun against this very son, who had his own misfortunes when he was young."

"The story is quite likely true in part," replied Wallace, "though it can't be quite accurate, as the old gentleman had but one leg, and running was altogether out of the question with him. It was probably old Tim Viner, who ran like a deer when a young man, as I've heard people say."

"Well, then, I suppose he ran his horse," added Jane, in the same quiet, drawling tone. "Something must have run, or they would not have got up the story."

I wondered if Miss Jane Hitchcox had ever taken the trouble to ascertain who they were! I happened to know both the Viners, and to be quite certain there was not a word of truth in the report of the twenty thousand dollars, having heard all the particulars of the late failure from one of my former owners, who was an assignee, and a considerable creditor. Under the circumstances, I thought I would hint as much.

"Are you quite sure that the failure of Viner & Co. was owing to the circumstance you mention, Mr. Brigham?" I inquired.

"Pretty certain. I am 'measurably acquainted' with their affairs, and think I am tolerably safe in saying so."

Now "measurably acquainted" meant that he lived

within twenty or thirty miles of those who did know something of the concerns of the house in question, and was in the way of catching scraps of the gossip that fell from the disappointed creditors. How much of this is there in this good country of ours! Men who live just near enough to one another to feel the influence of all that rivalry, envy, personal strifes, and personal malignancies can generate, fancy they are acquainted, from this circumstance, with those to whom they have never even spoken. One half the idle tales that circulate up and down the land, come from authority not one tittle better than this. How much would men learn, could they only acquire the healthful lesson of understanding that nothing, which is much out of the ordinary way, and which circulates as received truths illustrative of character, is true in all its material parts, and very little in *any*. But, to return to my passengers, and that portion of their conversation which most affected myself. They continued commenting on persons and families by name, seemingly more to keep their hands in, than for any discoverable reason, as each appeared to be perfectly conversant with all the gossip that was started ; when Sarah casually mentioned the name of Mrs. Bradfort, with some of whose supposed friends, it now came out, they had all a general visiting acquaintance.

"Dr. Hosack is of opinion she cannot live long, I hear," said Jane, with a species of fierce delight in killing a fellow-creature, provided it only led to a gossip concerning her private affairs. "Her case has been decided to be a cancer, now, for more than a week, and she made her will last Tuesday."

"Only last Tuesday?" exclaimed Sarah, in surprise. "Well, I heard she had made her will a twelvemonth since, and that she left all her property to young Rupert Hardinge ; in the expectation, some persons thought, that he might marry her."

"How could that be, my dear?" asked the husband ; "in what would she be better off for leaving her own property to her husband?"

"Why, by law, would she not? I don't exactly know

how it would happen, for I do not particularly understand
these things ; but it seems natural that a woman would be
a gainer if she made the man she was about to marry her
heir. She would have her thirds in his estate, would she
not ? ''

" But, Mrs. Brigham," said I, smiling, " is it quite certain Mrs. Bradfort wishes to marry Rupert Hardinge, at
all ? ''

" I know so little of the parties, that I cannot speak with
certainty in the matter, I admit, Captain Wallingford.''

"Well, but Sarah, dear,'' interposed the more exacting
Jane, " you are making yourself unnecessarily ignorant.
You very well know how intimate we are with the Winters,
and they know the Greenes perfectly well, who are next-
door neighbors to Mrs. Bradfort. I don't see how you can
say we have n't good means of being 'measurably' well
informed.''

Now I happened to know through Grace and Lucy, that
a disagreeable old person of the name of Greene did live
next door to Mrs. Bradfort ; but that the latter refused to
visit her, firstly, because she did not happen to like her, and
secondly, because the two ladies belonged to very different
social circles ; a sufficient excuse for not visiting in town,
even though the parties inhabited the same house. But
the Brighams, being Salem people, did not understand that
families might reside next door to each other, in a large
town, for a long series of months, or even years, and not know
each other's names. It would not be easy to teach this
truth, one of everyday occurrence, to the inhabitant of one
of our provincial towns, who was in the habit of fancying
he had as close an insight into the private affairs of all his
neighbors, as they enjoyed themselves.

" No doubt we are all as well off as most strangers in New
York,'' observed the wife ; " still, it ought to be admitted
that we may be mistaken. I have heard it said there is an
old Mr. Hardinge, a clergyman, who would make a far better
match for the lady, than his son. However, it is of no
great moment, now ; for, when our neighbor, Mrs. John
Foote, saw Dr. Hosack about her own child, she got all the

particulars out of him about Mrs. Bradfort's case, from the highest quarter, and I had it from Mrs. Foote, herself."

"I could not have believed that a physician of Dr. Hosack's eminence and character would speak openly of the diseases of his patients," I observed, a little tartly, I am afraid.

"Oh! he didn't," said Sarah, eagerly; "he was as cunning as a fox, Mrs. Foote owned herself, and played her off finely; but Mrs. Foote was cunninger than any half dozen foxes, and got it all out of him by negations."

"Negations?" I exclaimed, wondering what was meant by the term, though I had understood I was to expect a little more philosophy and metaphysics, not to say algebra, in my passengers, than usually accompanied petticoats in our part of the world.

"Certainly, negations," answered the matron, with a smile as complacent as that which usually denotes the consciousness of intellectual superiority. "One who is a little practised can ascertain a fact as well by means of negatives as affirmatives. It only requires judgment and use."

"Then Mrs. Bradfort's disease is only ascertained by the negative process?"

"So I suppose—but what does one want more?" put in the husband; "and that she made her will last week I feel quite sure, as it was generally spoken of among our friends."

Here were people who had been in New York only a month, looking out for a ship, mere passengers, as it might be, who knew more about a family with which I had myself such an intimate connection, than its own members. I thought it no wonder that such a race was capable of enlightening mankind, on matters and things in general. But the game did not end here.

"I suppose Miss Lucy Hardinge will get something by Mrs. Bradfort's death," observed Miss Jane, "and that she and Mr. Andrew Drewett will marry as soon as it shall become proper."

Here was a speculation, for a man in my state of mind. The names were all right; some of the incidents, even, were probable, if not correct ; yet how could the facts be known to these comparative strangers ? Did the art of gossiping, with all its meannesses, lies, devices, inventions, and cruelties, really possess so much advantage over the intercourse of the confiding and honest, as to enable those who practise it to discover facts hidden from eye-witnesses, and eye-witnesses, too, that had every inducement of the strongest interest in the issue, not to be deceived? I felt satisfied, the moment Mrs. Greene's name was mentioned, that my passenger were not in the true New York set ; and, justly enough, inferred that they were not very good authority for one half they said ; and yet, how could they know anything of Drewett's attachment to Lucy, unless their information were tolerably accurate ?

I shall not attempt to repeat all that passed while the ship dropped down the bay ; but enough escaped the gossips to render me still more unhappy than I had yet been, on the subject of Lucy. I could and did despise these people—that was easy enough ; but it was not so easy to forget all that they said and surmised. This is one of the curses attendant on the habit of loose talking ; one never knowing what to credit, and what not. In spite of all my disgust, and a firm determination not to contribute in any manner to the stock in trade of these people, I found great difficulty in evading their endless questions. How much they got out of me, by means of the process of negations, I never knew ; but they got no great matter through direct affirmatives. Something, however, persons so indefatigable, to whom gossiping was the great aim of life, must obtain, and they ascertained that Mr. Hardinge was my guardian, that Rupert and I had passed our boyhoods in each other's company, and that Lucy was even an inmate of my own house the day we sailed. This little knowledge only excited a desire for more, and, by the end of a week, I was obliged to submit to devices and expedients to pump me, than which even the thumb-screw was scarcely more efficient. I practised on the negative system, myself, with a good deal of dexterity, however, and threw my inquisitors off, very handsomely, more than once, until I discovered that Wallace Mortimer, determined not to be baffled, actually opened communications with Neb, in order to get a clearer insight into my private affairs! After this, I presume my readers will not care to hear any more about these gentry, whose only connection with my life grew out of the misgivings they contributed largely to create in my mind touching the state of Lucy's affections. This much they did effect, and I was compelled to submit to their power. We are all of us, more or less, the dupes of knaves and fools.

All this, however, was the fruits of several weeks' intercourse, and I have anticipated events a little in order to make the statements in connection. Meeting a breeze, as has been said already, the Dawn got over the bar about two o'clock, and stood off the land, on an easy bowline, in company with the little fleet of square-rigged vessels that went out at the same time. By sunset Navesink again dipped, and I was once more fairly at sea.

This was at the period when the commerce of America was at its height. The spirit shown by the young republic in the French affair had commanded a little respect, though the supposed tendencies of the new administration were causing anything but a cordial feeling toward the country to exist in England. This powerful nation, however, had made a hollow peace with France the previous March, and the highway of nations was temporarily open to all ships alike, a state of things that existed for some ten months after we sailed. Nothing to be apprehended, consequently, lay before me, beyond the ordinary dangers of the ocean. For these last I was now prepared by the experience of several years passed almost entirely on board ship, during which time I had encircled the earth itself in my peregrinations.

Our run off the coast was favorable, and the sixth day out we were in the longitude of the tail of the Grand Bank. I was delighted with my ship, which turned out to be even more than I had dared to hope for. She behaved well under all circumstances, sailing even better than she worked. The first ten days of our passage were prosperous, and we were mid-ocean by the 10th of the month. During this

"There are moments when the haven of New York does present pictures on which the artist would seize with avidity." Engraving after a painting by William Birch showing the New York waterfront as it appeared to Miles Wallingford when he set out on his voyages across the seas.

(p. 420)

time I had nothing to annoy me but the ceaseless *cancans* of my passengers. I had heard the name of every individual of note in Salem, with certain passages in his or her life, and began to fancy I had lived a twelvemonth in the place. At length I began to speculate on the reason why this morbid propensity should exist so much stronger in that part of the world than in any other I had visited. There was nothing new in the disposition of the people of small places to gossip, and it was often done in large towns, more especially those that did not possess the tone of a capital. Lady Mary Wortley Montagu and Horace Walpole wrote gossip, but it was spiced with wit, as is usual with the scandal of such places as London and Paris ; whereas this, to which I was doomed to listen, was nothing more than downright impertinent, vulgar meddling with the private affairs of all those whom the gossips thought of sufficient importance to talk about. At Clawbonny we had our gossip, too, but it was innocent, seldom infringed much on the truth, and usually respected the right of every person to possess certain secrets that might remain inviolate to the world. No such rules prevailed with my passengers. Like a certain editor of a newspaper of my acquaintance, who acts as if he fancied all things in heaven and earth were created expressly to furnish materials for "paragraphs," they appeared to think that everybody of their acquaintance existed for no other purpose than to furnish them food for conversation. There must have been some unusual cause for so much personal *espionnage*, and at length I came to the following conclusion on the subject. I had heard that church government among the Puritans descended into all the details of life ; that it was a part of their religious duty to watch over each other, jog the memories of the delinquents, and serve God by ferreting out vice. This is a terrible inducement to fill the mind with the motes of a neighborhood, and the mind thus stowed, as we sailors say, will be certain to deliver a cargo. Then come the institutions with their never-ending elections, and the construction that had been put on the right of the elector to inquire into all things ; the whole consummated by the journals, who assume a power to penetrate the closet, ay, even the heart, and lay bare its secrets. Is it any wonder if we should become, in time, a nation of mere gossips? As for my passengers, even Neb got to consider them as so many nuisances.

From some cause or other, whether it was having these loose-tongued people on board or not, is more than I can say, but certain it is, about the time Salem was handsomely cleaned out, and a heavy inroad had been made upon Boston, that the weather changed. It began to blow in gusts, sometimes from one point of the compass, sometimes from another, until the ship was brought to very short canvas, from a dread of being caught unprepared. At length these fantasies of the winds terminated in a tremendous gale, such as I had seldom then witnessed, and such, indeed, as I have seldom witnessed since. It is a great mistake to suppose that the heaviest weather occurs in the autumnal, spring, or winter months. Much the strongest blows I have ever known, have taken place in the middle of the warm weather. This is the season of hurricanes, and, out of the tropics, I think it is also the season of the gales. It is true, these gales do not return annually, a long succession of years frequently occurring without one ; but when they do come, they may be expected, in our own seas, in July, August, or September.

The wind commenced at southwest on this occasion, and it blew fresh for several hours, sending us ahead on our course at the rate of eleven knots. As the sea got up and sail was reduced, our speed was a little diminished perhaps, but we must have made more than a hundred miles in the first ten hours. The day was bright, cloudless, genial, and even bland, there being nothing unpleasant in the feeling of the swift currents of the air that whirled past us. At sunset I did not quite like the appearance of the horizon ; and we let the ship wade through it under her three topsails, single reefed, her fore-course, and fore-topmast staysail. This was short canvas for a vessel that had the wind nearly over her taffrail. At nine o'clock second reefs were taken in, and at ten the mizzen-topsail was furled. I then turned in, deeming the ship quite snug, leaving orders with the mates to reduce the sail did they find the ship straining or the spars in danger, and to call me should anything serious occur. I was not called until daylight, when Talcott laid his hand on my shoulder, and said, "You had better turn out, Captain Wallingford ; we have a peeler, and I want a little advice."

It was a peeler, indeed, when I reached the deck. The ship was under a fore-course and a close-reefed main-top-sail, canvas that can be carried a long time while running off, but which I at once saw was quite too much for us. An order was given immediately to take in the topsail. Notwithstanding the diminutive surface that was exposed, the surges given by this bit of canvas, as soon as the clews were eased off sufficiently to allow the cloth to jerk, shook the vessel's hull. It was a miracle that we saved the mast, or that we got the cloth rolled up at all. At one time I thought it would be necessary to cut it from the yard. Fortunately the gale was steady, this day proving bright and clear like that which had preceded it.

The men aloft made several attempts to hail the deck, but the wind blew too heavily to suffer them to be heard. Talcott had gone on the yard himself, and I saw him gesticulating in a way to indicate there was something ahead.

The seas were running so high that it was not easy to obtain much of a look at the horizon, but by getting into the mizzen-rigging I had a glimpse of a vessel's spars, to the eastward of us, and directly on our course. It was a ship under bare poles, running as nearly before us as she could, but making most fearful yaws ; sometimes sheering away off to starboard, in a way to threaten her with broaching-to ; then taking a yaw to port, in which I could see all three of her masts, with their yards pointing nearly at us. I got but one glimpse of her hull as it rose on a sea at the same instant with the Dawn, and it actually appeared as if about to be blown away, though I took the stranger to be a vessel at least as large as we were our-

selves. We were evidently approaching her fast, though
both vessels were going the same way.

The Dawn steered beautifully, one of the greatest vir-
tues in a ship, under the circumstances in which we were
then placed. A single man was all that we had at the
wheel, and he controlled it with ease. I could see it was
very different with the ship ahead, and fancied they had
made a mistake on board her, by taking in all their canvas. Talcott and the gang aloft, had not got out of the
top, however, before we had a hint that it would be well
to imitate the stranger's prudence. Though our vessel
steered so much better than another, no ship can keep on
a direct line while running before the wind, in a heavy
sea. The waves occasionally fly past a vessel, like the
scud glancing through the air ; then they seem to pause,
altogether, as if to permit the ship to overtake them.
When a vessel is lifted aft by one of these torrents of
rushing waters, the helm loses a portion of its power ;
and the part of the vast machine that first receives the
impulse, seems intent on exchanging places with the bows,
vessels often driving sideways before the surges, for spaces
of time that are exceedingly embarrassing to the mariner.
This happens to the best-steering ships, and is always one
source of danger in very heavy weather, to those that are
running off. The merit of the Dawn was in coming under
command again, quickly, and in not losing so much of the
influence of her helm, as is frequently the case with wild-
steering craft. I understand there is a sloop-of-war now
in the navy, that is difficult to get through a narrow passage, in a blow, in consequence of her having this propensity to turn her head first one way, then another, like a gay
horse that breaks his bridle.

The hint given just as Talcott was quitting the top,
and to which there has been allusion, was given under the
impulsion of one of these driving seas. The Dawn still
carried her fore-topmast staysail, a small triangular piece
of stout canvas, and which was particularly useful, as leading from the end of the bowsprit toward the head of the
fore-topmast, in preventing her from broaching-to, or

pressing up with her bows so near the wind as to produce the danger of seas breaking over the mass of the hull, and sweeping the decks. The landsman will understand this is the gravest of the dangers that occur at sea, in very heavy weather. When the ship is thrown broadside to the sea, or comes up so as to bring the wind abeam, or even forward of the beam, as in lying-to, there is always risk from this source. Another danger, which is called pooping, is of a character that one, who is ignorant of the might of the ocean when aroused, would not be apt to fore-see. It proceeds from the impetuous velocity of the waves, which, rushing ahead so much faster than the ves-sel that is even driving before the gale, breaks against the quarter, or stern, and throws its masses of water along the deck, in a line with its keel. I suppose the President steamer to have been lost by the first of these two dangers, as will appear in the following little theory.

There is no doubt that well-constructed steamers are safer craft, the danger from fire excepted, than the ordi-nary ship, except in very heavy weather. With an ordi-nary gale, they can contend with sufficient power; but it is an unfortunate consequence of their construction, that exactly as the danger increases, their power of meeting it diminishes. In a very heavy swell, one cannot venture to resort to a strong head of steam, since one wheel may be nearly out of water, while the other is submerged, and thus endanger the machinery. Now the great length of these vessels renders it difficult to keep them up to the wind, or head to sea, the safest of all positions for a ves-sel in heavy weather, while it exposes them to the addi-tional risk of having the water break aboard them near the waist, in running dead before it. In a word, I sup-pose a steamer difficult to be kept out of the trough, in very heavy weather; and no vessel can be safe in the trough of the seas, under such circumstances; one of great length less so than others. This is true, however, only in reference to those steamers which carry the old-fashioned wheel; Erics-son's screw, and Hunter's submerged wheels, rendering steam-ships, in my poor judgment, the safest craft in the world.

28

The Dawn was overtaken by the seas, from time to time; and, then, like everything else that floats, she yawed, or rather, had her stern urged impetuously round, as if it were in a hurry to get ahead of the bows. On these occasions, the noise made by the fore-topmast staysail, as it collapsed and filled, resembled the report of a small gun. We had similar reports from the foresail, which, for moments at a time, was actually becalmed, as the ship settled into the trough, and then became distended with a noise like that of the shaking of a thousand carpets, all filled with Sancho Panzas, at the same instant. As yet, the cloth and gear had stood these violent shocks admirably; but, just as Talcott was leading his party down, the ship made one of her sidelong movements; the staysail filled with a tremendous report, and away it flew to leeward, taken out of the bolt-rope as if it had been cut by shears, and then used by the furies of the tempest. Talcott smiled. as he gazed at the driving canvas, which went a quarter of a mile before it struck the water, whirling like a kite that has broken its string, and then he shook his head. I disliked, too, the tremendous surges of the foresail, when it occasionally collapsed, and as suddenly filled, menacing to start every bolt, and to part every rope connected with block or spar.

"We must get in that fore-course, Mr. Talcott," I said, "or we shall lose something. I see the ship ahead is under bare poles, and it were better we were as snug. If I did not dislike losing such a wind, it would be wiser to heave-to the ship; man the buntlines and clew-garnets, at once, and wait for a favorable moment."

We had held on to our canvas too long; the fault of youth. As I had determined to shorten sail, however, we now set about it in earnest, and with all the precautions exacted by the circumstances. Everybody that could be mustered, was placed at the clew-lines and buntlines, with strict orders to do his best at the proper moments. The first mate went to the tack, and the second to the sheet. I was to take in the sail myself. I waited for a collapse; and then, while the ship was buried be-

tween two mounds of water, when it was impossible
to see a hundred yards from her in any direction,
and the canvas was actually dropping against the mast,
I gave the usual orders. Every man hauled, as if for
life, and we had got the clews pretty well up, when the
vessel came out of the cavern into the tempest, receiving the whole power of the gale, with a sudden surge, into
the bellying canvas. Away went everything, as if the
gear were cobwebs. At the next instant, the sail was in
ribbons. I was deeply mortified, as well as rendered uneasy, by this accident, as the ship ahead unquestionably
was in full view of all that happened.

It was soon apparent, however, that professional pride
must give place to concern for the safety of the vessel.
The wind had been steadily increasing in power, and had
now reached a pass when it became necessary to look
things steadily in the face. The strips of canvas that remained attached to the yard, with the blocks and gear attached, threshed about in a way to threaten the lives of all
that approached. This was only at the intervals when
the ship settled into the troughs; for, while under the full
influence of the gale, pennants never streamed more directly from a mast, than did these heavy fragments from
the fore-yard. It was necessary to get rid of them; and
Talcott had just volunteered to go on the yard with this
end, when Neb sprang into the rigging without an order,
and was soon beyond the reach of the voice. This daring
black had several narrow escapes, more especially from
the fore-sheet blocks; but he succeeded in cutting everything adrift, and in leaving nothing attached to the spar,
but the bolt-rope of the head of the sail. It is true, little
effected this object, when the knife could be applied, the
threads of the stout canvas snapping at the touch.

As soon as the ship was under bare poles, though at the
sacrifice of two of her sails, I had leisure to look out for
the other vessel. There she was, more than half a mile
ahead of us, yawing wildly, and rolling her lower yard-
arm to the water's edge. As we drew nearer, I got better
glimpses of this vessel, which was a ship, and as I fan-

cied, an English West Indiaman, deep-loaded with the produce of the islands. Deep-loaded, as I fancied, for it was only at instants that she could be seen at all, under circumstances to judge of this fact ; sometimes her hull appearing to be nearly smothered in the brine, and then, again, her copper glistening in the sun, resembling a light vessel, kept under the care of some thrifty housewife.

The Dawn did not fly, now all her canvas was gone, as fast as she had previously done. She went through the water at a greater rate than the vessel ahead ; but it required an hour longer to bring the two ships within a cable's length of each other. Then, indeed, we got a near view of the manner in which the elements can play with such a mass of wood and iron as a ship, when in an angry mood. There were instants when I fancied I could nearly see the keel of the stranger for half its length, as he went foaming up on the crest of a wave, apparently ready to quit the water altogether ; then, again he would settle away into the blue abyss, hiding everything beneath his tops. When both vessels sunk together, no sign of our neighbor was visible, though so near. We came up after one of these deep plunges into the valleys of the ocean, and, to our alarm, saw the English ship yawing directly athwart our course, and within fifty fathoms of us. This was about the distance at which I intended to pass, little dreaming of finding the other ship so completely in our way. The Englishman must have intended to come a little nearer, and got one of those desperate sheers that so often ran away with him. There he was, however ; and a breathless minute followed, when he was first seen. Two vehicles dashing along a highway, with frightened and runaway teams, would not present a sight one half as terrific as that which lay directly before our eyes.

The Dawn was plunging onward with a momentum to dash in splinters, did she strike any resisting object, and yawing herself sufficiently to render the passage hazardous. But the stranger made the matter tenfold worse. When I first saw him in this fearful proximity, his broadside was nearly offered to the seas, and away he was flying,

on the summit of a mountain of foam, fairly crossing our
fore-foot. At the next moment, he fell off before the wind
again, and I could just see his tops directly ahead. His
sheer had been to-port, our intention having been to pass
him on his larboard side ; but, perceiving him to steer so
wild, I thought it might be well to go in the other direction.
Quick as the words could be uttered, therefore, I called out
to port our helm. This was done, of course ; and just as the
Dawn felt the new influence, the other vessel took the same
sheer, and away we both went to-starboard, at precisely the
same instant. I shouted to right our helm to "hard a-starboard," and it was well I did ; a minute more would have
brought us down headlong on the Englishman. Even now
we could only see his hull at instants ; but the awful proximity of his spars denoted the full extent of the danger.
Luckily we hit on opposite directions, or our common destruction would have been certain. But it was one thing in
that caldron of a sea to determine on a course, and another
to follow it. As we rose on that last wave that alone separated us from the stranger, he was nearly ahead ; and as we
glanced onward, I saw that we could barely clear his larboard quarter. Our helm being already a-starboard, no
more could be done. Should he take another sheer to-port,
we must infallibly cut him in twain. As I have said, he
had jammed his helm to-port, and slowly, and with a species
of reluctance, he inclined a little aside. Then we came up,
both ships rolling off, or our yards must have interlocked,
and passing his quarters with our bows, we each felt the
sheer at the same instant, and away we went asunder, the
sterns of the ships looking at each other, and certainly not a
hundred feet apart. A shout from Talcott drew me to our
taffrail, and, standing on that of our neighbor, what or
whom should I see, waving his hat, but the red countenance
of honest Moses Marble !

CHAPTER XXVI.

" At the piping of all hands,
When the judgment signal's spread—
When the islands and the lands,
And the seas give up the dead,
And the south and the north shall come ;
When the sinner is dismayed,
And the just man is afraid,
Then Heaven be thy aid,
Poor Tom."

BRAINARD.

THE two ships, in the haste of their respective crews to get clear of each other, were now running in the troughs ; and the same idea would seem to have suggested itself to me and the other master, at the same instant. Instead of endeavoring to keep away again, one kept his helm hard a-port, the other as hard a-starboard, until we both came by the wind, though on opposite tacks. The Englishman set his mizzen-staysail, and though he made bad weather of it, he evidently ran much less risk than in scudding. The seas came on board him constantly ; but not in a way to do any material damage. As for the Dawn, she lay-to, like a duck, under bare poles. I had a spare staysail stopped up in her mizzen-rigging, from the top down, and after that the ship was both easy and dry. Once in a while, it is true, her bows would meet some fellow heavier than common, and then we got a few hogsheads of water forward ; but it went out to leeward as fast as it came in to windward. At the turn of the day, however, the gale broke, and the weather moderated sensibly ; both sea and wind beginning to go down.

Had we been alone, I should not have hesitated about bearing up, getting some sail on the ship, and running off on my course, again ; but the desire to speak the stranger and have some communication with Marble, was so strong, that I could not make up my mind to do so. Including myself, Talcott, Neb, the cabin steward, and six of the people forward, there were ten of us on board, who knew the ex-mate ; and, of the whole ten, there was not a dissenting voice concerning his identity. I determined, therefore, to stick by the Englishman, and at least have some communication with my old friend. As for myself, I own I loved Marble, uncouth and peculiar as he sometimes was. I owed him more than any other man living, Mr. Hardinge excepted ; for he had made me a seaman, having been of use to me professionally, in a hundred ways. Then we had seen so much in company, that I regarded him as a portion of my experience, and as in some measure identified with my own nautical career.

I was afraid at one moment, that the Englishman intended to remain as he was, all night ; but, about an hour before sunset, I had the gratification to see him set his foresail, and keep off. I had wore round, two hours before, to get the Dawn's head on the same tack with him, and followed under bare poles. As the stranger soon set his main-topsail, close-reefed, and then his fore, it enabled us to make a little sail also, in order to keep up with him. This we did all that night ; and, in the morning, both ships were under everything that would draw, with a moderate breeze from the northward, and no great matter of sea going. The English vessel was about a league to leeward of us, and a little ahead. Under such circumstances, it was easy to close. Accordingly, just as the two ships' companies were about to go to breakfast, the Dawn ranged up under the lee-quarter of the stranger.

"What ship's that?" I hailed, in the usual manner.

"The Dundee ; Robert Ferguson, master. What ship's that?"

"The Dawn ; Miles Wallingford. Where are you from?"

"From Rio de Janeiro, bound to London. Where are you from?"

"From New York, to Bordeaux. A heavy blow we have just had of it."

"Quite; the like of it I've not seen in many a day. You've a pretty sea-boat, yon!"

"She made capital weather, in the late gale, and I've every reason to be satisfied with her. Pray, have n't you an American on board, by the name of Marble? We fancied that we saw the face of an old shipmate on your taffrail, yesterday, and I have kept you company in order to inquire after his news."

"Ay, ay," answered the Scotch master, waving his hand, "the chiel will be visiting you prasently. He's below, stowing away his dunnage; and will be thanking you for a passage home, I'm thinking."

As these words were uttered, Marble appeared on deck, and waved his hat, again, in recognition. This was enough; as we understood each other, the two ships took sufficient room, and hove-to. We lowered our boat, and Talcott went alongside of the Dundee, in quest of our old shipmate. Newspapers and news were exchanged; and, in twenty minutes, I had the extreme gratification of grasping Marble once more by the hand.

My old friend was too much affected to speak, for some little time. He shook hands with everybody, and seemed as much astonished as he was delighted at finding so many of us together again; but not a syllable did he utter for several minutes. I had his chest passed into the cabin, and then went and took my seat alongside of him on the hen-coops, intending to hear his story, as soon as he was disposed to give it. But it was no easy matter to get out of ear-shot of my passengers. During the gale, they had been tongue-tied, and I had a little peace; but no sooner did the wind and sea go down, than they broke out in the old spot, and began to do Boston, in the way they had commenced. Now Marble had come on board in a manner so unusual, and it was evident a secret history was to be revealed, they all three took post in the companion-way, in a manner to render it impossible anything material could escape them. I knew the folly of attempting a change of position on deck ; we should certainly be followed up ; and people of this class, so long as they can make the excuse of saying they heard any part of a secret, never scruple about inventing the portions that happen to escape their ears. Consequently, I desired Marble and Talcott to follow me ; and, incontinently, I led the way into the main-top. I was obeyed, the second mate having the watch, and all three of us were soon seated with our legs over the top-rim, as comfortable as so many gossips, who have just finished their last cups, have stirred the fire, and drawn their heads together to open a fresh budget. Neither Sarah nor Jane could follow us, thank God !

" There, d——n 'em," said I, a little pointedly, for it was enough to make a much more scrupulous person swear, " we 've got the length of the main-rigging between us, and I do not think they 'll venture into the top, this fine morning, in order to overhear what shall be said. It would puzzle even Wallace Mortimer to do that, Talcott."

" If they do," observed Talcott, laughing, " we can retreat to the cross-trees, and thence to the royal-yard."

Marble looked inquisitive, but, at the same time, he looked knowing.

" I understand," he said, with a nod ; " three people with six sets of ears—is it not so, Miles ? "

" Precisely ; though you only do them credit by halves, for you should have added to this inventory forty tongues."

" Well, that is a large supply. The man, or woman, who is so well provided, should carry plenty of ballast. However, as you say, they 're out of hail now, and must guess at all they repeat, if repeating it can be called."

" Quite as much as nine tenths of what they give as coming from others," observed Talcott. " People never can tell so much of other persons' affairs, without bailing out most of their ideas from their own scuttle-butts."

" Well, let them go to—Bordeaux," said I, " since they are bound there. And now, my dear Marble, here we are, and dying to know all that has happened to you. You have firm friends in Talcott and myself, either of us ready to give you his berth for the asking."

"Thank'ee, my dear boys—thank'ee, with all my heart and soul," returned the honest fellow, dashing the moisture from his eyes, with the back of his hand. "I believe you would, boys ; I do believe you would, one or both. I am glad, Miles, you came up into this bloody top, for I would n't like to let your reg'lar 'long-shore harpies see a man of my time of life, and one that has been to sea, now, man and boy, close on to forty years, with as much blubber about him as one of your right whales. Well—and now for the log ; for I suppose you 'll insist on overhauling it, lads."

"That we shall ; and see you miss no leaf of it. Be as particular as if it were overhauled in an insurance case."

"Ay ; they 're bloody knaves, sometimes, them under-writers, and a fellow need be careful to get his dues out of them—that is to say, some ; others, ag'in, are gentlemen down to their shoe-buckles, and no sooner see a poor ship-wrecked-devil, than they open their tills, and begin to count out before he has opened his mouth."

"Well, but your own adventures, my old friend ; you forget we are dying with curiosity."

"Ay ; your cur'osity 's a troublesome inmate, and will never be quiet as long as one tries to keep it under hatches ; especially female cur'osity. Well, I must gratify you, and so I 'll make no more bones about it, though it 's giving an account of my own obstinacy and folly. I reckon, now, my boys, you missed me the day the ship sailed from the island ? "

"That we did, and supposed you had got tired of your experiment before it began," I answered, " so were off, be-fore we were ourselves."

"You had reason for so thinking, though you were out in your reckoning, too. No—it happened in this fashion. After you left me I began to generalize over my situation, and I says to myself, says I, ' Moses Marble, them lads will never consent to sail and leave you here on this island, alone, like a bloody hermit,' says I. ' If you want to hold on,' says I, ' and try your hand at a hermitage,' says I, ' or

to play Robinson Crusoe,' says I, 'you must be out of the
way when the Crisis sails'—boys, what's become of the old
ship? Not a word have I heard about her, yet!''

" She was loading for London when we sailed, her owners
intending to send her the same voyage over again."

" And they refused to let you have her, Miles, on account
of your youth, notwithstanding all you did for them?"

" Not so ; they pressed me to keep her, but I preferred a
ship of my own. The Dawn is my property, Master Moses !''

"Thank God ! then there is one honest chap among the
owners. And how did she behave? Had you any trouble
with the pirates?''

Perceiving the utter uselessness of attempting to hear
his own story before I rendered an account of the Crisis and
her exploits, I gave Marble a history of her voyage from
the time we parted down to the day we reached New York.

"And that scaramouch of a schooner that the Frenchman gave us in his charity?''

"The Pretty Poll? She got home safe, was sold, and is
now in the West India trade. There is a handsome balance,
amounting to some fourteen hundred dollars, in the owners'
hands, coming to you from prize money and wages."

It is not in nature for any man to be sorry he has money.
I saw by Marble's eyes that this sum, so unusually large for
him to possess, formed a new tie to the world, and that he
fancied himself a much happier man in possessing it. He
looked at me earnestly for quite a minute, and then remarked, I make no doubt with sincere regret,—

" Miles, if I had a mother living, now, that money might
make her old age comfortable ! It seems that they who have
no mothers have money, and they who have no money have
mothers."

I waited a moment for Marble to recover his self-command,
and then urged him to continue his story.

" I was telling you how I generalized over my sitiation,"
resumed the ex-mate, " as soon as I found myself alone in
the hut. I came to the conclusion that I should be carried
off by force, if I remained till next day ; and so I got into
the launch, carried her out of the lagoon, taking care to give

the ship a berth, went through the reef, and kept turning to windward until daybreak. By that time the island was quite out of sight, though I saw the upper sails of the ship as soon as you got her under way. I kept the topgallant-sails in sight, until I made the island again ; and as you went off I ran in and took possession of my dominions, with no one to dispute my will, or to try to reason me out of my consait.''

"I am glad to hear you term that notion a conceit, for, certainly, it was not reason. You soon discovered your mistake, old messmate, and began to think of home.''

"I soon discovered, Miles, that if I had neither father nor mother, brother nor sister, that I had a country and friends. The bit of marble on which I was found in the stone-cutter's yard, then seemed as dear to me as a gold cradle is to a king's son ; and I thought of you, and all the rest of you—nay, I yearned after you, as a mother would yearn for her children.''

"Poor fellow, you were solitary enough, I dare say ; had you no amusement with your pigs and poultry ?''

"For a day or two they kept me pretty busy. But by the end of a week I discovered that pigs and poultry were not made to keep company with man. I had consaited that I could pass the rest of my days in the bosom of my own family, like any other man who had made his fortune and retired, but I found my household too small for such a life as that. My great mistake was in supposing that the Marble family could be happy in its own circle.''

This was said bitterly, though it was said drolly, and while it made Talcott and myself laugh, it also made us sorry.

"I fell into another mistake, however, boys,'' Marble continued, "and it might as well be owned. I took it into my head that I should be all alone on the island, but I found, to my cost, that the devil insisted on having his share. I'll tell how it is, Miles, a man must either look ahead or look astarn ; there is no such thing as satisfying himself with the present moorings. Now this was my misfortune, for ahead I had nothing to look forward to, and astarn what comfort had I in overhauling past sins ?''

" I think I can understand your difficulties, my friend ;
how did you manage to get rid of them ? "

" I left the island. You had put the Frenchman's launch
in capital condition, and all I had to do was to fill up the
breakers with fresh water, kill a hog and salt him away,
put on board a quantity of biscuit, and be off. As for
eatables, you know there was no scarcity on the island, and
I took my choice. I make no doubt there are twenty
hogsheads of undamaged sugars at this very moment in the
hold of that wreck and on the beach of the island. I fed
my poultry on it the whole time I stayed."

" And so you abandoned Marble Land to the pigs and
the fowls ? "

" I did, indeed, Miles, and I hope the poor creatures will
have a comfortable time of it. I gave 'em what the lawyers call a quit-claim, and sailed two months to a day after
you went off in the Crisis."

" I should think, old shipmate, that your voyage must
have been as solitary and desperate as your life ashore."

" I 'm amazed to hear you say that. I 'm never solitary
at sea, one has so much to do in taking care of his craft,
and then he can always look forward to the day he 'll get in.
But this generalizing, night and day, without any port
ahead, and little comfort in looking astern, will soon fit a
man for Bedlam. I just weathered Cape Crazy, I can tell
you, lads, and that too in the white water ! As for my
v'y'ge being desperate, what was there to make it so, I
should like to know ? "

" You must have been twelve or fifteen hundred miles
from any island where you could look forward to anything
like safety, and that is a distance one would rather not
travel all alone on the high seas."

" Pshaw ! all consait. You 're getting notional, Miles,
now you 're a master and owner. What 's a run of a thousand or fifteen hundred miles, in a tight boat, and with
plenty of grub and water ? It was the easiest matter in
the world, and if it war n't for that bloody Cape Horn, I
should have made as straight a wake for Coenties' Slip as
the trending of the land would have allowed. As it was, I

turned to windward, for I knew the savages to leeward weren't to be trusted. You see it was as easy as working out a day's work. I kept the boat on a wind all day, and long bits of the night, too, until I wanted sleep, and then I hove her to under a reefed mainsail, and slept as sound as a lord. I hadn't an uncomfortable moment after I got outside of the reef again, and the happiest hour of my life was that in which I saw the tree-tops of the island dip."

"And how long were you navigating in this manner, and what land did you first make?"

"Seven weeks, though I made half a dozen islands, every one of them just such a looking object as that I had left. You weren't about to catch me ashore again in any of them miserable places! I gave the old boat a slap, and promised to stick by her as long as she would stick by me, and I kept my word. I saw savages, moreover, on one or two of the islands, and gave them a berth, having no fancy for being barbecued."

"And where did you finally make your landfall."

"Nowhere, so far as the launch was concerned. I fell in with a Manilla ship, bound to Valparaiso, and got on board her; and sorry enough was I for the change, when I came to find out how they lived. The captain took me in, however, and I worked my passage into port. Finding no ship likely to sail soon, I entered with a native who was about to cross the Andes, bound over on this side, for the east coast. Don't you remember, Miles, monsters of mountains that we could see, a bit inland, and covered with snow, all along the west side of South America? You must remember the chaps I mean."

"Certainly; they are much too plain, and objects much too striking, ever to be forgotten, when once seen."

"Well, them's the Andes; and rough customers they be, let me tell you, boys. You know there is little amusement in a sailor's walking on the levellest 'arth and handsomest highways, on account of the bloody ups and downs a fellow meets with; and so you may get some idee of the time we had of it, when I tell you, had all the seas we saw in the last blow been piled on top of each other, they would have made but a large pancake, compared to them 'ere Andes. Natur' must have outdone herself in making 'em; and when they were thrown together, what good comes of it all? Such mountains might be of some use in keeping the French and English apart; but you leave nothing but bloody Spaniards on one side of them Andes, and find bloody Spaniards and Portugeese on the other. However, we found our way over them, and brought up at a place called Buenos Ayres, from which I worked my passage round to Rio in a coaster. At Rio, you know, I felt quite at home, having stopped in there often, in going backward and forward."

"And thence you took passage in the Dundee for London, intending to get a passage home by the first opportunity?"

"It needs no witch to tell that. I had to scull about Rio for several months doing odd jobs as a rigger, and the like of that, until, finding no Yankee came in, I got a passage in a Scotchman. I'll not complain of Sawney, who was kind enough to me as a shipwrecked mariner; for that was the character I sailed under, hermits being no way fashionable among us Protestants, though it's very different among them Catholic chaps, I can tell you. I happened to mention to a landlady on the road, that I was a sort of a hermit on his travels; when I thought the poor woman would have gone down on her knees and worshipped me."

Here then was the history of Moses Marble, and the end of the colony of Marble Land, pigs and poultry excepted. It was now my turn to be examined. I had to answer fifty curious inquiries, some of which I found sufficiently embarrassing. When, in answer to his interrogatories, Marble learned that the major and Miss Merton had actually been left at Clawbonny, I saw the ex-mate wink at Talcott, who smiled in reply. Then, there was Rupert, and how came on the law? The farm and mills were not forgotten; and, as for Neb, he was actually ordered up into the top, in order that there might be another shake of the hand, and that he might answer for himself. In a word, nothing could be more apparent than the delight of Marble at finding himself among us once more. I believed even

then, that the man really loved me; and the reader will
remember how long we had sailed together, and how
much we had seen in company. More than once did my
old shipmate dash the tears from his eyes, as he spoke of
his satisfaction.

"I say, Miles—I say, Roger," he cried, "this is like being
at home, and none of your bloody hermitages! Blast me, if
I think, now, I should dare pass through a wood all alone.
I'm never satisfied unless I see a fellow-creatur', for fear
of being left. I did pretty well with the Scotchman, who
has a heart, though it's stowed away in oatmeal, but this is
home. I must ship as your steward, Miles, for hang on to
you I will."

"If we ever part again, until one or both go into dock,
it will be your fault, my old friend. If I have thought of
you once, since we parted, I have dreamed of you fifty
times! Talcott and I were talking of you in the late gale,
and wondering what sail you would advise us to put the
ship under."

"The old lessons have not all been forgotten, boys; it
was easy enough to see that. I said to myself, as you stood
down upon us, 'That chap has a real sea-dog aboard, as is
plain by the manner in which he has everything snug, while
he walks ahead like an owner in a hurry to be first in the
market.'"

It was then agreed Marble should keep a watch, whenever it suited him, and that he should do just as he pleased
aboard. At some future day, some other arrangement
might be made, though he declared his intention to stick by
the ship, and also announced a determination to be my first
mate for life, as soon as Talcott got a vessel, as doubtless
he would, through the influence of his friends, as soon as he
returned home. I laughed at all this, though I bade him
heartily welcome, and then I nicknamed him commodore,
adding that he should sail with me in that capacity, doing
just as much and just as little duty as he pleased. As for
money, there was a bag of dollars in the cabin, and he had
only to put his hand in, and take what he wanted. The
key of the locker was in my pocket, and could be had for

asking. Nobody was more delighted with this arrangement than Neb, who had even taken a fancy to Marble,
from the moment when the latter led him up from the
steerage of the John, by the ear.

"I say, Miles, what sort of bloody animals are them
passengers of yours!" Marble next demanded, looking
over the rim of the top, down at the trio on deck, with a
good deal of curiosity expressed in his countenance. "This
is the first time I ever knew a shipmaster driven aloft by
his passengers, in order to talk secrets!"

"That is because you never sailed with the Brigham
family, my friend. They 'll pump you till you suck, in the
first twenty-four hours, rely on it. They 'll get every fact
about your birth, the island where you first saw me, what
you have been about, and what you mean to do; in a word,
the past, present, and future."

"Leave me to overlay their cur'osity," answered the ex-
mate, or new commodore; "I got my hand in, by boarding
six weeks with a Connecticut old maid, once, and I 'll defy
the keenest questioner of them all."

We had a little more discourse, when we all went below,
and I introduced Marble to my passengers, as one who was to
join our mess. After this, things went on in their usual train.
In the course of the day, however, I overheard the following
brief dialogue between Brigham and Marble, the ladies being
much too delicate to question so rough a mariner.

"You came on board of us somewhat unexpectedly, I
rather conclude, Captain Marble?" commenced the gentleman.

"Not in the least; I have been expecting to meet the
Dawn, just about this spot, more than a month, now."

"Well, that is odd! I do not comprehend how such a
thing could well be foreseen?"

"Do you understand spherical trigonometry, sir?"

"I cannot say I am at all expert—I 've looked into
mathematics, but have no great turn for the study."

"It would be hopeless then, to attempt to explain the
matter. If you had your hand in at the spherical, I could
make it as plain as the capstan."

"You and Captain Wallingford must be somewhat old acquaintances, I conclude?"

"Somewhat," answered Marble very dryly.

"Have you ever been at the place that he calls Clawbonny? A queer name, I rather think, captain!"

"Not at all, sir. I know a place, down in the Eastern States, that was called Scratch and Claw, and a very pretty spot it was."

"It's not usual for us to the eastward, to give names to farms and places. It is done a little by the Boston folk, but they are notional, as everybody knows."

"Exactly; I suppose it was for want of use, the chap I mean made out no better in naming his place."

Mr. Brigham was no fool; he was merely a gossip. He took the hint, and asked no more questions of Marble. He tried Neb, notwithstanding; but the black having his orders, obeyed them so literally, that I really believe we parted in Bordeaux, a fortnight later, without any of the family's making the least discovery. Glad enough was I to get rid of them; yet, brief as had been our intercourse, they produced a sensible influence on my future happiness. Such is the evil of this habit of loose talking, men giving credit to words conceived in ignorance and uttered in the indulgence of one of the most contemptible of all our propensities. To return to my ship.

We reached Bordeaux without any further accident or delay. I discharged in the usual way, and began to look about me for another freight. It had been my intention to return to New York, and to keep the festivities of attaining my majority, at Clawbonny; but, I confess, the discourse of these eternal gossips, the Brighams, had greatly lessened the desire to see home again so soon. A freight for New York was offered me, but I postponed an answer, until it was given to another ship. At length an offer was made to me to go to Cronstadt, in Russia, with a cargo of wines and brandies, and I accepted it. The great and better informed merchants, as it would seem, distrusted the continuance of the hollow peace that then existed, and a company of them thought it might be well to transfer their

liquors to the capital of the Czar, in readiness for contin-
gencies. An American ship was preferred, on account of
her greater speed, as well as on account of her probable
neutral character, in the event of troubles occurring at any
unlooked-for moment.

The Dawn took in her wines and brandies accordingly,
and sailed for the Baltic about the last of August. She
had a long, but a safe passage, delivering the freight according to the charter-party, in good condition. While at
Cronstadt, the American consul, and the consignees of an
American ship that had lost her master and chief mate by
the small-pox, applied to me to let Marble carry the vessel
home. I pressed the offer on my old friend, but he obsti-
nately refused to have anything to do with the vessel. I
then recommended Talcott, and after some negotiation, the
latter took charge of the Hyperion. I was sorry to part
with my mate, to whom I had become strongly attached ;
but the preferment was so clearly to his advantage, that I
could take no other course. The vessel being ready, she
sailed the day after Talcott joined her ; and sorry am I to be
compelled to add, that she was never heard of, after clearing the Cattegat. The equinox of that season was tremendously severe, and it caused the loss of many vessels ; that
of the Hyperion doubtless among the rest.

Marble insisted upon taking Talcott's place, and he now
became my chief mate, as I had once been his. After a
little delay, I took in freight on Russian government account, and sailed for Odessa. It was thought the Sublime
Porte would let an American through ; but, after reaching
the Dardanelles, I was ordered back, and was obliged to
leave my cargo in Malta, which it was expected would be
in possession of its own knights by that time, agreeably to
the terms of the late treaty. From Malta I sailed for
Leghorn, in quest of another freight. I pass over the details
of these voyages, as really nothing worthy of being recorded occurred. They consumed a good deal of time ; the
delay at the Dardanelles alone exceeded six weeks, during
which negotiations were going on up at Constantinople,
but all in vain. In consequence of all these detentions,

and the length of the passages, I did not reach Leghorn until near the close of March. I wrote to Grace and Mr. Hardinge, whenever a favorable occasion offered, but I did not get a letter from home, during the whole period. It was not in the power of my sister or guardian—*late* guardian would be the most accurate expression, as I had been of age since the previous October—to write, it being impossible for me to let them know when, or where, a letter would find me. It followed, that while my friends at home were kept tolerably apprised of my movements, I was absolutely in the dark as respected them. That this ignorance gave me great concern, it would be idle to deny ; yet I had a species of desperate satisfaction in keeping aloof, and in leaving the course clear to Mr. Andrew Drewett. As respects substantials, I had sent a proper power of attorney to Mr. Hardinge, who, I doubted not, would take the same care of my temporal interests he had never ceased to do since the day of my beloved mother's death.

Freights were not offering freely at Leghorn, when the Dawn arrived. After waiting a fortnight, however, I began to take in for America, and on American account. In the meantime, the cargo coming to hand slowly, I left Marble to receive it, and proceeded on a little excursion in Tuscany, or Etruria, as that part of the world was then called. I visited Pisa, Lucca, Florence, and several other intermediate towns. At Florence, I passed a week looking at sights, and amusing myself the best way I could. The gallery and the churches kept me pretty busy, and the reader will judge of my surprise one day, at hearing my own name uttered on a pretty high key, by a female voice, in the Duomo, or Cathedral of the place. On turning, I found myself in the presence of the Brighams ! I was overwhelmed with questions in a minute. Where had I been ? Where was Talcott? Where was the ship? When did I sail, and whither did I sail? After this came the communications. They had been to Paris ; had seen the French Consul, and had dined with Mr. R. N. Livingston then negotiating the treaty of Louisiana ; had seen the Louvre ; had been to Geneva ; had seen the Lake ; had seen Mont

Blanc ; had crossed Mont Cenis ; had been at Milan ; Rome ; had seen the Pope ; Naples ; had seen Vesuvius ; had been at Pæstum ; had come back to Florence, and *nous voici!* Glad enough was I, when I got them fairly within the gates of the city of the Lily. Next came America ; from which part of the world they received such delightful letters ! One from Mrs. Jonathan Little, a Salem lady then residing in New York, had just reached them. It contained four sheets, and was full of news. Then commenced the details ; and I was compelled to listen to a string of gossip that connected nearly all the people of mark, my informants had ever heard of in the great Commercial Emporium that was to be. How suitable is this name ! Emporium would not have been sufficiently distinctive for a town in which " the merchants " are all in all ; in which they must have the post-office ; in which they support the nation by paying all the revenue ; in which the sun must shine and the dew fall to suit their wants ; and in which the winds, themselves, may be recreant to their duty, when they happen to be foul ! Like the Holy Catholic Protestant Episcopal Church, Trading Commercial Trafficking Emporium should have been the style of such a place ; and I hope, ere long, some of the " Manor Born " genii of that great town will see the matter rectified.

" By the way, Captain Wallingford," cut in Jane, at one of Sarah's breathing intervals, that reminded me strongly of the colloquial Frenchman's " S'il crache il est perdu," " you know something of poor Mrs. Bradfort, I believe ? "

I assented by a bow.

" It was just as we told you," cried Sarah, taking her revenge. " The poor woman is dead ! and, no doubt, of that cancer. What a frightful disease ! and how accurate has our information been in all that affair ! "

" I think her will the most extraordinary of all," added Mr. Brigham, who, as a man, kept an eye more to the main chance. " I suppose you have heard all about her will, Captain Wallingford ? "

I reminded the gentleman that this was the first I had ever heard of the lady's death.

"She has left every dollar to young Mr. Hardinge, her cousin's son," added Jane, "cutting off that handsome, genteel young lady, his sister, as well as her father, without a cent,"—in 1803, they just began to speak of cents, instead of farthings,—"and everybody says it was so cruel!"

"That is not the worst of it," put in Sarah. "They do say, Miss Merton, the English lady has made so much noise in New York—let me see, Mr. Brigham, what earl's granddaughter did we hear she was?"

This was a most injudicious question, as it gave the husband an opportunity to take the word out of her mouth.

"Lord Cumberland's, I believe, or some such person; but no matter whose. It is quite certain General Merton, her father, consents to let her marry young Mr. Hardinge, now Mrs. Bradfort's will is known; and as for the sister, he declares he will never give her a dollar."

"He will have sixteen thousand dollars a year," said Jane, with emphasis.

"Six, my dear, six," returned the brother, who had reasonably accurate notions touching dollars and cents, or he never would have been travelling in Italy; "six thousand dollars a year was just Mrs. Bradfort's income, as my old school-fellow Upham told me, and there is n't another man in York who can tell fortunes as true as himself. He makes a business of it, and don't fail one time in twenty."

"And is it quite certain that Mr. Rupert Hardinge gets all the fortune of Mrs. Bradfort?" I asked, with a strong effort to seem composed.

"Not the least doubt of it in the world. Everybody is talking about it; and there cannot well be a mistake, you know, as it was thought the sister would be an heiress, and people generally take care to be pretty certain about that class. But, of course, a young man of that fortune will be snapped up, as a swallow catches a fly. I've bet Sarah a pair of gloves we hear of his marriage in three months."

The Brighams talked an hour longer, and made me promise to visit them at their hotel, a place I could not succeed in finding. That evening I left Florence for Leghorn, writing a note of apology, in order not to be rude.

Of course I did not believe half these people had told me; but a part, I made no doubt, was true. Mrs. Bradfort was dead, out of all question; and I thought it possible she might not so far have learned to distinguish between the merit of Lucy, and that of Rupert, as to leave her entire fortune to the last. As for the declaration of the brother that he would give his sister nothing, that seemed to me to be rather strong even for Rupert. I knew the dear girl too well, and was certain she would not repine; and I was burning with the desire to be in the field, now she was again penniless.

What a change was this! Here were the Hardinges, those whom I had known as poor, almost as dependents on my own family, suddenly enriched. I knew Mrs. Bradfort had a large six thousand a year besides her own dwelling-house, which stood in Wall Street, a part of the commercial emporium that was just beginning to be the focus of banking, and all other moneyed operations, and which even then promised to become a fortune of itself. It is true, that old Daniel M'Cormick still held his levees on his venerable stoop, where all the heavy men in town used to congregate, and joke, and buy and sell, and abuse Boney; and that the Winthrops, the Wilkeses, the Jaunceys, the Verplancks, the Whites, the Ludlows, and other families of mark, then had their town residences in this well-known street; but coming events were beginning "to cast their shadows before," and it was easy to foresee that this single dwelling might at least double Rupert's income, under the rapid increase of the country and the town. Though Lucy was still poor, Rupert was now rich.

If family connection, that all-important and magical influence, could make so broad a distinction between us, while I was comparatively wealthy and Lucy had nothing, what, to regard the worst side of the picture, might I not expect from it when the golden scale preponderated on her side? That Andrew Drewett would still marry her, I began to fear again. Well, why not? I had never mentioned love to the sweet girl, fondly, ardently as I was attached to her; and what reason had I for supposing that one in her situation could reserve her affections for a truant sailor? I am afraid I was unjust enough to regret that this piece of good fortune should have befallen Rupert. He must do something for his sister, and every dollar seemed to raise a new barrier between us.

From that hour I was all impatience to get home. Had not the freight been engaged, I think I should have sailed in ballast. By urging the merchants, however, we got to sea May 15th, with a full cargo, a portion of which I had purchased on my own account, with the money earned by the ship within the last ten months. Nothing occurred worthy of notice until the Dawn neared the Straits of Gibraltar. Here we were boarded by an English frigate, and first learned the declaration of a new war between France and England; a contest that, in the end, involved in it all the rest of Christendom. Hostilities had already commenced, the First Consul having thrown aside the mask just three days after we left port. The frigate treated us well, it being too soon for the abuses that followed, and we got through the pass without further molestation.

As soon as in the Atlantic, I took care to avoid everything we saw, and nothing got near us until we had actually made the Highlands of Navesink. An English sloop-of-war, however, had stood into the angles of the coast formed by Long Island and the Jersey shore, giving us a race for the Hook. I did not know whether I ought to be afraid of this cruiser or not, but my mind was made up not to be boarded if it could be helped. We succeeded in passing ahead, and entered the Hook while he was still a mile outside of the bar. I got a pilot on the bar, as was then very usual, and stood up against the town with studding-sails set, it being just a twelvemonth, almost to an hour, from the day when I passed up the bay in the Crisis. The pilot took the ship in near Coenties' Slip, Marble's favorite birth, and we had her secured and her sails unbent before the sun set.

CHAPTER XXVII.

"With look like patient Job's, eschewing evil ;
With motions graceful as a bird's in air ;
Thou art, in sober truth, the veriest devil
That e'er clinched fingers in a captive's hair."

HALLECK.

THERE was about an hour of daylight, when I left the counting-house of the consignees, and pursued my way up Wall Street, to Broadway. I was on my way to the City Hotel, then, as now, one of the best inns of the town. On Trinity Church walk, just as I quitted the Wall Street crossing, whom should I come plump upon in turning, but Rupert Hardinge! He was walking down the street in some little haste, and was evidently much surprised, perhaps I might say startled, at seeing me. Nevertheless, Rupert was not easily disconcerted, and his manner at once became warm, if not entirely free from embarrassment. He was in deep mourning ; though otherwise dressed in the height of the fashion.

"Wallingford ! " he exclaimed—it was the first time he did not call me " Miles "—" Wallingford ! my fine fellow, what cloud did you drop from ? We have had so many reports concerning you, that your appearance is as much a matter of surprise as would be that of Bonaparte, himself. Of course your ship is in ? "

"Of course," I answered, taking his offered hand ; "you know I am wedded to her, for better, for worse, until death or shipwreck doth us part."

"Ay, so I've always told the ladies : 'There is no other matrimony in Wallingford,' I've said often, 'than that

which will make him a ship's husband.' But you look con-
foundedly well ; the sea agrees with you, famously."

"I make no complaint of my health—but tell me of that
of our friends and families. Your father—"

"Is up at Clawbonny, just now—you know how it is
with him. No change of circumstances will ever make him
regard his little smoke-house-looking church as anything
but a cathedral, and his parish as a diocese. Since the
great change in our circumstances, all this is useless, and I
often think—you know one would n't like to say as much
to him—but I often think, he might just as well give up
preaching, altogether."

"Well, this is good, so far ; now for the rest of you, all.
You meet my impatience too coldly."

"Yes, you were always an impatient fellow. Why, I
suppose you need hardly be told that I have been admitted
to the bar."

"That I can very well imagine ; you must have found
your sea-training of great service on the examination."

"Ay, my dear Wallingford—what a simpleton I was !
But one is so apt to take up strange conceits in boyhood,
that he is compelled to look back at them in wonder, in
after life. But which way are you walking ? "—slipping an
arm in mine ; "if up, I 'll take a short turn with you.
These 's scarce a soul in town, at this season ; but you 'll see
prodigiously fine girls in Broadway, at this hour, notwithstanding—those that belong to the other sets, you know ;
those that belong to families that can't get into the country
among the leaves. Yes, as I was saying, one scarce knows
himself, after twenty. Nor, I can hardly recall a taste, or
an inclination, that I cherished in my teens, that has not
flown to the winds. Nothing is permanent in boyhood ;
we grow in our persons, and our minds, sentiments, affections, views, hopes, wishes, and ambition all take new directions."

"This is not very flattering, Rupert, to one whose acquaintance with you may be said to be altogether boyish."

"Oh ! of course I don't mean that. Habit keeps all right
in such matters : and I dare say I shall always be as much

attached to you as I was in childhood. Still, we are on diverging lines, now, and cannot forever remain boys.''

'' You have told me nothing of the rest,'' I said, half choked, in my eagerness to hear of the girls, and yet unaccountably afraid to ask. I believe I dreaded to hear that Lucy was married. '' How and where is Grace ? ''

'' Oh ! Grace !—yes, I forgot her, to my shame, as you would naturally wish to inquire. Why, my dear captain, to be as frank as one ought with so old an acquaintance, your sister is not in a good way, I 'm much afraid ; though I 've not seen her in an age. She was down among us in the autumn, but left town for the holidays, for them she insisted on keeping at Clawbonny, where she said the family had always kept them, and away she went. Since then, she has not returned ; but I fear she is far from well. You know what a fragile creature Grace ever has been—so American ! Ah ! Wallingford ! our females have no constitutions—charming as angels, delicate as fairies, and all that ; but not to be compared to the English women in constitutions.''

I felt a torrent of fire rushing through my blood, and it was with difficulty I refrained from hurling the heartless scoundrel who leaned on my arm, into the ditch. A moment of reflection, however, warned me of the precipice on which I stood. He was Mr. Hardinge's son, Lucy's brother ; and I had no proofs that he had ever induced Grace to think he loved her. It was so easy for those who had been educated as we four had been, to be deceived on such a point, that I felt it unsafe to do anything precipitately. Friendship, habit, as Rupert expressed it, might so easily be mistaken for the fruits of passion, that one might well be deceived. Then it was all important to Grace's self-respect, to her feelings, in some measure to her character, to be careful that I suppressed my wrath, though it nearly choked me.

'' I am sorry to hear this,'' I answered, after a long pause, the deep regret I felt at having such an account of my sister's health contributing to make my manner seem natural, '' very, very sorry to hear it. Grace is one that requires the

tenderest care and watching ; and I have been making passage after passage in pursuit of money, when I am afraid
I should have been at Clawbonny, discharging the duties of
a brother. I can never forgive myself ! ''

" Money is a very good thing, captain," answered Rupert, with a smile that appeared to mean more than the
tongue expressed, " a surprisingly good thing is money !
But you must not exaggerate Grace's illness, which I dare
say is merely constitutional, and will lead to nothing. I
hope your many voyages have produced their fruits ? ''

"And Lucy," I resumed, disregarding his question concerning my own success as an owner, " where and how is
she ? ''

" Miss Hardinge is in town,—in her own—that is, in our
house,—in Wall Street, though she goes to *the place* in the
morning. No one likes to remain among these hot bricks,
that has a pleasant country-house to fly to, and open to
receive him. But I forgot—I have supposed you to know
what is very likely you have never heard ? ''

" I learned of the death of Mrs. Bradfort while in Italy,
and seeing you in black, at once supposed it was for her.''

" Yes, that's just it. An excellent woman has been
taken from us, and, had she been my own mother, I could
not have received greater kindness from her. Her end, my
dear Wallingford, was admitted by all the clergy to be one
of the most edifying known in the place for years.''

"And Mrs. Bradfort has left you her heir? It is now
time to congratulate you on your good fortune. As I understand her estate came through females to her, and from
a common ancestor of hers and yours, there is not the
slightest reason why you should not be gratified by the
bequest. But Lucy—I hope she was not altogether forgotten ? ''

Rupert fidgeted, and I could see that he was on tenter-
hooks. As I afterwards discovered, he wished to conceal
the real facts from the world ; and yet he could not but
foresee that I would probably learn them from his father.
Under all the circumstances, therefore, he fancied it best to
make me a confidant. We were strolling between Trinity

Cooper in middle age. From a sketch by Henry Inman.

and Paul's Church walks, then the most fashionable promenade in town ; and before he would lay open his secret,
my companion led me over by the Oswego Market and
down Maiden Lane, lest he might betray himself to the
more fashionable stocks and stones. He did not open his
lips until clear of the market, when he laid bare his budget
of griefs in something that more resembled his old confidential manner, than he had seen fit to exhibit in the earlier
part of our interview.

"You must know, Miles," he commenced, "that Mrs.
Bradfort was a very peculiar woman—a very peculiar sort
of a person, indeed. An excellent lady, I am ready to
allow, and one that made a remarkably edifying end—but
one whose peculiarities, I have understood, she inherited
with her fortune. Women do get the oddest conceits into
their heads, you know, and American women before all
others ; a republic being anything but favorable to the con-
tinuation of property in the same line. Miss Merton, who
is a girl of excellent sense, as you well know yourself,
Miles, says, now, in England I should have succeeded, quite
as a matter of course, to all Mrs. Bradfort's real estate."

"You, as a lawyer, a common-law lawyer, can scarcely
require the opinion of an Englishwoman to tell you what
the English laws would do in a question of descent."

"Oh ! they 've a plaguey sight of statutes in that country
as well as ourselves. Between the two, the common law is
getting to be a very uncommon sort of a law. But, to cut
the matter short, Mrs. Bradfort made a will."

"Dividing her property equally between you and Lucy,
I dare say, to Miss Merton's great dissatisfaction."

"Why, not just so, Miles, not exactly so ; a very capricious, peculiar woman was Mrs. Bradfort—"

I have often remarked, when a person has succeeded in
throwing dust into another's eyes, but is discarded on being
found out, that the rejected of principle is very apt to
accuse his former dupe of being capricious, when in fact he
has only been deceived. As I said nothing, however, leaving Rupert to flounder on in the best manner he could, the
latter, after a pause, proceeded.

"But her end was very admirable," he said, "and to the last degree edifying. You must know she made a will, and in that will she left everything, even to the town and country houses, to—my sister."

I was thunderstruck! Here were all my hopes blown again to the winds. After a long pause, I resumed the discourse.

"And whom did she leave as executor?" I asked, instantly foreseeing the consequences should that office be devolved on Rupert himself.

"My father. The old gentleman has had his hands full between your father and mother and Mrs. Bradfort. Fortunately, the estate of the last is in a good condition and is easily managed. Almost entirely in stores and houses in the best part of the town, well insured, a few thousands in stocks, and as much in bonds and mortgages, the savings from the income, and something like a year's rents in bank. A good seven thousand a year, with enough surplus to pay for repairs, collections, and other charges."

"And all this, then, is Lucy's!" I exclaimed, feeling something like the bitterness of knowing that such an heiress was not for me.

"Temporarily, though of course I consider Lucy as only my trustee for half of it. You know how it is with the women ; they fancy us all young men spendthrifts, and so between the two they have reasoned in this way : 'Rupert is a good fellow at bottom, but Rupert is young, and he will make the money fly ; now, I'll give it all to you, Lucy, in my will, but of course you'll take care of your brother, and let him have half, or perhaps two thirds, being a male, at the proper time, which will be as soon as you come of age and can convey.' You understand Lucy is but nineteen, and cannot convey these two years."

"And Lucy admits this to be true? You have proof of all this?"

"Proof! I'd take my own affidavit of it. You see it is reasonable, and what I had a right to expect. Everything tends to confirm it. Between ourselves, I had quite $2,000 of debt, and yet you see the good lady did not leave me a

dollar to pay even my honest creditors, a circumstance that
so pious a woman, and one who made so edifying an end,
would never think of doing without ulterior views. Considering Lucy as my trustee, explains the whole thing."

"I thought Mrs. Bradfort made you an allowance,
Rupert; some $600 a year, besides keeping you in her
own house?"

"A thousand; but what is $1,000 a year to a fashion-
able man in a town like this? First and last, the excellent
old lady gave me about $5,000, all of which confirms the
idea that at the bottom she intended me for her heir.
What woman in her senses would think of giving $5,000 to
a relative to whom she did not contemplate giving more?
The thing is clear on its face, and I should certainly go
into chancery with anybody but Lucy."

"And Lucy! what says she to your views on the subject
of Mrs. Bradfort's intentions?"

"Why, you have some acquaintance with Lucy—used
to be intimate with her, as one might say, when children,
and know something of her character." This to me, who
fairly worshipped the earth on which the dear girl trod!
"She never indulges in professions, and likes to take people
by surprise when she contemplates doing them a service,"
—this was just as far from Lucy's natural and honest mode
of dealing, as it was possible to be,—"and so she has been
as mum as one who has lost the faculty of speech. However, she never speaks of her affairs to others; that is a
good sign, and indicates an intention to consider herself as
my trustee; and, what is better still, and more plainly
denotes what her conscience dictates in the premises, she
has empowered her father to pay all my debts; the current
income and loose cash being at her disposal at once. It
would have been better had she given me the money, to
satisfy these creditors with it, for I knew which had waited
the longest, and were best entitled to receive the dollars at
once; but it's something to have all their receipts in my
pocket, and to start fair again. Thank Heaven, that much
is already done. To do Lucy justice, moreover, she allows
me $1,500 a year, *ad interim.* Now, Miles, I've conversed

with you, as with an old friend, and because I knew my
father would tell you the whole, when you got up to Clawbonny; but you will take it all in strict confidence. It
gives a fashionable young fellow so silly an air, to be
thought dependent on a sister; and she three years younger
than himself! So I have hinted the actual state of the
case round among my friends; but it is generally believed
that I am in possession already, and that Lucy is dependent
on me, instead of my being dependent on her. The idea,
moreover, is capital for keeping off fortune-hunters, as you
will see at a glance.''

"And will the report satisfy a certain Mr. Andrew
Drewett?" I asked, struggling to assume a composure
I was far from feeling. "He was all attention when I
sailed, and I almost expected to hear there was no longer a
Lucy Hardinge.''

"To tell you the truth, Miles, I thought so, too, until
the death of Mrs. Bradfort. The mourning, however, most
opportunely came to put a stop to anything of the sort,
were it even contemplated. It would be so awkward, you
will understand, to have a brother-in-law before everything
is settled, and the trust is accounted for. *Au reste*—I am
very well satisfied with Andrew, and let him know I am
his friend; he is well connected; fashionable; has a pretty
little fortune; and I sometimes tell Lucy that he is intended for her, as Mrs. Bradfort, no doubt, foresaw, inasmuch as his estate, added to just one third of that of our
dear departed cousin, would just make up the present
income. On my honor, now, I do not think the difference
would be $500 per annum.''

"And how does your sister receive your hints?''

"Oh! famously—just as all girls do, you know. She
blushes, and sometimes she looks vexed; then she smiles,
and puts up her lip, and says 'Nonsense!' and 'What
folly! Rupert, I'm surprised at you!' and all that sort of
stuff, which deceives nobody, you'll understand, not even
her poor, simple, silly brother. But, Miles, I must quit
you now, for I have an engagement to accompany a party
to the theatre, and was on my way to join them when we

met. Cooper plays, and you know what a lion he is; one would not wish to lose a syllable of his Othello."

"Stop, Rupert—one word more before we part. From your conversation, I gather that the Mertons are still here?"

"The Mertons! Why, certainly; established in the land, and among its tip-top people. The colonel finds his health benefited by the climate, and he has managed to get some appointment which keeps him among us. He has Boston relatives, moreover, and I believe is fishing up some claims to property in that quarter. The Mertons here, indeed! what would New York be without the Mertons?"

"And my old friend the major is promoted, too—you called him colonel, I think!"

"Did I? I believe he is oftener called General Merton, than anything else. You must be mistaken about his being only a major, Miles; everybody here calls him either colonel, or general."

"Never mind; I hope it is as you say. Good-by, Rupert; I'll not betray you, and—"

"Well—you were about to say—"

"Why, mention me to Lucy; you know we were acquainted when children. Tell her I wish her all happiness in her new position, to which I do not doubt she will do full credit; and that I shall endeavor to see her before I sail again."

"You will not be at the theatre this evening? Cooper is well worth seeing—a most famous Othello!"

"I think not. Do not forget to mention me to your sister; and so, once more, adieu!"

We parted; Rupert to go toward Broadway, at a great pace, and I to lounge along, uncertain whither to proceed. I had sent Neb to inquire if the Wallingford were down, and understood she would leave the basin at sunrise. It was now my intention to go up in her; for, though I attached no great importance to any of Rupert's facts, his report concerning my sister's health rendered me exceedingly uneasy. Insensibly I continued my course down Maiden Lane, and soon found myself near the ship. I went on board, had an explanation with Marble, gave some

30

orders to Neb, and went ashore again, all in the course of the next half hour. By a sort of secret attraction, I was led toward the Park, and soon found myself at the door of the theatre. Mrs. Bradfort had now been dead long enough to put Lucy in second mourning, and I fancied I might get a view of her in the party that Rupert was to accompany. Buying a ticket, I entered and made my way up into the Shakespeare box. Had I been better acquainted with the place, with the object in view, I should have gone into the pit.

Notwithstanding the lateness of the season, it was a very full house. Cooper's, in that day, was a name that filled every mouth, and he seldom failed to fill every theatre in which he appeared. With many first-rate qualifications for his art, and a very respectable conception of his characters, he threw everything like competition behind him ; though there were a few, as there ever will be among the superlatively intellectual, who affected to see excellences in Fennel, and others, to which the great actor could not aspire. The public decided against these select few, and, as is invariably the case when the appeal is made to human feelings, the public decided right. Puffery will force into notice, and sustain a false judgment, in such matters, for a brief space ; but nature soon asserts her sway, and it is by natural decisions that such points are ever the most justly determined. Whatever appeals to human sympathies, will be answered by human sympathies. Popularity too often gains its ascendency behind the hypocrite's mask in religion ; it is usually a magnificent mystification in politics ; it frequently becomes the patriot's stalking-horse, on which he rides to power ; in social life, it is the reward of empty smiles, unmeaning bows, and hollow squeezes of the hand ; but with the player, the poet, and all whose pursuits bring them directly in contact with the passions, the imagination, and the heart, it is the unerring test of merit, with certain qualifications connected with the mind and the higher finish of pure art. It may be questioned if Cooper were not the greatest actor of his day, in a certain range of his own characters.

I have said that the house was full. I got a good place, however ; though it was not in the front row. Of course, I could only see the side boxes beneath, and not even quite all of them. My eyes ran eagerly over them, and I soon caught a glimpse of the fine, curling hair of Rupert. He sat by the side of Emily Merton ; the major—I knew he was a colonel or general, only by means of a regular Manhattan promotion, which is so apt to make hundreds of counts, copper captains, and travelling prodigies of those who are very small folk at home—the major sat next, and, at his side, I saw a lady, whom I at once supposed to be Lucy. Every nerve in my system thrilled, as I caught even this indistinct view of the dear creature. I could just see the upper part of her face, as it was occasionally turned toward the major ; and once I caught that honest smile of hers, which I knew had never intentionally deceived.

The front seat of the box had two vacant places. The bench would hold six, while it had yet only four. The audience, however, was still assembling, and, presently, a stir in Lucy's box denoted the arrival of company. The whole party moved, and Andrew Drewett handed an elderly lady in, his mother, as I afterwards ascertained, and took the other place himself. I watched the salutations that were exchanged, and understood that the new-comers had been expected. The places had been reserved for them, and old Mrs. Drewett was doubtless the *chaperone;* though one having a brother and the other a father with her, the two young ladies had not hesitated about preceding the elderly lady. They had come from different quarters of the town, and had agreed to meet at the theatre. Old Mrs. Drewett was very particular in shaking hands with Lucy, though I had not the misery of seeing her son go through the same ceremony. Still he was sufficiently pointed in his salutations ; and during the movements, I perceived he managed to get next to Lucy, leaving the major to entertain his mother. All this was natural, and what might have been expected ; yet it gave me a pang that I cannot describe.

I sat, for half an hour, perfectly inattentive to the play, meditating on the nature of my real position toward Lucy.

I recalled the days of childhood and early youth ; the night of my first departure from home ; my return, and the incidents accompanying my second departure ; the affair of the locket, and all I had truly felt myself, and all that I had supposed Lucy herself to feel, on those several occasions. Could it be possible I had so much deceived myself, and that the interest the dear girl had certainly manifested in me had been nothing but the fruits of her naturally warm and honest heart—her strong disposition to frankness— habit, as Rupert had so gently hinted in reference to ourselves ?

Then I could not conceal from myself the bitter fact that I was, now, no equal match for Lucy, in the eyes of the world. While she was poor, and I comparatively rich, the inequality in social station might have been overlooked ; it existed, certainly, but was not so very marked that it might not, even in that day, be readily forgotten ; but now, Lucy was an heiress, had much more than double my own fortune—had a fortune, indeed ; while I was barely in easy circumstances, as persons of the higher classes regarded wealth. The whole matter seemed reversed. It was clear that a sailor like myself, with no peculiar advantages, those of a tolerable education excepted, and who was necessarily so much absent, had not the same chances of preferring his suit, as one of your town idlers ; a nominal lawyer, for instance, who dropped in at his office for an hour or two, just after breakfast, and promenaded Broadway the rest of the time, until dinner ; or a man of entire leisure, like Andrew Drewett, who belonged to the City Library set, and had no other connection with business than to see that his rents were collected and his dividends paid. The more I reflected, the more humble I became, the less my chances seemed, and I determined to quit the theatre, at once. The reader will remember that I was New York born and bred, a state of society in which few natives acted on the principle that " there was nothing too high to be aspired to, nothing too low to be done." I admitted I had superiors, and was willing to defer to the facts and opinions of the world as I knew it.

In the lobby of the building, I experienced a pang at the idea of quitting the place without getting one look at the face of Lucy. I was in an humble mood, it is true, but that did not necessarily infer a total self-denial. I determined, therefore, to pass into the pit, with my box-check, feast my eyes by one long gaze at the dear creature's ingenuous countenance, and carry away the impression, as a lasting memorial of her whom I so well loved, and whom I felt persuaded I should ever continue to love. After this indulgence, I would studiously avoid her, in order to release my thoughts as much as possible from the perfect thralldom in which they had existed, ever since I had heard of Mrs. Bradfort's death. Previously to that time, I am afraid I had counted a little more than was becoming on the ease of my own circumstances, and Lucy's comparative poverty. Not that I had ever supposed her to be in the least mercenary— this I knew to be utterly, totally false—but because the good town of Manhattan, even in 1803, was *tant soit peu* addicted to dollars, and Lucy's charms would not be likely to attract so many suitors, in the modest setting of a poor country clergyman's means, as in the golden frame by which they had been surrounded by Mrs. Bradfort's testamentary devise, even supposing Rupert to come in for quite one half.

I had no difficulty in finding a convenient place in the pit ; one from which I got a front and near view of the whole six, as they sat ranged side by side. Of the major and old Mrs. Drewett it is unnecessary to say much. The latter looked as all dowager-like widows of that day used to appear, respectable, staid, and richly attired. The good lady had come on the stage during the Revolution, and had a slightly military air—a parade in her graces, that was not altogether unknown to the *élèves* of that school. I dare say she could use such words as " martinets," " mohairs," " brigadiers," and other terms familiar to her class. Alas ! how completely all these little traces of the past are disappearing from our habits and manners !

As for the major, he appeared much better in health, and altogether altered in mien. I could readily detect the influence of the world on him. He was evidently a

so much greater man in New York than he had been
when I found him in London, that it is not wonderful he
felt the difference.   Between the acts, I remarked that all
the principal persons in the front rows were desirous of
exchanging nods with the " British officer," a proof that
he was circulating freely in the best set, and had reached
a point, when " not to know him, argues yourself unknown.'''

Emily certainly looked well and happy.   I could see
that she was delighted with Rupert's flattery, and I confess I cared very little for his change of sentiment or his
success.   That both Major and Emily Merton were different persons in the midst of the world and in the soli-
tudes of the Pacific, was as evident as it was that I was a

' The miserable moral dependence of this country on Great Britain,
forty years since, cannot well be brought home to the present generation.   It is still too great, but has not a tithe of its former force.
The writer has himself known an Italian prince, a man of family and
of high personal merit, pass unnoticed before a society that was eager
to make the acquaintance of most of the " agents " of the Birming-
ham butter dealers ; and this simply because one came from Italy and
the other from England.   The following anecdote, which is quite as
true as any other fact in this work, furnishes a good example of what
is meant.   It is now a quarter of a century since the writer's first
book appeared.   Two or three months after the publication, he was
walking down Broadway with a friend, when a man of much distinction in the New York circles was passing up, on the other sidewalk.
The gentleman in question caught the writer's eye, bowed, and
crossed the street, to shake hands and inquire after the author's
health.   The difference in years made this attention marked.   "You
are in high favor," observed the friend, as the two walked away,
"to have —— pay you such a compliment—your book must have done
this."   "Now mark my words—I have been puffed in some English
magazine, and —— knows it."   The two were on their way to the
author's publishers, and, on entering the door, honest Charles Wiley
put a puff on the book in question into the writer's hand.   What rendered the whole more striking, was the fact that the paragraph was
as flagrant a puff as was ever written, and had probably been paid for,
by the English publisher.   The gentleman in question was a man of
talents and merit, but he had been born half a century too soon to
enjoy entire mental independence in a country that had so recently
been a colony.

different personage in command of the Crisis and in the pit of the Park Theatre. I dare say, at that moment Miss Merton had nearly forgotten that such a man as Miles Wallingford existed, though I think she sometimes recalled the string of magnificent pearls that were to ornament the neck of his wife, should he ever find any one to have him.

But Lucy, dear, upright, warm-hearted, truth-telling, beloved Lucy! all this time I forget to speak of her. There she sat in maiden loveliness, her beauty still more developed, her eye as beaming, lustrous, feeling, as ever, her blush as sensitive, her smile as sweet, and her movements as natural and graceful. The simplicity of her half mourning, too, added to her beauty, which was of a character to require no further aid from dress, than such as was dependent purely on taste. As I gazed at her, enthralled, I fancied nothing was wanting to complete the appearance but my own necklace. Powerful, robust man as I was, with my frame hardened by exposure and trials, I could have sat down and wept, after gazing some time at the precious creature, under the feeling produced by the conviction that I was never to renew my intercourse with her, on terms of intimacy at least. The thought that from day to day we were to become more and more strangers, was almost too much to be borne. As it was, scalding tears forced themselves to my eyes, though I succeeded in concealing the weakness from those around me. At length the tragedy terminated, the curtain dropped, and the audience began to move about. The pit, which had just before been crowded, was now nearly empty, and I was afraid of being seen. Still, I could not tear myself away, but remained after nine tenths of those around me had gone into the lobbies.

It was easy, now, to see the change which had come over Lucy's position, in the attentions she received. All the ladies in the principal boxes had nods and smiles for her, and half the fashionable-looking young men in the house crowded round her box, or actually entered it to pay their compliments. I fancied Andrew Drewett had a self-

satisfied air that seemed to say, "You are paying your
homage indirectly to myself, in paying it to this young
lady." As for Lucy, my jealous watchfulness could not
detect the smallest alteration in her deportment, so far
as simplicity and nature were concerned. She appeared
in a trifling degree more womanly, perhaps, than when I
saw her last, being now in her twentieth year, but the
attentions she received made no visible change in her
manners. I had become lost in the scene, and was standing in a musing attitude, my side face toward the box,
when I heard a suppressed exclamation, in Lucy's voice.
I was too near her to be mistaken, and it caused the blood
to rush to my heart in a torrent. Turning, I saw the
dear girl, with her hand extended over the front of the
box, her face suffused with blushes, and her eyes riveted
on myself. I was recognized, and the surprise had produced a display of all that old friendship, certainly, that
had once existed between us, in the simplicity and truth of
childhood.

"Miles Wallingford!" she said, as I advanced to shake
the offered hand, and as soon as I was near enough to
permit her to speak without attracting too much attention
—"you arrived, and we knew nothing of it!"

It was plain Rupert had said nothing of having seen
me, or of our interview in the street. He seemed a little
ashamed, and leaned forward to say,—

"I declare I forgot to mention, Lucy, that I met Captain Wallingford as I was going to join the colonel and
Miss Merton. Oh! we have had a long talk together,
and it will save you a history of past events."

"I may, nevertheless, say," I rejoined, "how happy I
am to see Miss Hardinge looking so well, and to be able
to pay my compliments to my old passengers."

Of course I shook hands with the major and Emily,
bowed to Drewett, was named to his mother, and was
invited to enter the box, as it was not quite in rule to be
conversing between the pit and the front rows. I forgot
my prudent resolutions, and was behind Lucy in three
minutes. Andrew Drewett had the civility to offer me

his place, though it was with an air that said plain enough,
"What do I care for him? he is a shipmaster, and I am a
man of fashion and fortune, and can resume my seat at
any moment, while the poor fellow can only catch his
chances, as he occasionally comes into port." At least, I
fancied his manner said something like this.

"Thank you, Mr. Drewett," said Lucy, in her sweetest
manner. "Mr. Wallingford and I are very, very, old
friends—you know he is Grace's brother, and you have
been at Clawbonny"—Drewett bowed, civilly enough—
"and I have a thousand things to say to him. So, Miles,
take this seat, and let me hear all about your voyage."

As half the audience went away as soon as the tragedy
ended, the second seat of the box was vacated, and the
other gentlemen getting on it, to stretch their limbs, I had
abundance of room to sit at Lucy's side, half facing her,
at the same time. As she insisted on hearing my story,
before we proceeded to anything else, I was obliged to
gratify her.

"By the way, Major Merton," I cried, as the tale was
closed, "an old friend of yours, Moses Marble by name,
has come to life again, and is at this moment in New
York."

I then related the manner in which I had fallen in with
my old mate. This was a most unfortunate self-interrup-
tion for me, giving the major a fair opportunity for cutting
into the conversation. The orchestra, moreover, giving
notice that the curtain would soon rise for the after-piece,
the old gentleman soon got me into the lobby to hear the
particulars. I was supremely vexed, and I thought Lucy
appeared sorry ; but there was no help for it, and then we
could not converse while the piece was going on.

"I suppose you care little for this silly farce," observed
the major, looking in at one of the windows, after I had
gone over Marble's affair in detail. "If not, we will continue our walk, and wait for the ladies to come out.
Drewett and Hardinge will take good care of them."

I assented, and we continued to walk the lobby till the
end of the act. Major Merton was always gentleman-like ;

and he even behaved to me as if he remembered the many
obligations he was under. He now communicated several
little facts connected with his own circumstances, alluding
to the probability of his remaining in America a few years.
Our chat continued some time, my looks frequently turning toward the door of the box, when my companion suddenly observed,—

"Your old acquaintances the Hardinges have had a
lucky windfall—one, I fancy, they hardly expected, a
few years since."

"Probably not ; though the estate has fallen into excellent hands," I answered. "I am surprised, however,
that Mrs. Bradfort did not leave the property to the old
gentleman, as it once belonged to their common grandfather, and he properly stood next in succession."

"I fancy she thought the good parson would not know
what to do with it. Now, Rupert Hardinge is clever and
spirited, and in a way to make a figure in the world ; and
it is probably in better hands than if it had been left first
to the old gentleman."

"The old gentleman has been a faithful steward to me,
and I doubt not would have proved equally so to his own
children. But does Rupert get all Mrs. Bradfort's property ?"

"I believe not ; their is some sort of a trust, I have
heard him say ; and I rather fancy that his sister has
some direct, or reversionary interest. Perhaps she is
named as the heir, if he die without issue. There was
a silly story, that Mrs. Bradfort had left everything to
Lucy ; but I have it from the best authority, that that is
not true." The idea of Rupert Hardinge's being the
"best authority" for anything ; a fellow who never knew
what unadulterated truth was, from the time he was in
petticoats, or could talk ! "As I know there is a trust,
though one of no great moment, I presume Lucy has some
contingent interest, subject, most probably, to her marrying with her brother's approbation, or some such provision.
The old lady was sagacious, and no doubt did all that was
necessary."

It is wonderful how people daily deceive themselves on the subject of property; those who care the most about it, appearing to make the greatest blunders. In the way of bequests, in particular, the lies that are told are marvellous. It is now many years since I learned to take no heed of rumors on such subjects, and least of all, rumors that come from the class of the money-gripers. Such people refer everything to dollars, and seldom converse a minute without using the word. Here, however, was Major Merton evidently Rupert's dupe; though with what probable consequences, it was not in my power to foresee. It was clearly not my business to undeceive him; and the conversation getting to be embarrassing, I was not sorry to hear the movement which announced the end of the act. At the box door, to my great regret, we met Mrs. Drewett retiring, the ladies finding the farce dull, and not worth the time lost in listening to it. Rupert gave me an uneasy glance, and he even dragged me aside to whisper, " Miles, what I told you this evening is strictly a family secret, and was entrusted to a friend."

" I have nothing to do with your private concerns, Rupert," I answered; " only let me expect you to act honorably, especially when women are concerned."

" Everything will come right, depend on it; the truth will set everything right, and all will come out just as I predicted."

I saw Lucy looking anxiously around, while Drewett had gone to order the carriages to advance, and I hoped it might be for me. In a moment I was by her side; at the next, Mr. Andrew Drewett offered his arm, saying, her carriage " stopped the way." We moved into the outer lobby, in a body, and then it was found that Mrs. Drewett's carriage was up first, while Lucy's was in the rear. Yes, Lucy's carriage!—the dear girl having come into immediate possession of her relative's houses, furniture, horses, carriages, and everything else, without reserve, just as they had been left behind by the last incumbent, when she departed from the scene of life, to lie down in the grave. Mrs. Bradfort's arms were still on the chariot,

I observed, its owner refusing all Rupert's solicitations to supplant them by those of Hardinge. The latter took his revenge, however, by telling everybody how generous he was in keeping a carriage for his sister.

The major handed Mrs. Drewett in, and her son was compelled to say good night, to see his mother home. This gave me one blessed minute with Lucy, by herself. She spoke of Grace ; said they had now been separated months, longer than they ever had been before in their lives, and that all her own persuasions could not induce my sister to rejoin her in town, while her own wish to visit Clawbonny had been constantly disappointed, Rupert insisting that her presence was necessary, for so many arrangements about business.

"Grace is not as humble as I was in old times, Miles," said the dear girl, looking me in the face half sadly, half reproachfully, the light of the lamp falling full on her tearful, tender eyes, "and I hope you are not about to imitate her bad example. She wishes us to know she has Clawbonny for a home, but I never hesitated to admit how poor we were, while you alone were rich."

"God bless you, Lucy !" I whispered, squeezing her hand with fervor. "It cannot be that—have you heard anything of Grace's health ? "

"Oh ! she is well, I know—Rupert tells me that, and her letters are cheerful and kind as ever, without a word of complaint. But I must see her soon. Grace Wallingford and Lucy Hardinge were not born to live asunder. Here is the carriage ; I shall see you in the morning, Miles, at breakfast, say eight o'clock precisely."

"It will be impossible. I sail for Clawbonny with the first of the flood, and that will make at four. I shall sleep in the sloop."

Major Merton put Lucy into the carriage, the goodnights were passed, and I was left standing on the lowest step of the building, gazing after the carriage, Rupert walking swiftly away.

CHAPTER XXVIII.

"Hear me a little;
For I have only been silent so long,
And given way unto this course of fortune,
By nothing of the lady: I have marked
A thousand blushing apparitions start
Into her face; a thousand innocent shames
In angel whiteness bear away those blushes."

SHAKESPEARE.

I REACHED the Wallingford before eleven, where I found Neb in attendance with my trunks and other effects. Being now on board my own craft, I gave orders to profit by a favorable turn in the wind, and to get under way at once, instead of waiting for the flood. When I left the deck the sloop was above the State prison, a point toward which the town itself had made considerable progress since the time I first introduced it to the reader. Notwithstanding this early start, we did not enter the creek until about eight in the morning of the second day.

No sooner was the vessel near enough, than my foot was on the wharf, and I began to ascend the hill. From the summit of the latter I saw my late guardian hurrying along the road, it afterward appearing that a stray paper from town had announced the arrival of the Dawn, and that I was expected to come up in the sloop. I was received with extended hands, was kissed just as if I had still been a boy, and heard the guileless old man murmuring his blessings on me, and a prayer of thankfulness. Nothing ever changed good Mr. Hardinge, who, now that he could command the whole income of his daughter, was just as well satisfied to live on the three or four hundreds he got from his glebe and his parish, as he ever had been in his life.

"Welcome back, my dear boy, welcome back!" added Mr. Hardinge, his voice and manner still retaining their fervor. "I said you must—you would be on board, as soon as they reported the sloop in sight, for I judged your heart by my own. Ah! Miles, will the time ever come when Clawbonny will be good enough for you? You have already as much money as you can want, and more will scarce contribute to your happiness."

"Speaking of money, my dear sir," I answered, "while I have to regret the loss of your respectable kinswoman, I may be permitted to congratulate you on the accession to an old family property. I understand you inherit, in your family, all of Mrs. Bradfort's estate—one valuable in amount, and highly acceptable, no doubt, as having belonged to your ancestors."

"No doubt—no doubt—it is just as you say; and I hope these unexpected riches will leave us all as devout servants of God as I humbly trust they found us. The property, however, is not mine, but Lucy's; I need not have any reserve with you, though Rupert has hinted it might be prudent not to let the precise state of the case be known, since it might bring a swarm of interested fortune-hunters about the dear girl, and has proposed that we rather favor the notion the estate is to be divided among us. This I cannot do directly, you will perceive, as it would be deception; but one may be silent. With you, however, it is a different matter, and so I tell you the truth at once. I am made executor, and act, of course; and this makes me the more glad to see you, for I find so much business with pounds, shillings, and pence, draws my mind off from the duties of my holy office, and that I am in danger of becoming selfish and mercenary. A selfish priest, Miles, is as odious a thing as a mercenary woman!"

"Little danger of your ever becoming anything so worldly, my dear sir. But Grace—you have not mentioned my beloved sister?"

I saw Mr. Hardinge's countenance suddenly change.

The expression of joy instantly deserted it, and it wore an air of uncertainty and sadness. A less observant man than the good divine, in all the ordinary concerns of life, did not exist; but it was apparent that now he saw something to trouble him.

"Yes, Grace," he answered doubtingly; "the dear girl is here, and all alone, and not as blithe and amusing as formerly. I am glad of your return on her account, too, Miles. She is not well, I fear; I would have sent for a physician last week, or the moment I saw her; but she insists on it there is no need of one. She is frightfully beautiful, Miles! You know how it is with Grace—her countenance always seemed more fitted for heaven than earth; and now it always reminds me of a seraph's that was grieving over the sins of men!"

"I fear, sir, that Rupert's account, then, is true, and that Grace is seriously ill?"

"I hope not, boy—I fervently pray not! She is not as usual—that is true; but her mind, her thoughts, all her inclinations, and, if I may so express it, her energies, seem turned to heaven. There has been an awakening in the spirit of Grace, that is truly wonderful. She reads devout books, meditates, and, I make no doubt, prays, from morn till night. This is the secret of her withdrawal from the world, and her refusing of all Lucy's invitations. You know how the girls love each other—but Grace declines going to Lucy, though she knows that Lucy cannot come to her."

I now understood it all. A weight like that of a mountain fell upon my heart, and I walked on some distance without speaking. To me, the words of my excellent guardian sounded like the knell of a sister I almost worshipped.

"And Grace—does she expect me, now?" I at length ventured to say, though the words were uttered in tones so tremulous, that even the usually unobservant divine perceived the change.

"She does, and delighted she was to hear it. The only thing of a worldly nature that I have heard her express of late, was some anxious, sisterly wish for your speedy return. Grace loves you, Miles, next to her God!"

Oh! how I wished this were true, but, alas! alas! I knew it was far from otherwise!

"I see you are disturbed, my dear boy, on account of what I have said," resumed Mr. Hardinge; "probably from serious apprehensions about your sister's health. She is not well, I allow; but it is the effect of mental ailments. The precious creature has had too vivid views of her own sinful nature, and has suffered deeply, I fear. I trust my conversation and prayers have not been without their effect, through the divine aid, and that she is now more cheerful—nay, she has assured me within half an hour, if it turned out that you were in the sloop, she should be happy!"

For my life, I could not have conversed longer on the painful subject; I made no reply. As we had still a considerable distance to walk, I was glad to turn the conversation to other subjects, lest I should become unmanned, and sit down to weep in the middle of the road.

"Does Lucy intend to visit Clawbonny this summer?" I asked, though it seemed strange to me to suppose that the farm was not actually Lucy's home. I am afraid I felt a jealous dislike to the idea that the dear creature should have houses and lands of her own; or any that were not to be derived through me.

"I hope so," answered her father, "though her new duties do not leave Lucy as much her own mistress as I could wish. You saw her and her brother, Miles, I take it for granted?"

"I met Rupert in the street, sir, and had a short interview with the Mertons and Lucy at the theatre. Young Mr. and old Mrs. Drewett were of the party."

The good divine turned short round to me, and looked as conscious and knowing as one of his singleness of mind and simplicity of habits could look. Had a knife penetrated my flesh, I could not have winced more than I did; still I affected a manner that was very foreign to my feelings.

"What do you think of this young Mr. Drewett, boy?" asked Mr. Hardinge, with an air of confidential interest, and an earnestness of manner that, with him, was inseparable from all that concerned his daughter. "Do you approve?"

"I believe I understand you, sir ; you mean me to infer that Mr. Drewett is a suitor for Miss Hardinge's hand."

"It would be improper to say this much even to you, Miles, did not Drewett take good care, himself, to let everybody know it."

"Possibly with a view to keep off other pretenders," I rejoined, with a bitterness I could not control.

Now Mr. Hardinge was one of the last men in the world to suspect evil. He looked surprised, therefore, at my remark, and I was probably not much out of the way in fancying that he looked displeased.

"That is not right, my dear boy," he said gravely. "We should try to think the best, and not the worst, of our fellow-creatures." Excellent old man, how faithfully didst thou practise on thy precept ! "It is a wise rule, and a safe one ; more particularly in connection with our own weaknesses. Then it is but natural that Drewett should wish to secure Lucy ; and if he adopt no means less manly than the frank avowal of his own attachment, surely there is no ground of complaint."

I was rebuked ; and, what is more, I felt that the rebuke was merited. As some atonement for my error, I hastened to add,—

"Very truly, sir ; I admit the unfairness of my remark, and can only atone for it by adding, it is quite apparent Mr. Drewett is not influenced by interested motives, since he certainly was attentive to Miss Hardinge previously to Mrs. Bradfort's death, and when he could not possibly have anticipated the nature of her will."

"Quite true, Miles, and very properly and justly remarked. Now, to you, who have known Lucy from childhood, and who regard her much as Rupert does, it may not seem so very natural that a young man can love her warmly and strongly, for herself alone ; such is apt to be the effect of brotherly feeling ; but I can assure you, Lucy is really a charming, as we all know she is a most excellent, girl ! "

"To whom are you speaking thus, sir ? I can assure you, nothing is easier than for me to conceive how possible it is for any man to love your daughter. As respects Grace,

31

I confess there is a difference ; for I affirm she has always seemed to me too saintly, too much allied to heaven already, to be subject, herself, to the passions of earth.''

" That is what I have just been telling you, and we must endeavor to overcome and humanize—if I may so express it—Grace's propensity. There is nothing more dangerous to a healthful frame of mind, in a religious point of view, Miles, than excitement—it is disease, and not faith, nor charity, nor hope, nor humility, nor anything that is commanded ; but our native weaknesses taking a wrong direction, under a physical impulse, rather than the fruits of repentance, and the succor afforded by the Spirit of God. We nowhere read of any excitement, and howlings, and wailings among the apostles.''

How could I enlighten the good old man on the subject of my sister's malady ? That Grace, with her well-tempered mind, was the victim of religious exaggeration, I did not for a moment believe ; but that she had had her heart blighted, her affections withered, her hopes deceived, by Rupert's levity and interestedness, his worldly-mindedness and vanity, I could foresee, and was prepared to learn ; though these were facts not to be communicated to the father of the offender. I made no answer, but managed to turn the conversation toward the farm, and those interests about which I could affect an interest that I was very far from feeling, just at that moment. This induced the divine to inquire into the result of my late voyage, and enabled me to collect sufficient fortitude to meet Grace, with the semblance of firmness, at least.

Mr. Hardinge made a preconcerted signal, as soon as he came in view of the house, that apprised its inmates of my arrival ; and we knew, while still half a mile from the buildings, that the news had produced a great commotion. All the blacks met us on the little lawn—for the girls, since reaching womanhood, had made this change in the old dooryard—and I had to go through the process of shaking hands with every one of them. This was done amid hearty bursts of laughter, the mode in which the negroes of that day almost always betrayed their joy, and many a " Welcome home, Masser Mile!" and "Where a Neb got to, dis time, Masser Mile?" was asked by more than one; and great was the satisfaction, when I told his generation and race that the faithful fellow would be up with the cart that was to convey my luggage. But Grace awaited me. I broke through the throng, and entered the house. In the door I was met by Chloe, a girl about my own sister's age, and a sort of cousin of Neb's by the half-blood, who had been preferred of late years to functions somewhat resembling those of a lady's maid. I say of the half-blood; for, to own the truth, few of the New York blacks, in that day, could have taken from their brothers and sisters, under the old *dictum* of the common law, which declared that none but heirs of the whole blood should inherit. Chloe met me in the doorway, and greeted me with one of her sweetest smiles, as she courtesied, and really looked as pleased as all my slaves did, at seeing their young master again. How they touched my heart, at times, by their manner of talking about "ole Masser, and ole Missus," always subjects of regret among negroes who had been well treated by them! Metaphysicians may reason as subtly as they can about the races and colors, and on the aptitude of the black to acquire, but no one can ever persuade me out of the belief of their extraordinary aptitude to love. As between themselves and their masters, their own children and those of the race to which they were subject, I have often seen instances which have partaken of the attachment of the dog to the human family; and cases in which the children of their masters have been preferred to those of their own flesh and blood, were of constant occurrence.

"I hope you been werry well, sah, Masser Mile," said Chloe, who had some extra refinement, as the growth of her position.

"Perfectly, my good girl, and I am glad to see you looking so well—you really are growing handsome, Chloe."

"Oh! Masser Mile—you so droll!—now you stay home, sah, long time?"

"I am afraid not, Chloe, but one never knows. Where shall I find my sister?"

" Miss Grace tell me come here, Masser Mile, and say she wish to see you in de family room. She wait dere, now, some time."

"Thank you, Chloe; and do you see that no one interrupts us. I have not seen my sister for near a year."

"Sartain, sah; all as you say." Then the girl, whose face shone like a black bottle that had just been dipped in water, showed her brilliant teeth, from ear to ear, laughed outright, looked foolish, after which she looked earnest, when the secret burst out of her heart, in the melodious voice of a young negress, that did not know whether to laugh or to cry. " Where Neb, Masser Mile? what he do now, de fel-ler? "

" He will kiss you in ten minutes, Chloe; so put the best face on the matter you are able."

"Dat he won't—de sauce-box—Miss Grace teach me better dan dat."

I waited to hear no more, but proceeded toward the triangular little room, with steps so hurried and yet so nervous, that I do not remember ever before to have laid my hand on a lock in a manner so tremulous—I found myself obliged to pause, ere I could muster resolution to open the door, a hope coming over me that the impatience of Grace would save me the trouble, and that I should find her in my arms before I should be called on to exercise any more fortitude. All was as still as death, however, within the room, and I opened the door, as if I expected to find one of the bodies I had formerly seen in its coffin, in this last abiding place, above ground, of one dead. My sister was on the *causeuse*, literally unable to rise from debility and agitation. I shall not attempt to describe the shock her appearance gave me. I was prepared for a change, but not one that placed her, as my heart instantly announced, so near the grave !

Grace extended both arms, and I threw myself at her side, drew her within my embrace, and folded her to my heart, with the tenderness with which one would have embraced an infant. In this situation we both wept violently, and I am not ashamed to say that I sobbed like a child. I dare say five minutes passed in this way, without either of us speaking a word.

"A merciful and all-gracious God be praised! You are restored to me in time, Miles?" murmured my sister, at length. I was afraid it might be too late."

"Grace! Grace! what means this, love? My precious, my only, my most dearly beloved sister, why do I find you thus?"

"Is it necessary to speak, Miles?—cannot you see?—do you not see, and understand it all?"

The fervent pressure I gave my sister, announced how plainly I comprehended the whole history. That Grace could ever love, and forget, I did not believe; but that her tenderness for Rupert—one whom I knew for so frivolous and selfish a being, should reduce her to this terrible state, I had not foreseen as a thing possible. Little did I then understand how confidingly a woman loves, and how apt she is to endow the being of her choice with all the qualities she could wish him to possess. In the anguish of my soul I muttered, loud enough to be heard, " The heartless villain!"

Grace instantly rose from my arms. At that moment she looked more like a creature of heaven, than one that was still connected with this wicked world. Her beauty could scarcely be called impaired, though I dreaded that she would be snatched away from me in the course of the interview; so frail and weak did it appear was her hold of life. In some respects I never saw her more lovely than she seemed on this very occasion. This was when the hectic of disease imparted to the sweetest and most saint-like eyes that were ever set in the human countenance, a species of holy illumination. Her countenance, now, was pale and colorless, however, and her look sorrowful and filled with reproach.

"Brother," she said solemnly, " this must not be. It is not what God commands—it is not what I expected from you—what I have a right to expect from one who I am assured loves me, though none other of earth can be said to do so."

"It is not easy, my sister, for a man to forget or forgive the wretch who has so long misled you—misled us all, and then turned to another, under the impulse of mere vanity."

"Miles, my kind and manly brother, listen to me," Grace rejoined, fervently pressing one of my hands in both of hers, and scarcely able to command herself, through alarm. "All thoughts of anger, of resentment, of pride even, must be forgotten. You owe it to my sex, to the dreadful imputations that might otherwise rest on my name—had I anything to reproach myself with as a woman. I could submit to any punishment; but surely, surely, it is not a sin so unpardonable to be unable to command the affections, that I deserve to have my name, after I shall be dead, mixed up with the rumors connected with such a quarrel. You have lived as brothers, too—then there is good, excellent, truthful, pious Mr. Hardinge, who is yet my guardian, you know; and Lucy, dear, true-hearted, faithful Lucy—"

"Why is not dear, true-hearted, faithful Lucy here, watching over you, Grace, at this very moment?" I demanded huskily.

"She knows nothing of my situation—it is a secret, as well as its cause, from all but God, myself, and you. Ah! I knew it would be impossible to deceive your love, Miles! which has ever been to me, all that a sister could desire."

"And Lucy! how has her affection been deceived? Has she, too, eyes only for those she has recently learned to admire!"

"You do her injustice, brother. Lucy has not seen me, since the great change that I can myself see has come over me. At another time, I will tell you all. At present I can only say, that as soon as I had certain explanations with Rupert, I left town, and have studiously concealed from dear Lucy the state of my declining health. I write to her weekly, and get answers; everything passing between us as cheerfully, and, apparently, as happily as ever. No, do not blame Lucy; who, I am certain, would quit everything and everybody to come to me, had she the smallest notion of the truth. On the contrary, I believe she thinks I would rather not have her at Clawbonny, just at this moment, much as she knows I love her; for one of Lucy's observation and opportunities cannot but suspect the truth. Let me lie on your breast, brother, it wearies me to talk so much."

I sat holding this beloved sister in my arms, fully an hour, neither of us speaking. I was afraid of injuring her, by further excitement, and she was glad to take refuge in silence, from the feelings of maiden shame that could not be otherwise than mingled with such a dialogue. As my cheek leaned on her silken hair, I could see large tears rolling down the pallid cheeks; but the occasional pressure of the hands, told me how much she was gladdened by my presence. After some ten or fifteen minutes, the exhausted girl dropped into feverish and disturbed slumbers, that I would have remained motionless throughout the night to maintain. I am persuaded it was quite an hour before this scene terminated. Grace then arose, and said, with one of her most angelic smiles,—

"You see how it is with me, Miles—feeble as an infant and almost as troublesome. You must bear with me, for you will be my nurse. One promise I must have, dearest, before we leave this room."

"It is yours, my sister, let it be what it may; I can now refuse you nothing," said I, melted to feminine tenderness. "And yet, Grace, since you exact a promise, I have a mind to attach a condition."

"What condition, Miles, can you attach, that I will refuse? I consent to everything, without even knowing your wishes."

"Then I promise not to call Rupert to an account for his conduct—not to question him—nay, even not to reproach him," I rejoined, enlarging my pledges, as I saw by Grace's eyes that she exacted still more.

The last promise, however, appeared fully to satisfy her. She kissed my hand, and I felt hot tears falling on it.

"Now name your conditions, dearest brother," she said, after, a little time taken to recover herself; "name them, and see how gladly I shall accept them all."

"I have but one—it is this. I must take the complete direction of the care of you—must have the power to send for what physician I please, what friends I please, what advice or regimen I please!"

"Oh! Miles, you could not—cannot think of sending for him!"

"Certainly not; his presence would drive me from the house. With that one exception, then, my condition is allowed?"

Grace made a sign of assent, and sunk on my bosom again, nearly exhausted with the scene through which she had just gone. I perceived it would not do to dwell any longer on the subject we had been alluding to, rather than discussing; and for another hour did I sit sustaining that beloved form, declining to speak, and commanding silence on her part. At the end of this second little sleep, Grace was more refreshed than she had been after her first troubled repose, and she declared herself able to walk to her room, where she wished to lie on her own bed until the hour of dinner. I summoned Chloe, and, together, we led the invalid to her chamber. As we threaded the long passages, my sister's head rested on my bosom, her eyes were turned affectionately upward to my face, and several times I felt the gentle pressure of her emaciated hands, given in the fervor of devoted sisterly love.

I needed an hour to compose myself after this interview. In the privacy of my own room I wept like a child over the wreck of the being I had left so beautiful and perfect, though even then the canker of doubt had begun to take root. I had yet her explanations to hear, and resolved to command myself so far as to receive them in a manner not to increase the pain Grace must feel in making them. As soon as sufficiently calm, I sat down to write letters. One was to Marble. I desired him to let the second mate see the ship discharged, and to come up to me by the return of the sloop. I wished to see him in person, as I did not think I could be able to go out in the vessel on her next voyage, and I intended him to sail in her as master. It was necessary we should consult together personally. I did not conceal the reason of

this determination, though I said nothing of the cause of
my sister's state.   Marble had a list of physicians given him
and he was to bring up with him the one he could obtain,
commencing with the first named and following in the order
given.   I had earned ten thousand dollars, net, by the labors
of the past year, and I determined every dollar of it should
be devoted to obtaining the best advice the country then
afforded.   I had sent for such men as Hosack, Post, Bayley,
M'Knight, Moore, etc., and even thought of procuring
Rush from Philadelphia, but was deterred from making the
attempt by the distance and the pressing nature of the
emergency.   In 1803, Philadelphia was about three days'
journey from Clawbonny, even allowing for a favorable time
on the river ; with a moderately unfavorable, five or six ;
whereas the distance can now be passed, including the
chances of meeting the departures and arrivals of the different lines, in from twelve to fifteen hours.   Such is one of
the prodigious effects of an improved civilization ; and in
all that relates to motion, and which falls short of luxury,
or great personal comfort, this country takes a high place in
the scale of nations.   That it is as much in arrears in other
great essentials, however, particularly in what relates to
tavern comforts, no man who is familiar with the better
civilization of Europe can deny.   It is a singular fact that
we have gone backward in this last particular within the
present century, and all owing to the increasing gregarious
habits of the population.   But to return to my painful theme,
from which, even at this distance of time, I am only too
ready to escape.

I was on the point of writing to Lucy, but hesitated.   I
hardly knew whether to summon her to Clawbonny or not.
That she would come, and that instantly, the moment she was
apprised of Grace's condition, I did not in the least doubt.
I was not so mad as to do her character injustice, because I
had my doubts about being loved as I had once hoped to be.
That Lucy was attached to me, in one sense, I did not in the
least doubt ; this her late reception of me sufficiently proved,
and I could not question her continued affection for Grace,
after all the latter had just told me.   Even did Lucy prefer

Andrew Drewett, it was no proof she was not just as kind-hearted, as ready to be of service, and as true in her friendship, as she ever had been. Still, she was Rupert's sister, must have penetration enough to understand the cause of Grace's illness, and might not enter as fully into her wrongs as one could wish in a person that was to watch the sick pillow. I resolved to learn more that day, before this portion of my duty was discharged.

Neb was summoned and sent to the wharf with an order to get the Wallingford ready to sail for town at the first favorable moment. The sloop was merely to be in ballast, and was to return to Clawbonny with no unnecessary delay. There was an eminent but retired physician of the name of Bard, who had a country residence on the other bank of the Hudson, and within a few hours' sail from Clawbonny. I knew his character, though I was not acquainted with him personally. Few of us of the right bank, indeed, belonged to the circles of the left in that day ; the increasing wealth and population of the country have since brought the western side into more notice. I wrote also to Dr. Bard, inclosing a check for a suitable fee, made a strong appeal to his feelings—which would have been quite sufficient with such a man—and ordered Neb to go out in the Grace and Lucy immediately to deliver the message. Just as this arrangement was completed, Chloe came to summon me to my sister's room.

I found Grace still lying on her bed, but stronger, and materially refreshed. For a moment I began to think my fears had exaggerated the danger, and that I was not to lose my sister. A few minutes of close observation, however, convinced me that the first impression was the true one. I am not skilled in the theories of the science, if there be any great science about it, and can hardly explain even now the true physical condition of Grace. She had pent up her sufferings in her own bosom for six cruel months in the solitude of a country-house, living most of the time entirely alone, and this, they tell me, is what few even of the most robust frames can do with impunity. Frail as she had ever seemed, her lungs were sound, and she spoke easily and with almost all her original force, so that her wasting away was not the consequence of anything pulmonary. I rather think the physical effects were to be traced to the unhealthy action of the fluids, which were deranged through the stomach and spleen. The insensible perspiration was affected also, I believe, the pores of the skin failing to do their duty. I dare say there is not a graduate of the thousand and one medical colleges of the country who is not prepared to laugh at this theory, while unable, quite likely, to produce a better—so much easier is it to pull down than to build up ; but my object is merely to give the reader a general idea of my poor sister's situation. In outward appearance, her countenance denoted that expression which the French so well describe by the customary term of "*fatigué*," rather than any other positive indication of disease—Grace's frame was so delicate by nature, that a little falling away was not as perceptible in her as it would have been in most persons, though her beautiful little hands wanted that fullness which had rendered their taper fingers and roseate tint formerly so very faultless. There must have been a good deal of fever, as her color was often higher than was formerly usual. It was this circumstance that continued to render her beauty even unearthly, without its being accompanied by the emaciation so common in the latter stages of pulmonary disease, though its tendency was strongly to undermine her strength.

Grace, without rising from her pillow, now asked me for an outline of my late voyage. She heard me, I make no doubt, with real interest, for all that concerned me, in a measure concerned her. Her smile was sweetness itself, as she listened to my successes ; and the interest she manifested in Marble, with whose previous history she was well acquainted, was not less than I had felt myself, in hearing his own account of his adventures. All this delighted me, as it went to prove that I had beguiled the sufferer from brooding over her own sorrows ; and what might not be hoped for, could we lead her back to mingle in the ordinary concerns of life, and surround her with the few friends she so tenderly loved, and whose absence, perhaps, had largely contributed to reducing her to her present state? This thought recalled Lucy to my mind, and the wish I had to ascertain how far it might be agreeable to the latter, to be summoned to Clawbonny. I determined to lead the conversation to this subject.

"You have told me, Grace," I said, "that you send and receive letters weekly, to and from Lucy?"

"Each time the Wallingford goes and comes; and that, you know, is weekly. I suppose the reason I got no letter to-day was owing to the fact that the sloop sailed before her time. The Lord High Admiral was on board; and, like wind and tide, he waits for no man!"

"Bless you—bless you, dearest sister—this gayety removes a mountain from my heart!"

Grace looked pleased at first; then, as she gazed wistfully into my face, I could see her own expression change to one of melancholy concern. Large tears started from her eyes, and three or four followed each other down her cheeks. All this said, plainer than words, that, though a fond brother might be momentarily deceived, she herself foresaw the end. I bowed my head to the pillow, stifled the groans that oppressed me, and kissed the tears from her cheeks. To put an end to these distressing scenes, I determined to be more business-like in future, and suppress all feeling, as much as possible.

"The Lord High Admiral," I resumed, "is a species of Turk, on board ship, as honest Moses Marble will tell you, when you see him, Grace. But now, for Lucy and her letters—I dare say the last are filled with tender secrets, touching such persons as Andrew Drewett, and other of her admirers, which render it improper to show any of them to me!"

Grace looked at me, with earnestness, as if to ascertain whether I was really as unconcerned as I affected to be. Then she seemed to muse, picking the cotton of the spotless counterpane on which she was lying, like one at a loss what to say or think.

"I see how it is," I resumed, forcing a smile; "the hint has been indiscreet. A rough son of Neptune is not the

"My sister was on the *causeuse*, literally unable to rise from debility and agitation." Wallingford is reunited with Grace, pining away for love of Rupert. *Drawing by Clara Cawse.*   (p. 484)

proper confident for the secrets of Miss Lucy Hardinge.
Perhaps you are right ; fidelity to each other being indispensable in your sex.''

"It is not that, Miles. I doubt if Lucy ever wrote me
a line that you might not see ; in proof of which, you shall
have the package of her letters, with full permission to read
every one of them. It will be like reading the correspondence of another *sister*."

I fancied Grace laid an emphasis on the last word she
used ; and I started at its unwelcome sound—unwelcome,
as applied to Lucy Hardinge, to a degree that I cannot express. I had observed that Lucy never used any of these
terms, as connected with me, and it was one of the reasons
why I had indulged in the folly of supposing that she was
conscious of a tenderer sentiment. But Lucy was so
natural, so totally free from exaggeration, so just and true
in all her feelings, that one could not expect from her most
of the acts of girlish weakness. As for Grace, she called
Chloe, gave her the keys of her secretary, and told her to
bring me the package she described.

"Go and look over them, Miles," said my sister, as I received the letters ; "there must be more than twenty of
them, and you can read half before the dinner hour. I will
meet you at table ; and let me implore you not to alarm
good Mr. Hardinge. He does not believe me seriously ill ;
and it cannot benefit him or me to cause him pain."

I promised discretion, and hastened to my own room with
the precious bundle of Lucy's letters. Shall I own the
truth ? I kissed the papers, fervently, before they were
loosened, and it seemed to me I possessed a treasure, in
holding in my hand so many of the dear girl's epistles. I
commenced in the order of the date, and began to read with
eagerness. It was impossible for Lucy Hardinge to write
to one she loved, and not exhibit the truth and nature of
her feelings. These appeared in every paragraph in which
it was proper to make any allusions of the sort. But the
letters had other charms. It was apparent throughout, that
the writer was ignorant that she wrote to an invalid, though
she could not but know that she wrote to a recluse. Her

aim evidently was to amuse Grace, of whose mental sufferings she could not well be ignorant. Lucy was a keen
observer, and her epistles were filled with amusing comments on the follies that were daily committed in New
York, as well as in Paris or London. I was delighted with
the delicate pungency of her satire, which, however, was
totally removed from vulgar scandal. There was nothing
in these letters that might not have been uttered in a drawing-room, to any but the persons concerned; and yet they
were filled with a humor that rose often to wit, relieved by
a tact and taste that a man never could have attained.
Throughout, it was apparent to me, Lucy, in order to
amuse Grace, was giving full scope to a natural talent—
one that far surpassed the same capacity in her brother, being as true as his was meretricious and jesuitical—which
she had hitherto concealed from us all, merely because she
had not seen an occasion fit for its use. Allusions in the
letters, themselves, proved that Grace had commented on
this unexpected display of observant humor, and had expressed her surprise at its existence. It was then as novel
to my sister as it was to myself. I was struck also with
the fact, that Rupert's name did not appear once in all
these letters. They embraced just twenty-seven weeks
between the earliest and the latest date; and there were
nine-and-twenty letters, two having been sent by private
conveyance; her father's, most probably, he occasionally
making the journey by land; yet no one of them contained
the slightest allusion to her brother, or to either of the Mertons. This was enough to let me know how well Lucy
understood the reason of Grace's withdrawal to Clawbonny.

"And how is it with Miles Wallingford's name?" some
of my fair readers may be ready to ask. I went carefully
through the package in the course of the evening, and I set
aside two, as the only exceptions in which my name did not
appear. On examining these two with jealous care, I found
each had a postscript, one of which was to the following
effect: "I see by the papers that Miles has sailed for Malta,
having at last left those stubborn Turks. I am glad of
this, as one would not wish to have the excellent fellow

shut up in the Seven Towers, however honorable it may
have been." The other postscript contained this : " Dear
Miles has got to Leghorn, my father tells me, and may be
expected home this summer. How great happiness this will
bring you, dearest Grace, I can well understand ; and I need
scarcely say that no one will rejoice more to see him again
than his late guardian and myself."

That the papers were often looked over to catch reports
of my movements in Europe, by means of ships arriving
from different parts of the world, was apparent enough ;
but I scarce knew what to make of the natural and simply
affectionate manner in which my name was introduced. It
might proceed from a wish to gratify Grace, and a desire to
let the sister know all that she herself possessed touching
the brother's movements. Then Andrew Drewett's name
occurred very frequently, though it was generally in connection with that of his mother, who had evidently constituted herself a sort of regular *chaperone* for Lucy, more
especially during the time she was kept out of the gay world
by her mourning. I read several of these passages with the
most scrupulous attention, in order to detect the feeling with
which they had been written ; but the most practised art
could not have more successfully concealed any secret of
this sort, than Lucy's nature. This often proves to be the
case ; the just-minded and true among men daily becoming
the profoundest mysteries to a vicious, cunning, deceptive,
and selfish world. An honest man, indeed, is ever a para-
dox to all but those who see things with his own eyes.
This is the reason that improper motives are so often imputed to the simplest and seemingly most honest deeds.

The result was, to write, entreating Lucy to come to
Clawbonny ; first taking care to secure her father's assent
to aid my request. This was done in a way not to awaken
any alarm, and yet with sufficient strength to render it
tolerably certain she would come. On deliberate reflection,
and after seeing my sister at table, where she ate nothing
but a light vegetable diet, and passing the evening with her,
I thought I could not do less injustice to the invalid or her
friend. I took the course with great regret on several ac-

counts ; and, among others, from a reluctance to appear to draw Lucy away from the society of my rival, into my own. Yet what right had I to call myself the rival or competitor of a man who had openly professed an attachment, where I had never breathed a syllable myself that might not readily be mistaken for the language of that friendship, which time, and habit, and a respect for each other's qualities, so easily awaken among the young of different sexes ? I had been educated almost as Lucy's brother ; and why should she not feel toward me as one ?

Neb went out in the boat as soon as he got his orders, and the Wallingford sailed again in ballast that very night. She did not remain at the wharf an hour after her wheat was out. I felt easier when these duties were discharged, and was better prepared to pass the night in peace. Grace's manner and appearance, too, contributed to this calm ; for she seemed to revive, and to experience some degree of earthly happiness, in having her brother near her. When Mr. Hardinge read prayers that night, she came to the chair where I stood, took my hand in hers, and knelt at my side. I was touched to tears by this act of affection, which spoke as much of the tenderness of the sainted and departed spirit, lingering around those it had loved on earth, as the affection of the world. I folded the dear girl to my bosom, as I left her at the door of her own room that night, and went to my own pillow, with a heavy heart. Seamen pray little ; less than they ought, amid the rude scenes of their hazardous lives. Still, I had not quite forgotten the lessons of childhood, and sometimes I practised on them. That night I prayed fervently, beseeching God to spare my sister, if in his wisdom it were meet ; and I humbly invoked his blessing on the excellent divine, and on Lucy, by name. I am not ashamed to own it, let who may deride the act.

CHAPTER XXIX.

"Wherever sorrow is, relief would be ;
If you do sorrow at my grief in love,
By giving love, your sorrow and my grief
Were both extermined."

As You Like It.

I SAW but little of Grace, during the early part of the succeeding day. She had uniformly breakfasted in her own room, of late, and, in the short visit I paid her there, I found her composed, with an appearance of renewed strength that encouraged me greatly as to the future. Mr. Hardinge insisted on rendering an account of his stewardship, that morning, and I let the good divine have his own way ; though, had he asked me for receipt in full, I would cheerfully have given it to him, without examining a single item. There was a singular peculiarity about Mr. Hardinge. No one could live less for the world generally ; no one was less qualified to superintend extensive worldly interests, that required care, or thought ; and no one would have been a more unsafe executor in matters that were intricate or involved : still, in the mere business of accounts, he was as methodical and exact as the most faithful banker. Rigidly honest, and with a strict regard for the rights of others, living moreover on a mere pittance, for the greater part of his life, this conscientious divine never contracted a debt he could not pay. What rendered this caution more worthy of remark, was the fact that he had a spendthrift son ; but even Rupert could never lure him into any weakness of this sort. I question if his actual cash receipts, independently of the profits of his little glebe, exceeded $300 in any one year ; yet he and his children were ever well

32

dressed, and I knew from observation that his table was always sufficiently supplied. He got a few presents occasionally, from his parishioners, it is true ; but they did not amount to any sum of moment. It was method, and a determination not to anticipate his income, that placed him so much above the world, while he had a family to support ; whereas, now that Mrs. Bradfort's fortune was in the possession of his children, he assured me he felt himself quite rich, though he scrupulously refused to appropriate one dollar of the handsome income that passed through his hands as executor, to his own uses. It was all Lucy's, who was entitled to receive this income even in her minority, and to her he paid every cent, quarterly ; the sister providing for Rupert's ample wants.

Of course, I found everything exact to a farthing ; the necessary papers were signed, the power of attorney was cancelled, and I entered fully into the possession of my own. An unexpected rise in the value of flour had raised my shore receipts that year to the handsome sum of nine thousand dollars. This was not properly income, however, but profits, principally obtained through the labor of the mill. By putting all my loose cash together, I found I could command fully $30,000, in addition to the price of the ship. This sum was making me a man quite at my ease, and, properly managed, it opened a way to wealth. How gladly would I have given every cent of it, to see Grace as healthy and happy as she was when I left her at Mrs. Bradfort's, to sail in the Crisis !

After settling the figures, Mr. Hardinge and I mounted our horses, and rode over the property to take a look at the state of the farm. Our road took us near the little rectory and the glebe ; and, here, the simple-minded divine broke out into ecstasies on the subject of the beauties of his own residence, and the delight with which he should now return to his ancient abode. He loved Clawbonny no less than formerly, but he loved the rectory more.

" I was born in that humble, snug, quiet old stone cottage, Miles," he said, " and there I lived for years a happy husband and father, and I hope I may say a faithful shepherd of my little flock. St. Michael's, Clawbonny, is not Trinity, New York, but it may prove, on a small scale as to numbers, as fitting a nursery of saints. What humble and devout Christians have I known to kneel at its little altar, Miles, among whom your mother, and your venerable old grandmother, were two of the best. I hope the day is not distant when I shall meet there another Mrs. Miles Walingford. Marry young, my boy ; early marriages prove happier than late, where there are the means of subsistence."

"You would not have me marry, until I can find a woman whom I shall truly love, dear sir?"

"Heaven forbid ! I would rather see you a bachelor to my dying day. But America has enough females that a youth like you could, and indeed ought to love. I could direct you to fifty, myself."

"Well, sir, your recommendations would have great weight with me. I wish you would begin."

"That I will, that I will, if you wish it, my dear boy. Well, there is a Miss Hervey, Miss Kate Hervey, in town ; a girl of excellent qualities, and who would just suit you could you agree."

"I recollect the young lady ; the greatest objection I should raise to her, is a want of personal attractions. Of all Mrs. Bradfort's acquaintances, I think she was among the very plainest."

"What is beauty, Miles? In marriage, very different recommendations are to be looked for by the husband."

"Yet, I have understood you practised on another theory ; Mrs. Hardinge, even as I recollect her, was very handsome."

"Yes, that is true," answered the good divine, simply ; "she was so ; but beauty is not to be considered as an objection. If you do not relish the idea of Kate Hervey, what do you say to Jane Harwood—there is a pretty girl for you."

"A pretty girl, sir, but not for me. But, in naming so many young ladies, why do you overlook your own daughter?"

I said this with a sort of desperate resolution, tempted by

the opportunity, and the direction the discourse had taken. When it was uttered, I repented of my temerity, and almost trembled to hear the answer.

"Lucy!" exclaimed Mr. Hardinge, turning suddenly toward me, and looking so intently and earnestly in my face, that I saw the possibility of such a thing then struck him for the first time. " Sure enough, why should you not marry Lucy? There is not a particle of relationship between you, after all, though I have so long considered you as brother and sister. I wish we had thought of this earlier, Miles ; it would be a most capital connection—though I should insist on your quitting the sea. Lucy has too affectionate a heart, to be always in distress for an absent husband. I wonder the possibility of this thing did not strike me, before it was too late ; in a man so much accustomed to see what is going on around me, to overlook this !"

The words, " too late," sounded to me like the doom of fate ; and had my simple-minded companion but the tithe of the observation which he so much vaunted, he must have seen my agitation. I had advanced so far, however, that I determined to learn the worst, whatever pain it might cost me.

"I suppose, sir, the very circumstance that we were brought up together has prevented us all from regarding the thing as possible. But, why ' too late,' my excellent guardian, if we who are the most interested in the thing should happen to think otherwise?"

"Certainly not too late, if you include Lucy, herself, in your conditions ; but I am afraid, Miles, it is ' too late ' for Lucy."

"Am I to understand, then, that Miss Hardinge is engaged to Mr. Drewett? Are her affections enlisted in his behalf?"

"You may be certain of one thing, boy, and that is, if Lucy be engaged, her affections are enlisted—so conscientious a young woman would never marry without giving her heart with her hand. As for the fact, however, I know nothing, except by inference. I do suppose a mutual attachment to exist between her and Andrew Drewett."

" Of course with good reason, sir. Lucy is not a coquette, or a girl to encourage when she does not mean to accept."

" That 's all I know of the matter. Drewett continues to visit ; is as attentive as a young man well can be, where a young woman is as scrupulous as is Lucy about the proper forms, and I infer they understand each other. I have thought of speaking to Lucy on the subject, but I do not wish to influence her judgment, in a case where there exists no objection. Drewett is every way a suitable match, and I wish things to take their own course. There is one little circumstance, however, that I can mention to you as a sort of son, Miles, and which I consider conclusive as to the girl's inclinations—I have remarked that she refuses all expedients to get her to be alone with Drewett ; refuses to make excursions in which she must be driven in his curricle, or go anywhere with him, even to the next door. So particular is she, that she contrives never to be alone with him, even in his many visits to the house."

" And do you consider that as a proof of attachment ?— of her being engaged ? Does your own experience, sir, confirm such a notion ? "

" What else can it be, if it be not a consciousness of a passion—of an attachment that she is afraid every one will see ? You do not understand the sex, I perceive, Miles, or the fineness of their natures would be more apparent to you. As for my experience, no conclusion can be drawn from that, as I and my dear wife were thrown together very young, all alone, in her mother's country-house ; and the old lady being bedridden, there was no opportunity for the bashful maiden to betray this consciousness. But if I understand human nature, such is the secret of Lucy's feelings towards Andrew Drewett. It is of no great moment to you, Miles, notwithstanding, as there are plenty more young women to be had in the world."

" True, sir ; but there is only one Lucy Hardinge ! " I rejoined, with a fervor and strength of utterance that betrayed more than I intended.

My late guardian actually stopped his horse this time, to look at me, and I could perceive deep concern gathering around his usually serene and placid brow. He began to penetrate my feelings, and I believe they caused him real grief.

" I never could have dreamed of this ! " Mr. Hardinge at length exclaimed. " Do you really love Lucy, my dear Miles ? "

" Better than I do my own life, sir—I almost worship the earth she treads on—love her with my whole heart, and have loved, I believe, if the truth were known, ever since I was sixteen—perhaps I had better say, twelve years old ! "

The truth escaped me, as the torrent of the Mississippi breaks through the levee, and a passage once open for its exit, it cleared a way for itself, until the current of my feelings left no doubt of its direction. I believe I was a little ashamed of my own weakness, for I caused my horse to walk forward, Mr. Hardinge accompanying the movement, for a considerable distance, in a profound, and I doubt not, a painful silence.

"This has taken me altogether by surprise, Miles," my late guardian resumed ; " altogether by surprise. What would I not give could this have been known a year or two since ! My dear boy, I feel for you, from the bottom of my heart, for I can understand what it must be to love a girl like Lucy, without hope. Why did you not let this be known sooner—or, why did you insist on going to sea, having so strong a motive for remaining at home ? "

" I was too young, at that time, sir, to act on, or even to understand my own feelings. On my return, in the Crisis, I found Lucy in a set superior to that in which I was born and educated, and it would have been a poor proof of my attachment to wish to bring her down nearer to my own level."

" I understand you, Miles, and can appreciate the generosity of your conduct ; though I am afraid it would have been too late on your return in the Crisis. That was only a twelvemonth since, and, then, I rather think, Andrew Drewett had offered. There is good sense in your feeling on the subject of marriage in unequal conditions in life, for they certainly lead to many heart-burnings, and greatly lessen the chances of happiness. One thing is certain ; in all such cases, if the inferior cannot rise to the height of the superior, the superior must sink to the level of the inferior. Man and wife cannot continue to occupy different social positions ; and as for the nonsense that is uttered on such subjects, by visionaries, under the claim of its being common-sense, it is only fit for pretending theories, and can have nothing to do with the great rules of practice. You were right in principle, then, Miles, though you have greatly exaggerated the facts of your own particular case."

"I have always known, sir, and have ever been ready to admit, that the Hardinges have belonged to a different class of society from that filled by the Wallingfords."

"This is true, but in part only ; and by no means true to a degree that need have drawn any impassable line between you and Lucy. You forget how poor we then were, and how substantial a benefit the care of Clawbonny might have been to my dear girl. Besides, you are of reputable descent and position, if not precisely of the gentry ; and this is not a country, or an age, to carry notions of such a nature beyond the strict bounds of reason. You and Lucy were educated on the same level ; and, after all, that is the great essential for the marriage connection."

There was great good sense in what Mr. Hardinge said ; and I began to see that pride, and not humility, might have interfered with my happiness. As I firmly believed it was now too late, however, I began to wish the subject changed ; for I felt it grating on some of my most sacred feelings. With a view to divert the conversation to another channel, therefore, I remarked with some emphasis, affecting an indifference I did not feel,—

"What cannot be cured, must be endured, sir ; and I shall endeavor to find a sailor's happiness hereafter, in loving my ship. Besides, were Andrew Drewett entirely out of the question, it is now ' too late,' in another sense, since it would never do for the man who, himself at his ease in the way of money, hesitated about offering when his mistress was poor, to prove his love, by proposing to Mrs.

Bradfort's heiress. Still, I own to so much weakness as to wish to know, before we close the subject forever, why Mr. Drewett and your daughter do not marry, if they are engaged? Perhaps it is owing only to Lucy's mourning?''

'' I have myself imputed it to another cause. Rupert is entirely dependent on his sister, and I know Lucy so well as to feel certain—some extraordinary cause not interposing—that she wishes to bestow half her cousin's fortune on her brother. This cannot be done until she is of age, and she wants near two years of attaining her majority.''

I made no answer ; for I felt how likely this was to be true. Lucy was not a girl of professions, and she would be very apt to keep a resolution of this nature a secret in her own breast, until ready to carry it into execution. No more passed between Mr. Hardinge and myself, on the subject of our recent conversation ; though I could see my avowal had made him sad, and that it induced him to treat me with more affection, even, than had been his practice. Once or twice, in the course of the next day or two, I overheard him soliloquizing—a habit to which he was a good deal addicted —during which he would murmur, '' What a pity !''— '' How much to be regretted !''—'' I would rather have him for a son than any man on earth !'' and other similar expressions. Of course, these involuntary disclosures did not weaken my regard for my late guardian.

About noon, the Grace and Lucy came in, and Neb reported that Dr. Bard was not at home. He had left my letter, however, and it would be delivered as soon as possible. He told me also that the wind had been favorable on the river, and that the Wallingford must reach town that day.

Nothing further occurred, worthy of notice. I passed the afternoon with Grace, in the little room ; and we conversed much of the past, of our parents in particular, without adverting, however, to her situation, any further than to apprise her of what I had done. I thought she was not sorry to learn I had sent for Lucy, now that I was with her, and it was no longer possible her illness could be concealed. As for the physicians, when they were mentioned, I could see a look of tender concern in Grace's eyes, as if she regretted that I still clung to the delusion of hoping to see her health restored. Notwithstanding these little drawbacks, we passed a sweet eventide together. For more than an hour, Grace lay on my bosom, occasionally patting her hand on my cheeks, as the child caresses its mother. This was an old habit of hers, and it was one I was equally delighted and pained to have her resume, now we were of the age and stature of man and woman.

The next day was Sunday, and Grace insisted on my driving her to church. This was done, accordingly, in a very old-fashioned, but very easy Boston chaise, that had belonged to my mother, and with very careful driving. The congregation, like the church edifice, of St. Michael's was very small, being confined, with some twenty or thirty exceptions, to the family and dependents of Clawbonny. Mr. Hardinge's little flock was hedged in by other denominations on every side, and it was not an easy matter to break through the barriers that surrounded it. Then he was not possessed with the spirit of proselytism, contenting himself with aiding in the spiritual advancement of those whom Providence had consigned to his care. On the present occasion, however, the little building was full, and that was as much as could have happened had it been as large as St. Peter's itself. The prayers were devoutly and fervently read, and the sermon was plain and filled with piety.

My sister professed herself in no manner wearied with the exertion. We dined with Mr. Hardinge, at the rectory, which was quite near the church; and the irreverent, business-like, make-weight sort of look, of going in to one service almost as soon as the other was ended, as if to score off so much preaching and praying as available at the least trouble, being avoided, by having the evening service commence late, she was enabled to remain until the close of the day. Mr. Hardinge rarely preached but once of a Sunday. He considered the worship of God, and the offices of the Church, as the proper duties of the day, and regarded his own wisdom as a matter of secondary importance. But one sermon cost him as much labor, and study, and anxiety, as most clergymen's two. His preaching, also, had the high qualification of being addressed to the affections of his flock, and not to its fears and interests. He constantly reminded us of God's love, and of the beauty of holiness; while I do not remember to have heard him allude half a dozen times in his life to the terrors of judgment and punishment, except as they were connected with that disappointed love. I suppose there are spirits that require these allusions, and the temptations of future happiness, to incite their feelings; but I like the preacher who is a Christian because he feels himself *drawn* to holiness, by a power that is of itself holy; and not those who appeal to their people, as if heaven and hell were a mere matter of preference and avoidance, on the ground of expediency. I cannot better characterize Mr. Hardinge's preaching, than by saying, that I do not remember ever to have left his church with a sense of fear toward the Creator; though I have often been impressed with a love that was as profound as the adoration that had been awakened.

Another calm and comparatively happy evening was passed, during which I conversed freely with Grace of my own intentions, endeavoring to revive in her an interest in life, by renewing old impressions, and making her participate in my feelings. Had I been with her from the hour spring opened, with its renewal of vegetation, and all the joys it confers on the innocent and happy, I have often thought since, I might have succeeded. As it was, she listened with attention, and apparently with pleasure, for she saw it served to relieve my mind. We did not separate until I insisted Grace should retire, and Chloe had made more than one remonstrance about her young mistress' exceeding the usual time. On leaving my sister's chamber, the negress followed me with a light, lest I should fall, among the intricate turnings, and the ups and down of the old building.

"Well, Chloe," I said, as we proceeded together, "how do you find Neb? Does he improve by this running about on the ocean—especially do you think he is tanned."

"De *fel*-ler!"

"Yes, he is a fellow, sure enough, and let me tell you, Chloe, a very capital fellow, too.   If it can be of any advantage to him in your favor to know the truth, I will just say, a more useful seaman does not sail the ocean than Neb, and that I consider him of as much importance as the mainmast."

"What be dat, Masser Mile?"

"I see nothing, Chloe—there are no spooks at Clawbonny, you know."

"No, sah! What be 'e t'ing Neb like, de *fel*-ler?"

"Oh! I ask your pardon—the mainmast, you mean. It is the most important spar in the ship, and I meant that Neb was as useful as that mast.   In battle, too, Neb is as brave as a lion."

Here Chloe could stand it no longer; she fairly laughed outright, in pure, natural admiration of her suitor's qualities. When this was performed, she ejaculated once more, "De *fel-ler!*" dropped a courtesy, said "Good night, Masser Mile," and left me at my own door.   Alas! alas! among the improvements of this age, we have entirely lost the breed of the careless, good-natured, affectionate, faithful, hard-working, and yet happy blacks, of whom more or less were to be found in every respectable and long established family of the State, forty years ago.

The next day was one of great anxiety to me.   I rose early, and the first thing was to ascertain the direction of the wind.   In midsummer this was apt to be southerly, and so it proved on that occasion.   Neb was sent to the point, as a lookout; he returned about ten, and reported a fleet of sloops in sight.   These vessels were still a long distance down the river, but they were advancing at a tolerable rate. Whether the Wallingford were among them, or not, was more than could yet be told.   I sent him back to his station, as soon as he had eaten ; and unable to remain quiet in the house, myself, I mounted my horse, and rode out into the fields.   Here, as usual, I experienced the happiness of looking at objects my ancestors loved to regard, and which always have had a strong and near interest with me.

Perhaps no country that ever yet existed has been so little understood, or so much misrepresented, as this Amer-

ica of ours. It is as little understood, I was on the point
of saying, at home as it is abroad, and almost as much misrepresented. Certainly its possessors are a good deal
addicted to valuing themselves on distinctive advantages
that, in reality, they do not enjoy, while their enemies
declaim about vices and evils from which they are comparatively free. Facts are made to suit theories, and thus it is
that we see well-intentioned, and otherwise respectable
writers, constantly running into extravagances, in order to
adapt the circumstances to the supposed logical or moral
inference. This reasoning backward has caused Alison,
with all his knowledge and fair-mindedness, to fall into
several egregious errors, as I have discovered while recently
reading his great work on Europe. He says we are a
migratory race, and that we do not love the sticks and
stones that surround us, but quit the paternal roof without
regret, and consider the play-grounds of infancy as only so
much land for the market. He also hazards the assertion,
that there is not such a thing as a literal farmer—that is,
a tenant who farms his land from a landlord—in all America. Now, as a rule, and comparing the habits of America
with those of older countries, in which land is not so abundant, this may be true ; but as literal fact, nothing can be
less so. Four fifths of the inhabited portion of the American territory has a civilized existence of half a century's
duration ; and there has not been time to create the long-
lived attachments named, more especially in the regions
that are undergoing the moral fusion that is always an
attendant of a new settlement. That thousands of heartless speculators exist among us, who do regard everything,
even to the graves of our fathers, as only so much im-
provable property, is as undeniable as the fact that they are
odious to all men of any moral feeling ; but thousands and
tens of thousands are to be found in the country, who do
reverence their family possessions from a sentiment that is
creditable to human nature. I will not mention Clawbonny
and its history, lest I might be suspected of being partial
but it would be easy for me to point out a hundred families,
embracing all classes, from the great proprietor to the plain

A view of the Hudson River as it appeared when the *Wallingford* made her cruises from Clawbonny. *Drawing by W. H. Bartlett.*

yeoman, who own and reside on the estates of those who
first received them from the hand of nature, and this after
one or two centuries of possession.   What will Mr. Alison
say, for instance, of the Manor of Rensselaer?   A manor,
in the legal sense, it is no longer, certainly, the new institutions destroying all the feudal tenures ; but, as mere property, the late patroon transmitted it as regularly to his
posterity, as any estate was ever transmitted in Europe.
This extensive manor lies in the heart of New York, a State
about as large and about as populous as Scotland, and it
embraces no less than three cities in its bosom, though their
sites are not included in its ownership, having been ex-
empted by earlier grants.   It is of more than two centuries'
existence, and it extends eight-and-forty miles east and west,
and half that distance, north and south.   Nearly all this
vast property is held, at this hour, of the Van Rensselaers,
as landlords, and is farmed by their tenants, there being
several thousands of the latter.   The same is true, on a
smaller scale, of the Livingston, the Van Cortlandt, the
Philipse, the Nicoll, and various other old New York
estates, though several were lost by attainder in the Revolution.   I explain these things, lest any European who may
happen to read this book, should regard it as fiction ; for,
allowing for trifling differences, a hundred Clawbonnys are to
be found on the two banks of the Hudson, at this very hour.[1]
   But to return to the narrative.

   [1] Even the American may learn the following facts with some
surprise.   It is now about five-and-twenty years since the writer,
as tenant by the courtesy, came into possession of two farms, lying
within twenty-three miles of New York, in each of which there had
been three generations of tenants, and as many of landlords, without a scrap of a pen having passed between the parties, so far as the
writer could ever discover, receipts for rent excepted ! He also stands
in nearly the same relation to another farm, in the same county, on
which a lease for ninety years is at this moment running, one of the
covenants of which prescribes that the tenant shall "frequent divine
service according to the Church of England, when opportunity offers."
What an evidence of the nature of the tyranny from which our ancestors escaped, more especially when it is seen that the tenant was
obliged to submit to this severe exaction, in consideration of a rent
that is merely nominal !

My curiosity increased so much as the day advanced that I rode towards the point to look for the sloop. There she was, sure enough, and there was Neb, too, galloping a young horse, bareback, to the house with the news. I met him with an order to proceed to the wharf with the chaise, while I dashed on in the same direction myself, almost devoured with an impatience to learn the success of my different missions as I galloped along. I could see the upper part of the Wallingford's sails gliding through the leaves that fringed the bank, and it was apparent that she and I would reach the wharf almost at the same instant. Notwithstanding all my anxiety, it was impossible to get a glimpse of the vessel's deck.

I did not quit the saddle until the planks of the wharf were under the horse's hoofs. Then I got a view of the sloop's decks for the first time. A respectable-looking, tall, slender, middle-aged man, with a bright dark eye, was on the quarter-deck, and I bowed to him, inferring at once that he was one of the medical gentleman to whom I had sent the message. In effect, it was Post, the second named on my list, the first not being able to come. He returned my bow, but before I could alight and go on board to receive him, Marble's head rose from the cabin, and my mate sprang ashore and shook me cordially by the hand.

"Here I am, Miles, my boy," cried Marble, whom, off duty, I had earnestly begged to treat me with his old freedom, and who took me at my word, "here I am, Miles, my boy, and farther from salt water than I have been in five-and-twenty years. So this is the famous Clawbonny! I cannot say much for the port, which is somewhat crowded while it contains but one craft, though the river outside is pretty well, as rivers go. D' ye know, lad, that I 've been in a fever all the way up lest we should get ashore, on one side or the other? your having land on both tacks at once is too much of a good thing. This coming up to Clawbonny has put me in mind of running them straits, though we have had rather better weather this passage, and a clear horizon. What d' ye call that affair up against the hillside yonder, with the jig-a-merree that is turning in the water?"

"That's a mill, my friend, and the jig-a-merree is the very wheel on which you have heard me say my father was crushed."

Marble looked sorrowfully at the wheel, squeezed my hand, as if to express sorrow for having reminded me of so painful an event, and then I heard him murmuring to himself, "Well, I never had a father to lose. No bloody mill could do me that injury."

"That gentleman on the quarter-deck," I remarked, "is a physician for whom I sent to town, I suppose."

"Ay, ay, he's some such matter, I do suppose, though I've been generalizing so much about this here river, and the manner of sailing a craft of that rig, I've had little to say to him. I'm always a better friend to the cook than to the surgeon. But, Miles, my lad, there's a rare 'un in the ship's after-cabin, I can tell you!"

"That must be Lucy!" and I did not stop to pay my compliments to the strange gentleman, but almost leaped into the vessel's cabin.

There was Lucy, sure enough, attended by a respectable-looking elderly black female, one of the half dozen slaves that had become hers by the death of Mrs. Bradfort. Neither spoke, but we shook hands with frankness, and I understood by the anxious expression of my companion's eye, all she wished to know.

"I really think she seems better, and certainly she is far more cheerful, within this last day or two," I answered to the appeal. "Yesterday she was twice at church, and this morning, for a novelty, she breakfasted with me."

"God be praised!" Lucy exclaimed, with fervor. Then she sat down and relieved her feelings in tears. I told her to expect me again, in a few minutes, and joined the physician, who, by this time, was apprised of my presence. The calm, considerate manner of Post gave me a confidence I had not felt for some days; and I really began to hope it might still be within the power of his art to save the sister I so dearly loved.

Our dispositions for quitting the sloop were soon made, and we ascended the hill together, Lucy leaning on my arm. On its summit was the chaise, into which the doctor and Marble were persuaded to enter, Lucy preferring to walk. The negress was to proceed in the vehicle that had been sent for the luggage, and Lucy and I set out, arm and arm, to walk rather more than a mile in company, and that, too, without the presence of a third person. Such an occurrence, under any other circumstances than those in which we were both placed, would have made me one of the happiest men on earth ; but, in the actual situation in which I found myself, it rendered me silent and uncomfortable. Not so with Lucy ; ever natural, and keeping truth incessantly before her eyes, the dear girl took my arm without the least embarrassment, and showed no sign of impatience or of doubt. She was sad, but full of a gentle confidence in her own sincerity and motives.

" This is dear Clawbonny again ! " she exclaimed, after we had walked in silence a short distance. " How beautiful are the fields, how fresh the woods, how sweet the flowers. Oh ! Miles, a day in such a spot as this is worth a year in town ! "

" Why then do you, who have now so much at your command, pass more than half your time between the heated bricks of Wall Street, when you know how happy we should all be to see you here, among us again ? "

" I have not been certain of this ; that has been the sole reason of my absence. Had I known I should be welcome, nothing would have induced me to suffer Grace to pass the last six sad, sad months by herself."

" Known that you should be welcome ! Surely you have not supposed, Lucy, that I can ever regard you as anything but welcome here ? "

" I had no allusion to you—thought not of you, Miles, at all," answered Lucy, with the quiet manner of one who felt she was thinking, acting, and speaking no more than what was perfectly right ; " my mind was dwelling altogether on Grace."

" Is it possible you could doubt of Grace's willingness to see you at all times and in all places, Lucy ? "

" I have doubted it ; have thought I was acting pru-

dently and well in staying away just at this time, though I
now begin to fear the decision has been hasty and unwise.''

'' May I ask why Lucy Hardinge has come to so singular
and violent an opinion, as connected with her bosom friend
and almost sister, Grace Wallingford ? ''

'' That almost sister ! Oh ! Miles, what is there I possess
which I would not give that there might be perfect confidence
again between you and me on this subject ; such confidence as
existed when we were boy and girl—children, I might say.''

'' And what prevents it ? Certain I am the alienation
does not, cannot come from me. You have only to speak,
Lucy, to have an attentive listener ; to ask, to receive the
truest answers. What can, then, prevent the confidence
you wish ? ''

'' There is one obstacle ; surely, Miles, you can readily
imagine what I mean ? ''

'' Can it be possible Lucy is alluding to Andrew Drewett ? '' I thought to myself. '' Has she discovered my
attachment, and does she, will she, can she regret her own
engagement ? '' A lover who thought thus, would not be
apt to leave the question long in doubt.

'' Deal plainly with me, I implore of you, Lucy,'' I said
solemnly. '' One word uttered with your old sincerity and
frankness may close a chasm that has now been widening
between us for the last year or two. What is the obstacle
you mean ? ''

'' I have seen and felt the alienation to which you allude
quite as sensibly as you can have done yourself, Miles,'' the
dear girl answered, in her natural, simple manner ; '' and I
will trust all to your generosity. Need I say more, to
explain what I mean, than mention the name of Rupert ? ''

'' What of him, Lucy ?—be explicit ; vague allusions may
be worse than nothing.''

Lucy's little hand was on my arm, and she had drawn
its glove on account of the heat. I felt it press me, almost
convulsively, as she added, '' I do, I must think you have
too much affection and gratitude for my dear father, too
much regard for me, ever to forget that you and Rupert
once lived together as brothers ? ''

33

"Grace has my promise already, on that subject. I shall never take the world's course with Rupert, in this affair."

I heard Lucy's involuntary sob, as if she gasped for breath; and, turning, I saw her sweet eyes bent on my face with an expression of thankfulness that could not be mistaken.

"I would have given the same pledge to you, Lucy, and purely on your own account. It would be too much to cause you to mourn for your brother's—"

I did not name the offence, lest my feelings should tempt me to use too strong a term.

"This is all I ask—all I desire, Miles; bless you—bless you! for having so freely given me this assurance. Now my heart is relieved from this burden, I am ready to speak frankly to you; still, had I seen Grace—"

"Have no scruples on account of your regard for womanly feeling—I know everything, and shall not attempt to conceal from you, that disappointed love for Rupert has brought my sister to the state she is in. This might not have happened, had either of us been with her; but, buried as she has been alone in this place, her wounded sensibilities have proved too strong for a frame that is so delicate."

There was a pause of a minute, after I ended.

"I have long feared that some such calamity would befall us," Lucy answered in a low, measured tone. "I think you do not understand Grace as well as I do, Miles. Her mind and feelings have a stronger influence than common over her body; and I fear no society of ours, or of others, could have saved her this trial. Still, we must not despair. It is a trial—that is just the word; and by means of tenderness, the most sedulous care, good advice, and all that we two can do to aid, there must yet be hope. Now there is a skilful physician here, he must be dealt fairly by, and should know the whole."

"I intended to consult you on this subject—one has such a reluctance to expose Grace's most sacred feelings!"

" Surely, it need not go quite as far as that," returned Lucy, with sensitive quickness ; " something—much—must be left to conjecture ; but Dr. Post must know that the mind is at the bottom of the evil ; though I fear that young ladies can seldom admit the existence of such a complaint, without having it attributed to a weakness of this nature."

" That proceeds from the certainty that your sex has so much heart, Lucy ; your very existence being bound up in others."

" Grace is one of peculiar strength of affections—but, Miles, we will talk no further of this at present. I scarce know how to speak of my brother's affairs, and you must give me time to reflect. Now we are at Clawbonny again, we cannot long continue strangers to each other."

This was said so sweetly, I could have knelt and kissed her shoe-ties ; and yet so simply, as not to induce misinterpretation. It served to change the discourse, however, and the remainder of the way we talked of the past. Lucy spoke of her cousin's death, relating various little incidents to show how much Mrs. Bradfort was attached to her, and how good a woman she was ; but not a syllable was said of the will. I was required, in my turn, to finish the narrative of my last voyage, which had not been completed at the theatre. When Lucy learned that the rough seaman who had come in the sloop was Marble, she manifested great interest in him, declaring, had she known it during the passage, that she would have introduced herself. All this time, Rupert's name was not mentioned between us ; and I reached the house, feeling that something like the interest I had formerly possessed there, had been awakened in the bosom of my companion. She was, at least, firmly and confidingly my friend.

Chloe met Lucy at the door with a message—Miss Grace wanted to see Miss Lucy alone. I dreaded this interview, and looked forward to being present at it ; but Lucy begged me to confide in her, and I felt bound to comply. While the dear girl was gone to my sister's room, I sought the physician, with whom I had a brief but explicit conference. I told this gentleman how much Grace had been alone, permitting sorrow to wear upon her frame, and gave him to understand that the seat of my sister's malady was mental suffering. Post was a cool, discriminating man, and he ventured no remark until he had seen his patient; though I could perceive by the keen manner in which his piercing eye was fixed on mine, that all I said was fully noted.

It was more than an hour before Lucy reappeared. It was obvious at a glance that she had been dreadfully agitated, and cruelly surprised at the condition in which she had found Grace. It was not that disease, in any of its known forms, was so very apparent; but that my sister resembled already a being of another world, in the beaming of her countenance—in the bright, unearthly expression of her eyes—and in the slightness and delicacy of the hold she seemed, generally, to have on life. Grace had always something of this about her—much, I might better have said; but it now appeared to be left nearly alone, as her thoughts and strength gradually receded from the means of existence.

The physician returned with Lucy to my sister's room, where he passed more than an hour; as long a time, indeed, he afterward told me himself, as he thought could be done without fatiguing his patient. The advice he gave me was cautious and discreet. Certain tonics were prescribed; we were told to endeavor to divert the mind of our precious charge from her sources of uneasiness, by gentle means and prudent expedients. Change of scene was advised also, could it be done without producing too much fatigue. I suggested the Wallingford, as soon as this project was mentioned. She was a small sloop, it is true, but had two very comfortable cabins; my father having had one of them constructed especially in reference to my mother's occasional visits to town. The vessel did little, at that season of the year, besides transporting flour to market, and bringing back wheat. In the autumn, she carried wood, and the products of the neighborhood. A holiday might be granted her, and no harm come of it. Dr. Post approved the idea, saying frankly there was no objection but the expense; if I could bear that, a better plan could not possibly be adopted.

That night we discussed the matter in the family circle, Mr. Hardinge having come from the rectory to join us. Everybody approved of the scheme, it was so much better than leaving Grace to pine away by herself in the solitude of Clawbonny.

"I have a patient at the Springs," said Dr. Post, "who is very anxious to see me; and, to own the truth, I am a little desirous of drinking the waters myself, for a week. Carry me to Albany, and land me; after which you can descend the river, and continue your voyage to as many places, and for as long a time, as the strength of Miss Wallingford, and your own inclinations, shall dictate."

This project seemed excellent in all our eyes ; even Grace heard it with a smile, placing herself entirely in our hands. It was decided to put it in practice.

CHAPTER XXX.

"And she sits and gazes at me,
With those deep and tender eyes,
Like the stars, so still and saint-like,
Looking downward from the skies."

LONGFELLOW.

THE next morning I set about the measures necessary for carrying out our plan. Marble was
invited to be of the party, the arrangements
concerning the ship allowing of his absence for a few days.
Once engaged, he was of infinite service, entering into the
plan as my mate. The regular skipper was glad to have a
furlough ; and I retained on board no one of the proper
crew but the river-pilot ; a man who could not be dispensed
with. By this arrangement, we cleared the cabin from company that was not desirable for the circumstances. Neb and
three of the Clawbonny blacks were delighted to go on such
an excursion, and all were more or less familiar with the little
duty that would be required of them. Indeed Marble, Neb,
and myself were every way able to take care of the vessel.
But we chose to have plenty of physical force ; and a cook
was indispensable. Clawbonny supplied the latter, in the
person of old Dido of that ilk.

By noon, the whole party were ready to embark. Grace
was driven to the wharf, and she walked on board the sloop,
supported by Lucy and myself ; more, however, from solicitude than from absolute necessity. Every precaution, however, was taken by order of the physician to prevent anything
like excitement ; the blacks, in particular, who would have
followed "Miss Grace" to the water's edge, being ordered
to remain at home. Chloe, to her manifest satisfaction, was

permitted to accompany her "young mistress," and great was her delight. How often that day did the exclamation of " De feller ! " escape her, as she witnessed Neb's exploits in different parts of the sloop. It was some little time before I could account for the black's superfluous activity, imputing it to zeal in my sister's service ; but, in the end, I discovered Grace had to share the glory with Chloe.

No sooner was everybody on board than we cast off. The jib was soon up ; and under this short sail we moved slowly out of the creek, with a pleasant southerly breeze. As we passed the point, there stood the whole household arrayed in a line, from the tottering, gray-headed, and muddy-looking negro of seventy, down to the glistening, jet-black, toddling things of two and three. The distance was so small, it was easy to trace even the expressions of the different countenances, which varied according to the experience, forebodings, and characters of the different individuals. Notwithstanding the sort of reverential attachment all felt for "Miss Grace," and the uncertainty some among these unsophisticated creatures must have experienced on the subject of her health, it was not in nature for such a cluster of "niggers" to exhibit unhappiness at a moment when there were so many grounds of excitement. The people of this race know nothing of the word, perhaps; but they delight in the thing quite as much as if they did nothing but electioneer all their lives. Most pliant instruments would their untutored feelings make in the hands of your demagogue ; and, possibly, it may have some little influence on the white American to understand how strong is his resemblance to the "nigger," when he gives himself up to the mastery of this much approved mental power. The day was glorious, a brighter sun never shining in Italy, or on the Grecian islands ; the air balmy ; the vessel was gay to the eye, having been painted about a month before, and every one seemed bent on a holiday ; circumstances sufficient in themselves to make this light-hearted race smiling and happy. As the sloop went slowly past, the whole line doffed their hats, or courtesied, showing at the same time a row of ivory that

shone like so many gay windows in their sable faces. I
could see that Grace was touched by this manifestation of
interest ; such a field-day in the Clawbonny corps not having
occurred since the first time my mother went to town, after
the death of my father. Fortunately, everything else was
soothing to my sister's spirits ; and, so long as she could sit
on the deck, holding Lucy's hand, and enjoy the changing
landscape, with her brother within call, it was not possible
she should be altogether without happiness.

Rounding the point as we entered the river, the Wallingford eased-off sheet, set a studding-sail and flying-top-
sail, and began to breast the Hudson, on her way toward its
sources.

In 1803, the celebrated river we were navigating, though
it had all the natural features it possessed to-day, was by no
means the same picture of moving life. The steamboat did
not appear on its surface until four years later ; and the
journeys up and down its waters were frequently a week in
length. In that day, the passengers did not hurry on board,
just as a bell was disturbing the neighborhood, hustling his
way through a rude throng of porters, cartmen, orange-
women, and news-boys, to save his distance by just a minute and a half, but his luggage was often sent to the vessel
the day before ; he passed his morning in saying adieu, and
when he repaired to the vessel, it was with gentleman-like
leisure, often to pass hours on board previously to sailing,
and not unfrequently to hear the unwelcome tidings that
this event was deferred until the next day. How different,
too, was the passage from one in a steamboat ! There was
no jostling of each other, no scrambling for places at table,
no bolting of food, no impertinence manifested, no swearing
about missing the eastern or southern boats, or Schenectady,
or Saratoga, or Boston trains, on account of a screw being
loose, nor any other unseemly manifestation that anybody
was in a hurry. On the contrary, wine and fruit were provided, as if the travellers intended to enjoy themselves ; and
a journey in that day was a *festa*. No more embarked than
could be accommodated ; and the company being selected,
the cabin was taken to the exclusion of all unwelcome in-

truders. Now, the man who should order a bottle of wine
to be placed at the side of his plate, would be stared at as a
fool ; and not without reason altogether, for, did it escape
the claws of his *convives* and the waiters, he would probably
reach the end of his journey before he could drink it.

In 1803, not only did the dinner pass in peace, and with
gentleman-like deliberation ; not only were the cooler and
the fruit taken on deck, and the one sipped and the other
eaten at leisure in the course of an afternoon, but in the
course of many afternoons. Passages were certainly made
in twenty-four hours in the sloops ; but these were the exceptions, a week being much more likely to be the time
passed in the enjoyment of the beautiful scenery of the river.
The vessel usually got aground, once at least, and frequently
several times in a trip ; and often a day or two were thus
delightfully lost, giving the stranger an opportunity of visit'
ing the surrounding country. The necessity of anchoring,
with a foul wind, on every opposing tide, too, increased these
occasions, thus lending to the excursion something of the
character of an exploring expedition. No, no ; a man would
learn more in one passage, up or down the Hudson, forty
years since, than can be obtained by a dozen at the present
time. I have a true seaman's dislike for a steamboat, and
sometimes wish they were struck out of existence ; though
I know it is contrary to all the principles of political economy,
and opposed to what is called the march of improvement.
Of one thing, however, I feel quite certain : that these inventions, coupled with the gregarious manner of living that has
sprung up in the large taverns, is, as one of our writers ex-
presses it, " doing wonders for the manners of the people " ;
though, in my view of the matter, the wonder is that they
have any left.

There might have been thirty sail in sight, when the Wallingford got fairly into the river, some turning down on a
young ebb, making their fifteen or twenty miles in six hours,
and others, like ourselves, stealing along against it at about
the same rate. Half a dozen of these craft were quite near
us, and the decks of most of those which were steering north,
had parties including ladies, evidently proceeding to the

"Springs." I desired Marble to sheer as close to these different vessels as was convenient, having no other object in
view than amusement, and fancying it might aid in divert-
ing the thoughts of my sister from her own sorrows, to the
faces and concerns of others. The reader will have no difficulty in understanding, that the Wallingford, constructed
under the orders of an old sailor, and for his own uses, was a
fast vessel. In this particular she had but one or two competitors on the river ; packets belonging to Hudson, Pough-
keepsie, and Sing Sing. She was now only in fair ballast-
trim, and being admirably provided with sails, in the light
wind we had, she actually went four feet to most of the
other vessels in sight's three. My request to Marble—or,
order, as he chose to call it—was easily enough complied
with, and we were soon coming up close on the quarter of a
sloop that had its decks crowded with passengers who evidently belonged to the better class ; while on the forecastle
were several horses, and a carriage ; customary accompani-
ments to such a scene in that day.

I had not been so happy in a long time, as I felt at that
moment. Grace was better, as I fancied at least, and it was
certain she was more composed and less nervous than I had
seen her since my return ; and this of itself was removing
the weight of a mountain from my heart. There was Lucy,
too, her rounded cheek rosy with the pleasure of the moment, full of health, and with eyes that never turned on me
that they did not beam with confidence and kindness—the
sincerest friendship, if not love—while every look, movement, syllable, or gesture that was directed toward Grace,
betrayed how strongly the hearts of these two precious
creatures were still knit together in sisterly affection. My
guardian, too, seemed happier than he had been since our
conversation on the state of my own feelings toward his
daughter. He had made a condition, that we should all
—the doctor excepted—return to Clawbonny in time for
service on the ensuing Sunday, and he was then actually
engaged in looking over an old sermon for the occasion,
though not a minute passed in which he did not drop the
manuscript to gaze about him, in deep enjoyment of the

landscape. The scene, moreover, was so full of repose, that even the movements of the different vessels scarce changed its Sabbath-like character. I repeat, that I had not felt so perfectly happy since I held my last conversation with the Salem Witches, in the Duomo of Firenze.

Marble was excessively delighted with the behavior of the Wallingford. The latter was a sloop somewhat smaller than common, though her accommodations were particularly commodious, while she was sparred on the scale of a flyer. Her greatest advantage in the way of sailing, however, would have been no great recommendation to her on a wind ; for she was nearly start light, and might not have been able to carry full sail in hard November weather, even on the Hudson—a river on which serious accidents have been known to occur. There was little danger in midsummer, however ; and we went gliding up on the quarter of the Gull, of Troy, without feeling concern of any sort.

"What sloop is that?" demanded the skipper of the Gull, as our boom-end came within a fathom of his rail, our name being out of his view.

" The Wallingford of Clawbonny, just out of port, bound up on a party of pleasure."

Now, Clawbonny was not then, nor is it now, what might be called a legal term. There was no such place known in law, beyond the right which usage gives ; and I heard a low laugh among the passengers of the Gull, as they heard the homely appellation. This came from the equivocal position my family occupied, midway between the gentry and yeomanry of the State, as they both existed in 1803. Had I said the sloop came from near Coldenham, it would have been all right ; for everybody who was then anybody in New York, knew who the Coldens were ; or Morrisania, the Morrises being people of mark ; or twenty other places on the river , but the Wallingfords were as little known as Clawbonny, when you got fifteen or twenty miles from the spot where they had so long lived. This is just the difference between obscurity and notoriety. When the latter extends to an entire nation, it gives an individual, or a family, the note that frees them entirely from the imputation of existing under the first condition; and this note, favorably diffused through Christendom, forms a reputation—transmitted to posterity, it becomes fame. Unfortunately, neither we nor our place had even reached the first simple step in this scale of renown; and poor Clawbonny was laughed at, on account of something Dutch that was probably supposed to exist in the sound—the Anglo-Saxon race having a singular aptitude to turn up their noses at everything but their own possessions, and everybody but themselves. I looked at Lucy, with sensitive quickness, to see how she received this sneer on my birthplace; but, with her, it was so much a matter of course to think well of everything connected with the spot, its name as well as its more essential things, that I do not believe she perceived this little sign of derision.

While the passengers of the Gull felt this disposition to smile, it was very different with her skipper; his Dutch pilot, whose name was Abrahamus Van Valtenberg, but who was more familiarly known as 'Brom Folleck, for so the children of New Netherlands twisted their cognomens in converting them into English [1] ; the black cook, the mulatto steward, and the "all hands," who were one man and a boy. There had been a generation of sloops which bore the name of Wallingford, as well as generations of men, at Clawbonny; and this every river-man knew. In point of fact, we counted four generations of men, and six of sloops. Now, none of these vessels was worthy of being mentioned, but this which my father had caused to be built; but she had a reputation that extended to everybody on the river. The effect of all this was to induce the skipper of the Gull to raise his hat, and to say,—

[1] A story is told of a Scotchman of the name of Farquharson, who settled among the High Dutch on the Mohawk, some time previously to the Revolution; where, unable to pronounce his name, the worthy farmers called him Feuerstein (pronounced Firestyne). The son lived and died under this appellation; but the grandson, removing to a part of the country where English alone was spoken, chose to Anglicize his name; and, by giving it a free translation, became Mr. Flint!

"That, then, I suppose, is Mr. Wallingford himself—you are welcome back on the river ; I remember the time well, when your respected father would make that boat do anything but talk. Nothing but the new paint, which is different from the last, prevented me from knowing the sloop. Had I taken a look at her bows, this couldn't have happened."

This speech evidently gave me and my vessel an estimation with the passengers of the Gull that neither had enjoyed the moment before. There was some private conversation on the quarter-deck of the other vessel, and then a highly respectable and gentleman-like looking old man, came to the rail, bowed, and commenced a discourse.

"I have the pleasure of seeing Captain Wallingford, I believe," he remarked, "with whom my friends, the Mertons, came passengers from China. They have often expressed their sense of your civilities," he continued, as I bowed in acquiescence, "and declare they should ever wish to sail with you, were they again compelled to go to sea."

Now, this was viewing my relation to the Mertons in any point of view but that in which I wished it to be viewed, or indeed was just. Still it was natural ; and the gentleman who spoke, a man of standing and character, no doubt fancied he was saying that which must prove particularly acceptable to me ; another proof how dangerous it is to attempt to decide on other men's feelings or affairs. I could not decline the discourse ; and, while the Wallingford went slowly past the Gull, I was compelled to endure the torment of hearing the Mertons mentioned, again and again, in the hearing of Lucy and Grace ; on the nerves of the latter of whom I knew it must be a severe trial. At length we got rid of this troublesome neighbor, though not until Lucy and her father were recognized, and spoken to by several of the ladies in the other party. While my late guardian and his daughter were thus engaged, I stole a glance at my sister. She was as pale as death, and seemed anxious to go below, whither I led her, most happily, I have every reason to think, as things turned out.

When the Wallingford had left the Gull some little dis-

tance astern, I returned to the deck, and Lucy went to take
my place by the side of Grace's berth. She reappeared,
however, in a very few minutes, saying that my sister felt
an inclination to rest herself, and might fall asleep. Feeble,
almost, as an infant, these frequent slumbers had become
necessary, in a measure, to the patient's powers. Chloe
coming up soon after with a report that her young mistress
seemed to be in a doze, we all remained on deck, in order
not to disturb her. In this manner, half an hour passed,
and we had drawn quite near to another sloop that was
going in the same direction with ourselves. At this moment, Mr. Hardinge was deeply immersed in his sermon,
and I perceived that Lucy looked at him, from time to time,
as if she expected to catch his eye. I fancied something
distressed her, and yet it was not easy to imagine exactly
what it could be.

"Do you not intend to go nearer the other sloop?" Lucy
at length inquired, alluding to the vessel that was almost in
a line with us; but to which I had ordered Neb to give a
respectable berth.

"I thought the gossip of the last quite sufficient; but, if
you like these interviews, certainly."

Lucy seemed embarrassed; she colored to her temples,
paused a moment, and then added, affecting to laugh—and
it was so seldom Lucy affected anything, but this time she
did affect to laugh—as she said,—

"I do wish to go near that sloop, though it is not exactly
for the reason you suppose."

I could see she was distressed, though it was not yet easy
to imagine the cause. Lucy's requests were laws to me, and
Neb was ordered to sheer down on the quarter of this second sloop, as we had done on that of the first. As we drew
near, her stern told us that she was called the "Orpheus
of Sing Sing," a combination of names that proved some
wag had been connected with the christening. Her decks
had also a party of both sexes on them, though neither carriage nor horses. All this time, Lucy stood quite near me,
as if reluctant to move, and when we were sufficiently near
the sloop, she pressed still nearer to my side, in the way in

which her sex are apt to appeal to those of the other who possess their confidence, when most feeling the necessity of support.

"Now, Miles," she said in an undertone, "you must 'speak that sloop,' as you call it; I can never hold a loud conversation of this sort in the presence of so many strangers."

"Very willingly, Lucy; though you will have the goodness to let me know exactly what I am to say."

"Certainly; begin, then, in your sailor fashion, and when that is done, I will tell you what to add."

"Enough; Orpheus, there!" I called out, just raising my voice sufficiently to be heard.

"Ay, ay; what's wanted?" answered the skipper, taking a pipe from his mouth, as he leaned with his back against his own tiller, in a way that was just in accordance with the sleepy character of the scene.

I looked at Lucy, as much as to say, "What next?"

"Ask him if Mrs. Drewett is on board his sloop—Mrs. Andrew Drewett, not Mr.—the old lady, I mean," added the dear girl, blushing to the eyes.

I was so confounded—I might almost add appalled—that it was with great difficulty I suppressed an exclamation. Command myself I did, however, and observing that the skipper was curiously awaiting my next question I put it.

"Is Mrs. Andrew Drewett among your passengers, sir?" I inquired, with a cold distinctness.

My neighbor nodded his head, and spoke to some of his passengers, most of whom were on the main deck, seated on chairs, and concealed from us, as yet, by the Wallingford's mainsail, her boom being guyed out on the side next the Orpheus, with its end just clear of her quarter.

"She is, and wishes to know who makes the inquiry?" returned the Sing Sing skipper, in the sing-song manner in which ordinary folk repeat what is dictated.

"Say that Miss Hardinge has a message to Mrs. Drewett from Mrs. Ogilvie, who is on board that other sloop," added Lucy, in a low, and, as I thought, tremulous tone.

I was nearly choked; but made out to communicate the

fact as directed. In an instant I heard the foot of one who leaped on the Orpheus' quarter-deck, and then Andrew Drewett appeared, hat in hand, a face all smiles, eyes that told his tale as plain as any tongue could have uttered it, and such salutations as denoted the most perfect intimacy. Lucy took my arm involuntarily, and I could feel that she trembled. The two vessels were now so near, and everything around us was so tranquil, that by Lucy's advancing to the Wallingford's quarter-deck, and Drewett's coming to the taffrail of the Orpheus, it was easy to converse without any unseemly raising of the voice. All that had been said between me and the skipper, indeed, had been said on a key but little higher than common. By the change in Lucy's position I could no longer see her face; but I knew it was suffused, and that she was far from being as composed and collected as was usual with her demeanor. All this was death to my recent happiness, though I could not abstain from watching what now passed with the vigilance of jealousy.

"Good morning," Lucy commenced, and the words were uttered in a tone that I thought bespoke great familiarity, if not confidence; "will you have the goodness to tell your mother that Mrs. Ogilvie begs she will not leave Albany until after her arrival? The other sloop, Mrs. Ogilvie thinks, cannot be more than an hour or two after you, and she is very desirous of making a common party to—ah! there comes Mrs. Drewett," said Lucy, hastily interrupting herself, "and I can deliver my message myself."

Mrs. Drewett coming aft at this instant, Lucy certainly did turn to her, and communicated a message which it seems the lady in the Gull had earnestly requested her to deliver in passing.

"And now," returned Mrs. Drewett, when Lucy had ceased, first civilly saluting me, "and now, my dear Lucy, we have something for you. So sudden was your departure, on the receipt of that naughty letter"—my letter, summoning the dear girl to the bedside of her friend, was meant—"that you left your work-box behind you, and as I knew that it contained many notes besides bank-notes, I would not allow it to be separated from me until we met. Here it is; in what manner shall we contrive to get it into your hands?"

Lucy started, and I could see that she both felt and looked anxious. As I afterward learned, she had been passing a day at Mrs. Drewett's villa, which joined her own, both standing on the rocks quite near to that spot which a mawkish set among us is trying to twist from plain, homely, up-and-down, old-fashioned Hell-Gate, into the exquisite and lackadaisical corruption of *Hurl*-Gate,—Heaven save the mark! What puny piece of folly and affectation will they attempt next? But Lucy was paying this visit when she received my letter, and it appears such was her haste to get to Grace, that she quitted the house immediately, leaving behind her a small work-box, unlocked, and in it various papers that she did not wish read. Of course one of Lucy's sentiments and tone could hardly suspect a lady, and Mrs. Drewett was strictly that, of rummaging her box or of reading her notes and letters; but one is never easy when such things can be supposed to be in the way of impertinent eyes. There are maids as well as mistresses, and I could see in a moment that she wished the box was again in her own possession. Under the circumstances, therefore, I felt it time to interfere.

"If your sloop will round-to, Mr. Drewett," I remarked, receiving a cold salutation from the gentleman, in return for my own bow, the first sign of recognition that had passed between us, "I will round-to, myself, and send a boat for the box."

This proposal drew all eyes toward the skipper, who was still learning against his tiller, smoking for life or death. It was not favorably received, extorting a grunt in reply, that any one could understand denoted dissent. The pipe was slowly removed, and the private opinion of this personage was pretty openly expressed, in his Dutchified dialect.

"If a body couldt get a wint for der askin', dis might do very well," he said; "but nobody rounts-to mit a fair wint."

I have always remarked that they who have used a dialect different from the common forms of speech in their

34

youth, and come afterwards to correct it, by intercourse with
the world usually fall back into their early infirmities in
moments of trial, perplexity, or anger. This is easily
explained. Habit has become a sort of nature, in their
childhood, and it is when most tried that we are the most
natural. Then, this skipper, an Albany—or Al*bon*ny man,
as he would probably have styled himself, had got down the
river as far as Sing Sing, had acquired a tolerable English ;
but, being now disturbed, he fell back upon his original
mode of speaking, the certain proof that he would never
give in. I saw at once the hopelessness of attempting to
persuade one of his school, and had begun to devise some
other scheme for getting the box on board, when to my surprise, and not a little to my concern, I saw Andrew Drewett,
first taking the box from his mother, step upon the end of
our main-boom, and move along the spar with the evident
intention to walk as far as our deck and deliver Lucy her
property with his own hands. The whole thing occurred so
suddenly, that there was no time for remonstrance. Young
gentlemen who are thoroughly in love, are not often discreet
in matters connected with their devotion to their mistresses.
I presume Drewett saw the boom placed so favorably as to
tempt him, and he fancied it would be a thing to mention to
carry a lady her work-box across a bridge that was of so
precarious a footing. Had the spar lain on the ground, it
would certainly have been no exploit at all for any young
man to walk its length, carrying his arms full of work-
boxes ; but it was a very different matter when the same feat
had to be performed on a sloop's boom in its place, suspended
over the water, with the sail set, and the vessel in motion.
This Drewett soon discovered, for, advancing a step or two,
he grasped the topping-lift, which luckily for him happened
to be taut, for a support. All this occurred before there was
time for remonstrance, or even for thought. At the same
instant Neb, in obedience to a sign previously given by me,
had put the helm down a little, and the boom-end was
already twenty feet from the quarter-deck of the Orpheus.

Of course, all the women screamed, or exclaimed, on some
key or other. Poor Mrs. Drewett hid her face, and began

to moan her son as lost. I did not dare look at Lucy, who remained quiet as to voice, after the first involuntary exclamation, and as immovable as a statue. Luckily her face was from me. As Drewett was evidently discomposed, I thought it best, however, to devise something not only for his relief, but for that of Lucy's box, which was in quite as much jeopardy as the young man, himself; more so, indeed, if the latter could swim. I was on the point of calling out to Drewett to hold on, and I would cause the boom-end to reach over the Orpheus' main deck, after which he might easily drop down among his friends, when Neb, finding some one to take the helm, suddenly stood at my side.

"He drop dat box, sartain, Masser Mile," half whispered the negro; "he leg begin to shake, already, and he won'erful skear'd!"

"I would not have that happen for a good deal. Can you save it, Neb?"

"Sartain, sir. Only hab to run out on 'e boom and bring it in, and gib it Miss Lucy; she mighty partic'lar about dat werry box, Master Mile, as I see a hundred time, and more too."

"Well, lay out, boy, and bring it in, and look to your footing, Neb."

This was all Neb wanted. The fellow had feet shaped a good deal like any other aquatic bird, with the essential difference, however, that no small part of his foundation had been laid abaft the perpendicular of the tendon Achilles, and being without shoes he could nearly encircle a small spar in his grasp. Often and often had I seen Neb run out on a topsail-yard, the ship pitching heavily, catching at the lift, and it was a mere trifle after that to run out on a spar as large as the Wallingford's main-boom. A tolerably distinctive scream from Chloe, first apprised me that the negro was in motion. Looking in that direction, I saw him walking steadily along the boom, notwithstanding Drewett's loud remonstrances and declarations that he wanted no assistance, until he reached the spot where the young gentleman stood grasping the lift, with his legs submitting to more tremor than was convenient. Neb now grinned, looked as amiable as possible, held out his hand, and revealed the object of his visit.

"Masser Mile t'ink 'e gentleum better gib me Miss Lucy box," said Neb, as politely as he knew how.

I believe in my soul that Drewett could have kissed Neb, so glad was he to obtain this little relief. The box was yielded without the slightest objection, Neb receiving it with a bow, after which the negro turned around as coolly as if he were on deck, and walked deliberately and steadily in to the mast. He stopped an instant just at the small of the spar to look back at Drewett, who was saying something to pacify his mother, and I observed that, as he stood with his heels in a line, the toes nearly met underneath the boom, which his feet grasped something in the manner of talons. A deep sigh reached my ear as Neb bounded lightly on deck, and I knew whence it came by the exclamation of "De *fel*-ler !"

As for Neb, he advanced with his prize, which he offered to Lucy with one of his best bows, but in a way to show he was not conscious of having performed any unusual exploit. Lucy handed the box to Chloe, without averting her eyes from Drewett, in whose situation she manifested a good deal more concern than I liked, or fancied he deserved.

"Thank you, Mr. Drewett," she said, affecting to think the box had been recovered altogether by his address ; " it is now safe, and there is no longer any necessity for your coming here. Let Mr. Wallingford do what he says "—I had mentioned, in a low voice, the practicability of my own scheme—" and return to your own sloop."

But two things now interposed to the execution of this very simple expedient. The first was Drewett's pride, blended with a little obstinacy, and the other was the "Al*bon*ny " skipper's pride, blended with a good deal of obstinacy. The first did not like to retreat, after Neb had so clearly demonstrated it was no great matter to walk on the boom, and the latter, soured by the manner in which we had outsailed him, and fancying Andrew had deserted to get on board a faster vessel, resented the whole by sheering away from us to the distance of a hundred yards. I saw

that there remained but a single expedient, and set about
adopting it without further delay.

"Take good hold of the lift, Mr. Drewett, and steady
yourself with both hands ; ease away the peak halyards to
tauten that lift a little more, forward. Now, one of you
stand by to ease off the guy handsomely, and the rest come
aft to the mainsheet. Look out for yourself, Mr. Drewett,
we are about to haul in the boom, when it will be a small
matter to get you in upon the taffrail. Stand by to luff
handsomely, so as to keep the boom as steady as possible."

But Drewett clamorously protested against our doing anything of the sort. He was getting used to his situation,
and intended to come in Neb-fashion in a minute more.
All he asked was not to be hurried.

"No, no—touch nothing, I entreat of you, Captain
Wallingford," he said earnestly. "If that black can do it,
surely I ought to do it, too."

" But the black has claws, and you have none, sir ; then
he is a sailor, and used to such things, and you are none,
sir. Moreover, he was barefooted, while you have got
on stiff, and I dare say slippery boots."

"Yes, the boots are an encumbrance. If I could only
throw them off, I should do well enough. As it is, however,
I hope to have the honor of shaking you by the hand,
Miss Hardinge, without the disgrace of being helped."

Mr. Hardinge here expostulated, but all in vain ; for I saw
plainly enough Drewett was highly excited, and that he was
preparing for a start. These signs were now so apparent
that all of us united our voices in remonstrances ; and Lucy
said imploringly to me, " Do not let him move, Miles—I
have heard him say he cannot swim."

It was too late. Pride, mortified vanity, obstinacy, love,
or what you will, rendered the young man deaf, and away
he went, abandoning the lift, his sole protection. I saw,
the moment he quitted his grasp, that he could never
reach the mast, and made my arrangements accordingly.
I called to Marble to stand by to luff ; and, just as the
words passed my lips, a souse into the water told the
whole story. The first glance at poor Drewett's frantic

manner of struggling told me that Lucy was really aware
of his habits, and that he could not swim. I was in light
duck, jacket and trousers, with seaman's pumps; and
placing a foot on the rail, I alighted alongside of the
drowning young man, just as he went under. Well
assured he would reappear, I waited for that, and presently
I got a view of his hair, within reach of my arm, and I
grasped it, in a way to turn him on his back, and bring
his face uppermost. At this moment the sloop was gliding away from us, Marble having instantly put the helm
hard down, in order to round-to. As I afterward learned,
the state of the case was no sooner understood in the other
sloop, than the Albonny men gave in, and imitated the
Wallingford.

There was no time for reflection. As soon as Drewett's
hair was in my grasp, I raised his head from the water,
by an effort that forced me under it, to let him catch his
breath ; and then relaxed the power by which it had been
done, to come up myself. I had done this to give him a
moment to recover his recollection, in hope he would
act reasonably ; and I now desired him to lay his two
hands on my shoulders, permit his body to sink as low as
possible and breathe, and trust the rest to me. If the
person in danger can be made to do this, an ordinarily
good swimmer could tow him a mile, without any unusual
effort. But the breathing spell afforded to Drewett had
the effect just to give him strength to struggle madly for
existence, without aiding his reason. On the land, he
would have been nothing in my hands ; but in the water,
the merest boy may become formidable. God forgive me,
if I do him injustice ! but I have sometimes thought, since,
that Drewett was perfectly conscious who I was, and that
he gave some vent to his jealous distrust of Lucy's feelings
toward me. This may be all imagination ; but I certainly
heard the words "Lucy," "Wallingford," "Clawbonny,"
"hateful," muttered by the man, even as he struggled there
for life. The advantage given him, by turning to allow
him to put his hands on my shoulders, liked to have cost
me dear. Instead of doing as I directed, he grasped my

neck with both arms, and seemed to wish to mount on my head, forcing his own shoulders quite out of water, and mine, by that much weight, beneath it. It was while we were thus placed, his mouth within an inch or two of my very ear, that I heard the words muttered which have been mentioned. It is possible, however, that he was unconscious of that which terror and despair extorted from him.

I saw no time was to be lost, and my efforts became desperate. I first endeavored to swim with this great encumbrance ; but it was useless. The strength of Hercules could not long have buoyed up the under body of such a load, sufficiently to raise the nostrils for breath ; and the convulsive twitches of Drewett's arms were near strangling me. I must throw him off, or drown. Abandoning the attempt to swim, I seized his hands with mine, and endeavored to loosen his grasp of my neck. Of course we both sank while I was thus engaged ; for it was impossible to keep my head above water, by means of my feet alone, with a man of some size riding, from his shoulders up, above the level of my chin.

I can scarcely describe what followed. I confess I thought no longer of saving Drewett's life, but only of saving my own. We struggled there in the water like the fiercest enemies, each aiming for the mastery, as, if one were to live, the other must die. We sank, and rose to the surface for air, solely by my efforts, no less than three times ; Drewett getting the largest benefits by the latter, thus renewing his strength ; while mine, great as it was by nature, began gradually to fail. A struggle so terrific could not last long. We sank a fourth time, and I felt it was not to rise again, when relief came from an unexpected quarter. From boyhood, my father had taught me the important lesson of keeping my eyes open under water. By means of this practice, I not only felt, but saw the nature of the tremendous struggle that was going on. It also gave me a slight advantage over Drewett, who closed his eyes, by enabling me to see how to direct my own exertions. While sinking, as I believed, for the last time, I saw a large object approaching me in the water, which, in the confusion of the moment, I took for a shark, though sharks never ascended the Hudson so high, and were even rare at New York. There it was, however, swimming towards us, and even descending lower, as if to pass beneath in readiness for the fatal snap. Beneath it did pass, and I felt it pressing upward, raising Drewett and myself to the surface. As I got a glimpse of the light, and a delicious draught of air, Drewett was drawn from my neck by Marble, whose encouraging voice sounded like music in my ears. At the next instant my shark emerged, puffing like a porpoise ; and then I heard,—

"Hole on, Masser Mile—here he nigger close by !"

I was dragged into the boat, I scarce know how, and lay down completely exhausted ; while my late companion seemed to me to be a lifeless corpse. In a moment Neb, dripping like a black river-god, and glistening like a wet bottle, placed himself in the bottom of the boat, took my head into his lap, and began to squeeze the water from my hair, and to dry my face with some one's handkerchief— I trust it was not his own.

"Pull away, lads, for the sloop," said Marble, as soon as everybody was out of the river. "This gentleman seems to have put on the hatches for the last time—as for Miles, he 'll never drown in fresh water."

THE END.

GREAT ILLUSTRATED CLASSICS

Adam Bede—*Eliot*
Afloat and Ashore—*Cooper*
The Arabian Nights
Around the World in Eighty Days—*Verne*
The Autobiography and Other Writings of Benjamin Franklin
Ben-Hur—*Wallace*
The Black Arrow—*Stevenson*
Black Beauty—*Sewell*
The Call of the Wild and Other Stories—*London*
Captains Courageous and Other Stories—*Kipling*
Christmas Tales—*Dickens*
The Cloister and the Hearth—*Reade*
A Connecticut Yankee in King Arthur's Court—*Clemens*
The Cruise of the Cachalot—*Bullen*
David Copperfield—*Dickens*
The Deerslayer—*Cooper*
Emma—*Austen*
Famous Tales of Sherlock Holmes—*Doyle*
From the Earth to the Moon—*Verne*
Great Expectations—*Dickens*
Green Mansions—*Hudson*
Gulliver's Travels—*Swift*
Hawthorne's Short Stories—*Hawthorne*
Henry Esmond—*Thackeray*
The House of the Seven Gables—*Hawthorne*
Huckleberry Finn—*Clemens*
The Hunchback of Notre-Dame—*Hugo*
Ivanhoe—*Scott*
Jane Eyre—*Brontë*
A Journey to the Centre of the Earth—*Verne*
Kenilworth—*Scott*
Kidnapped—*Stevenson*
Kim—*Kipling*
King Arthur—*Malory*
The Last Days of Pompeii—*Bulwer-Lytton*
The Last of the Mohicans—*Cooper*
Lord Jim—*Conrad*
Lorna Doone—*Blackmore*
The Luck of Roaring Camp and Other Stories—*Harte*
The Man in the Iron Mask—*Dumas*
The Mill on the Floss—*Eliot*
The Moonstone—*Collins*

The Mysterious Island—*Verne*
Nicholas Nickleby—*Dickens*
The Odyssey—*Homer*
The Old Curiosity Shop—*Dickens*
Oliver Twist—*Dickens*
The Oregon Trail—*Parkman*
The Pathfinder—*Cooper*
Père Goriot—*Balzac*
Pickwick Papers—*Dickens*
The Pilot—*Cooper*
The Pioneers—*Cooper*
The Prairie—*Cooper*
Pride and Prejudice—*Austen*
Quentin Durward—*Scott*
Quo Vadis—*Sienkiewicz*
The Red Badge of Courage and Other Stories—*Crane*
The Return of the Native—*Hardy*
The Rise of Silas Lapham—*Howells*
Robinson Crusoe—*Defoe*
The Scarlet Letter—*Hawthorne*
The Scarlet Pimpernel—*Orczy*
Sense and Sensibility—*Austen*
Silas Marner—*Eliot*
The Sketch Book—*Irving*
The Spy—*Cooper*
The Strange Case of Dr. Jekyll and **Mr.** Hyde and Other Famous Tales—*Stevenson*
A Tale of Two Cities—*Dickens*
Tales—*Poe*
The Talisman—*Scott*
Tess of the D'Urbervilles—*Hardy*
The Three Musketeers—*Dumas*
Tom Sawyer—*Clemens*
Treasure Island—*Stevenson*
Twenty Thousand Leagues Under the Sea—*Verne*
Twenty Years After—*Dumas*
Two Years Before the Mast—*Dana*
Typhoon and Other Tales of the Sea—*Conrad*
Uncle Tom's Cabin—*Stowe*
Vanity Fair—*Thackeray*
Walden—*Thoreau*
The Way of All Flesh—*Butler*
Westward Ho!—*Kingsley*
The White Company—*Doyle*
White Fang and Other Stories—*London*
The Wreck of the Grosvenor—*Russell*
Wuthering Heights—*Brontë*

GREAT ILLUSTRATED CLASSICS—TITANS

Autobiography of Benvenuto Cellini
Barnaby Rudge—*Dickens*
Bleak House—*Dickens*
Crime and Punishment—*Dostoevsky*
Dombey & Son—*Dickens*

Don Quixote—*Cervantes*
Everybody's Plutarch
Little Dorrit—*Dickens*
Martin Chuzzlewit—*Dickens*
Our Mutual Friend—*Dickens*

Short Novels of Henry James—*James*